FESTIVAL

By J. B. Priestley

FICTION

FESTIVAL
JENNY VILLIERS
BRIGHT DAY
THREE MEN IN NEW SUITS
DAYLIGHT ON SATURDAY
BLACK-OUT IN GRETLEY
LET THE PEOPLE SING
THE DOOMSDAY MEN

THEY WALK IN THE CITY
FARAWAY
ANGEL PAVEMENT
THE GOOD COMPANIONS
WONDER HERO
BENIGHTED
ADAM IN MOONSHINE

PLAYS

SEVEN PLAYS
THE LINDEN TREE AND
    AN INSPECTOR CALLS
FOUR PLAYS
JOHNSON OVER JORDAN
I HAVE BEEN HERE BEFORE
TIME AND THE CONWAYS
WHEN WE ARE MARRIED

BEES ON THE BOAT DECK
DUET IN FLOODLIGHT
CORNELIUS
EDEN END
DANGEROUS CORNER
LABURNUM GROVE
THE ROUNDABOUT

MISCELLANEOUS

DELIGHT
POSTSCRIPTS
RAIN UPON GODSHILL
MIDNIGHT ON THE DESERT
ENGLISH JOURNEY
FOUR-IN-HAND
I FOR ONE
TALKING: AN ESSAY
OPEN HOUSE

APES AND ANGELS
SELF-SELECTED ESSAYS
THE BALCONINNY
THE ENGLISH COMIC CHARACTER
MEREDITH (E.M.L.)
PEACOCK (E.M.L.)
THE ENGLISH NOVEL
HUMOUR (E. HERITAGE SERIES)
BRIEF DIVERSIONS

FESTIVAL

by J. B. Priestley

Harper & Brothers

PUBLISHERS   NEW YORK

This story is published in England
under the title of *Festival at Farbridge*

FOR

A. S. FRERE

FRIEND, PUBLISHER

CONTENTS

PART ONE

PART TWO

PART THREE

FESTIVAL

PART ONE

CHAPTER ONE

Laura Casey

I

ON A bleak and gusty Saturday afternoon in March, the 2:45 bus from Market Square, Farbridge, arrived at the corner of Mayton Park Avenue, and stopped just long enough to allow a young woman carrying a portable typewriter to descend, which she did gracefully but grumpily. She was a small, dark and rather fierce young woman; and was wearing her old blue coat and felt hat, her old red dress that had never recovered from the cleaners, stockings that had laddered and not been too well repaired; and she was sure she was looking terrible, and did not care much, having no immediate joy in life. Her name was Laura Casey.

Up Mayton Park Avenue, which rises steeply, the typewriter soon seemed less portable than the advertisements suggest. Laura scowled at every name on the gateposts of the detached villas, until at last she came to Rosebank, the residence of Major G. D. Bulfoss, Member of Parliament for Farbridge. Passing a monkey tree on her way up the short drive of Rosebank, she told it what she thought of it; and then, thankfully putting down her typewriter, she gave a vicious twist to one of those spring bells that sound like a fire alarm. While she waited, the March wind proved once again that her old blue coat had had it. This front door had been recently painted a nasty dark chocolate, and Laura took an instant dislike to it. Nothing seemed to be happening inside the house, so she rang the bell again, making a noise sufficient for two fire alarms.

The woman who peeped around the door, probably clutching at a wrap, must have had a terrific hair-do that morning, for her head seemed to be covered with brass shavings. She had a tiny silly nose, large and wavering eyes; and was fortyish. Apparently in a panic about something. "Oh!" she gasped. "Oh dear! What is it?"

Laura was patient with her. "I work in the office—Bulfoss and Sons —and I was told to come here this afternoon and do some letters for Major Bulfoss. At three o'clock."

"Oh dear! This is awkward. I'm Mrs. Bulfoss."

Laura said that she had guessed that.

"Actually," and Mrs. Bulfoss clutched at this word as she clutched at her wrap, "Major Bulfoss isn't getting back until about five. He sent a telegram."

"Not to the office, he didn't," said Laura severely. "I'd better wait, if you don't mind. I'm not very keen on going away and coming back."

"No, of course not. Poor you!" And Mrs. Bulfoss suddenly smiled and stopped dithering. "Come in."

The hall had been done in a metallic green, first cousin to the dark chocolate on the front door. Mrs. Bulfoss caught Laura disliking it. "I wanted it a nice stone color—but Gerald—Major Bulfoss—insisted on this wretched color. Why, I can't imagine," she added, with a surprising tartness. "But I'm so sorry, I ought to have asked your name."

But as Laura told her, it was clear that Mrs. Bulfoss was not really listening but was now dithering again, quite unable to make up her mind about something. There seemed to be a queer atmosphere about Rosebank this afternoon. Something had gone wrong. This was not how people behaved in Mayton Park Avenue, Laura was sure. Mrs. Bulfoss had not the look of a woman who was the confident wife of Major G. D. Bulfoss, M.P. Why was she half-dressed and dithering at this hour?

"Actually," and Mrs. Bulfoss clutched again, "I'm quite alone. I sent the maids out." And she gave Laura an imploring look, as if to beg her to declare that maids should be sent out on Saturday afternoons.

Laura stared hard and said nothing. Nine times out of ten this technique worked.

"Oh dear!" And Mrs. Bulfoss looked round the hall, but no help came from there, only that wrong shade of green. So she gave Laura another imploring glance.

But Laura was nothing but a little statue, a miniature female Buddha with untidy hair and a miserable old red dress.

"I'm trying to decide what to pack," said Mrs. Bulfoss, in a different tone now. "You see, Miss Tracey, I'm going away."

"I see." Laura was disappointed. The queerness, then, was a swindle. "By the way, it's not Tracey but Casey. Where shall I wait, Mrs. Bulfoss?" It was the perfect secretary who spoke; the cold career woman, aloof from feminine dithering. Pack the gray or the blue—who cares?

"Miss Casey, I wish—I wish you'd help me. You see—actually—I'm —well, I'm leaving my husband—*really* going away."

The statue came to life at once. She had been right all the time. This was a crisis, drama. "Of course I'll help you. Where do we go?"

They went up to Mrs. Bulfoss' bedroom, all very dainty and pink, with no evidence of Major Bulfoss there; but now in a state of deplorable confusion.

"Isn't it awful? I really can't decide what to take," said Mrs. Bulfoss, picking up a folded skirt and then putting it down somewhere else. Laura suspected that the poor woman had been doing this for the past hour. "The fact is, I don't really know whether I shall be staying in London or in the country. Isn't it ridiculous?"

"Let's put some of each kind in," said Laura. "Decide what you *must* have, and then fill up with odds and ends. Are these the cases you're taking?"

Once they had started packing systematically, Mrs. Bulfoss became very confidential indeed, as if she needed to talk and had had nobody to confide in. "I still keep wondering if I'm doing the right thing. It's not as if we had children, of course. And I do feel that Arthur needs me in a way that Gerald doesn't. I suppose you've met Gerald at the office, Miss Casey."

"Only once or twice. He's been out of it since I joined the firm. His elder brother is my boss."

"Ah—yes, Beverly. What do you think of him?"

"I can't bear him," said Laura.

Mrs. Bulfoss was delighted to hear this. "Neither can I. Of course he's quite different from Gerald, apart from being much older."

Laura wondered whether to admit that she could not bear Gerald, but decided against it, even if Mrs. Bulfoss was running away from him.

"But sometimes I think Gerald's growing more like him. Aren't these lovely? I bought them in Italy two years ago but haven't really worn them yet. Actually, I've known Arthur for ages. He's never *looked* at anybody else, and he's not strong—he's something to do with chemicals, you know, and that must be bad for him although he says it isn't—and he *needs* somebody. Not like Gerald, who only seems to need an audience now. It was bad enough before he won the election, but since then, although I've not seen a lot of him, of course, he's been *so* stuffy and pompous—I just couldn't stand it. Arthur's quite different—very sweet—just adores everything I say and do. And, after all, we've only one life to live, haven't we?"

"I don't know," said Laura.

"Oh dear!" Mrs. Bulfoss was quite dismayed. She stopped packing, to stare open-mouthed; but Laura impatiently passed her four pairs of full-fashioned nylons. Whether it was Gerald or Arthur or independent enterprise, Mrs. Bulfoss appeared to have done pretty well for herself.

"What I mean," said Laura, looking about her for more things to pack, "is that sometimes I feel we've only one life to live, and then at other times I feel we must have dozens at least, or it's all so silly that it's not worth bothering about. Just as sometimes I feel I'm nothing at all really—no more than a beetle or a wasp—and then sometimes I feel I'm tremendously important and that everything's been got up for my benefit."

"I know just what you mean," said Mrs. Bulfoss vaguely. She was looking at a pink-and-oyster jacket that seemed to Laura particularly revolting. "I don't know whether to take this. I've always been rather attached to it, and I know Arthur adores it. What do you think?"

"No. And if he asks, tell him it was ruined by the cleaners. What's this other one—Arthur—like? Tall, short, fat, thin, older or younger than Major Bulfoss? Or don't you want to talk about him?"

"Why, my dear, I don't mind. He's about ten years older than I am—rather plump—I tease him about that, but I don't care really—and rather pale, I think that's the chemicals but he says not, and with splendid eyes—really splendid—a sort of hazel. Quite different from Gerald's."

"Good!" And so it was, because the Bulfoss brothers had eyes like boiled cod. "How are you going? Train?"

Mrs. Bulfoss lit up like a lighthouse at dusk. "My dear," she cried triumphantly, "you'll never guess. Arthur's arranged for a car to take me the whole way. The man's been waiting at the White Hart since this morning, and I telephoned as soon as Gerald's telegram came, saying that he'd better call at four o'clock. Then he takes me *the whole way*." It was all wonder and glory, and the least Laura could do was to exclaim in admiration and envy, although the thought of plump pale old Arthur waiting at the other end left her cold, even though it might be a nice change from Major Bulfoss.

"A Daimler, I think," Mrs. Bulfoss murmured, still lost in the enchantment of these wonderful arrangements.

"You'd better get dressed then. Perhaps I could make some tea."

"My dear, *could* you? I'll come down the moment I'm ready."

"Are you leaving a note on a pincushion or anything?" said Laura.

"I've been wondering about that. Because Gerald doesn't know, of course. Some men might have guessed what might happen, but not Gerald—oh no! What do *you* think I ought to do?"

"Well, if you like," said Laura slowly, "I can tell him. I'll have to stay on until he comes. Anyhow you can decide while I'm making the tea." And off she went.

The tea had not been brewed more than a minute before Mrs. Bulfoss arrived in the kitchen. She was wearing a beige costume and a leopard-skin coat and a Daimler-all-the-way look, and appeared much taller and grander than before. Her manner too was more aloof at first, although it thawed a little over the second cup. Laura sat on a hard little kitchen chair, and nibbled some rather mournful biscuits; Mrs. Bulfoss remained standing, with an eye on the clock.

"I think if you just say that I've gone away and will be writing to him in a few days," said Mrs. Bulfoss, "that will do, Miss Casey."

"What about Arthur?" said Laura, who did not appreciate this new manner.

Mrs. Bulfoss frowned, hesitated, bit her lip. "Actually, they've never met. Though of course he's heard me mention Arthur now and then. But Gerald won't want any *scandal*, of course."

"I'll bet he won't. But I don't mention Arthur, you think?" Laura lit a cigarette and puffed away at it, half-closing her eyes, as if she had been assisting at scandalous elopements for years and years.

"Knowing Gerald, I don't think he'll want to discuss this with you, Miss Casey. But don't forget to tell him I'll be writing in a few days. There are sure to be dozens of things I've forgotten. Perhaps we'd better bring the bags down now."

Laura felt like telling her to bring them down herself or make use of Arthur's chauffeur, but then decided that all this sudden grandeur only meant that poor Mrs. Bulfoss was trying to keep up her courage. But it did seem to be an afternoon for lugging things around. On the way down a grandmother clock on the half-landing received a nasty bump.

"You're not married or engaged or anything, are you?" said Mrs. Bulfoss, when they were both breathing hard together in the hall, with the luggage all ready for the Daimler.

Laura replied briefly that she wasn't.

"Is your home here in Farbridge?" Mrs. Bulfoss sounded as if she had just opened a bazaar and Laura had just presented her with a bouquet.

"No, it isn't. I came here from London, only about three months ago, for a change. As a matter of fact, I haven't got a home. There's only my father, and he's somewhere in Central America, treasure-hunting."

"Treasure-hunting?" Mrs. Bulfoss sounded shocked.

"That's right—looking for treasure," said Laura cheerfully.

"But surely they don't let you do that nowadays, do they? I mean—currency and permits and things."

"Dad does it. He was a marine engineer and then decided he must start looking for all this treasure the old pirates are supposed to have buried. At least that's what he was doing when I last heard from him —but it may be something else now. He's a bit mad, of course, but a darling. After we lost my brother in the war and then Mother died, he didn't bother about living a steady respectable life any longer—and just did what he liked. And quite right too. Listen—I believe that's your car."

"Oh dear!" Mrs. Bulfoss was immediately back in her original fluster. "I wonder if I'm doing the right thing. Just see if it's a Daimler, will you, dear?"

Laura at the window reported that it was one of the largest Daimlers she had ever seen, and that now a very important-looking chauffeur was stepping out of it. This threw Mrs. Bulfoss into a panic.

"Can you remember if we packed my little red velvet bag?"

"I'm sure we did," said Laura firmly, although she had not the least recollection of any such bag. "I'll answer the door, shall I? It'll look better."

"My walking shoes—?"

"Remember them distinctly," said Laura, as she went to the door.

"By the way, where have you put the Major's correspondence? After all, that's why I'm here."

"In the study," said Mrs. Bulfoss. "Oh dear! I'm sure there are dozens of things I ought to have done that we've forgotten—"

The chauffeur was a broad, red-faced man who looked like the captain of a liner, perfect for a colored Cunard advertisement in an American magazine. At the sight of him, Mrs. Bulfoss was all dignified condescension, as if some gigantic bazaar would have to be opened at the end of the journey. Laura wondered what Arthur was doing—chemicals, golf, or pacing about somewhere, pale and plump and tense. Gerald would be dozing in a first-class carriage from Euston, blissfully unaware that nobody but a malicious secretary was waiting for him at Rosebank.

"Is this everything, merdom?" said the chauffeur.

"Everything, thank you," said Mrs. Bulfoss. "Well, goodbye—Miss Casey."

As Mrs. Bulfoss sailed through, the chauffeur, standing respectfully in the doorway, turned toward Laura and gave her an enormous slow wink. It was like a friendly signal from whole generations of coachmen, grooms, ostlers, chauffeurs, all the sardonic men of the Road. Laura stood at the door while the car majestically negotiated the drive. She caught a last glimpse of Mrs. Bulfoss' inadequate nose, those desperate curls, now on their way from Gerald to Arthur, from portentous political speeches to mysterious moods influenced by still more mysterious chemicals, from pink-plump and high blood pressure to waxy-plump and possible kidney trouble; and in that glimpse she discovered all the silliness, eternal hopefulness, grandeur, of her adventurous sex, inhabitants of a territory long occupied by the armies of the male. She waved, although there was nobody to wave back at her. The Daimler made an important All-the-way-to-Arthur noise, and vanished.

2

There was something at once silly and intimidating, Laura found, in being alone in a strange house. She caught herself tiptoeing about, and had to fight hard to resist a desire to open drawers and ransack cupboards, like a detective. The study was a sad little room at the back, and it had a smell of stale cigars and old magazines. Too much of it was taken up by a bookcase filled with books that were either oldish and all about sport and travel (*Safari Days* and *With Rod and Gun on*

the Border Country, that kind of thing), or very new and warning
everybody against Russia and Socialism. There was one large leather
armchair, which was too cold, and there were two upright chairs,
studded with brass knobs, that were too hard. There was a photograph
of Winston Churchill, looking as if he had won the last three or four
wars all by himself; and some very dull groups, political, social, sporting. And as Major Bulfoss was still a partner in Bulfoss and Sons,
Estate Agents, Valuers and Auctioneers, there was a lot of stuff about
the place that reminded Laura of the office in which she had spent the
last three months. Nothing happened except two telephone calls, both
asking for Major Bulfoss (nobody wanted Mrs. Bulfoss except Arthur),
and the arrival of the postman, which added five letters to the pile on
the study table. Laura began opening all the letters that were not
marked *Personal* or *Private*; they were nearly all invitations to address
meetings or give prizes; and the only one in which she could take any
interest was an involved but passionate complaint about a kitchen range
from a woman who appeared to think that Questions in the House
ought to be asked about it. Several preatomic centuries seemed to pass.

Then history began again. Nothing seemed to be lacking except drums
and trumpets. Doors banged, voices roared, and the place seemed to
be packed with noisy large men. The Member for Farbridge, accompanied by three prominent members of the Conservative Club, had
returned. Laura felt herself blown about like a leaf in a gale.

"Sent you up from the office, did they?" Major Bulfoss shouted.
"Good! Shan't be long. Just sort out the letters and that sort of thing
while I give these fellas a drink. Where are the maids? All right, tell
me later, must attend to these chaps. Do it all myself, of course, as
usual." He had the Bulfoss boiled eye with an angry complexion,
clipped thick mustache, a meaty butcher's look, and one of those voices
that always seemed to Laura like rude stares. "Don't want a drink
yourself, I imagine? Better not, eh? Well, shan't be long, Miss—er—"

He left the study door open behind him, and soon Laura could
hear from the drawing room the sound of glasses tinkling against
decanters and much guffawing. The voice of the Honorable and Gallant Member, who apparently had been attending an important private
meeting of his party, rose triumphantly above the rest; but a good time,
Laura decided sourly, was being had by all. And at least an equally
good time, she promised herself, would shortly be had by Laura Casey,
looking up from her typewriter to break the news about Mrs. Bulfoss.

"Well, gentlemen," she heard the Major cry, "I hate to break up this session but I've a hell of a pile of letters to attend to and a secretary waiting in my study." And after more guffawing and talk of "One for the road," and cries of: "You're dead right there, old boy," and: "I couldn't agree with you more, my dear chap," with the balloon of masculine complacency becoming more perilously inflated every second, Major Bulfoss bustled them out. It occurred to him then, as well it might, that the study was rather a cold melancholy sort of place in which to examine his correspondence; so Laura was commanded to leave her typewriter behind her and bring the letters and her notebook into the drawing room, which had now the atmosphere of a superior saloon bar.

The Major, settling down with another whisky and soda, grunted his way through more than half the letters before he spoke to Laura again. "Suppose I ought to ask my wife about one or two of these affairs." He looked across at Laura, who was sitting up on a chair much too tall for her, very demure with notebook and pencil. "I take it she's out. Did you happen to see her before she went out?"

"I did," said Laura carefully. "She left about four o'clock. I've been here since three."

"Oh, have you? Too bad. Meant to get through to the office this morning about that, but just couldn't manage it." Major Bulfoss took another pull at his whisky. "Did Mrs. Bulfoss mention where she was going?"

"No, she didn't."

"Humph! She might have left a message."

"She did leave a message."

"Then you ought to have told me."

"I hadn't forgotten," said Laura, again with much care, "but I was trying to decide what would be the best time to tell you."

Major Bulfoss stared at her. "Look, Miss—er—"

"Casey."

"Of course—Casey. Well—look, Miss Casey—I'd just as soon you didn't try to be funny. Do you mind?"

"Not at all." And Laura stared back at him.

"Thanks very much. Well, what was the message?"

"She asked me to tell you that she's gone away and would be writing in a few days."

"Nonsense! You must have misunderstood her."

Laura shook her head. "I don't think so, Major Bulfoss."

"Look, Miss—er—Casey, I've had rather a long day and I've still a good deal to do, whether you help me to do it or not. So no argument, please. And by the way, why didn't Miss Benson come today? That was the arrangement I had with the office—that Miss Benson should do my letters here."

"Miss Benson thinks she might be getting flu—so I was asked—as a favor—if I'd take her place here today."

"Oh well, pity about that. And I suppose you're annoyed because you've been kept so long. Don't blame you entirely, Miss Casey, but I'll be obliged if you won't try to be funny or argue the point quite so much. There isn't time, and I don't happen to be in the mood for it. Eh?"

As Laura made no reply, he glanced at several more letters in a stern fashion. She watched him like a very small cat watching a very large mouse. Something in her level gaze made him uneasy. He had to stop reading. "Look here, you must have got that message all wrong. I mean to say, Mrs. Bulfoss didn't take any luggage when she went."

Laura was very precise. "She took two large cases, one small case, and a hat box."

He sat up, staring. "What?"

"In a large Daimler," she continued, with a certain dreaminess now, "that was going All The Way."

"All the way—where?"

Laura smiled. "She didn't tell me that. She just said she was leaving you but would write in a few days. Probably to ask you to send on all the things she'd forgotten to pack."

"All the things—" cried the Major, on his feet but stupefied. "My God!"

The telephone was ringing in the hall. If Major Bulfoss heard it, he gave no sign of having done so.

"Shall I answer the telephone, Major Bulfoss?" Laura inquired demurely.

"What? Yes, yes, answer the dam' thing. Tell 'em anything."

A massive contralto informed Laura that she was being spoken to by Mrs. Whatmore, Chairman of the Women's Executive Committee of the Farbridge Conservative Party. Major Bulfoss was there, was he? Then Mrs. Whatmore, with a deputation of the Farbridge Conservative Women, would shortly arrive at Rosebank.

Looking more glazed than before, Major Bulfoss was drinking whisky without soda. But as he saw Laura, a hopeful thought occurred to him. "My wife?"

"No. Mrs. Whatmore, Chairman of the—"

"Oh, damn an' blast Mrs. Whatmore! Don't tell me, I don't want to know. But—look here—did you gather from anything my wife said that she was going to stay with her sister?"

"I gathered very definitely that she was *not* going to stay with her sister." Laura was so firm that he had to believe her.

He swallowed about a third of a tumbler of neat whisky, and this, following all the drinks he had had before, made him goggle a little. "By George, this is pretty thick, I must say. Just going off like that. Look here, are you *sure*? Or is this something you've cooked up between you?"

"No cooking up, Major Bulfoss," she assured him.

He wagged a finger at her. "I don't trust you. You come here, taking Miss Benson's place without anything being said to me—which is sus-er-spicious, to say the least of it, and then you immediately spin me this yarn. Not funny." He glared at her, squinting in an effort to keep her in focus. "Not funny at all, young woman. Well—see for myself." Out he marched, and a moment later Laura could hear him shouting: "Madge! Madge!" on the stairs. She sat down, this time in a more comfortable chair, and wondered where the Daimler was and what Mrs. Bulfoss was feeling and how impatient Arthur felt; and then she remembered that Mrs. Whatmore and her Conservative Ladies were probably on the way. It sounded as if a rogue elephant were loose upstairs.

The front door produced its startling fire-alarm ring. Mrs. Whatmore? Too early, Laura decided as she crossed the hall. She could still hear Major Bulfoss upstairs, and it now sounded as if he were looking for Mrs. Bulfoss in all the wardrobes and chests of drawers.

"The Member is in," said a deep voice, "because I saw him arrive." And the man walked straight into the hall without waiting for any invitation to enter. He was an unusual and rather frightening type, dressed in old-fashioned dark clothes; as stiff as if he were made out of wood; and not unlike a small-scale moving and talking version of an Easter Island statue. "The name is Abel Stang," he announced in his pulpit voice. "I wish to see the Member."

"He's rather busy," said Laura, turning into a mere secretary again in this formidable presence.

"I shall not keep him long," Mr. Stang intoned. He needed Covent Garden to do himself justice.

"What's this?" cried Major Bulfoss, glaring over the banister rail. "What's this? Can't see anybody, y'know. Much too busy."

"I have written several letters to you," said Mr. Stang severely, "and sent you some of our pamphlets—"

"Yes, yes, yes, yes. But some other time, my dear sir."

Mr. Stang pointed a very long forefinger, apparently stained yellow by some acid, and now achieved a tone as resonant as six double-basses. "The name is Abel Stang. The subject of the letters and the pamphlets was the Single Tax—"

"Yes, yes, we know all about that—"

"You do not know all about it. You prefer to remain in ignorance of the one measure which, constructively applied, would reduce all our economic problems to mere matters of minor adjustment." It was obvious that Mr. Stang had made use of this tremendous sentence many times before; it rolled out of him without hesitation or flaw, like a superb armored division going into action. "Major Bulfoss, I have challenged you before. Now I challenge you again. The Single Tax—"

"Go away." The Major was almost screaming now.

"The noble efforts of Henry George," Mr. Stang continued.

But the Major came charging down the stairs, blasting Henry George on the way. Whatever his defects might be, lack of courage was not among them, although no doubt the whisky helped. "Outside! Before I kick you out." And he shook his fist about six inches from Mr. Stang's immense Easter Island nose. Laura, who felt like a trembling pigmy, stared at them, fascinated.

"Threats of violence, Major Bulfoss," said Mr. Stang, with an infuriating calm, "have no effect upon me."

"Oh haven't they?" And the Major drew back a little, but not because he was any calmer. "Well, what about this, then?" And he threw himself forward, possibly with the idea of rushing Mr. Stang off his feet. The next moment, without Laura knowing quite how it had happened, the Major was flat on his back; and the moment after, Mr. Stang was calmly putting a pamphlet into her hand. "Read. Digest. Learn. Speak to others," he told her, and then unhurriedly departed.

"Did he hurt you?" she asked, as she tried to help Major Bulfoss to his feet. But he waved her away.

"Not much. Strong as a bull, that chap. Barmy, of course." He limped back into the drawing room and immediately helped himself to another large whisky. Laura wondered whether to tell him that he was drinking too much, but decided against it.

"Now then, Miss—er," said the Major, giving her one of his suspicious squinting glares. "Want the truth about my wife. Gone away? Right. Where?"

"I don't know. Honestly, I don't, Major Bulfoss. I gave you the exact message she gave me."

"Never mind about messages. Don't tell me she packed up and left without saying anything more than that. Couldn't do it. I know Madge." He hesitated a moment, took a quick gurgling drink, then stopped glaring and gave Laura a look of appeal. "Do you think she just went off in a huff—or is it serious?"

"Serious, I'm afraid."

He took a step toward her, offering a close-up of bloodshot bewilderment. His tone dropped to a hoarse whisper. "Think there's a man in it? All right, I can see you know there is." He pondered heavily for a moment. "Good God!—it's that dam' blighter—Arthur Hatchet-Ferrers. Isn't it?"

"It's Arthur Somebody."

"Hatchet-Ferrers. West British Chemicals." The Major nodded slowly, and, as if the situation called for slow-motion, very slowly drained his glass, leaned forward and peered at the decanter, which was almost empty now, and then, like a man giving an exhibition under water, appeared to float out of the room, apparently going in the direction of the pantry. Laura took this opportunity of nipping into the study and putting her typewriter back into its case. Whatever else happened now, letters were out. When she returned to the drawing room, Major Bulfoss, still in slow-motion, was opening a bottle of whisky.

"Do you think you ought to have any more?"

"Yes. Not a drinking man as a rule," he explained very slowly and gravely. "Can take a drink or leave it alone. Ask anybody. But this is different. Very different. You have a drink, eh?"

"No, thank you," said Laura, trying not to sound prim.

"Yes, yes. Small glass of sherry."

"All right, then."

"Help yourself," said the Major, who by this time had already started on the new bottle. He sat down with great care, placed the hand with the glass on one knee and rested the other hand on his other knee, looked darkly at Laura and said slowly: "Arthur Hatchet-Ferrers. A pipsqueak if there ever was one. What does she see in him, tell me that, Miss Lacey."

"Not knowing him, I can't tell you exactly," said Laura, sipping her sherry. "But women are often attracted by men who they think need them badly. Often it's silly, but that's how it works."

He ignored this. "She thinks I don't know him. But I do—met him once—lunch at a club in town. Arthur Hatchet-Ferrers—fat chap—face like an underdone pie—never see fifty again—might be nearer sixty—takes pills with his lunch. Made a packet, no doubt—probably in the war. But what is he? Nothing. Who is he? Nobody. And haven't I said to her, over and over again: 'Just wait, old girl. Be patient, that's all. Title soon—Lady Bulfoss. What's the matter with that? Just back me up, that's all, old girl,' I said. And now just because I've had to be away a lot—in the House—meetings—public service—that sort of thing —no fun, y'know; dashed hard slogging, lot of it—as soon as my back's turned, she goes running off to a fella like Hatchet-Ferrers. Sent a dam' great car for her, eh?"

"Enormous. A hired Daimler, I'd say."

"It'll go on his expense account and he'll get it off tax. That's the way these fellas do it. But women don't know—don't care. All the same to them. Bit of fuss, bit of palaver—and they'll swallow anybody and anything, hook, line and sinker." He did some swallowing himself and came up for air more goggly than ever. But now he was dignified, disillusioned, melancholy. "I don't pretend to be as well-off as Hatchet-Ferrers. Wouldn't think of it. No pretense about me. But within limits—rea-son-nable limits—and I think you'll agree, Miss Er, that there have to be rea-son-nable limits—I've given my wife everything she ever asked for." He waved broadly at the room, and the look he gave it suggested that it was five hundred feet long and crammed with ivory, jade, ropes of pearls. "Everything she ever asked for. Know my brother Beverly?"

"Yes, of course," said Laura. "I work for him."

The Major had to give this a moment's thought. "That's right. Know his wife, my sister-in-law?"

"No, I don't."

"Always been jealous of Madge, my wife. Why? Knew that Madge had only to ask me, and there it was—pronto! Television set last Christmas—no use to me, no time for it, all for her. And what does Beverly's wife get? You can imagine."

"I can. By the way, would you like to ring him up?"

"Certainly not." The Major looked annoyed. "Dam' silly idea. Keep this to ourselves. Sure you don't know where she went? Yes, yes, I know the car was taking her to Hatchet-Ferrers, but he might be anywhere—just kind of chap who would. Old admirer of hers, of course. Known that all along. But after I met him, never took him seriously. Couldn't—fella like that—face like a white elephant's backside—"

"Hasn't he got splendid hazel eyes?" said Laura.

"No, he hasn't," the Major shouted. "Little pig's eyes and big bags under 'em. But *she* told you that, I'll bet my boots. Talking about him while she was packing up to go! No decency. No what-is-it—reticence. Women!"

"Well, what about women?" said Laura, with some asperity and not very wisely.

The Major came up spluttering from the middle of a drink to answer her. "I'll tell you what about women," he bellowed, rising very unsteadily. "And don't answer back. You're too young yet to know what your sex gets up to. Or perhaps you're not, but that doesn't matter. Well, to begin with, most of 'em are a feather-headed bunch of gibbering nitwits. No balance. No judgment. No staying power. No dam' common sense. Don't interrupt. Just listen for once. Learn something. Women! Like a set of spoiled kids. Nowadays they are. Don't say they always were. But now we've gone an' spoiled 'em past mending—"

"I haven't noticed it," said Laura, almost at the top of her voice.

"I said—don't interrupt. I tell you, I've had a hundred times more trouble with women—in business, social life, politics—than I've ever had with men. You know where you are with a man—put your point of view, have a drink or two, and you can get along, barring a few barmy Socialists. But women—and I don't care who they are, what they are, whose side they think they're on, whether they're trying to sell a house, buy a house, use their vote, give a party—they're just a big bloody nuisance—"

"I think you'd better stop now," said Laura, who in spite of the noise Major Bulfoss was making had heard something else.

"Certainly not. Stop when I've finished—an' not before." He glared at her suspiciously. "Where you going?"

"Just opening the door," Laura told him, on her way.

"Leave door alone." But he was too late.

"Well, here we are," cried Mrs. Whatmore, a massive woman with a purple face and a maroon costume. Five other members of the Women's Executive Committee came crowding in after her. "And how are you, Major Bulfoss? Tired?"

He glowered at them, swaying perceptibly. The only sound that came from him was rather like the noise made by a collapsing tire.

The shy smiles had withered from the faces of the five women behind Mrs. Whatmore. Some looked alert, others anxious. But Mrs. Whatmore was still the smiling confident leader, firm but pretending to archness. "I'm sure you must be," she sang in her best contralto. "But not *too* tired, I hope, to receive our little deputation, as you promised, and to admit that you have been a *weeny* bit naughty. Eh?"

Major Bulfoss continued to glower and sway. But the sound now suggested that the tire was being pumped up again. It was too much for Laura, who, with a sense of disaster curling over them all like a great black wave, felt she had stopped breathing.

"Major Bulfoss," she said in a little breathless voice, "hasn't been able to do his letters yet."

If a mouse had popped out and spoken to her, Mrs. Whatmore could not have looked more painfully surprised. "I dare say," she said, with an annihilating glance. Then she turned to the Major again, restoring her broad false smile. "Yes, a *weeny* bit naughty, Major Bulfoss. Because you did agree—didn't you?—to have a regular meeting with our Women's Committee. We women feel there is much more we can do if we have your co-operation, as the Sitting Member, in our efforts. That is so, isn't it?"

"Go home," said the Major.

"I beg your pardon!"

"Go home." This was still said in a tone that was calm and clear, if loud.

The women exchanged looks, and the sight of them doing this blew up any self-control the Major may have had left. He stamped and roared. "Don't stand gaping and twittering there. Just buzz off. Go on. Get cracking."

There were murmurs of dismay and alarm from the supporting five, who began to shuffle backwards; but their redoubtable Chairman stood her ground, and, a brighter purple now, glared back at the Major. "I shall report this to the General Committee," she told him. "In my opinion, Major Bulfoss—and I'm sure these ladies will support me— you're drunk."

A strange smile, the first of any kind Laura had seen him wear so far, illuminated the Major's face, like moonlight on a ruined city. And he spoke now as a man might from such a city, softly, coldly, and with a kind of lunatic precision. "And in *my* opinion, Mrs. Whatmore —and whether anybody supports me is neither here nor there, though a lot of people would if I mentioned it—you're a poisonous old wind-bag. And now—" and the sudden bellow arrived with a grand sense of tone and tempo—"*get out!*"

As they fled, the Major dropped down into his chair, stretched out his legs, and began humming some unrecognizable tune. Then he looked in a glazed fashion at Laura, who was standing in the doorway. "Not you, of course. Do letters—or p'r'aps have a nice drink. Li'l' glass sherry?"

Shaking her head, Laura wondered whether she ought to point out to him that he had loosed upon Farbridge six of the most active and dangerous tongues the town possessed.

"Arthur Hatchet-Ferrers," he muttered, without rancor but in a last spasm of wonder. "Pills for lunch . . . one foot in the grave . . ." He seemed to be dropping off to sleep but he opened his eyes wide for a moment and murmured: "All between ourselves . . . can't have any scandal, eh? . . . Quite right." And then his eyes closed, he slumped farther down in the chair, he grunted, bubbled, and finally began to snore. Wondering what she ought to do now, Laura waited for several minutes. Sometimes she looked at the Major; not a pretty sight, but he appealed to her more in this helpless innocence of sleep than he did when awake. Sometimes she stared at a large Victorian landscape, of an impossible world made of colored cottonwool, that had a grim fascination for her. The Major snored away. Perhaps he was now play-ing cricket, a small boy again, or noticing pretty Madge for the first time at the tennis club. Poor Major Bulfoss!

There was a noise in the hall and then the drawing-room door, which Mrs. Whatmore had slammed behind her, was opened cautiously. A girl with a cheeky fat face looked in. As she stared, Laura made a sign to her and quietly joined her in the hall.

"Looks bottled to me," said the girl.

"He is a bit," said Laura.

"I'll bet it's her," said the girl. "Has she popped off? Knew that's what she was up to. Told Cook, but she wouldn't have it. She owes me two bob now."

"Well," said Laura, "I'm off. I'll get my typewriter."

"What'll happen when he wakes up?" the girl asked, as she followed Laura. "Ructions?"

"Ructions," said Laura softly.

3

Ever since her first few days in Farbridge, Laura had had a bed-sitting room and board at the Saxons', in the end house in Alma Street. Ernest Saxon was the science master at the County School; and his wife, Hilda, had been a teacher too. They had two children, Peter, eleven, and Ann, nine. A despairing woman called Mrs. Foster came in four mornings a week to help. The trouble about Ernest and Hilda, who were kind and sweet, was that you could not laugh at anything with them. They had not a glimmer of humor between them. They could not bother about jokes or nonsense. At the same time, they never looked for, never expected, any kind of magic in things. Before she had met them, Laura had often wondered who the people were who were supposed to listen to and to enjoy all those discussion programs on the wireless, all that arguing and nagging about Industry and Agriculture and Wages and Savings and Science and Councils of Europe and What Was Happening to Youth and The Truth About Bulgaria. Now she knew. It was the Saxons. They could not listen as often as they wished, of course, for both of them had a lot to do; but Laura felt that if they had the Leisure (a favorite word, and there were frequent talks about what people ought to do with it) and a regular supply of dull wholesome food, Hilda and Ernest could have listened happily for hundreds of years. They would listen to plays and music too, but in an anxious sort of way, never for fun and magic but as if at some time they might have to pass an examination on cultural subjects. Mostly they made Laura feel very young and frivolous, although now and again she listened to them and suddenly felt very old and wise, just as if somehow they were really new on this planet whereas she had known it and its tricks for thousands of years. They did not care much about comfort and coziness, preferring coldish rooms and hard chairs, scraggy meals with salads and no appetizing smells, and always discussing rather than talking; but they were immensely kind, without a single evil thought or impulse, and Laura, while she laughed at them, regarded them with both respect and affection. Hilda was rather tall, and had a bony but scrubbed face, a long reddish neck, and enormously wide hips that seemed all wrong. Ernest was smaller, rounder, had a ginger mustache and gold spectacles, and laughed a lot in a serious conscientious sort of way, as if they had taught him to do it at college.

It was typical of Hilda and Ernest that they immediately saw this Bulfoss adventure of hers as a political event. They were discussing it after supper, when the children were in bed and before Hilda and Ernest felt it was time to settle down to grapple with the Third Program.

"And I must say," said Ernest, "that unless you're exaggerating the whole thing, Laura—and I know you *do* exaggerate at times—Bulfoss may be asked to resign."

"That would mean a by-election," said Hilda, delighted at the prospect.

"It would. And this time perhaps the Labour Party could find a better man than Prince. Not a strong candidate, as I said at the time." Ernest was a hard-working supporter of Labour, although critical of it from a Keep-Farther-Left point of view. In fact, he did not like anybody to be farther Left than he was, and considered the Communists to be much nearer the Right.

"I never thought Prince good enough," said Hilda. "A poor speaker. Mrs. Coote would have been much better. Ernest, why don't you suggest Mrs. Coote?"

"Because I doubt if she's sound. Especially," he added, putting on a look that Laura had come to recognize as being bound up mysteriously with international relations, "about Foreign Policy."

"Don't let's get on to Foreign Policy," said Laura. "Please, not tonight."

Ernest smiled indulgently, as he often did with his small daughter, Ann. "As I've pointed out before, my dear Laura, we live in a world—"

"I know, I know," cried Laura. "Atom bombs, hydrogen bombs, biological warfare! You needn't tell me."

"Surely then it's worth discussing?"

"Call it silly if you like—I can't help it—but I always feel that all this discussing and Foreign Policy business just make it worse. I mean, why can't everybody just let it all alone for a few years?" Laura sat up straight and stared hard at a large photograph on the wall. "Yes, I know what you're going to say—but I can't help what I feel. And that is, that the more plotting and fuss and talk and Articles by our Special Correspondent there are, the worse everything becomes. And I can't help feeling too that, for some reason or other, the people who make the most fuss, who are always giving us solemn warnings, are really enjoying it and would hate a world that was quiet and peaceful, perhaps because they wouldn't know what to do in it.

"Perhaps so. Perhaps not," said Ernest, who always said this when he could not be bothered with what you said. "But fundamentally, it resolves itself into a problem of power." He was off now, with Hilda, who was very good and wifely about listening, looking attentive and nodding from time to time. But Laura let her mind wander, and was secretly startled when, as it crossed some vague desert, it encountered the glaring purple image of Mrs. Whatmore. Like a surrealist picture.

"Do you know this Mrs. Whatmore?" she asked them. It was always difficult to pin the Saxons down to people, but worth trying.

Ernest made his laughing noise, a kind of bark. "What a woman! Talk about reactionaries! Used to be Vice-Chairman of the Education Committee. I've had several tussles with her."

Laura tried to imagine Ernest and Mrs. Whatmore tussling, but found it difficult. "Yes, but who is she? Remember, I haven't been here long."

"They're Whatmores, the artificial silk people," said Hilda, who, unlike Ernest, had been brought up in Farbridge and so knew about everybody. "I suppose they're about the richest family in Farbridge. She's been furious for years because she expected her husband to be given a title and he didn't get one."

Ernest made his laughing noise again. Titles indeed!

"That's what everybody says," added Hilda. "I have a friend— you've met her, Laura—Helen Weeks, who's now the personnel manager at Whatmore's; and she knows a lot of gossip about them. Mrs. Whatmore isn't Farbridge. I forget where she came from. He's a bit better—Colonel Whatmore—he was in the army in the First War, with the Farbridge Territorials."

"These colonels," Ernest began.

But Laura, determined to avoid a discussion of militarism, drowned him. "It's odd to think you've been here always. I always keep forgetting it. Very odd."

"What's odd about it?" asked Hilda, reasonably enough.

"Tell me what you really think of it," said Laura.

While Hilda hesitated, Ernest jumped in. "Farbridge is a typical specimen," he began; but Laura would not have it.

"No, Ernest, I don't want any *typical specimen* stuff. Besides, I wasn't asking you. It's Hilda's town, not yours."

Hilda gave her a wide clear look. Hilda's eyes, a lightish hazel, were her best feature. "You know," she said slowly, "I love it. I can see all the faults it has, and I can understand other people, like you and Ernest, not caring about it much, thinking it dull and messy. But it's all mixed up with my life. And I love it. Really love it—as you do a person." And she looked at Ernest now, and he nodded and smiled, not to show that he agreed with her—he had a poor opinion of Farbridge—but perhaps in recognition of a womanly warmth and depth of feeling in her.

"I think that's wonderful," cried Laura. "I wish I felt like that about any place. I do a bit about a village where I used to stay with my grandmother when I was small. But I've moved about too much—like you, Ernest." She hurried on so that he would not break in with some dreary generalization. "I can't make anything out of Farbridge. It doesn't seem to me to have a character at all. It just misses everything. If it were gayer and better-looking, it would begin to be exciting. If it were much uglier and sinister, at least it would be a challenge. But as it is, it isn't anything—and doesn't want to be anything. It's—it's like the food you get at the White Hart and the Oak Nook and other places. You can't exactly say it's bad—it fills you up and you can keep going on it—but it isn't real food. Well, Farbridge is like that to me. It's just a town, a place. I can't hate it, I can't love it. Perhaps," she ended rather mournfully, "I can't really live in it."

It was Ernest's opinion, expressed at some length, that Farbridge represented Edwardian bourgeois values, and that even the working class clung to these values. Ernest could always see people clearly marked out into classes, as if they wore special uniforms. This always puzzled Laura.

Hilda might be Mrs. Ernest Saxon and a discusser, but after all she was a woman too. "You've only been here three months," she told

Laura, smiling but a little sharp, "and nothing has happened to you yet."

"How do you mean that nothing has happened to her?" Ernest demanded. "She's spent nearly a hundred days here—"

"No," said Laura, ignoring Ernest, who was not really on in this scene. "Nothing's happened. And nothing will. It's that kind of place —I mean, for me it is," she added hastily.

It was at that moment that Eric Longshaw arrived. But as his voice was heard greeting Ernest in the hall, Laura exhibited no symptoms either of confusion or excitement, and clearly there was nothing about this arrival that seemed to her to contradict anything she had said. Indeed, she muttered hastily to Hilda: "You see what I mean? Eric."

Eric Longshaw, who worked in the South Midland Bank, where Laura had first made his acquaintance, was Laura's most persistent admirer. She could not help feeling grateful to him for this devotion, and sometimes, when she thought little of herself, being rather touched by it. As if a melancholy talking dog had attached itself to her. At the same time she often felt impatient with him because he was merely Eric Longshaw, and not some wonderful man quite different from Eric and impossible to imagine in the South Midland Bank, a man whose very presence would strike the rock and release the miraculous waters of her own admiration and devotion. There were even moments when she found herself disliking poor Eric because he seemed then to be the reality mocking her vague dreams. Even while he shrank from her glares and snubs and jeers—unlike the dream figures, who had a short way with such rubbish—his very persistence made him formidable, rather sinister: it was like a cold coming on. Sometimes, in the middle of the night, there seemed no escape. Sooner or later she would have to take Eric and settle down in Farbridge. Not that there was anything really wrong with Eric. Joyce and Myrtle, the other girls at Bulfoss and Sons (for you could not count old Miss Thring as a girl), would have jumped at him. He was rather tall, if not very wide; almost handsome in a dim way; polite, considerate, not stupid; and was said to be doing well at the Bank. But then Laura did not want a young man who was said to be doing well at a bank.

Grinning, Ernest ushered him in. So far as anybody or anything really could be a joke to Ernest, Eric was one, partly because he was Laura's admirer, and partly because Ernest, with whom Eric hardly ever ventured to argue, regarded him as a weak-kneed wobbly reactionary, a groggy specimen of the Capitalist class. Hilda, who was not above matchmaking, was well disposed toward Eric and saw him married to Laura and then rapidly converted to the Saxon point of view.

"I thought I'd just look in," said Eric in his cautious way. "Rather cold out." He produced his very respectable cigarette case and offered it round. Ernest did not smoke cigarettes but made a continual nuisance of himself with a mixture of shag and coltsfoot in one of three filthy little pipes. Laura and Hilda each accepted a cigarette, and a light from Eric's neat little lighter, which, like Eric, never went wrong. Both Hilda and Eric smoked in the same way, very carefully, as if the cigarette might blow up. Laura always puffed hard. She did not really enjoy smoking but sometimes enjoyed the idea of herself smoking. Ernest, in his cloud of shag and coltsfoot, now turned himself into the sardonic Thinker. He asked some of his usual questions about the Bank, and Eric replied in his customary polite but noncommittal fashion. It was all very dull.

Finally the talk came round to the Festival of Britain. Some months before, the Farbridge Council had rejected the proposal that the town should do anything special about the Festival. The Council had declared, through a large majority, that Farbridge could not afford to celebrate the Festival. Laura knew all about this because here the Saxons for once had not agreed. Ernest had jeered at the idea of a Festival but he had jeered equally hard at the Council's decision not to spend any money on it. Though severely economical himself, Ernest always seemed to think that public bodies should spend money like drunken sailors. Hilda felt that here was an opportunity for more culture, with the Third Program materialized and let loose in the street, and so had been in favor of the Festival idea; but, remembering the rates, she would not join Ernest in jeering at the Council.

"Old Jordan," said Eric, "was in the Bank this morning. He told me that some of them are trying to persuade the Mayor and the Town Clerk to push something through about the Festival. But of course it's too late now."

"Months and months too late," said Ernest, delighted to point this out. "Not that it matters, except that it just shows you what idiots these chaps are. Couldn't afford it!"

"Well, it wouldn't have been easy," said Hilda.

"However, this country's got more important things to think about and to do than fooling around with festivals."

"Quite so," said Eric.

"I don't see it," said Laura.

"And it might have been very pleasant." Hilda looked wistful. "Some good drama, music, exhibitions of modern art, and lectures."

"Oh—would there have to be lectures?" cried Laura. "That's not my idea of a festival—lectures."

"What's wrong with lectures?" said Ernest.

"I suppose there's nothing wrong with them, just as there's nothing wrong with algebra or Commercial Spanish or First-Aid Training. But they don't seem to me part of a festival. If I'm festifying, then I don't want lectures."

"I doubt," said Eric cautiously, "if most people round here want a Festival. At least, that's my impression."

Hilda and Ernest agreed, and Eric looked rather smug.

"They may not want one," said Laura, "but—by golly—they need one. And not the lecturing kind either."

"Lecturing is just what they do need," said Ernest. "They don't know enough. That's what's the matter with most people here."

Eric thought so too.

"And I don't agree," cried Laura, rather crossly. "Not knowing enough—in your sense—isn't what's wrong with people. What's wrong with us now is that we don't *feel* enough. Life ought to be wonderful, and now for most people it isn't."

"It never was," said Ernest, who would never keep quiet long, although there was nothing ill-tempered about his interruptions. "You read—"

But Laura cut in sharply: "I know. Mountains of miseries. And now we've got penicillin and pensions. But it's what people feel inside themselves that I'm thinking about. And even all their betting and boozing and sex are dreary, just another kind of routine."

"That may be." This was Ernest again, of course. "But—well—though I grumble a lot—I must say I enjoy my life. Eh, Hilda?"

"Yes, dear, I think you do."

"And I believe you do, Ernest," said Laura, who knew he did. "But you're rather a special case, I think. A lot of things now that don't suit other people are just your cup of tea. Anyhow, the point is, if festivals will break this dreary routine, then let's have festivals."

"But suppose we can't afford it?" said Hilda.

"Exactly," said Eric, nodding like an Oriental sage a hundred years old. But there in the Bank, of course, Eric knew what hundreds of people could or could not afford.

They made Laura feel desperate. "Well, suppose we can't afford to be sensible much longer? What if we're all busy wasting something much more important than money and materials and labor?" She flashed a look all round. "What if we've stopped understanding the kind of people we are?"

"If the community," Ernest began heavily.

But Laura had jumped up. "Sorry, Ernest, but I want a walk." She turned to Eric, now rising hopefully. "Like a walk, Eric?"

His delight brought back that familiar mixture of shame and irritation. This dull little walk, just so much fresh air before going to bed, would be magic for him—poor Eric—blast him!

A coldish night, indigo, spacious, with a remote glitter of stars. They went the length of Alma Street, then along Inkerman Place, through a mid-Victorian bit of Farbridge to which electricity and the B.B.C. Light Program had been added. They turned into Baldwin Road, one of the town's main thoroughfares that had been reconstructed between the wars. It had an up-to-date urban look. The Elite Cinema sparkled down the road, as if a hundred feet of Los Angeles had been dropped there. The King's Head, a big bogus pub, was pretending to look as cozy as a Christmas card. A dazzle of white light and stainless metal, like a quick glimpse of an operating theater, was Barker's Fish Restaurant. The furniture shop at the corner was still lighting up a foul bedroom suite in lilac and gamboge oak. At the North Farbridge Social Club they were holding a dance, spilling into the night the melancholy *thump-a-thump* of American folk music.

"When you hear them like this, those dance bands," said Laura as they walked past, "they always sound so damned sad."

Eric agreed. He agreed with everything she said. If she had attacked the South Midland Bank—and she had half a mind to try it—he would have agreed with her. Poor Eric! But why wasn't he somebody else? But who, for instance? There was a young man somewhere—perhaps a hundred young men, which was somehow a humiliating thought—who could probably switch on the magic for her too. A huge Saturday night sadness descended upon Laura. They passed a little pub that sounded like a zoo at feeding time.

"You can't really blame people for downing a lot of double gins they can't afford," said Laura unhappily.

"In a way you can't." Eric was making a cautious Bank job out of this. "But then again—"

"Yes, I know, Eric. Let's go back, shall we?" She squeezed his arm, and was annoyed to find it tighten excitedly, and then was annoyed with herself for being annoyed.

"Would you," he inquired humbly, "like to do anything tomorrow?"

"I can't think of anything at the moment, Eric," she said, restraining an impulse to make his hair stand on end by telling him a hundred daft things she would like to do. "I've a lot of silly things I must do at home. Things like washing my hair, and bits of ironing, and odd chores."

All the way home, Eric, who had been made treasurer of the Mayton Park Tennis Club, explained very sensibly but at wearying length some crisis at the club in which he had neatly put that nuisance, Miss Rawson, in her place. Laura thought about Saturdays, Sundays, various people, the Festival of Britain, her father, Central America, ships and the sea, the Milky Way, and God. After receiving a peck on the cheek from a trembling Eric, she went indoors and found the Saxons sipping cocoa and up to their necks in a Greek play on the Third Program, with a lot of refined persons intoning and moaning. She accepted a slice of cake, and took it up to bed.

4

Sunday morning had a steely flashing look that suggested a northeast wind and possible sleet later on. But the Saxons, who were above discomfort, had decided on a country walk and a picnic; so Laura had the house to herself. She washed her hair, did some ironing, and dusted her room, for Mrs. Foster was not only desperate but careless; after that she crouched in front of her gasfire reading the *Sunday Times* and the *Observer*. She was just beginning to wonder what she ought to try her hand at for lunch—it was then about noon—when she heard the front door bell ringing. Putting a short coat over her slacks and then tying a scarf round her head as she went downstairs, she answered this summons. It was Major Bulfoss, pouchy but still pink.

"Morning, Miss Casey. Like a word or two with you. Had some trouble getting your address." He said this as if it were her fault. Evidently he was going to take a high line. But whatever line he proposed to take, it was obviously better that he should do it indoors; so she ushered him into the Saxons' sitting room, which at that moment was about as cozy as a poached egg in a refrigerator.

Major Bulfoss looked about him with gloomy distaste. "Bit cheerless, isn't it?"

"Yes," said Laura. "But it isn't my house. I just have a room here."

The Major sat down, lit a cigarette, looked at it with some surprise, as if it were a new kind with quite a different flavor, cleared his throat, then looked at Laura.

"Look here, Miss Casey." He paused a moment. "What exactly happened last night?"

"Well, after telling Mrs. Whatmore she was a poisonous old windbag and telling all of them to get out, you fell asleep; and then, as your maid had come back, I cleared out. I couldn't see any point in staying."

"No, no, quite so. Made rather an ass of myself, eh?"

"I don't know, Major Bulfoss. I'm just telling you what happened."

"Humph!" He cleared his throat again. "Rather a strain, y'know, being in the House these days. Late nights—all that sort of thing. Tells on a chap. Then I'd had a good lunch and a few drinks on the train. Might happen to anybody. And then this business about my wife. Look here—did you tell me she'd gone off to Arthur Hatchet-Ferrers?"

Laura nodded. "Though I didn't know he was Mr. Hatchet-Ferrers. You supplied that bit."

The Major frowned. "Needn't be funny about it, y'know. Had a notion last night you were being funny about it."

"That was when you couldn't believe Mrs. Bulfoss had really gone."

"All right, needn't go into that. Point is—no joke, y' know. I mean, the whole thing's pretty serious. Particularly for a man in my position. By the way," and now he looked apologetic, "haven't such a thing as a drink here, have you?"

"Cider."

"Good God, no." He shuddered. "Look the sort of people who would drink cider. I've got my car outside. Would you like me to run you as far as the White Hart, and then we could continue our talk there?"

"No, I shouldn't."

"Any particular reason, Miss Casey?"

"Yes. My hair isn't dry yet. I'm not dressed for the White Hart. And anyhow I think it's a bad idea."

Major Bulfoss gave her a schoolboy grin. "You wouldn't if you were me." Then, fatally, he remembered who he was, or who he thought he was. "All right, we stay here. Shan't keep you long. But wanted to remind you there's such a thing as loyalty."

Laura stared at him. "I'm not running round the town talking about you, if that's what you mean, Major Bulfoss."

"Told these people probably, haven't you?"

"I couldn't help telling them some of it. Their name's Saxon, by the way."

"Teacher chap? Heckled me at one of my meetings. Why, he's a redhot Socialist. You a Socialist, Miss Casey?"

"No. I think I'm an Anarchist. And that comes of living with Socialists and working for Conservatives."

"Give you one word of advice. Not about this business—though it comes into it—but generally. Better watch that tongue of yours. My brother mentioned that when I spoke to him this morning about you. He doesn't care for it. Said he'd been meaning to speak to you about it himself. But I said: 'Look here, never mind about that. I'll just put it to her on the ground of loyalty.' That's what I said. And that's what I'm doing, Miss Casey."

"Major Bulfoss," cried Laura, sparkling and flushing, "I'd no intention of talking to people about you and your affairs. I'm not that sort of person. But it's nothing to do with any loyalty to Bulfoss and Sons. I haven't any loyalty to Bulfoss and Sons."

"You haven't, eh?"

"No, why should I? You talk as if I'd been with them for years. I've only been here three months. I only came here because I happened to run into a girl called Potter I'd known in the Wrens, and she was leaving your office to get married, and said the job was going if I wanted a change from London, which I did—God knows. And if Mr. Beverly Bulfoss doesn't like the way I talk, he'd better speak to me about it. As a matter of fact, I don't like the way *he* talks."

"Look here, don't be cheeky."

"I'm not being any cheekier than you are," said Laura, in a temper now. "I did my best for you last night—and if you'd come round this morning and simply said you'd been an idiot and would I keep quiet about it, I'd have said of course I would. But what's all this about loyalty and watching my tongue—whatever that means—and Mr. Bulfoss talking to me about it? What's the idea?"

"The idea is—you talk too much and in the wrong way. And," the

Major added, pushing himself out of his chair, not without a grimace, "you're doing it now."

There was a noise outside, and Laura went to the window to see what was happening. An angry little car had arrived, and out of it sprang a tubby man, mistakenly dressed in golfing tweeds. He charged into the house as if he owned it and had just heard it was on fire. Before Laura could reach the sitting-room door, he had opened it and bounced in. He wore no hat, was very red and almost bald, and appeared to be steaming. Laura hastily stepped back, as if from a smoking bomb.

"Captain Mobbs, Conservative agent," he shouted. "Where's Major Bulfoss? Ah—there you are. My godfathers!"

He sat down, put his little fat legs together, and then with both hands began drumming hard on his little fat thighs. Beads of sweat gathered on his forehead and ran down his pendulous cheeks. He took out an enormous yellow handkerchief and mopped himself with it. Laura stared at him, fascinated.

"Glad you found me, Mobbs." But Major Bulfoss sounded uneasy. "Meant to get in touch with you sometime today."

Captain Mobbs came out of his yellow handkerchief. "Meant to get in touch with me sometime!" he shouted. "I heard the yarn out at the West Farbridge Golf Club. Drove like hell to your house. Drove like hell to your brother's house. Drove like hell here, where they said you were calling. Dropped everything—bang! Now then."

But Major Bulfoss was glaring at Laura. "You see? Can't keep quiet, and already it's all over the place—West Farbridge Golf Club."

"*Me* keep quiet?" Laura was furious. "Do you realize you insulted all the most prominent members of the Conservative Women's Executive Committee? Of course it's all over the town."

Captain Mobbs jumped up and seemed to do a stepdance. "My godfathers! So it's true, then? Mrs. Whatmore?"

"Mrs. Whatmore."

"Who were the others?"

"I don't remember," the Major told him sulkily.

"You know?" And he looked at Laura, who noticed now that his piggy little eyes were hot too.

"I don't know," she said, "and I don't care."

Captain Mobbs plumped down again and this time patted one thigh very hard, like a dairyman with butter. "Who does care? Just tell me that. Who does care? Only the Agent. Only poor Captain Bloody Mobbs, that's all. Only the man who sweated his guts out working miracles in this division. That's all. Does the Member care? Does his girl friend care?"

"I'm not his girl friend," said Laura hastily.

"Beside the point, beside the point," said Captain Mobbs, drumming away again with both hands. "Question now is—what's to be done. And we must work fast. Mrs. Bulfoss ought to be seeing those women now. Telling 'em you've worked so hard you're on the edge of a nervous breakdown. Long days—late nights—all devoted to the interests of Farbridge Conservatives, especially the women. That's the line. To a man in such a state of nervous exhaustion a drink or two can tip him over the edge. Don't do it yourself. Get her to run round—anxious wife, no sleep. Might get a doctor's certificate. I'd better talk to her myself."

"You can't."

"Why not?"

"She's away."

"All right then," yelled Captain Mobbs, who seemed to have no respect for his Member. "Get her back. Ring her up at once. Where is she—and what's the number?"

"Look here, Mobbs, will you kindly stop shouting at me? And anyhow this wife business is out."

"Out? It's the only possible move. Did it years ago when Pensworth-Jones, who was Member then for South Burmanley, got stinking paralytic at the annual ball."

"Well, you can't work it this time," said the Major gloomily. "The fact is, Mobbs, between ourselves, my wife's left me."

"Left you?"

"Yes, for another chap."

Captain Mobbs, who was extraordinarily good value, like a super-mechanical toy, now made a moaning sound, closed his eyes, and rocked violently.

"So there it is, Mobbs. Didn't expect it, of course. No idea it would happen. Quite a shock. That's why I had a few more drinks."

It was as if somebody had pressed another button. Captain Mobbs stopped rocking, opened his eyes, and jumped up. "And that's the line we take. Only possible line."

"What—and tell everybody?"

"Tell these women. Wife ran away. Probably in Paris now—champagne, flowers, new clothes, jewelry bought with black market francs —all sense of duty forgotten—to hell with Farbridge. That might work."

"Why should it?" said the Major, who was evidently not in the picture.

"They'll be jealous. Be on your side. Poor Major Bulfoss—that woman let him down badly—we mustn't be too hard on him now. That's what they'll tell each other and everybody else? Eh?" He turned to Laura for confirmation.

"Yes, that's how it might work," she admitted.

"Would with you, eh?"

"No, it wouldn't. But we're not talking about me."

"No, what we're doing is wasting time. Come on, Bulfoss. We'll go to my office first. Then ring up Mrs. Whatmore, arrange to see her, and find out who the others were. Need an aspirin? Or a drink? Both at the office. Come on." And out he went, charging back to his car, banging the door and the gate.

Major Bulfoss lingered a moment, no doubt feeling that he had to assert himself with somebody. He gave Laura a hostile look. "Just remember what I said."

"What was that?"

"Look here—that won't do. You know very well. Loyalty—and that sort of thing." He made a movement with his lips as if tasting something unpleasant. "Devil of a head this morning—otherwise I'd have put that little blighter Mobbs in his place."

Over a sketchy sort of lunch that did not turn out too well, Laura brooded darkly over Bulfoss and Sons, with special reference to the senior partner, Mr. Beverly Bulfoss. She had a feeling now that her relations with Mr. Bulfoss, never very happy, would soon rapidly deteriorate. And after lunch, in the huge emptiness of the afternoon, darkened by clouds heavy with sleet, she went to the length of finding the last issue of the *Farbridge Weekly Record* and staring sleepily at its two columns of *Situations Vacant*. If there were any openings for cheeky secretaries who answered back, they had not been mentioned to the *Weekly Record*. Hailstones rattled at the windows, trying to get at her. She felt very small, lonely, and longed passionately to be making tea and toast for some huge smiling man who adored her.

5

Laura had never settled down with Bulfoss and Sons. At the end of the first week there she had realized that it had been a mistake to accept the job, but out of loyalty to her ex-Wren chum, whose place in the office she had taken, she felt she could not walk out so soon, and after that she had hung on because nothing more attractive offered itself. Laura was very ambitious about life itself, fiercely demanding a great deal from it, as if promises had been made to her at birth and so far had not been kept; but like many quite intelligent girls who learn shorthand and typing she was not ambitious about her work and tended to drift into any job that was going. But she cared about the atmosphere of a place and the kind of people she had to work with; and at Bulfoss' neither of them was right. It gave her no pleasure at all to help on this business of estate agenting, valuing, and auctioneering. Clearly somebody had to do it, but Laura soon discovered it was not for her. And the people there were not her sort. Joyce Benson, now down with flu, was pleasant enough in her own dim fashion; but Myrtle Tetlow was a silly girl, one of the silliest girls Laura had ever known. It was like working with an enormous hen. Miss Thring, a short, thick, spectacled woman, who had been there for ages, was essentially the Old Retainer, who saw the universe revolving round Bulfoss and Sons. She regarded Laura as a flippant and untrustworthy type who would never make a good Bulfossian. Then there was Percy Fitch, who had just been made a junior partner and was doing most of the work that Major Bulfoss did before he became a Member of Parliament. He had modeled himself on the Bulfoss brothers, roughly combining some of Beverly's gentility with the military brusqueness of Major Bulfoss, and adding to the mixture a rather cheap sauce of his own. He took all but the most important auctions now, and Laura could imagine that he had a rattling good time with them. He was assisted by a faded old clerk called Linny, like a ghost in a shiny dark suit: probably the real Linny died years ago. And at the head of them all, the presiding genius, was Beverly Bulfoss.

Before she met Mr. Bulfoss, Laura, idly looking at advertisements, had often wondered who lived in the strange world they seemed to describe, a world of gentleman's residences all tastefully arranged and replete with all possible conveniences and comforts, with Morning Rooms opening into Libraries and giving onto Magnificent Terraces and Well-Stocked Gardens, with Ornamental Staircases leading from Ornate Halls by way of Superb Landings to no fewer than eight Master Bedrooms. Now she knew. It was Beverly Bulfoss, Esquire. He was at heart, she felt, a cunning old meanie. But this was glossed over with a marzipan paste of old-world gentility, tastefully replete with every effective mannerism. He was like a repertory actor playing a straight Earl. His appearance was just right, for he was tall and thin and had a long bony face. His clothes artfully suggested both the businessman and the country squire. He had a high whinnying voice, as if a horse had once found its way into the family. His manner with well-to-do women, whether they came to buy or sell, was perfect. If they came to buy and he had to defend high prices, he made them feel that an aristocratic tradition was still keeping at bay the snarling lower orders. If they came to sell and he had to excuse low prices, he created an atmosphere in which they felt they were comtesses and princesses during the French and Russian revolutions. When he told them a mortgage could be arranged, he seemed to be gently interposing a carpet between a silk petticoat and the mud. He handed over an Order To View as if it were a *laisser-passer* for the Captain of the Swiss Guard at Versailles. It was impossible to imagine him asking for bids for *Lot 231: Bedroom Toilet Set (damaged) together with One Set Fire Irons, Black Rug, Three Blankets.*

On Monday morning he never arrived in the office, and Laura wondered whether Captain Mobbs—and she could not help liking Captain Mobbs, although Ernest, when he returned later on Sunday, had denounced him with unusual ferocity—had swept him into his campaign for restoring the prestige of Major Bulfoss with the Conservative Women's Executive Club. But on Monday afternoon, as Miss Thring announced with pride and joy, a very important client was coming to see Mr. Bulfoss, who certainly could not fail her. This was Lady Barth, a rich old barmpot who, probably because she had nothing else to do, was always either buying and selling property or threatening to buy and sell it. She had tremendous rows with everybody, from neighboring landowners to the Ministry of Town and Country Planning; and every few weeks she stumped in and out of the office, screeching like a giant cockatoo. She was deaf herself, and apparently thought everybody else was. She was due at three on Monday afternoon, and at five minutes to three Mr. Bulfoss arrived, in a flurry and obviously perturbed. At five past, Lady Barth's ancient Rolls-Royce came sailing up; and out she popped like a jangling old witch.

No door could have been more firmly closed than the door of Mr. Bulfoss' private office. But Lady Barth's screech came through it like a circular saw. "Heard at lunch your brother's making an ass of himself."

Mr. Bulfoss undoubtedly had to raise his voice to make himself heard, but he contrived to keep it on his side of the door. Perhaps, Laura thought, he bent down and mouthed it carefully into her ear.

"Well, what if she did?" was the next installment from Lady Barth. "Seemed a silly little woman to me. He's well rid of her. But I never understood why he had to go into Parliament. Why didn't he stay here and do some work? Oh—of course, he's better than these colliers and engine-drivers who call themselves politicians now. Just to plunder us. Downright robbery! But now—what about that miserable fellow who works for the County Council? Told you what he wrote to me, didn't I?"

Laura overheard nothing else for several minutes because she had to rescue Myrtle from a telephone message. Myrtle could hold long private talks on the telephone, but any business call always found her bewildered and halfway to tears. "They always sound so *serious*," she complained once to Laura. "And then I get all flustered and don't understand what they mean."

Then Lady Barth was yelling like a madwoman. "You're shuffling, Bulfoss. Wriggling and shuffling. Are you on my side, man, or aren't you? Stop beating about the bush. I know very well you're not a solicitor—I'm not an idiot. When I need a lawyer, I know where to find several excellent men—men who understand their business, which seems to me more than I can say of you." She came jangling and screeching out, followed by a scarlet Mr. Bulfoss, vainly expostulating, his usual character performance in ruins.

"Miss Thring," said Mr. Bulfoss sharply, on his return. "Speak to you in my room. Important."

"Now what's up?" said Myrtle, when Miss Thring, trembling with anxiety and importance, had waddled out. "There's something up, y'know. Felt it all day. Haven't you noticed?"

Laura said she had.

"So have I," continued Myrtle. "Felt it ever since this morning. Went to the Grand last night with a terrible boy—the one with curly hair in the music department at Crawley's—wouldn't keep his hands to himself a minute. Aren't they awful? 'Oh, for goodness' sake, do stop it,' I said. Last time he takes me to the pictures. How do you get on with that chap in the Bank?"

"We're just friendly."

"That's what you say. But he's ever so nice, isn't he?" Myrtle brought out a sigh that shook her overripe bosom. "Why can't I find one like that? I mean, a nice quiet gentlemanly chap—steady and all that—and not one of these all-in wrestlers like that boy last night."

"You're too luscious, Myrtle. Nature overdid it a bit with you, and then you piled it on yourself. If you go round looking like two big helpings of turkey and Christmas pudding, you must expect to attract the hungry types and perhaps put off those who aren't quite so hungry. So either you ought to let it rip, which I wouldn't advise in Farbridge, or try cutting down the sex appeal."

"There's no need to talk like that," said Myrtle sulkily.

"Sorry, Myrtle, I wasn't trying to be unpleasant."

"Besides, I do meet some interesting chaps. Like that one I told you about who travels in wines and spirits. Married of course. They nearly always are—when you can get it out of them. Huffy too if you ask 'em about their wives. But very interesting. Witty too, some of 'em. I'll bet that Eric Who's-it at the Bank isn't very witty."

"No, I wouldn't call him very witty."

"Do you think our Percy's witty?"

"No," Laura replied decisively. She knew all about Percy Fitch's wit and humor, and, in fact, regarded them as one of the drawbacks of the job.

"That's because you don't know him like I do. Sometimes he's a scream."

"I don't like screams."

"In a way," said Myrtle reflectively, staring at Laura with her swimming foolish cow's eyes, "you're very conceited, aren't you?"

Laura was startled. "Am I? It never occurred to me."

"In a way you are. One or two people have said that to me about you. I suppose it's because you've lived in London and traveled about to different places—abroad and all that. Anyhow, I never see why you came here—not having anything to do with Farbridge and not knowing anybody here. Why did you?"

"I don't know, Myrtle. A sudden impulse. I thought a town like this, not too big and easy to get out of into the country, might be a nice change after London. I'd got so tired of queues and crowded buses and tube trains and millions of people all looking so worried. And my father had gone away again, and I hadn't any close friends left in London—and—oh—I'd just had enough of it."

"Smashing shops and shows, though. That's what I'd like. And plenty of chaps to choose from, all taking you out. Didn't they take *you* out?"

"Yes, sometimes. But if they had enough money to do it properly, I nearly always found I didn't like them very much—and it was a nuisance pretending I did. Or if they hadn't enough money, then it got embarrassing, and I felt sorry for them, and then they were cross or sulky because they knew I felt sorry for them."

"Touchy, that's right," said Myrtle, contemplating the mystery of the male. "Talk about us, we're not in it with *them*. One wrong word —and they're off. Terribly touchy. My two brothers are just the same. Mum and me have to laugh sometimes. I've seen us—"

But this was never to be revealed. At that moment Miss Thring returned, loaded down with responsibility, already careworn with it, and told Myrtle to take her work out to the counter of the Inquiries Room. "I wish to speak privately to Miss Casey," she added, for the benefit of both girls.

"Mr. Bulfoss will see you in a few minutes," she told Laura, standing very close to her, so close indeed that Laura was engulfed by the musty smell, like that of a second-hand clothes shop, that Miss Thring carried about as part of her private atmosphere. "I wanted to have a word or two with you first."

Laura disliked Miss Thring, but now, looking at the faded red-rimmed eyes magnified by the thick glasses, she felt sorry for her. "Yes, what's the matter, Miss Thring?" she said gently.

"I don't know if you remember," said Miss Thring, softly and very carefully, "but I was talking on the telephone this morning to Miss Slingsby of Porritt and Worsnop, Birmingham. And as a matter of fact she was telling me how shorthanded they are in their office. Of course they don't do the class of business we do. Hardly any County work. But it might suit you, Miss Casey."

"Are you telling me I ought to go and work in Birmingham?" Laura was bewildered.

"I believe a word from me to Miss Slingsby would be quite sufficient," said Miss Thring, with some complacency.

"I dare say it would. But I don't want to go to Birmingham."

Miss Thring closed her eyes. "I'm only trying to help you, Miss Casey."

"I don't get this. Wait a minute! Does it mean that Bulfoss wants to get rid of me?"

Miss Thring opened her eyes and now they looked like gray peas. "If you wish to continue in Estate Agency work—"

"Oh—blow Estate Agency work!" cried Laura rudely.

"I was only going to say—that if you wished to continue in Estate Agency work, then a recommendation from Bulfoss and Sons to Porritt and Worsnop would carry great weight. Without it, of course—well, that's a very different thing. And I think I ought to add—and one of my closest friends is Miss Thurston at the Ministry of Labour office here, so I know something about it—that if you want to stay in Farbridge, you'll probably find it difficult—*very* difficult indeed—to obtain another post. Which is why I mentioned Miss Slingsby and—"

"I know," Laura broke in, "and Porritt and Worsnop of Birmingham. Well, you've said your piece. Now I'm going to talk to Mr. Bulfoss."

"He hasn't sent for you yet," cried Miss Thring in alarm.

"I'm going to talk to him without being sent for."

When Laura dashed in—and the only way was to dash in—Mr. Bulfoss raised his long gray head and then raised his short gray eyebrows. "I don't remember ringing for you, Miss Casey."

Any shakiness she might have felt was now swept away by a further flood of indignation. Coming the grand manner over her, was he, the old phony!

"No, but I had to see you at once." She looked at him steadily, though feeling far from steady inside.

Mr. Bulfoss now raised the whole of himself and contrived to look down on Laura as if he were about fifty feet tall. "I understood that Miss Thring wanted to talk to you before I did."

"She has talked to me," said Laura. "Birmingham."

"I know nothing about Birmingham." He fingered his mustache in an important sort of way, as if he were about to sell the Suez Canal. "But I gathered that Miss Thring might have some helpful suggestion to make to you."

"Well, she wants to pack me off to Birmingham. For some reason or other," she added pointedly.

"There's no mystery about that, Miss Casey," he told her acidly. "Miss Thring has known for some time that I've not been satisfied with your work here. She felt herself you were not settling down with us. When Miss Potter, who'd been with us for several years, recommended you for her post and told us she'd known you in the—er—Service—Wrens, wasn't it?—we decided to give you a trial. It was a little experiment, and unfortunately it didn't succeed. We've known it for some time, and so, I think, have you, Miss Casey. There's nothing personal in all this," he continued, much pleasanter now and even trying to smile. "But obviously our kind of work isn't what you want. If Miss Thring, who's had great experience, very great experience, thinks you'd be better suited to—er—a firm like Porritt and Worsnop—those are the people she had in mind, I imagine, if she mentioned Birmingham—then I'm delighted to hear it. And I advise you to take advantage of her suggestion. Porritt and Worsnop are good people, in their way—and you'd probably like Birmingham —large city, lots for young people to do there. On the other hand, as no doubt Miss Thring told you, Farbridge isn't expanding—local business conditions are not too favorable—so that even if you wanted to stay here—and I can't imagine why you should—you would find it difficult to obtain a suitable post."

Mr. Bulfoss then sat down, looked severely at some papers on his desk, and did not glance again in Laura's direction until he noted, once more with the eyebrows well raised, that she too was sitting down. Not only was she tired of standing, but now her knees felt wobbly.

"What that amounts to," she said slowly, "is that you want me to go."

"We shall pay you for this week. But you needn't stay here, and I strongly advise you not to stay, but either to accept Miss Thring's suggestion or to begin immediately and look outside Farbridge for another post. If you dislike Birmingham, then you ought to go back to London. Your home's there, I understand."

"My home's not anywhere," said Laura, and suddenly, to her annoyance, she felt like crying.

"I shall be glad to give you a reference. That is, if you behave sensibly."

"How do you think you're behaving?"

"I beg your pardon!" It was not so much the question as her tone of voice and flashing eye that shook him.

"Like a mean stinker."

They jumped up together, both glaring now.

"I guessed this was coming," cried Laura, drowning some spluttering protest he was making, "from something your brother said yesterday morning. Only you couldn't have done it a worse way. If you'd said: 'Look, Major Bulfoss made an idiot of himself on Saturday when you were there, so now please forget about it all, will you?'— then I'd have been glad to. I don't like telling tales, and anyhow I was really rather sorry for the poor Major. But now you've torn it, you and silly old Thring between you. I wouldn't have minded if you'd just been honest and told me it embarrassed you having me around, after Saturday. But all this smooth false muck about not being satisfied with my work here, offers of Birmingham, threats about references, warnings about no other jobs going here—it just makes me sick. All right then—I'm sacked, and I'm going—now." She hurried to the door, but turned for one last word. "But don't think I'm leaving Farbridge. Because I'm *not*."

She bumped into Miss Thring, who had probably been listening just outside the door, but she ignored her and hurried blindly to collect her things. Percy Fitch, back from his sale, was guffawing over some story with Myrtle. Laura ignored them too. If they said anything to her, she did not hear them. On her way out, however, as she made haste to have a good little cry somewhere in private, she ran into poor old Linny, the ghost.

"Here, miss, what's the matter?" he said, peering at her.

She had to tell somebody, and he would do, poor old thing. "Had a row. Got the sack. Been calling Bulfoss names."

"Go on! Here," he whispered, "what names?"

"I called him a mean old stinker."

"You didn't!"

"I did."

A most astonishing smile illuminated Linny's face, transforming him at once from a ghost into a man. "I'd have given five quid to have heard it. Ten quid if I had it. Here—one day I'll tell you what this lot did to me—cruel! And good luck, miss! All the bloody best!"

6

That was how Laura Casey, in the middle of the following Wednesday morning, came to be sitting, alone, at a lopsided gate-legged table in the far corner of the Old Oak Nook in Peter Place, Farbridge. The café was crowded with middle-class matrons and their daughters, together with a sprinkling of businessmen, all so desperate in these times that by eleven o'clock they had temporarily abandoned the struggle to survive and were now consuming morning coffee, cakes, and cigarettes. Laura herself, hunched over her almost empty coffee cup, was smoking like an angry little engine. She looked as if she had turned her back not only upon the Old Oak Nook but also upon all Farbridge.

A voice broke through her indignant reverie. "May I sit here, please?" it inquired.

This voice spoke softly, humbly, but in a full baritone, hinting at a great sounding board of a chest. And Laura, as she looked up and nodded, saw that this was a very large young man indeed, almost a giant. As he descended massively into one of the other two chairs, she also discovered that he was very handsome. He had bronze hair, sun-bleached in places to a pale gold, and all of it much lighter than his face, which was deeply tanned. But what was odd and at the same time very attractive about him was the quality of his eyes. These were set queerly, and of a mahogany shade, yet not hard but soft and darkly clear. They seemed to look at her, most respectfully too, out of another continent. Meeting their alien but entrancing gaze, Laura instantly regretted a dozen faulty details of her appearance and cursed her luck. At that moment all sunlight vanished and the wild rain of March slashed at the heavily leaded windows of the Old Oak Nook, which was a catering establishment owned by a retired folk dancer.

"I didn't know this place would be so crowded," said the young man in a massive careful way. He did not talk like a foreigner, yet there was something in his speech that matched his eyes. "I'm a stranger here."

Laura, telling herself bitterly that he just would be a stranger, told him that she believed this place was nearly always crowded at this time. She tried to think of something else to say that would keep the conversation going and yet seem reasonably ladylike and aloof. But before she could think of anything suitable, he spoke again. Miraculously too.

"My name,' he said very solemnly and with a certain innocence, almost like a new small boy reporting to a teacher, "is Theodore Jenks."

Before she knew she was doing it, she was giving him a wide grin. "Laura Casey's my name."

"Miss Casey?"

"Yes, Miss Casey."

His nod was like a bow. Everything about him seemed to be on a large scale, but all very gentle, simple, innocently friendly. So far a heavenly type. It flashed across her mind that her father would like him. Now, after giving his order to the waitress, he smiled at Laura, who felt small, untidy, inadequate but somehow happy.

"You are not married," he said. "Neither am I. I come from the East Indies, and am visiting this country for the first time." He hesitated a moment, regarding her gravely. "We may be disturbed soon or you may have to go, so may I say one thing to you, please?"

"Yes, what is it?" And she stared at him, unable to imagine what was coming.

"I think you are very beautiful."

"Me?" she gasped, among the rockets and Catherine wheels. And as he nodded and looked wistful, this innocent giant with the gold hair and the strange dark eyes, she knew she was done for. This was it.

Theodore Jenks

I

THEODORE was staying at Renders Hotel, in Mayfair. It was like staying in a novel by Thackeray. Electricity had been smuggled in somehow, but apart from that everything there seemed to date from the Crimean War. In order to help the Victorian illusion, no air was admitted into the building, and there were times when Theodore felt that he was about to suffocate. All the people there, both guests and staff, were old. The waiters and porters were studies in senile decay. Ancient chambermaids tottered along the corridors carrying brass cans of tepid water. There was an early whimsical sketch of a lift. There was much blowing and bellowing down speaking tubes. Any meal taken up to a bedroom involved about a hundredweight of metal dish covers. To deal with two square inches of mutton, you were given a knife and fork big enough for a roasted ox. Everything in the dining room was gigantic except the helpings. To ask one of the waiters, probably suffering from an enlarged heart or rheumatoid arthritis, to bring a cruet was almost to commit manslaughter. The guests were no younger. Enameled Edwardian beauties went creaking through the public rooms. Wheezy popeyed old bucks dropped into the faded plush chairs, lit cigars, and called for large pink gins, while their blood pressures went rocketing up. These ancients ought to have been dying right and left, but there seemed to be something in the atmosphere of Renders, from which all oxygen had long been removed, that preserved them.

Among these wheezy old bucks was one Sir Gervais Chesbey, with whom Theodore had made friends. He had been sent on a special mission once to Singapore, and while there had met Theodore's grandfather, who had done him a service or two. Sir Gervais was a rather frightening companion, not because his manner was intimidating, for he was pleasant enough and had taken a fancy to Theodore, but because he was always purple and breathless, as if at the end of

a long wrestling bout with life, and did everything with great difficulty. To see him take out and light a cigar was seemingly to witness
a juggling feat of appalling skill. Merely unfolding a newspaper
looked a hard searching task to him; and he climbed into a taxi like
a man about to go down half a mile in a bathysphere. Theodore was
not merely a robust but an unusually powerful young man, but a
morning with Sir Gervais, in this world of intensely difficult slow-
motion, apparently in an element far denser than air, exhausted him.
Nevertheless, he had already spent several mornings and afternoons
with him, because it happened that Sir Gervais, surprisingly enough
(though Theodore had already discovered that English life is full of
these surprises), had an exceptionable knowledge and appreciation
of pictures and old furniture, silver and pottery, and was delighted
to take Theodore, who knew little about such things and was anxious
to learn, to museums and galleries. And to Theodore, who had been
stunned at first and then afterwards shockingly depressed by the gray
vastness of London and the sight of its joyless hurrying crowds, these
glimpses of its art and crafts had been entrancing.

On the morning after Theodore's visit to Cambridge, they were
paying a second visit to the Victoria and Albert Museum, where Sir
Gervais was well known and given preferential treatment as a con-
noisseur. At the end of an hour or so—and Sir Gervais, like a wise
man, always carefully restricted both the time and number of objects
to be examined—Sir Gervais mentioned lunch. "Fact is, m'boy," he
said, panting as usual and talking in staccato phrases, "want you to
join us. Nephew and niece lunching with me. Dull for 'em with only
me. Good for you too. Meet young people. Join us, eh? Good!"

In the taxi he explained, in his telegraphic fashion, who these young
people were and why they might be useful to Theodore. They were
the children of his younger brother, now dead; and their names were
Lionel and Clare. Lionel was a successful journalist, who now wrote
a daily column for the *Daily Echo*. "Beastly rag—never look at it
m'self—one of Lord Palmersgreen's beastly rags. Pays well, though,
Palmersgreen. Young Lionel's probably making a dam' good thing
out of it. Big expense sheet—all that. Goes everywhere. Useful to you if
you want to look around, m'boy." Clare Chesbey was an actress.
"Good-lookin' gal too," said Sir Gervais. "But doesn't seem to make
much of a go of it. Invited me once or twice—Sunday nights—
couldn't make head or tail of what they were doing. Don't let her

know you've got any money, m'boy. Be after it—not for herself, not that kind of gal—but to put on one of these dam' queer shows—gals with green faces moaning in front of black curtains or filthy daubs. Ought to get married—but never meets anybody—all these dam' pansies—place is full of 'em. Anyhow, there y'are—Lionel and Clare. Try to give you a decent lunch. Ordered a bottle of drinkable hock— hell of a price."

2

Both Lionel and Clare were late, to the annoyance of Sir Gervais, who had ordered four sherries and drank two of them himself and made Theodore drink the other two. The young people arrived separately but within a minute or two of each other, and Sir Gervais, ignoring Lionel's demand for a cocktail, insisted upon going straight into the dining room, where some tired little hors d'oeuvres were waiting for them. There was a basic family likeness between the brother and sister, but superficially they looked very different. Clare Chesbey was dark and mysterious, as if she had once played a young witch and had never quite relinquished the part. She did a good deal of impressive eye-opening and -shutting, mostly at Theodore. She said little, but did it in a remote contralto murmur, like a lost princess in a tower. Coarsely considered, she was a fairly luscious young woman, white-skinned and wide-mouthed, with a hearty appetite; and not, Theodore decided early, his type. Lionel, several years older, was a thin and nervous fellow with snapping black eyes. He was carelessly dressed, with a tie much lighter than his shirt, and he seemed to have modeled himself on the American newspapermen so often seen in films, even to the length of talking with a slight American accent. He kept bringing out a pad and pencil and scribbling a word or two. In spite of his knowingness, nervous tricks, New York atmosphere, there were times when he looked like an unhappy child who had been allowed for years to stay up too late.

"First visit, eh?" he said to Theodore. "What about some impressions? Might use 'em."

"Wish you'd use this lunch," Sir Gervais grumbled. "And put that dam' pad away."

"Don't call this lunch, do you, Gerry?"

"Best I can do, these days, m'boy."

"Sorry, I didn't mean it that way. But look at this place, these people—everybody ready for embalming—"

"Lionel, don't be squalid," said Clare.

"Well, Jenks, what about your impressions of London?" said Lionel.

"I've been thinking," said Theodore, in his slow easy way. He noticed Clare widening her eyes at him, and felt confused. "Never having been before, I've nothing to compare—"

"Put it this way," said Lionel. "Is London better or worse than you expected?"

"Better. Much better."

"How d'you account for that?"

"Because a lot of the papers, both English and American, make it out to be worse than it is."

"Doubt that, m'boy," said Sir Gervais. "Try this hock—very decent wine."

"I doubt it too," Clare murmured from her distant tower in the forest.

"Ever read my paper—*Daily Echo*?"

"Sometimes," said Theodore, trying the hock and finding it very decent indeed.

"What do you think of it?"

"I don't understand it," Theodore replied earnestly.

"No, thanks, Uncle Gerry—whisky please. What don't you understand about it, Jenks?"

"It's always saying it believes in Britain, and at the same time it always behaves as if London were a suburb of New York. All these columns about American films and film stars, vaudeville artistes, plays—"

"Perfectly true, Mr. Jenks," Clare murmured. "It never gives *us* any publicity. And you know it, Lionel."

"Okay, I know it. What are we eating, Gerry? Stewed parrot? Fact is, Jenks, we've gone American—bound to happen—that's where the real power is. Our boys on the news know it, act on it, but it's too early yet for the paper to say so in its editorials, so we go on printing all the old nonsense about believing in Britain."

"But I do believe in Britain," said Theodore. "I suppose I sound like a prig—"

"My dear, it's heavenly," said Clare, who was not too remote and languid to be able to cut in if she wanted to. "And I believe it's the very first time I've ever heard anybody say the word *prig*—off the stage, of course—"

"Don't go all whimsy on us, Clare," said her brother.

"Oh—shut up!"

"There's some sort of pudding," Sir Gervais wheezed. "Can't say what it's like. Never touch 'em m'self."

"Good God, no," said Lionel. "Lots of black coffee for me."

"I like pudding," said Theodore. "Even the pudding here."

Clare made her eyes enormous for him. "Then I'll have some too. Lovely pudding, please."

"The Edith Evans touch now, eh?" Lionel jeered. "Tell me, Jenks, what are you doing here?"

"He's seeing the sights," said Sir Gervais. "Sometimes with me. Good for him too. But thought you might like to take him round a bit, Lionel, eh?"

"Can do. And might be a good idea at that." Lionel whipped out a diary and glanced at it. "How are you fixed for the rest of today, Jenks? Manage it? Good! Must go and phone the office, Gerry. Join you outside when these two have finished mopping up their horrible pink puds."

"He may find it very boring carting me around," said Theodore.

"Not a bit, m'boy. Waiter—bill."

"Lionel will adore it," murmured Clare. "Lots of showing off. And he realizes you're somebody quite new and attractive. Did you say you're part Chinese? What a gorgeous idea! Darling Uncle Gervais, in ten minutes I must go and rehearse."

"One of these Sunday night shows again?"

"No, darling, we're opening tomorrow night at the Mermaid Theater Club—"

"Never heard of it—"

"My dear, you've never heard of anything." They were standing now, and she put a hand on Theodore's arm, drowned him in the fathomless night of her eyes while two ancient waiters halted shakily with their dishes upraised, and said with more animation than she had so far displayed: "And, Mr. Jenks, *you* must come and see us. Yes, tomorrow night at the Mermaid. I shall send you a ticket. Here, isn't it? That's settled then."

As they followed her out, Sir Gervais whispered: "Needn't go if you don't want to, m'boy. Might amuse you, though. Can't tell. Not as bad as they sound, y'know—these two. Enjoyed your lunch? Good man!"

When Clare had gone off to her rehearsal, the three men still lingered over their coffee, in a dim sleepy corner cut off from the general traffic of the lounge by a mysterious overgrown plant. Theodore and Sir Gervais, rather drowsy now, pulled contentedly at their cigars, and even Lionel did not draw smoke out of his cigarette as desperately as he had done when he first arrived. The Victorian air of Renders, with its high content of carbon dioxide, was having its effect on them. And the brandy that Sir Gervais had ordered, in defiance of both his doctor and his bank manager, did nothing to break the dreamy spell. As if it belonged, like the hotel, to a more spacious time, the afternoon seemed to broaden and deepen.

"But I've material for a column to find, chaps," said Lionel, half-protesting.

"Do you write it all now, m'boy?" his uncle inquired, stifling a yawn.

"Write about twice as much as they print. But that's fair enough. My own idea, actually. And I do it all now," he added, "except the smearing. Been taken off that."

"What's the smearing?" said Theodore.

"Dirty work, eh?" said Sir Gervais.

"It's necessary at times," said Lionel, with the air of a rather indolent lecturer, "chiefly for political reasons, that certain persons should be discredited. Hence the Smear, my friends. If a Socialist has no money, we point that out, suggesting that he envies the rich and is on the make. If he has money—and it's never been clear to me why he shouldn't have—then we point that out, and suggest he's a fake. One fellow I know makes a nice living by telling the public what shares are held by Labour Members of Parliament. I've never discovered if the public objects to Labour members owning shares. They might as well object to Conservative members using municipal gas and water. But then we assume on our paper that nobody thinks. Which is all right. But where we're wrong—and of course I'm not really including myself, but mean the top boys—is in thinking that our readers, dumb as they are, take us seriously. It's all haywire. We work like hell to bring out a good comic paper, brighter and funnier every year, getting up to all kinds of monkey tricks, and yet imagine we're still an organ of public opinion, the fourth estate, and directly descended from Milton. Oh yes—we can start the adolescents and nitwits talking about film stars and fashions, cut a slice off a radio comic, or build up a dance-band leader. But when it's a serious issue, what we say doesn't mean a thing. And why should it? We can't have it both ways. Either we're clowning or we're not."

"Then the Smear, as you call it, doesn't work," said Theodore.

"Well, you can't push out that gluey stuff all over the country without some of it sticking. The trick is, of course, to make it as nasty as you can without risking a libel action. That's where my new colleague, Freddy Trout, is a maestro. I used to be too slapdash. Nevertheless," Lionel added mischievously, "I could do one or two quite good smear paragraphs on Uncle Gervais here."

"Doubt it, m'boy, doubt it very much."

"You do, eh, Gerry?" Lionel was thoughtful for a moment or two. "Well, how's this? Very rough, of course, and would have to be polished—but not bad. 'In these hard times, when most of us are worrying about production and crushing taxes, Sir Gervais Chesbey is a fortunate man. He divides his time between his country house in Oxfordshire, with its well-stocked home farm, and the snug Renders Hotel in Mayfair. He is a familiar figure in the Bond Street galleries—' "

"Why, confound it!" Sir Gervais looked as if he were about to explode. "That'll do. Anybody'd think—to hear that nonsense—I'd millions—instead of being nearly broke." He turned to Theodore. "Got a country cottage—and about a hundred acres of stinking pasture I can't afford to clean up. Give me special rates here—and haven't bought a picture or anything else for years—can't afford to. Never heard such dam' bosh."

Lionel grinned. "And I happen to know that you come up to town when you can't endure that old woman's horrible cooking and the smell of paraffin for another single day. But the readers don't. And there isn't a single statement I made you could use as the basis of an action against us. That's the Smear, gentlemen."

"Well," and puffing and blowing, Sir Gervais pushed himself out of his chair, "this fortunate man feels like a nap. And you lads can get on with your nonsense."

3

In the taxi, Lionel explained the first item on their program. "It's a meeting of something called the New Empire Group. We shall have a reporter covering it, but the office thought I might find something there for my column. We're very hot on the Empire at the *Echo*."

"I know you are," said Theodore earnestly, "and I've never understood what it's about. You seem to blame everybody for letting down the Empire, but I've never grasped what it is everybody fails to do that ought to be done."

"Well, I don't know," said Lionel grinning. "And the editor doesn't know. And the proprietor doesn't know. So of course the readers don't know. But it looks as if something's badly wrong, and we're trying to put it right. So what more do you want?"

"I want a lot more."

"Jenks, my dear chap," criel Lionel, "you are to my thirsty soul like a spring of clear cold water in the desert. Promise not to leave my side until I call it a day, which usually, I must warn you, is pretty dam' late. I owe Uncle Gerry something for introducing us. Dear old boy, isn't he? Look out for Clare, though. Have you any money?"

Theodore explained that his grandfather had left him a few thousand pounds.

"Well, don't let Clare and her gang get their hands on any of it. Otherwise it'll go down the drain—and when I say *drain* I mean it, because it's as good a name as any for their kind of drama. Not that she isn't a nice kid, behind all that fancywork, but where her precious art's concerned, she could skin a Greek moneylender. So watch out and keep your checkbook out of sight."

Theodore promised to be careful, and then asked: "What will happen, do you think, at this New Empire Group meeting?"

"Nothing but blah blah blah blah," replied Lionel cheerfully. "But I might get a nice little personal angle. Ties, for instance. What sort of ties do our politicians wear in the afternoon? Might be something in that. But the speeches, I warn you, won't mean a sausage."

Five minutes later, Theodore found himself in the gloomy ballroom of a large hotel. There was a scattering of people, many of them obviously reporters, in the thicket of gilt chairs; and facing them was a very long table, behind which sat about twenty very solemn persons, of varying ages, sizes, and color. The Chairman, an immensely tall, thin, melancholy man who never stopped fussing with his eyeglasses, was announcing that they were here to talk about the Empah, had a wonderful list of speakahs, and that he would first call upon the Right Honorable Percival Bullan, the distinguished Conservative membah.

Mr. Bullan, who looked very cold and unhappy and might have been suffering from kidney trouble, thanked the Chahman, reminded the audience that the Conservative Partay had always believed in the Empah, was ready at all times to put the Empah first, did not hesitate at any time or any place to denounce those who would pull down the Empah, sneer at the Empah, neglect the Empah. He told them how they all knew how their Chahman had served the Empah, and said that he considered it a privilege to be appealing for the Empah under such a Chahman, that they all realized what excellent work could be performed by the New Empah Group, of which he was proud to be a membah; and added, as a happy afterthought, that just as there would always be an England, so too there would always be an Empah. Then Mr. Bullan sat down and stared with some severity at the nearest empty chairs.

Lord Cokehurst, the next speaker, announced that he spoke for Liberal opinion. He was a fat man who seemed to imagine he was in a Turkish bath and not in an underheated ballroom on a cold March afternoon. If his oratory did nothing to warm up the meeting, he himself did, for just to look at him mopping himself was to feel the temperature being raised. He declared, behind his cascade of perspiration, that the Liberals had always been the friends of Empire and, if they should be restored to power, which might be sooner than many people imagined, they would prove themselves once again to be staunch supporters of Empire. He too, like his Right Honorable friend, was delighted to support the New Empire Group. And he finally reminded his listeners, just as his handkerchief was obviously sopping and useless, that this was an Empire on which the sun never set. After which he sat down and whispered urgently to his neighbors, perhaps to ask for a towel.

And now the voice of the People was heard at the meeting. It came from the Right Honorable Fred Duck, that stalwart Labour leader, at whom Theodore stared hard, for the fame of Fred Duck had traveled round the world, and, as Theodore knew, had been discussed over the tea in the back rooms of Chinese stores and on the decks of Malay schooners. Mr. Duck was a burly irritable man who, to the dismay of the Chahman, thumped the table with vast meaty hands. He appeared to be in sharp disagreement with the other speakers, and indeed with everybody anywhere, but did not explain why. He had little schooling, no privileges, had had to go out and work at the age of thirteen, Mr. Duck declared, but for all that he was a better friend of the Empy-yer than most people who had lived in luxury all their lives. He was ready to support this New Empy-yer Ger-roup, and promised that most of his mates would do the same, but warned the audience, who could lump it if they didn't like it, that his back was against the wall. But even so he was ready to stand up and fight the good fight for the Empy-yer. And then, as if he felt a lot better, he slapped the Chahman on the back and, to the sound of applause as scattered as the audience, he hurried out.

Wearing a grimace that was perhaps intended to be an arch smile, the Chahman observed that a movement of this kind would not be complete without the support of the Ladies, a statement that brought some applause from several ladies on the little gilt chairs. There was nobody, he thought, who better represented the woman's point of view than their friend, Lady Tirle, who was with them that afternoon and would now speak. Lady Tirle, who was at once commanding and twittering, and suggested a battle-cruiser beflagged for a party, announced right off that she was a woman. She gave the impression—and Theodore remembered how he had been bewildered for years by a similar point of view in the popular newspapers—that she was not a member of a sex that is lavishly distributed throughout the world but something quite different, astoundingly rare, perhaps a live but tame mastodon. Lady Tirle also announced that as a woman she believed in the Empire. As a woman, she was careful to point out, she had visited many parts of the Empire. All these other women believed in the Empire. And here she would like to pay a tribute to the Royal Family, who also believed in the Empire. She was glad and proud to know there was a place in the New Empire Group for women.

"I don't understand this," said Theodore, while the Chahman was staring at his agenda, first with his eyeglasses on, then with them off. "They all seem to agree about something. But what is it?"

"It's the Empah," Lionel whispered. "We'll push off in about five minutes."

The Chahman, now in a muddle, called up his reserves. One of them was a beaming little colored man, who asked everybody to visit West Africa. Another was an elderly man who declared that they were all neglecting the "Great Dominion of Kenneda," and appeared to imagine that Canada had been offering us all her products for years, without reference to dollar payments or any balance of trade, and that we simply would not accept the stuff. Then a thin brown man arose, muttered something about Australia, told a funny story that made the Chahman and three other persons laugh heartily but failed to reach anybody else, made a remote reference to cricket, and tried to sit on Lady Tirle's lap. Before the Chahman could call on anybody else, a madwoman, looking like a dilapidated bird's nest, popped up from nowhere, and shouted that unless the New Empire Group came out strongly against vivisection, it would receive no support from her. The Chahman pretended that she had never existed and called upon the Secretary, a commando type, who roared that he was ready to take names of new members and that tea would be served.

"We've had it, chum," said Lionel. "Let's get cracking, as the Hon. Sec. is about to say."

On their way to the Savoy Hotel, where Lionel had his next engagement, he refused to tell Theodore what would happen there. "Just stick around, pal." He became very American. "From now on it's big-time stuff."

They went upstairs to a suite that was crowded with youngish men rather like Lionel and about an equal number of women, some of them young and smart and others middle-aged and rather anxious. Theodore came to the conclusion that they were nearly all journalists, and Lionel introduced him to several of them, but would not explain himself nor allow any of the others to explain the purpose of this gathering. Clearly it was a very important occasion. The atmosphere was very different from that of the Empah meeting. Something tremendous was about to happen. No food or drink was being served: that would come later, Lionel said.

Then two Americans, with exhausted pallid faces and gaudily painted ties that seemed somehow to belong to two other men, were busily clearing a few square yards of carpet before the bedroom door, and begging the company to sit down and be quiet for half a minute. "Glad to see you here, folks," one of them shouted, "but just give us a break, will you?" A break was given them. "All set, I guess, Benny," the other shouted. Nobody stirred, nobody spoke. The great moment had arrived.

Out of the bedroom came a young woman, like a fabulous doll out of its case. She was an astonishingly handsome young woman, but so metallically finished, streamlined and engine-turned, so glossily done over, so inhumanly completed, so lacking in warmth and charm, that she seemed to Theodore quite repulsive. She stood motionless for a second or two, wearing a smile that might have been stenciled on her face. No meaning could be found in that smile, nor in the eyes above it.

"Well, folks," cried one of the Americans triumphantly, looking almost phosphorescent in his attempt to conjure up some enthusiasm out of his ebbing vitality, "here she is—paying her first visit to you British. My pleasure and privilege to present—Miss Ilba Cram."

And then he and the other American, although now nearly green with excitement and fatigue, clapped so hard that many of the others there had to clap too. The rest appeared to make a buzzing sound; but it helped.

Certain faint flickerings disturbed Miss Ilba Cram's exquisite mask. Her eyes were no longer without meaning. She seemed wary, rather frightened; as if somewhere inside that superb structure and its matt finish was a small-town girl who found herself a long way from home. Her lips moved soundlessly, as if she were rehearsing. Then, not without an effort, she looked very haughty indeed, like a queen of some iron dynasty visiting a distant province; and she made her little speech. "Thanks a lawt. I warnt yew people to know how vurry pleased I am to be here today and to attaind the premeer of my new picture tonight. Most of yew have already seen me in my pictures and now I am seeing yew and your country, having come all the way frawm Hallywood and had quite a trip. But I believe that motion pictures can help folks all over the wurld to unnerstan' one anawther. And that's all, I guess."

Now that her majesty had spoken, the crowd could feast; and in came the waiters bearing food and drink, of which Theodore, whose appetite and thirst were in proportion to his size, claimed his share. Lionel had vanished, probably to fight his way to the side of Miss Ilba Cram. But Theodore no longer felt shy; and joined in the general chatter.

"I've never seen her in a film," he said to his neighbor, a bleary man who was polishing off whiskies with astonishing speed. "Is she a good actress?"

"Terrible. I hear Mayersnick isn't renewing her contract."

"But why all this fuss, then?"

"They've sunk two and a half million dollars in this new stinkaroo that opens tonight, so they got to give it a build-up. I hear it's terrible. What do you hear, Agnes?"

"I don't hear it's terrible," said Agnes, who was a severe-looking middle-aged woman, "I *know*. I've seen it." She looked inquiringly at Theodore. "Aren't you in films?"

"No, I'm not. I don't know anything about them."

"They could do with you, with those looks. And I don't believe you're a newspaperman. Eh?"

"No, I came here with Lionel Chesbey. He's—well—showing me round."

"He'll do that all right," said Agnes. "But I ought to warn you—he's apt to get plastered at these parties, and then stay quietly plastered the rest of the night. So watch out. Hello, George, who let you in?"

There was a kind of slow swirling movement in the packed room that gradually took Theodore from one corner to the other, and though better able than most of them there to resist any pressure, Theodore did not trouble to resist it because to him one part of the room was as good as any other. Finally, after several cocktails and bits to eat, he found himself next to one of the exhausted Americans, who was mournfully sipping soda water. "Boy, am I tired," he muttered to Theodore. "See what I'm drinking? Charged water. If I got started on hard liquor, I'd never make that premeer tonight—no, sir, not Benny." Then his glance, hollow with fatigue, sharpened. "Say, you're quite a fella. They got you signed up here?"

"Signed up?" Theodore was puzzled for a moment. "Oh—I'm not a film actor."

"Benny," a voice wailed high above the chatter. "Benny."

"That's little Ilba," said the American. "Been that way ever since we left the Coast. Handsome, you've gotta meet her—and I won't take no." He grabbed hold of Theodore's sleeve and pulled him toward the bedroom door where Miss Cram was still holding her court. Two minutes later he was inside the bedroom, as a member of a very small select party that included the two American men, Lionel, a wiry and restless American woman, a mysterious oldish man rather like a yellow frog, and, of course, Miss Cram herself. The American who was not Benny was pouring out champagne.

"Oh phooey, Benny," he was shouting. "This don't count as a drink. Just a tonic—what we all need."

"He is ker-vite righd, my dears," said the yellow frogman in a very deep foreign bass. "Chost a toneeg."

"Now quit beefing, Ilba," said Benny. "You were swell, and they ate it."

"I forgot that bit about dee-moc-rac-ee, Benny—you remember?"

"Give it to me, Miss Cram," said Lionel. "For the *Daily Echo*."

"Afterwards, Mr. Chesbey," said the other American, handing out the glasses of champagne. "We need a tonic."

"Ker-vite righd."

"And, Ilba," shouted Benny, "I want you to meet—" he turned to Theodore "—who is it, Handsome?"

"I'll do this," cried Lionel, in a tone that made Theodore remember Agnes' warning. "He's my friend. Miss Cram—meet Theodore Jenks, one of the richest men in Indonesia, grandson of the Governor of the Malay States and great-grandson of the last Empress of China."

"My, my!" cried the wiry American woman, staring.

But Ilba was all dignity and graciousness. As she put a small firm hand in Theodore's outstretched paw and let it remain there, she said: "Mr. Jenks, this is a great pleasure to me, and I want to tell you that after that Bali picture I made—although I never went there, only a camera unit for the back projection shots—I'm crazy about your part of the world."

"Me too," cried the wiry woman.

"I haf been dere vonce," said frogman in his sleepy bass. "For oil beeznos. No goot."

"You ought to make a film on one of Theodore's plantations," Lionel shouted. "What do you say, old boy?"

Even if Theodore had not by this time felt that nothing was worth saying in this lunatic bedroom, he would not have been heard, for they were all talking at once, from the screaming high pitch of the wiry American woman to the mysterious double-bass of the frogman. Ilba Cram had released his hand but was now standing very close to him, so that the blackened spikes of her eyelashes were like railings round a pond, and she seemed to be explaining, like a hypnotized schoolgirl, her passion for culture and travel. Finally, there was a banging on the door, which somebody had locked, and Benny went to see who was trying to outrage the royal privacy.

"Well, well," cried Benny. "Look who's here."

The young woman who pushed him aside was a brunette, whereas Miss Cram was a blonde, but otherwise she was a duplicate, having exactly the same artificial look, the same metallic finish and cold perfection.

"Ilba dahling!" she cried, dramatically extending her arms.

"Moona!" screamed Miss Cram. And they rushed to embrace, like sisters driven apart by twenty years of war and ruin.

"Can you beat it?" said Benny to Theodore. "It's not two weeks since they were both eating together at Mike Romanoff's. Actresses!"

"Moona 'as gone vairy beeg 'ere," observed the frogman. "Ilba veel do vell doo."

Theodore crossed to Lionel, who was helping the other American to pour out more champagne. "I'm sorry, but I can't stand any more of this."

"Neither can I," cried Lionel cheerfully. "Let's beat it. See you later, Wilbur. Benny, we've had it."

"Mr. Jenks," said Benny, shaking hands and suddenly very solemn, "Lionel says you're with him tonight. Well, that's fine. I want to talk to you, Mr. Jenks, about motion pictures. Now don't forget. It's a date."

There was still some kind of a party going on in the other room, but Lionel waved aside several people who wanted to talk to him, much to Theodore's relief.

"You needn't have come with me," said Theodore when they were outside. "But I'd had enough of it."

"Quite right. Besides, we must change. A dinner jacket will do. Look —I'll pick you up at Renders in about an hour. Better have a quick sandwich or something. We'll eat properly after the show."

"What show?"

"Why—Ilba Cram's 'premeer.'"

"Well, I don't know," said Theodore dubiously. "I'm beginning to feel I've had enough of—"

"Now, now," said Lionel, "you might as well see the whole performance for once. That was only the First Act. And you've come to have a look at English life, and this is part of English life."

"I call it American life. And I can't see why anybody wants it here."

"You wait, chum. Then you'll see. Renders in an hour then—and a black tie."

4

High on the gigantic façade of the cinema were letters of gold and fire, spelling ILBA CRAM IN HOMETOWN KID. Searchlights played restlessly on the cleared space in front of the doors, where scores of police were holding back an immense dark swarm of folk. Now and then there came from the inner ring of this swarm, as new arrivals were recognized and welcomed, a huge sigh, sometimes sharply rising to a cheer, while the mob in the blind outer darkness grunted and screamed and pushed. Doomsday might have been breaking in Leicester Square; and perhaps it was. In spite of their eagerness, noise, and energy, there seemed to Theodore something somnambulistic about these people, as if they were shoving and staring in a dream. He had seen plenty of crowds before, had sometimes been frightened, at other times uplifted, by the sight and sound of them; but this was different, new and evilly strange, outside any tradition of human assembly, all dark and blind, somehow mechanical, not sustained and enlivened by any of the forces of a genuine great event, of which it was a mockery, yet with a sinister life of its own. He had a sudden fancy that even the people who thought they were pulling the strings here, manipulating the mass so that they came crowding and screaming to this place, were themselves only marionettes, whose strings vanished into a darkness of mysterious and menacing power. Ilba Cram, Benny and Wilbur, the frogman (whoever he was), Lionel and his employers and his colleagues, might be larger pieces on the board where these nameless thousands were pawns; but the game itself was being played, perhaps for stakes of an appalling magnitude, by beings not to be found in any directory, perhaps outside our time and space. But then, what with one thing and another, Theodore was, he knew, rather excited himself.

In the golden cavern of the foyer, the bulbs of the press photographers popped and flashed. Film celebrities were being photographed on their way to see moving photographs of other film celebrities. There were many famous faces. Cabinet ministers, who no doubt had been working hard all day for the glory and prosperity of Britain, arrived, nodding and smiling, to work for nothing for the glory and prosperity of Hollywood. All the people Theodore had left in that bedroom made a triumphal appearance, looking much the same except they had changed their clothes. Ilba and Moona now proved that their shoulders and bosoms were as superbly engine-turned and finished as their faces. Benny and his colleague Wilbur wore magnificent tuxedos, but were so far gone in fatigue that they looked like glazed-eyed dying fishes. The wiry American woman was there, waving and screaming. So was the mysterious frogman, in full evening dress and dribbling away at a vast cigar. And very soon it was impossible to move, the foyer was so densely packed. Theodore could hardly breathe, but began to wonder, if this occasion were one of the triumphs of this life, whether there was much to be said for breathing.

The auditorium, when they came to it at last, was large and cool, quite sensible after the foyer, receiving them almost ironically. There was still a good deal of staring and waving, but in here the important personages looked considerably less important and more like real people. The film itself—the cause of all this fuss, or the apparent cause —was a notable anticlimax. There was nothing wrong with it, as a mild bit of mass entertainment; but nobody who had not taken part in it would remember it for four days. It showed Ilba, still as immaculate as ever, as a girl in a shop in a small Middle Western town filled with character actors. A rich young man, accompanied by a comedian, had crash-landed his aircraft just outside this town; he made the acquaintance of Ilba; he was visited by an uncle richer still and rather more entertaining; he deliberately worked up a misunderstanding followed by a quarrel with poor Ilba; and then, a haunted man, he left hurriedly to drink and gamble in hot spots and sit up very late, looking bored, with sneering blondes and heavy-eyed night club proprietors. But—you folks know how it is—he was just as crazy about Ilba as she was about him—my, my! So he rushed back to the little town and listened to a speech by Ilba on the American way of life and dee-moc-rac-ee; a speech that was heard on this occasion with the deepest respect by the British, in spite of their ancient caste system, their old-fashioned political and economic set-up, their fabulous dukes and ragged crossing-sweepers, their remoteness in castle or cottage from the life of these rugged pioneers. When the film had gone its way, several fussy men appeared on the stage, followed by a tiny glittering Ilba, who said that she was very pleased to attend the premeer of her new picture there, had come all the way from Hollywood and had quite a trip, and that she believed that motion pictures could help folks all over the world to understand one another.

Then the foyer nonsense began all over again, and Theodore could not breathe and wondered about breathing but found enough breath to tell Lionel that he had had quite enough of this performance. Outside there seemed to be more people than ever. Lionel suggested walking, and Theodore, glad to have some air, readily agreed; so they pushed their way out through the crowd, which appeared to regard them with contempt because they were not behaving properly and not waiting haughtily for some gigantic car to carry them away.

"Can't help it," said Lionel, as they emerged, "but I really dislike all those half-witted twerps who can find nothing better to do than wait like that. I'd shout for joy one night if all this nonsense was laid on and nobody turned up to gape at it. I know—they're my readers, my public. But I can't help it—that's what I feel, Jenks."

"Have we finished now?" Theodore inquired.

"No, no, there's still the Third Act. But that won't be so bad. We're going now, for supper, to what is at the moment the most fashionable and successful of our night clubs—the Glass Slipper."

"I've never been to a real night club," said Theodore.

"London's the wrong place for 'em. Not like Paris or New York. Here everybody wants to go to bed."

"I want to go to bed," Theodore admitted, "except that I'm hungry."

"There'll be food," said Lionel. "And it mightn't be bad. They usually look after me. Pinky Creech, who does their publicity, is a pal of mine."

They discovered Pinky Creech, who looked rather like an enormous boiled ham that had found its way into a dinner jacket, drinking champagne cocktails with some friends in the bar. All the lights in there were illuminated glass slippers. They could hear the dance orchestra playing in the next room.

"Well, Lionel, you filthy old sausage," cried Pinky, who had immediately left his friends, "how does it go? And who's this?"

Theodore was introduced to him, but this time without any nonsense about governors and Chinese empresses, much to his relief.

"Between ourselves and off the record and all that," said Pinky, beckoning to the waiter, "you've arrived years too late, Jenks. London's dull nowadays. We've had it, eh Lionel? What are you drinking? Give it a name, chaps—there's everything here." After they had given it a name, he continued mournfully: "We may perk up a bit soon— Festival business—but it won't last. Isn't the money about. Not like the old days. We can't be gay any more. Dunno why, but there it is— even money apart, and of course we're all broke—we can't be gay. I'm not gay. Lionel here's not gay, though he sometimes pretends to be. And you won't be gay. So don't expect it, old boy, just put it right out of your mind. Well—cheers!"

"Cheers!" they echoed somberly.

"It'll be a pretty big night tonight, though," said Pinky. "Lot of well-known people coming. Got a good new act too—Italian bloke who imitates a cat and a mouse. Great talent. Going better than Lulu, though he's only drawing a tenth of her salary. Tony overpays that bitch. She's just bought five Siamese cats. You might mention that Lionel."

"I might," said Lionel gloomily. "But it's corny, Pinky, corny to hell."

"He's sad," said Pinky turning to Theodore. "What have you done to him?"

"Fair enough," said Lionel, with a faint grin. "What have you done to me, Jenks?"

"I've just been with you, that's all," said Theodore, rather bewildered. "But all this film palaver seemed to me rather boring and depressing."

"Couldn't agree with you more, old boy," cried Pinky.

"He was making a hit with Ilba Cram, though," said Lionel.

"Well, look at him," said Pinky.

"I didn't notice the hit," said Theodore. "And she seemed to me like a mechanical doll. Nobody could be interested in a woman like that. And all this crowding round just to have a look at her. In a great old city like London. It seemed wrong to me. It gave me a queer feeling."

"Hoy, steady, old boy," cried Pinky in mock alarm. "We live here. Can't pop back to the East Indies."

"We're hungry, that's our trouble," said Lionel. "See you later Pinky."

By the time their supper was served, the place was filling up. Many of the people had attended the film show. At a table not far away the frogman was entertaining Ilba, Moona, the wiry American woman, Benny, and Wilbur. From time to time people came up to their table and talked to Lionel, and between these visits he would ask Theodore to excuse him and would slip across to other tables. The late hour, the drinks, and a half-excited tiredness, together gave Theodore a feeling of heightened consciousness, sharpening every impression. He felt he was witnessing a badly rehearsed performance of gaiety, with no genuine high spirits, no vitality and joy, anywhere. When they were not jerked into activity, swaying and grinning and nodding, the men in the band drooped and yawned. So did the waiters, who merely sketched a smiling willingness. He sensed behind her bright mask the weary contempt of the singer they called Lulu, and the melancholy of the Italian clown who imitated a cat and a mouse. Among the guests only an occasional young girl, proud and beaming, or a young man obviously in love with his dancing partner, suggested real enjoyment; the others appeared to be there to see and be seen, to kill another couple of hours, to postpone tomorrow. At the table of his film acquaintances, Ilba and Moona still seemed to be immaculate, securely lacquered as they were against late hours; the wiry American woman still waved and screamed; Benny was getting tight and Wilbur falling asleep; and the presiding frogman, yellowed and carved by the night, began to look gigantically grotesque, like an idol dug out of ancient mud.

During one of Lionel's absences, Theodore spoke to a waiter who was leaning on the back of a chair at the next table, deserted during this particular dance. He was an elderly man, beak-nosed and hollow-eyed, who might have been a veteran of some forgotten Roman legion watching the frontier of the barbarians.

"Yes, sare?" he said wearily.

"I don't want anything, thank you," said Theodore, smiling. "I was just wondering about you."

"You vunder about me? Nobody do t'at for a long time. What do I tell you, sare?"

"How long have you been here?"

"Since it open. Before, ot'er clobs, hotels." His shrug suggested centuries of waiting.

"Do you like it?"

"Like it? 'Ow can a man like it. Not possible."

"Then why do you do it?"

"Mak' money. Save money. Soon I retire."

"And where will you retire to?"

A tragic light threw into relief the hawklike mask, as the waiter moved forward and bent a little. "You ask t'at," he said slowly. "I ask it also. Soon I retire. But to vhere do I retire? By Jesus—I 'ave fooled myself. I save money—I write letters—I ask many people. Vhere to go? An' all time I know I 'ave fooled myself. No bloddy place at all. Pardon me, sare."

Lionel returned, all a wide grin. "Got a nice story. See those two." He pointed out a tall actor type and a very young girl whose face seemed vaguely familiar to Theodore. "Here they are again—and this time it looks as if there's something in it—and anyhow it's a good story." Seeing that Theodore still looked bewildered, Lionel explained that these were two of the best-known British film stars and that now, after many rumors, it seemed certain that they imagined themselves to be in love.

"Well, what about it?" asked Theodore, puzzled.

"Oh—for God's sake, Jenks!" cried Lionel. "Don't overdo it."

"I'm sorry," said Theodore, who saw that Lionel was really annoyed with him. "I'm not pretending anything. And I'm grateful for the trouble you've taken. But I simply don't understand why it's important whether these two are in love or not."

"Look, pal, I don't care about 'em. They don't mean a sausage to me, on or off the screen. But it happens that millions of *Echo* readers, mostly women, *do* care about 'em. A nice little item about that romance will be exciting news throughout our brave new Britain."

"How do you know it will?"

"Because we know our public," Lionel replied with some irritation. "We know our business, chum."

"Yes, I suppose so," said Theodore dubiously. "But it may be all going round in a circle. I mean, they think it's important because *you* think it's important, and you get excited about it because you think *they'll* be excited about it. And perhaps really, at heart, nobody cares. Just as I don't, and I'm an ordinary kind of chap."

"No, you're not. But that's beside the point. Look—you saw that mob swarming round the cinema tonight. Why were they there?"

"I've been thinking about that. Perhaps they were there because the *Daily Echo* and other papers told them, as if it were very important and something not to be missed, that Miss Ilba Cram would be there. If I went to a place and all the papers, with millions of readers and only so much very valuable space, announced with great excitement that Tilly the Black Kitten would be on view at a certain time at a certain spot, I might be tempted to go there because I might think there was something very special about Tilly or about black kittens in general that I'd missed."

"And I don't care which way it works, so long as it works. Have another drink."

"No, thank you. I think I've had too many already."

"Either too many," said Lionel grinning, "or not enough. Just in the wrong mood."

"I'm sorry," said Theodore. "But, you see, in the long run it may be working very badly. It can't be good for people to be deliberately worked up all the time about trivialities. I mean—"

But Lionel stopped him, at the same time taking out his little pad and a pencil. "If you're trying to tell me we don't like our readers to think, you needn't. I know. Old Palmersgreen has been against it for years. But then our readers have always met him halfway. After all, they needn't buy and read his papers. But hang on, I want to make a note or two—and then telephone the office."

It was then that Benny, deathly pale, glassy-eyed, and with his magnificent tuxedo furry with tobacco ash, descended upon Theodore. He fell into a chair, put an elbow into an ashtray, leaned his head against one hand, and with the other tapped Theodore hard on the shirt front. "Been looking for you everywhere, Handsome," he began, with immense drunken solemnity. "Been thinking it over. An' I can't let you do it."

"Let me do what?"

With an enormous effort, Benny stared in surprise. "I can't let you go into motion pictures."

"But I don't want to go into motion pictures," said Theodore.

"Don't be that way, Handsome," said Benny reproachfully. "None o' that starchy limey stuff. Be a pal. Nothing against me, have you, Handsome?" he inquired anxiously.

Theodore assured him that he had not.

"Fine! Then what we want's some good Scotch." He beckoned to the elderly waiter, and would have lost his balance if Theodore had not hastily put out a hand. "Jewseppy, what we want's some good Scotch. None of your hooch an' cut stuff. Good Scotch. In fact, *very* good Scotch. Get going, Jewseppy, an' let's have some snappy service. Now then—" and he turned to Theodore, and began tapping his front again "—I can't let you do it. Could if I wanted to. Like that." And he tried to snap his fingers, failed to make any sound, and stared at them in disgust.

Theodore now decided there was no point in his declaring that he had never any intention of going into films. But he thought he might risk changing the subject. "By the way, who is that queer-looking man who's giving you supper, the one who looks rather like a frog."

"Not a frog," said Benny. "Some kind o' Squarehead or Bohunk, I guess. Or maybe Polack. Holds the European end for Mayersnick. Just an old Weisenheimer. Forget him, Handsome, and let's keep to the point. Which is—I'm warning you off motion pictures—see? Against my own interest, but what of it? When I talk straight to a guy, I talk straight. And I say—keep away from this crap."

"Oh—Benn-ee!" a voice wailed reproachfully. And there was the beautiful Ilba standing beside them. "Oh—Mr. Jenks—I never noticed you here. You look gorgeous all formal. How'm I lookin'?"

"From where I'm sitting," said Benny, before Theodore could reply, "you look terrible, Ilba. Take a look at yourself in the powder room."

"I'm tired. I wanna go back to the hotel."

"*You're* tired. Me, I'm not tired. How could I be, just carting you from the Coast to New York and then from New York here, doing every goddam thing—"

"Benny, let's go."

"See what I mean?" he said to Theodore. "And she's not the worst." The drinks arrived now. "Thanks, Jewseppy. Charge 'em up to my friend over there—the fat old guy who's looking this way. Care for some Scotch, Ilba?"

"No. I wanna go home. And you've had enough."

"Now, now, now, Beautiful! Well—the toast of the evening will be proposed by Mr. Benny Gentz, of the Mayersnick Picture Corporation." And Benny staggered to his feet despite the attempt of Miss Cram to keep him in his chair. "The Motion Picture Industry —international understanding—and Democracy!" He emptied his glass in one huge gurgling swallow, stared wildly at nothing for a moment, and then fell crashing across the table. "Crap," he muttered among the ruins, "crapola."

5

Next morning Theodore found a note for him from Miss Clare Chesbey, and with it was a ticket for the first performance of *Why Should the Nightingale?* by Derek Boon at the Mermaid Club, Kensington. In this note, a dashing affair in violet ink, Miss Chesbey begged him to accompany her to a little party given for the cast and various friends by the leading spirit of the club, Mrs. Hungerford. and he was on no account to dress.

The Mermaid Club was on the ground floor of a large dingy corner house not far from Kensington High Street. A room at the back, which looked as if it might have once been a studio, had been converted into the theater, with a small stage and narrow uncomfortable seats for about a hundred people. When Theodore arrived, five minutes before the curtain was advertised to rise, most of these hundred people were in the bar, which was conveniently situated between the front entrance and the theater proper. Theodore had a seat in the third row. He spent several minutes carefully reading the program, from which he gathered that the principal performers were Philippa Hookwood and Bettison Phelps, with Clare Chesbey one of the five supporting players. The scene of the drama was the garden of a Cardinal de Cortrai in Avignon, during the later Middle Ages. Various details about wigs, costumes, furniture, lighting, and musical effects, were added, and Theodore had ample time to read and mark these before any of the seats near him were occupied. Somewhere a bell began ringing angrily, but it did not seem to worry anybody. There were strange sounds from behind the curtain, which bulged and shook from time to time, rather as if an obstinate elephant were being dragged on to the stage and then balanced on its hind legs.

Two solemn young men took the seats immediately in front of Theodore, and he was able to overhear their talk. From it he gathered that the author of the piece, Derek Boon, was one of the new school of poetic dramatists who realized that London audiences had had more than enough of the dreary old naturalistic stuff, with its cups and saucers and wet mackintoshes and problems and prose dialogue. Boon, they assured each other, was undoubtedly a coming man, who with this, his third play, might be expected to dazzle the West End like a sunburst as soon as a good theater could be found for him. Boon had color and glamour and fire. Boon would do much to restore to our Theater some of its Elizabethan splendor. They had both had their eye upon Boon from the first. All of which Theodore noted with satisfaction, and began to feel impatient when the bell still went on ringing and the curtain refused to rise, although it was now well past the time of starting. A little weary of London now, Theodore eagerly waited for Boon to take him to medieval Avignon.

Two men came along the row, bringing with them a smell of gin and ginger ale, and after some confusion, during which they politely refused to accept Theodore's seat, they sat down one on each side of him and talked across him. One was an oldish fellow, who had

an abrupt manner and a high-pitched voice; the other was square
and solid, a ginger chap with a hard glance.

"I see Philippa's playing some kind of princess," said the oldish
man.

"Good show," said the square man.

"And this chap Bettison Phelps is in it again."

"Wet," said the square man.

"Avignon—that's where the scene is, Trevy."

"There in 'Forty-four, Hooky." And then, after some deliberation,
he added: "Liked it."

"Pardon me, sir," said Theodore to the older man, "but I'm new
to London. Is Miss Hookwood a good actress?"

"One of the best, sir. My daughter. My name's Hookwood."

"My name's Jenks—Theodore Jenks."

"No relation of Matthew Jenks, used to be in the Federated
States?"

"He was my father, Mr. Hookwood."

"Not surprised," said Mr. Hookwood. "I was wondering who you
reminded me of. Trevy, you've heard me talk of Matthew Jenks,
whom I knew out East—this is his son. Group Captain Trevone,
Mr. Jenks."

"Nice work," said the Group Captain. The lights began to fade.
"They're off."

Cardinal de Cortrai had not been very fortunate in his garden,
which appeared to consist of two mysterious egg-shaped statues, some
black hedges, and a miniature pavilion made of barley sugar. Lolling
there, not at ease but with many a twist and wriggle, was a youth
with butter-colored locks and a pink-and-white-striped costume. Two
bright lights from the front suddenly illuminated the eggy statues
and then went out again. A radio-gramophone made a noise like a
circular saw but was faded down to a faint scraping of stringed instruments, straight from the Middle Ages. Then a very handsome medieval
serving maid darted into the garden—and Theodore saw at once that
it was Clare Chesbey—and put her head back and threw out a hand
towards the pink-and-white youth, who wriggled himself up and
assumed a very fantastic attitude indeed, as if he had been mercilessly
struck with paralysis while trying to get out of his tights. It looked
now as if these two were about to perform a ballet.

"Highbrow," the Group Captain muttered.

Then Clare broke into speech, not in the voice she had used the day before at lunch but in a special tone more suitable for Boon's winged neo-Elizabethan manner of playwriting:

> *Oh sir, thinking my mistress sent me here,*
> *You look at me with an expectation*
> *Larger than life can bear. No message*
> *Answers it, unless I am myself an answer*
> *Written in hot blood, my quivering tongue*
> *Its pen.*

At which she rolled her eyes at him provocatively and amply displayed her charms.

"Bit spicy," said the Group Captain.

The pink-and-white youth, though admitting that her bosom was white enough to be the paper of any message, did not respond to her advances. He was not, he confessed at some length, in the mood.

"A screaming queer, anyhow," said the Group Captain.

With many a wriggle and twist and odd tossings of the head, the youth continued:

> *It is a mood*
> *In which all events slither to the brink*
> *Of bored incredibility. The world's*
> *An empty pie dish, a blown egg, the tankard*
> *Of a tippler whose chalked score outruns*
> *The landlord's slate. Here in my brain's*
> *An old spider spinning a web of nothing*
> *To catch the one fly that left the ointment...*

They were interrupted by the impressive entrance of the Princess and the Cardinal.

"My daughter," said Mr. Hookwood.

"Looks smashing," said the Group Captain, whose massive frame, to Theodore's discomfort, expanded with wonder and joy.

Miss Hookwood had a classical profile, dark auburn hair, a generous figure, a rich low voice, and was altogether a most attractive young woman. Bettison Phelps, the actor who played the Cardinal, was much older; a dignified man with a saturnine look and a 'cello concerto of a voice. He might dress up as a cardinal on Thursday and a banker on Monday but would never be mistaken for anything but a

romantic actor. But whereas he would demand a stiff salary for pulling on gray-striped trousers, he would be ready to put on red robes
for almost nothing.

The Cardinal told Clare and the pink-and-white youth, in Boon's
best manner, that here in his garden he wanted only air and not
their company. So they departed, as if about to perform a ballet
somewhere else. Miss Hookwood then announced with considerable
charm that she found a green canker in the moon and so many bright
brittle scabs in the stars. To which Mr. Phelps, after carefully working himself farther upstage and finding a spotlight, declared that
the wine he had drunk was fountaining a perfumed poison from belly
to heart and heart to mind, and gave it as his opinion that Miss Hookwood's eye and the white tower of her throat had between them
contrived this. Miss Hookwood, replying with spirit, told him that
she was a woman, and a woman out of love, and that a woman out
of love was an empty court, an inn with bolted shutters, the dark
side of the moon, and a great many other things that were fine
to say. But Mr. Phelps was able to prove that a cardinal in love,
and especially one whose wine was charged with perfumed poison,
was a great many other things equally fine to say. This duet was
broken by an armored Count, who was obviously intended to be a
fierce commanding figure but unfortunately suggested the last sardine
peering out of its tin. The two soldiers who accompanied him, though
carrying pikes, had an unmedieval air and looked like two furniture
removers who had been asked, at the last minute, to take away the
statues, with which indeed they had some trouble. The Group Captain mistakenly supposed all this to be welcome comic relief, and
bellowed with laughter, to the annoyance of the two solemn young
men sitting in front of him who turned and shushed at him, whereupon he tapped them both on the shoulder, pushed forward his formidable jaw, and told them that if they wanted any trouble they could
have it—pronto. Mr. Phelps, glaring at all three front rows, paused
pointedly, and then, when he had silence, informed the Count that
hell waited for him with a couch of burning brass.

There was a long scene between the Cardinal and the Count,
followed by an equally long scene between Miss Hookwood and
Clare and the pink-and-white youth, after which a drunken steward
turned up to get in everybody's way. The act ended with a neo-

Elizabethan song by the steward. During the applause the Group Captain, a resolute man of action, charged along the row.

"Gone to get our drinks," Mr. Hookwood explained. "Trevy's very quick at that sort of thing. Somebody has to be in these places. Now you come along with me, Jenks."

They arrived in the bar with at least half the audience, but Group Captain Trevone, wearing a grim smile, was keeping a corner for them and had already secured three large gins and ginger ales and a plate of sausage rolls. "Service," he said with some complacency. "Tuck in, chaps."

"Smart work, Trevy," said Mr. Hookwood in his abrupt high-pitched voice, which had something of a military ring. He was quite unlike his handsome daughter, and was a beaky, brown-faced man, clean-shaven and with short but untidy white hair. He had restless gleaming eyes, and looked like a mad general. "So you're Matt Jenks's son, eh? Died years ago, didn't he? What about *his* father, your grandfather? Dead? Great character—only met him once. What are you doing here?"

Theodore explained that he had come into a modest inheritance and, following a suggestion in his grandfather's will, was taking his first look at England. He added that he was there at the play at the invitation of Clare Chesbey, whose uncle he knew at Renders.

"Ah—yes, old Gerry Chesbey," cried Mr. Hookwood. "Known him for years. And the niece is a friend of Philippa's. Nice girl. What do you think of my daughter?"

"Smashing, eh?" said the Group Captain, and then looked very grim indeed. But this was because the two solemn young men had unwittingly become their neighbors in the crush.

"It's genuine Boon, of course," one of them was saying. "But I'm not going to say yet whether it's an advance on his *Give Me Arcturus*. That remains to be seen, Eric. But it's definitely more sustained than *When Will Great Orpheus*? Don't you agree?"

"I think Miss Hookwood's splendid," said Theodore. "Easily the best."

"Every time," said the Group Captain, regarding Theodore with approval.

"Is this a good play?" Theodore asked.

"Haven't the least idea," said Mr. Hookwood. "Don't understand these things. Never did. Never shall. Neither does Trevone here. Eh, Trevy?"

"Seems a lot of guff to me," said the Group Captain, "except when Philippa's on. Stone me—what a wench!"

"And I must say," cried the solemn young man who was Eric, "that Archie's done a lovely production—quite lovely. Mrs. Hungerford," he called. "I'm just saying to Charles that Archie's done a lovely production."

Mrs. Hungerford—who was to be his hostess later, Theodore now remembered—was a fuzzy little woman about fifty who seemed to bounce about in her excitement and to have no words with which to express her exalted emotions.

"My dears," she was crying, "it's all so—I mean, it simply gives one *everything*—I'm just—you know—simply—ah, Mr. Hookwood, isn't dear Philippa absolutely—and the whole thing—I mean, really beginning to—to soar."

"Quite," said the Group Captain, biting off half a sausage roll.

"This is Mr. Jenks," said Mr. Hookwood, seeing that Mrs. Hungerford, so far as she could be said to be with anybody anywhere in her present condition, had now joined them.

"I might have known," Mrs. Hungerford gasped, as if Theodore had just been awarded to her as a prize. "And isn't our dear little Clare bringing you to my party? Oh—splendid! And don't you all feel—what shall I say?—the *surge* of the whole thing? Dear Derek's play—surely his best—and darling Archie's production—and Philippa, *so* beautiful—and wonderful Bettison Phelps—such authority and yet so—so—I must find Derek and Archie." And off she bounced.

"Flames coming out of the top," said the Group Captain. "Let's have another round."

"Can't I do it?" Theodore asked, although he did not want another drink.

"No, take you too long," said Mr. Hookwood. "Trevy has the technique. Look at him." And they saw the square solid form of the Group Captain shouldering its way to the counter. "My partner. Wonderful chap. Fine war record and now a first-class man in industry, though quite new to it. You ought to come down and see what we're doing, Jenks. Remind me about it later, if we're all going to that woman's party. Said I'd go to please my daughter. Trevy and I are up in town just for the night."

The bell began ringing angrily again. The two solemn young men, Eric and Charles, put down their light ales and hurried out. Mrs. Hungerford could be seen bouncing against people to start them off toward the exit. The Group Captain returned with three large gins and ginger ales. The bell rang furiously. "Oughtn't we to be going in?" said Theodore.

"Lots of time," said Mr. Hookwood.

"Down the hatch," said the Group Captain, raising his glass.

"That Hungerford woman," said Mr. Hookwood, "puts up the money for these capers."

"Excitable type," said the Group Captain. "Guff, mostly. But Philippa rings the bell. Every time."

"Trevone's very devoted to my daughter," said Mr. Hookwood. "As you may have observed, Jenks."

"Cut it out, Hooky," said the Group Captain gruffly. Then, as if reminded of his duty, he swallowed the rest of his drink, took a step toward a lingering huddle of dim types between him and the exit, barked: "Gangway!" and went out. Theodore and Mr. Hookwood hurried after him.

It was not easy for Theodore to give the second—and concluding—act the attention that possibly it deserved. Soon after it started Mr. Hookwood fell asleep and immediately produced a strange high bubbling sound, like some dangerous liquid coming to the boil. On the other side of him, the Group Captain was even more disturbing, for now not only did his passion for Miss Hookwood audibly increase, so that he seemed about to explode whenever she appeared, but he also refused to conceal his dislike of all the male performers, at whom he grunted and snorted and muttered menacingly. A further protest from Eric and Charles, rather half-hearted this time, created a scene that was superior in its immediate effect to anything that Boon and his company were offering on the stage. It was only toward the end that the play came to life for Theodore. The Cardinal had been out-witted and humiliated by the naughty Princess and the pink-and-white youth, and now, picturesquely disordered, he was left with Clare, who, robbed of the pink-and-white youth, was ready to offer him such consolation as he might require, within the surprisingly wide limits of ecclesiastical manners in medieval Avignon. Mr. Bettison Phelps, an old hand, made the most of this situation, looking at once pathetic and noble, and using his voice as if Casals himself were at the 'cello there. Putting a hand on Clare's dark bowed head as she crouched at his feet, he cried:

> *My time runs out;*
> *The blue-gold years and the rose gardens,*
> *My young blood promised me, where are they now?*
> *A scent of roses in the dust, a jewel*
> *On the ringed hand drawing the last curtain*
> *Round my bed. These dreams are in our blood;*
> *The heart's a treachery, and only the mind*
> *Keeps faith to play the executioner,*
> *Spilling this dreaming blood upon the ground* ...

and for a moment or two Theodore did not hear Mr. Hookwood's bubbling snores or the grunts of the Group Captain.

Then all was over except for applause and bows and speeches. Mr. Phelps and Miss Hookwood said that the audience had been wonderful and that they themselves owed everything to the genius of Mr. Boon, who was then pushed on looking rather like an unmade bed. Mr. Boon, white-faced and croaking, said that the cast had been wonderful but that they all owed everything to the skill and patience of the producer, Mr. Archie Mossat. Mr. Mossat, who had a long whimsical face and a few damp gingerish curls, and looked like a rather aristocratic Scots clown, said that everybody had been wonderful, quite wonderful, and that they were all particularly grateful to their friend, Mrs. Hungerford, who then succeeded in bouncing on and off the stage before the curtain came down for the last time.

It was fortunate for Theodore that he had now been adopted by Mr. Hookwood and Group Captain Trevone, for, left to himself, he would not have known how to reach Clare Chesbey in the mysterious regions backstage. But the other two were old hands at this business, and they took him round to the stage door and through the press of excited twittering folk in the narrow corridors and stairways. The Group Captain led the attack, showing no mercy to the screaming and fluttering Erics and Charleses and their like who were in the way. Miss Hookwood and Clare were in adjoining dressing rooms, showing greasy smiling faces to all the friends and admirers and students of the drama who screeched: "But, darling, you were *marvelous.*" After about quarter of an hour of this, during which Theodore felt deeply embarrassed and in the way, the actresses announced that they really must change and closed their doors on the admiring world. In the corridor outside, the Group Captain suddenly appeared with two thick and not very clean glasses, giving one of them to Theodore. "Large gin and ginger ale," he said, like a conjuror concluding a trick. "Everything under control. Hooky's finding a cab."

"There'll be five of us with Miss Chesbey," said Theodore.

"He'll have to take five," said the Group Captain darkly. "Can't think what they had in these glasses. Hellish flavor. Filthy types, these stage types." Then he scowled, for Eric and Charles came by, still in solemn discussion.

"Mind you, Charles," Eric was saying, "if it goes into the West End—and of course it *must*—Archie must relight the whole production. The lighting is *wrong*, Charles."

"Wet hens," said the Group Captain. "Hear you're coming down to have a look at us, Jenks."

"Oh am I?" said Theodore, surprised.

"That's the idea, according to Hooky. Everything laid on. Light industry, y'know. Early days yet, but already a nice set-up—you'll like it, Jenks. Come on, you frippets," he bellowed at the two closed doors. "Get weaving."

"I must say," Theodore confided, "I'm hungry. I always seem to be hungry here in London. Not that there's anything wrong with the food—it's much better than I expected—but on nights like this one seems to go so long without any solid food."

"Couldn't agree with you more," said the Group Captain. "Every time I come up with Hooky to see one of Philippa's plays, I rumble like the devil half the night. That's why the plays are so barmy now. Everybody's hungry and feeling half-witted. Ah—here you are." This was addressed to the young women, who with a nice instinctive sense of timing now emerged together, all sleek smiling femininity.

In the taxi Theodore found himself sitting between them, while Mr. Hookwood and the Group Captain faced them in the occasional seats; and he had to tell them how he had enjoyed the play. "I liked it very much," he said.

"Clare darling," said Miss Hookwood, wailing like a clarinet, "he's just as gorgeous as you said. But he didn't like us."

"I know, darling," said Clare, lower still and equally exquisite and desolated, "and I'm so disappointed."

"But I *said* I liked it," he protested.

"Oh—no—we know."

"Quite right, darling."

"Fact is," said Mr. Hookwood, in his abrupt high-pitched way, "to tell these creatures you like something of theirs means nothing to 'em. That's so low down in the scale of praise, in their world, that it amounts to condemnation. Where we'd say *passable*, they'd say *wonderful*. When they mean *fairly good*, they say *absolutely marvelous*—"

"What happens," Theodore asked, "if you really want to say you enjoyed something enormously?"

"You couldn't do it in their language," said Mr. Hookwood. "All the words would have been used up. To do it properly you'd have to scream and beat your head against a wall. Eh, Phil?"

"Poppy Hungerford nearly does that." Philippa began giggling, and Clare, probably feeling that she could descend from her dignity too, giggled with her. And then Philippa turned herself into Mrs. Hungerford: "I mean—honestly, darlings—it's just—well, there aren't words really—but it does, the whole thing, add up to—just—*everything*—Heavens, yes—*more* than everything . . ."

"Bang on, Phil," said the Group Captain admiringly.

"Gorgeous, darling," said Clare. "Do you think anything happens between her and Archie?"

"I don't believe anybody knows about Archie," said Philippa. "But don't you think he's a genius, Mr. Jenks?"

"No, I don't," said Theodore, and had his arm squeezed hard by Clare, who pressed herself even closer to him. Whether this was a reward or a punishment, or had nothing to do with their conversation, he could not decide.

"But then," said Philippa rather loftily, "I don't suppose you know very much about the Theater, do you, Mr. Jenks?"

"I don't know anything about it," he replied cheerfully.

"And I think you're very sweet," said Clare.

"Darling, don't frighten the poor man," said Philippa.

"Shut up, Phil," said her father. "Seems to me anyhow there's a lot of damned humbug written and talked about the Theater. It's a little thing puffed out with hot air. We do far more astonishing things in industry, but don't all run screaming at each other every night.

Childish nonsense. Exhibitionism. You look at and listen to 'em at this party we're going to."

"Every time," said the Group Captain. "By the way, need we go?"

"Yes, of course we must," said Miss Hookwood sharply. "At least Clare and I must. You can please yourself, Trevy."

"Yes, yes, just burbling on," said the Group Captain apologetically. "Wouldn't think of not going—eh, chaps? Hello, must be there."

"Yes. Look, Clare—Charles and Eric."

"Yes. And is that Mona going in with Harold?"

"Peculiar thing," said Mr. Hookwood, as the taxi slowed up, "how parties affect you young women. Booze is nothing to it. Kind of empty nervous high spirits. I can hear it already in your voices."

"Dead right, Hooky," said the Group Captain. "No, I'll pay the cab." But Theodore, who could be masterful at times, insisted upon settling with the taxi driver, and told the others not to wait. "I want an extra five bob for that fifth passenger," the man said.

"I was going to give you an extra half-crown," said Theodore mildly.

"Wait a minute! Wait a minute! Another five bob's what I want—see?" He was very fierce.

"Were you promised five bob?"

"Never mind what I was promised or not promised," he snarled. "I've told you—another five bob. Come on—look sharp! Or else—"

"Or else what?" Theodore inquired, gently.

Rashly assuming that this young man concealed the heart of a chicken within his large frame, the taximan spat out several unpleasant words and added that for two bloody pins he'd get out of his cab. The next moment he was out of his cab, for Theodore, very angry now, had pulled him out, and, pinning both arms in a terrible grip, was shaking him violently. Helpless and terrified, the man heard the strangest and most fearsome words coming from this enraged giant, words like the hissing of serpents, the sharpening of knives, cracks of thunder, words of infinite menace, inevitable black doom.

"Now, are you sorry?" said Theodore, releasing him.

"Sorry? Course I'm sorry," the man cried, between his gasps. "Serves me right too. Oughta've known I'd talk about getting out o' me cab once too often. Have to pick a bloke big as a bull. And language—what was it? Malay? Serves me right—and if you say it's half a crown, then it's half a crown."

"My dear," and Theodore turned in surprise to find Clare at his elbow, "I've longed to do that for years. You were gorgeous." And she took his arm and led him into the entrance hall of the mansion flats. "Lucky I decided to wait, otherwise I'd have missed that. You know," she added slowly, "I think I adore you. And I don't propose to let you out of my sight at this party. Thank goodness you're so large, Jenks. You don't mind if I just call you Jenks, darling, do you? Because I think it's sweet—just like you."

Feeling rather foolish, and also a little dazed, Theodore allowed himself to be thus taken possession of and conducted up to Mrs. Hungerford's flat on the third floor. It looked a rum place, but Theodore had no time to decide what made it look so odd before the party, which was the Mermaid Club all over again, broke over him. Clare behaved as if she were a hunter newly arrived from the mountains of Yünnan and had succeeded in capturing there, in Theodore, a giant golden panda. It was she who took him round the room and introduced him to Derek Boon and Archie Mossat, Eric and Charles, Bettison Phelps and the rest. The refreshments, which included some odd Central European delicacies and a greenish punch that looked and tasted like embrocation, were chiefly served by two Austrian women, who had turned on so much Viennese charm that they seemed almost out of their minds. Mrs. Hungerford bounced her fuzzy little person in and out of every group, and was well-nigh speechless with glory.

"He adores the play," Clare told Boon, in her capacity as trainer-interpreter. And Theodore did not resent this because it saved him a lot of trouble.

"Jolly good of you, jolly good," said Boon, a nice youngish chap, all tidied up now and looking more like a farmer than the passionate chronicler of amorous cardinals. "We're trying to get clean away from all that dreary old drawing-room and back-kitchen stuff. Eh, Archie?"

"Ay. Nae more cocktails an' cups o' tea," cried Mr. Mossat, whose accent was as Scots as his appearance. "Believe it or not, but Ah prayed every neet, barrin' Sundays, for twenty yearrs to be reed o' these screepts filled wi' cocktails an' cups o' tea. An' droll butlers an' comic maids. An' all the daft fuss wi' telephones."

"Absolutely," said Clare, and took Theodore away. "Don't you agree, Jenks darling?"

"I don't know," said Theodore, who might be feeling dazed, partly

as a result of the evening's events and partly because of the Group
Commander's large gins and ginger ales, but who still kept a certain
detachment, based on an obstinate solidity of character. "In this play
of Boon's there aren't any cocktails or cups of tea, but everybody
keeps drinking imaginary wine out of imitation goblets and tankards.
And though there aren't any comic butlers and maids, there's a comic
steward and a semi-comic handmaiden or something, the girl you
played. And though there isn't a telephone, of course, there are several
messengers, who take up more time and aren't particularly interesting.
It all gets away from life today, of course—"

"But that's the point, my dear. The whole point."

"Which means it's a nice change for people," he continued thoughtfully, "and I suppose that's what they like. But wouldn't they possibly
feel a lot more, be hit harder where they live, if the curtain went up
on life as it is today and they saw themselves instead of a lot of fancy
cardinals and princesses?"

"But it's all so *dreary*," cried Clare. "Everything's so dreary now."

"I don't believe it is," said Theodore firmly. "And I don't believe
people really think so. It's frightening sometimes—and that's what
people really feel, only they're pretending not to."

"Don't touch that stuff, Jenks." It was the Group Captain, and he
carried two big tumblers. "Only meant for a horse's hindquarters.
Here you are, chaps. Two large gins and ginger ales. See you later."

"I can never decide," said Clare dreamily, "whether that Trevone
man is rather sweet or rather sinister—or both. But then he's madly
devoted to Philippa, of course. And at the moment she's rather concentrating on Bettison Phelps—quite a mistake, in my view."

"And if I could write a play," said Theodore, ignoring her remarks
and refreshed by a long pull at the gin and ginger ale, "I'd write a play
showing people secretly frightened and pretending everything was
dreary."

"And it would run a week," said Clare, who was shrewder than she
generally appeared to be. "Besides being very dull and difficult for the
actors. We adore putting on fancy clothes and spouting gorgeous lines.
Don't we, Bettison?" For now they had been joined by the actor, who
somehow contrived to look almost as noble and melancholy in blue
serge as he had done in his red robe.

"The Theater, Mr. Jenks," he announced, as if opening the slow
movement of a 'cello sonata, "belongs to the Actors. It always did, my

dear boy. But for about forty years we foolishly allowed it to be taken
from us by authors and producers, who compelled us to do what they
wished, making us *work* instead of *play,* contracting instead of expanding our personalities; and the old magic vanished. Now—taking possession of the playhouse once again—we are bringing it back. Clare, dear
heart, you look so ravishing tonight that I believe you must be falling
in love. Is this the fortunate fellow? My dear boy, I congratulate you."
And he sauntered away, toward one of the few bottles of whisky on
view.

"He's rather sweet, isn't he?" said Clare. "Though of course he wears
stays and elevators, and dyes like mad, and has to be massaged and
daren't eat properly—and is probably hundreds of years old, poor old
sweet. But a *real* actor."

"And could never be mistaken for anything else," said Theodore.
"Just as if he could act but only act an actor."

"Drink that up, and don't be tiresome, Jenks. I'm still hungry."

"So am I. Shall we try over there?"

Near the table where most of the food was—and now the two
middle-aged Viennese soubrettes had vanished—Eric and Charles were
eating apple strudel and explaining the subtleties of her part to Philippa
Hookwood. Not far away the Group Captain, who had not been mellowed by his mysterious and endless supply of gin and ginger ale, was
glowering at them. At his side were Mr. Hookwood and the young
actor with butter-colored hair, who had exchanged his pink-and-white
costume for a green tweed suit and a lilac shirt that were equally picturesque. Clare was dragged into the Eric-and-Charles discussion by
Philippa, and Theodore felt himself free to obey a signal from Mr.
Hookwood.

"I'm simply a frightful mass of nerves," the young actor was hissing,
closing his eyes and throwing his head back. "It's a maddening nuisance
but there it is—just a mass of nerves. Aren't you?"

"No, I'm not," said Mr. Hookwood. "No nerves at all. Same with
him." And he indicated the Group Captain, who had turned to be
busy at a little table, which he appeared to have concealed from the
general gaze by screening it with his massive body. "You ought to
take a three-mile run every morning."

"My dear, I'd *die,*" the young actor screamed.

"There's a fellow over there waving at you," said Mr. Hookwood,
winking at Theodore.

"Tank up, chaps," said the Group Captain. "The old gin and ginger. Had to keep it covered or some of these queers would have had it mopped up long since. Hear you had a turn-up with the taxi bloke, Jenks. Nice work. Now, when are you coming down to see us?"

"That's the point," said Mr. Hookwood. "Trevy and I must go in a minute. Ought to see what some of us are trying to do in light industry, Jenks. What about coming down on Monday and staying a day or two? We can put you up right on the spot."

Theodore thanked them, adding that Monday would suit him.

"Good show," said the Group Captain. "But drink up, old boy. I can just squeeze another round out of it."

"I don't think I can manage this, let alone another one," said Theodore apologetically. "How do I get to you?"

"Trevy'll explain," said Mr. Hookwood. "I must have a word with Phil before we go."

"Take the 10:35 to Farbridge," said the Group Captain. "Change at Farbridge for local slow train to Brant-in-the-Hollow. That's where we are—Hookwood and Trevone Limited, Light Alloy Products, Brant Manor, Brant-in-the-Hollow. If you get the 10:35, you'll be in at about one. I'll be there. Let's drink to it. All the best!"

"All the best!" And with one vast gulp, Theodore put away most of the gin and ginger ale in his glass. When he looked at the party again, it seemed to have retreated and to have dwindled and yet to be both brighter in color and noisier than before, as if it were now on a stage. "Very odd," he heard himself saying. "And why is this room so rum?"

"Because," said Clare, who had unaccountably taken the place of the Group Captain, "poor Poppy Hungerford was mad about advanced nonrepresentational art and then got a craze for Early Victorian, and now they're both mixed up and don't fit at all. And I think we ought to be going home."

In the taxi he found himself kissing Clare from time to time, but failed to discover any particular point in it. A nice girl, who improved on further acquaintance, but not, it appeared, the one he was looking for; which was sad, very sad, very very sad. . . .

6

The little slow train from Farbridge went rumbling along between low rounded hills and fields still sullen with winter. To Theodore, still haunted by the glare and splendor of the East, this Midland landscape seemed gray, dull, almost lifeless. Now and then he caught a glimpse of a pleasant stone village or an old mansion, but there was no sun to give them warmth and color. He had been glad to leave London, of which he had suddenly tired, but he began to wonder if this visit to Mr. Hookwood and the Group Captain, which had somehow been thrust upon him, would not prove to be a mournful mistake. However, it was all experience, another and quite different look at the English scene.

Brant-in-the-Hollow, when it came, looked exactly like the other five stations they had stopped at since Farbridge. The Group Captain was not on the platform. Perhaps he had forgotten all about this visit. But when Theodore reached the station entrance, he heard a vast roar and hooting coming up the hill; then he saw the Group Captain driving up in a long low open car, of an old pattern, very dirty but lavishly furnished with lamps and plaques and gadgets, and looking as if it had just been driven across Asia.

"Not kept you waiting? Good!" cried the Group Captain. "Shove your bag in the back. Old bus, of course, but still goes like hell."

They shot down the hill, making as much noise as if they were splitting it in two. "Giving you a bite at the pub, if you don't mind," the Group Captain shouted above the din. "Be there in a tick."

The village street went whizzing past, so many flashes of weathered stone. At the bottom the Group Captain turned and shot them up to a pub door. A moment later they were standing in a small saloon bar, where a very fat man was pouring out two large gin and ginger ales.

"Service, George," the Group Captain shouted. "Nice work. Meet Mr. Jenks from Indonesia or thereabouts. This is George."

"How do?" said George. "Come to see what they're doing up at the Manor? My youngest girl works for 'em up there, an' she says they're crackers. That's her word for it—crackers."

"She's crackers," said the Group Captain. "So are you, George. And so is this one." And he made a rush at a plump young woman who had just entered the bar from the back, embraced her, and shouted: "Where's the steak and kidney pud you promised me, frippet?"

"Go on, Groupie," she cried, pushing him away. "I told you it was steak and kidney Thursday. Today it's meat pie, roast potatoes, and greens."

"What the hell are greens? Drink up, Jenks. Two more, George."

"If you don't mind," Theodore protested, "I think I'll wait until I've eaten something—"

"Get weaving, frippet," the Group Captain shouted at the plump young woman. "Bring in the meat pie and greens. We're busy men."

"You're off your chump, and it's ready now," the young woman shouted, all in high good humor.

As she went bustling out, a little old man, brown and hard as a nut, came bustling in. "I've fixed 'im, Cap'n," he cried triumphantly. "Fixed 'im proper."

"Fixed what? Give him a drink, George."

"Rum," said the old man promptly. "Yes, Cap'n, it's all doddled up proper. Young Joe Farley'll bring 'is concertina—that's Joe who's over at Warbley's—an' a nice 'and with the concertina, as good as you could wish for—an' 'im an' me we'll 'ave a bit of a practice like first, we will—"

"What *is* this?" demanded the Group Captain. "Here—swallow this rum."

"Thankin' you kindly, Cap'n. An' as for Joe's concertina an' me singin'—that's for the concert you're 'avin' up at the Manor—"

"Never heard of it."

"Mr. Hookwood it was that asked about it," said the ancient.

"Oh well, that's his pigeon. I'm not in the picture."

"I got one or two ol' songs a bit on the free side, you might say," said the old man, winking rapidly at Theodore.

"Go on, you nasty old man," cried the plump young woman, who now returned with a loaded tray.

"Don't tell nothin' you don't know about—"

"That'll do."

"Better hold 'em back, Grandpa," said the Group Captain. "You can sing 'em to me afterwards."

"You're as bad as he is," said the plump young woman, busy at the table.

"Not 'im," said the old man, chuckling. "At 'is age I was just makin' a start. Well—'ave to see Frank Mokes 'bout one of 'is young pigs. 'E'll 'ave one breakin' its leg any day now, Frank will. Mornin', Cap'n. Mornin', sir." And out he went, still chuckling.

"The wicked old sausage," said George.

"Now if you want some more," said the plump young woman, "just ask—and there won't be any. Now stop it," for the Group Captain was trying to land a slap on her magnificent behind, "or you won't get any bread and butter pudding. And what will your friend think? Nice manners!"

"Glad you could come down, Jenks," said the Group Captain, over the meat pie. "Don't see anything in London. All right for a razzle, but that's all. Philippa won't come down because she says it's dull here. Doesn't seem dull to me."

Theodore said that so far it had not seemed dull to him.

"You're dead right. All very matey and lively. Changed a lot in the last ten years, of course. I came down here first early in the war, teaching blokes to fly. Took a fancy to it, and when I went into partnership with old Hooky, I persuaded him to see what we could find round here."

"I don't understand about Mr. Hookwood," said Theodore. "I thought he'd been in the Colonial Service."

"Colonial Service, then Indian. When they retired him, he was still full of beans and had some capital, so he joined me. I'd a couple of good foreman types from the Raf, so we all got weaving. Hooky didn't know anything about industry, of course, but he was sound on Admin. and turned out to be a cracking organizer. We organize like hell up at the Manor. It'll rock you, Jenks old boy."

"This manor is your factory, is it?"

"Workshops, offices, everything. Hooky—he's a widower—and I and a few other unmarried types live there, bang on the spot. Huge barn of a place, mind you. Nobody could live—" But now he broke off, then muttered: "Hold it."

Two people had arrived. One of them was a tall man in very old riding clothes. He had a long melancholy face, a drooping mustache, and a look of perpetual and slightly pained surprise. His companion was a dumpy middle-aged woman who stared indignantly at the world from under an outrageous purple hat.

"Good morning, Sir Barclay," said George respectfully.

"Good morning, George." Sir Barclay turned to the woman, bent down and shouted: "What will you have, Mrs. Porter? I say—what will you have?"

"Stout," said the woman in a loud blank voice, and then waddled grumpily into a corner.

"A stout, George," said Sir Barclay mournfully, "and—er—a glass of bitter for me—"

"Nonsense!" the Group Captain called to him. "What you want's a socking big gin and ginger ale."

"Oh—hello—Trevone! Quite agree, but can't afford it—must look to the pennies, my dear chap."

"George, a large gin and ginger ale for Sir Barclay."

"Much obliged." Sir Barclay came over to them, and was introduced to Theodore as Sir Barclay Gishforth, Lord and owner of Brant Manor. "We rent it from him," the Group Captain explained.

"And a dam' good job too," said Sir Barclay. "Otherwise, with that place on our hands, we'd be sunk. As it is, we're foundering by inches."

"Who's the lady friend?" the Group Captain whispered.

"Needn't lower your voice. She's deaf as a post. She's the cook—and she's going, and I'm supposed to be taking her to the station. But I thought I'd try softening her up with a drink and then making a last desperate appeal. Daphne and I can manage the cleaning and that sort of thing, but neither of us can cook, and if this woman goes, then we live on boiled eggs and tinned muck. Bit thick, isn't it? I say that Daphne ought to have learned how to cook, and she says why not me. What's this?"

"Bread and butter pud," said the plump young woman, who had just arrived with two large helpings of it. "And very nice, though I say it as shouldn't, gents."

"Very fond of it," said Sir Barclay wistfully. "Oughtn't to be hard to do."

"It isn't, if you know how. Have some."

"I say, that's good of you," cried Sir Barclay, brightening for a second. But then the complications of this life darkened the air again, and restored to him his look of pained surprise. "Rather difficult to manage at the moment, though. Trying to persuade Mrs. Porter there to stay with us," he explained to the plump young woman.

"I'll have a go," she said, "while you have some pud."

"Oh, I say, could you?"

"If Maggie can't, nobody can," said George, who had brought Sir Barclay's gin and ginger ale. All four men watched Maggie approach Mrs. Porter, who was now grimly removing froth from her lips.

"Mrs. Porter," Maggie shouted, "you know that nasty hard American pork?"

Mrs. Porter nodded, her face impassive in the shade of that monstrous purple hat.

"Well, I don't know what to do with it," Maggie continued at the top of her voice. "I wish you'd have a look and tell me."

"There's ways," Mrs. Porter announced, like an oracle.

"I wish you'd show me."

"You young women don't know everything, do you?" Mrs. Porter was almost conversational.

"That's right."

Mrs. Porter rose. "I'll have a look." And she waddled after Maggie, who returned a moment or two later with a helping of bread and butter pudding for Sir Barclay.

"I've got her interested," Maggie announced. "Leave it to me."

The three men settled down to their pudding and gin and ginger ale. "Wonderful life you fellows have," said Sir Barclay. "You'll have to find me a job, Trevone. You really will. Must be something I can do. What about this personnel management game—seeing the chaps and girls are all happy—what? Something in that, isn't there?"

The Group Captain looked thoughtful. "Could be. Hooky and I have been doing it ourselves up to now. But we've been wondering lately about a personnel manager. But are you the type, old boy?"

"Possibly not," said Sir Barclay modestly. "But good old family and all that, you know. Lot of these people are still snobs—if it is snobbery."

The Group Captain shook his massive head. "Young uns aren't. Grown up in a new world. Wouldn't give a sausage for your baronetcy, not even the girls. New types—you'd be surprised."

"No, wouldn't be surprised," said Sir Barclay, denying his permanent look. "But always get on damned well with these local chaps and girls. So does Daphne. Might take it in turns or something, eh?" he added hopefully.

"I'll talk it over with Hooky."

"Do, my dear chap. Don't want to be a nuisance, but something'll have to be done." He looked at Theodore. "You in this industry game, Mr. Jenks?"

Theodore explained that he was a mere visitor.

"You'll be astonished to see what these amazing chaps have done up at my old place. Can never get over it myself. I just remember it in my grandfather's time when he had the whole place going—scores of bedrooms and servants by the dozen and supplies arriving by the cartload. Couldn't last, of course. Even in my governor's time about half the place was shut off, and then, before Trevone and Hookwood turned up to take it off our hands, my wife and I were living in a corner of it, perishingly cold most of the time. No children, thank God. Now we live in the old head gamekeeper's cottage—no birds now, just a few rabbits—and can keep it fairly warm and clean but can't feed ourselves properly. Walk over for a cup of tea tomorrow, if you're staying. Glad to see you. Glad to see anybody so long as they don't expect to be dined and wined." Sir Barclay carefully drained his glass. "Daphne was reminding me last night how her governor—he was in shipping and took a hell of a toss at the end—commandeered most of Claridge's when we were married and filled about five hundred people up to the neck with the best Bollinger. The old man used to have his cigars specially made for him in Havana—used to come in cabinets, thousand at a time. Couldn't last, of course. Had a good innings, perhaps too good, because I always suspected he was a wrong un. Daphne gets bitter sometimes—you know how women are—but I tell her we can't grumble. We had our innings when we were young and could enjoy it. Now then." He rose expectantly, for the plump Maggie was ushering in Mrs. Porter.

"I'll stop on," said Mrs. Porter, "if I gets another ten shillings a week."

"Best I could do," said Maggie. "Can't shift her from that. You'll have to cough up, Sir Barclay."

"I say, you've done wonders," said Sir Barclay. "Well, Mrs. Porter," he bellowed, "I suppose I ought to talk to Lady Gishforth—"

"My last word," Mrs. Porter announced, the purple hat bobbing. "Take it or leave it."

"Then we'll have to take it," Sir Barclay shouted. He turned to the Group Captain. "Dashed awkward. Have to manage somehow, I suppose."

"Shopping to do if I do come back," said Mrs. Porter.

"Shopping—yes—well, better get on with it, eh?" the Baronet roared at her. Then, after thanking the Group Captain for his drink, he reminded Theodore he would be welcome to walk over and take tea with them. "Might have scones now," he added hopefully.

The Group Captain took Theodore rattling and jolting up a long drive that showed many signs of wear and tear. On each side was a ruined park broken here and there into allotments. Then came some old Army huts, a collection of shabby cars, bicycles and some lorries, and finally the great ghostly façade of Brant Manor, which was an enormous Jacobean mansion. They took Theodore's bags up the dilapidated main staircase, along a corridor that was sad and draughty, then up a narrow winding staircase, and finally into a remote room that contained nothing but some inadequate distemper, a camp bed, one naked electric bulb, two coathooks and a torn towel, a piece of cracked linoleum, a peculiar smell, and a temperature just above freezing point. Theodore had seen nothing so grim since he left the Army.

"You'll be fairly snug in here," said the Group Captain cheerfully. "Bathroom of sorts at the end of the corridor. But I'd advise the lav downstairs. You'll find Hooky and me on the first floor—*Admin*. Show you round whenever you're ready.

Theodore had brought two large bags, not because he had expected to stay long at Brant Manor, but so that he could remain away from London if necessary for several weeks. But how he could do any unpacking in this room, he could not imagine; unless he merely transferred the contents of one bag to the other. He unstrapped them, took out a few things for the night, and then sat on the bed, which immediately sagged and groaned alarmingly. He lit a cigar in the hope of warming the place up and hiding that peculiar smell. After the hearty knockabout business in the pub, which he had enjoyed, this cold little room seemed very cheerless; and he began to regret that he had not decided to stay at the pub. Sleepily he pulled away at his cigar, and half-lost himself in a somber reverie.

It was broken by the entrance, following immediately upon a knock, of a short untidy young woman. "You're Mr. Jenks, aren't you? Groupie sent me up. I'm his secretary. Call me Liz. Everybody does. Nice cigar. Mind giving me a light from it?" She had eyes like gooseberries and a mouth as wide as a clown's; and she wore a puce jumper stained with ink and dingy corduroy slacks. After she had lit her cigarette, she stared hard at him and said: "Groupie said you were a smashing type. And for once he's dead right."

If there was any adequate reply to this, Theodore did not know it. So he looked down at her in silence. For a moment or two she was busy expelling smoke through her left nostril.

"I was sent up to look after you and show you round if you want to see anything," she said. "A Board of Trade chap has just arrived, so Groupie and Mr. Hookwood are tied up. What do you think of this room they've given you?"

"Well—between ourselves, Liz—not much."

"They've no idea. Mr. Hookwood's ancient and doesn't care—that's how you get, I suppose. But Groupie ought to get married. You keen on industry?"

"No, I'm not."

She stared at him in astonishment. "Why did you come here then?"

"I don't know. I'm looking around, and as they seemed anxious for me to come here, I thought I might as well see what they were doing. I still don't understand what you make here."

"Anything small you can make out of these alloys," said Liz. "Some of its sub-contracting work, but we're developing a few lines of our own. Let's go, shall we?"

All the main workshops were on the ground floor, and what had once been the drawing room, the dining room, the library, the morning room, was now filled with little machines and workers, mostly girls in green or brown overalls. Above the whirr and clatter in each workshop, and beating hard against what remained of the old paneling, was the sound of popular songs and dance tunes issuing relentlessly from loud-speakers. Mad giants proclaimed out of throats of brass their most intimate sentiments. "Ah ree-a-lize," they moaned with frightening emphasis, "all yew meant toe me-yer"; "Ah'm feeling blew," the monsters whined, "becarze of yew"; and there was no escape from the love life of these sentimental demons, who all appeared to live in the South or West of the United States. Theodore felt that hell might be something like this. Yet nobody looked unhappy. The matrons who could be seen bending with a prodigal curve of buttocks, the young girls who peeped out of dark-fringed eyes as clear and innocent as dewponds, all seemed content, sometimes even happy, as they tended their machines and hummed those monstrous melodies.

Liz had left Theodore in the care of one of the Group Captain's foremen, a lean character called Fred, who explained every technical process at great length, usually at about an inch from Theodore's ear. Throughout this tour, in which he was spared nothing, he never understood what Fred was talking about or what all these women and girls were supposed to be making. It was like being in a confused dream that might at any moment turn sinister.

"Well, that's it, chum," said Fred, after he had taken Theodore to the foot of the main staircase. "Gives you a rough idea."

"Yes, thanks very much."

"Mind you," Fred continued, "I think we've broken the jobs down too far. Me and the Group's working at a plan to build 'em up in teams. Worth trying."

Liz came scampering down the great stairs, a perky incongruous figure against their remnants of grace and style. "Cuppa for you in a minute, Mr. Jenks," she announced. "How did it go, Fred? Give him the works?"

"You're a cheeky little basket," Fred told her. "This place is full of 'em, but you get the prize." He winked solemnly at Theodore, then stalked away.

"I'm not your type, am I?" said Liz, as they went up the stairs.

"I hadn't thought about it," Theodore began.

"Go on. Of course you had. Everybody does—I mean, while they're still young." She gave him a sharp nudge. "Come off it—you can't kid me."

Which was true enough, he decided. "All right then, Liz—you're not."

"That's better." She was obviously not offended. "Take a look at Dulcia—she's Mr. Hookwood's secretary. She might be more your style. Tall and refined—and a bit dim. Drinks sherry and cider—and reads books."

"Don't you read books?"

"Never. What's the point when there's so much real life going on? And when you're tired of that, there's always television and the flicks. This way—cuppa's in the Planning Room."

In this room many a Lady Gishforth must have trembled as a young bride, shrieked with the birth pangs, and stared with a glazing eye at the last daylight on earth. Across the ceiling there were cupids smiling among blotched and cracked roses. The lower panels on the walls were covered with charts boldly colored in poster paints. On a long table near the window Mr. Hookwood was comfortably perched, smoking a cherrywood pipe. He was wearing a thick blue jersey, old flannel pants, and sandals, and the thatch of white hair above his brown beaky face was very untidy. He looked like a cozy old yachtsman.

"Liz, help Dulcie with the tea," he said. "Well, Jenks, what do you think of us?"

"Very interesting," said Theodore. "But I was just thinking how happy you looked."

Mr. Hookwood took his pipe out of his mouth, tapped the end of his nose with the mouthpiece, then puffed away again. "So I am, my boy, so I am. Haven't made any money yet—but that'll come. And that's not the point. I spent thirty years being an official—and a good one too, let me tell you—and there I was, having to be careful—and now I don't give a damn. By the way, Trevy'll be back in a minute. It was a great stroke of luck for me running into him, then going into this business. Haven't enjoyed myself so much since I was a boy. Look at those charts."

"I was noticing them," said Theodore. "Very impressive."

"The fun Trevy and I have had with those things—why, it's rolled fifty years off my back. Sometimes we've stayed up half the night doing 'em. This is our latest." He went across and pointed with his pipe. "Export analysis in terms of currencies. Useful, you know, Jenks. Don't think it isn't useful. Gives you the whole situation at a glance. Essential for planning."

But there was a twinkle behind his surface solemnity. He knew—and knew that Theodore knew he knew—that at the root of all this was a boyish impulse to use poster paints on the largest sheets of paper obtainable. And as he caught Theodore's glance, he laughed. "Trevy loves 'em too."

The Group Captain came in at that moment, and with him were the two secretaries and the tea. Dulcie was a rather tall girl, older and neater than Liz; and she had a long neck, downy cheeks, and pretty eyes that had a mixed look of apprehension and gentle reproach. After dispensing the tea, Liz sprawled on the only rug in the place while Dulcie drooped herself elegantly against a chart headed *Raw Material Breakdown*. The tea, served in thick chipped cups, had been stewed into a black bitterness; the cake was stale. The painted cupids among their roses seemed to stare in pale astonishment. The voices of the sentimental giants could still be heard from below. Outside the window, against a bleached chill sky, the rooks flapped and cawed. The Group Captain, nearly choking with fury and stale cake, denounced the Board of Trade. Nothing he saw or heard made much sense to Theodore, who still felt he was fixed in a dream.

There was no escaping from this dream after tea. The Group Captain, still bristling, took Liz off to write what he called some "snorters." All fire and energy and organizing genius, Mr. Hookwood, accompanied by the gentle apprehensive Dulcie carrying a large card- board plan so highly colored and intricate that it looked like a master- piece of modern art, marched Theodore up and down stairs and along corridors, demonstrating some elaborate system he had evolved so that everybody in the firm knew where everybody else could be found. This meant following variously colored arrow signs in every part of the huge decaying mansion, often far from any evidence not only of industrial enterprise but of human life itself. It was like play- ing a huge mysterious game. After red, blue, yellow, and green arrows had been observed and followed in turn, they tackled the brown, which in the fading light were harder to discover, and they ended at a remote door labeled EXPORT: LATIN AMERICA that led them into a former linen room occupied by one boy, two new files, and a homemade dartboard on which the boy was trying his skill. While Mr. Hookwood remonstrated with the boy, Theodore and Dulcie re- tired to the landing, along which a green dusk was creeping.

They looked at each other for a moment. The vague apprehension fled from Dulcie's eyes, and something glimmered in its place. She smiled. This was enough for Theodore, who began roaring with laughter until he was leaning against the wall, helpless, with tears rolling down his cheeks. Infected by this huge merriment, the girl laughed too; so that when Mr. Hookwood came out, the pair of them were roaring and screeching, their faces scarlet, their eyes screwed up and wet, the landing lost in a crimson fog.

"Hello, hello, you two!" cried Mr. Hookwood smiling. "What's the joke? Come on, now."

"I don't know," Theodore gasped, and went off into a fresh peal.

"Oh—do stop," cried Dulcie, as helpless as he was.

"I know—my fault—sorry—can't help it."

Mr. Hookwood stared from one to the other, frowned for a second, then began laughing too; and now the three of them were shaken by an ecstasy of idiotic mirth. Round the corner of the door EXPORT: LATIN AMERICA came the face of the boy, his eyes widening, his face broadening into a grin. Theodore pointed to him, and the other two saw what he saw, and off the three of them went again, this time joined by the boy.

Later, after all the employees had gone and there had been large gins and ginger ales in the Planning Room, Theodore was taken by

Mr. Hookwood and the Group Captain to a corner of the canteen (blue arrow) on the ground floor, where a heavily breathing indignant woman brought them tepid mutton, potatoes and drowned cabbage, soggy apple pie and custard, a brute of a meal. Mr. Hookwood then decided to do some work, so the Group Captain took Theodore blaring and rattling through the dark and the rain to the pub where they had had lunch; and there George produced more large gins and ginger ales, the plump smiling Maggie came and went, and various representatives of Brant-in-the-Hollow talked about nothing in particular with that huge solemnity and unnecessary emphasis generally to be discovered in crowded saloon bars. Then they went blaring and rattling back to the Manor, now so much deeper darkness in the dark; and Theodore, in a stupor of gin, ginger ale, cigar smoke, indigestion and weariness, stumbled into his cold little room and his cold little bed, fell asleep at once, woke up sharply after about two hours, and then spent an Ice Age alternately wrestling and dozing.

At breakfast, which arrived nearly cold on trays in the Planning Room, Theodore told the partners that he ought to go, but, to his dismay, they would not hear of it. Mr. Hookwood said there was to be an entertainment that night in the canteen, and that Theodore must on no account miss it. So he agreed to stay another night. "And perhaps you could do something," said Mr. Hookwood, who was in charge of the program. "Sing—recite—anything."

"I can do a few little conjuring tricks," said Theodore.

"Good man! What about apparatus?"

"I have a pack of cards and one or two other things in my bag," said Theodore. "And I could collect anything else I need—quite ordinary things—during the day. But I ought to have an assistant—a girl preferably."

"When I've done my letters, you can take Liz," said the Group Captain. "I'll be out the rest of the day. Back for dinner and the show, of course."

"I meant to ask the Gishforths to come and eat with us tonight," said Mr. Hookwood.

Theodore remembered Sir Barclay's invitation to tea. "I'll walk across the park this afternoon and tell them about tonight."

"Good show," said the Group Captain. "Now we're all set. And if you want to rehearse your tricks with Liz, come down to my office about half-past eleven. I'll be through then."

Theodore hardly recognized Liz when he discovered her in the Group Captain's office. The stained jumper and dingy slacks had been replaced by a neat gray dress with a white collar, and her hair had been carefully done.

"Partly for tonight," she explained, "and partly for your sake."

"My sake?"

"Yes," she said gloomily, "I've gone and fallen for you. Don't tell me it's silly, because I know it is. But that's me all over. Now let's see these tricks. And what do I do?"

He went through the tricks he proposed to perform, and showed her carefully what she had to do to help him. She was very quick, and soon understood what was required of her. "It's a smashing turn," she declared. "We ought to make a variety act of it. Dulcie'll be as jealous as blazes. Those tall refined girls are hell inside. She told me about that giggling do you had last night. I was jealous then. My God —aren't we a bright lot? I don't see how you do that trick with the Queen of Spades."

"I have several of them," said Theodore, showing her.

"What a sell! Why, I could conjure at that rate. Let me try."

"It's not quite as easy as it looks."

"Nothing ever is, except getting into mischief. Well, I'll try." Which she did, several times. "I must say, you're a gorgeous chap. Groupie thinks you're not married. Is he right? Good! Any special girl friend?"

"No, not at present." And then Theodore yawned.

"Well, don't yawn about it. Oh—I suppose you didn't get much sleep up in that stinking little room. What do you think about us here —honestly now?"

"I think—I'm sorry," for he was yawning again "—I think you're all very pleasant—but—"

"But a bit barmy. That's what I think too," she said cheerfully. "And they can say what they like about what women want—and you ought to hear my Mum on what happens when Mr. Right Comes Along—but if you ask me it'll be a bit grim after this, getting married and washing nappies and queuing for fish. I like it here, though I'm beginning to fancy some passionate love somewhere in my life. When are you leaving us?"

"Early tomorrow, Liz."

"You would, wouldn't you? Oh—well—back to the old slacks then.

Still, there's tonight—and we ought to be the best turn there. I say, you haven't fallen for that daughter of Mr. Hookwood's, like Groupie, have you?"

Theodore assured her he had not.

"Glamorous," said Liz severely. "But expensive, would never take to industry, and in a few years she'll weigh tons. Look—honeyboy— go up and have a nap, and either Dulcie or me'll try to find something decent to eat at lunch and bring it up on a tray. It's blue murder down there anyhow. Go on—pop off."

He was dreaming of gold islands in dark seas when a tap came at his door. But it was the gentle Dulcie, her downy cheeks aflame, who entered with his tray. "We tossed for it," she announced, without adding who had won. "I'm afraid it's not very nice, but it's the best we could do. Do you want me to go?"

"No, please don't. If you don't mind my eating."

"No, of course not. Besides, I can take the things back." She regarded him earnestly, with pretty startled eyes. "Mr. Jenks, I wish you'd tell me what you think of the people you've met here. Your honest opinion."

"I don't understand them," said Theodore, struggling with a piece of sausage embedded in tough batter. "They seem quite different from any people I've met before. Like a new race."

"Oh—I'm so glad. I began to think it must be me."

"Well, it may be, but it's me too," he told her. "I don't know whether they belong to a new civilization or a new barbarism, but whatever it is, it's new—and quite strange to me."

"That's what I feel," she cried. "I've tried to explain to my father and mother, but I can't make them understand. These people don't care for any of the things we like at home—and yet they're not just stupid. For instance, Liz is better at her work than I am. But they seem to live in a strange world, not the one I know, and to feel differently inside about everything. Sometimes I feel they're childish and I'm grown-up. At other times they seem to me grown-up and I feel childish. I thought there must be something wrong with me."

"No, I feel the same. And I'm sure there's nothing wrong with me." He smiled at her confidently.

"I used to wonder about the audiences you hear at B.B.C. variety programs," she said, still worried and looking not unlike a tall good-looking rabbit. "They never laugh at the jokes—they just clap them.

Now I think they're these people. It's what Liz and Fred would do, I'm sure. I'm sorry your sweet looks so horrid." It was a mixture of tinned peaches and pink blancmange. "I have to play the piano to-night—though I'm not very good. I'm glad you're staying, Mr. Jenks."

He stopped eating, to stare at her speculatively. "I'm just wondering if I can endure another night in that little brute of a bed. How do you all get home after this show? And where do you live?"

"Well, I live just this side of Farbridge," she told him. "And a lot of the others live that way too, and there'll be at least one special bus. If you'd like me to, I could ring up the White Hart at Far-bridge—it's quite a nice hotel—and book a room for you there."

"That's it," he cried enthusiastically. "Please do."

"Just for one night?"

"I suppose so." And he remembered afterwards how wrong he was to suppose so.

At about quarter-past four, after wandering round the park, he came to a cottage squatting among tall trees noisy with rooks. Sir Barclay Gishforth must have been looking out of a window, for he was opening the door before Theodore had quite reached it. His long drooping face had not been designed to express delight, but he gave Theodore the impression that he was very pleased to see him. "I hoped you'd look in, my dear fellow. Dull day, isn't it? Not bad here in summer but the winter seems to last forever. Tedious at times."

He led Theodore into a sitting room so crowded with things, many of them much too large for it, that there seemed to be no place for people in there. "Dashed cramped, I know," he said ruefully; and then went out and shouted to his wife and Mrs. Porter, while Theodore exchanged stares with an Early Victorian Major-General Sir Adrian Gishforth, who looked as if at any moment he might pull down the wall.

"I've left Barclay to bring in the tea," said Lady Gishforth, after introducing herself. "He told me what happened yesterday in the pub and I'm much obliged to you, Mr. Jenks."

"Oh—it had nothing to do with me," said Theodore.

"Certainly it had. That young woman Maggie managed it, of course, but she was probably showing off for your benefit. I know these girls. The minute an attractive strange young man appears, they show off like mad. Do sit down."

She was still a handsome woman, with clear hard eyes, but she looked as if she had gone through some process that had converted flesh and blood into a mysterious indestructible material somewhere between leather and china. Her voice too must have been transformed by this alchemy, for it had no softness and none of the usual feminine inflections; it came out, as if from a larynx constructed of whip-cord and porcelain, equally harsh and strong in every syllable it pronounced. She made him feel that while he was not personally un-welcome there, he was nevertheless a representative of the mad and evil world that imprisoned the Gishforths in that cottage, if only a very minor and almost innocent official employed by the vast Anti-Gishforth Combine now ruling this planet.

"Barclay said you were only a visitor, but as he always gets every-thing wrong, I didn't take much notice of that."

Theodore assured her that that was all he was and that even now he was not clear about what happened at the Manor.

"They tried to show me once," she said severely, "but I couldn't believe anybody would want those silly little things they were making. All the local girls rush off there, of course. Quite absurd. Not that I dislike Mr. Hookwood or Group Captain Trevone, but I can't believe they couldn't find something more sensible to do. What's it like now in the East?"

Theodore told her that things were difficult now in the East, and even attempted to explain why. But she brushed aside his tentative references to politics and economics.

"No, don't tell me. I can't bear it." But the way she said this and the look she gave him suggested there was nothing she could not bear. "In my opinion it's simply that most people are now quite mad. It won't last, of course, though Barclay sometimes talks as if it will. In a few years, you'll see, people will be quite sensible again. They'll be tired of all this nonsense." And with a casual little gesture she apparently cleaned twenty years of history off the face of this planet. Then, until her husband brought in the tea, she examined him closely about his stay in London.

"Scones," cried Sir Barclay. "Pretty good, eh?"

"Don't stand there dithering, darling—" and there was no differ-ence between her *dithering* and her *darling* "—but hand Mr. Jenks a plate."

"I forgot to tell you," said Theodore. "I have a message from Mr.

Hookwood, who asks you to come over and have dinner and then stay on for the entertainment tonight in the canteen."

"Jolly good," cried Sir Barclay before his wife could say anything. "I might sing my song again, eh, Daphne? You won't remember it," he told Theodore. "Before your time. But it's a comic song—*The Galloping Major*—tomtitty-tomtitty-tomtitty-tom—"

"Oh—do stop your tomtittying!" Then, as she looked at him, a wintry gleam crept into the clear hard gaze. "Barky, you are an ass."

"I know, my love, I know." Sir Barclay, delighted by this invitation, was quite jovial. "But there it is. Better or worse and all that." He turned to Theodore. "Is the food up there any better?"

"It's been horrible so far," Theodore replied, "but I understand a special effort will be made tonight."

"And about time too," said Lady Gishforth. "Though what can you expect, when there isn't a civilized woman near the place—just a few old village sluts and all those idiotic young girls? But they seem to obtain plenty of drink from somewhere, have you noticed?"

Theodore said that he had, and received a wink from Sir Barclay, who went on to say that some of these industrial chaps were quite extraordinary chaps in their drinking habits. "Few years ago, lunched at a place where a cousin of mine's a director—some kind of metal business—and we drank a mixture of gin and kümmel, glasses of it— at lunch, mark you. All goes down to business expenses, I suppose. I really must persuade these chaps to give me a job of some kind."

"My dear, there's nothing useful you could do," his wife told him.

"That's the catch," Sir Barclay admitted.

"What they need is a woman of some experience to make them reasonably comfortable. You found it dreadfully uncomfortable, didn't you, Mr. Jenks? If that girl of Hookwood's left the stage— where I can't believe she's doing any good; I never hear of her—she might help, though of course she probably knows nothing, living in lodgings and all that sort of thing. Have you met the girl? You have? Did you find her attractive?"

"I thought her rather a charmer," said Sir Barclay.

"Be quiet, darling. You think anybody's a charmer. I want to know what Mr. Jenks thinks of her. You've met her, haven't you?"

Theodore gave them an account of his evening at the Mermaid Club and at Mrs. Hungerford's party.

"Wish I could get up to Town these days," said Sir Barclay,

wistfully. And later, when he took Theodore out to show him a short cut back to the Manor, he said: "You might inquire whether they'd like me to do my song again. I have the music, of course, and there's rather a nice little secretary girl plays the piano. Just mention it, my dear fellow, and say we'll be along about half-past seven. Between ourselves, Daphne'll love it. Pretends not to, but you know how they are."

They met for dinner in the Planning Room. The Gishforths arrived looking trim and rather distinguished. Everybody put away several large pink gins while Mr. Hookwood and the Group Captain explained the charts to Sir Barclay, and Lady Gishforth, who refused to look at the charts, talked to Theodore. "Used to be my bedroom, of course," she said as she sipped her third pink gin, "and of course it looked heavenly before the war. But always shockingly cold and draughty. Look at Barclay—poor darling! Hasn't the least idea what they're talking about. Thank goodness you're here, so I haven't to pretend."

The dinner was very different from the sad muck of the evening before; and it was not served by the indignant heavily breathing woman but by two young women, brisk and smiling, who brought them smoked salmon, soup, roast duck, ice cream. Theodore, remembering that he would have to conjure soon, drank nothing; Lady Gishforth and Mr. Hookwood finished a bottle of hock between them; the Group Captain kept on with his gin and ginger ale; and Sir Barclay, his eyes no longer lost in slightly pained surprise, dealt methodically and persistently with a bottle of whisky and a syphon of soda water. "And I must say," he declared more than once, "you're doing us extraordinarily well here, you really are. Capital."

While they were having coffee, the door flew open and there burst upon them the little old man Theodore had seen the previous day in the pub. "Come on in, Joe," he cried. "Don't be shy, Joe. No occasion to be shy." But Joe, hugging his concertina, stayed in the doorway. "Just to let you know we're 'ere an' willin', masters. 'Ev'nin', Mr. Hookwood! Ev'nin', Cap'n! Ev'nin', Sir Barclay an' lady! Ev'nin', young sir!'"

"Ev'nin', all," cried Joe desperately.

"Luffy," said Sir Barclay genially, "you're an old scoundrel."

"No rum here, you know," said the Group Captain.

"Wasn't expectin' it, Cap'n," cried old Luffy. "Drop o' anythin' short'll do. Young Joe don't take it—do you, Joe? Got 'is concertina all ready—see? Ah—thank yer, Mr. Hookwood sir. Just to wet the ol' whistle afore we get's goin', as yer might say. An' a good 'ealth to you, Lady Gishforth, ma'am!"

"Never mind about my good health," said Lady Gishforth severely. "What about my eggs?"

"Never seen a sight o' one, as true as I'm 'ere. Don't never touch an egg, let alone someone else's eggs not my property. Well, Mr. Hookwood, sir, I 'ad to tell you they're all sittin' in their places below, ready for to make a start—and as nice a lookin' a lot as ever I see for miles around—eh, Joe?"

"That is so," said Joe.

"Well, here we are," cried Mr. Hookwood, a few minutes later to the packed canteen. "I hope you'll enjoy yourselves. I know I shall. First-class program tonight—best we've had, I think."

"Hear, hear!" Sir Barclay called from the front row. He had had his share at last of good whisky, was smoking an excellent cigar, had accepted an invitation to sing *The Galloping Major,* and for the time being had forgotten the bewildering desert that still called itself a world.

Miss Dulcie Whittle, pink and apprehensive, opened the program with a piano solo full of maidenly arpeggios. She was followed by a wooden young man who stared at the ceiling and sang in a choky tenor. Next came two girls, so heavily powdered that they looked deathly, who sang mournfully about Alabama, and then, when they were encored, sang mournfully about Kentucky. The boy who had been discovered in the linen room labeled EXPORT: LATIN AMERICA now took the stage, produced a broad grin, was immediately cheered and whistled at, produced a broader grin, then suddenly looked terrified, swallowed hard, muttered something about the Klondike, was told by colleagues at the back to speak up, and then shouted in despair: "So you want a Klondike story, sir, as it was in 'Ninety-eight," and narrowly escaped falling off the platform. By this time Theodore was behind the little curtain at the side, giving a few final instructions to a palpitating Liz, who kept muttering: "Gosh—am I terrified?" and squeezing his hand with her own wet little paw.

Theodore had often performed these tricks at home and at Army entertainments, and now, perhaps because he was among strangers, he felt more confident than usual. His turn was a great success, and he was compelled to do some extra tricks, for which he summoned Sir Barclay on to the stage. His last feat was to deal Sir Barclay, who, fumbling and open-mouthed, had shuffled the cards, a poker hand consisting of four aces and a joker. This concluded the first part of the show; whereupon Theodore joined the Group Captain behind the little curtain, where he was waiting with large gins and ginger ales; and Sir Barclay, before his whisky and soda arrived, contrived in an absent-minded but not ineffective fashion to embrace both Liz and Dulcie, who were busy exchanging their fears and joys.

In the second half of the entertainment, Sir Barclay's major, though unquestionably very much like the real thing, did not perhaps gallop quite as hard as the composer intended him to gallop; but the chorus, in which Lady Gishforth joined in a loud, clear but detached manner, went with a fair swing. The triumph of this half, and indeed of the whole evening, belonged to old Luffy, enthusiastically accompanied by Joe, who within five minutes appeared to be steaming. Old Luffy had not much of a voice; he often forgot his words, and was not always clear about the tune; but he had the true hypnotic quality of the great popular artist. Although there were times when nothing more than a hoarse cackle seemed to emerge from his toothless gap, the glittering eye above it (and he generally closed the other eye, as though the whole song were one colossal wink) belonged to a magician. After *Bacon and Beans* and *Two Lovely Black Eyes* and a few other old music-hall ditties, he plucked from his memory all manner of rural ballads and lyrics about poaching and ploughing, beer and cider, maidens and haystacks, sometimes artless, sometimes sly, while Joe swayed and steamed in the background; and then it was as though some ancient bucolic spell, remote from the world of institutions and social planning, some magic of the cornfield and the moonlit copse forever dying and yet never lifeless, gathered strength to hold and to inspire them all. And Theodore, looking and listening in the fog of smoke and through his own interior haze of gin and ginger, suddenly felt then that what was new and bewilderingly different here did not really matter at all, that here were people as people had always been, packed and sweaty and grinning, bellowing and screaming all manner of foolish stuff, but uplifted together by a large innocent happiness. Afterwards, thinking back, he realized how he had carried this feeling, and the vague thoughts that clustered about it, like a tiny germinating seed, first through all the mutual

thanks and farewells of the evening's end, then through the mysterious
night journey of the bus that finally deposited him and his two bags
at the door of the White Hart in Farbridge, through the sleep that
followed close upon the midnight chimes and did not allow him to
catch the early fast train to London. So that it was there, this seed,
and perhaps already beginning to sprout, when he went out next
morning and took his first look at Farbridge.

<h1 style="text-align:center">7</h1>

In the middle of that Wednesday morning, Theodore found himself in Peter Place, old and built of stone, much of it rather quaint,
but at that hour packed thick with parked cars and noisy with buses.
One of its oldest houses, he saw, had been turned into a café calling
itself the Old Oak Nook. He was rather tired of wandering about,
and the low sky was darkening for rain. It was not until he had
reached the far room that he realized that the place was almost full.
Still wondering whether he ought to retreat, he noticed in the far
corner a table for three where only one young woman was sitting.
Even then he hesitated, for she looked as if she might resent being
disturbed. But already the first spatter of rain was on the window.

"May I sit here, please?" he said to her, speaking quietly and rather
formally, chiefly because he felt absurdly conspicuous, like a stranded
giant, standing there among all those seated women.

The young woman looked up, nodded, and then seemed to stare
at him, not rudely but somehow delightfully. She had soft dark hair,
almost sooty; a vivid face, delicate and eager; and eyes of an intense
blue, like that of some flowers that seem to have a flicker of fire in
their blueness.

"I didn't know this place would be so crowded," he heard himself
saying, still in an embarrassed stilted way. But now it was not because
he felt conspicuous, for he had forgotten all the other people there,
but because of that small upturned face, with its soft night, its burning
blue. "I'm a stranger here."

"It's nearly always crowded at this time," the girl replied, not
smiling and sounding rather sulky, yet somehow not unfriendly.
Then she hesitated a moment.

It flashed upon him then that there was not a second to be wasted,
that if there was another pause she might as well be in China. So as

he sat down he said the first thing that came into his head. "My name is Theodore Jenks."

There must have been something about the way he said this that pleased or amused the girl, for she smiled delightfully and said at once: "Laura Casey's my name."

"Miss Casey?" He had to know.

"Yes, Miss Casey."

He nodded, and then ordered some coffee from the waitress who appeared at that moment. When she had gone, he smiled across the table at Laura Casey, out of a happy excitement. But he noticed that she had finished her coffee and her cigarette and therefore might walk away forever before he could say anything else. Something must be said at once. "You are not married. Neither am I. I come from the East Indies, and am visiting this country for the first time." But that was not enough. "We may be disturbed soon or you may have to go, so may I say one thing to you, please?"

She looked rather startled. "Yes, what is it?"

Well, he had to tell her. "I think you are very beautiful."

"Me?" she cried, as if astonished, though now she looked more beautiful than ever.

And now the silence between them, though anything but empty, brought an embarrassed self-consciousness. Theodore did not know what to say next. Laura Casey was looking at him strangely. What happened now? It was awkward.

Then the problem was solved for them because they were no longer alone. The third chair was being claimed. "Now I'm sorry, very sorry. I know exactly how you feel," said the newcomer, who had a rather deep, hoarse voice that had an oddly insinuating quality, which hinted at a mock-solemn devilment in the speaker. "But take my word for it that this is the only vacant seat in the whole establishment, and I had to come in out of the weather. But don't mind me. In fact, pretend I'm not here. Waitress," he called masterfully, as if the room were empty or he owned the place.

Theodore took a good look at him. He was an oldish fellow, somewhere between fifty-five and sixty-five probably; and he was bulky, perhaps all the bulkier because he had not taken off an enormous and rather shabby green overcoat. He was clean-shaven, florid, with a lot of white hair; and he had a piratical nose and tiny bright eyes as busy and wicked as mice. He looked something between a clever old actor and a rather raffish admiral. And whatever else he might be, he was obviously a character, a personality. Now, having dismissed the waitress, who had responded at once to his imperious summons, he turned to them again. "Say the word," and the little eyes twinkled away, "and I obliterate myself."

"It's not necessary," said Laura Casey, half-annoyed, half-amused. "We're not together."

"We had just exchanged names, sir," said Theodore.

"Very sensible too. What names?"

"This is Miss Laura Casey. My name's Theodore Jenks."

"Good! Well, Miss Casey, Mr. Jenks, my name's Tribe—Commodore Tribe. And I'll tell you one thing—you're a devilish good-looking pair. Neat contrast too. Only thing that's given me any pleasure so far in this town. To say nothing of this damnably depressing Oldy Englishy Tea Shoppy. I'm much obliged to you—by George, I am!" He whipped out a little black pipe that looked as if it had been gnawed by rats, and blew through it vigorously.

Laura Casey broke out of her confusion to begin laughing. "I'm sorry. I don't know why it's so funny." She suddenly glanced at Theodore as if he were not a stranger but someone she had known for years. And Theodore, remembering the awkwardness of that sudden silence between them, was grateful now to this Commodore Tribe, who had not separated him from this girl but somehow brought them closer together. A sleety rain still battered away at the leaded windows. The packed room had a thick atmosphere of coffee, smoke, and damp raincoats. But the three of them at this table seemed to be living in their own tiny world. A wonderful mixed feeling of coziness and excitement, better than anything he had known for some time, took possession of him. And he had an idea, itself exhilarating, that Laura Casey felt all this too, and that her glance had told him that she did, was meant to tell him so.

"Well now," said the Commodore, who was now smoking his little black pipe, "let's talk about ourselves. Who'll begin?"

"I think Miss Casey should begin," said Theodore.

"So do I," said the Commodore.

"You make it sound like *Alice in Wonderland*," she said.

"What's wrong with that?" said the Commodore.

CHAPTER THREE

Commodore Tribe

I

WITH an unfinished paragraph on the desk in front of him, Commodore Tribe was slumped back in his chair, dozing. It was the dead middle of the afternoon; he had lunched heartily at the Bell and then smoked a pipe or two; and now he had quietly taken leave of this uninspired and profitless hour. He was sitting at the far end of the upper floor of a large converted barn, which was in fact the editorial and general office of that monthly publication, *M.F.A.*— that is, *Mostly Foreign Affairs.* The room was furnished and decorated in a rough-and-ready fashion, with files and books, mostly review copies, round the walls. A small oil stove was giving out more smell than warmth. The roof was leaking in two or three places. Altogether it was a cheerless place in which to pass a wet March afternoon; but Commodore Tribe was now comfortably drifting away from it.

He was restored, though slowly, to full consciousness by the sound of an unusually unpleasant grating voice coming from the next room. "Miss Church," he called sleepily, "send that fellow away. Don't listen to him. Take no excuses. Send him away."

But the next moment the caller was inside the room, fuming and glaring not two yards away. Commodore Tribe sat up and regarded him with frank distaste. He was a small elderly man, with a long waxy nose and a clipped gray beard and mustache; a scraggy mean fellow.

"Go away, sir," said Commodore Tribe. "If you want to see us, choose some other time."

"You can't talk to me like that," the newcomer shouted. "Who are you?"

Lifting his bulk still higher in the chair, the Commodore saw that little Miss Church, the secretary, was making alarmed motions at him through the doorway. But this meant little or nothing because poor

Miss Church existed in a perpetual state of alarm, living in this world like a rabbit in a kennel of hounds.

"I said—who are you?"

"And I heard you," said the Commodore, frowning at him. "But for that matter—and it's really more to the joint—who the devil are *you*? As you can see—or would see if you only stopped jigging about and blinking and blowing—I work here. Whereas you've just come charging in, uninvited, disturbing us, making a nuisance of yourself—"

"My name's Crandry—and I happen to be the proprietor of this publication." And clearly he thought the Commodore would be overwhelmed, following Miss Church's example. In fact, he waited for some sign of abasement, probably living for such signs. This time he was disappointed.

"Ah, Mr. Crandry—allow me to introduce myself—Tribe—Commoder Horace Tribe—"

"Commodore?" Mr. Crandry sounded as if he could not believe his ears. "Commodore? What d'you mean—Commodore?" He sat on the edge of the only other chair, and glared away. He had eyes like scratched marbles, and his green tie looked as if it had been dyed in some metallic poison that was already beginning to turn his nose into dead wax.

The Commodore closed his eyes and assumed an air of immense patience, as though he were a lama a hundred years old. "If you must know—after serving for some years in the Royal Navy, I—er—was attached, chiefly in an advisory capacity, to the Navy of one of the South American republics and had the honorary rank of Commodore." He opened his eyes. "By the way, you haven't any tobacco on you— or a cigar—have you? I'm clean out."

"Don't smoke. Never have done. Let's come to the point. What are you doing here?"

The Commodore stared at him reproachfully. "Don't you know? I'm here as assistant editor and special adviser to our friend, Thoken, who, as you probably know, is away at present."

"No, didn't know," Mr. Crandry snapped. "Been abroad myself. Business in South Africa. Only just got back. Where is Thoken?"

"He's in France. Or Italy," said the Commodore vaguely. "Keeping in touch with the situation, you know."

"What situation?"

"Why, the situation in France or Italy, as the case may be. Must keep in touch, Mr. Crandry. Offered to go myself, but Thoken insisted upon going—and don't blame him with the damnable weather we have here. Roof leaks too. You're attending to these things, I imagine. Anyhow, Thoken went off, and that left me here in charge. As you see."

"Don't know anything about you. Should have been told. Can't see why you should have been taken on. All extra expense. What salary are you getting?"

"Nominal—purely nominal," said the Commodore, shaking his white locks. "You'll hardly believe it. Twelve pounds a week."

But there was no pleasing Mr. Crandry. "I don't call that nominal. What are you doing for that?"

The Commodore stared at him and then raised his formidable eyebrows. "My dear sir, you sound as if you were catechizing an office boy. At the moment I'm completing the editorial notes for the next issue." He waved a hand at the desk but then realized that this had been a mistake, for Crandry, before he could be stopped, made a dive for the writing pad there.

"*Early last month*," Crandry read out slowly, "*it was decided at an emergency meeting at the Kremlin to double the number of long-range submarines under construction in the Soviet yards. We are informed that this decision—*" He stared over the writing pad. "Well, what about this decision?"

"What do *you* think?" the Commodore inquired smoothly. "Let's have *your* ideas, Mr. Crandry." His manner suggested they were a pair of easy conspirators.

Crandry flung down the pad, jumped up, and looked as if he were about to do a stepdance on it. In his fury his voice became a harsh scream. "What do *I* think? Never heard such confounded impudence! And this emergency meeting at the Kremlin—how the blazes do *you* know what happened in the Kremlin?"

"Guesswork, my dear sir. Pure guesswork."

"But I'm not going to waste good money printing and circulating your guesswork. You must be out of your mind, man. We want facts—facts—facts." And he thumped the desk.

The Commodore ignored him. "Miss Church," he called, "please nip across to the grocer for some tobacco. It'll be muck, but better than nothing. If I'm to have all this noise and fuss in here, I must smoke." He then looked at Mr. Crandry, who seemed to be stunned by these tactics, and asked: "And where do we get these facts from?"

"Where—where—well, that's your job—and Thoken's."

"You're being unreasonable," said the Commodore easily. "Come now, you must see that. *M.F.A.* has been giving its readers these secret items from the Kremlin—and of course, other places—ever since it started. Look at the files—they're just behind you."

"But we can't print guesswork. Thoken assured me he had sources of information—"

Smiling, the Commodore raised a large hand and pushed it out towards Crandry's waxy nose, which was now turning a very unpleasant pink. "My dear Crandry—"

"I'm not your dear Crandry."

"You're not," and now the Commodore showed some sign of irritation, "and I wish to God you'd stop jigging and mopping. The point is—Thoken's guessing, I'm guessing, and if you were bringing out this monthly, you'd have to be guessing too. Come, come, use your commonsense. I doubt if the combined intelligence services of Britain, the United States and Western Europe can penetrate into the Kremlin. So how do you expect me to do it, on twelve pounds a week, sitting here in a damned wet barn in the South Midlands? What do you think I have—second sight?"

"But our readers—"

"Our readers, whoever they are, like to feel they're being taken behind the scenes, listening to hidden microphones in Moscow, wearing false beards in Teheran, peering at messages in invisible ink in the back rooms of Stamboul night clubs. For that they're willing to pay half a crown a month, and if you happen to have that sort of mind, it's probably a bargain."

"I'll bargain you—you—you charlatan," Crandry screeched. "I don't care what terms you arranged with Thoken, I'm the proprietor—and here and now you're discharged."

"You mean that?" And the Commodore stared at him in some surprise. "Careful now. You're obviously a livery, peppery sort of fellow—that nose—"

"I tell you—you're discharged."

"And remember you're due to go to press next Tuesday. Do you propose to edit the thing yourself, Crandry?"

"No, I don't," he snapped. "It's no longer any business of yours, but you might as well know that I'm also the proprietor of the *South Mid-*

land Gazette and the *Weekly Record and Advertiser,* and until I get Thoken back, one of their fellows can take charge of this publication."

The Commodore rose, lofty, contemptuous. "Their idea of foreign affairs is a dispute in the cattle market at Moreton-on-the-Marsh. So you own those two miserable papers, eh, Crandry? In that case, accept my resignation." He turned to greet Miss Church. "Thank you very much, my dear."

"I got an ounce of Newmown Hay Mixture and an ounce of Hedger Flake," she announced breathlessly.

"They're both muck. But better than nothing. I think you heard me tell Mr. Crandry that he must accept my resignation, eh?"

"Yes, Commodore Tribe," she replied, looking at him mournfully.

"Resignation? I told you you were discharged." Crandry was bending over the desk, making out a check. "And out you go."

The Commodore went across to the shelves and began removing books from them with admirable speed and dexterity.

Crandry looked up. "What are you doing with those books?"

"These books, which I've reviewed," replied the Commodore with dignity, "are my property."

"Nothing of the kind. They stay in this office."

"Miss Church, is it or is it not the custom for reviewers to keep the books they've reviewed? Speak up, my dear, so that Mr. Crandry can hear you."

"Well, yes—that's right," Miss Church stammered. "I mean, reviewers usually keep the books."

"It's not worth arguing about," said Crandry. "And here's your check—for two weeks' salary—and you can clear out at once."

The Commodore examined the check. "This is simply for twenty-four pounds. What about expenses?"

"You'll get no expenses out of me," shouted Crandry, doing a little jig of rage. "And if there's any more argument, I'll cancel that check, and defy you to sue me." He turned away, making for the door.

"You seem to me a singularly unpleasant little man," said the Commodore severely. "I was right to resign. We could never work together happily."

Crandry wheeled round and wagged a forefinger. "I shall be here again tomorrow, and if I find you still here, I'll have you thrown out."

"I weigh sixteen and a half stone," said the Commodore, "so I take some throwing out. But if you find me here tomorrow—by George—I'll undertake to throw myself out."

The proprietor stayed long enough in the other room to inform Miss Church, who had followed him in there, that he was far from satisfied and that she had better be careful. Lighting a pipe of the Newmown Hay Mixture, which had the smell of cheap pomade, the Commodore looked out of the window and saw Crandry climb into a landaulette of the same poisonous green shade as his tie. He departed into the sullen damp afternoon. The Commodore collected some more books.

"Oh, I'm so sorry, Commodore Tribe," cried Miss Church, a few minutes later. There were tears in her eyes, which were large, brown, and bulgy. "It's—oh—it's such a pity. I ought to have warned you about Mr. Crandry and how difficult he is. I feel it's all my fault."

"Nonsense, Miss Church. You're always thinking everything's your fault—it's a form of egoism. This isn't your fault at all. As a matter of fact, I couldn't work with any man who's ass enough to own a publication like this, not even if he turned out to be a pleasant ass. Whereas this fellow comes screeching and flapping like a wounded cockatoo."

She regarded him tearfully. "But what will you do now?"

"Look around, look around," he replied vaguely but cheerfully. "Something'll turn up. Incidentally, I'd do the same if I were you, my dear."

"Why—do you think—?"

"I think he'll chuck it soon."

"Oh, good gracious!" She stared at him, dismayed.

"Why worry? You can do better than this. We can all do better than this. Well, perhaps not poor Thoken—though I don't know why we should pity him when probably at this moment he's basking in the square at Arles, with a bottle of Château neuf-du-pape inside him, inventing a paragraph or two about Yugoslavia. He ought to have let me go. Now, let me see. Is that all?" He glanced round the room, which was already beginning to reek of Newmown Hay. "Can't see anything else worth taking. Except you, my dear Miss Church— Lettice, isn't it?" He gave her a look at once droll and fond.

"Oh—I'm so *miserable*," cried poor Miss Church, girlishly distressed for all her forty years. And now she wept copiously.

The Commodore embraced and comforted her in a large avuncular manner; she was not badly shaped. "Now, now, my dear. This won't do. Dry those tears."

"I know, I know. I'm being silly, Commodore Tribe. But I've enjoyed everything here so much more since you came. It's been quite *different*."

"Naturally," he murmured, "naturally. Well now, if anything should turn up for me, not too far away, and there's a place for you, then I'll send for you."

She lit up at once. "Really? You promise?"

"Certainly. A definite promise. And now—if any letters come—"

"Yes, yes—where shall I send them?"

"Nowhere," said the Commodore promptly. "Burn 'em. Well—Crandry and Company can finish that note about the Soviet submarines, about which they can't know less than I do. And I'll stagger along to the Bell with these books. There ought to be somebody I can persuade to buy 'em. I'll be at the Bell over the week end, I imagine, if you notice anything else here I ought to have. And now—Miss Church—Lettice—*Au revoir—Auf wiedersehn—Hasta la vista*—Be seeing you. Even that's American, you notice, not strictly English. Apparently, as a nation we never want to see anybody again. Too much piracy and looting."

"If there's anything—anything at all—I can do," said Miss Church, ignoring his impersonal observations, "I shall be very glad, Commodore Tribe—"

"I shan't forget. And don't let that fellow Crandry bully you. Not good for him, and very bad for you." And with that, the Commodore took final leave of the more intimate journalism of foreign affairs.

2

The parcel of books was heavy and so was his old green ulster. It was not a warm afternoon but it began to feel like one to the Commodore, making a stately progress down Tredberrow's straggling main street on his way back to the hotel. When he reached a trim little Georgian house and heard a tapping on one of its windows, he was glad to halt. It was Mrs. Watson beckoning him in; and in he went.

"Stay to tea," said Mrs. Watson. "The Vicar's coming. I shall enjoy entertaining you both." Mrs. Watson was very old, a widow who shared the house with a grim elderly maid called Birkett. She was the most intelligent person in Tredberrow, and probably for miles around. She looked a small clean witch, was forever exchanging spectacles, sometimes wearing two pairs at a time, knew everybody and everything belonging to the whole neighborhood, and, with the doubtful exception of Lucy York at the Bell, she was the only real friend the Commodore had made in Tredberrow. "Why are you carrying all those books? I can see they're books, and while we're having tea I think that Birkett had better make a proper parcel of them, otherwise you'll spill them in the road."

Seating himself at the other side of the hearth in a chair much too small for him, the Commodore explained what had happened between himself and Crandry that afternoon. "So I insisted upon taking these books away," he concluded, "in the hope of selling 'em to somebody. May make a few pounds. And I can do with a few pounds." He was always frank with Mrs. Watson, having realized from the first that here was somebody who could not be fooled.

"You're not to try to sell them to the poor Vicar," she said sharply. "I know you probably could, but you're not to. He's even poorer than you are, Mr. Tribe." She would never give him his fancy rank, and told him at their first encounter that she did not believe in it, although she was willing to let him have it in public.

"Nobody could be poorer than I am," he told her.

"Nonsense. The Vicar is. He's got nothing but his wretched stipend—and all those great maddening daughters—and though you may have nothing but your wits—and I know you live on them—they're a better financial asset than his stipend."

"I doubt it," he said gloomily.

"Come, come, this isn't like you. And surely you must have known from the first that you wouldn't last long with that absurd review. Mr. Thoken's different—he's half a fool—and you're not. So you must have known, and of course you did. Not that I think you haven't been foolish."

He gave her a fat slow rueful grin, which she recognized with a spectral little grin of her own, but then she returned to her brisk severity, wagging a tiny swollen finger at him.

"Where you've made your mistake, my friend," she continued, "is that you've carried your wits to the wrong market. You're out-of-date, far more than I am although I'm years and years older than you. You don't understand what's happening here. Probably it's this easy boozy life abroad that's done it. Do you want me to speak frankly?"

"I thought you were doing, my dear Mrs. Watson. But I can take a stiffer dose, if that's what you mean."

"Very well. I say—you're carrying your wits to the wrong market. Nowadays the place for an adventurer like you, with nothing to offer but a touch of charm and plenty of impudence, is in public affairs. That's where the easy money, the fat, is in these days, and not where you're trying to find it, among the Crandrys, who count every penny. This isn't America, where no doubt you'd make a fortune humbugging a few millionaires. Two out of three of my young relatives, who are mostly idiots, are earning a living at the public expense and out of the taxes I pay, as I keep reminding them. And if they can do it, so could you, my friend. Now then, what do you say to that?"

"The answer's quite simple," said the Commodore, with a heavy sigh. "I ought to have come back sooner. Now I'm too old. There's the rub. Most of your young relatives may be in the trough, but they're young. I'm not. I may seem young to you, but to the average Appointments Committee I look a hundred—and a damned dubious raffish hundred at that. No doubt I could talk 'em out of worrying about that side of it, but not out of looking at these white hairs."

"You could dye them."

"Yes—and look like a retired Mexican brigand. I've tried it. And—by George—I even frightened myself every time I shaved."

She nodded briskly. "You have a point there, I'll admit. But with all this Festival of Britain nonsense, there ought to be something, if it's not too late. What are your immediate plans?"

"I haven't any," he confessed, "though I've not had much time to think yet, having been turfed out of that job only half an hour ago. The truth is, I haven't been bothering—just drifting along here—"

"I know. And being given a lot of fat meals and free drinks by Mrs. York at the Bell. I know what you've been up to there, Mr. Tribe. And that's one reason why I called you in, and I must deal with this before the Vicar arrives, so please don't interrupt. My maid Birkett," she continued, lowering her voice, "is very friendly with the sister of Mrs. York's husband, Frank York. And I gather that Frank York may be coming back any day now, and I imagine that he hasn't told his wife, who, whatever she may have told you, is terrified of him. Now, do you see?"

The Commodore gave her a slow nod, and pushed out his lower lip. "Not so good," he admitted. "Why does everything come at once?"

"Because that's how life works—in fits and starts and sudden jumps. I discovered that long ago. And so ought you."

"I did. It was really a rhetorical question. I've never been told much about the husband—I discouraged talk about him as being in bad taste—but I did gather he was obstinate and bad-tempered, that they quarreled about how the place should be run, and that he went off, just before I came here, to let her run it herself for a time while he went back to some job he'd had in the war. And now he's coming back, eh? Humph—awkward!"

"It might be—very," she said dryly. "So I thought I'd better warn you, for both your sakes—though I couldn't begin to talk to her—she's really a stupid woman, as you must have discovered, although I don't suppose you cared, with everything there revolving round you. Oh—I know."

The Vicar, Mr. Hobson, arrived. He always gave the Commodore the impression that he had once been a large pink hearty clergyman but was now being rapidly melted down, perhaps by black magic. Recently the melting must have been fiercer than ever, for this afternoon his features were running and blurring and his voice sounded remote and not quite belonging to him, as if ventriloquism came into it somewhere. But he shook hands vigorously, almost triumphantly, as though all three had been on a desert island for several years and now saw a ship's boat crossing the lagoon.

"And what a magnificent tea!" he cried. "Mrs. Watson always gives us a magnificent tea—doesn't she, Commander?"

"I've been giving Mr. Tribe some good advice too," she said dryly.

"Quite right, quite right," said the Vicar, eating buttered toast very quickly. "I've had rather a curious afternoon. Potts was taking his motor as far as Little Erwick and back, so I went with him to pay a call on the Vicar there—poor old Stanch. There's hardly anybody in Little Erwick now, of course, and nobody goes to church, which is just as well as the roof's fallen in, and I found poor Stanch playing the organ—he used to be an excellent musician—up to the knees in docks and nettles. Yes, the whole place a ruin. And poor Stanch really a ruin too. Always rather eccentric, but now quite unbalanced. He told me his housekeeper's mad. Oddly enough, in the circumstances, I think he's quite right. Half the vicarage—on the ground floor, of course— is full of pigs, and poor Stanch and his housekeeper don't seem to know to whom they belong. But I'm talking too much—as usual. Any news, Mrs. Watson?"

"Let me see. And do help yourself to that orange cake. Birkett makes it specially for you." She thought for a moment. "Bert Stiles's son, Alec, has been drunk for three days, as you probably know. The young man staying with Mrs. Ogden *is* her nephew—that's definitely settled. Old Fawcett has broken his leg again. The man's bicycle has been seen outside Miss Wainwright's again. Mr. Trump wants to organize an indignation meeting to denounce Dr. Pulross. Frank York is probably returning to the Bell. And our friend here has just resigned from that absurd review."

"Dear me! This cake is really splendid—I must tell Birkett." He turned his pulpy red face, his watery eyes, toward the Commodore. "I'm sorry to hear this, Commander. But I never thought you'd settle in our quiet little backwater. I always felt you'd soon be making for fresh woods and pastures new, as Milton calls them. A detestable man but a great poet of course, one of our greatest. And now what will you do, Commander? Or is it a secret?"

"I'm thinking of applying to one of Mrs. Watson's young relatives for a job," he replied pointedly.

"And why not?" she cried. "As a matter of fact I was just deciding to write to my nephew Daubenny—Daubenny Stevens, who is the only son of my youngest sister, who married a man in the Home Office— to suggest he should give you lunch next week. Could you go up to town on Tuesday, if necessary, Mr. Tribe? Very well, I'll write to Daubenny. He's in that ministry of progaganda or information, or whatever it's called."

"He must be very clever," said the Vicar, humbly and from far away.

"If he is, he's kept it from me. More tea?"

They sipped and munched and looked at the winking fire while the afternoon faded and died. It was cozy and friendly, the Commodore reflected, but damnably old. He could almost feel himself melting down like the Vicar. Perhaps the same influences might be at work on him. "Any witches round here?" he inquired. "Not counting you, Mrs. Watson."

"If I'd known how to become one, I might have been one," she said, not displeased. "That is, once I'd got the family settled."

"Not now," said the Vicar. "There used to be two—cousins, I believe—out at Little Erwick. Incidentally, poor Stanch told me he

believes that hell will shortly be established here on earth. We're
making it ourselves, which explains, in his view, poor fellow, why
there are now so many people in the world."

"He might be right at that," said the Commodore.

"It's not a view I can accept of course," said the Vicar gravely.

"You know, it's an odd thing," cried Mrs. Watson, "but when the old
religious writers and preachers had to describe hell, they had to invent
the most fantastic and unlikely settings and goings-on, something quite
different from anything people saw around them then. Whereas now—
well, I've just been reading a story by this man C. S. Lewis and his
hell is just an industrial suburb, full of quarrelsome people, that goes
on and on, probably with tram journeys lasting weeks—and it's quite
convincing. Now, compared with the old religious writers, he's hardly
had to imagine anything, only to exaggerate a little what's here already.
So perhaps your poor Mr. Stanch may be right after all. In any case,
I've always thought that too many people just *are* hell. That, and
being sorry when it's too late. My idea of hell would be to have hurt
all the people I'm fondest of, to discover that they'd gone for good and
I was in the middle of a perpetual Bank Holiday crowd. What's heaven
like, by the way?"

"You can't be asking me," said the Commodore.

"Certainly not, Mr. Tribe. Vicar? Or is it too difficult?"

"Heaven," the Vicar began slowly, "is like what you want it to be
like, only always just a bit better."

"Now I call that clever of you," cried Mrs. Watson. "Do you believe
in it?"

"Certainly I do." The Vicar was very positive. "And I trust you do,
Mrs. Watson."

"I'm afraid not. The scale of it defeats me. Too many people, far too
many to be catered for. Though Swedenborg said the English had a
special heaven, which always seemed to me very sensible of him. What
do *you* think, Mr. Tribe?"

"I've been up and down and roundabout," said the Commodore,
"and I've seen a lot of religions at work. And I don't like them. With
all due respect, padre. As a matter of fact I'm not thinking about the
Church of England, which is something different, something intended
to keep the English decent and fairly comfortable and not likely to go
tearing off into religion and making nuisances of themselves—"

"Now, one moment, Commander," the Vicar began.

"No, let him go on," said Mrs. Watson. "Unless, of course, it's making you feel too uncomfortable, Mr. Hobson."

"Not at all," he murmured. "Please continue, Commander. You were saying you don't like religion—or was it religions?"

"I put it in the plural because I've seen so many of 'em, hard at it all over the place. Gods, idols, churches, temples, altars, all shapes and sizes." The Commodore drew a long reflective breath. "Now it seems to me that when the original fire's died out of them, they're just an expensive racket, hardly ever giving the people their money's worth. But when the fire and conviction are still in them, as you discover here and there, I like them even less. All this concentrating on saving one's soul, slaving away at it, and despising anything else, I don't like the look of it, the sound of it, the smell of it. You get unpleasant people who are busy running a mad obstacle race they've invented for themselves, and into which, if you're not careful, they'll enter you. They're throwing this world away for the next, and if they reach the next, then they'll throw that away for the one after that. And if I were their Creator, I'd make 'em start again and try to enjoy one of my worlds at a time. Mind you, I'm roughly lumping all the holy men together now, whether they cry to Jehovah, Allah, Brahma, seven assorted Buddhas, or Mumbo Jumbo. And it's ten to one they end by inventing a system of rules and regulations, rewards and punishments, that enables any debilitated railway clerk to pass with honors straight into paradise and would instantly rule out every great man and woman the world's ever seen. They talk about a universe of Divine Love so narrow, mean, and vindictive that any man thought capable of helping to put it together would be shunned in a dockside beerhouse. I've met people so busy leading the life of the spirit and saving their souls that they haven't in them as much fun, joy and lovingkindness as a Levantine moneylender. I've seen—"

"All this," cried the Vicar, jumping up, pulling his features together, and bringing back his voice so that it rattled the ornaments, "all this, my dear sir, is entirely beside the point. Are you aware of that?"

The Commodore heaved himself out of his chair, nodded amiably, and said: "Now, now, Mr. Hobson. Take it easy. We're making too much noise."

"Indeed we are," said the Vicar. "And I must run away. A magnificent tea, Mrs. Watson, really magnificent. I don't know how you do it. My poor girls can't—though they try hard. Thank you, thank

you, thank you!" There may have been several more, but by this time
he was out in the street.

"I shall write to my nephew now, asking him to reply at once,"
said Mrs. Watson. "Telephone me on Monday morning."

"I will—and many thanks."

"You're a rascal, you know," she continued, "and twenty years ago
I would have strongly disapproved of you. Now I don't care—and even
wish you well."

He took the swollen claw, with its deeply embedded gems, she
held out. "I was thinking, my dear Mrs. Watson, that you're the only
real friend I've made here, and that it's you—and only you—I shall
miss when I go."

The sharp old glance softened for a moment. Then she laughed.
"There's enough female left in me, you rogue, to respond a little to
that whisky-sodden hoarse voice of yours, my friend. That's how you
do it, I suppose. Why we women are so susceptible to voices, I've
never understood. By the way, my nephew Daubenny, unless he's
radically changed just lately, is rather a conceited prig. But then so
many of them are now. Telephone me on Monday."

He thanked her and departed, in an unusually somber mood, perhaps
knowing already that he would never see her again.

3

Late in the evening, after the Bell had been closed to the local
public, he was enjoying a last whisky in Mrs. York's little sitting
room. She was looking at him, as she frequently did, with wonder and
affection mistily mingled in her large hazel eyes, which, in spite of her
forty-odd years, her semisophisticated patter, her smart gowns, were
those of a plump daft country lass. He was wondering whether to tell
her that her husband might return any day now—or, what was more
important, perhaps any night—and was rapidly reviewing the arguments for and against this move. After being asked twice what he was
thinking about, he decided against telling her, chiefly because she
might then want him to clear out at once, and that would be very
inconvenient. Then he remembered the books.

"My dear Lucy, I was thinking about all those books I brought
from the *M.F.A.* office. They're worth at least ten pounds, and I could
do with ten pounds. Now is there anybody coming here who has the

money and is fool enough to buy those books? You know your customers. Can you think of anybody?"

She was delighted to help him, but as usual was rather vague. "You
see, I don't know about books," she confessed, her full lower lip
drooping in apology. "And people don't talk about them much here,
do they?"

"Most of them don't talk about anything except racing and football,
heifers in calf and gilts in pig. And once I'd understood what gilts in
pig were—and the mystery of it kept me going here the first few weeks
—there wasn't much conversation left."

"Oh—go on with you—"

"But there must be somebody," he continued, "who'd like to own
some impressive-looking volumes and could afford a few pounds for
'em. Think now, my dear."

"I am thinking." And she was, for every feature suggested a challenging mental effort. "Let's see—tomorrow's Saturday, isn't it? Well now,
I've a dinner for four ordered—by that young Geoffrey Middleham, up
at Low Hall. I believe that him and Admiral Broadwater are playing
a golf match with two gentlemen from Farbridge—and I know he told
Walter he wanted a very special dinner. I'm getting them some very
nice hors d'oeuvres and a chicken to follow and—"

"Yes, yes, a very special dinner. But you think he's a likely customer? Plenty of money? Not much sense?"

"You could try him, couldn't you, dear? And he'll probably bring
them in early, to have some cocktails. He came in for quite a lot of
money, and doesn't mind spending it, specially when he's had a few
drinks—you know the sort."

"I know them well," said the Commodore, finishing his whisky,
"but—unfortunately—in rapidly decreasing numbers. Mr. Geoffrey
Middleham, eh? Thank you, my dear Lucy." Smiling at her, he
hoisted himself to his feet.

"I must lock up." And as she rose, she gave him a glance he knew
well. "Shall I—?"

"Not tonight," he said softly. He took her plump rosy face between
his hands and kissed her. "You're tired. So am I. Goodnight, my dear."

The Bell was one of those innumerable smallish country hotels
that now help to bring urban refinements and gaieties into rural life.
Lucy York might be a fond and foolish woman, at least so far as the
Commodore was concerned, but she was not without a business sense

and some understanding of the great social trends. The taproom and modest saloon bar were left undisturbed, but the dining room had been enlarged, and in the far corner of the lounge, where Walter, the decayed waiter, served coffee, was a small cocktail bar, complete with colored lights, rows of fancy liqueur bottles, and a blonde barmaid who looked like a rough sketch of a Hollywood film star and more than hinted at the depravity of the age we live in, though in private life she was the chaste and devoted wife of a corporal in the Royal Army Medical Corps. Almost monopolizing this little bar and the services of the blonde barmaid, early on Saturday evening, were four men in golfing tweeds. They had the solidly complacent look of well-to-do Englishmen who had taken exercise and were now taking alcohol. Between them they had created at once the atmosphere of a decent club with a fairly stiff entrance fee and a secretary who could wear a regimental tie. They were behaving like sound clubmen, straddling their legs, talking in loud uninflected voices, guffawing and roaring at very small jokes or no jokes at all; being so manly that they hardly seemed human. And to them, like an enormous smiling pike after minnows, came Commodore Tribe.

He remembered now having already met Mr. Geoffrey Middleham, who was a sandy, bulbous young man, as though a fox had been crossed with a frog. "A-ha!" he cried, striking the right note immediately. "Middleham, eh?"

"What? Oh yes—Commodore Tribe, eh?"

"It is. And how's it going?"

"Pretty good. Have a drink. Know Admiral Broadwater, do you?"

"Run across you somewhere, I think," said the Admiral, a short, thick, leather-and-mahogany old boy, who began to frown and was obviously one to be avoided. The Commodore turned sharply to the other two, a stiff middle-aged fellow, proud and bloodshot, and a tubby little chap as red and bald as a new baby.

"From the West Farbridge Club," said Middleham. "Colonel Whatmore. Captain Mobbs. Commodore Tribe."

"Commodore?" said the Admiral.

"Courtesy rank," said the Commodore hastily. "Tell you about it later. Well—gentlemen—happy days! From Farbridge, eh? Don't know it yet but I've been meaning to have a look at it one day."

"Captain Mobbs," said Colonel Whatmore, "is our Conservative agent there—and he's done a remarkably fine job."

"Bravo, Captain!" cried the Commodore, who had no political convictions of any kind. "Thought you had a True Blue look about you."

"He had a bluer look this afternoon when the Admiral here had finished with him," said Middleham guffawing.

"My godfathers—yes!" cried Captain Mobbs, bouncing a bit. "What the Good Old Navy did to me! Ow!"

Nobody roared louder at this than the Commodore, who could hardly finish his drink.

"Live here, Commodore?" Colonel Whatmore asked.

"In this very pub, don't you?" said Middleham.

"At the moment, yes, gentlemen," said the Commodore. "I've been giving a hand to the *M.F.A.* people here—as special adviser—"

"That's it, of course," said Middleham, suddenly proud of his acquaintance. "Dashed clever stuff too."

"I subscribe," said Colonel Whatmore, looking at the Commodore with a new respect, "and read it regularly. Very sound publication. Eh, Mobbs? You see it, don't you?"

"Never miss it. Those reports from Russia," cried the Captain. "First-class. You've got a good man there."

"Between these four walls, gentlemen," said the Commodore, lowering his voice and half-closing his eyes, although he was able to notice that even the Admiral looked impressed, "we have a remarkable man there. And when the whole story comes to be told—well, no more of that. Have to be careful, even here. You understand?" They nodded gravely, every face weighing a ton. The Commodore, without losing his grasp of them, now gradually brought his voice to a normal level. "We've agents everywhere, of course. It's taken some organizing. But now I've resigned, having seen them through the worst of it and left everything ticking over nicely. In strict confidence, if you don't mind, gentlemen. It's as well not to say too much about these things. We're living, as you fellows know only too well," he concluded impressively, "in very difficult times."

"Gosh—yes," said Middleham, and ordered another round.

"If you don't mind my asking," said Colonel Whatmore, "have you any particular plans?"

"It's been suggested," the Commodore replied quite truthfully, "that I should join one of the public services. I have to go up to town on Tuesday to see a man. Then—well, we'll see. I might find it amusing for a few months to handle some special form of public relations—plan a national campaign perhaps—that sort of thing."

"Quite," cried little Captain Mobbs. "Do a sound job too, I imagine."

"I've had a certain amount of experience," the Commodore observed modestly, "in various parts of the world. Excuse me a moment." He took Middleham on one side. "Something's just occurred to me, Middleham old man," he whispered impressively. "I've accumulated rather a remarkable little collection of absolutely first-class recent books on foreign affairs, just the sort of stuff a fellow like you ought to have by him, to keep himself well informed. You know—*France at the Crossroads*—*The Italian Problem*—*The Aftermath of Potsdam*—*After MacArthur, What?*—"

"*After MacArthur, What?*" Middleham repeated, bewildered but respectful.

"Yes—*What*. That's the kind of thing. Packed with important information, official secrets given away right and left. Can't pick these things up in any bookshop, you know." Which was true enough. "Now the trouble is, my place is closed for the time being, I'm traveling light for a few months, and I don't want to leave these books here—no room for 'em and besides they'd be wasted. Now, my dear chap, after dinner—not now but after dinner—I want you to pop up to my room with me and take a look at those books. Apart from the value of the collection itself, their ordinary market value is round about forty pounds—"

"Forty pounds!" Middleham was scared.

The Commodore put a reassuring hand upon his shoulder. "Forty pounds at least. You can see for yourself when you look at 'em. *But*—" and now he leaned forward and most delicately delivered every syllable into Middleham's left ear—" I'll let them go—to *you*—and I'll be obliged if you'll keep this quiet—for fifteen pounds. Fifteen, that's all." Here he stopped behaving like a Sicilian conspirator. "Just give me five minutes after dinner. Agreed? Fine!" He restored the young man, already solemn, his face lengthening with the weight of international secrets, to his golfing companions; after which he tactfully withdrew himself, to eat as good a dinner as they would have, in private and at no cost.

About nine, refreshed and jovial, the Commodore returned to the smoke and babble of the Saturday night lounge, then marched Middleham upstairs to his bedroom, where the review copies were on display on the dressing table. "There you are, my dear fellow. And I don't think I need tell you that it's a superb collection, which, of course, I could never have got together if it hadn't been for my work on *M.F.A.*"

"On what?" said Middleham, who had clearly done himself very well and was now looking rather froggier than foxier.

"*M.F.A.*—you know, *Mostly Foreign Affairs.* We were talking about it before dinner, and the other fellows were saying some very nice things about it. Intelligent fellows, by the way." The Commodore was feeling in excellent form, and he found it a pleasure to listen to his own mellifluous tone.

"Very intelligent fellows," said Middleham slowly, goggling a little. "Colonel Whatmore is a very big man in Farbridge. Very large factory there. Art-fissal shilks."

"Artificial silks? Really?"

"Yes—art-fissal shilks. Very big business." Middleham now turned his attention to the books again. He bent down and looked as if he were about to smell one of the largest volumes, a massive work, unreadable and unsaleable, entitled *Crosscurrents in Swedish Foreign Policy*, then hastily jumped back as though it might bite him. Then, with a considerable effort, he became foxier rather than froggier, put up a forefinger and squinted at it, and said with an enormous air of low cunning: "Before dinner you said fifteen pounds. Remember?"

Yes, the Commodore remembered.

"No good," said Middleham, using the forefinger now to prod the Commander's tie, which was his second best and had pale pink and gray stripes and had been given to him in 1937 by the wife of a Peruvian lawyer. "Not having any, old boy. Twelve pound ten—or you can keep 'em. My last word. But cash, mind you."

"It's a sacrifice," said the Commodore, "but if you want to settle for 'em here and now for twelve pound ten, then I'll agree."

In a kind of graceful slow-motion, as if he were transacting business deep under water, Middleham produced twelve pound notes and a ten-shilling note from his wallet, looked about him wonderingly, giving the impression that he thought his companion had suddenly vanished, and then carefully placed the money on the bed. "And what we'll do now is this," he said weightily, as though already burdened with the foreign policy of Sweden. "We'll put the books in

my car outside—only just outside, not far—and then we'll come in
and have a drink. What do you say, old boy?"

When they returned to the lounge, now uncomfortably crowded,
the Admiral was about to leave, clearly having had quite enough of it
all. While the four of them had a final session on their golf, the
Commodore sought out Mrs. York, who was much too busy to use
her little sitting room, and then went back to the remaining three.
"I can get you out of this," he told them. "Follow me. But better tell
Walter or the girl what you want first."

As Colonel Whatmore and Captain Mobbs, scarlet and damp, had
been keeping pace with their host before, during, and after dinner, all
was roaring good-fellowship in the little sitting room. After half an
hour of talk among the four of them, with more drinks, the Commodore found himself drawn away from the other two by Colonel
Whatmore, who pulled his chair as close as possible and glared in his
bloodshot fashion at the Commodore's right eye. His manner suggested the commanding officer of the old school, big business, public affairs, together with the even heavier seriousness of the oldish
man who had drunk too much and must at all costs carry his load
with dignity.

"Tell you what, Tribe," he said. "Notice I'm dropping the *Commodore*? Quite deliberate. Think you ought to drop it too. Have my
reasons, of course. Always have my reasons."

"I'm sure you have, Colonel," said the Commodore heartily. "Call me
Tribe—or Horace, for that's my name—or anything you fancy. But
I think you were going to say something else," he added, anxious
to steer the talk away from the subject of his mysterious rank.

"Right, I was. Clever of you to spot it. But doesn't surprise me.
Had my eye on you tonight. Know that?"

"I suspected it once or twice, Colonel. And I said to myself: 'Careful,
my boy. That's a dam' sharp eye too.' I warned myself: 'No nonsense
about that eye, Horace, my lad.' And was I right or was I wrong?"
The Commodore gave him a quick glance, wondering if he had not
gone too far, but saw that all was well.

"You were right." Colonel Whatmore picked up his glass, looked
severely at the Commodore over the top of it, drained it and gave a
flick or two to his bristling gray mustache. "Tribe, I'm a man who has
had to make quick decisions. In the Service. In business. In political
matters. For example, our present Member—Major Bulfoss. Had to

decide which of three candidates—all good candidates—we'd take. I said: 'We'll take Bulfoss.' Like that. 'We'll take Bulfoss.'"

"'We'll take Bulfoss,'" the Commodore repeated admiringly. "It's a great gift, Colonel. Sometimes I feel I have it, sometimes I feel I haven't. But you were saying?"

"I was saying that I'm a man used to making quick decisions. Have to be. Now I've had my eye on you, and I believe you're a man I could use in my business. Public relations perhaps. Or personnel management. That sort of thing—not the technical side, of course."

"Of course," said the Commodore. "Artificial silk, isn't it?"

"It is. Now a lot of men," and the Colonel glared as if his hearer might be one of them, "would think you were too old. Nonsense! Prime of life, like me. Don't you agree?"

The Commodore agreed most fervently. And added that it was a pleasure to meet a man of the Colonel's independence of mind and sound judgment.

"Quite so," said Colonel Whatmore solemnly, nodding a gracious acceptance of the tribute. "See what you mean. Now—tell you what I want you to do. Go up to Town and see your man, if you like. No harm in that. But don't settle anything until you've seen me." He fumbled in his inside pocket and finally produced a card, which he handed over, and a diary, at which he stared for some time, looking vaguely surprised, as if the entries had been written in some foreign language. "Away Monday and Tuesday," he announced at last, "but could see you early on Wednesday morning in my office—Farbridge. Think you said you didn't know the town. Very decent sensible sort of place. Conservative Member, local man, not bad fellow. Unionist Club—modest sort of place, rather provincial, of course—but they do their best. Golf at the West Farbridge—I'm president so you'd be all right there. Any family—no?" The Colonel's utterance had been thick and monotonous in tone for some time, but now it dropped to a woolly mumble that was hard to hear. "Have son and daughter myself. Son's a very steady lad—doing quite well. Daughter's much younger —clever girl, doing well at Oxford—but at moments seems to me off her head—never heard such nonsense—" He seemed on the point of falling asleep, but after a moment or two of nothing but heavy breathing, he jerked himself upright, glared at the Commodore, then suddenly shouted: "The bosh these youngsters talk. Absolute bloody bosh!"

"Car's ready when you are, Colonel Whatmore," said Captain Mobbs, who looked as if somebody had been trying to boil him alive but was altogether more alert than the Colonel, probably because he was his own Turkish bath. "Better get going, eh?"

"One for road?" said Middleham, a pure pink frog now.

"None for road," said Colonel Whatmore. Then he jerked himself sharply round in his chair, as if dodging a huge missile, remained in that curious posture for a moment or two, during which he turned purple, and then heroically pushed himself onto his feet. "Don't forget," he said to the Commodore. "Want to see you. Matter of fact, taken a great fancy to you."

"So have I," cried Captain Mobbs, enthusiastically shaking hands. "Any time you're in Farbridge, old boy, look me up. Captain Mobbs, Conservative Office."

"Don't worry, Mobbs. He'll be in Farbridge," the Colonel announced magnificently. "I'll bring him there." Then he looked suspiciously at Middleham, who was holding out a trembling hand.

"Goodni', ol' man," cried Middleham. "An' thanks for game."

"What game?" asked the Colonel severely. "Time we were off, Mobbs. Fellows we dined with gone long ago."

4

Mrs. Watson's nephew, Daubenny Stevens, had sent a message asking the Commodore to meet him for lunch on Tuesday at the New Half Century Club. After some difficulty, the Commodore found it in the Wigmore-Welbeck region just north of Oxford Street, a part of London he did not know very well and did not believe he would ever come to love. The New Half Century Club was very new indeed, and in fact still looked sticky and reeked of varnish. The Commodore had spent much of his life in clubs in various parts of the world, and was always prepared to enjoy another club; but he felt at once that the New Half Century had no hope of ever becoming a favorite of his. It could not help being new, of course, but it seemed to have overdone its newness, to have allowed itself to be opened long before it was ready to welcome anybody, to be still a contractor's work-in-progress rather than a civilized establishment. It was also a mixed club, with women and girls apparently in the majority. And the

Commodore, although far from being a misogynist, did not like the look or the sound of these women and girls, who seemed to incline too much either to fat or to bone and made a noise like radio feature programs out of control. Moreover, he guessed at once that the food and drink would be bad.

Daubenny Stevens was a long thin youngish fellow, with a pale fixed gaze, a drooping nose, and a mouth that promised nothing. He had the mean administrator's trick of deliberately cutting out all helpful small talk, all the little ejaculations that lubricate conversation, of just staring and saying nothing, waiting for the other man to commit himself. He brought two small glasses of a watery mixture that he described as "a decent dry sherry," and as soon as they had emptied them he led the way into a very crowded dining room with a scheme of decoration that suggested a cheap coffin. Here three angry waitresses were banging down minute portions of food, as if they had been press-ganged into helping at a dolls' tea party. And here, over two tiny sodden helpings of cottage pie and tumblers of mournful bitter beer, the Commodore met the pale inquiring gaze of his host and wished he was anywhere else.

"What sort of people use this club?" he asked desperately.

"People from our ministry," said Daubenny Stevens, "and some B.B.C. people. You might say we're all engaged in one form or another of mass communications. Some documentary film people too. Mass communications on an official level, you might say."

This was his longest speech so far, and the Commodore wondered if he might be warming up. After all, this was the fellow's idea of a lunch, the Commodore reflected, and so perhaps it might warm the fellow up. So he waited a few moments, but nothing happened. Nothing, that is, between him and Daubenny Stevens, although much was happening all round them. This included some violent motions of the elbow of a fat woman who was sitting far too close to him, bellowing about a feature program from Cornwall, and jabbing and sawing away at some bit of meat as if she had been given a whole roast goose.

"Mass communications, eh?" said the Commodore. "But on an official level, as you say. Sort of thing your aunt was mentioning to me." He looked across for the tiniest signal, the merest token of help, of co-operation, of interest. Not a glimmer. "Yes, the sort of thing your aunt was mentioning to me." What made it worse was that at every other table people were talking as though they had just been taken off a foundering liner. Communication was in full swing everywhere but at this table of theirs. "I was having tea with her, the other day," he continued, "and I happened to say that I was looking for something amusing to do—I was with *Mostly Foreign Affairs,* you know, but resigned—and she told me I ought to talk to you."

"Yes," said Daubenny Stevens.

"She wrote to you, of course," the Commodore said idiotically. But all he received this time was the merest sketch of a nod. He tried another sip of the watery beer and then wondered what would happen if he asked for a large whisky and soda. "Very good of you to ask me to have lunch with you."

"Not at all," said Daubenny Stevens. "Apple Charlotte or cheese?"

"Do you know," said the Commodore, calling up some of the last reserves, "I think I'll have cheese."

"My dear," said a man with a beard, "you can't possibly let poor old Mac do it."

"My God—no!" cried a girl with a stock and shortish hair. She looked like a minor character in the French Revolution. "Not Mac, darling!"

"I know, I know, I know," the fat woman shouted, her elbow working away. "But you see how it is, don't you? If it isn't Mac, then what's Ronnie going to say?"

The Commodore felt like turning round and joining them, perhaps to defend poor old Mac. And what about poor old Horace Tribe, sitting across from this pale-eyed oyster?

"What your aunt suggested," said the Commodore, "was that I ought to try some form of public service, of the kind that a lot of you seem to be in. She seemed to think there were openings, epecially now with this Festival of Britain business. It was her idea, you know, not mine. I wouldn't know. Been abroad a lot. Out of touch, as she pointed out." He looked hopefully across the table, now groaning under two square inches of Apple Charlotte, a square inch of cheese, and two biscuits.

"Quite," said Daubenny Stevens.

"By the way, I'm not boring you, am I?"

"Irony?" There might have been a ghost of a smile trying to haunt that unpromising little mouth. Or perhaps the Apple Charlotte was too hot.

"Well now," said the Commodore, feeling it was now or never, "I can easily imagine that an account of my difficulties isn't very interesting to you. And—if you don't mind my saying so—you aren't opening out very much, are you?"

"The trouble is, I have to see a lot of people," said Daubenny Stevens, "and as most of them talk too much, I've got into the habit of not being too encouraging and responsive."

"What do you do?" asked the Commodore, immensely responsive and encouraging.

"I was in Pamphlets but at the moment I'm doing Home Lectures."

"You mean, you arrange for people to go round and lecture the public on various official subjects?"

"Yes."

"Nothing for me there, I suppose?"

"There might be in the autumn. Not before. But I don't advise it as a full-time job."

"What about this Festival of Britain business?"

"I think my aunt was misleading you there."

"No jobs going, eh?"

"Much too late now. I've nothing to do with the Festival, but I've made some inquiries, and we're joining a man for coffee who knows all about it."

"Good!" said the Commodore, and meant it. "Might as well wait then, eh?"

"Yes. But I don't think there's much chance. I'm afraid my aunt talks a lot of nonsense about official jobs."

The Commodore grinned. "She thinks they're a bit of a racket. All this mass communicating on an official level—she wouldn't understand it. Neither do I, by the way. What's it all about anyhow?"

There were distinct signs of life in Daubenny Stevens. "We have to educate and influence the mass of the people. Make them understand what's happening. We do it through documentary film, wireless features and talks, press releases, mass publications, and lectures. And there's bound to be more and more of it, as time goes on, no matter what government we have. Government by consent in the modern world really implies a conditioned electorate."

"It does, does it?" said the Commodore rather dubiously.

"The people you see here are all busy creating public opinion."

"Yes, well, no doubt that explains a good deal," said the Commodore vaguely, giving a quick glance round at the creators of public opinion. "I'd just as soon they didn't, myself, and there wasn't so much communicating and conditioning, but I dare say I'm prejudiced. Born too early perhaps."

"I shouldn't be surprised," said Daubenny Stevens, with some severity. "Shall we move into the other room?"

It was rather more comfortable than the dining room, although it appeared to have been decorated by the same inexpensive undertaker. At a table in a corner the Commodore was introduced to a Mr. Bilst and a Mrs. Peck. Mr. Bilst was a warm pudgy chap, with an odd manner that was both jovial and furtive, as if he were an intellectual gangster. Mrs. Peck was a very young woman who wore a dirty yellow sweater and a thick tweed skirt. She had a face like underdone pastry, but beautiful sad eyes, which stared over her thick muddy cheeks out of some lost world.

"Couldn't you do with some brandy?" Mr. Bilst asked.

"I could indeed," cried the Commodore.

"So could I and we'll have some," said Bilst, adding mysteriously: "Nobody here's signed a contract with us, so it all goes down on the sheet. None for you two? All right—two bigs uns for us." And he winked at the Commodore; but before the Commodore could wink back, he had turned to Daubenny Stevens. "By the way, old man, my spies tell me that Dewhirst doesn't want the F.O. to send him to Ec. and Soc. but would like to get back to the C.O.I. He says he wouldn't have minded either the I.L.O. or F.A.O., but there's not a chance."

As Bilst looked like continuing in this strain and his manner suggested that it was all highly confidential, the Commodore lit his pipe and then looked through the smoke at Mrs. Peck, who was sitting next to him. "If you don't mind my saying so," he said to her, "you look very young to be married."

"I've two brats. Married for ages."

"Then you're not one of these—er—mass communication experts, humph?"

"Yes, documentary films. Oh—hello, Rogers!"

This was addressed to a young man who looked as if he had just left a fishing fleet. "Just one word, Claudia ducks, that's all," he said, putting an arm round her shoulder. "Don't let friend Norman foist that bloody cutter on you. Dig those little toes in, Claudia."

"I mean to, Rogers."

"That's the girl! How's it going?"

"Dimmish, so far. I'm worried."

The young man withdrew his arm to pat her cheek with an enormous red hand. "Sorry but not surprised, ducks. We're a shambles as is. But don't forget to tell Norman what he can do with his editor. Couldn't cut a sponge cake. 'Bye!"

"Documentary films?" asked the Commodore, indicating the retreating back of the young man, who now gave the impression he was returning to the Arctic Circle.

"Yes, I used to be his assistant," said Mrs. Peck. "Now I'm producing. It's all rather difficult." She sighed, gathering into her great mournful eyes all the despair of mankind. "Bim Toulec—you know his work, do you?—quite gorgeous—has written a heavenly little score for me, but I'm having a fiendish time trying to get the right rhythmical balance into the visuals. I want them dynamic, of course, but with a sort of scherzo effect, bringing everything significant dancing out of a velvety spacial depth. You see what I mean?" She looked as if she were about to cry.

"I do," said the Commodore, shaking his head. "And, as you say, it's all rather difficult. What's the film about, by the way?"

"It's a short, of course," she replied. "To remind housewives to be careful about turning off their gas taps. I produced *Save on Washing*. Did you happen to see it? We got some lovely filter and scrim shots into that. Quite gorgeous. What foul coffee!"

"Are you," and the Commodore leaned forward and lowered his voice, "a member of this club?"

"No, I'm just lunching with Bilst. Why?"

"I've been popping in and out of clubs for well over forty years. And I think this is the worst. If this is the New Half Century, give me anything in the old half century."

"Try the brandy," said Bilst, who must have had sharp ears and probably made considerable use of them in his career as an intellectual conspirator.

"I must go," said Daubenny Stevens.

"So must I," said Claudia Peck.

"Bilst will explain about the Festival," Stevens continued. "I'm afraid there's nothing more I can do for you at present, Commodore Tribe. No, not at all. Goodbye!"

Left to themselves, the Commodore and Bilst relaxed over their brandy. "Couldn't help overhearing what you said to Claudia about the club," Bilst observed. "And I agree it's pretty bad. But it must be much worse when you have the bad luck to be Daubenny Stevens' guest."

"I oughtn't to grumble," the Commodore confessed, feeling a little better now. "I suppose he only saw me at all because his old aunt insisted. I don't know if he's a friend of yours, and if so, I'm sorry, but she warned me that he was a conceited prig and even then she didn't tell me the half of it. If I'd met that young man in any other circumstances, I'd have told him one or two things. As it was, I couldn't. The brandy isn't bad, by the way, though I oughtn't to be drinking it on what amounts to an empty stomach. Now tell me about this Festival business."

"It's not really my pigeon," said Bilst, a conspirator at once, "but I know about it, and pull a few strings in a quiet way. And if you'd come to me about a year ago, even six months ago perhaps, I might have arranged for you to have something. Perhaps as one of the provincial organizers, running a local Festival season. Could you have managed that?"

"Certainly," replied the Commodore promptly. "Often done that sort of thing abroad—all over the place. Far East, West Indies, South America. Nothing in it."

"Just the man, I've no doubt," said Bilst, finishing his brandy. "Let's have another, shall we? Just a minute." He lumbered off like an agile little bear to waylay the waitress, then returned, beaming and winking. "All laid on. Well, about the Festival. You see, the festivities are due to begin in most places in about five or six weeks, which means, of course, that all the places that are running their own shows appointed their organizers months ago. Of course a lot of towns aren't doing anything special for the Festival."

"Then they ought to be," said the Commodore warmly. "Miserable devils—what's the matter with 'em?"

"They'd probably tell you they couldn't afford it," said Bilst. "But even if one of them changed its mind, which isn't likely, you can see that there simply isn't time to get yourself appointed and push on with the job now."

"As a matter of fact, my dear fellow, I can't see it. There's plenty of time if the right man sets about it. And I could—if necessary—be that man. By the way, you don't happen to have a list of these towns that have their own special organizers, do you?"

"I brought one along, after Stevens rang me this morning," said Bilst, and produced it. "Any particular place you want to know about?"

"The nearest town of any size to where I am at the moment," said the Commodore, "is Farbridge. Know anything about Farbridge and the Festival?"

Bilst consulted his documents. "It's one of the towns that refused to appoint an organizer or to make any plans for the Festival. Must be hard nuts there. Though it's no size, of course. About fifty thousand, I imagine." He looked up and grinned. "Thinking of asking 'em there to give you a last-minute appointment?"

"I have to see a man there in the morning about a possible job in his business," the Commodore replied slowly. "But this Festival thing is just worth remembering. And if I did have a go at it, might I let you know, just to see if you could still pull one or two of those strings you mentioned?"

Bilst made a note. "Why not? Commodore Tribe, isn't it? And here's my address and telephone number. Let's finish this brandy. I'm due elsewhere."

They left the club together and walked as far as Oxford Street, where Bilst, who was late for his next appointment, took a taxi. The Commodore felt better than he had done at lunchtime, but as he battled his way along Oxford Street, into which the female population of a fair-sized town seemed to have been decanted, he was far below his usual level of good spirits. Originally he had intended to take the afternoon train back to Tredberrow, but now, after that dismal miniature of a lunch and the depressing society of Daubenny Stevens, he felt he owed himself a good evening in the West End. This meant catching the very late train that reached Tredberrow in the small hours, and then a two-mile walk from the station, all at the end of a long day too; but he could manage it. But he did not want to spend the evening alone; so now he looked for a telephone box.

He rang up three old acquaintances. From the first there was no reply at all. He was told that the second man had gone abroad. The third call brought him worse news: "The Captain died just five weeks ago, sir—didn't you hear?" And suddenly he felt old and very tired, squashed into that smelly little box, with the traffic grinding and hooting past in a London that had grown strange and cold, full of mass communicators and empty of friends. The sour taste in his mouth seemed the unfamiliar flavor of defeat. But a tapping on the glass reminded him that this was no place in which to lose himself in self-pity.

"I beg your pardon, madam," he said, taking off his old black hat. "I heard some disturbing news, and didn't hear you at first, I imagine."

"It's quite all right," the woman said. "But do you think you could change two shillings. I lost my last two pennies in that stupid machine next door. There was nobody in, where I was ringing, and then I pressed the wrong thing—I always do."

"I think I've been pressing the wrong button all my life, madam," he told her. "But here are two pennies."

She gave him a look in which speculation was mixed with concern. She had good gray eyes in a pleasant middle-aged face, a face that seemed less experienced, more innocent, than the rather smart clothes she wore. Her accent too, though she spoke briskly enough, had something provincial about it, perhaps even rustic, earthy. "Do put your hat on—you'll catch cold," she said. "I oughtn't to ask—a perfect stranger too—but I could see something was wrong. Did you say it was bad news?"

"I rang up an old friend," he said slowly; and though he had been genuinely shocked, he could not help dramatizing the situation now. "I was told he died five weeks ago."

She was all concern now, and made the *t-t-t-t* noise that most rather old-fashioned comfortable women like to make at these moments.

"I came up for the day," the Commodore continued, with a fine tragic cadence, "and hoped to spend the evening with him. It was hard to realize that we'd already spent our last evening on earth together. And—well, I was beginning to feel sorry for myself in there—and kept you waiting, I'm afraid."

"I know just how you feel," she said, regarding him earnestly. "I had just the same experience only last week, just after I arrived here."

"Skews *me*!" cried a cheerful voice, and the owner of it, a young man in a hurry, dived between them into the call box. They looked at each other, prepared to be either annoyed or amused. Then they laughed.

"My name is Tribe—Commodore Tribe—"

"Oh yes," and she nodded and smiled, as if recognizing that this was a sensible move of his.

"And I'd be much obliged," he continued, "if you'd overlook the informality of these proceedings—and take a cup of tea with me."

"Well, you know," she cried in a rather excited but still quietly confidential way, "I don't see why I shouldn't—do you? In the circumstances—I mean, you hearing your friend has gone, and the very same thing happening to me only last week. I expect there's a teashop near here."

"Sure to be." And they found one not three hundred yards away, all very cozy indeed, and there in a corner, with a pink-shaded little light between them, they ate toasted tea-cakes and drank three cups each, and never stopped talking. The Commodore did most of the talking, and was very much the seasoned traveler, to his listener's great content, for she was one of those untraveled but romantic souls who see the world as a box of delights and wonders. Nevertheless, he gave her plenty of opportunity to talk about herself, and the curious thing was that, apart from a few little reminiscences, which established that her name was Grace, she seemed deliberately to avoid giving him any definite information. She never mentioned her surname, where she had spent most of her life, what her circumstances were, what she was doing in London or even where she was staying. He laid little traps for her, but, naive though she might be, she contrived to escape them. It was all the more curious and tantalizing because this reticence seemed completely out of character, for she was clearly an easy friendly creature, not at all the type of woman who would pretend to be mysterious about herself for an obvious effect.

"Well," she said regretfully, when it was clearly time to go, "this has been very nice."

"It's a pity we can't make an evening of it," he said. "Dine and go to a show."

"I have two tickets for one," she told him. "That's what I was going to ring up about. I'll be glad if you'll come with me, Commodore Tribe."

"Delighted! That is, if you'll dine with me first. You will? Good! Now—let me see. I'm rather out of touch. What's the show?"

She told him—it was a revue, and it started later than the straight plays—and then he named a restaurant not too far away from the theater, and they agreed to meet there at seven. After she had gone, he strolled along to the restaurant, to make sure of a table, and then, at ease and with time pleasantly on his hands, he drank two pink gins in a pub and glanced through the evening paper. He had no job and owed more money than he possessed, and three hours before he had been feeling older, lonelier, more forgotten and useless, than he ever remembered feeling at any other time; but now, with a few pounds still in his pocket and his evening agreeably planned, he felt himself again. The newspaper he had bought appeared to snarl at everybody and everything in a downright vindictive fashion; and he raised his eyebrows over it. What was the matter with these people?

At five-past seven, waiting in the restaurant, he reminded himself that women were always like that. At ten-past he began to see his evening in ruins and himself a victim of a false lying Grace, whose pleasing and innocent appearance covered depths of deceit. Two minutes later, an admirable rosy person now in dark blue, she was breathlessly apologizing. Dinner was a rather more intimate and riper version of tea. They were friends now, not afraid of a teasing remark or two, and sometimes they were content to exchange looks and smile companionably; but the general pattern of talk was as before, with the Commodore pulling delights and wonders out of the world's great box for her, while she still contrived to tell him nothing about herself.

"I shall have to call you Grace," he said rather pointedly, "as I've nothing else to call you."

"Yes, well—that's all right." And, rosy though she was, she now had a heightened color. "Call me Grace. It's my name."

At the theater they both enjoyed the same funny bits, and enjoyed each other's enjoyment too. It was very snug in this multicolored glittering cave with the howling dark world shut out and nearly forgotten. The interval arrived, and she smilingly refused a drink but begged him to go out for one. And when he returned, there she was, looking up eagerly from her program, ready to welcome him back, as though they had known each other for years and this was some anniversary. Nothing could have been pleasanter, and the Commodore began to see this as the first of many such evenings and wondered how to find some job that would make these evenings possible. And then it happened, as these things always happen; as though that almost forgotten howling dark world outside had sent one of its tigers crashing through the paper wall of illusion.

The comedians of the revue were rollicking through the chief comic sketch of the second half. And nobody there was laughing louder than the Commodore, who, in a final spasm, which hurt him, lost the stage in a bloodshot haze and for a minute was conscious of nothing but his own coughing and choking and agony of merriment. Then, coming out of it, he turned to Grace to apologize. She was not there. Remembering there are more ways than one of reacting to violent laughter, he was not alarmed and waited easily for her return. When the show went on and on, and began to draw to its close, and she had not come back, he concluded that she probably did not want to disturb the other people along the row and was content to stand somewhere behind. But when the show was over, he could not see her anywhere. He waited in the foyer, but she did not appear. Finally, he asked the attendant if he remembered seeing her. "That's right, sir," the man said, with the nonchalance of those who not only stand, wait, and serve but are occasionally called upon to pronounce doom. "Lady in blue, wasn't it—left about the middle of the second half? I remember 'cos I got a taxi for her. No, she didn't leave no message."

It was like a sinister fairy tale. After all that sudden friendliness, those soft and warming glances, those smiles and dimples, the wonder and the admiration and the teasing, she had vanished as unexpectedly as she had arrived, an unknown woman tapping at a call box; vanished into the huge stone wilderness and mystery of London, leaving behind, so far as he could remember, not a single clue to her identity. Huddled in his corner of the late train, as it went screeching and flashing through the darkening suburbs and then the wastes of the night, he tried to remember everything she had told him but failed to find a single fact that would help him to trace her. She had gone, and now he would never even know why she went like that, without a word, while he was laughing his head off. All the way to Tredberrow Junction and then along the two-mile trudge to the Bell, he examined and questioned the mournful riddle; and now the lost Grace was no longer a pleasant little provincial woman, mere company for an evening that promised nothing, but, he came to persuade himself, the last and best woman in his life. And if she had been a dead matchstick he had flicked away anywhere between Welbeck Street and Leicester Square, she could not be more irretrievably lost, more hopelessly gone.

There was no night porter at the Bell, but the old waiter, Walter, sometimes sat up for a latecomer. The Commodore found the back door unlocked, and then found Walter, looking like one of Rembrandt's old men, snoring under one dim bulb in the kitchen. And at once he felt in his bones that something was wrong. He was careful to waken the old man very gently.

"Everything all right, Walter?" he whispered.

"Not by a long chalk, Commodore," said Walter softly, shaking his head. "Read this. She asked me specially to sit up to give it to you. And it's my guess, sir, you won't like it."

Lucy York had written: *Frank is back—very suspicious and difficult —and I am dreadfully worried. He musn't meet you—so if you do decide to stay tonight you must leave very early in the morning—I've told Gladys to waken you at six in case you do stay—but do be careful!*

"Walter," he said softly, "could you put your hand on some whisky? If so, we'll have a drink together. It'll be the last."

They sat upright on the two kitchen chairs, under the sad dim bulb, and had their drink. "I'm leaving early in the morning, Walter. I'll go to Farbridge—I have to see a man there anyhow. Not possible to arrange transport now, so I'll take one small bag and leave the other two to be sent on, when I know where I'm staying. Keep an eye on them for me, will you, Walter? Here's a pound. I wish it was more, but the fact is I doubt if I've enough left to pay my bill here and God knows where the next check's coming from—it's like that."

The weary old face crinkled into a sly grin. Without saying very much, Walter and the Commodore had always understood each other. "Wouldn't worry about the bill here, sir. Have an idea not much'll be said about that."

"You may be right, Walter."

"Won't be the same without you, Commodore," the old man said slowly. "Brightened us all up, you have, and I've said so many a time. But it couldn't last, of course, sir. Nothing lasts—but the bad seems to last a bit longer than the good. Though my idea of what's good and what's bad mightn't be some people's."

"Nor mine." He sipped his whisky. "I've been feeling old today, Walter—which isn't like me—so perhaps I need a change—"

"Old? Not you. I could give you years and years." The old man chuckled softly but triumphantly. Tell you a secret. None of 'em here know. I'll not see seventy-five again—and that's the truth. I'd already got a good regular job with Spiers and Ponds back at the time of the Diamond Jubilee—think of that. Wouldn't like a sandwich or anything, Commodore?"

"No, thanks, Walter. Too tired to eat—so this whisky'll do me. But I hope Gladys can scratch me up some breakfast early in the morning. There's a bus that runs to Farbridge at some unearthly hour—pick it up at the crossroads, don't you?—and I must catch it. Well!" He rose, yawning. "Good luck, Walter! You've been a friend."

"And the same to you, sir, the very same to you."

And they shook hands, one frail and one bulky figure under that dim bulb in the great shadowy kitchen.

5

As the Commodore, weighed down with his heavy overcoat and a bag, hurried toward the crossroads, it was daylight and the sun was up somewhere, but all Tredberrow and the meadows beyond it were coldly shrouded in mist, thickening in places to fog, and it was impossible to see anything clearly ahead. As he puffed and grunted along, feeling very drawn about the eyes, the Commodore reflected gloomily that it was a ghostly and inhospitable-looking world into which he was hurrying his bag. And he also had an uneasy feeling that he was cutting it very fine for that bus, the only one for several hours. At one moment he thought he heard a distant hooting in the mist.

When he arrived at the little shelter at the crossroads, there were no passengers waiting there and no sign of the bus. After sitting down for a minute or two and recovering his breath, he heard voices. Peering round the shelter he saw what appeared to be a pair of very dumpy centaurs, but after a moment or two these resolved themselves into two men who were each holding by the horns some kind of sheep. When he approached them he saw that these were rams, as low and broad as sofas and with huge curved horns that might have come out of Greek mythology. The men holding them were alike in having brown and rather wooden faces, but one was clearly much older than the other, and presumably was a senior and superior shepherd. They were staring at their beasts, almost lost in some antique spell; and seemed to be performing a strange duet.

"Yes, Charlie, her's a proper ship."

"Her's a proper ship indeed, Jebb."

"Look at that back and head on ern, Charlie."

"An' this ern too, Jebb."

"Egad, her'll be a ram afore his mother, Charlie."

"A proper ship, Jebb."

"An' this un'll be a better man than his father, Charlie."

"A better man than his father, Jebb."

"Good morning," said the Commodore heartily.

They came out of their duet and dream to stare at him. The massive rams protested in a sonorous bass. Then Jebb, taking charge, said good morning, and Charlie, following his lead, said good morning too. The rams had faces like intellectual clowns. The two shepherds, deprived of their duet, looked more wooden than ever. It seemed preposterous to inquire about a bus in this company.

"I fancy her's been an' gone," Jebb replied.

"Ay, been an' gone," Charlie echoed.

"For Farbridge you said?"

"That's it—the Farbridge bus," said the Commodore, rather irritable now.

"I fancy gen'l'man has missed un, Charlie."

"He's missed un, Jebb."

"All right then, I've missed it," said the Commodore. "Now what do I do? Isn't another one for hours, eh?"

The elder shepherd brought out an enormous old silver watch and stared at it gravely. The younger one looked steadily in the direction of the watch, as if that might help. The rams attempted the opening movement of a double sonata for bass bassoons. The Commodore felt that he was marooned with this quartette in another kind of time, in which a minute of ordinary time might seem like an hour and yet the Norman Conquest be only a week or two away.

"Twenty-past eleven the next bus be," said the elder shepherd, putting away his watch. "Or thereabouts, eh, Charlie?"

"Twenty past or thereabouts, Jebb," said the faithful Charlie.

"I can't wait until twenty-past eleven," cried the Commodore, now in despair.

"Charlie and me's taking these two ship to Farbridge market."

"Ay, to Farbridge market."

"Billy Porson's van. Eh, Charlie?"

"Billy Porson's van, Jebb."

"Well now," cried the Commodore, seeing the light at last, "do you think you could give me a lift?"

"Had it in mind," replied the elder shepherd very cautiously.

This was too bold a stroke for young Charlie, who for once had nothing to say and could only stare, with perhaps just a suggestion of a nod.

"The van's coming here, is it? Good! Thanks very much. Fine animals you have here."

He was commanded to feel their wool, to dig his fingers deep into it, and this he did with a knowing air. The broad backs looked more like sofas than ever. "Very fine indeed. I congratulate you. Magnificent sheep."

"Ay, her's a proper ship."

"Her's a proper ship indeed, Jebb."

They were back in the duet, but just as Jebb was declaring once again that his ram would be a better man than his father, the van came hooting through the mist. It was arranged that the Commodore should sit up in front with Porson, a smelly little man, while the two shepherds traveled inside the van with their beasts. Now and again, chiefly when the van had to stop, the Commodore could overhear them continuing their duet. After questioning Billy Porson, the Commodore learned that the White Hart was the best hotel in Farbridge—for those who could afford it—and there he was driven, for the Commodore had made it a rule always to stay at the best possible hotel, whatever his circumstances might be. A good address, he argued, helped a man to make money; and if there was no money to be made, then you might as well owe a large bill to a good hotel as owe a smaller one to a bad hotel. Indeed, it was easier to live on credit at the more superior establishments. He had known in his time some men who could only afford to stay at the most expensive hotels in London, Paris, and New York.

He had just time to deposit his bag in his room and have a wash before going to keep his appointment with Colonel Whatmore. The artificial silk factory, which was on the outskirts of the town, covered a good deal of ground and suggested a large and prosperous enterprise. The offices occupied a central block, five storys high; and there the Commodore gave his name to a young woman at the Inquiries Counter and told her he had an appointment with Colonel Whatmore. After a few minutes the young woman returned, looking rather flustered, and said the Colonel wanted to know what his business was. The Commodore then found the card Colonel Whatmore had given him on Saturday night, scribbled a few words on it, and handed it over to the young woman. After another wait, she came back, looking downright miserable now, and conducted him along a corridor and into a small office, to confront a woman who might have been the principal of a women's college. She refused to return his smile and appeared to regard him as a suspicious character. The Commodore, who began to feel that he was a long way from the hearty good-fellowship of Saturday night, waited for this severe woman to announce him. A large electric clock and a number of little signaling lamps, flashing on and off, did nothing to reassure him. Lucy York's little sitting room at the Bell was now receding with the velocity of light.

The man sitting behind the wide desk bore a close physical resemblance to the Colonel Whatmore who had kept an eye on him and taken such a fancy to him on Saturday night. There was the same stiff old-school military carriage, the same red face and bristly gray mustache, and more or less the same bloodshot eyes. But it was painfully clear at once that this was not a golfer who had been dined and wined generously, but the Chairman of Whatmore and Company, Limited. The two were as far apart as drinking late on Saturday is from working early on Wednesday.

"I think there's some mistake—er—Commodore—er—Tribe," said Colonel Whatmore, without asking his visitor to sit down.

"Is there? You asked me to call here, you know," said the Commodore, sitting down without being asked. "It was your idea."

The Colonel looked annoyed and then cleared his throat very sharply, as if that might help. "I don't think so."

The Commodore looked hard at him. "I do. Otherwise I wouldn't be here, you know. You suggested there might be something I could do here—public relations or personnel management."

"We're not thinking of making any changes in our present staff," said the Colonel, grasping at this familiar phrase with some relief.

If the man had admitted he had been tight on Saturday and had probably made all manner of ridiculous promises he could not possibly keep when sober, all would have been well; and the Commodore would have forgiven him at once. It was this attempt to bluff it out and put him in the wrong that made him angry.

"You said—and I've quite a clear recollection of it, even if you haven't—you said that you'd been keeping your eye on me, that you prided yourself on making quick decisions—about a Major Bulfoss, for instance—and had taken such a fancy to me that I had to come here and see you as soon as possible. Which," the Commodore added, "was this morning."

"Well, I'm sorry you've had this journey for nothing," said the Colonel, very red now and looking along his desk. "And I can only repeat that there's been some mistake and that we're not thinking of making any changes in our present staff. And that's all, I think." He rang a bell, and tried to pretend that he was now alone in his office.

"No, not quite all," said the Commodore as he stood up. He turned to see that the severe secretary had now come in and was looking inquiringly at the Colonel.

"Yes, I want you, Miss Moseley," said the Colonel, still pretending that the Commodore had vanished.

"Yes, Colonel Whatmore." She was helping him with his pretense.

"It's obvious now," said the Commodore in a loud clear voice, "that you were even tighter, more pickled, plastered and bottled, on Saturday night at Tredberrow than I thought you were. You didn't look too bad outside, being one of these stiff shut-in types, but I see now that inside you must have been mere mush and slosh. All right, if you can't hold your liquor, then you can't."

Colonel Whatmore, furious, pushed himself up from the desk, and began shouting. "If there's any more of this—"

"There isn't much more," and the Commodore easily shouted him down. "I'm not blaming you for Saturday, when you were only a conceited donkey who'd had three or four whiskies too many. But this morning's performance is just a piece of insufferable, wooden-headed, damnably stupid masquerading that's an insult both to my intelligence and to any sense and good manners you may have ever possessed. And if I ever have the bad luck to meet you again, just look out, Whatmore, because I'll do my best to make you look the pompous ass you are, drunk or sober. And that's a promise, a real one, not like yours. Good morning." And he clapped his hat on the back of his head, thrust his hands deep into the pockets of his voluminous old green overcoat, and strode out of the office, out of the whole works, like a conqueror.

It was raining when the bus stopped in the old-fashioned square, so the Commodore went into the oldy quainty café in the corner. The place seemed to be full, but finally he spotted an empty chair. It belonged to a table already occupied by a strikingly handsome pair, a little dark girl with fine eyes, and a massive young man who had something at once odd and magnificent about him. To them, chiefly because he liked the look of them, he apologized at some length, and, after dealing with the waitress, he added: "Say the word, and I obliterate myself."

Obviously the girl could not decide whether to be annoyed or amused. "It's not necessary," she told him. "We're not together."

"We had just exchanged names, sir," said the young man, grandly but with a youthful charm.

"Very sensible too," said the Commodore, who felt the need of company and talk. "What names?"

"This is Miss Laura Casey. My name's Theodore Jenks."

So he told them his name, and complimented them on their looks, concluding: "I'm much obliged to you—by George, I am!" And took to his pipe.

The girl, a lively little poppet, began laughing, and cried: "I'm sorry. I don't know why it's so funny." She exchanged some dancing looks with young Theodore Jenks, who was clearly much taken with her, as well he might be. And indeed, as she well might be with him too, for although there might be something a trifle too exotic about him for all tastes, he was undoubtedly a noble specimen of young manhood. And any minute now, if it had not already happened, the pair of them would be falling in love. He could give them a hand.

"Well now," he said, his pipe going nicely, "let's talk about ourselves. Who'll begin?"

"I think Miss Casey should begin," said Theodore Jenks, with deepest respect.

"So do I," said the Commodore, to help him along.

"You make it sound like *Alice in Wonderland*," she told them.

"What's wrong with that?" said the Commodore.

"Nothing. I adore it," she replied, smiling. Then she looked serious, with the huge tender solemnity of the young. "I don't really live here but I've been working here—as a secretary at an estate agent's. And now I've lost my job. I won't go into all the details, but on Saturday night I went out to do some letters for one of the partners of my firm who's the M. P. for Farbridge. His name's Bulfoss—"

"Major Bulfoss?" cried the Commodore, remembering Colonel Whatmore.

"Yes. Do you know him? Anyhow, he got tight—and insulted some women who came to call on him, particularly a very important rich woman, Mrs. Whatmore—"

"Wife of Colonel Whatmore?" cried the Commodore.

"Yes. Why?"

"So Major Bulfoss insulted the wife of Colonel Whatmore! On Saturday night too! *'We'll take Bulfoss.'*" And the Commodore sat back and bellowed and shook with laughter, to the astonishment of the other two. "I'm sorry, Miss Casey," he said finally, wiping his eyes. "Please go on."

"There isn't much more. Except that these Bulfosses, instead of asking me to be quiet about it in a decent sort of way, tried to pack me off and pretend that my work wasn't satisfactory, so we had a flaming row and I marched out. And now, although I haven't a job, I just feel like staying on here to annoy them."

"My dear child," said the Commodore, leaning forward to pat her hand. "I know exactly how you feel. And now it's your turn, Mr. Jenks. Tell us who you are and what you're doing here. And don't tell us you're from Birmingham and traveling in cheap jewelery and fancy goods, or I'll be disappointed, and so, though she'll not admit it, will Miss Casey here."

"I come from Indonesia," he began slowly. "I'm mostly English, but one of my grandmothers was Chinese. Which explains why I probably don't look entirely English. Incidentally," and he gave them both a challenging look, "I'm very proud of my Chinese grandmother, who was the wisest person I've ever known."

"I believe you," said the Commodore. "I know the Chinese and have a great liking and respect for 'em."

"I think it's a lovely idea to have a Chinese grandmother," said Miss Casey thoughtfully. "Perhaps everybody ought to have one."

"I fought in the war out there," said Theodore. "My parents died. Then my grandfather died, and left me his money. In his will he said he wanted me to spend some of the money on a visit to England. So I came here and have been looking about, chiefly in London. Then I met some rather eccentric chaps who run a kind of factory in the Manor at Brant-in-the-Hollow, and I came from there last night. I'm just looking round."

"Enjoying it?" the Commodore asked.

"Well, to tell you the truth, I'm just beginning to get a little bored."

"You'd like something to do?"

"If it was worth doing and I could do it—yes. Now what about you, Commodore Tribe?"

"Now that you know about each other, you don't want to hear about me," said the Commodore shrewdly. "But I've two suggestions to make. First, as I can't take much more of this place, but don't want us to part—and I'll explain why in a minute—I suggest that you and I, Mr. Jenks, spin a coin to decide which of us stands the three of us lunch at the White Hart—"

"But I'd be delighted to," cried Theodore; and clearly meant it. He glanced quickly at Miss Casey and was reassured by her answering smile.

"No, must toss for it." The Commodore had now spun his coin. "Heads or tails? Heads? Hard luck! It's tails. Lunch for three then at the White Hart at one o'clock sharp. Agreed? Good! Then I shall leave you two to talk over my second and more important suggestion." He looked at them in silence for a moment. "It happens that I'm at a loose end—and had an idea about this town. Now here are you, Miss Casey, an experienced secretary, an attractive personality, with some knowledge of the town—right? Here are you, Mr. Jenks, with plenty of money to be going on with—and I wish I could say the same for myself, but let that pass—but wondering what to do, and anxious, unless I'm losing my faculties, to keep in touch with Miss Casey— right? Very well. Then I suggest we all work together. What do you say?"

"I don't understand," said Miss Casey. "Work together at what? Some business you have in mind? What is it you're suggesting we do, Commodore?"

"Oh that," he replied casually, waving a hand. "You've heard, no doubt, that there's to be no Festival here."

"Yes, they decided against it. They would!"

"Well," said the Commodore slowly, "what I suggest is that we make them change their minds and then run the Festival for them. In short, we have here—Commodore Tribe, chief organizer; Mr. Theodore Jenks, assistant organizer; Miss Laura Casey, secretary or head of secretarial services altogether, the power house, the brains, the inspiration, of the Farbridge Festival."

"But they'll never agree," cried Miss Casey.

"Never mind about them for the moment. Do *you* agree?"

"*I* do," said Theodore eagerly, with an appealing glance at Laura Casey.

"I'd love it," she told them.

"Excellent," said the Commodore, standing up. "I shall begin making my plans and doing some reconnaissance. We meet at one for lunch. And let me assure you," he added, leaning on the table but without lowering his voice, "although there may be opposition, difficulties, obstacles of many kinds, lions in the path, Farbridge will now have a Festival."

PART TWO

CHAPTER ONE

Early Developments

I

ON THE evening of the Wednesday when Laura first met Theodore Jenks, the Saxons had company. They were entertaining Hilda's friend, Helen Weeks, and Ernest's friend and colleague from the County School, Paul Ravenstreet. Miss Weeks, who was the personnel manager at Whatmore's, was a tall, dark, rather intense woman of thirty-five, who had been engaged to a man who was killed in the war. She had fine eyes but a rather ugly despairing sort of mouth, as if she came out of one of those Greek tragedies on the Third Program. Sometimes Laura was afraid of her; at other times she was sorry for her. Paul Ravenstreet was a thin restless type, very untidy and argumentative, with a lopsided face, so that when you looked at him from one side he seemed fierce and when you saw him from the other side he looked mild. He was a Communist and was passionately devoted to Russia, which he never seemed to regard as a country full of people pretty much like other people elsewhere—perhaps because he had never been there—but thought of it as another and far better world, from which all the vile plotting and intriguing and greed he denounced in Britain and America had been banished forever. He and Ernest could argue for hours and hours, and the great thing was to jump in and stop them right at the beginning, otherwise the evening was ruined. Laura had done it on this Wednesday evening by describing her meeting with Theodore Jenks and Commodore Tribe in the Old Oak Nook and the lunch at the White Hart that followed it.

"I don't get this, Laura," said Ernest. "Why should these two chaps come here to Farbridge simply to try to run a Festival? Doesn't make sense to me."

"Sounds rather peculiar," said Miss Weeks, looking thoughtfully at Laura. Probably she had guessed, as Hilda certainly had, that Theodore Jenks was already rather a special person to Laura. "By the way, I have an idea your Commodore man called to see Colonel Whatmore this morning and was very rude to him. I heard the Colonel's secretary, Miss Moseley, burbling about it."

"Then he's all right," said Ravenstreet. "And I'm for him. And any-how this town ought to have its Festival. In Russia—"

Hilda charged in at once. "Nobody here's bothering to do it, although plenty of people wanted one. So why shouldn't these two?"

"That doesn't answer my question," said Ernest. "The point is, they're not Farbridge men, so why should they bother? If they imagine there's any money in it, they're in for a shock, even supposing they could per-suade the Council to reverse its decision. I just don't see what their game is." And he stared almost accusingly at Laura.

She was sorry now she had told them anything, but it was too late to drop the subject. "If I try to explain," she began slowly, "then I shall expect you all to help us. As a matter of fact, I promised to do that when we were discussing what we ought to do when we were having lunch. I think Commodore Tribe wants a job of some kind. He's rather old and hasn't much money, I fancy. And he's the kind of man who'd enjoy persuading a lot of people to do things for him. He's a sort of adventurer in a way, I think, and probably rather a wicked old boy, the kind you feel you ought to disapprove of but can't help liking. Mr. Jenks—" she hesitated a moment, feeling embarrassed, then continued hastily "—he's quite different. He has money and he's over here to have a look at English life, and I think he feels he'd rather do something like this than just wander about like a tourist. And I can quite under-stand that."

To her relief, all the others agreed. The women probably did it to please her; while the two men, who clearly did not suspect the presence of any personal feeling in her statement, agreed because they liked to see people hard at it arguing and organizing and making something and were dead against young men spending time and money on mere sight-seeing.

"And I've said I'll help," Laura continued, with one of her chal-

lenging flashing looks, "because I think it's a good idea, and I've nothing to do at present and can just afford to carry on for a few weeks,
helping them without being paid."

"I was going to ask about that," said Hilda. "I suppose that if they
land the job, then you'll be properly employed, eh?"

"Yes. We agreed about that. Mr. Jenks says he won't take anything.
In fact, he offered to put some money up, to cover our initial expenses,
but I was against that and then the Commodore pretended to be against
it too, though I doubt if he really was. But of course if we can persuade
the people here to run a Festival and to give us a grant, then I'll get
paid."

"Not a hope, my dear girl," said Ernest.

"I'm afraid not, Laura," said Miss Weeks. "It's already been tried,
and several of us made quite a fuss about it. And if the local people
who want a Festival can't do anything, how are two strangers going
to manage it?"

"Now wait a minute," cried Ravenstreet. "I'm not so sure about that
argument. These stupid bourgeois types are often more impressed by
strangers than they are by people they know."

"That's quite true, Paul," said Hilda. "It may be somebody from outside who's needed. And if this Commodore man is clever—"

"I don't know that he's exactly clever," said Laura slowly, thinking
it over. "But I have a feeling he's very artful and persuasive. He's got
an impressive manner."

"And what about this Jenks chap?" Ernest inquired, with a sudden
and hateful grin. "Attractive?"

Laura resolutely faced those winking gold spectacles. "He's very
large, very good-looking, simple, and sincere."

"O-ho! He is, is he?" And Ernest made his mechanical laughing
noise, for which Laura could have brained him.

But Hilda came to the rescue. "When you talk about our helping
you," she said hastily, "I suppose you'd like us to give you the names
of people who might support you—humph? Well, let's think." She
looked inquiringly at Helen Weeks.

"I'd better make a note of their names," said Laura. "I don't suppose
I shall know many of them." And as she found pencil and paper, she
saw that a great contentment had settled upon the company. Hilda and
Miss Weeks were happy to discuss personalities; and the two school-
masters, though innocent enough themselves, and sharply opposed on

the question of Socialism versus Communism, were cozily at home together in an atmosphere of conspiracy, of nudges and winks and
whispering Back Room Boys. In fact, they began to look like two
character actors in a revolutionary drama, and seemed to turn the
Saxons' sitting room into *A Cellar in Bryst, the Capital of Moldonia—
Late at Night.*

"You ought to have three columns," said Ernest. "Those who are
For. Those who are *Against.* And *Neutrals* or *Wobblers.*"

"If there are any," said Ravenstreet. "Which I doubt, my friends."

"No, I know two," said Miss Weeks. "Don't forget that I was mixed
up in this Festival business when it was first discussed. I was a co-opted
member of that special committee."

Laura could not imagine what "a co-opted member" might be, but
it sounded so official and grand that she looked at Helen Weeks
with increased respect. And the two men nodded gravely and allowed
her to continue, so no doubt that "co-opted" had done something to
them too.

"The chief neutrals or wobblers," said Miss Weeks, "happen to be
very important indeed. The Mayor and the Town Clerk."

"Quite right," said Ernest.

"I'd have said myself—*Against*," said Ravenstreet, turning so that the
fierce side of his face could be clearly seen. It looked almost diabolical
in its cynicism.

"No, wobblers—born wobblers, Paul," said Ernest, holding up a
conspiratorial finger. "Put them down, Laura. The Mayor. The Town
Clerk. Key men too, of course."

Laura, feeling rather silly, put them down.

"What about the Borough Treasurer—what's his name—Coverack?"
Hilda inquired, looking up from her knitting. It is not easy to be a
perpetual knitter and a keen intellectual at the same time, but Hilda
just managed it.

"Dead against," Miss Weeks replied. "One of the worst. And with
him is the Chairman of Finance—Alderman Tanhead. Both dead
against it."

"Tanhead would be," said Ernest. "Bad Tory type."

"Quite so," said Ravenstreet. Then he dropped his voice as though
the political police were already in the café above their cellar. "But
I'll bet your Labour stalwart, Alderman Muleford, isn't any better.

My guess is that our T.U.C. friend, Muleford, in this matter as in many others, thinks along the same lines as Boss Tanhead."

"Now wait a minute," cried Ernest. But both Laura and his wife told him there was to be no political argument.

"Actually, you're quite right," Helen Weeks told Ravenstreet. "We had a lot of trouble with Alderman Muleford, who unfortunately carries a great deal of weight."

"Look—I've put these people down," said Laura. "But I don't really see the point of these *Againsts*. They're no use to us. It's the other people—the *Fors*—we want. Isn't it?"

Hilda agreed. Miss Weeks was busy lighting a cigarette. The two conspiratorial males did not agree and exchanged glances that wondered at Laura's naïveté. How had she found her way, these glances asked, into that Moldonian cellar?

"You have to know who the Enemy is," said Ernest gravely.

"And where he is," said Paul, shaking his head, "and what strong points he occupies."

"To understand where you must bring your maximum pressures," said Ernest.

"Where to concentrate your forces," added Marshal Ravenstreet.

"Well, I don't care," cried Laura, rather wildly. "It seems all silly and depressing to me. What we want to know first is the sort of people who were in favor of a Festival here, and then we can go to them and persuade them to try again."

"I'm sure that's sensible," said Hilda, probably backing up Laura because she had guessed about Theodore Jenks.

"Very well," said Ernest indulgently. "What about our esteemed Chief Education Officer—friend Huntley?"

"Wobbler," said Ravenstreet. "Wobbling written all over him."

"No, he wasn't. He was very much on our side." Miss Weeks was admirably businesslike now. "So you can put him down. Also, Mrs. Coote, who's Chairman of the Education Committee—and very keen. Also, the Medical Officer—Dr. Barr, who might be useful. Then there's Councillor Gisburn, one of the best of the younger Labour men, who didn't understand much about it but stood up to Muleford. Then there's old Jordan, who used to be on the Council—I believe he was mayor once—but then resigned. He was a co-opted member too. He pressed hard for the Festival, and though he's old and rather eccentric he still has some influence."

"I doubt it," said Ravenstreet. "Off his head, I'm told. Buddhist or something. Typical old bourgeois Liberal escaping to mysticism. Once heard him give a lecture—all escapism."

"I was there too," said Ernest. "And I agree with you, Paul. Just trying to escape."

"It's a funny thing," said Laura, who knew nothing about this old Jordan but felt she was on his side now, "but the more prisons and police and arrests and concentration camps and labor settlements there are in the world, the more we seem to denounce people for trying to escape. I mean, at one time people used to be sympathetic about escaping—romantic stories used to be written about escapers—but now you mustn't escape. It's queer."

"We're talking about something quite different," said Ernest severely.

"We're talking about the Farbridge Festival," said Hilda, even more severely, and frowning at her husband.

"I'm sorry—it's my fault," said Laura. "And I've got Mr. Jordan down. Please go on, Miss Weeks. Is there anybody else you can think of who might be useful?"

Helen Weeks hesitated a moment. "There's a rather nice Arts Council woman who spoke to our committee. Her name's—Ayton— yes, Miss Irene Ayton. I can't think of anybody else. No—there was a boy called Michael Seacombe—he's a journalist—not on the *Farbridge Weekly Record*—but a sort of free lance—I think he collects local news for some of the London papers. He wasn't on the committee, of course, but he got hold of me afterwards. I suppose he'd like a Festival because it would be something for him to report—but he might be very useful. By the way, don't expect any sympathy from the *Weekly Record*. The editor—a silly man called Corby-Smith—"

The two men groaned in chorus. They knew Corby-Smith.

"And Corby-Smith," Ravenstreet added, "writes what his proprietor tells him to write. And that fellow—like your Colonel Whatmore, Miss Weeks—has his tentacles all over the place in this town. I believe he and Whatmore control the Palace and one of the other two cinemas."

"I've heard that too," said Ernest, back in the cellar again and almost ready to insert the fuse into the bomb. "You can't get away from him. What's his name?"

"I'm trying to remember," said Ravenstreet, half-closing his eyes and rubbing the end of his nose with a long forefinger. "A secret Capitalist octopus—that's the type."

"I think the man you mean," said Helen Weeks, "is Crandry."

That was the man, they all agreed; and Laura was told to add him, in large black letters, to the *Againsts*.

"We're back at them again," Laura sighed; and then examined her lists.

"How does it look, dear?" Hilda asked.

Before she could reply, Ernest spoke. "It looks better on paper than it really is. And I'll tell you why. The people who are for the Festival haven't the power of the people who are against it."

"Exactly," cried Ravenstreet. "The same old story."

They gave each other one of their get-the-bomb-ready looks. Laura could have slapped them. She looked inquiringly at Helen Weeks, who suddenly pulled her despairing mouth into a smile and looked not merely handsome but almost beautiful. "It's true, Laura. The other side had the weight, and that's why we lost the decision."

"Oh dear!" cried Laura, thinking of Theodore and not the Festival.

"Nevertheless," Helen continued, "I had a feeling then—and still have it now—that if there'd been some extra push, from somebody determined to see the Festival through, we might have got it."

"Not a hope," said Ernest.

"Oh—shut up, Ernest," said Laura crossly.

"It needed somebody to rouse the town," said Helen. "Jordan's too old, though he'd help, I'm sure. Mrs. Coote's too busy. Joe Gisburn's a bit young and really doesn't know enough about it. Huntley and Dr. Barr would be good allies, but after all they're Council employees and can't take the lead. It needs—something—somebody—we hadn't got on that committee—and it's just possible your two friends can pull it off. Anyhow, I think they ought to try. And tell them I'll do anything I can, although I'm afraid it isn't much." She smiled again as she stood up, and Laura longed to embrace her, particularly as the smile soon began to fade and the despair crept back into her face again.

Ravenstreet was going too, and Ernest said he would accompany both visitors as far as the bus stop.

"Well, Laura," said Hilda as soon as the others had gone, "I think I understand about this Commodore man, but I don't quite see the young man. Tell me more about him. What's his name? Jenks?"

"Hilda darling," said Laura firmly, "I hope you can meet him quite soon. But I haven't anything more I can tell you about him at present. After all, we've only just met, and though we talked for hours, the

Commodore was there all the time. But now I've got this list, which is just what they wanted, and I'll take it along to the White Hart in the morning. And I'm terribly grateful to Helen Weeks. You know, Hilda, I suddenly felt quite fond of her tonight."

Hilda look at her for a moment or two. Then, with an impulsiveness rare with her, Hilda put down her knitting, sprang out of her chair, and crossed the hearth to embrace Laura, who was standing near the fire. "And I am very very fond of you, Laura darling," she said softly, "and I long for you to be happy."

"Oh—Hilda!" And Laura stared at her, not knowing whether to laugh or to cry. "I know you do. But how wonderful of you to say so! Let's wash up now, shall we?"

And then they both laughed. It was as though there was so much magic about that even Hilda could feel it. As for Laura, she was half-drowned in it.

2

The Commodore knocked on the door marked *Private* and then, on being told to enter, found that Mr. Hull appeared to be going over some accounts with the young woman from the cashier's desk below. "I'm sorry. You're busy, I see."

"No, no, Commodore," said Mr. Hull. "Just. finished. What's the time? Gone twelve? Then yer'll take something with me. All right, me dear." And the young woman departed with her accounts.

"If you're having something," said the Commodore.

"Always do about this time," said Mr. Hull, with the solemnity of men who do have something about that time. "Gin or a drop o' Scotch, Commodore?"

"A drop of Scotch," said the Commodore, smiling his approval. He had liked Mr. Hull the night before, when they had had some pleasant talk, and he was prepared to like him even more this morning. Here was a good solid man in a good solid room. There were two armchairs, capacious and leathery, meant for solid men; and the Commodore sank into one of them gratefully. Mr. Hull, who believed in doing one thing at a time but doing it well, was silent, being busy pouring out the two drops of Scotch, both of gigantic dimensions.

Mr. Seth Hull was the proprietor of this White Hart hotel, owned the largest garage in Farbridge, and was reputed, as the Commodore had already discovered. to be a partner in a flourishing Commission

Agency and to have a thick finger in many other pies. He was also the chairman of the Farbridge United Football Club, and the President of the Farbridge and District Billiards Association. He was a strongly built man about sixty, with a square, clean-shaven, mottled face, out of which two tiny blue eyes stared like indignant forget-me-nots. His rusty bass voice did not belong to the South Midlands but suggested an origin north of the Trent. He and the Commodore had first met on the previous evening, and had at once taken to each other. But now he presented the Commodore with a tricky problem. Here was a man not easily or safely humbugged. But could the Commodore afford to be frank with him? It was tricky: this was a man to have on your side.

"Well," said Mr. Hull, holding up his glass, a tumbler built like himself, "here's how!"

"Here's how!" said the Commodore with equal solemnity, knowing that men like Hull do not admire sketchy casual drinkers. He took a good pull, then smacked his lips. "I say—that's uncommonly good Scotch—uncommonly good. I haven't tasted better for years."

Mr. Hull nodded complacently. "It's a drop o' the real stuff. Don't give it to everybody, yer know."

"Glad to hear it, Mr. Hull. Keep it for men who can appreciate it—like me." And he winked.

Mr. Hull winked back, quite slowly. "Like a cigar, Commodore?"

"I would, thank you, but not to smoke immediately. Too near lunch-time."

"Never touch one before lunch meself," said Mr. Hull, rising heavily. "But just the same yer'll have one, to smoke later. I'd like your opinion o' these cigars." And then, like a man giving prizes, he gave the Commodore a large cigar enclosed in a white metal tube and awarded one to himself.

"Now I hope I'm not wrong," the Commodore began, when they had settled themselves down after this prize-giving, "but I have an idea, Mr. Hull, that I couldn't do better than talk to you before talking to anybody else—I mean anybody else of importance—in this town."

"If you're selling something, Commodore," said Mr. Hull, "it's no go. Money's too tight just now."

"No, I've nothing to sell. Except an idea—and I'm not asking you to pay for that."

"Then I'll buy it," said Mr. Hull, and wheezed for a few moments like a grandfather clock. The Commodore laughed politely with him, and then waited. "What is this idea?"

"Most towns are celebrating this Festival of Britain this spring," said the Commodore. "Farbridge isn't."

"That's right. Turned it down. Couldn't afford it."

"Well, I want to persuade the local authorities to change their minds."

"Why?" said Mr. Hull.

"For one reason, I think people ought to celebrate festivals—"

"Go on!" And Mr. Hull closed his eyes and wagged his head slowly, as if in an ecstasy of skepticism.

The Commodore finished his Scotch in one tremendous gulp. He needed a bit of help, and it would do this talk no harm if Hull decided to refill the glasses. "Look—I'll be perfectly frank with you, and I can only hope you'll keep it to yourself. I'm nearly broke—oh, I can pay my hotel bill, but you know what I mean—and I happen to like this neighborhood—I've been running a monthly review not far from here —and don't feel like moving on just now. And when I've persuaded 'em here they ought to have a Festival, I want to persuade 'em that I'm the man to run it. I've two nice youngsters who want to help me— you've met one of them, he's staying here, young Jenks. Mind you, I don't expect to get fat on it—I've no illusions about that—but it'll keep me going until something else turns up—and this might encourage that something to turn up—and it'll keep me amused. You see, Mr. Hull, I'm putting my cards on the table. Just for your sake. I daren't talk to anybody else here like this. So please keep this to yourself."

Mr. Hull equaled the Commodore's great gulp, then took the glasses to the desk. As before he said nothing while engaged in the solemn task of filling the glasses.

"Here's how!"

"Here's how!"

There was a pause. "And do I look like a chap that goes blabbing round the place?" Mr. Hull inquired.

"No, you don't," the Commodore told him, truthfully enough.

"And I'm not. I'll tell yer another thing, Commodore. If yer'd talked any other way but what yer did, I wouldn't have given yer this second glass o' Scotch. I'd have said to meself: 'Bloody poppycock!' that's what I'd have said. Now I'll ask yer two questions."

As he stopped and stared at the Commodore expectantly, like an actor waiting for his cue, the Commodore said: "Good! What are they?"

"Number One," Mr. Hull announced, as if he were running some sort of quiz program. "What d'yer thing is going to amuse yer running one o' these dam' festivals?"

The Commodore grinned. "Honest to God I don't know. But after being stuck in a damp barn for months, writing nonsense about foreign affairs, I think a Festival would be a nice change. Shows, music, bright lights, fun and games. And don't forget you won't do badly out of it, with people pouring into the place. No, don't tell me they won't— because I'll see to that—"

"And how will yer see to it?"

"Showmanship, ballyhoo, banging the big drum. I've had some experience, you know, though not lately here at home."

"Question Number Two," Mr. Hull announced, staring hard. "Yer say you're nearly broke, but yer can pay your hotel bill. How long do yer think yer can pay it at your present rate—bedroom, meals, drinks?"

The Commodore returned the hard stare. "Bit personal that, isn't it?"

"No, it's not a bit personal, it's a lot personal. Needn't answer if yer don't want. Please yerself, Commodore."

This was it. Now, which way? The Commodore hesitated a moment, then suddenly grinned again. "After a couple of weeks, at the present rate, I shan't be feeling too happy. And I may add that I owe money elsewhere, though I don't think I need worry about that."

"Why?"

"A woman comes into it."

"Ar—she does, does she?"

The Commodore stood up. "And now I've answered your questions, Mr. Hull, freely and frankly, and thrown in some thanks for this excellent whisky, just let me say this—damn and blast your impudence!"

"That's right." And Mr. Hull brought out his rusty wheezy laugh again. "Put yer through it properly, didn't I?" He rose ponderously, holding out a hand like several pounds of sirloin. "Yer'll do, Commodore. Shake hands."

"Certainly. But what does this mean?"

"It means I'm on. And if yer've got Seth Hull with yer in this town, yer've not made a bad start. Now finish yer Scotch an' come with me."

He led the way up a flight of backstairs to the second floor, where he moved massively and in silence along the landing. Near the end he

turned into a dark little passage and there opened a door. The room
they entered was fairly long and very narrow, and appeared to be a
sitting room that had not been used for a long time. It had one small
and grimy window. As Mr. Hull did not speak, the Commodore, who
did not know what to say and was waiting to learn why he had been
brought there, had time to take stock of the place. It contained a table
covered with a worn dark-green tablecloth, a lopsided armchair up-
holstered in rubbed leather, three chairs that had once been part of a
dining-room set, and a little old yellowish upright piano. The carpet
was a faded brown. The walls seemed to have been decorated with dirty
pickled cabbage, and on one of them was General Sir Redvers Buller,
V.C. and on another was a large misty Victorian maiden. The smell
was a mixture of soot and old clothes.

"What d'yer think of it, Commodore?"

"Forlorn and neglected sort of hole, isn't it?" said the Commodore
lightly.

"Dare say. Some chaps would have made a bedroom out o' this, but
not me. Just not bothered with it." Mr. Hull then looked accusingly at
him. "Well, take it or leave it."

"Take it—as what?"

"Office. Festival job. Have to have something, won't yer? Won't
charge yer anything."

"Oh—well, of course," cried the Commodore, much relieved. "We'll
be delighted, Mr. Hull. Very good of you. I'll get these two young
people of mine up here as soon as I can. Probably they can brighten it
up a little, somehow. The girl will probably have some ideas—they
usually have, and she's a bright little thing. No telephone, of course."

"No, and can't fix that. But there's one not far off on the landing.
Right then—and here's the key. That's settled."

On the way down the Commodore began to talk freely of his plans.
"Miss Casey, who's acting as my secretary, has produced a very useful
little list of people here who are known to be for and against the
Festival scheme. I propose to see some of them as soon as I can, but I
may send my assistant, Mr. Jenks, to interview several of the less
important types. We have to work fast, of course, Mr. Hull."

"Right. And while yer at it, just call me Seth—saves a bit o' time."

"Certainly, Seth. A good idea."

"And I'll stick to Commodore," said Seth. "Tickles me fancy. Never met one before. Now we'll go downstairs. I've a lunch date, but I want to do a bit o' telephoning for yer first. So just hold on."

They separated in the lounge entrance, where the Commodore found his two young assistants still in the corner they had occupied when he left them earlier. They were talking earnestly, clearly absorbed in one another, and the Commodore felt he had almost to break through an invisible shell, designed to cut them off from the ordinary world, before he could get at them.

"First game to us," he announced triumphantly, tossing the key on the little table. "I've won over the landlord, now Seth to me, and he's given us a room on the second floor that we can use as an office. There's the key. It's a horrible dingy little brute of a place that nobody's had any fun in for years and years, but while I'm out and about this afternoon, I want you two to do what you can to clean and brighten the place up. Think you could manage it?"

"We'll try," said Theodore, and looked at Laura, who was flashing her excitement like a little lighthouse. She nodded eagerly, her eyes blazing away.

"Do what you can with it," continued the Commodore, secretly hoping that Theodore, in his present exalted state, might be inspired to spend some money improving that room. "You understand that sort of thing much better than I do. Especially you, Miss Casey—or is it time I made it Laura?"

"Yes, of course," she cried. "It's silly bothering about these misters and misses. Can we go up and look at it now?"

He graciously wafted them upward with one large gesture. No sooner had they hurried away than Seth emerged from the office, and the Commodore crossed the lounge to meet him.

"Have to be off now," said Seth. "Meet yer here just after three, Commodore. Then we go and see the Mayor and the Town Clerk. I'll go along to give yer support."

"Now that's very kind of you, Seth."

"Not it. I've a fancy to see yer in action against them two. We'll have a good afternoon wi' them."

"What are they like?"

"Couple o' twerps. Well, I'm off."

The Commodore gazed at the broad retreating back with considerable satisfaction. This was a bulldozing ally. His instinct had not failed him when he had decided to start first with Seth Hull. He moved with complacent dignity toward the dining room, where a cool sparkle of March sunlight was illuminating not ungenerous helpings of Lancashire hotpot.

3

Alderman Herbert Walmer, Mayor of Farbridge, was a prosperous ironmonger, a Liberal and Wesleyan, who had arrived at the Mayor's Parlor, where he was sitting now, by way of long and cautious service in municipal affairs. He was a gaunt whiskery man, who looked like a Victorian celebrity seen on a television screen, the general outline of him being impressive, but the details blurred and jellying. He was probably the most respectable man between Birmingham and Bristol. He had a powerful clanging voice, admirable for public speaking, but he suffered from two defects: some peculiar relation between his breathing, his bushy mustache, his dentures, compelled him to make a sound somewhere between a buzz and a hiss, a sort of loud *Pzzzz*; and, like many other public men who are mainly self-educated, who talk a great deal but are always anxious not to commit themselves, he had much trouble with his syntax, often entangling himself beyond help in relative clauses.

Whatever might have happened outside, the Mayor's Parlor with its waxed pine, its civic insignia, its huge photographs of previous mayors, never failed to soothe Alderman Herbert Walmer. Sitting at ease now in its largest chair, he looked around him with unwearied satisfaction. The objective world, that smoothly treacherous scene, gave no sign that trouble might be on its way. All was well, it seemed. His Worship was a nonsmoker as well as a teetotaler, otherwise he might have puffed away in great contentment; as it was, he gave himself a boiled sweet, and sucked it with noisy abandon.

After a few minutes of this lotus-eating flavored with peppermint, the Town Clerk arrived. Mr. Meare was a small man, neat as an expensive doll, with an oversized head and a wistful expression, so that, with his rather dim coloring, he looked not unlike a water-color sketch of J. M. Barrie. He spoke with a certain nervous precision, rather like a don, but as he was nearly always both timid and anxious, he was apt to leave sentences and even phrases trembling unfinished in the air; so that listening to him was like hearing a precise little judge summing up a difficult case, but hearing it on a very faulty radio set.

"I was wondering, Mr. Mayor," he began apologetically, "what might be behind—visit of Mr. Hull—"

The Mayor did not share his anxiety. "*Pzzzz*. Probably wants me to attend a football match or present some of his billiard prizes, which I might be willing to undertake, other things being equal, which they may not be, of course. We'll see, Mr. Meare. We'll see." And he waved a long arm negligently.

Mr. Meare stared at the hand at the end of this arm as if it might produce a rabbit. "Yes, of course, Mr. Mayor. Something of that sort— though in that case I don't quite see—that is, why he should ask for me—nothing to do with my department."

The Mayor heavily crunched what remained of his boiled sweet, wiped his mouth with an enormous handkerchief, settled his mustache, and observed: "Seth Hull never understood public business, the way we have to run things, which he never had nothing to do with, he's had no experience, Seth Hull hasn't."

"Never served on the Council, I believe?"

"Not him. *Pzzzz*. Couldn't be induced, which is not saying he ought to have been. He's been useful from time to time, in his own way, which isn't a way I'd always approve of, on the contrary, but he's nicely off. *Pzzzz*. He's very nicely off," he added, dropping his voice. The Mayor had that deep respect for money which is generally found among old-fashioned Nonconformist shopkeepers. "I wouldn't like to say what Seth Hull is worth today, which is a tidy sum, a very tidy sum, though no wife and family, nobody but himself."

"Not a Farbridge man—been given to understand—Mr. Mayor— eh?" The Town Clerk himself was not a local man, and indeed had only been in the borough a few years.

"*Pzzzz*. No. Came here, from somewhere up North, just after the First War, which it might be nearly thirty years since or more, and bought the White Hart that had been going down for some time."

"A good hotel," the Town Clerk ventured, for like most nervous people he felt compelled to keep a conversation going.

The Mayor frowned, and even brought a kind of disapproval into his opening *Pzzzz*. "In a way, I suppose it is, never recommending it myself, not caring to be seen there myself either, which is all between ourselves, Mr. Meare." He hesitated a moment, held the Town Clerk's troubled glance, then whispered: "*Pzzzz*. Goings on. In the war he was lucky not to have got into trouble, what with a lot of talk and Goings On. *Pzzzz.*"

The Town Clerk might be an overconscientious and worried official, but he was human, and he happened to belong to that larger category of persons who, unlike the Mayor, are at once fascinated by and rather wistful about Goings On. So now he asked: "What—er—exactly—sort of—?"

"*Pzzzz,*" replied the Mayor severely. "Don't think you need ask, Mr. Meare. You can imagine what they were up to."

"Oh—yes, of course—naturally—" The Town Clerk had been a scholar in his youth and now had a vision of rose petals falling into purple wine, flushed cheeks, and white arms, the clashing of cymbals; then hurriedly dismissed it for the idiocy it was. The subject must be changed. "Shall I—or would you prefer to deal with him or them yourself, Mr. Mayor—or shall we wait until—how to handle it?"

"*Pzzzz.*" The Mayor was an alarm clock now. Both men looked at the door. The visitors were announced. At once the Parlor seemed crowded, with all its peace and quiet gone forever, as if half the world had marched in. Mr. Meare knew at once that trouble had arrived. Seth Hull looked more formidable than usual; and his companion, who was introduced to them as Commodore Tribe, was a tall bulky man, whose manner, affable but slightly condescending, suggested he was a person of some consequence. He seemed to give the Parlor one quick glance, then dismiss it as a third-rate room in a third-rate town hall. Mr. Meare felt very small, fragile, anxious.

"Now, gentlemen," said this Commodore Tribe, as soon as they were all seated, "I'll explain at once—and as briefly as possible—why I asked our friend Mr. Hull to bring me here." His tone was curt, authoritative; his glance challenging. "A few days ago I attended a small conference in London. We discussed the plans for the Festival of Britain, with particular reference to the provinces. I was shown, at my request, a list of those towns that have made no special arrangements for holding a local celebration. Among those towns was Farbridge." He looked at them accusingly. Then, relenting, he smiled. "As I have friends in this neighborhood, I agreed to come down here to discover if I could persuade you people here to fall·into line with all the more important municipal authorities in the country. It was felt in London that you may not have realized your responsibility in this matter of the Festival. No doubt you concluded that an independent celebration could safely be left to the cities and a few of the larger towns."

"*Pzzzz*," the Mayor began.

"I beg your pardon." And the Commodore looked surprised.

"That was the decision we—after careful consideration," said the Town Clerk, hurriedly intervening. "Into the question—the question thoroughly—last year."

"*Pzzzz*. We appointed a special committee, with the power to co-opt various interested persons, which decided against having a Farbridge Festival, and which we have a report of its findings. You have one, Mr. Meare?"

"Certainly—of course—at once," and the Town Clerk scurried off like a rabbit.

"*Pzzzz*. Better wait till the Town Clerk brings that report," said the Mayor, not quite comfortable because the Commodore was staring at him severely again.

"Well, I think yer were wrong," Seth Hull announced with a leaden finality.

"Unquestionably, Mr. Hull," said the Commodore, as smooth and rich as satin, "but no doubt it was easy, as I shall prove, to misunderstand the situation. But let us wait for the report." He now produced the cigar that Seth had given him before lunch, slowly removed it from its metal cylinder, pierced it with great care, blew down it thoughtfully like a woodwind player tuning up, and then lit it, just as the Town Clerk returned with the report. The Town Clerk hesitated, looking at the cigar with some respect. Here was a man setting fire, in the middle of the afternoon, to about fifteen shillings.

"I'm sorry, my dear sir," said the Commodore, almost as if he had slipped away to Havana itself. "Thank you." He accepted the typewritten sheets, glanced at them rather disdainfully as though he were used to handling much better reports, and casually whipped over the pages. "I see that the chairman of this committee was an Alderman Tanhead," he observed, with some hint of distaste.

"Chairman of Finance," said the Town Clerk.

"*Pzzzz*. And as Chairman of Finance, which seemed to us the proper person to run this special committee, which was appointed for this particular job."

"Indeed," murmured the Commodore, blowing smoke at the report and giving the impression that he was gently disinfecting it. "And what does Alderman Tanhead do when he's not being Chairman of Finance or otherwise assisting the Council?"

"Corn merchant," said Seth Hull, before the other two could reply, "in a smallish way."

"A corn merchant," the Commodore repeated, in a tone of quiet melancholy. "Well, no doubt a sound man."

"We all have great confidence in Alderman Tanhead," said the Mayor. "*Pzzzz*. That isn't to say I've always agreed with him on all questions, which I haven't, and on some questions he's not capable of taking a broad liberal view, and that he can be narrow at times, I dare say—"

The Commodore promptly rescued the talk from this morass. "Yet a sound man. A good Chairman of Finance." He tapped the report. "But the right man for this? I doubt it, gentlemen. I've had dealings with public authorities in many parts of the world, and it's been my experience that so-called sound men in charge of finance have only one object —to prevent money being spent."

"Every time," said Seth.

"Well," said Mr. Meare, even more hesitant and tentative than usual, "I think perhaps—in the special circumstances—the object of the committee—to have reference to a Festival—then perhaps—"

"*Pzzzz*." This was an angry one, like a hornet in the room. "With all due respect, I say it's our business, which it always has been, who we make a chairman of when arranging a committee. *Pzzzz*. Which amounts," he added crossly, "to it not being necessary to have any further discussion under this head."

"What head? Tanhead?" And Seth slapped a thigh, and wheezed away in the depths.

Although he was aware of the change in the Mayor's manner, the Commodore blandly ignored it. He looked at the report again, noting privately that it confirmed the list that Laura had prepared. "Well now, I see that there was a small majority in favor of not holding a Festival, on the ground that Farbridge is not a sufficiently large town and would find it difficult to afford a special Festival grant. In short, Farbridge is too small and too poor."

"Poppycock an' bunkum," said Seth.

"Put like that, no doubt it may be," said the Mayor, "but I must say that though I was willing to be guided by the finding of the committee, which I'd appointed, that had been my opinion from the first. *Pzzzz*.

And the Town Clerk felt the same, which there's no harm in admitting now."

"Well—there were some people—apparently some feeling—Festival might be held here," said the Town Clerk. "But—as you say, Commodore—Farbridge too small—cannot afford it."

"I don't say it," said the Commodore with some asperity, giving the Town Clerk a severe glance. "I was merely summarizing the argument here in this report. For my part, I agree with Mr. Hull in thinking it nonsense. The chief point has been missed. Astonishing but true, gentlemen,—it's been clean missed. Size is relative. In comparision with Manchester, Birmingham, Liverpool, Bristol, then Farbridge is a small town, with its modest fifty thousand or so."

"About fifty-six thousand three hundred now," the Town Clerk observed, with a touch of pride.

"Very good." The Commodore gave him an approving nod, then looked hard at the Mayor. "Now, while advising a well-known editor on foreign affairs, I've been staying lately in the village of Tredberrow. And nobody in Tredberrow would think of Farbridge as a small town. And the same applies to scores of villages and hamlets in these parts. To all those good folk, quite apart from your fifty-six thousand here, Farbridge represents the urban life, with all its luxuries, its glitter and glamour. To them it is—*The Town*. Look at your map, and it will prove my point. And if Farbridge has no Festival, then for most of these people, including your own, there *is* no Festival."

"Un-con-tra-dict-able," cried Seth surprisingly.

The other two would have spoken, but the Commodore, rising impressively, would not allow it. "By George, gentlemen, I came here, more or less under instructions, to appeal to your patriotism, to remind you that you are in Britain when there is to be a Festival of Britain. But now I'll say nothing about that. For now I ask—where's your civic pride, gentlemen? The people looked to you. Not only your own people but all the people for scores of miles around, who come to your markets and spend their money here—some of it on Alderman Tanhead's corn, I have no doubt. They imagined that all the celebrations throughout the country would be duplicated, perhaps excelled, here in Farbridge for them. They saw themselves living like princes for a week or two, with all the arts and graces of life waiting on them. And what do you do? You mutter that you're a small town and can't afford it, like a miserly housewife refusing a beggar, and slam the door in their faces."

"That's the stuff," crid Seth. "Now what are yer going to say, chaps?"

Mr. Meare glanced at the Mayor, who seemed to be brooding. "I must confess," said Mr. Meare, "—point about the importance of Farbridge—large rural area—not previously raised so not taken into consideration—though, of course—"

"*Pzzzz.*" The Mayor came to life. "I see your argument, which I'm not saying was taken into consideration by our committee, which didn't, and it's a good point, a very good point. *Pzzzz.* We here in Farbridge, which is an ancient borough, that's proud to offer the—er facilities and conveniences—to the people of the rural areas, which haven't got what we've got, but of course we must consider our own ratepayers first, and that doesn't mean we can't fulfil our obligations to the County, while at the same time we have to meet the reasonable demands of our townspeople, though I won't agree we think of Farbridge as either a small town or as a poor town, which it—"

"Here, Mr. Mayor," Seth cut in brutally, "can't yer make it shorter?"

"*Pzzzz.* I didn't notice your friend here making it short."

"No, but he was saying something. You're just tying yerself in knots."

For a moment all the tufts of iron-gray hair on the Mayor's face—and they sprouted everywhere humanly possible—seemed to quiver with rage. But he recovered himself, ignored Seth, and turned to the Commodore. "*Pzzzz.* The point I was about to make, which contradicts your argument, with all due respect, is there's been no wide public demand for a Festival, not here or in the surrounding districts. *Pzzzz.*" There appeared to be more of these buzzings when he was agitated.

"Are you sure, Mr. Mayor?" the Commodore inquired politely. He saw that he could leave the rough stuff to Seth, who, he suspected, had shrewdly decided that this was how they should both play their parts.

"*Pzzzz.* Take the press. A few letters have appeared, that asked what we were doing, but the local press decided against the Festival from the first. *Pzzzz.* Which you would agree with me there, Mr. Town Clerk?"

"From the very first—yes. Mr. Corby-Smith—editor of our *Weekly Record*—co-opted by the committee—"

"Half a minute," cried Seth unpleasantly. "Why did yer have him on if yer knew what he thought before yer started? Know what I call that, chaps? Hanky-panky."

"Certainly no strong public feeling," the little Town Clerk continued hurriedly, addressing himself to the Commodore. "No noticeable wide demand at all—really none."

But the redoubtable Seth Hull could not be ignored in this fashion. "No wide demand! Course there wasn't. The only wide demand yer'll ever find round here—or in most other places—is for drinks, cigs, fish and chips, winners at ten to one, and slap and tickle and roly-poly. Wide demand! Strong public feeling! Don't come that stuff wi' me."

"*Pzzzz. Pzzzz.* Nobody is coming any stuff with you," shouted the Mayor. "But haven't we just been told by this gentleman we've been shutting doors in people's faces, which was all because they wanted a festival here and we decided against it, that isn't true when in fact nothing of the kind has happened? *Pzzzz.* You can't shut doors in people's faces if the people aren't there to have the doors shut in their faces."

"A mere metaphor, of course," said the Commodore smoothly, "and I think we shall do well to forget it." He returned the cigar to his mouth for a moment, but kept his command over his audience. "But allow me, Mr. Mayor, to say something about public demand. Our friend Mr. Hull is perfectly right, in my opinion. Most people only want what they understand, what they've already acquired a taste for, the familiar pleasures. If, when they do not even know what a festival is, they are warned that their money may be spent on one, they will probably say no. Or at best be indifferent. Nobody knows better than I do," he continued grandly, like an elder statesman, "what the press can accomplish, one way or the other. Or how a few well-chosen phrases, spoken by respected public figures like yourself, Mr. Mayor, can influence the people's opinion."

"Very true, of course," said Mr. Meare, glancing nervously at the Mayor. "Though—must make it clear—all we wished was—to ascertain—the Council—and representative opinion—felt about—"

"*Pzzzz.*" A sharp one. And now it looked as if the prosperous ironmonger rather than the civic dignitary was taking charge. He stared hard at the Commodore. "With all due respect, Commodore Tribe, it isn't clear to me yet what your interest is in this matter."

"Now that's a dam' nice way to talk," Seth growled. "I bring along an important—"

"No, please, Mr. Hull," said the Commodore smiling, though he much disliked this new turn the conversation had taken. From now on it could be tricky. "Let me make myself clear, gentlemen. After this talk in London, some of it official, some of it quite informal, I felt curious about Farbridge and the Festival. I felt in a way almost responsible, having stayed for some time not far from here. Now I had some time on my hands, so I came here to find out for myself. I spoke to several people, including our friend Mr. Hull here, and found they were all sorry that no Festival had been arranged. Actually I had a list of influential people who want one. No doubt you'll tell me it's too late now."

"Well—yes," said the Town Clerk hurriedly. "I'd hoped to make that point."

"Much too late. *Pzzzz*. We were told over six months ago, which was by this—*Pzzzz*—what's-it?—Arts Council, that said it would take us all our time then, which means it's much too late now. *Pzzzz*." A higher and almost triumphant hiss-buzz.

The Commodore, who had planned to encounter this moment, now sprang from his chair and waved his cigar. "By George, gentlemen— that's what I thought you'd say. In fact, they told me in London it was too late. And now I'm going to say to you what I said to these London fellows, and it's this." He paused artfully. "For two pins, just to prove I'm right and you're wrong, I'll cancel my engagements, put everybody off no matter what it costs, and stay here and *run the Festival myself*."

"Yer won't!" Seth's cry of delighted astonishment was superb, suggesting that a first-class character actor had been lost in him. "By crumpets! Now that's talking like a man." And he shook hands so warmly, with such manifestation of pride and joy, that the Commodore was almost deceived himself.

"Now don't say another word, Commodore," Seth continued. "Leave this to me."

The other two had said nothing. Mr. Hull's masterly little bravura performance had not given them much opportunity to speak; but apart from that, as was now evident when he and the Commodore turned to face them, it was clear that they did not know what to say.

Seth regarded them stonily. "After thirty years," he began slowly, every word heavy with doom, "I reckon meself a Farbridge man. And I've got big interests i' this town, as yer ought to know by this time. And I'm ashamed of yer. Mayor and Town Clerk o' Farbridge— and I'm ashamed of yer. Nothing—not a word—to say, the pair of yer. An offer like that and not even a thank yer. Nothing but bloody poppycock and hanky-panky, that's all yer get round here."

"*Pzzzz,*" the Mayor began, excitedly.

"Don't buzz at me, Herbert Walmer," Seth shouted. "Where's me hat? I'm off."

"Now, now, Mr. Hull," said the Commodore blandly, "you're not being fair—"

"If you've still got patience to talk to 'em, well and good," cried Seth. "But not me. And they haven't heard last o' this." And he stumped out, banging the door behind him.

"*Pzzzz. Pzzzz. Pzzzz.*" The Mayor was swarming rather than talking, but after a moment or two some words began to emerge. "Disgraceful! In the Mayor's Parlor too! And in front of the Town Clerk—an official! I'll have him kept out of the Town Hall from now on, mark my words."

"Now, gentlemen," and the Commodore, who had been enjoying his fine cigar, spoke soothingly, "I'm sorry about that little scene, for which you can't blame me—"

"No, no, Commodore—of course not—we're only sorry—"

"*Pzzzz.* You've behaved like a perfect gentleman throughout, which anybody can see you are too, Commodore." The Mayor was calming down now. "And what you said just took us by surprise, that's all—"

"Of course it did. And I thought it would." The Commodore smiled at them. "Now then, I've taken enough of your valuable time, gentlemen. What I suggest is this. If I can prove to you, within the next week or two, that there is in fact a very considerable demand for a Farbridge Festival and that your committee was mistaken, you will reconsider its unfortunate decision. On the understanding—because otherwise I leave you in an unhappy position—that, given a suitable grant, and of course we can go into all that later, I will make myself responsible for the whole Festival program and arrangements. And these, of course, can be submitted for the approval of any committee you care to set up, if you should think that necessary. And in this way, gentlemen," he concluded grandly, "I keep my word, I make good my boast."

The Mayor and the Town Clerk exchanged troubled glances. They looked like men who felt obscurely that they had been manipulated into occupying a false position; but somehow there was nothing they could do about it now.

"Well, Mr. Mayor," said the Town Clerk, "I feel—very fair and reasonable offer—depending, of course, upon whether any demand really exists—ought to accept—grateful to Commodore Tribe—"

"*Pzzzz.* I agree with you, Mr. Meare, which doesn't mean we can commit ourselves or the Council at this stage, but we can promise to regard this as still an open question, which it is if the public feeling is what you say it is, Commodore, and you can prove it."

"That's all I ask, gentlemen," said the Commodore, smiling. "Incidentally, I can be found at the White Hart, but if you have any message and I don't happen to be there, then my secretary, Miss Casey, or my personal assistant, Mr. Jenks, can deal with any inquiry. Just ask for my office. Oh!—and as you probably don't know anything about me—I've spent so much time abroad that I've been overlooked recently by *Who's Who*—I'll let you have some details of my career. You'd probably like to have them, wouldn't you? Well, good afternoon, gentlemen. We shall meet again soon, I trust. Good afternoon."

Seth Hull was waiting below, as the Commodore thought he would be. "Worked, didn't it?"

"Admirably," said the Commodore. "Thanks to you chiefly, I imagine, Seth. They're not committed to much, and it's ten to one they'll try to uncommit themselves if there's strong opposition. Though it's possible we may have hooked the Mayor, who looks to me a vain obstinate fellow and won't easily admit he's been made a fool of. The other chap's more intelligent—but very weak."

"Couple o' twerps, like I told yer," said Seth complacently. "Well, now yer'd better start running round a bit and starting up this public demand they talk so much about. Might run a meeting."

"I have it in mind," said the Commodore. "By the way, you were quite right about these cigars. They're quite uncommonly good. You're a man of taste and judgment, Seth."

4

That melancholy disused sitting room on the second floor of the White Hart was already looking better. Its one window had been cleaned and now offered a clear view of the Soft Furnishings Department of Jordan's Stores across the way. There was a fire in the grate and a faded but not unpleasant rug on the hearth. The original table, minus its sad green cloth, was still there, but there was another table now, set across the opposite corner, also another armchair and a modest chest of drawers. A cream-colored shade had been found for the electric bulb that hung in the center of the room. General Buller and the Victorian maiden had vanished from the walls, although as yet nothing had been done to hide their pickled cabbage wallpaper. But further plans had been made.

"We haven't really done very much to it," said Theodore, just after he arrived that morning. "Yet it's surprising how different it looks."

"I thought that," said Laura, from behind her portable typewriter. "It's because the room's alive now. I believe rooms have feelings and like to be taken notice of. And this room's responding very nicely."

"I believe it is," said Theodore, smiling at her in his large shy way. "But there must be other things I could get for it."

"There are," she told him promptly. "But you're not to. Not yet. You remember what I said yesterday? It isn't fair for you to start buying things right and left when we don't really know what's going to happen. As it is, you must have spent about ten pounds, perhaps all for nothing."

"No, not for nothing, whatever happens. I'm enjoying this, and after all I came over here to enjoy something as well as to learn something."

"I don't know about enjoying," she said darkly, "but I'll bet you'll learn plenty about good old England before we're through with this." She looked at him speculatively for a moment or two, and then, before he could ask her what was the matter, she went swiftly to the door, glanced out and listened there, and returned to stand looking at him again.

"What's the matter, Laura?"

"Have you lent the Commodore any money?"

"No. He's never asked me to lend him any. Why?"

"Well, you're not to, that's all." She listened a moment, then continued hurriedly in a low voice. "Look—I like the Commodore. He's fun, and in a way a darling old boy. But I wouldn't trust him a yard with any money. I don't mean he'd deliberately swindle anybody. But

I'm sure he's careless and extravagant and rather unscrupulous about borrowing and never paying back. I've met the type before."

"Well," he said, almost apologetically, "so have I. Plenty of them out East, you know, Laura."

"I nearly took him on one side on Wednesday afternoon, after we first talked about this Festival scheme, to tell him he wasn't to start borrowing your money. But then I thought I didn't know him well enough."

"I'm glad you didn't, Laura. It might have spoiled everything."

"No, it wouldn't," she said shrewdly. "He can take it. But it was too soon then." She waited a moment, looking hard at him. "It would spoil everything for me, though, if I knew he'd begun borrowing your money. I know—it's *your* money. But it would make everything here seem *ugly*. So—will you do something for me?"

"Of course."

"Promise me—solemnly—you won't lend him any money."

"All right," he told her. "I promise—solemnly—I won't lend him anything."

"Thank you, Theodore." She put paper in her machine, and began typing hard.

"What are you typing?"

"Just trying the machine. This is rotten paper we bought, but I suppose it'll do until we've landed the Festival. If and when we do land it."

"I think we'll pull it off." He sounded confident. "I've no reason for saying this. Just a feeling I have."

"You don't know them here. I don't know them very well, but enough to be doubtful. And Ernest Saxon—you're meeting him on Saturday night, remember?—swears we haven't a hope, and he's been here for years and knows nearly everybody. Is that your notebook?"

"Yes." He held out for her better inspection an orange-colored school exercise book on which was printed boldly: *University Composition Book*. "It's all right, isn't it?"

"A nuisance to carry around. You'll have to have one of those boring dispatch cases."

"I've thought of buying one," said Theodore solemnly.

She began laughing. "Don't ask me why it's funny, because I don't know." As she continued, he began laughing too. Then the pair of them laughed away, and perhaps the room laughed a little too. They were still laughing when the Commodore arrived.

He was wearing another old suit—and he had confessed that he had no new suits—but it was quieter than the one they had seen him in before; and now he was also wearing a stiff linen collar with immense wings and a gray tie so fat that it was almost a stock. Possibly he had also done something to his fine shock of hair. The total effect was not only more urban but had something senatorial about it. He suggested a distinguished Dominion Premier on holiday but not above discussing Commonwealth relations over lunch at Chequers.

"And what," he inquired, "are we laughing at? Or is it simply that we are young and high-spirited and foolish and fascinated by each other?" Receiving no answer to this except a glare from Laura, he continued: "Well, children, to work. A conference—a conference! And by the way, I must congratulate you on having improved this place. But a few touches are still lacking."

"It's this horrible wallpaper," said Laura.

"What we want, to cover it up, are posters of other Festivals," said the Commodore. "Make a note of it, please, Laura. Then let's look at your list of friends and enemies." After smoking at his copy for a minute or so, he said: "To save time we'll have to tackle people separately. Now I'd better take the political personages, the Town Hall gang, because I already know the atmosphere. But this chap Jordan, for instance. He's a possibly ally, and he has money and influence. But he's an eccentric old boy, I'm told. Now he won't want to see me—I'm nearly an eccentric old boy myself. You two ought to tackle him. Laura, my dear, pop along and ring him up, and explain what we're trying to do in your most dulcet and fascinating tones, then ask if you and Theodore can see him. Humph?"

"I'll try," said Laura, and went out to telephone.

"Let me see," said the Commodore, "who's the local M.P.?"

"Major Bulfoss," Theodore replied. "Don't you remember—Laura told us about him?"

"So she did. Better leave him to me, then. And I might use that little fat man, Captain Mobbs, his agent. Well, that's that. And I'll get round among these damned aldermen and councillors and officials. But next week, Theodore, you'd better find somebody with a car who knows this part of the world—Mobbs might do—and then rope in

some of the local nobs and gentry. We may be up to our neck in a
social revolution, as we keep being told, but my guess is that there's
still any amount of good old-fashioned snobbery about, so that it
would be useful to have a few titles on our side. Make a note of it,
my boy. Find out who they are and how you get to 'em. It's your
job not mine. You're young and handsome and you'll take their
fancy better than another old geezer like me. Agreed?"

"I'll do my best," said Theodore modestly. "I suppose they'll be
patrons or something of that sort?"

"Something of that sort," said the Commodore, waving a hand.
"I leave it to you, my boy."

"But what are they to be patrons of?"

The Commodore stared at him. "The Farbridge Festival. Naturally."

"Yes, but what happens at the Farbridge Festival?"

"I haven't the foggiest notion, Theodore. That can come later."

"Can it?"

"Well, can't it? Anyhow it must. For instance, we don't know what
we can give them until we know what they will give us."

"Yes, but—we must have some idea what we're going to do."
Theodore looked obstinate. "Laura made that point yesterday, and
obviously she's quite right. We must have a program of some sort—"

He stopped now because Laura returned, looking triumphant.
"He sounds a sweet old poppet and he's asked Theodore and me to
lunch."

"Good work," cried the Commodore. "I knew you had a way with
you, Laura. Keep it up."

"What's this about a program of some sort?" she asked hastily, pink-
cheeked.

"I was saying," said Theodore, "that you and I had agreed that we
must have some rough idea of what ought to happen at the Festival."

"Of course we must," she cried. "I was talking about it last night to
Hilda Saxon, where I live, because she's a sound Festival type of the
more serious sort. And we decided there must be about a week of good
music in the Corn Exchange, and a really good theatrical company at
the Palace, and perhaps some decent films, and Hilda says lectures—"

"Lectures!" The Commodore stared at her in horror. "Good God!"

"I know—but people like Hilda want them. I'm all for processions
and fun in the parks and fireworks—"

"Fireworks certainly," cried the Commodore. "Must have fireworks. Eh, Theodore?"

Theodore, who was looking at his *University Composition Book,* merely nodded. "Exhibitions," he announced. "Pictures perhaps, and local industries, and so on. And perhaps the schools could produce a pageant."

"They can produce a dozen, for all I care," said the Commodore, "so long as I can keep well away from 'em. Druids with cottonwool beards. Haven't seen a pageant for years, and I'd be quite happy never to see another. But you've got quite a program there. Laura, just type a list of these attractions for us—several copies, please. Have you any of that copying stuff?"

"Carbon paper?" she said demurely. "Yes, I remembered that. Though very soon, if we make any progress, we may need a duplicator of some sort. And I may need some help."

She began typing. Theodore entered more notes into his *University Composition Book.* The Commodore, who preferred the spoken to the written word, lolled back in the newer armchair and smoked at the ceiling while no doubt planning the broader strategy of his campaign. And nothing more happened for several minutes.

Then a young man burst in. He was tallish and thin, had a blue chin and an impudent nose, and was wearing a yellow ocher tie and an indigo shirt and a rumpled light suit. "Well," he cried cheerfully, "what's the idea?"

The Commodore regarded him severely. "One idea, popular in my time, was to knock."

"Have it your own way," said the young man. He went out, knocked hard, then marched in again, grinning broadly. "How's that?"

Now he noticed Laura, and it seemed to Theodore that his glance brightened at once. Tolerant though he was, Theodore found himself disliking this impudent stranger. But now both Laura and the Commodore were smiling.

"The name," he announced, "is Michael Seacombe, Journalist, free lance. Nothing to do with the local rag. Send stories to some of the national dailies and Sundays. Seth Hull here's a good friend of mine. He's just dropped me a hint about you people. Like to introduce yourselves?"

"Miss Laura Casey, our secretary," said the Commodore. "Mr. Theodore Jenks, my assistant. And I'm Commodore Tribe."

"Hello, hello, hello," cried Seacombe. "And now—going back to the beginning—what's the idea?"

"Well," the Commodore began.

But Theodore stopped him. "I'm sorry, Commodore. But do we want, at this stage, to say anything to Mr. Seacombe?"

"Theodore," cried Laura, "don't be stuffy."

"I beg your pardon," said Theodore stiffly. And found himself, for the first time for years, wanting to sulk.

Seacombe gave them a quizzical look. "Now I'll tell you something about the press. It's simple but a lot of people—even experienced public men—never grasp it. I don't say it always works—there are stinkers in every profession—but forty-nine times out of fifty it does. Confide in us, be frank with us, bring us on your side, and, apart from a few stinkers, we'll print what you want us to print and ignore the rest. But be cagey, try to keep us out, tell us to pop off, be grand and haughty with us, and you're sunk. For instance, there's a juicy little story going round about our Member here, and it would be worth quite a few pennies to me in the right quarter. But two nights ago, little Mobbs, the Tory agent, spilled the beans over a few Scotches, and I agreed not to touch it. That's how it works, good people—begging yours, Miss Casey," he concluded drolly.

"Granted as soon as asked," said Laura in the same style.

"So now—who talks?" said Seacombe, looking from Laura to the Commodore.

The Commodore explained their plan, adding that he had the Mayor's promise to reopen the question of a Farbridge Festival if it could be proved there was a strong public demand for one. "And now we're busy getting in touch with various people," he said, giving the journalist a few names.

"You must count me in on this," said Seacombe. "It's not a bad little story as it stands now, but I'll leave it for a few days. With any luck, you ought to provide me with plenty of good stories soon, so I'll do what I can to help. When you've got a few useful people on your side, you ought to organize a public meeting."

The Commodore said he had thought of that.

"Early next week," Seacombe continued briskly, "the B.B.C. is running its *Next Question, Please* program from the Corn Exchange here. Only a few questions are chosen, of course, but you want to make sure that one of them is 'Should Farbridge have a Festival?' and I think I can help you to fix that one. They're sure to say yes, and if there's plenty of applause—and B.B.C. audiences applaud anything—it'll make rattling good publicity."

"Make a note of it, Laura," cried the Commodore, delighted.

"And when you really get cracking, you'll need a good publicity man," said Seacombe. "And that's me. I accept your offer."

"We haven't made one yet," said Theodore.

Seacombe looked at him, lifting one eyebrow quizzically. "Correct me if I'm wrong, but I have an idea you don't like me very much."

Theodore gave him a long look but said nothing.

"Theodore!" cried Laura reproachfully.

"We're striking the wrong note," said the Commodore, hoisting himself out of his chair. "I'll take Mr. Seacombe below. We might have a word or two with our friend Seth. Just exchange notes," and he looked from Laura to Theodore, twinkling away, "and prepare yourselves for lunching with Jordan."

"Be seeing you, Miss Casey," cried Seacombe as they went out.

For the next five minutes Laura typed away with marked severity, a model for any school of stenographers. Theodore, behind the other table, stared intently at his *University Composition Book* as though some urgent message, originally written in invisible ink, might now be deciphered in its pages. The room began to take on again its forlorn look.

"He said half-past twelve," said Laura, at the end of these five gigantic minutes.

"Who did?" Theodore inquired politely.

"Old Mr. Jordan, of course. Or have you forgotten we're supposed to lunch with him?"

"That's very early, isn't it?"

She looked hard at the pickled cabbage on the wall just above his head. "I don't suppose it's really necessary we should both go."

"If you'd prefer to go alone," he began heavily.

"I think this is very silly."

"I'm sorry." And then wondered what he was sorry about.

"So you ought to be, Theodore," she said warmly. "I thought you were very rude to that Seacombe man, who might be very useful to us. I never imagined you could be so unpleasant to anybody."

He gave this some thought. "I didn't mean to be. The fact is, I don't think I like journalists. Can't stand that cheeky know-all manner they cultivate."

"It's nothing."

"Barging in like that! Annoyed me. However, I'll try to do better next time, if there has to be a next time." Every word weighed about a ton.

She ignored them all. "As I don't quite understand where the house is, we'd better start off about twelve." She put another sheet into her machine, although she had no idea what to type on it. Then, her heart banging away, she looked up to see him towering above her table, a humble bewildered giant, too humble, too easily bewildered. He plucked her hand from the side of the typewriter, as if it were a flower, held it a moment, then gently put it down on the table.

"I feel this room can't hold us both just now," he said slowly and softly, the vast adorable idiot. "I'll meet you downstairs at twelve."

As soon as he had closed the door behind him, she threw at it the *Emgee Type Eraser Made in England*, and felt much better.

5

Old Mr. Jordan's house was a dingy villa that had a semicircular drive and some neglected laurels and rhododendrons. It looked like a house in one of our more somber detective stories; it's owner ought to have been lying not far from one of the bay windows, with an Oriental paper knife buried in his cold breast. But in fact Mr. Jordan, who answered the door himself, was very much alive. He was a stringy brownish old man with a big nose and a thin beard, and might almost have been an Arab chieftain. He was wearing carpet slippers, stained flannel trousers, a brown cardigan above a gray cardigan, a faded plaid shirt, and no tie. Shabby and messy but very clean. He had a high staccato voice.

"Come in, come in," he cried. "Nice young people, I should think. Good eyes. I'm very untidy here. Old man. Can't be bothered."

The hall was like part of a second-hand shop. There was only just room to pass between odd pieces of furniture and piles of books. But the dining room, into which he led the way immediately, was very bare. There were no pictures on the walls and only the necessary minimum of furniture. On the table, which had been roughly laid for three, were a jug of some pale-yellow liquid, a whole-wheat loaf, and an enormous wooden bowl.

"Lunch," said Mr. Jordan, pointing. "Salad—made it myself. Good bread. Mead. All I have. All you'll get."

"It sounds very nice," said Laura. "And I've never had mead. It's mixed up in my mind with Anglo-Saxons."

"We're mixed up with Anglo-Saxons," said Mr. Jordan. "But this young man's got some exotic strain in him. Inquire later." These remarks were made in exactly the same tone in which he had replied to Laura, but obviously they were not addressed to her and were really a thinking aloud. "This mead's young. Not very strong. Do you good. Pretty child but probably doesn't eat properly. Sit down, sit down, sit down."

He dumped great helpings of his salad onto their plates. It consisted of lettuce, tomatoes, grated carrot, potatoes, beetroot, spring onions, dates, and hard-boiled eggs. The whole-wheat bread, cut in thick slices, was delicious. The mead tasted like a sweetish wine, and seemed to Laura, who had had great hopes of it, rather disappointing.

"Don't mind me," said Mr. Jordan. "I'm seventy-five. For fifty years I was a shopkeeper. Had to please everybody. Did well. You know the place, eh?"

The young people nodded. "It's a very good shop," said Laura. "The best in Farbridge."

"Never go near it now," said Mr. Jordan. "Had to please everybody for fifty years. When I retired, I decided I'd done enough, so now I just please myself. Don't care a rap. One advantage of being old—you don't care. Not if you've any sense. In love with him?"

"What? Oh—no—" stammered Laura, scarlet.

"None of my business." He looked at Theodore. "Not a Communist?"

"No, I'm not," Theodore replied firmly. "In fact, I don't like Communists."

"High Tory perhaps?"

"No, not at all," said Theodore.

"Most young men seem to go to one extreme or the other," said Mr. Jordan. "I've a grandson—up at Oxford—talks and behaves as if he were the last of some ancient family—blue blood, Crusades, moldering castles. Keep telling him he's the grandson of a shopkeeper who made a little money. No need to give himself airs. Young donkey. Probably don't like this salad."

"Yes, I do," said Laura, who did.

"Too much lemon juice in the dressing. Radical Liberal myself. Empirical, pragmatic. Too much theory in politics. All wrong. If it works, keep on with it. If it doesn't, try something else. Politics is a sort of housekeeping and shopkeeping. Too much solemn bunkum about it. *The Honorable and Gallant Member for Farbridge!* Fiddle-de-dee! Like undergraduates. My grandson talks like that—heard him once at the Union. This young man seems rather a solemn fellow."

"He's not really," said Laura, to Theodore's confusion. "But we had rather a stupid little quarrel this morning, and he hasn't quite got over it. But can we talk to you about the Farbridge Festival, please, Mr. Jordan?"

"Sensible girl. Certainly. Remember what you said on the telephone —I've an excellent memory, though probably I don't look as if I had— but just enlarge on it."

So Laura explained what the three of them were trying to do and what little had already been done. Much to her relief, for she had ex-pected him to be chiming in all the time, Mr. Jordan listened attentively and did not interrupt her once.

"I'll do what I can," he said. "Might even add something to the Council grant, if they give you one. Not a penny if they don't. Don't propose to waste money. Might help you with them though if they knew I'd supplement their grant. Might be ready to give thirty-five pounds for every hundred they give you, but don't tell them that. Coverack—he's the Borough Treasurer—would sit up all night work-ing out how much he could cut down the grant on that basis. Honest industrious man, Coverack, but too fond of power because he doesn't enjoy life. You probably think I don't enjoy life but I do. One reason why I want a Festival. Give people a jerk—start them enjoying life. Need something. Too worried, most of them. Or half-asleep. Most of these girls in shops now are half-asleep."

"Yes, they are," said Laura. "I've noticed that. They haven't any interest in serving you, so they're making it drearier and drearier for themselves. Is that politics? Some people seem to think it is."

"I don't think it is," said Theodore.

"Of course it isn't," cried Mr. Jordan. "Nothing to do with govern-ment. Psychological. Drift of the times. Bad influence of the press too. Hate the press. Wrong values all the time. Glorifying rubbish. What are you going to do with yourself?" he asked Theodore. "Can't spend your life organizing festivals?"

"No, I'm merely on a visit here," said Theodore; and then explained how he came to be in England and what had happened to him before. Mr. Jordan was delighted when he heard that Theodore had a Chinese grandmother.

"I've read a lot about the Chinese," said Mr. Jordan. "Trying to understand Zen Buddhism now. Very difficult. Just catch hold of something, then it goes. Finished? Had enough? Then I'll make some tea—Chinese tea."

"Couldn't we wash up?" Laura asked.

"Yes," he replied promptly. "Kitchen at the end of the hall. I'll be there."

When he had gone and they began to clear the table, Laura said: "He *is* eccentric, isn't he? But I like him. Don't you?"

"Yes," said Theodore. "In the East many old men, after they have been in business for years and have brought up families, go off to live simply by themselves, in the jungle or in a cave in the mountains. I think that is what Mr. Jordan has done. This house is now his cave in the mountains."

"Do you think he lives here by himself? It's rather a waste of a house if he does."

But after they had washed up in a large bare kitchen, and had then followed Mr. Jordan, with the tea, into a back room, a young parson came in. He was nearly as big as Theodore, and looked and spoke like an enormous schoolboy.

"Reginald Perkins," said Mr. Jordan, introducing him. "Had any lunch, Reginald? You have? Well, get yourself a cup and have some tea."

"Jolly good!" said Perkins, and went out, shutting the door behind him with such vigor that a whole pile of books went slithering down. This back room was like the hall, crammed with books, files, portfolios.

"New curate at St. John's," Mr. Jordan explained. "Lives here. Mrs. Coote sent him. Paid a pittance. No brains and makes a lot of noise, but fine young fellow. Now this," he continued, passing their cups, "is tea—clear, fresh, invigorating—and not brown mud. Young fellow should appreciate it. Don't know about the girl. Sensible child, though. Here you are, Reginald. Take this—and I'll take that cup."

"Tophole!" said Perkins, beaming. He sat down in a small chair that began to creak ominously.

"We'll smoke," Mr. Jordan announced. Laura had a cigarette and

Theodore one of his cigars, but Mr. Jordan and Reginald Perkins filled pipes from a paper bag labeled *Herbal Mixture*. When their pipes were alight, there was an autumnal smell of burning leaves.

"What pictures today?" Mr. Jordan asked Perkins, as if this were part of some daily ritual.

"I think those ripping water colors, please, Mr. Jordan," said Perkins. "Shall I get them out?"

Mr. Jordan nodded, then turned to Laura and Theodore. "Always look at a few pictures after lunch. Sensible idea, eh? Spread them out, Reginald."

Laura was afraid that the water colors that Perkins was taking out of a portfolio might be miserable daubs, for there was no evidence anywhere that Mr. Jordan might have any taste. But these were exquisite things.

"They're lovely," she cried.

"Don't talk—look. Can't help it, I suppose—they *must* talk."

So they sipped their tea and smoked and stared at the sketches, which conjured the rough paper into the light of a June morning or a heavy August afternoon. Laura was enchanted by them. There was one of a Dutch barn against low hills, caught in the green magic of the time between sunset and twilight, that made her want to cry out at the wonder of this world.

"Right," said Mr. Jordan. "All by one man, of course. Yardlow. Can't make any money. Help to keep him going. Which do you like best? Any preference?"

"That one," said Theodore, pointing to the barn.

"Oh, Theodore!" cried Laura, forgetting they were not on those terms at the moment. "So do I."

"Very well," said Mr. Jordan, almost irritably. "Take it, take it."

"Do you mean—we can have it?" she gasped.

"Yes, yes, yes. Sold things for fifty years. Now I give 'em away. Nice change. Pack it carefully."

"Oh—I'll do it," said Laura eagerly. "And thank you a thousand times—it's a wonderful present." With some rather clumsy assistance from Perkins, she packed the sketch in cardboard and brown paper.

"Mr. Jordan," said Theodore earnestly, "if you've other things as good as this, couldn't we have a show of them for the Festival?"

"Certainly. Just find the right place to hang them. Come round again and we'll choose the best and have them framed."

"Topping scheme," said Perkins.

"Make some more tea," said Mr. Jordan. "All fresh and clear." And off he went with the teapot.

"Does anybody else live here?" Laura asked.

"Rather," said Perkins, beaming. "Very nice couple who work at the hospital. They're out all day, of course. And a crotchety deaf old man called Summers, but he's away at present. Mr. Jordan never comes to church—doesn't get on with my vicar—and pretends he isn't a Christian at all. But I know jolly well he is—and about the best round here. Do you do any boxing?" he asked Theodore, who replied that he didn't. "Pity! I'd have asked you to come along to my boy's club. Football and boxing are the only way I can find of arousing their interest. Fortunately, I'm not bad at them myself. If you and I could have had a good go at each other, we could have packed the place and brought in all sorts of nasty little spivs. How are you on drama, Miss Casey?"

"Useless," she told him. "I believe most girls think they can act, even when they won't admit it. I *know* I can't. I'm terrible."

"So am I," said Perkins. "Though in my last parish, everybody said I was very funny as a drunken tramp. All the plays we did there had tramps in them. French windows in libraries—with tramps creeping in, sometimes drunk and funny, sometimes sinister. Would there be anything in your Festival for the girls to do? I'm simply rotten with girls."

"We'll think of something. Won't we, Theodore?"

"Procession and pageant," said Theodore.

"Jolly good," cried Perkins. "Anything with dressing up in it. Hello, somebody's here." He dashed into the hall, banging the door again so that more books went slithering down.

Laura began laughing, and laughed so much that she had to sit down. "He's sweet—but like a sort of big talking dog, banging about."

"When I was a small boy," said Theodore, "I used to read a lot of books that my father had kept from the time he was a boy. And some of them were school stories. They were full of characters just like Mr. Perkins. I feel he's just stepped out of one of them. It's funny about England," he continued, thoughtfully. "Once you're outside London, you seem to meet all kinds of people you never expect to meet, people you can't imagine meeting just from reading about England in the papers or most of the books. Not only odd characters, but people who seem to belong to other periods. You never imagine, when you live a long way off, that all the other Englands—Victorian and Edwardian, for instance—still survive in certain people."

"I wish I thought all this Festival business was going to be like this," said Laura. "But I know it won't be. We're having the best bits first. You'll see."

"There's no point," he told her, "in not enjoying a good bit because you think the other bits won't be as good."

"I think we all do that now. It's not trusting things—feeling somebody or something will get at you if you allow yourself to be happy. Still, don't think it'll be all like this. What's happening out there? Ought we to go, do you think? Mr. Jordan may have forgotten he's supposed to be making some fresh tea for us all."

But Mr. Jordan not only brought in the tea but also the visitor, who was a warm, reddish sort of woman, about forty-five, with a quick eye and a large determined mouth. "Mrs. Coote," he announced. "Told her about you. Very helpful woman. Likes her own way, of course."

"I've been wanting to meet you," said Laura. "Helen Weeks said you'd want to help us."

"She's quite right," said Mrs. Coote. "Tell me what you propose to do, while I drink this delicious tea."

With some assistance from Theodore, Laura sketched a possible program for the Festival.

"That's more or less what we had in mind originally," said Mrs. Coote. "Have you any idea what it'll cost? Or haven't you worked that out yet?"

"It's very difficult to work it out," said Theodore. "It seems to me to depend on the scale of the thing, and also on what people are ready to do to help it out. For instance, if we have to pay a heavy rent for a concert hall or a theater, then the drama or music part of it will cost more. I think we need a little more time. I'd like to try to work out some possible figures with the Commodore."

"And I'd better meet this Commodore," said Mrs. Coote briskly. "I don't really understand what a Commodore's doing trying to organize a Festival here. Or even quite where you two come in."

"Nice woman really," cried Mr. Jordan. "Don't mind her. Overdoes this official businesslike manner. Women always do, once they've got the hang of it. Tell her you're doing it for fun. If she doesn't like that, let her lump it."

"In my case that would be quite true," said Theodore firmly. "And if somebody here tells me to mind my own business, I don't know what my answer would be."

"And I'll bet somebody will," said Laura darkly.

"Probably several people will," said Mrs. Coote, smiling. "Nevertheless, you might succeed where we failed, just because we were all very busy people and not one of us could make the Festival a special target."

"Not target. Let's have no targets." Mr. Jordan shook his head in disgust. "Everybody talks about targets now. Reaching targets. Passing targets. Idiotic jargon."

"Shut up," said Mrs. Coote amiably. "They know what I mean. You'll certainly have it thrown at you, probably by the wretched *Weekly Record*, that you're not Farbridge people and ought to go away and mind your own business. You must be prepared for that—and even worse things than that. But I have a meeting of the Education Committee—I'm Chairman—this afternoon, and I'll tell them what's happening. The Director, Mr. Huntley, will be on our side, and although he's not a very forceful character, he's very useful. What's this man going to do for you?" And she indicated Mr. Jordan.

"Never mind about that," said Mr. Jordan, before Laura or Theodore could reply. "You do your part, I'll do mine. Tell you this, though. I was going away for a few weeks. But now I won't go until something's arranged about this Festival. And I can pull a string or two. Don't look it, but I can."

"You didn't last time," said Mrs. Coote reproachfully.

"This is different. Taken a fancy to these two. Don't know about this Commodore. Might be a charlatan. But perhaps we need a charlatan, an adventurer, a showman. Why not?"

"I must go," said Mrs. Coote.

"They're going too," said Mr. Jordan. "I want to have a nap. You're all going. Come again—tomorrow—any time—ring me up. Girl got the water-color sketch? Good! Off you go."

Outside, Mrs. Coote said: "One of you ought to see Councillor Joe Gisburn. And as soon as possible. How do you like Mr. Jordan?"

"I adore him," cried Laura.

"I like him," said Theodore. "But I must confess I'm terribly hungry. The next time I see him I shall go between meals. Just ask for tea," he added thoughtfully.

"Greedy pig," said Laura.

Mrs. Coote laughed. "Most of them are. And those who aren't—somehow—are even less lovable. Look—there's a bus. We must fly."

6

It was the Commodore who saw Councillor Joe Gisburn, later that afternoon. Councillor Gisburn was a fair, stocky chap about thirty-five, aggressive but essentially amiable, and the owner of an extremely loud angry voice, like that of an overworked bus conductor. He was eating cold meat pie and washing it down with gulps of strong tea. His little living room was the noisiest apartment the Commodore had known for years. The radio was on at full strength, although nobody seemed to be listening to it. Two Gisburn children were playing some mysterious shouting game in one corner. In another corner a younger child was hammering away. Mrs. Gisburn, a plump smiling woman, kept popping in and out, carrying a healthy-looking baby that must have roared and howled merely to contribute to the family din. None of them seemed to notice the noise, although everybody had to shout to be heard at all. But after twenty minutes of it, bellowing replies to Gisburn's questions, the Commodore felt exhausted.

"What about that sponge, Joe?" Mrs. Gisburn shouted.

"Well, what about it?" he shouted back at her.

"Do you want some or not?"

"Same we had yesterday?"

"Yes—can't make it every day."

"Keep it," he shouted, all in good humor.

"I want some," cried the hammering child.

"Well, you can't have any," shouted Mrs. Gisburn.

The child hammered harder than ever.

What the hell am I doing here? the Commodore asked himself, and longed for a deserted smoke room, a deep leather chair, a whisky and soda.

"We'll be with you again next week at the same time," roared the radio.

"Okay. We're off," shouted Gisburn. He drained his cup, wiped his mouth, sprang to his feet, whipped out a cigarette and a lighter, lit the cigarette, took three quick strong puffs at it, handed it to his wife, who took two quick strong puffs at it and fended off the baby, who was bellowing like a miniature bull, and then smilingly returned the cigarette to her husband. The Commodore felt dizzy. A week of this family and he would have to crawl into a nursing home.

"Pleased to have met you, Commander," shouted Mrs. Gisburn, who had wide eyes and was as ripe and innocent as a plum.

"Thank you, Mrs. Gisburn," he roared, hardly knowing what he was saying. "And the same to you."

The street outside, which was lined with little houses all exactly like the Gisburns', seemed wonderfully quiet and restful. But there was to be no loitering in it. Joe Gisburn, though loaded down with meat pie, set off at a very sharp pace, his cigarette burning like a quick fuse.

"With any luck," he said, "we'll just catch Alf Muleford in his office. An' if we do, we'll go for him. Only thing to do. Go for him. He'll be against it, like you said, but we go for him."

"Do I go for him or do you go for him?" the Commodore asked.

"We both go for him. Only thing with Alf. I wanted to do it last time, when we had that special committee, but I didn't see who was going to do this Festival job even if we pushed it through. Mrs. Coote's too busy. So am I—even if I knew what to do, which I don't. And there's nobody at the Town Hall could take it on. Town Clerk doesn't know whether he's coming or going. And you know what our Mayor's like—poor old Herbert Walmer—just a stuffed shirt with a little saw-mill attached—*Pzzzz*. This town wants livening up, and if you or anybody else can help to do it, good luck to you, I say. We'll get the bus here. Alf Muleford's office is just behind the Town Hall."

They were there in ten minutes. Alderman Muleford's office, which was the district headquarters of one of the big trade unions, was on the first floor, above a tobacconist's shop, and was the musty wreck of a Victorian parlor. Alderman Muleford was a bald man in the fifties. He had a long upper lip and a formidably obstinate chin. He was smoking, without any apparent enjoyment, a short pipe. He nodded to Gisburn in a not unfriendly fashion, but turned a slaty little eye on the Commodore.

"Now look, Alf," Joe Gisburn began, "this is Commodore Tribe and he's trying to get this Festival thing going before it's too late, and this time I want you to back me up and not go along with all the old Tories."

"It came up for consideration," said Muleford very deliberately, "and was turned down." His voice was heavy but curiously flat, and every word arrived with an air of cold finality. He seemed to the Commodore to be perfectly equipped for pronouncing a death sentence.

"Well, we can consider it again and change our minds," said Gisburn.

"Why?" It fell like a lead weight.

"Now turn it up, Alf. If the people here want a Festival, like other places are having, then they ought to have one."

"Who says they want one? Nobody's asking me for one." Ten lead weights.

"Oh—for God's sake!" And Gisburn, leaning against some files, fished out a cigarette from a crumpled packet and set fire to it, all with a kind of contemptuous flourish.

"I can assure you, Alderman Muleford," said the Commodore as smoothly as he could, "there's a considerable demand both here in the town and in the surrounding district that Farbridge should follow the example of other towns—"

"Just a minute," said Muleford. He stared hard at the Commodore before he spoke again. "Joe here's a colleague of mine. Councillor. Labour man. Right. But I don't have to argue the point with you, y'know. And as a matter of fact," he added portentously, "I think Councillor Gisburn might have done better—much better—to have asked my permission before he brought you along here. Very irregular. *Very* irregular."

"I see," said the Commodore. "Well, that's my fault—not his. In my ignorance, I didn't realize that there might be certain formalities to be observed before I had the privilege of talking to you, Alderman Muleford."

"No need to be sarcastic," said Muleford. "That'll get you nowhere. And another thing. I'm not Herbert Walmer, y'know. Nor the Town Clerk."

"What are you getting at, Alf?" Gisburn asked.

"What I'm getting at, Joe, is this. I don't see where this chap comes in. I'm only saying now what I've already told 'em in the Town Hall. I don't get the idea. I don't see where this chap comes in. I don't see why he's got to come along an' tell us we ought to have a Festival or anything else when we've already decided not to have one. We're responsible—and he's not."

"Look—will you just come down off your high horse for a minute, Alf? You're a Labour man—"

Muleford brought his hand down flat on the table. "Yes, I'm a

Labour man, an' I was working for the Movement before you first went to school, Joe Gisburn. I've fought for a decent living wage and for proper hours and conditions, an' I'll go on fighting for 'em. I stand where I've always stood," he continued, in a louder and more singsong style that suggested election oratory, "for the welfare of the Working Class, a better standard of living for the Workers, and for the Trade Union and Labour Movements. I still say today what I said thirty years ago—"

"Yes, Alf, we know. This isn't a meeting."

"Very well," said Muleford, as though he had made a generous concession. "But in the present case, what it comes down to is this—I'm not voting public money for Fancywork just because some toff comes down from London to talk us into it. No fear. We can do without Fancywork. There's been too much of that already."

"Go on," cried Gisburn derisively. "Where?"

"Not here," said Muleford. "In other places, not here. Fancywork. And all wrong, in my opinion. Not what the Movement was ever for. Hours an' wages—"

"Damn it, Alf!" shouted Gisburn. "There's something else in life besides hours and wages."

"I never said there wasn't. And don't shout at me, Joe. I'm not deaf. What I'm saying is that with rates as they are, we don't want to be paying out good money for flag-waving an' singing an' play-acting an' all this Fancywork. I'm not against people enjoying themselves. I like my game o' bowls in the park—"

"Some people would call that Fancywork," said the Commodore. "No doubt good money's been spent on that."

Before Muleford could reply, a secretary or clerk, a woman with thick spectacles and some evidence of sinus trouble, came in from the back office and placed some papers on the table.

"One moment," said the Commodore, in his most winning style. "Let me put it to this young lady. Now then—wouldn't you like to see the Festival of Britain celebrated here in Farbridge—processions, fireworks, a pageant, plays, music, exhibitions—bringing gaiety, grace, color into your life? Wouldn't you?"

"No, I wouldn't. Will that be all, Mr. Muleford?"

"That's all," said Muleford, watching her depart with a faint smile on his face, like a pale gleam of January sunshine illuminating a granite sarcophagus. The Commodore, who could think of nothing else to do at this moment, blew his nose importantly.

"So you're against us, Alf?" said Gisburn in despair.

"That's right, Joe," said Muleford with some complacency.

"Joining some of the worst Tories, eh?"

"Can't help that. No Party line on this question, Joe. And they know me. I stand by my principles. What I fought for yesterday, I'll fight for tomorrow. But no Festivals and Fancywork."

The Commodore reached for his hat. "Councillor Gisburn, I think we're wasting time." He looked down at Muleford, who was now relighting his pipe, which appeared to contain some wet Newmown Hay Mixture. "Speaking as a toff from London, whatever that might be," he began softly, "I should just like to say this, Alderman Muleford. I've seen several people already about this Festival business, and so far you're the only person who's received me with deliberate discourtesy. But it's been in private, and I came uninvited to see you in this office of yours, so I'll let it pass. But now I warn you that if you try the same tactics in public, I'll show you up for the conceited woodenhead you are, if it's the last thing I do. Good day, Alderman."

The Farbridge Town Hall is not one of those pretentious stone pseudo-Gothic or baroque buildings that many of our cities erected during their Victorian heyday. It was built between the wars, to replace an older structure that was much too small, and it is a square brick building, four stories high, that might be a rather dignified factory. In the steely sunset of this March day, it looked both grim and wary, and unhappily reminded the Commodore, as he and Gisburn hurried toward the main entrance, of Alderman Muleford. It was as though they were hurrying toward a vast image, flattened and powerfully reinforced, of the Alderman.

"Don't think I'm leaving it at that," Gisburn was saying. "I'll tackle Alf Muleford at the next Party meeting. Mrs. Coote'll be glad to join in. She and Alf have never got on. And our chaps won't like it when they find him lined up with Tanhead and that Tory lot. Leave it to me. Now you want to see Huntley—Chief Education Officer—don't you? No guts, but means well. I'll take you along there—might just catch him in—then leave you to it."

The Chief Education Officer, was still hard at work when they arrived. (The Commodore now began to realize that the popular notion of official hours at work was about fifty years out of date.) He was a very refined man, about fifty, melancholy and debilitated, who spoke in a low murmur, and had a trick of closing his eyes after he had ventured any statement, and then taking such a deep breath that not only his nostrils but his whole head quivered. It seemed cruel that such a fastidious being should be imprisoned in the laborious machinery of municipal government; you wanted to give him an aspirin and send him home to read T. S. Eliot. He was certainly not the Commodore's idea of a doughty ally, but nevertheless he was a pleasant change from Alderman Muleford.

"Erce," he murmured, after Joe Gisburn had shouted an introduction and rushed off, "my chairman—Mrs. Coote—a splendid woman, by the way—had a word with me about it this afternoon, Commodore. If there's still time—it's a capital idea, of course—capital—erce." He closed his eyes, breathed, quivered.

Still smarting from Muleford, the Commodore decided to give his scheme the air of an official mission. "I was up in town talking to Bilst, Daubenny Stevens, and some of the other Back Room Boys about the Festival of Britain. When they knew I'd been living near here this winter and had some—er—good contacts, they suggested I ought to do something about Farbridge. Between these four walls, of course, Mr. Huntley."

This was the right line. Huntley opened his eyes, then half-closed them, and nodded several times. "I thought something of that sort must have happened." His murmur took on a knowing Back Room Boy tone. "Only way of doing it, of course. I think you might pull it off—erce. You're not worried about the lack of time?"

"Not if we can get things moving here," said the Commodore. "And they are moving already. Very much between ourselves," and now he imitated the other's murmur, "I've already had at least one promise to supplement any official grant on a very liberal scale. You'll keep that to yourself, Mr. Huntley, please."

The other produced two of the slowest nods the Commodore had ever seen. And what with these slow-motion movements and the whispering and murmuring and eye-closing, he felt he was taking part in an elaborate deathbed scene. A few muted strings in the background, the toplights switched off, and perhaps several guttering candles in their place, and they had it all.

"Strong opposition, of course," Mr. Huntley murmured. "Mostly— in confidence, Commodore—from the same people who try to cut us down in Education. Finance here is sticky—very sticky—but I'm very fortunate in my Chairman. Mrs. Coote is splendid—really splendid. Erce. With Mrs. Coote—Gisburn—old Jordan—you're not doing badly at all. And I'll do what I can. It might help, of course, if you brought the schools in to do something." And then he went under the anesthetic again.

"My assistant, Jenks—very keen intelligent fellow—" and the Commodore found it impossible to raise his voice and be brisk—"suggests the schools shoud be asked to produce a Farbridge Pageant."

Mr. Huntley returned to consciousness. "First-rate idea—first-rate—first-rate—" It was like a cradle song. "We could do it like a shot, of course—like a shot. They'd all be keen—desperately keen. Only thing that worries me there is the time. Two months or so. Not long, of course."

Making a considerable effort, the Commodore managed to break the spell. "Help me to push this business through in the next week or ten days, and you're all right for time. And you might risk it and make a start anyhow."

"Erce," Mr. Huntley murmured. "I was thinking along the same lines. And I've one or two very very keen youngish Heads—really first-class people—"

But now a round red-faced little man, almost smoking hot, burst into the room. He was introduced to the Commodore as Dr. Barr, the Medical Officer of Health. Nothing could be farther removed from Huntley's manner than Dr. Barr's. He was one of those Scots who seem to exist in a perpetual state of amazement and gleeful wonder. He had a loud high voice that went up and up in astonishment.

"Ay, ay, Commodore, Ah've been hearing tell of you. An' you're going to try an' gie us a Farbridge Festival after all? Well, well, well! An' you're seeing Huntley here. Ye couldn't find a better man under this roof. An' Ah hear you've got Seth Hull workin' for ye. Ay, the news travels round in a wee place like this. Well, good luck to ye, good luck to ye, Commodore."

"Thank you, Dr. Barr," said the Commodore. "And don't you think, as a medical man, something like a Festival might do these people a bit of good?"

"Ay, Ah do, Ah do, Ah do," cried Dr. Barr. "There's half o' them away to their doctors for want of something to put their minds on.

They're bored stiff, man, an' that's a fact. You're plannin' to give us some music, Ah take it?"

"Certainly. As good as we can get, I promise you."

"Do ye hear that, Huntley? Ay, ay," and Dr. Barr rubbed his hands together delightedly. "Well, Ah'll be there, Commodore, Ah'll be there—and the wife and the two girls alongside me. An' the Corn Exchange is no so bad for sound, Ah'm tellin' ye. Ye could do a lot worse in many a bigger place. Ay, ay, a lot worse. Have ye seen our Member o' Parliament—Major Bulfoss?"

"No, I've been wondering about him."

"Worth trying," Huntley murmured.

"Juist what Ah was goin' to say maself," cried Dr. Barr in the highest wonder and glee. "The very words. Worth tryin'. Ah had it on the tip o' ma tongue."

"Between ourselves," Huntley crooned sadly, "not a first-class fellow—"

"Och, no! Where would the Tories here be gettin' a first-class fellow from?"

"But Bulfoss could be useful." Huntley was now a whispering ventriloquist, or the ghost of a particularly refined Back Room Boy, and the Commodore found it difficult to hear him at all. "Erce—Bulfoss could be useful. Especially at this moment. Dr. Barr will explain. I must look through this stuff." And he closed, breathed, quivered, went under.

"Ay, ay, that's true," cried Dr. Barr. "Well, Commodore, come away to ma office an' Ah'll explain. We're away, Huntley, we're away, we're away." Along the corridor, he continued: "Commodore, ye look like a man who could take a dram. Ye are, eh? Ay, ay—well thanks to the wife's brother, Ah'm never without—though it's a Malt whisky Ah've got in ma office just now. Could ye take a Malt whisky?"

"I can take—and have taken—every kind of whisky that was ever poured in and out of a bottle," said the Commodore. "Brown, yellow, white, Scotch, Irish, Rye, Bourbon, Moonshine, gasoline and burned sugar. In my time I've drunk so-called whisky made out of diesel oil and bananas by black magicians and Chinese sorcerers."

"Ye have, ye have, eh?" cried Dr. Barr, delighted. "Ay, ay, well, it's a great thing to have traveled—an' Ah'll tell ye a tale or two maself when we're better acquainted. Here's ma office."

Over a dram of the Malt, Dr. Barr explained about Major Bulfoss.

"He's in trouble just now with Whatmore an' a few o' the stiffer Tories, who'll no want your Festival. Ah heard it this day at the Club, wi' two or three o' them clittering an' clattering. An' Ah'm thinking— an' it's what Huntley would have told ye only he's overcautious—ye might get Bulfoss to take a different line. Do ye know wee Mobbs, the Agent? Ye do? Ay, ay, well Mobbs might be your man to bring the Member in, ye understand, Commodore? Over a drink or two Ah'm thinking ye could persuade wee Mobbs to come in wi' ye, Commodore." And Dr. Barr winked gigantically, screwing his round red face into a look of cunning that made him appear like a man in agonies of neuralgia.

"I'm very grateful for the tip," said the Commodore. "To say nothing of this excellent whisky."

"Ay, ay, it's a good Malt," cried Dr. Barr, beaming. But then he was interrupted.

The Enemy arrived. The Commodore knew at once that here was the Enemy. The look he gave Dr. Barr, the Commodore, the drams of Malt; his cold little eye; his long nose; his tightening lips; his chill and grating tone; the tremendous atmosphere of disapproval, suspicion, resentment, he brought with him—all these belonged to the Enemy.

"Ay, ay," cried Dr. Barr, a shadow across his heartiness, "ye'll not have met Mr. Coverack, our Borough Treasurer. Commodore Tribe. Mr. Coverack'll be the man ye'll be wanting to talk to soon, Commodore—ay."

"About what?" said Coverack.

"Don't tell me ye've not heard of it. The Farbridge Festival, man."

"I don't know anything about a Farbridge Festival," said Coverack, ignoring the Commodore. "You promised to let me have those figures this afternoon, Dr. Barr."

"Ah did, Ah did. An' if they're not in your office this minute, they're on their way. Ah gave them to Miss Worsley a good two hours since. Though there was a wee bit o' copying for her to do."

"Miss Worsley hasn't been near my department," said Coverack.

"Ay, well—ye know how it is—"

"All I know is that I ought to have had those figures last Monday—"

"Ay, ay, but Ah explained at the time—" Dr. Barr was still apologetic and good-humored.

The other man mistakenly assumed this to be weakness. "I've told you before, Dr. Barr," he began, severely.

But he was not allowed to continue. Dr. Barr put down his glass with a bang. He was puce and bristling. "A' Ah'm telling you, man, ye'll not take that tone wi' me. Ah'm the Medical Officer o' Health for this borough, not one o' your clerks, Coverack. Ye'll oblige me by leaving ma office, into which ye came uninvited."

"I came on official business," said Coverack, white with anger. "And it's not my fault if I interrupt your convivial session with this—er—gentleman." He looked at the Commodore. "Who, by the way, ought to be told by somebody that he's wasting his time—as well as other people's."

"If you don't know anything about a Farbridge Festival," said the Commodore, "then how do you know I'm wasting my time? Illogical, isn't it, Mr. Coverack?"

"It may interest you to know," said Coverack, with a malicious gleam, "that since you came blustering in here the other day, we've put through an inquiry about you to the Festival of Britain authorities, who have replied that you have no standing with them and that, in fact, they don't know anything about you."

This was unexpected and very nasty, but the Commodore gave no outward sign of being disturbed. He merely raised his eyebrows. "If this had been mentioned to me, I could have saved you the trouble. I've never suggested that I was sent here by the Festival of Britain people in London. I merely said I came here after having some talk in London, quite informal talk, with a few men like—er—Bilst. Furthermore, if you propose to take this narrow official line, then you ought to know that the provincial cities and towns have made their independent arrangements for Festivals, appointing local organizers, without reference to the Festival of Britain authorities in London. So these remarks of yours—which incidentally you made quite unnecessarily offensive—"

"Hear, hear!" cried Dr. Barr.

"Are quite beside the point."

"We shall see," said Coverack unpleasantly.

"Man, ye want a liver pill," said Dr. Barr.

"Or is it dyspepsia?" said the Commodore looking thoughtfully at Coverack's long nose.

"You can waste your own time—and Dr. Barr's," said Coverack angrily, "but there's no reason why you should waste mine." And left.

"Ay, ay, ay," Dr. Barr chuckled, "Ah'm thinking ye had him there.

Mind ye, Commodore," and now he looked serious, "yon's an able man an' he's carrying great influence wi' his chairman, Tanhead, who's another o' the same kidney."

"So I gather. I haven't tried him yet, but I had a go at Alderman Muleford this afternoon, with disastrous results. I ended by calling him a conceited woodenhead."

"Ye didn't!" Dr. Barr was delighted. "Ah've had it on the tip o' ma tongue these last two years. Conceited woodenhead! Ah must remember that. Well, well, you're away to catch wee Mobbs, no doubt." And they shook hands warmly.

Wee Mobbs was about to close his office, which was two rooms above a sports shop just off Peter Place, when the Commodore arrived. He was not the lively figure he had been at the Bell, that Saturday night, and in fact was looking disconsolate, like a baby that had cried hard and attracted no attention. But he seemed glad to see the Commodore.

"Heard you were around, old boy," he said. "And glad you remembered my invitation to look me up here. Though how any of us remembered anything after that night, I can't imagine. My godfathers! We had a load on. Old Whatmore was paralytic. What happened about you and him, old boy?"

The Commodore briefly but vividly described the scene in Whatmore's office, and Captain Mobbs, brightening up, listened to it, entranced.

"I'd have given a fiver to have been there," he declared, when the other had finished. "Serve him right too, though don't tell anybody I said so. We ought to have a drink on it, old boy."

"Well, why not? And I want to have a talk with you."

"Stout fella. Any time. But when you looked in I was just about to pop across to the Palace—first house."

"Music hall?"

"Yes, old boy. Second-rate, of course. But the fact is, I've had quite a spot of trouble this week—and later tonight, after dinner, I have to go and talk to my Member, Major Bulfoss, out at his place—and, to be candid, old boy, I'm not looking forward to it, what with one thing and another, so I thought I'd have an hour or so at the Palace. Know the manager, and he always looks after me. Believe it or not, Commodore, I find it relaxes me—jugglers, acrobats, comics, song-and-dance, that sort of thing. Silly, but there it is." He peered at the Commodore quite anxiously, his red bald face very comical.

"I'll come with you," said the Commodore. "Then you must dine with me at the White Hart, and after that, if you don't mind, I'd like to see Major Bulfoss with you. I've a scheme that might help you both."

The tubby little man was delighted, and said so. "Let's go, old boy. And explain your scheme afterwards, if you don't mind. I've had a week of it—right up to the neck in the Brown Windsor. I'd like to forget about local politics for a couple of hours. Just relax—trapeze act—Indian clubs—stepdancing—that's what I want."

The Palace was the old-fashioned type of small theater-cum-music hall, with leaded lights in the swing doors, thick brass handrails, worn dark-red carpet, plenty of plaster decoration in faded gilt, rubbed plush seats, a stale smoky-beery atmosphere, and a general air of being fixed forever in the year 1913. The manager was a very old man with a waxen face, hair and mustache dyed blue-black, and a very old evening suit, so that he looked like a villain in a film of the 1913 period. In a sad hoarse whisper he said he would be glad to accommodate Captain Mobbs and Friend with a box, and would also be glad to accept a drink from them first. As the orchestra was already playing the overture, and this was the sedate First House, there was nobody in the bar except two glum men in bowler hats and check coats who gave the impression they were not in a theater but probably waiting for a horse. An Edwardian lady, dyed auburn and so heavily rouged that she looked feverish, was in attendance. Captain Mobbs and Friend had whisky; the manager had a gin and peppermint.

"Touring revue," said the manager, replying to Mobbs. "Fair. I wouldn't say more than that. We have to book what we can get, of course. And business isn't what it was. It's no good pretending it is. There isn't the money about now. Ask Mrs. Montgomery." He looked at the Edwardian barmaid.

"There is not indeed," said Mrs. Montgomery, who sounded like an embittered duchess. "They have not the Money. To Say Nothing of Wireless and the Television. Not that we get the Shows We Did. We do not get the Shows We Did. And that, if I may say so, is Commented Upon. Here in this bar I have heard Remarks Passed."

"You can't get blood out of a stone," said the manager, looking as if he had been trying and failing for about forty years.

"We'll go in," said Mobbs hastily. "Probably see you in the interval."

When they arrived in the little box, which was almost on the stage, the touring musical director, who looked about nineteen, was tossing back his long flaxen locks and waving his baton at the orchestra, which consisted of seven phlegmatic men and a fat woman at the piano, as if he had brought the Vienna Philharmonic to the finale of the *Eroica*. The house was about half full. Remembering that he would need this place as his Festival Theater, the Commodore stared about him, and saw that the auditorium was divided into stalls and pit, a dress circle, and above that a gallery, and probably seated about nine hundred. He could see nothing wrong with it as a possible playhouse for the Festival.

But there was a great deal wrong with what was happening in it on this evening. If this show was fair, he could not imagine what the manager's idea of a bad show would be. Everybody in this touring revue seemed to be either too young to have learned anything or too old to be still performing. The eight skinny girls in the chorus looked as if they ought to be immediately packed off to some home where they would be given hot baths, nourishing food, adequate sleep, and a few remedial exercises. Three of the principals were like horrible schoolchildren who had been allowed to do their worst with a make-up box and a hamper of costumes. On the other hand, the older members of the company—a comedian, a massive soprano, and a severe elderly couple who played various instruments but always came on as though they had been sent by some ecclesiastical authority to close the building —looked years older than the Commodore himself, in fact like contemporaries of the manager. The old comedian, wheezing away at his gags, desperately pretending at times to be capable of making fun of this unreal new world of radio, atomic energy, and government controls, was nothing less than a tragic figure, hobbling about in grotesque out-of-date costumes, despair and death glaring above the red nose, the painted grin. The Commodore, feeling like one old clown taking advantage of another, hated to look at the man, yet found it impossible not to look at him. The whole show, together with the response of the audience, had no life, no hope, no soul in it, but was like some mumbling automatic ritual of entertainment, mechanically mimicking something that had once been zestful, creative, freely expressive of a people's life; and the audience, in their instinctive wisdom, were aware of all this, knew it to be a shadowy relic of something once vital and now lost and gone, and what they clapped and laughed at most, indeed the only things they enjoyed, were old tunes, long-remembered words, that caught a faint gleam of life from reminiscence, like ghosts recollecting a lost Maytime.

"Terrible show," said Captain Mobbs, as the curtain came down at the interval. "I'm sorry, old boy. Much worse than usual. Needn't tell me. I can see what you're thinking, and quite agree with you."

"I'll tell you what I was thinking," said the Commodore, on their way out of the box. "And it'll explain why you needn't be sorry you brought me here. I'm trying to run a Farbridge Festival, to light the place up a bit, and—by George—after what I've seen here this last hour, nothing's going to stop me. If I can't give 'em something better than that, I'll set fire to the town and bring 'em to life that way."

"My godfathers!" cried little Mobbs. "I know just how you feel, old boy. But can you do it?"

"With a bit of help, I can do it. Let me tell you, Mobbs—between us, my two assistants and me, we have the ideas, the enthusiasm, the energy. Just a bit of help, that's all we need. And after tonight, after what we've just seen in there, my dear chap, I expect it from you. I meant to talk you into it anyhow—and I have one or two arguments you'll appreciate too—but it's my belief you're on to it now without a word from me. Though you shall have the arguments later. But aren't you, my dear chap?"

"I am, old boy. I'm with you. Count on Archie Mobbs. Ah—here's the manager—poor old blighter!"

"I thought, gentlemen," said the manager, whose shirtfront had acquired a tomato stain, "you'd prefer to step into my room for a little refreshment." And there was nothing wrong with the manager's room; it was a good solid 1913 room; its walls covered with old bills and signed photographs of vanished comedians and forgotten soubrettes; with a mahogany desk and a carpet and two armchairs and a safe; and on the desk three glasses and a bottle and a siphon.

"Only fair, isn't it?" This was after the manager had poured out their drinks and taken one himself, probably on the strength of having Captain Mobbs and Friend there. "Only fair, as I warned you. Not one of our better attractions."

"Frankly, we thought it terrible, old boy," said Mobbs, bouncing about a little and mopping himself. "With all due respect—a bloody awful show."

"I have to agree," said the Commodore. "It's pathetic. And the audience know it is. But I like your theater—nothing wrong with it at all."

"A good house," said the manager, with mournful pride, touching his blue-black mustache delicately. "Always been well looked after. Behind as well as in front. We can take a fairly big show here. Plenty of room behind. Flies in good order. Good switchboard. And we seat just under a thousand."

The Commodore put a hand on the shiny black shoulder. "I'm Commodore Tribe. If you haven't heard of me, you soon will, because I propose to organize a Farbridge Festival. And we shall want to make use of this theater. One of our key buildings. Now, my dear sir, how would you like to see your theater packed night after night with the best people from miles around, all expectant, enthusiastic, ready to shout when the curtain finally comes down? And on the stage something exciting, full of drama, color, life, straight from London. Every night an event."

"My godfathers—now you're talking, old boy!" cried Mobbs, seizing the manager's bottle.

"Now who owns this place?" the Commodore continued, without waiting for the manager to say anything.

"A local company," the manager replied. "Farbridge Theater Company, Limited. Some very important local men on the board. You'd have to talk to the chairman."

"I'll make an appointment to see him next week."

"He's usually here on Wednesday morning," said the manager. "You can catch him then."

The Commodore, who was in high spirits, probably because he was no longer seeing that revue, made a note of the time and place. Then he and Mobbs went off to see what Seth Hull could provide for them at the White Hart. On the way there, the Commodore told himself that this had been quite a day. Yet most of the evening, together with Major Bulfoss, M.P., was still before him.

7

"Now, my dear Mobbs," said the Commodore comfortably, from behind one of Seth Hull's cigars, "tell me about this Bulfoss."

"Right, old boy," said Mobbs. "As soon as we're out of this traffic."

With a good dinner and a few more drinks inside them, they were now rattling along in Mobbs's little car, climbing the west road on their way to Mayton Park Avenue and the residence of the Member for Farbridge. At Mobbs's request, they had not discussed local affairs during dinner but had fleeted the time with an exchange of reminiscences, during which they had discovered several common acquaintances to the delight of Mobbs, who made no secret of his pleasure in the Commodore's company. No admirer of life in the South Midlands, little Mobbs felt he was making friends with another—and more traveled and impressive—exile from the great world.

"Bulfoss, old boy, is a chump," Mobbs began. "I'm talking off the record, of course, completely off the record. He wasn't a bad candidate—I've handled much worse—and he started off fairly well as a Member. But he's out of his depth. He drinks and can't hold it. He flies off the handle. His wife's run away. Didn't look the type but of course you can't tell with women. Then he gets tight and insults a deputation from the Women's Executive Committee—my godfathers!"

"I know about that," said the Commodore. "My secretary, Miss Casey, was there. She worked for the Bulfoss firm."

"Oh—that one. Pretty little dark girl, eh?"

"Yes, and a nice intelligent child. Very fond of her myself, and, so far as I can gather, my assistant, young Jenks, has gone and fallen in love with her. But why did these Bulfoss fellows turn her out?"

"Because the older brother, Beverly, is an even bigger chump than Gerald. I raised Cain when I knew what had happened. She could have made it very awkward for 'em—and for all of us. But she's kept quiet about it, hasn't she?" he inquired, rather anxiously. They were now on the outskirts of the town, and there was little traffic about.

"She has," said the Commodore. "But—they'd better be careful. She's set her heart on this Festival—perhaps because of young Jenks—and I'd like to give Major Bulfoss a tip that he'd be safer on our side than he would be against us. Unless you mention it, my dear Mobbs. We'll see. But go on about Bulfoss."

"A chump, as I told you, old boy. I can make him see reason and he'll do what I tell him to do, if I keep at him. But the minute he's left to himself, God knows what he's up to. Because of their wives, Whatmore and his crowd are pressing for his resignation. I had to dash up to the Central Office the other day, and pile it on thick about Mrs. Bulfoss popping off, though of course that doesn't look too good. I tell you, I've had a hell of a time this week, old boy. Now we'll be there in a minute, and I'll have to explain why I've brought you along, Commodore, so give me a line on your scheme. Not," he added, "that I couldn't make a dam' good guess, old boy."

"I expected it, my dear chap," said the Commodore. "A man of your experience. I want to propose that he back our Festival scheme. At once—bang! That gives us the support of the local Member, very useful. It gives him a chance to assert himself and take what might easily become a very popular line."

"I'll buy it," cried Mobbs. "The people who'll be against it are mostly against him anyhow. Can do. It's what I've been looking for, old boy. Now here we are—up in the front line. Hold your fire until I give the signal."

The lights were on in the hall, and they could hear a gramophone or radio set playing loud dance music, so loud that Mobbs had to ring several times before the door was opened. "What the blazes is he up to now?" Mobbs muttered, as they waited.

The door was opened by a red-haired girl with a cheeky fat face, who was wearing a very tight emerald-green dress that looked as if it might burst at any moment. She was out of breath. She also had an offhand, flouncing manner that did not suggest the better type of domestic service.

"Oh—well," she said, tossing her head, "I'll tell him. But I don't think he expected you so soon." And off she went across the hall, with much unnecessary jiggling of the hips. A radio-gramophone, now silent, accounted for the dance music.

"Monkey business here, I'd say," Mobbs whispered, as they took off their overcoats. "Awkward—but can't let it pass."

Major Bulfoss received them in the drawing room. He was looking hot and blown, and was refreshing himself hastily with a large whisky and soda. He looked unpleasantly surprised to see the Commodore.

"Don't look like that," said Mobbs, attacking at once. "This is Commodore Tribe, a friend of mine and an old friend of my old friend, the Maharajah of Swindi. And he's the man we want—at least I want, and you will if you have any sense. But that'll keep. Whisky, Commodore? Whisky for me too, please, Major."

"Help yourself," said the Major rather sulkily. He was still breathing hard and his pink face glistened. He made a rather furtive dab or two at it with his handkerchief, then blew his nose hard.

"Been dancing?" asked Mobbs, over the decanter.

The Major looked guilty. "Just trying out a few steps with Anita. Find I'm a bit rusty."

"Calls herself Anita, does she? I'll bet that's not what her mother calls her. Happy days!" And Mobbs raised his glass, winking at the Commodore above the Major's bowed head. "I'd be careful with that piece, if I were you."

"Well, you're not me," said the Major sulkily. "And leave the girl out of it. She's a good-hearted lively kid, and she was only trying to cheer me up a bit."

"No concern of mine, old boy," said Mobbs cheerfully. "Only— you've enough spots of bother on hand without getting entangled with red-headed parlormaids who waggle their hips."

"Now look, Mobbs," said the Major despairingly. "You tell me to stay on here, won't let me go up to Town. So here I am, stuck in this damned dull house, with my wife God knows where. How would you like it?" He appealed to the Commodore now. "Bit thick, y'know, Commander—Er—"

"Commodore Tribe is the name, Major Bulfoss," he was told firmly.

"Sorry. But you see how it is? I dare say Mobbs has explained how things are round here." And he helped himself to another drink.

"He has," said the Commodore. "And that's why I'm here. You can help me. I can help you."

"Absolutely," cried Mobbs. "Listen carefully to this, Bulfoss, old man."

"I'm prepared to run a Farbridge Festival if I'm given a reasonable grant," said the Commodore. "The Mayor's ready to reopen the question. I've talked to him and the Town Clerk. I've got Mrs. Coote, Councillor Gisburn, Jordan, the Chief Education Officer, and some others on my side. To say nothing of Seth Hull at the White Hart. And young Seacombe, who reports local news for some of the London dailies."

"We know him," said Mobbs. "Useful bloke too."

"Very soon I propose to hit the big drum hard. Question on the B.B.C. program here next week. Public meeting. Deputations to the Mayor. Now I want you. We can do without you, but it'll help if the local Member joins us, perhaps takes the chair at our public meeting." The Commodore stopped for a moment, staring hard at the Major. "Now look at it from your point of view, Major Bulfoss. You're in trouble, chiefly with the people who'll oppose the Festival."

"Couldn't agree with you more," cried Mobbs, drumming on his fat little thighs.

"By coming out good and strong for the Festival, you assert yourself, you take a popular line, you win some friends you didn't have before, and though you don't get the support of the local press—"

"We've lost that anyhow, old boy," said Mobbs hastily. "Whatmore's too strong there."

"But you have a chance of a friendly line or two in the national press. In short, my dear sir, you've nothing to lose and everything to gain."

"He's right, you know, dead right," Mobbs told his Member. "It's what I was looking for, just the very thing."

The Major finished his drink and tried to look thoughtful. "But what is this Festival? What do you want to do?"

The Commodore sketched their program, while Mobbs began refilling the glasses. "Incidentally," he concluded, "it's not just for Farbridge but for a fairly big stretch of country on every side of us, where there won't be anything else of this sort. I'm arranging for support from influential people in the neighborhood, people my assistant, Jenks, and I know pretty well. Not your constituents, of course, but if they find you giving a lead here, their gratitude might be useful. Eh, Mobbs?"

"Happy Days!" cried Mobbs.

"Cheers!" said the Major gloomily.

The Commodore refreshed himself in silence, but looked inquiringly at Mobbs, who now, like the Major, was beginning to show signs of wear and tear. He was very red and moist; his eyes were so carefully focused that they glared; and his speech and movements began to take on a slow solemnity.

Now he held up a little fat forefinger, as if offering the Major a sausage for careful inspection, and said slowly: "I endorse everything my friend the Commodore has said, Bulfoss. I endorse it freely. And there's a further point. Of great interest to you, Bulfoss, old boy, and to me. If they're arguing about a Festival here, then they won't be talking so much about other things. In fact, we spike Whatmore's guns. His and other people's. We spike their guns."

"Well, you'll certainly take the wind out of their sails," said the Commodore.

"We take the wind out of their sails," said Mobbs. "We spike their guns."

"Never mind about these guns and sails," cried the Major irritably. "You think it's a good thing for me to do, Mobbs? All right. But I'm not very clear about it, not yet, I'm not. Not quite sure what I'm letting myself in for. After all," and he stared at the Commodore, "I don't know you."

"I don't know you," said the Commodore pleasantly. "By the way, talking about knowing people, you'll be interested to learn that Miss Casey, the girl who was here last Saturday night, is now my secretary."

"I thought she'd cleared out." The Major looked worried.

"No, no. She told me that she made it very plain to your brother that she intended staying in Farbridge. An intelligent attractive girl, but with a will of her own."

The Major said nothing but walked slowly to a bell and pressed it. Then he returned to his chair, still saying nothing.

"You'd oblige me, Bulfoss," said Mobbs severely, "by pulling yourself together and coming to life."

"I've had a long day—I don't know what doing—and am rather tired," the Major confessed, "and a bit confused. What with one flaming thing and another!"

Anita came flouncing in, looking like a Montmartre type as represented in a third-rate touring company. "Well, what do you want?" she demanded.

Her master smiled weakly, apologetically, and waved a hand toward the small table. "Oh—er—some more whisky and another siphon, please, Anita."

"Been shifting it, haven't you?" And she went out before one of them could reply.

"Upset about something," said the Major uneasily. "She's a sensitive type."

"Bulfoss, old boy," said Mobbs. "If you fancy her, then you fancy her—and it's all up to you. But don't tell us she's a sensitive type. Not that one. Not Anita."

"Drop it, Mobbs," shouted the Major, thoroughly out of temper.

The little agent took this rebuke quite calmly, merely raising his eyebrows at the Commodore. The Major brooded, not looking at either of them. Then Anita returned with a bottle and a siphon, which she dumped noisily on the small table. "I'd go easy if I was you," she remarked. She waited a moment. "Nobody got anything to say?"

"Yes," Mobbs grunted. "Pop off."

"Manners!"

"I'd like to ask you a question," said the Commodore, smiling at her.

"Wouldn't you like a Farbridge Festival in May or June—pageant, processions, fireworks, dancing, music, plays?"

"Would I?" cried Anita. "Just you try me."

"Thank you. That's all."

Before she could reply, there was a ringing from the front door. It took her swaying out.

"You see what I mean?" said the Commodore to the Major.

"Very neat," cried Mobbs. "Convincing. Anita—the Voice of the People."

"All right," said the Major, pushing himself up. "I'm with you. Farbridge wants a Festival, and it ought to have one. That's my line."

"Spoken like a man," cried Mobbs, delighted. "We'll drink to that."

Anita looked in, cheekier than ever. "It's your brother and Old What's-it. And don't all get bottled. Cheery-bye."

"Steady the Buffs," said Mobbs, busy with the drinks again. "And mark this, old boy—if they ask me to go, I'm not going. So keep calm. Poor old Captain Archie Bloody Mobbs will see you through."

The two visitors entered. They had the air of men about to break the gravest news, with just a suggestion that it probably served everybody else right. The first man was a longer, bonier, older version of Major Bulfoss, and clearly was his brother, Beverly. The other was a man about sixty, not very tall but large and impressive about the head.

"Alderman Tanhead," Mobbs muttered as the Major rather sulkily welcomed these new arrivals.

So this was the Chairman of the Finance Committee, the chief Tory Enemy, as Alderman Muleford was the chief Labour Enemy, and Coverack the chief Official Enemy. The Commodore stared at him searchingly. He had a high but narrow, worried forehead, a large Roman nose, and a sad boiled eye. He wore a stiff collar of an old-fashioned type, a tie like a piece of dark tape, and a black coat cut with short narrow lapels, a mean garment. He was a rather miserable figure, years out of date and very provincial, but nevertheless, as the Commodore forced himself to admit, somehow looked a genuine character, a personality.

"Now, Gerald," Beverly Bulfoss was saying, "I've been talking to Alderman Tanhead, and we decided we ought to see you. Alone, of course."

"It's a ticklish situation, Major Bulfoss," said Alderman Tanhead.

"Very ticklish." This word could never have been pronounced with more gravity in all its history.

"Either of you having a drink?" asked Mobbs, still in charge of that department. "No? Well—Happy Days!"

"In my opinion," said Beverly Bulfoss, "there have been too many happy days round here already."

"What do you mean, Bev?" the Major blustered.

"Uncalled for," said Mobbs, wagging a finger. "Distinctly uncalled for."

"I don't think we need detain this gentleman," said Alderman Tanhead, indicating the Commodore.

"I've no wish to stay," said the Commodore cheerfully. He paused a moment, timing it artfully. "I only came here to enlist the support of Major Bulfoss for my Farbridge Festival scheme. Now that he's promised it—"

"Now that he's *what?*" cried Tanhead.

"Promised his support," the Commodore continued smoothly, "then there's no point in my staying, fascinating though your talk will be, I'm sure. Just as you were ringing the front door bell, gentlemen, Major Bulfoss, with his profound political instinct, gave my little movement its slogan. Listen carefully, and see if you can improve on it—I can't. *Farbridge wants a Festival, and it ought to have one.* Splendid—eh, Mobbs?"

"A winner, old boy. Pulled right out of the bag."

"I think there's some mistake," said Beverly Bulfoss anxiously.

"No mistake, old boy. And don't look like that. Remember the old kitbag—and smile, smile, smile." And Mobbs, essentially a First War type, began humming the familiar tune.

"You can't do that, you know, Major Bulfoss," said Alderman Tanhead severely. "We don't propose to have a Festival. I dealt with that some months ago. I've heard some talk about this man at the Town Hall, but of course he has no standing here, none whatever. And you can't possibly allow him to use your name."

"Quite impossible," said Beverly Bulfoss. "Really—Gerald, I can't imagine what you've been thinking—if you *have* been thinking." His glance at the whisky was full of meaning. "Captain Mobbs and his friend had better leave us to talk things over with you."

"And the sooner the better," said Tanhead. "It's late now."

"What did I tell you?" cried Mobbs to the Major. "Poor old Archie Mobbs always knows. Well, Steady the Buffs."

Not unlike a pink bull pitchforked and prodded into a corner, the Major glowered at his brother and then at the Alderman, both of whom were staring at him reproachfully.

"Now, now, Gerald," said his brother anxiously.

"Don't *now, now* me, you fathead," shouted the Major. "I didn't ask you to come here badgering me. Or telling me what I can do and what I can't do. They elected me, not you. And if I want to support a Festival—or twenty festivals—then that's my business."

"On the contrary," Tanhead began.

"And don't you chip in, Tanhead," the Major roared. "You were never one of my supporters anyhow. I don't owe you anything."

"On the contrary," cried Mobbs, winking at the Commodore.

"I am Vice-chairman of the Farbridge Conservative Association," Tanhead declared with some force. "Do you realize that the Chairman, Colonel Whatmore, and several members of the Executive Committee, are already demanding your resignation? And now that you're proposing to lend your name to this Festival nonsense, to some gang of adventurers and mountebanks—"

"Hoy, hoy, hoy," Mobbs shouted. "I resent that, on behalf of my friend, the Commodore here. And there's such a thing as slander."

"We'll leave that out," said the Commodore quietly. He thought he heard a sound from the hall, but decided to ignore it. "I've had a few insults of this kind already, but I can take them. On the other hand, Alderman, I don't think you'll be able to bully Major Bulfoss out of doing what he considers to be a public duty. He's not made of such poor stuff."

"I think there's somebody out in the hall," said Beverly Bulfoss uneasily.

"Don't evade the issue," Mobbs told him sharply. "Stick to the point. If you have one, which I doubt. And you're quite right, old boy," he said, turning to the Commodore. "The Member for Farbridge—and I ought to know, because I got him elected—can't be bullied like that. He can't be taken advantage of, just because he's run into a little trouble."

"Just what I was about to say, my dear Mobbs."

"Another drink, old boy? This is thirsty work."

"They're quite right," said the Major, addressing his brother and the Alderman. "I won't have it. Coming here badgering an' bullying! Just when a fellow feels down. Stuck in a dam' dreary house. All alone, nobody caring a damn." He picked up his glass, which contained whisky but no soda, and hurriedly drained it. There was a mixed scuffling-and-giggling sound from the hall, but he did not appear to hear it. "I want a Festival. Nice girls want a Festival—they've told me —processions, fireworks, dancing. We all want a Festival, except you two, who wouldn't know what to do with one. And if Farbridge wants a Festival," he bellowed, scarlet and goggle-eyed now, "then it ought to have one. And if you miserable shuffling old sausages don't like it, then lump it. Like this." And seizing a blue-and-white vase from the mantelpiece, he sent it crashing into fragments in the hearth.

"Smashing the home up now," said a voice in the doorway. It was Anita, and with her, grinning broadly, was that enterprising young journalist, Michael Seacombe.

"Local Member Takes Strong Line on Festival Issue," cried Seacombe, enjoying himself. "Farbridge Wants Festival, Says Major Bulfoss. M.P. Denounces Local Killjoys. Urgent Demand for Farbridge Festival. Bulfoss Speaks for People."

"Who let you in here?" demanded Major Bulfoss.

"I did," said Anita sharply. "Newspaper chap, isn't he? And don't go smashing anything else. Proper waste. If you don't want 'em, I do."

The Major, his brother, and Alderman Tanhead all began speaking at once, but the Commodore, whose sheer bulk, rich experience, and personality came to his aid at such moments, swept them aside commandingly and took charge of the situation. "Mobbs, Seacombe, we'll take ourselves off. Major Bulfoss has had a long day, and he's had enough of us all. Come on, gentlemen. The Major has shown us plainly where he stands, we're grateful to him for the lead he's given us, and we ought not to inflict ourselves on him any longer. Goodnight, goodnight, goodnight."

Two minutes later they were in Mobbs's car. "Mine's bust," said Seacombe. "But I think I'd better drive, if you don't mind, *Capitaine*. You've hoisted a few, you know, old warrior. We'll go straight to the White Hart. I can do some telephoning from there, and old Seth will probably let me use his private office. Now we're moving, eh, Commodore?"

"It marches, my boy, it marches."

"*What's the use of worrying*," sang little Mobbs, "*it ne-ever was worth while—So-o-o—*"

8

At three minutes to eight on Saturday night, Theodore arrived at the Saxons' for dinner. The amount he did not know about this occasion would be material enough for a long chapter. In his male innocence he had no idea that both Laura and Hilda had been planning, scheming, intriguing, cajoling, and bullying for the past two and a half days, that all Saturday had been sacrificed to this dinner, that the Saxon children, after being taken out by their father, had been sent to bed early, that Ernest Saxon, grumbling and rebellious, had been victimized right and left by the women, did not see what all the fuss was about, and was now ready to be sharp with his visitor, that gin and vermouth and ginger ale had been bought specially for the occasion. He arrived, large, calm, handsome, knowing nothing. Not that he was indifferent, for he was excited enough inside, longing to see Laura at home, anxious to like the Saxons, about whom he had heard a good deal from her.

After a hasty greeting from Laura, who then disappeared, he was left alone with Ernest Saxon, who suggested in an off-hand way that he should mix his own gin and vermouth. Then Ernest had one too, having noted with a laboratory eye how Theodore had mixed his drink.

"Laura's told us about you, of course," said Ernest, when they had settled down. "But I'm still rather puzzled why you should bother with this Farbridge Festival scheme."

"It's purely an accident that I happen to be here," said Theodore carefully. "It might easily have been any other place. But I suppose I felt I'd get to know more by actually taking part in something than by merely staring at everything from the outside."

"That's reasonable," Ernest conceded. "But Farbridge isn't a very interesting place."

"I'm finding it quite exciting," said Theodore, with a smile. "And I think Laura is now."

"She's excited enough tonight," said Ernest, then added hastily. "But don't tell her I said so. What about Communism in the East—in China, for instance?"

"China will swallow it and then turn it into something else. China has done that before."

"I'm not sure I agree with that argument," said Ernest. "A modern dictatorship can use new methods—for propaganda, oppression, and so on. So history may not repeat itself. I doubt if it does."

"It's hard to explain," said Theodore. "But there's a kind of psychological density about the Chinese—I don't mean stupidity, of course—whereas I feel, though I don't know much about them, that this is just what the Russians hadn't got. There was a sort of emptiness there when the Revolution arrived. They wanted to believe in something passionately, but mostly had nothing to believe in. They were really a new people, like the Americans, whereas the Chinese are a very old people."

"What about the English? Yes, I know you're English too, but you've not been brought up here and I suppose you can look at us in a fairly detached way." Ernest was enjoying this, his kind of conversation, and although he was hungry he hoped the women would not come charging in for a few minutes yet.

"I think the English are much more like the Chinese than they are like the Russians and the Americans," said Theodore reflectively. "They live by a kind of instinct. And I have a feeling that what is happening now, the sharp political divisions, the way in which political thinking is beginning to be made a test, the political angle on everything, isn't quite right for England."

"Can't agree with that, I'm afraid, Mr. Jenks," said Ernest warmly.

"No, I thought you mightn't," said Theodore calmly. "But you asked me what I thought."

"We have a choice," Ernest began, but then, to his hardly disguised annoyance, his wife and Laura came in, to announce that dinner was on the table.

"I've heard so much about you," Hilda told Theodore.

"And I've heard a lot about you too, Mrs. Saxon," he said with a smile.

Laura felt at once that they were ready to like each other. About Ernest she was not sure. He was still looking ruffled, irritable. Poor Ernest—all this fuss!

"No politics, gentlemen, please," she told them, as they all sat down to dinner.

"When you came in," said Ernest, "I was about to convince our friend that he was wrong in thinking that England had become too politically-minded. As a matter of fact, most people still don't care—"

"No, Ernest, please," cried Laura. "This is going to be political too. And I refuse to have it, just for tonight."

"Don't forget," said Ernest, with a grin, "that Paul Ravenstreet may be looking in later."

"No," she cried in horror. "We don't want him. Not tonight. Oh—let's hope he doesn't come—that he's out with the Comrades somewhere. Theodore, you like gin and ginger ale, don't you?"

"I seem to have acquired a taste for it," said Theodore. "It really started with a Group Captain." And he told them about Group Captain Trevone and Mr. Hookwood, the Mermaid Club, Mrs. Hungerford's party, and his visit to Brant-in-the-Hollow. To all of which Laura and Hilda listened with that apparent entrancement which belongs to the ancient art of feminine flattery; while Ernest at least listened too and did not interrupt. And the dinner, which included roast mutton and ginger pudding and was deliberately designed to be on a Theodore rather than an ordinary Saxon scale, was turning out to be quite good. Laura was flashing away with excitement and happiness. Magic had been brought to Alma Street and the Saxons', and had survived.

"You know," Hilda said to Theodore, after he had finished his Group Captain reminiscences, "I'm simply longing for this Festival to happen. We get so little here—one begins to feel quite cut off. If it wasn't for the Third Program, I don't know what we'd do. Just stagnate. I don't suppose you've had much chance of listening to the Third Program, living in hotels."

"I don't like radio," said Theodore, not aggressively but in his large calm way that was miraculously free from any suggestion of superiority. "I never did."

"But you get so many good things that otherwise you'd miss," Hilda protested.

"Undoubtedly," said Ernest, "there's a lot of rubbish, but at its best it's a great educational force."

"I don't think I care much about great educational forces," said Theodore, smiling. "Perhaps I'm intellectually rather lazy."

"Perhaps you are," said Ernest, with a touch of schoolmasterish severity. He contrived not to receive the warning glances shot at him by his wife and Laura. "Not a good thing to be, you know. I see too much of it."

Theodore handled this unnecessary rebuke with great skill, neither replying to it nor pointedly ignoring it, but acknowledging it with an easy smile and then continuing what he wanted to say. "I don't like radio probably because I don't like the idea of a very small number of people performing for a gigantic audience, millions and millions. There seems to me something all wrong about one singer or violinist and eight million listeners. I'd rather multiply the musicians or the actors and divide up the listeners into proper playgoers or concert-attenders. And I'd rather have live goodish things than the best things coming out of a machine."

"So would I," said Laura. "But you can't always, you know. You may have to be in bed or be a long way from anywhere."

"And radio doesn't stop people performing in theaters or concert halls. Probably it encourages them." This was Hilda.

"That's what we're told," said Ernest.

"But I wonder if it's true," said Theodore. "Most people now seem to think you can go on adding things to life without taking anything away, without anything dropping out. But can you? Take Laura's two instances. It's pleasant for people who have to be in bed to have the radio to amuse them. But perhaps they're missing something—an opportunity to think, to make discoveries about themselves—that bedridden people found valuable before radio came along. And then people who lived a long way from anywhere once had special qualities of their own, just because they were out of touch with the world and could develop in their own way."

"I doubt those special qualities," said Ernest. "It's the old noble-savage illusion."

"But the savagery now might be in the center," said Theodore, "and we might be piping it out to people who are really more civilized without it. Where I come from, the people had a better way of living and better manners when I was a boy than they have now. Change isn't necessarily improvement."

"Why should people make the change then?" Ernest demanded.

"Sometimes out of laziness or because they're like children and want a new toy or because they're wheedled or bullied into making the change. And if they believe they're just adding things to life—and not substituting—then it's all the easier. But I'm glad," he said to Hilda, "that you feel like that about the Festival. It might not be very good in itself—it's been left very late and there may not be much money for it—and yet without being very good it may have a tremendous effect upon people here. If only as a change from talking about wages, prices, taxes, regulations, shortages."

"You think there's too much of that?" said Ernest.

"I do, though of course it's easy for me to be critical," Theodore admitted. "But it seems to me that just when people are tired of talking about such things, they turn on the radio and hear more talk about them, or pick up a newspaper and begin to read about them. And then, when they're naturally beginning to feel bored and stale, they're told they oughtn't to feel bored and stale—and not because boredom and staleness narrow and numb experience, take the color and fire out of living, but because they're bad for wages, prices, taxes, regulations, shortages. And back they are again." He looked at them apologetically. "Perhaps that seems stupid to you. If so, I'm sorry. It's just—an outsider's view."

"And I can't agree with it," said Ernest. "You talk as if people were too responsible, whereas I'm sure most of them are still irresponsible. Look at all this betting."

"I know what Theodore means," cried Laura. "Betting and all that nonsense is just being silly in that colorless world Theodore meant. It's—it's—no, don't stop me, please, Ernest—merely reversing everything in the same way of living. It's not really trying to get away from those values."

"Ah, that's the point," said Hilda, who was attached to values. "Has everybody finished? Go into the sitting room then, while I make the coffee."

Laura sat on a low stool near the fire and watched Theodore, who looked gigantic, light a cigar. She had never felt like this about anybody before. Sometimes it seemed as if she had known him forever. Yet there were moments too when he seemed not merely a stranger, in the ordinary sense of the term, but strangeness itself, a whole opposite and mysterious form of life manifesting itself as an unusually large and good-looking young man. Again, a look, a tone, would suddenly dissolve her into tenderness; yet there were times when he not only irritated her but roused her to a fury. It was all very rum and terribly exciting, perhaps too exciting. And while the two men talked, in their impersonal way, she decided how the rest of the evening must take shape with no loud argument, no noisy generalizations, but just the four of them round the fire, with Theodore and herself rather more prominent than the Saxons, talking quietly and intimately, revealing their true selves as people so rarely do. She could almost hear the talk drifting exquisitely on. And—as she told herself later—what a hope she had!

No sooner had the coffee been poured out than Paul Ravenstreet arrived, and within two minutes he and Theodore were lost in an argument about Communism and the Far East. Ten minutes later, Eric Longshaw appeared. Poor Eric nearly always came about this time on Saturday night; but Laura had forgotten all about him, as anybody might forget a lighted candle in the glory of the morning. Now she was annoyed with him because he still existed and had his habits; she was annoyed with herself for being so unfair to the poor man; and still further annoyed with him for being the cause of all this disturbance.

"I thought I'd just look in," he said as usual. "It's rather warmer out."

The Communist argument was interrupted just long enough for him to be introduced to Theodore, who was then hauled by Ravenstreet back into the morass of dialectical Stalinism. Eric looked startled, and then directed several timid inquiring glances at Laura that did nothing to end her annoyance.

"I've heard rumors," said Eric in his cautious way, "that you're working for some people who want to organize a Farbridge Festival."

Well, she could explain all that to him, and she did, not without difficulty because Ravenstreet, Ernest, and Theodore seemed to be all talking at once, chiefly at the top of their voices.

"It's a good idea, of course," said Eric when she had finished, "but I'm afraid the opposition will be too strong for you, even with the support you've mentioned."

"Oh—don't be so pessimistic."

"I'm not being," said Eric, not unreasonably. "But the more influential men here—Whatmore, Crandry, Tanhead—"

"Oh—blow the more influential men!" cried Laura impatiently. "We know about them, but they don't own the place. We can fight 'em. You'll see."

And now there was another ring at the front door. Who could it be this time? Hilda went to answer it, and after a minute or two returned with—of all people—Michael Seacombe, looking wildly untidy, reckless, rather tight. And Laura was furious. He knew where she lived because he had asked for her address, saying that he might have to get in touch with her quickly when she could not be found in their office at the White Hart. Laura had suspected at the time that this was All Her Eye, very much so indeed because he was obviously attracted to her. This did not in itself displease her, and she actually liked Michael, not only for the help he was giving them but for his energy and zest and cheerful impudence. If there had been no Theodore, just blowing everything to smithereens and not even knowing he was doing it, she would have been glad to have seen a lot of Michael, who would have been a welcome change from the dim respectable Eric. But he and Theodore seemed to have disliked each other from the moment Michael marched into the office; and for Michael to arrive here now, uninvited, when Theodore was paying his first visit, this was simply infuriating. Intimate quiet talk indeed! The room seemed crammed with men, like a pub toward closing time.

"Hello, hello, hello!" cried Michael, silencing the debaters. "Good evening, Laura. Hope you don't mind my popping in like this? And you're Mr. Saxon, are you? Good! Hello, Jenks! Ah—Comrade Ravenstreet—we've met before, haven't we?"

"Yes," said Ravenstreet boldly. "After which you sold a few lies to the Capitalist Press."

"A lie," said Michael cheerfully, "being anything likely to damage the Communist Party, while the truth is anything that might do it a bit of good. And some chaps meet in Moscow to decide for you which is which. Forgive me, ladies."

"Oh—don't mind us," said Laura, with some bitterness. "We can go and wash up while you all try to shout one another down."

"Say the word, my dear Laura, and I'll join you at the sink."

"So will I," said Theodore, looking annoyed. There was something about Michael that always destroyed his usual easy calm.

"There isn't going to be any washing up just yet," cried Hilda Saxon, rather crossly. "Ernest, do something—"

"What do you mean—do something?" said Ernest with some irritation. "We were having a very interesting discussion, and I'd like to get back to it."

"Political?" Michael inquired. There was mischief in his voice and eye.

"Yes," Ernest replied.

"I'm afraid I must be going," said Eric Longshaw mournfully. "Only just looked in, you know."

Feeling sorry for him, Laura took him to the front door, where he gave her one of his long dim wistful looks.

"Looks as if you're going to be rather busy in the near future, Laura," he said, carefully arranging his silk scarf. Eric was a great scarf and muffler man.

"I'm afraid I am, Eric," she replied gently.

He took it for what it was, a dismissal. "Well, if there's anything I can do—"

"I'll let you know at once, of course," she said brightly. "Goodnight Eric." She closed the door behind him very slowly, wishing she could have been kinder to him and yet still irritated by him. In the sitting room they were still at it, of course; so many loud idiotic voices, more like contesting gramophones than persons. "No, no, you're quite wrong there, Seacombe," Ernest was shouting. In she went, and the room looked just as crowded. Poor Eric's departure did not seem to have made any difference.

"Seacombe wouldn't know what we were talking about," said Ravenstreet.

"Nark it, Comrade!"

"What are your politics, Seacombe?" Ernest demanded, sharply.

"Oh dear—oh dear—oh dear!" cried Laura. She tried to smile at Theodore, but he had put on a dull wooden look, which he seemed to keep specially for Michael Seacombe's visits.

"I'm a Tory Rebel," Michael announced.

"There isn't such a thing."

"There is—and I'm it. I'm not a Conservative—I'm against Big Business, the Fat Boys, and the Central Office. I'm a very old-fashioned poor Tory."

"Which means nothing," said Ravenstreet.

"Wrong, Comrade. It means—"

"Shut up!" Laura shrieked.

"Certainly, Miss Casey," he replied with mock dignity.

"I'm sorry," said Laura, addressing them all. "I know I oughtn't to have made that horrible noise. But if there's any more of this noisy argument and showing off, then I'm going straight to bed. Theodore, tell us something, anything."

"You know," said Theodore rather stiffly, "that isn't possible. As soon as I'm told to say something interesting, my mind becomes a blank."

"Mine doesn't," said Michael. "For instance, I can tell you that it's all fixed that in the B.B.C. *Next Question, Please* program next week, a question will be asked about a Farbridge Festival. I can also tell you, having spies everywhere, that Alderman Tanhead and Muleford, ignoring their political differences, have been in conclave, deciding their anti-Festival policy, and that Treasurer Coverack has been seen hobnobbing with them. Item Three: there's been a first-class row between Coverack and Barr, the Medical Officer. Item Four: Bully Bulfoss and Fatty Mobbs are defying Colonel Whatmore and other True Blue Mandarins on various issues, including your Festival. The Seacombe Service—always first with the hard hot news. Thank you, ladies and gentlemen. Any offer of liquid refreshment will be gratefully accepted."

That set them going, with Michael maintaining his leadership. Laura did a gay little act, replying to Michael's challenge, but at heart she was disappointed and rather miserable. It ought to have been Theodore's evening, and she was annoyed with him for failing to stand up to Michael. When, after half an hour or so, Ravenstreet announced that he was going, Ernest said that he would walk part of the way with him, as they had some school affairs to discuss. Then Laura, suddenly feeling tired, began to send out those little signals that suggest an evening is over; and after some obvious maneuvering, lively on Michael's part, rather glum on Theodore's part, to outstay each other, the young men decided to leave together.

"What an exciting evening!" cried Hilda, when she and Laura began clearing the dining table. "Laura, it's made such a difference your being here—so many things happening—and such interesting people! I like your Theodore."

"Darling, he's not my Theodore. But you didn't see him at his best, not after dinner. He doesn't like Michael Seacombe, and he doesn't seem to know how to cope with Michael's cheerful cheeky manner."

"He's jealous, of course," said Hilda placidly. "And as it's new to him and he doesn't know what to do about it, he gets worried and annoyed with himself. I saw that at once."

Laura thought how you could never tell with Hilda. Sometimes she seemed appallingly dense, and then the next minute she would be surprisingly perceptive. But then perhaps she herself was like that. "Any more, Hilda, while we're alone and you're in this mood? No—really—please tell me."

"Michael Seacombe, I believe, is quite seriously attracted, Laura dear, and I fancy that's new to him too, and he can't quite understand it and he's covering a sort of shyness with cheek and impudence. But of course there's no comparison between those two young men, as you must know very well, my dear."

"It's like having one's fortune told," cried Laura, not as easy and gay as she sounded. "Go on. What—what about Theodore?"

"But, of course, it's obvious."

"It isn't obvious to *me*. And I'm the one it ought to be obvious to— golly—yes!"

Meanwhile, the two young men, under a wild moon and scurrying thin veils of cloud, were taking long-legged strides together toward the town center. There were no eager confidences between these two. But the antagonism that Laura had noticed was no longer there. They were not friendly yet, but there was between them a sort of stiffish but not unamiable neutrality. This took all flow from their talk, leaving it spare and curt with plenty of pauses, as if they were characters in super-masculine fiction.

"Perhaps I ought to warn you, Jenks," said Michael. "I've gone and fallen for young Laura."

"So I imagined," said Theodore. *Left-Right, Left-Right*—long legs striding.

"I don't know why. Damned if I do."

"Well, you don't want me to tell you, do you?" said Theodore dryly.

"No. And you wouldn't know, if I did. Can't be explained. Some-thing clicks."

"There's an old locked door in the back of your mind, and some girl suddenly seems to have the key." Theodore marched in silence for half a minute, then added: "I'm staying here because of Laura. She has the key."

"I thought so. But I warn you, I'm going to have a hell of a good try." They cut their way in silence through a little mob of roarers and babblers emptying a pub. "With luck you may get your Festival. But the girl—no."

"The girl and the Festival," said Theodore. "You'll see." And then, after another fifty yards, he added: "And very pleasing that sounds too. The girl and the Festival."

Many Avenues Explored

I

THE only public hall of any consequence in Farbridge, and the one used for all important meetings, concerts, lectures, is the Corn Exchange. It is an eighteenth-century building, but the hall itself, rectangular, high-roofed, with a rather narrow balcony on three of its walls, was discreetly modernized between the wars. It can seat about fifteen hundred people. There were not fifteen hundred people there on that Tuesday night, when the B.B.C. did its *Next Question, Please* program, because for some technical reason the balcony was not open to the public. But every seat below was taken—there had been a great scramble for tickets—except in the very front row. This row was reserved for those privileged persons whose written questions had been chosen by the producer of the program. They sat in the front row so that they could easily step up to the microphone and tell several million listeners who they were and what their question was. There were eight of them—though the last two had been warned that they were only there as reserves—and Number Four was Miss Laura Casey, whose question was: *Don't the Team agree that Farbridge should celebrate the Festival of Britain?* When they had discussed it in the office, Laura had wanted either Theodore or the Commodore (and Michael Seacombe had said he ought to be called "Seadore" to complete the trio) to ask the question, but the two men had been uncertain, and then Michael, who knew the B.B.C. people, had settled it by declaring at once that Laura, with an ordinary Farbridge address, to say nothing of her sex and looks, was the best choice. It was Michael who had arranged it all and found tickets for the other two men, and for Mrs. Coote, Mr. Jordan, Captain Mobbs, Seth Hull, Joe Gisburn, the Saxons, and several other Festival supporters, all of whom were artfully distributed among the audience, ready to lead the applause on the Festival question. And now here she was, in her new dark blue with the heavenly gay collar, feeling hot and anxious and hollow inside. She had never spoken into a microphone before, and the prospect was terrifying. What if she couldn't speak or was sick or something? It was all very well to be grand and patronizing about the B.B.C., but now, when the program was only ten minutes away, she felt desperately alone and longed to be clutching Theodore's large cool hand. It was so bad that it began to be not quite real, like having an operation.

The other Questioners seemed to be equally nervous, though this cut both ways, being sometimes a comfort and at other moments an added menace. The fat man on her right, Number Five, seemed to be in a sweat of apprehension, and kept rereading his question, as if some evil magic might transform its few words into something appalling. So he went on muttering it to himself, to keep it in order, then looked hastily again at his crumpled bit of paper to catch the wizards at work. The woman on her left, Number Three and very proud of it, so that she condescended to Laura as Four, was oldish and large and tremendously made-up and wearing everything anybody had ever given her, and looked at a first glance like minor Royalty waiting to open something. But she was very nervous too, in her elderly and rather majestic way. "This is my First Time," she admitted to Laura. "But I know all about it because My Daughter has broadcast many times, from various studios. My Daughter has told me all about it. Not too close and be careful of the breathing, My Daughter says. Loose dentures are inconvenient." She looked sharply at Laura, who said that she hadn't any dentures, only teeth, and asked what the Daughter did. "My Daughter," said Number Three with immense pride, "is an Entertainer. For the last three seasons she was a great favorite at Ilfracombe. This year My Daughter will be at Colwyn Bay, where I shall see her. You're looking rather flushed, what about me? Pale? I had tea with a Friend who gave me tinned salmon, which was probably a Mistake. My Daughter eats nothing before the show, not even in Pantomime. My Daughter—"

After the producer, a young man with wet hair, a green shirt, and a slight stutter, had told them what would happen and warned them that the program was about to go on the air, the Question Master and his Team arrived on the platform, and were greeted with that enthusiasm which tickets of admittance from the B.B.C. appear to generate so easily. The Question Master, Reginald Wendron, a short parsonical-looking man, gravely delighted with himself, had been a news announcer during the war, so that most people remembered his voice and felt vaguely that he had had a considerable hand in destroying the Luftwaffe, sinking the *Bismarck*, chasing Rommel out of Africa, just as they felt that Gary Cooper had accounted for scores of bad Indians and cattle rustlers. Now the good people of Farbridge, whom he had safely delivered to V Day, regarded him with as much awe as he conjured up for himself. For this program he had, of course, a lighter touch, condescending to little jokes, bringing out a merry Ha-ha-ha of admirable pitch and resonance, a representative of that democratic way of life which is associated at home and abroad with the British Broadcasting Corporation. Now on the air, dripping honey into the microphone, he introduced the program.

"Here we are again, with *Next Question, Please*, and tonight it is coming to you from the Corn Exchange, Farbridge, where we seem to have a very eager audience, who look as if they know some very difficult questions are coming up." Laughter and applause, and a smile from Mr. Wendron lasting exactly three and a half seconds. "There is one change in our Team tonight. Sir Henry Labrador is indisposed and his place has been taken—you will be glad to know—by the Member of Parliament for Farbridge—Major Bulfoss." Much applause, led in dumb show by Mr. Wendron, and rather awkwardly acknowledged by the Major, who turned scarlet, bobbed up, bobbed down, and looked frightened. "The other three," Mr. Wendron continued, "have often been with us on this program and are known to you all. Lady Tirle, who gives us the woman's point of view; Dan Cobbley, who tells us what the countryman thinks; and last but not least—our old friend George Bray—sometimes known, I believe, as the Radio Plumber." Laughter, applause, ecstasy.

This rather uncertain reference to Mr. Bray as the Radio Plumber was of course one of Reginald Wendron's little jokes. Everybody knew Mr. Bray as the Radio Plumber. By the strange and perhaps rather sinister magnification of broadcasting, he had whizzed from obscurity into national fame. He was a personality to millions who would never know anything about the country's great artists, scientists, scholars. His familiar voice arrived in their dry empty lives like dew and manna. He was a sulky-looking middle-aged man, with a hectoring style and a Cockney accent; and simply as a plumber he had been given a chance broadcast, and this had been so notable a success that now he did nothing but broadcast, make personal appearances, write or sign articles, bullying his admiring countrymen on almost any subject. Dan

Cobbley was another radio personality, although he was on a lower listening figure level than the Plumber. He was a professional rural character, with a burry, clotted-cream accent, who gave the impression that he had just hurried through milking to reach the microphone; but in fact he had an agent, several books of press-cuttings, and a service flat in Bayswater. Lady Tirle looked like a grander version of Questioner Number Three; and Laura had heard her before, giving the woman's point of view. She had a vague idea too that Lady Tirle had appeared in a comic Empire meeting that Theodore had once described to her.

The first two questions, with all the answers and back-chat around them, seemed to Laura to flit past like a dream. It was only when her proud neighbor, Number Three, was summoned to the microphone that the evening steadied itself and almost went into a maddening slow-motion. Number Three announced herself as Mrs. Delacey and demanded to know if Popular Entertainment was as good as it used to be. She returned from the microphone wearing an immensely gracious smile and giving a series of little nods.

"Mrs. Delacey asks the Team," said Mr. Wendron, who was like a Bishop presenting prizes at an idiot school, "if Popular Entertainment is as good as it used to be. Lady Tirle?"

"Speaking as a woman," said Lady Tirle with decision, "I would say that Popular Entertainment is better than it used to be. And I have a very good reason for saying that, from a woman's point of view. In recent years Popular Entertainment has been brought more and more into the Home. And for that, of course, we have to thank the B.B.C. I am sure that many housewives, who—er—in other times— were cut off from Popular Entertainment, because their duties did not allow them to leave the Home, have now been given access to—er— many forms of Popular Entertainment. And television will undoubt- edly bring still more Popular Entertainment of many kinds into the Home. From the woman's point of view—"

But as it was obvious she was going round and round in a very small circle, Wendron adroitly cut in with a: "Thank you, Lady Tirle. I'm sure many listeners will agree with you. And so ought the B.B.C." Some laughter and applause. "Major Bulfoss?"

Unlike the others, the Major was not an experienced broadcaster and although he ought to have felt at home in the Corn Exchange, where he had spoken often enough, he was far from feeling at ease with this

Question and Answer business. "Well—Mr. Chairman—I mean, Mr. Question Master—I don't—er—pretend to know very much about Popular Entertainment. Unless—er—you include—the House of Commons." A laugh here, led by the Commodore, Laura suspected, for she thought she heard his laugh and she knew that he was anxious to encourage the Major. "On the whole—I'd say—that Popular Entertainment—was about the same. Better in some ways—as Lady Tirle has told us—but not so good in others. I mean, I seem to remember a lot of jolly good shows that we don't seem to get nowadays. But that's perhaps because I'm so busy these days. But about the same—weighing one thing with another—would be my answer." And the Major ran a handkerchief round his collar, and then tried to give the impression he was really somewhere else.

Dan Cobbley, the rural character, was now called upon. He looked like a plumper Mr. Punch, and the instant his name was called he went into his performance, coming out of an imaginary barn and putting on a sly old rustic grin, to the delight of the audience. "Az tew Papular Antertainmant," he drawled in his best Mummerset, "that's whaat volks down our way would caal a haard question. Zome zay one thing. Zome zay another thing. Now Lady Tirle, she tells us woives want tew stap at home. But down our way the woives don't want tew stap at home—they want tew go tew the pictures, that's what they want down our way, the woives dew." Much laughter and applause for this, and Dan responded by scratching his head slowly, hoping to milk them for another round. "Well, volks, that's how it is. Zome zay one thing. Zome zay another thing. What Oi zay is this—if this yer program we dew is Papular Antertainmant, then Oi declare yere an' now Papular Antertainment be gettin' better all the toime." A roar.

"Thank you, Dan," said Wendron, laughing heartily with correct pitch and tempo. "Now we know what they think in the country. But what about the cities? Here's the man to tell us—our old friend, the Radio Plumber." A nice build-up, to which the audience responded enthusiastically.

The Radio Plumber scowled heavily—it was part of his act—and made a disgusted noise, almost like a belch, that served as his signature tune. "Naow, not on yer life," he snarled. "Pop'lar Enterteinement better than it used to be? Gertcha! What d'yer get now? Comics like Leno, Little Tich, 'Arry Tite, George Rowbey? Naow. Yer get blokes like Dan Cobbley an' me—answerin' silly questions." A delighted roar shook the Corn Exchange. " 'Ere—when I was a youngster us plumbers gave 'em some real enterteinment, we did. Forgot our tools. Now 'alf of 'em's got none to forget. All they got's permits now. Ever tried to stop a leak with a permit?"

But now, even while the Radio Plumber was still getting his laughs (but not from Mrs. Delacey, who was regarding him with haughty distaste), Laura's awful moment was looming and threatening, and she felt her heart knocking as if it wanted to be let out and to run home. The producer was smiling at her and making little comforting gestures with his hands, none of which he had troubled to do for Mrs. Delacey; but Laura felt terrified and rather sick, and told herself she was mad to have volunteered for this ordeal, which the large calm Theodore or the artful old Commodore would have encountered without a qualm. And then it was here; she was on her feet; she was going to the microphone; and suddenly, magically, it didn't matter at all, she was just Laura Casey asking a question. And it would be all right.

"Don't the Team agree," she asked in an earnest clear tone, "that Farbridge should celebrate the Festival of Britain?"

Before Wendron, who was quick and clever at that sort of thing, could repeat the question, the building rang with applause. The Festival gang had gone into action at once. They were still clapping while she returned, flushed and bright-eyed, to her seat, with everybody smiling at her.

"Miss Laura Casey," Wendron announced, with rather more emphasis and less patronage than usual, realizing that here was a live issue, quickening the program, "asks the Team if they don't agree that Farbridge should celebrate the Festival of Britain. And, as listeners must have heard, it seems to be a question that is exciting our audience here. I think you will agree that the first member of the Team who ought to answer this question is the Member for Farbridge—Major Bulfoss."

This was the Major's opportunity. Up to this moment he had cut a poor figure in these proceedings, and now or never was his chance to impress his constituents. Moreover, he was now standing on much firmer ground. He knew this question was coming, and had been coached in his reply by Captain Mobbs and the Commodore, over double whiskies up in Seth Hull's office.

"I am very glad," he said firmly, "this question has been asked. It is—I believe—a question that many people not only here in Farbridge but also in the—er—large rural area served by Farbridge—have been asking. And quite right too. I understand that the Town Council decided last year not to celebrate the Festival of Britain here, unlike most of our cities and larger towns. I believe that decision was a mistake." He waited for applause, and did not wait in vain. And this time it was hardly necessary for the claque to function. "I've been told that it is now too late. But that—I gather—is not the opinion of people who are willing to organize a Farbridge Festival even now. And that seems to me the proper spirit. It's never too late to try and do something worth doing. As the Member for this constituency, I feel that it would be a crying shame if Farbridge were left out of the picture. We here in Farbridge, one of the oldest market towns in the land, and now also a center of—er—new industrial enterprise, are as proud of our country as any other townspeople. We should therefore—er—show that pride. So, in my opinion, and I feel quite strongly about this, this year there should certainly be a Farbridge Festival."

"Hurray!" cried the gang, leading the cheers. This was not mere applause but something like a riot. A lot of people, including all the gang, were standing up to cheer and clap. The producer and Wendron were waving their arms at the audience, to quieten them so that too much valuable time would not be wasted.

"Well, there's no doubt, as listeners will have heard for themselves, what the feeling here is. Everybody agrees with Major Bulfoss." There were several shouts of "No," but he ignored them, and, after a quick glance at Lady Tirle, who shook her head, probably because she felt that the atmosphere was now too uproarious for the woman's point of view, he called upon Dan Cobbley. That artful old codger, leaving his haymaking, knew too much to suggest any disagreement in the face of this enthusiasm; but he took his own line.

"Down our way," he began, "we're but zimple volks an' don't know nothin' 'bout big towns like Farbridge. In these big towns, they do be tellin' me, there's zome volks who's long-faced an' cautious like an' don't want to be a-spendin' their money on vun an' merrymakin' as yew might zay." They laughed at that, and he rubbed his Punch nose in acknowledgment. "But we're havin' a bit of a zimple zort o' Festival of Britain even down along our parts—some vlags 'ung out, an' a braaass band an' moight be zome dancin' an' zingin'—an' a barrel or two o' zoider. An' don't yew be askin' me to come to Farbridge then

—not loikely—'cos Oi like to be where volks is spendin' their money an' not zaving it. But yew volks please yourselves. Yew don't have no Festival if yew don't want one. Have a noice funeral instead." And he grinned and scratched his head throughout the tumult that followed; mostly cheers but with a few loud indignant protests.

It was now the Radio Plumber's turn, and this was an anxious moment. He had a habit, as every listener knew, of opposing the majority, or sharply or sullenly disagreeing with the customer, in old plumber fashion, to show his independence. But tonight he was not risking it. He went with the tide, though in his own fashion.

"Farbridge 'ave a Festival? Ev'ry time! Gow orn," he jeered. "What's the metter with yer? 'Ave a bash at it, people, an' mike yer mis'rable selves 'eppy for once. Don't tike no notice of Dan Cobbley. Ly off thet cider—turns you up proper inside. An' 'e can keep 'is bress bends far as I'm concerned. But yer don't want to let nobody talk yer out of 'avin' a Festival—Tarn Carncillers or no Tarn Carncillers—an' if they don't like it, tell 'em to go an' wipe a joint. Naow—but listen I'm serious. What's the use of always grumblin' an' grahsin'—the wy some of yer do—an' syin' it's all dreary in good old England these dyes—an' then when even the Government—yes, even the perishin' Government—asks yer to do a Festival—yer go an' turn it dahn? So I sy—mike yer minds up to 'ave one—sharp—see?"

"Well," said Wendron, when the applause was dying down, "the answer to that question is a very decided yes, and it won't be our fault if Farbridge still decides against a Festival. Now the next question—"

But the remaining ten minutes were an anticlimax: the great question had come and gone. Laura experienced that sudden descent from high to low spirits which is the lot of most performers and explains why so many of them take to drink, fornication, and poker for reckless stakes. She merely took to a cold supper that Seth Hull had laid on for his friends at the White Hart; but although everybody congratulated her, and there was a decided air of triumph about the occasion, she still felt depressed and wished she could have gone straight home. She sat next to Theodore, who was obviously bewildered and rather disappointed because she seemed so lifeless.

"I wish I was small," she told him finally.

"You are small," he said, smiling at her.

"No, I mean absolutely tiny—about so big." She raised a hand six inches above the table.

He stared. "Why?"

But she couldn't tell him that then she could crawl into his pocket, so she merely shook her head.

"In my opinion," Seth was saying in his flat heavy way, "this has done it, chaps. Yer'll see."

"Young Seacombe swears he'll get us some first-class publicity out of it," said Mobbs. "And if he can't, I will. Do it on my head—bingo!"

"So could I," said the Commodore, who was looking very pleased with himself. "And—by George—I must say I'm kicking myself for not having looked into this radio thing earlier. I was talking to that B.B.C. fellow, and he tells me that imitation farm laborer, Cobbley, is paid twenty guineas a time for that nonsense of his. I must look into it as soon as this Festival is off my hands." He looked majestically round the table, very sure of himself. "Laura, my dear, you were perfect. My instinct to let you do it was right. My dear, a drink. What's the matter?"

"I'm rather tired," said Laura, feeling silly and wanting to cry. And she did cry too, once Theodore had taken her home and she had been rather snappy with him and left him looking bewildered and had then exchanged a few remarks with Hilda and Ernest Saxon and hurried up to bed. Just the sort of idiotic way, she told herself fiercely, she would end what had been—or ought to have been—a wonderful evening.

2

The Commodore's self-satisfaction had not vanished with the night. Next morning, although not quite the expansive radiant being who had sat up exchanging reminiscences with little Mobbs and Seth Hull, he still felt that his luck was in, and that the world, on which the sun was shining at last, was a better place than he had lately imagined it to be. After a leisurely breakfast in his room, he dressed slowly and with unusual care, humming the compositions of Leslie Stuart. Then, lighting a pipe, he went along to the office, taking his time and stopping to have a chat with a fellow guest (trying to do business with Whatmore's) and one of the chambermaids, Poppy, who, though so far removed from the sea, had contrived to get herself engaged to the mate of a trawler. It was nearly eleven when he actually entered the office.

"Good morning, Laura," he cried cheerfully. "Spring at last, I think. And where's our friend Theodore?"

"He's gone round to see Captain Mobbs in his office."

"Oh—yes. They go together—when is it, tomorrow?—to enlist a few members of the nobility and gentry."

"And a silly idea, I think," said Laura crossly. "I told him so, this morning."

"I see nothing wrong with it, my dear. I don't say it's necessary— particularly after last night. By the way, I'm told we've had a few little paragraphs in the press. But some fancy names—County people—will all help."

"I doubt it. And Theodore doesn't know them, except some idiotic baronet he met. And nobody's going to tell me that fat little Mobbs is thick with the County or whoever they are. I know he's the Conserva- tive agent here in Farbridge, but that's different. And he's rather an awful boozy little man, as I told Theodore." She sounded quite peevish.

"Mobbs knows some of them," said the Commodore. "And he's used to handling nobility and gentry. You underrate him, my dear Laura. And incidentally, the sun's shining, the world is awakening, our cause advances, so why, in your youth and beauty, my child, are you so unresponsive this morning?"

She eyed him coldly. "For that matter, why are you so pleased with yourself?"

"Because, for once, I feel I've every right to be pleased with myself. And with you, if you'll let me. What's the time? I have an appoint- ment this morning at the Palace with the Chairman and Vice-chairman of the Farbridge Theater Company, which owns both the Palace itself and the largest cinema in the town."

"Who are these people?"

"I don't know," he replied carelessly. "I made the appointment through the manager. But it shouldn't be hard to make them under- stand that we want their buildings for our Festival. And probably after last night—and fellows like these must know what the public is feeling—they'll jump at the chance. Well, I suppose I must toddle along."

"Do you know what I think?"

"I don't, Laura, but I've a suspicion it may be something dark and unfriendly. I've noticed it before about your sex, my dear. There's a deep-rooted contrariness about you all, so that when we're up, you're

down, and when we're down, you're up. It isn't merely keeping a sort
of balance—it goes farther than that—though how, why or where I
don't pretend to know." He reached for his hat.

"Well, I think," she told him, completely ignoring everything he had
said, "you're too pleased with yourself, Commodore Tribe. So look out.
That's all." And she resumed the typing he had interrupted.

"That's exactly the kind of thing I mean. And you're much too
young and good-looking and in love—for I take it you're in love—"

"Oh—shut up!" And she banged away.

Still smiling, he sauntered down to the entrance lounge, had a word
with Miss Pratt about her mother (who had a complaint that defied
the whole National Health Service), and then strolled along High
Street. It was a delightful morning, filling the street with clear light
and soft warming air. The windows of Jordan's Stores had charm and
dignity. Spring had arrived at the haberdasher's. Woolworth's in its
scarlet and gold was as bright as a new toy. Even Walmer's iron-
mongery—Pzzzz—glittered invitingly. For the first time, the Commodore looked about him with a fond paternal eye. This morning he
no longer felt a stranger in Farbridge. It seemed almost home to him.
A pleasant town, not too big, not too small, and admirably balanced
between the old and the new. Friendly people too—a trifle provincial
perhaps, but probably none the worse for that—good sound types, well
turned-out and not bad-looking some of them, as he had leisure to
notice this morning. If he had to settle in England—and there were
times when he longed for more sun and fewer regulations—this was
probably the right sort of place. He saw himself as an admired Farbridge character. Our dear old Commodore! And no doubt, once he
had put the Festival on the map, they would offer him something good.
Before he could decide what that something good ought to be, and so
crown the pleasing little daydream, he had arrived at his destination.

Undoubtedly the Palace, clearly discovered in mid-morning, looked
both tawdry and forlorn. And the manager, even in the subdued light
of the foyer, looked horrible—the shiny suit, the shinier hair and
mustache, the waxiness of him, that resurrected corpse's whisper—as
if Edgar Allen Poe had tried his hand at creating a theater manager!
But the Commodore, hiding his distaste, was immensely affable if
condescending. "Your people all ready for me? Good! And I'm all
ready for them. This may prove to be a great moment in the history

of your theater, my dear fellow. You heard what happened last night in the B.B.C. show at the Corn Exchange?"

"No, did anything happen? We were down a bit, I noticed."

"Yes, yes—well, I imagine your Chairman and Vice-chairman know all about it," said the Commodore heartily, although he could not help feeling rather disappointed. "We're on the move. Yes, on the move. Well—lead the way, if you don't mind."

Humbly, sadly, the manager knocked on the office door, opened it very gently about six inches, said something that the Commodore could not catch, then sadly, humbly, stepped aside for the Commodore to make his grand entrance.

"Good morning, gentlemen," cried the Commodore; and then his bluff opening remark, rehearsed silently on the stairs, died in his throat. He could only gape and goggle. This was what the bright morning, in the infinite treachery of events, had been keeping for him. This was what he had hummed and smiled and daydreamed on his way to. The Old Ironist had been at work again. For there, behind the desk, was a small elderly man with a long nose and a thin beard and a scraggy mean look—Crandry. And by his side, scrubbed and shrimp-pink, proud and bloodshot, was Colonel Whatmore. The Chairman and the Vice-chairman of the Farbridge Theater Company, Limited!

Then the Commodore, who had his moments of greatness, sharply recovered himself. He settled heavily in an armchair, took out his pipe and pouch, and said, "Well, Mr. Crandry—how's the Kremlin?"

It was a clever move because the sheer audacity of it rattled Crandry, who had been sitting there grimly complacent. At their previous encounter, he had lost his temper while the Commodore had remained cool and impudent. No doubt he had hoped to do better this time; but the Commodore's opening remark was too much for him. He lost his temper again.

"I've just been telling Colonel Whatmore," he cried in his harsh scream, "that you're nothing but a confounded charlatan, and that I discharged you on sight from my *Foreign Affairs* monthly."

"Actually, I resigned, Whatmore," said the Commodore to that gentleman, who immediately looked as if his blood pressure had jumped to 180. "Now let's talk about these theaters. I was here the other night, by the way, and was quite shocked by the performance and the apathy of the audience and the whole atmosphere of the place. Even you two ought to do better than that."

"Now listen to me," Crandry screeched. "We decided to see you here this morning so that we needn't waste any more time on you. Now understand this." And he slapped the desk. "Three things, just three things. First—even if there was a Festival here, we wouldn't let you come near our theaters. Second—there won't be a Festival here. Third—you'd better stop mountebanking round this town and clear out as soon as you can. That's all."

"And let me add," said Colonel Whatmore frostily, "that I'm in entire agreement with Mr. Crandry."

The Commodore had his pipe going now, and appeared to be enjoying it. "I don't know what you mean by 'mountebanking,' but Crandry's always a little wild, so we'll let that pass. But I'd like to point out that the odds are now there will be a Farbridge Festival—you've probably heard what happened last night on that B.B.C. program—remarkable demonstration—and I'd also like to remind you that it's a mistake for men who run theaters to ignore public opinion. Clearly you don't like me. A pity, though I must confess that I don't like you fellows either. And do stop blowing and jigging and fussing, Crandry. We can't discuss things calmly—"

"There isn't going to be any discussion," Crandry shouted.

"Quite so," said Colonel Whatmore. "Nothing more to be said. And I strongly advise you to stop making a nuisance of yourself here in Farbridge—Mr.—Er—"

"Not Mr. Er. My name's Tribe. And if you wish to give me a courtesy title—it's Commodore—"

"Rubbish," said Crandry. "I've had that looked into, and there isn't any such rank, even if you ever served in the Navy, which I doubt."

The Commodore stared at him. "I must say, my dear sir, you go to extraordinary lengths to be offensive. Not only did I hold a commission in the Royal Navy—I was a Lieutenant-Commander when I resigned —but I can also give you proof that I'm entitled to the courtesy title of Commodore, a rank I had for some years in one of the major South American republics, to which I was sent, in the first place, by the Admiralty—in conjunction," he added grandly, "with the Foreign Office." He looked sternly from one to the other. "I'm much too busy at present to want to involve myself in an action for slander. But if there's much more of this, I'll bring an action and ask for damages that will surprise you. By George—some of you fellows who have saved a few pennies think you can say and do anything you like."

There was no time for them to reply because the manager looked in to announce that Mr. Corby-Smith had arrived, and was told to send him up.

"Mr. Corby-Smith," said Crandry, "is the editor of the *Weekly Record*, the only newspaper published here in Farbridge. You'll also be interested to know that I'm the managing director of the company that publishes the *Weekly Record* and that Colonel Whatmore is a member of the board and one of the chief shareholders. And the *Weekly Record* is the only advertising medium of any importance both in Farbridge and the surrounding districts. I thought you'd like to know, *Commodore*."

"Very interesting. By the way, there's a line or two in some of the national dailies this morning about Farbridge and its Festival. Just a beginning, of course. I see these newspapers in all the shops, so I presume they're read here. Every day too, not once a week—for the small advertisements."

Mr. Corby-Smith came in. He was a tall elderly man with a narrow skull and pince-nez, a high stiff collar and a spotted bow tie; and suggested a minor character actor having a shot at the editor of *The Times* in an Edwardian play.

"Good morning, Mr. Crandry," he said in a plummy voice. "Good morning, Colonel Whatmore. May I smoke? We old journalists, you know—slaves of the Weed." He fitted a gasper into a long holder, lit it, sat down, and half-closed his eyes, did some knowing business with his pince-nez and the cigarette holder, and looked as if he were about to help Disraeli with the Suez Canal problem. The Commodore wrote him off as a pompous ass.

"Corby-Smith," said Crandry, who clearly had no respect for him, "you attended this B.B.C. thing last night, didn't you?"

"I did, Mr. Crandry. I thought it wiser to go there myself and not merely send one of my reporters, though of course I had a reporter present—"

"Yes, yes, we don't need all that. Point is—you heard this talk about a Farbridge Festival and the clapping, you know what it amounted to, eh?"

"I did. And afterwards burned the midnight oil writing a leader about it, to catch this week's issue. I said there—"

"We don't want a leading article," Crandry interrupted rudely. "Just give us your opinion."

"Yes, of course, Mr. Crandry," said Corby-Smith hurriedly. "Well, in my opinion it was very easy to draw wrong conclusions from the apparently enthusiastic response. In the first place, a certain number of people had gone there with the intention of applauding this Festival question. No doubt about that. I took particular note of several of them, including this—er—gentleman." And he pointed his long holder at the Commodore, who merely raised his eyebrows at him. "These people encouraged the others, who, of course, were all excited as they generally are when they attend these B.B.C. functions. The broadcasters," he added, not without shrewdness, "saw which way the wind was blowing, and so followed the example—the deplorable example, I have ventured to call it—of Major Bulfoss."

"Dam' fool," Colonel Whatmore muttered.

"In short, didn't amount to anything really?" Crandry asked impatiently.

"No, Mr. Crandry. It was totally unrepresentative of considered Farbridge public opinion. There can be no question about that."

"And how much will you bet on it?" said the Commodore.

Corby-Smith looked at him as if he were only just there, perhaps a specter about twelve inches high. "I don't bet. But I know something about public opinion. It's my business to know, as editor of the only newspaper here. What your business is—"

"Never mind about that," said the Commodore, nettled by this hoity-toity manner. "But next week we'll hold a public meeting, without any B.B.C. to excite everybody, and then you'll see."

"You won't," Crandry shouted angrily.

The Commodore stood up. "Why, who'll stop us?" He looked hard at Crandry and Whatmore, ignoring Corby-Smith, the stooge. "I didn't want it like this. You're playing it your way, not mine. You've told me I can't touch these theaters, there won't be a Festival, and that I'd better clear out. Though why I ought to clear out when you're so sure I can't succeed, I can't imagine. You say last night didn't mean anything, and we can't even have a public meeting to prove it did. And I'm a charlatan." So far he had spoken quietly, but now he went nearer the desk, so that he began to tower above Crandry, and raised his voice. "You're playing it rough and tough, are you?" He brought his big fist down on the desk with such a bang that the other three jumped in alarm. "Well—by God—I'll play it rough and tough now. And we'll see how you like that."

He swung out, slamming the door, and was carried down the stairs and through the foyer by the sheer grandeur of his exit. But in the street he slowed up, and common sense began seeping back. It was all very fine, but what the blazes had he meant anyhow? How did he begin playing it rough and tough? For that matter, what did it mean? And a nice mess he'd be in if they called his bluff on that threat about slander, if they really began investigating his naval career!

Everything that had pleased him along High Street on his way to the Palace was still there: in fact, the sun was higher, the light clearer, the air even softer and warmer, and the friendly people of this pleasant town were still more in evidence. But the scene no longer pleased him, and there were no more daydreams. He remembered Laura's warning that he was too pleased with himself; and now that he was off his perch, he not only felt that she had been right—and he ought to have remembered that there are moments when all women are witches— but also had a gloomy suspicion that the day had not done with him yet. It was too much to hope that the Ironical Department, which attends to cocky egos, would be satisfied merely with installing Crandry and Whatmore in that Palace office. Once those Grim Boys went into action, they liked to make a good job of it. The Commodore who returned to the entrance lounge of the White Hart looked the same smiling large man who left it earlier, after discussing her mother with Miss Pratt; but inside he was anxious and already wincing, wondering when and how the next blow would come. Nor was he kept wondering long.

For it seemed that there was somebody waiting to see him, a Mr. York. At that moment the name meant nothing to him, and he imagined this was somebody on Festival business. Mr. York was a thick-set fellow with dull-brown eyes, rather like an angry bullock. He and the Commodore seated themselves in a quiet corner of the lounge.

"You don't know me," said Mr. York, staring hard, "but I know a good bit about you."

"Such is fame," said the Commodore in a playful tone, still outwardly easy and smiling. "Something about the Festival, no doubt."

"Festival? I don't know anything about Festivals. I'm Frank York, from the Bell at Tredberrow."

Here it was—wallop! The Commodore pulled himself together. "Oh —yes—the Bell. Very nice place you have there too, Mr. York."

"That's right," said the other grimly, producing a bill. "And you owe it thirty-six pounds, eighteen shillings, and sixpence. I can give you the details, if you like. But that's the total. Thirty-six pounds, eighteen and six. I don't know just what went on when you were there and I wasn't there—though I have my ideas—but I *do* know you owe me that money and if I don't get it—sharp—you're in for plenty of trouble."

The Commodore took the bill and pretended to examine it, to give himself time to think. He never doubted that York meant what he said. And he knew at once that he had not a hope of staying on in Farbridge if he ignored this bill and allowed York to do his worst. Any such course would be sheer idiocy. He had either to duck out, which meant abandoning the Festival scheme, or to pay up promptly, leaving himself broke but still having a sporting chance of pulling off the Festival. It took him ten seconds to make up his mind.

"Well, Mr. York," he said pleasantly, taking out his checkbook, "there's no necessity, you know, to take that tone. I had to leave early, the other morning, to keep an appointment here. I would, of course, have got in touch with you. But I've been very busy. Here you are— a check for thirty-seven pounds. As you see, it's a check on a bank here in Farbridge, and there's nothing to prevent you from going round with it now."

"Nothing *is* going to prevent me," said York, with sardonic emphasis. "And after I've been round there, I'll leave your receipt here at the desk. But I'll just make sure of it first. If you *don't* mind."

"Not in the least," said the Commodore airily, rising. "If you prefer to conduct your business on these lines, just go ahead. But don't imagine I'll ever come back to the Bell."

"I wouldn't advise you to try," said York. "At least not while I'm there, and I'll be there for some time now. A place like that," he added grimly, "needs a man about. You'd be surprised. Good morning, *Admiral*."

On his way upstairs, the Commodore calculated that now he had not enough even to pay what he owed here at the White Hart. And he remembered that talk with Seth Hull, when Seth had asked some very pointed questions. Seth was friendly enough—and looked like being a great help with the Festival—but a Seth who found his bills unpaid might be very awkward indeed. It would have to be Theodore now.

He found him in the office talking to Laura. "You were quite right, my dear," he said to Laura. "I was too pleased with myself, earlier this morning. I found an unpleasant character called Crandry, with whom I'm on terms of mutual dislike, waiting for me as Chairman of the Farbridge Theater Company. His Vice-chairman, also there, was Colonel Whatmore. They told me we couldn't have their theaters even if there should be a Festival, but that anyhow there wouldn't be a Festival, and finally warned me that I was a suspicious character and better clear out."

"Oh—I say," cried Laura. "The beasts!"

"What did you tell them?" asked Theodore.

"I defied them grandly. By this time the editor of the local paper had arrived, to tell them that last night's enthusiasm about the Festival was a fake. A pompous stooge called Corby-Smith, and definitely one of the Enemy."

"I was told that," said Laura. "But what exactly did you say to them, Commodore?"

He grinned, not without an effort. "Told them if they wanted to play it rough and tough, then I could play it rough and tough too. Don't ask what I meant, because I don't know, though no doubt we'll think of something. But I want to have a word with you, Theodore, my boy."

He nodded and smiled. "Here I am, sir. At your service."

The Commodore shook his head. "Not Festival business. Private. Let's go down to the bar."

"Theodore!" cried Laura warningly. And he gave her a reassuring nod; but the Commodore, who had already left, did not see it.

"I'll be perfectly frank with you, my boy," said the Commodore, over their drinks. "Half an hour ago I had to make a choice. A man dunned me for a bill that I didn't expect, and I had to pay it. I paid it because if I hadn't, I would have had to abandon this Festival idea. When I came here, I'd counted on not having to pay it, at least for some time. But there it is—and frankly, my boy, now I'm broke. Haven't even enough for my bill here this week. Now, after last night, I believe there's more than an even chance of our getting this Festival."

"So do I. In fact, I'm certain we'll do it. I was just saying that to Laura."

"In that case, my boy, you make it easier for me to say what I have to say. I want you to advance me a hundred or so to tide me over the next two or three weeks." He spoke with an easy confidence, smiling at the large earnest young man, of whom by this time he was genuinely fond.

Theodore, turning brick-red, looked at him in obvious distress. "I'm sorry, Commodore—but—" he stammered "—I can't—"

This was the worst blow of the morning. "I was under the impression you had plenty of money, Theodore. That's what you told me."

"Yes—it isn't that—it's—it's—"

"If you're trying to tell me it's not a good risk," said the Commodore slowly, "you needn't hesitate. I'll admit it. But I don't bilk my friends." Suddenly he felt old and tired and horribly alone. There came a time, it seemed, when you didn't know the world or the people in it any longer.

"No, you don't understand, Commodore," Theodore protested. "I don't care about risks. It's not that. It's—" But he could not say what it was. "Oh—damn and blast—" Then, without another word, he hurried out of the bar.

The Commodore sat on, staring at his drink without tasting it. He would have to make other plans, but at the moment he hadn't the heart to start making them. He found it hard even to wonder why young Jenks had behaved like that. Perhaps it was just the Grim Boys up in the Ironical Department giving him good measure.

After what might have been two minutes or twenty, a folded piece of paper was dropped near his glass. Seth Hull was standing there, a wide grin across his square meaty face. The piece of paper was the receipted bill from the Bell. The Commodore stuffed it into his pocket.

"I didn't take to him," said Seth.

"Who?"

"Chap that bought that for yer. Pleased with himself too. You're not so pleased with yerself this morning, Commodore."

"I was. Too pleased with myself. So then it all went wrong."

"Have another drink."

"No, thanks, Seth. But if you're getting yourself one, come back here with it."

"Well," said Seth a minute later, "what's up?"

The Commodore described his visit to the Palace. "I talked about playing it rough and tough with 'em," he said in conclusion, "but it wasn't a good bluff. Perhaps I ought to have climbed down."

"What's matter with yer?" Seth was quite indignant. "Climb down nothing! Listen—I've had a go at them two before today, an' I'm ready for another. But that's not what's wrong. Don't tell me them two got yer down 'cos I wouldn't believe yer."

"No, well let's leave it at that."

Seth pushed out his thick lower lip and then wagged his head, the effect being that of a heavy and rather droll shrug. "Please yerself, Commodore. Now—I'll bet yer've never seen the Three Black Boys, an' I've got to nip round there so yer'd better come along with me. Do yer good."

The Commodore did an ordinary shrug, but then, remembering his manners, said he would be glad to have a look at the Three Black Boys, of which, he confessed, he had never heard.

"Nicest little place in Farbridge," said Seth as they turned out of High Street, to cut through into Peter Place. "Been trying to buy it for years. But they won't come down to a proper price, though they're letting it go to wrack an' ruin. They're all old an' obstinate an' daft. Owner's an old woman about eighty, an' she's got oldest solicitor yer ever saw—an' I can't get no sense out of 'em. And they're not doing much of a trade and, as I say, place is going to wrack an' ruin. But yer'll see what I mean in a minute."

At the far side of Peter Place was a short cul-de-sac, which the Commodore had never noticed before, called Saddlers Row. On the corner was a small old wine and spirits shop, with a broad low doorway and an old-fashioned window, containing a few sample bottles of dry sherry, port, and spirits. The faded lettering above the window announced that the shop was owned by Inchbald and Wainfleet.

"Chap who serves in there," said Seth, "must be a good seventy. Takes him ten minutes to give yer sixpence change. If he ever has to find six bottles, he'll drop dead."

The Commodore peered into the dusky eighteenth-century interior. "It's got some style, hasn't it?"

"Classy," said Seth. "Knew yer'd like it."

"But where do these Three Black Boys come in?"

"It's all one property. At back there's a storeroom an' a bit of an office, with cellars underneath of course. Then there's a short passage that takes yer into the Three Black Boys. Entrance is down Saddlers Row here." He led the way round the corner.

The tavern belonged to the same period as the wine shop, and had probably been built by the same man. To the left of the little entrance, paneled in dark wood, was a public bar, and to the right a little snug.

Beyond the bar, which occupied a central position and must have been installed long after the tavern was first built, was a low-ceilinged wide smoke room, also paneled in dark wood and with squat bay windows that looked on to a tiny courtyard. Facing the bar, and still labeled COFFEE ROOM, was the best room of all, although it was obviously not much used now and was in a bad state of repair. This was a long narrow room, with four windows on the long outer wall, and a door in the center of it, and these windows overlooked an unexpected walled garden, now a tangle of weeds.

"What d'yer think?" asked Seth.

The Commodore took a deep breath. They were alone in this last room; and indeed there were only a few people in the whole tavern. "If I'd the money, I'd buy this place if I had to talk to that old woman and her old solicitor day and night for a month. I wouldn't buy it as a speculation, though I've no doubt it might be a good one. I'd buy it to live here—once I'd put it right."

Seth nodded and grinned. "And that 'ud cost yer three or four thousand. It was touch-and-go whether it was going to be condemned, but I played hell on the quiet with some of 'em about that. But I can't get owner to give me a decent price—for the whole property, of course, shop an' all. There's a big old kitchen an' eight bedrooms upstairs—room for everybody to live in an' a bit over—but it's all going to wrack an' ruin, worse than down here. Better have one, for the good of the house, while we're here."

At the bar a rather deaf old man, after some bellowed commands from Seth, served them two large gins from a green-and-gold china barrel. "Kept the best Old Plymouth in that for donkeys' years," said Seth, "an' yer can still taste it. Well, I'm glad yer like it, Commodore. Nobby little do, this eh?"

"Nobby's not the word, but I know what you mean, Seth. In a way I'm sorry I've seen this place," he went on, not without a trace of bitterness. "I've never known where I wanted to end my days. I've known for some time I couldn't go on wandering much longer. Getting too old, and ought to settle. Sometimes I've thought I ought to get back to the warm places, to sit in the sun somewhere and be where living's cheap and easy. But a lot of those places—perhaps most of 'em—aren't what they were. They don't want us there. And you don't know when they're going to blow up now. I'm thirty years too late. And I'm not really a countryman. I'd find it damned dull living in some village. Yet

I don't like our cities, except London on about five thousand a year. But now I've seen what I want—this is it—the old shop, the pub here, and a nice little restaurant going in that coffee room, with the garden all trimmed up and meals outside there in summer. And it isn't mine. It can't be mine. And that's why I say I'm sorry I've seen it. It's tantalizing. And I don't want to be tantalized this morning. I've taken enough already today."

Seth gave him an odd look. "I'll bet I know what's wrong with yer, Commodore. You're bust, aren't yer?"

"Here's luck." The Commodore drank half his gin. "Yes, there's still a flavor of the Old Plymouth. And you're quite right. I'm broke." He finished his drink.

Seth nodded complacently. "Thought so. Well," he added, quite amiably, "I've two rules. One is—nobody stops at White Hart for nothing. T'other is—I don't lend money." He picked up his glass and grinned at the Commodore over the top of it.

But this was one grin too many. "I'd keep on trying to buy this place if I were you, Hull. And thanks for the drink." And before Seth could stop him, the Commodore had gone.

3

At about five o'clock that afternoon, Laura, having finished a long letter to her father and finding nothing more to do, felt bored and rather discontented. Theodore had been away all the afternoon. The Commodore had not been in the office since before lunch. Nobody had called or rung up. It had been a blank afternoon. So when at last Theodore came in, though she was secretly relieved, she put to him sharply that question which women have been asking men, at every minute of each twenty-four hours, for the last fifty thousand years or so. "Where have you been?"

Theodore looked troubled. "The Commodore didn't turn up, so I've been arranging the public meeting next week with Mobbs."

Laura made a face. "Too much Mobbs."

"Did the Commodore come back here?"

"No. Nobody's been here. Nothing's happened at all. A horribly long, dreary afternoon. Tell me something interesting without Mobbs and the meeting in it."

But instead of sitting down and being cozy, Theodore moved about the room in a restless, irritating fashion. Like a lost elephant, Laura thought; and she was about to tell him so when she saw that he was seriously disturbed, and came to the conclusion that only something important could have jerked him out of his usual calm and ease.

"What's the matter?"

He stopped, gave her a look that turned her heart over, but then said: "It's about the Commodore."

"Oh!" She was disappointed rather than relieved.

"I meant to tell you earlier, Laura," he continued, very much in earnest, "but then I thought I'd better wait. You remember when the Commodore took me down to the bar this morning?"

"Yes. And I warned you about your promise. Because I knew somehow he was going to ask you to lend him some money. And that was it, wasn't it?"

Theodore sat down now. "Yes. And I kept my promise. And of course I couldn't tell him. I didn't like it. In fact, it was hateful."

"I'm not sorry, except for you," said Laura, with a touch of defiance. "I knew he'd try it on. And he's no right to."

"It wasn't like that, Laura. A man came here this morning and made him pay some bill he hadn't been expecting to pay, at least not yet. If he hadn't paid, he'd have had to abandon our Festival scheme. He was quite frank with me. And when I refused, and couldn't even explain why, he looked hurt—there was no pretense—he felt like hell about it. And so did I."

"What did you do, Theodore?"

"I ran away. I didn't know what else to do. I tell you, it was hateful." He did not look at her.

She went across to him. "It's all my fault, I suppose. I'm sorry. But I felt it would all be so ugly and wrong if he began deliberately sponging on you—"

"I tell you," he cried angrily, "it wasn't like that. Don't you understand?"

She turned away, winking back the threatening tears. The noises of the street invaded the room, which suddenly became tiny, sad, lost. Laura mumbled something.

"I'm sorry but I didn't hear you," said Theodore with that enormous melancholy patience which we apparently acquire at these times.

"I only said hell. I'm coming back." And she hurried out, snatching her bag from the table as she went.

After he had looked at his right shoe and then at his left and had then gone to the window and stared, without wonder or joy, at the Soft Furnishings Department of Jordan's Stores, she returned, tearless, freshly powdered, trim and gay, as if a party were being held in the office.

"I'm sure that's a madwoman who haunts the Ladies'. That's the third time she's asked me about Ethel, and I can't keep on telling her I don't know who Ethel is. What would you do?"

"I don't know," he said glumly.

"Don't be cross, Theodore. Let's talk sensibly about it. I don't suppose any real harm's been done. If you like, I'll explain to the Commodore that I made you promise not to lend him anything. And if it's quite genuine—and it sounds like it—and he only wants enough to keep him going until the Festival is settled, then of course you ought to lend him something. We couldn't go on without him. Or could we?"

"No, we couldn't. I know you and I will do a lot of the work, but even if we could manage it all between us, they'd never agree to our running it. No, we couldn't do without him. I wouldn't even like to try. I'm very fond of the Commodore."

"So am I, in a way," she said, "though he's rather an old scoundrel. Well, we can both see him, and explain everything. And that's settled —humph?"

But he did not return her smile, though clearly he was no longer annoyed or sulky. "I can't help wondering about him. He never turned up at Mobbs's office. He's not been here. Where is he?"

"Oh—he's probably chasing some alderman or councillors or officials," she said airily. "I'm not worried about him. Let's talk about something else. Or shall we go? I seem to have been here for days. Let's have some tea—and then walk."

They were just locking up when a chambermaid arrived with a message from Mr. Hull asking if the Commodore would go along to his private office.

"We'd better look in and see what it is," said Theodore. "It might be something important. The Commodore thinks that Hull might do a lot for us."

"He's never quite real to me," said Laura, as they went along. "He's like a huge piece of meat that walks and talks in a meaty sort of way. With very blue, angry little eyes. You can't imagine him married. Except that there are women like that too—not meaty but doughy, fat and white, with bootbutton eyes—born to be Mrs. Hulls, all keeping big pubs and going off to the races."

Seth Hull was not alone in his office. Old Mr. Jordan was there, dressed in tweeds so brown and hairy that he almost looked like a caterpillar. He was delighted to see them.

"Hello, hello! Nice young people again. Heard you the other night, young woman, asking your questions. Splendid, splendid. But what rubbish those broadcasting fellows talked! Everybody so excited about it too. People get sillier. Yes they do. Healthier, cleaner, better-looking than they used to be, but sillier—sillier and sillier."

"Sit down," Seth Hull grunted. Then he looked solemnly at them. "Will anybody take a drop of anything?"

"Nothing for me, Hull, thank you," cried Mr. Jordan. "But give these nice young people something. In love, I fancy. Nonsense to say that being in love makes you indifferent to food and drink. Always hungry and thirsty when I was in love. Glands, probably."

"We were going to have tea," said Laura hastily. She was also busy trying to imagine Mr. Jordan in love, and it was difficult.

"Two teas—an' look sharp," Hull told the telephone. Then he looked at Laura and Theodore suspiciously, as if he thought they might have been up to something fishy. "Where's Commodore?"

"We don't know," Theodore told him. "And I'm rather worried about him. I left him downstairs in the bar this morning, and we haven't seen him since."

Hull's jaw dropped and he stared at Theodore, looking like an older Tweedledee or Tweedledum. "I say!" he cried with obvious concern. "I say! It's me then. It's me."

"What's you?" asked Laura.

"Extraordinary fellow," said Mr. Jordan, thinking aloud again. "Mind seems to work slowly. You think he's stupid. Yet very artful at times. Good business head."

Hull ignored these remarks, and indeed may not have heard them. Ruefully he continued: "Took him to look at Three Black Boys. Taken with it. But something wrong, an' I guessed it right off. I says: 'You're bust, aren't yer?' He admitted it, straight out. Always been straight with me, Commodore has, that's why I took to him."

At this moment a waitress arrived with the tea. "I don't know if this is what you want, Mr. Hull," she began.

"Put 'em down, an' pop off, love, we're busy," he told her. Laura took the tray, which was generously supplied with sandwiches and cakes, and looked inquiringly at him. "Nay, start your tea, start your tea."

"It's all right," said Laura rather apologetically, "we can listen while—"

"Start your tea," he shouted, making her jump.

"Oh—damn the tea," cried Theodore angrily, getting up. "Who do you think you are, shouting at Miss Casey like that?"

"No, Theodore," cried Laura. But secretly she was thrilled by this formidable display of protection. There he was, bristling like a great golden lion.

"Nerves, you know," cried Mr. Jordan. "All nerves. These big fellows are very deceptive. They're worried, both of 'em, I can see that."

"Now, now," said Hull to Theodore, "keep calm, young man. An' I'm sorry, Miss Casey. Fact is, I'm a bit upset. Now, just get started, an' I'll go on."

"There," said Laura, a few moments later. "Now, Mr. Hull, please go on. You told him he was bust or broke or whatever it was, and he admitted it."

"That's right," said Hull, troubled. "So I told him I'd two rules, that nobody stops at White Hart for nothing, an' I don't lend money. Then he just gives me a look, makes a remark—cold like—an' walks straight out. An' I says to meself then an' there, I ses: 'Seth Hull, yer've gone too far.' Said it then an' there."

"And I should think so too," cried Laura indignantly, staring at him fiercely. "How could he stay after you'd talked to him like that?"

"I know, I know," said Hull unhappily. "Needn't rub it in, Miss Casey."

"You see," said Theodore, "he'd already asked me to lend him something—just to keep him going until the Festival—and I'd refused, and I couldn't tell him why—"

"It was because he'd promised me he wouldn't lend him anything," said Laura. "And he wouldn't tell him that."

"So he was already feeling terribly hurt," said Theodore.

"Oh—crummocks!" said Hull. And he drew in a deep breath and then blew it out noisily.

"I find all this very confusing," cried Mr. Jordan. "So either ignore me or explain it all properly. One or the other, please."

So Laura explained it all to him, while Theodore, though still eating and drinking, and Hull, still breathing hard, brooded monumentally.

"I see, I see, my dear," said Mr. Jordan, when she had done. "Very unfortunate. Only met him for a moment or two, the other night. Seemed to me the kind of man we want for this Festival business. Defects of course, but defects of his virtues. But now—where is he?"

"Another thing," said Theodore miserably. "He went to talk to the Farbridge Theater Company this morning—"

"We know," said Hull. "Saw Crandry and Whatmore. That's what Mr. Jordan and me wanted to see him about."

"Well," Theodore continued, "he told us they'd been very unpleasant—suggested he was a suspicious character and had better clear out. He defied them, said if they wanted to be rough, he could be rough too, but he admitted he was bluffing and I think he was worried about that too."

"It seems to me we've enough people against us," said Laura with some bitterness, "without beginning to quarrel among ourselves."

"Quite so. Look foolish now. Must go through with it properly," said Mr. Jordan.

"We're going through with it properly," said Hull grimly. "I'll show 'em." Then he looked severely at Laura. "But I don't know as you're one to talk. If yer hadn't made this young man promise not to lend Commodore anything—"

"Yes, I know. Now you're rubbing it in—"

"That's right. Well, now we've both done a bit o' rubbing. An' we'll leave it at that."

"But wait a minute, Mr. Hull," said Theodore. "There's something I'm not quite clear about. Did you mean it when you told the Commodore that nobody stayed here for nothing and that you never lent money?"

Hull looked rather sheepish. "In a general way I did. Couldn't keep hotel going if I didn't. Some of 'em would be trying it on all the time. But I talked like that to Commodore just to put him through it a bit."

"Was it necessary to put him through it?" said Theodore coldly.

"Now look, lad. I'll explain, an' just try an' understand. I meet all sorts, an' I wasn't born yesterday. Now this chap turns up here. He's good company, been all over, tried everything, yer might say—an' a bit fancy an' grand an' la-di-da—one o' them ready to talk yer into anything. So first time I talks to him properly—in here—I puts him through it. If he's goin' to try anything on wi' me, then he talks me into no Festival nor anything else, see? But he doesn't, he gives me a straight answer to a straight question, wi' no fancy bluffing. So we know where we are. But this morning I felt I just had to have another little go at him, to show him he couldn't pull *my* leg, an' I did it once too often. I was wrong. I can be wrong, yer know. Though not often. But this time I went an' put me foot in it. An' there yer are." And having concluded what must have seemed to him nothing less than an oration, and a deplorable lapse from his usual laconic manner, Mr. Hull breathed noisily and stared with some indignation at a photograph of the Farbridge United A.F.C.

"Mr. Hull, I understand exactly what you mean," said Laura. "And thank you very much for telling us. You do see, Theodore? I'd have done exactly the same, I think, in Mr. Hull's place. Like you, I'm very fond of the Commodore, but I felt from the first he just mustn't be allowed to do his stuff on us. That's it, isn't it, Mr. Hull?"

He grinned at her. "That's right, love. An' you an' me'll get on."

"All very delightful," cried Mr. Jordan. "But we're wasting time, wasting time. Now then. Propose we create a small Festival fund. Stop all this lending money nonsense. Three of us—Mr. Jenks, Hull, and myself—contribute a hundred pounds each."

The other two men agreed at once.

"This can be repaid if necessary from the Festival grant, if we receive one. From this fund Commodore Tribe receives a salary of, say, twenty pounds a week. and Miss Casey—no, no, my dear, allow me— a salary of seven pounds a week."

"That's way to do it," said Hull.

"But, Theodore, do you—" Laura began, but was immediately stopped both by the look he gave her and his: "Yes, I must be in this." And she realized that all three men would only be annoyed and not gratified by any protest from her about her salary, so she kept quiet and had more tea while the three of them wrote checks and arranged that Mr. Hull should be the treasurer of the fund. Then she had an idea, and slipped out.

Returning a few minutes later, she announced: "The Commodore hasn't left. I've just asked, and his things are still in his room."

"Oh—good!" Theodore sounded much relieved, and smiled at her.

"If yer'd asked, I could have told yer that," said Hull dryly.

"Oh—you knew?"

"Well, it's my hotel, yer know, Miss Casey. An' happen I'm not so green as I look."

"Not at all," cried Mr. Jordan. "Very deceptive really. Smart man when it comes to the point. Now where's Babley? Time he was here. Nearly time I was off."

"He'll be along, Mr. Jordan," said Hull. "Now—about Commodore. He may be just keeping out o' sight while he's feelin' down i' the mouth. Or he may have gone to see somebody. Anyway, soon as he comes back, we'll tell him what we've fixed. An' I'll try to make it up to him a bit. But you two might have a look round for him."

As Laura and Theodore were agreeing to do this, Mr. Babley arrived. He was a merry little man with a dispatch case—like a business gnome, Laura thought.

"Ah-ha!" he said as he came in, and when he was introduced to Laura and Theodore he said: "Ah-ha!"

"Fixed it?" Hull inquired.

"Think so. Ah-ha!" He began merrily diving into his dispatch case.

"Wonderful gardener, Babley is," said Mr. Jordan, partly addressing Laura, partly thinking aloud. "Grow anything. Like magic. You must see his carnations. Takes prizes every year."

"Ah-ha!" said Mr. Babley, pulling out documents.

"Now you two can pop off," said Hull. "Got a bit o' business to do here. But I'll give yer a tip, if yer'll keep it quiet," he added as they were about to leave. "If Crandry an' Whatmore think they can do what they like with Farbridge Theater Company, they'll soon have another think comin'. We'll show 'em."

"Ah-ha!" said Mr. Babley, who could make it fit anything.

As they turned to go downstairs, Theodore said: "I feel a lot better about everything now, Laura. Don't you?"

"Ah-ha!" said Laura, exactly like Mr. Babley; and then they both laughed all the way down to the lounge, where several people looked up and stared and frowned, life in a hotel being no laughing matter.

4

When the Commodore marched out of the Three Black Boys he had no idea where he was going. All he wanted to do was to get away from Seth Hull, whose grin, coming after those loutish remarks about stopping at his hotel for nothing and his not lending money, could not be tolerated. As he came out of Saddlers Row into Peter Place, he rejected the notion of returning to the White Hart for lunch, for there he might run into Hull again—or young Jenks, another embarrassment.

As usual, various buses were arriving and departing, for Peter Place
was the town's chief bus station. The nearest bus was already throbbing, and, without knowing or caring where it was going, the Commodore joined the half-dozen people who were boarding it. As it
lumbered along High Street and then turned toward West Farbridge,
he gave himself up to somber reflection. Crandry's threats, Frank
York's menacing triumph, the strange behavior of Theodore Jenks,
Seth Hull's jeers and grins, and that tantalizing vision of the Three
Black Boys, he reviewed them all, and remembered too, with much
self-derision, his large airy confidence before he set out, humming and
lording it, for the Palace. Then the conductor came for his fare, and
the Commodore asked how far the bus was going and was told that it
was going out past Mayton Park and the West Farbridge golf course
as far as Tonks Cross. He took a one-and-ninepenny return ticket to
Tonks Cross. Shortly afterwards, the bus stopped near a large hoarding,
at which he glanced incuriously. WHAT ARE YOU GOING TO DO? a blue
poster asked. FACE THE FUTURE, a red poster told him. As he left them
behind, he reminded himself that he had often been in far worse jams
than this, with debts piled up, all credit gone, nasty inquiries being
made, visas refused, passports vanishing, hotel managers calling for
detectives, husbands loading pistols, ladies of various tints but of similar
temperament screaming hell and damnation; and somehow he had
always found his way out of them. And now what was this? He was
merely broke again, that was all. But—and with the thought his
gloomy mood returned—he was getting on, that was the trouble; and
not as resilient as he used to be, tired of packing up and trying again,
longing at heart to settle down and make the best of one place. (And
he suddenly remembered Grace, that mysterious nice woman who
vanished; and he whisked her into a Three Black Boys, all trim and
lively; and then told himself to stop being a dam' fool.) Horace Tribe,
as the youngsters liked to say now, had just about had it. He could hear
them saying so as he dived into black despair. But then—and it was
just as the bus reached Tonks Cross—he perked up, and—by George—
defied 'em.

Straightening himself up and taking a deep breath or two, a large
commanding figure, he looked about him. Tonks Cross—or what he
could see of it—was a crossroads that had been widened into a traffic
roundabout. There were a few small shops, a garage, and a hotel, the
Bull, which looked like an old roadside inn that had been enlarged and

dolled up to catch the motor trade. An impressive symbol of that trade was visible there, in the shape of a gigantic Daimler that had been drawn up near the main entrance. It was now after one, and the Commodore was hungry. What was good enough for the Daimler was good enough for him. He entered the Bull and demanded lunch.

He was referred by the barman to a middle-aged woman, who was suffering from a cold and what appeared to be a profound distaste for catering. She looked at the Commodore as if he had burst in asking for ivory, apes, and peacocks. "Dinig roob's closed," she said. "Workmed id. Bud we cad do you a ludge id de liddle roob. Jusd wud, iz id?"

The little room, which was decorated with old whisky advertisements and yellowing photographs of the Tonks Cross Cricket Eleven all heavily mustached, was so small that there was only space in it for two tables. One of them was already occupied by two people, a prettyish woman about forty and an older man, who glared at the Commodore through outsize tortoise-shell spectacles. He could hardly have looked more indignant if the Commodore had invaded his bedroom to sell him a box of matches.

"I must say," the man said. He had a high querulous voice, admirably designed for such protests.

"Nuisance, isn't it?" said the Commodore, turning on the charm. "But I gather that their dining room's closed and this is all we have." He smiled at the woman, who had yellow curls, no nose, and enormous silly blue eyes that looked as if they might rain with tears at any moment. She smiled back, moistly.

"Yes, that's what they told us," she said. "You remember, Arthur?"

If Arthur remembered—and this could not have been difficult, for they were only just beginning lunch—he gave no sign. But he stopped staring at the Commodore, who now took a good look at him. He was a fat, white, Humpty-Dumpty sort of man, with a pouting underlip; and the Commodore knew at once that he was rich, although nothing about him definitely indicated wealth. But there are some men who exist in a perceptible aura of affluence, who seem to be surrounded everywhere by a spectral smiling host of fellow directors, shareholders, stockbrokers, solicitors and bank managers; and this Arthur was undoubtedly one of these men. He was now busy pushing his soup plate away. Few persons can be said to be busy performing such a simple action, but Arthur was one of these few. He made almost an elaborate ritual of it.

"Really, Madge, this soup!"

"I know, Arthur, but these places are always the same. Take one of your yellow things."

Looking like a vast bleached baby, Arthur took one of his yellow things. He appeared to have several bottles of colored tabloids and pills at his disposal. A waitress now appeared with meat and vegetables for Madge and Arthur, and soup for the Commodore.

"Waitress," said Arthur, "I want a large cognac, at least Three Star, and a bottle of Apollonaris, chilled, if possible."

She gave him one wild look and fled.

"I don't think she understood you, dear," said Madge.

"I made it perfectly plain what I wanted," he replied. "perfectly plain. Now—what's this?" And he began pushing his meat about with a fork.

"Oh dear—oh dear!" said Madge. "Arthur, you really can't be so particular in these places."

"It's a mystery to me," said the Commodore, trying to see how busy he could be pushing away his own soup plate, "why they bother pretending to serve soup. They're not interested in soup. They don't try to make real soup. So why don't they stop this soup nonsense and offer us a sardine or two, a few olives, a bit of potato salad, and so on? Don't you agree?"

They did agree, Madge with tentative little nods and smiles, Arthur a trifle reluctantly but with some signs of now being mollified. The woman with the cold came in and asked Arthur what he wanted, as the waitress was new and did not understand. Arthur repeated his order in a high indignant tone.

"Well, I could get you a braddy and soda, if thad would do."

"Yes, yes," said Arthur wearily, closing his eyes, "a brandy and soda. Anything for you, Madge?"

Madge hesitated. "Do you know, I think some wine would be nice."

"We have sub nize wide."

Arthur opened his eyes until they seemed to fill his giant spectacles, shuddered, and said: "A half-bottle of champagne, dry and a good year."

"We've no halve-boddles."

"Oh—a bottle then—a bottle, a bottle, a bottle." He almost screamed it.

"And bring me a large whisky and soda," said the Commodore.

The woman gave all of them a watery despairing look, then departed, after first holding open the door for the waitress, who now brought in some stewed beef, carrots, and mashed potatoes for the Commodore. He ate for several minutes without even glancing across at the other two. He was curious about them and felt that he would learn more by keeping quiet and thus encouraging them to talk to each other. They said nothing, however, until after the drinks had arrived; but then, perhaps stimulated by the brandy and champagne, perhaps no longer acutely conscious of not having the room to themselves, they began to exchange rather urgent whispers. Arthur did his best to whisper as she did, but he had not the voice for it, and the Commodore found it easy to overhear most of what he was saying. Several facts began to emerge. Their relation was an intimate one but they were not married. Some crisis was challenging them. Madge knew this part of the world and Arthur didn't. They had motored from somewhere near Bournemouth that morning, had not much farther to go but were uncertain about what they ought to do. A Gerald came into it. And then it was as though a great searchlight had been suddenly switched onto a tiny dark arena; and the Commodore knew that this was the runaway wife of Major Bulfoss.

He looked across at them now. Arthur, busy pushing away his pudding, was telling her that they ought to know more about the situation. Mrs. Bulfoss, rather flushed after several glasses of champagne, looked as though she were trying to decide whether to laugh or to cry. Arthur took two violet pills. Mrs. Bulfoss, still hesitating between laughter and tears, said that he ought to have a word with Parkinson and that while he was outside he might ask the woman to make some really nice coffee. Arthur agreed to do this, stood up, which elevated him only about six inches, since he had a long body and very short legs, and waddled out. He left the door ajar, and the Commodore went and closed it.

He looked down at Mrs. Bulfoss, who smiled shakily. "You must excuse me," he began, returning to his seat, "but I couldn't help overhearing a little of your conversation. By the way, my name is Tribe— Commodore Tribe. I've recently arrived in Farbridge, hoping to organize the Festival. Now," he continued with a winning, confidential air, "at the risk of appearing impertinent, I really think I might be of some help to you—if as I imagine, you need some information. You see, I've been in fairly constant touch with Major Bulfoss."

"Oh dear—oh dear!" cried Mrs. Bulfoss, generally excited rather than gratified or dismayed. "I'm sure it's very kind of you, Commodore Tribe. But of course it's all so difficult, isn't it?"

"Just as you please, of course," said the Commodore, waving a hand. "But if you want me to help, I'll do what I can."

"Yes—well—" and Mrs. Bulfoss hesitated, her eyes wide, her mouth open— "I'd like it very much, of course—we're finding it very difficult to decide what would be best to do—but—well, perhaps if I just had a word with Arthur—Mr. Hatchet-Ferrers—first." She rose, pulling her leopardskin coat round her shoulders, smiled weakly, and made for the door. Silly; but not a bad-looking little woman. Would it be better for all concerned if she returned to Bulfoss? The Commodore, finishing his cheese, had time to give this question some thought.

Finally, after the waitress had cleared both tables and brought in coffee for three, Hatchet-Ferrers appeared, looking immensely solemn and portentous, a Humpty-Dumpty-in-chief. "Commodore Tribe?" he began, almost as though there were dozens of chaps there and he must find the right one. "I'm Arthur Hatchet-Ferrers, sir. West British Chemicals. You're not by any chance in industry, sir?"

"No, sir," said the Commodore in much the same tone. "I'm a retired naval man. Engaged at the moment in—er—various public enterprises."

Hatchet-Ferrers now brought out the largest cigar case the Commodore had ever seen. "I have to be careful of my health, Commodore, but I still indulge myself in a good cigar. Would you care to accept one, Commodore?"

"I shall be delighted, Mr. Hatchet-Ferrers." And so he was, for it was a magnificent Havana. He lit it with the extreme care that it deserved.

"Mrs. Bulfoss reported to me what you said to her," said Hatchet-Ferrers, now seated and with his own cigar alight. "She told me your approach was made with great delicacy."

"I hope it was. I thought I might be able to give you a little useful information, Mr. Hatchet-Ferrers, but naturally the situation was—rather difficult." The Commodore sounded to himself even more solemn and portentous than the other man. But he was beginning to enjoy this.

"It is merely part of a wider situation that is even more difficult, Commodore. And Mrs. Bulfoss, I need hardly tell you, is an extremely sensitive woman. You might call her exceptionally fine-fibered."

"That's what I imagined," said the Commodore gravely. "And you yourself, Mr. Hatchet-Ferrers, I fancy, are a highly strung type. Or am I wrong?"

"You are not wrong, Commodore. Highly strung is correct. I've a great many responsibilities and important commitments, as anybody in the chemical industries will tell you. I have to take care of my health. If not exactly delicate, I am not robust. And, unlike so many people these days, Commodore, I concern myself with the thoughts and feelings of other persons. My secretary often says: 'Mr. Hatchet-Ferrers, you worry too much about other people.' And she's right. I do. I pride myself on still possessing a conscience. Now, Commodore, taking advantage of your very kind offer," he continued, leaning forward and staring hugely through his spectacles so that his eyes were like headlamps, "I should like to put to you one or two essential questions, before I ask Mrs. Bulfoss to join us for coffee. First—how is Bulfoss taking it? A frank reply, please, Commodore."

"Not too well. He's been drinking fairly hard, has had a row with some of his most important supporters, and when I called on him the other night, with his agent, he'd been dancing with the parlormaid."

Hatchet-Ferrers looked deeply shocked. "Then I have been wrong, and Mrs. Bulfoss quite right. A woman's intuition, Commodore. They don't know how they know, but they know, especially a woman like Mrs. Bulfoss. She even mentioned the parlormaid when we were discussing the situation, late last Sunday. Is there—er—any definite commitment there, do you think?"

"Not yet, unless there have been some rapid recent developments." The Commodore found it almost impossible not to imitate the other's style as well as his manner.

Hatchet-Ferrers nodded in an immense Humpty-Dumpty way. "My second question. What has been the public reaction?"

"On the whole, I think, not unfavorable to Bulfoss."

"You have reasonably good grounds for that opinion, Commodore?"

"He appeared last night on a B.B.C. question-and-answer program in Farbridge. I was interested because we had a question planted in it about the Farbridge Festival, to test public opinion. Bulfoss took the popular line, and was loudly applauded."

"I don't know how we missed that."

"He took somebody's place, almost at the last moment." The Commodore was silent for a moment, then added: "I'm very friendly with Captain Mobbs, his agent, and he doesn't seem to be worried about the

Major's position. That is, so far as the town's concerned. But he's had a row with some of the chief Conservatives because he got tight and abused their wives when they called as a deputation. Actually, I'm in very close touch with Mobbs on this Festival thing."

Hatchet-Ferrers nodded again; it was like a bow. "If you will allow me to say so, Commodore—I've formed an excellent opinion of your judgment and discretion, and I should like the opportunity of telling Mrs. Bulfoss this, while at the same time discussing the general situation with her in terms of your very valuable information." He made the Commodore feel like a shareholder at the annual general meeting. "But I'm depriving you of your coffee, Commodore, and I should like you to join me in a liqueur brandy. Will you excuse me for a minute or two? You have the time, I hope?"

"I've lots of time," said the Commodore, coming out of the spell and beginning to talk like himself again. "You go ahead. I won't explain now—but what happens to Bulfoss is rather important to me at the moment. Which is one reason why I spoke to Mrs. Bulfoss."

After Hatchet-Ferrers had gone, the Commodore poured himself a cup of coffee—and it was excellent, perhaps because Hatchet-Ferrers had told them how to make it—and he had just taken a sip or two when the woman with the cold brought in what looked like a very noble offering of old brandy. He gathered that it was the best they had in the place and that, in the woman's opinion, the gentleman was a fusspot but wonderfully free with his money. Left to enjoy this brandy, together with the coffee and the magnificent cigar, the Commodore felt better than he had done since early morning and looked forward to playing a greater part in the Bulfoss-Hatchet-Ferrers affair.

This time Mrs. Bulfoss entered alone. These two were apparently so sensitive and fine-fibered that they could not talk to him together. But all this popping in and out, like characters in a farce, was having a bad effect on the Commodore, who was beginning to feel more and more mischievous, although he looked grave enough and only wished he could achieve the immense Humpty-Dumpty solemnity of Arthur Hatchet-Ferrers.

There was no reserve now about Mrs. Bulfoss. She accepted—and indeed welcomed—the Commodore as a character in the plot. What was good enough for Arthur was more than good enough for her. She had probably been pining for a confidant.

"Tell me about that wretched girl," she began, sitting close to him.

"You mean Anita, of course, don't you? Fancy a name like that! I meant to get rid of her before I left, though of course poor Gerald had to have somebody there—I mean, to look after the house, though goodness knows that girl never did much. Arthur told me you said he'd been dancing with her. That doesn't sound like Gerald. Do tell me, please."

The Commodore, who was rather sorry now he had ever mentioned the parlormaid, briefly explained what had happened, when he and Mobbs had called on the Major. "I think," he concluded, trying to make amends, "the poor chap was feeling rather bored and lonely, you know, and I imagine she suggested it. Not important, Mrs. Bulfoss."

"Of course, I could never bear that horrid fat little Mobbs," she cried. "He may be clever at his work—but always drinking and so dreadfully common."

"I like Mobbs myself," said the Commodore. "And he really doesn't come into this, except that he's been trying to repair the damage. After all, he wasn't even there on Saturday night, when Major Bulfoss turned the Conservative women out of the house."

"You don't think that secretary girl—" she began.

"Miss Casey? No, she tried to stop him drinking and tried to warn him that these women were on their way. She's a splendid girl, and incidentally is acting as my secretary now."

"She seemed all right," Mrs. Bulfoss admitted. And then, a volatile creature, she suddenly began giggling and asked: "Do you know what Gerald actually said to that awful Mrs. Whatmore?"

"According to Miss Casey, who's quite reliable, he told them to buzz off, and when Mrs. Whatmore said he was drunk, he called her a poisonous old windbag, and then bellowed at them all, at the top of his voice, to get out."

"Oh—dear!" It is not easy to be both dismayed and delighted but somehow Mrs. Bulfoss contrived it. "Poor Gerald! But you must admit he's rather sweet."

That was not how the Commodore thought of him, but he let it pass, merely nodding and smiling.

"Did he guess it was Arthur—Mr. Hatchet-Ferrers—do you know?"

"I think Miss Casey said he did, but I'm not very certain on that point."

"Has there been—do you think, Commodore—any scandal—you know, people talking everywhere? Because I know what Farbridge is," she added bitterly. She evidently thought, as so many people appear to do, that the town she knew best was peculiarly addicted to talking scandal, as if malicious gossip were almost unknown elsewhere.

"Difficult to say," the Commodore told her gravely. "So far it's been kept fairly quiet. Mobbs has done his best there, by the way."

"Are they blaming Gerald or me?"

"You chiefly, I fancy."

"They *would*!" She blinked back a few angry tears, then leaned forward and put a hand on his arm. "It's so difficult to know what to do for the best, Commodore. You *do* understand, don't you? I mean, I felt sure that Arthur—Mr. Hatchet-Ferrers—needed me far more than Gerald did. He's adored me for years, literally for years and years, and he's so sensitive and of course rather delicate too—but you've seen for yourself what he's like. But," and now she lowered her voice, "he's much more set in his ways than I imagined, I must admit—though you mustn't say a word, of course. And then I've been thinking that perhaps I've been wrong about Gerald—there's his public position to be considered too, of course—and now I really don't know what to do for the best. We've talked and talked about it—and that's why we came up here today. And you've no idea what a relief it is, Commodore, to have somebody to talk to about it, because there's been nobody but Arthur, who sometimes says one thing and sometimes another and is quite *moody*, which I never expected, because he never seemed moody before. Gerald is dreadfully moody, of course. Perhaps all men are. Are they?"

"Yes. Men are moody. So are women. In fact, we're all moody. I'm moody myself at times," the Commodore added.

"Are you really? You don't look it somehow. But Arthur—"

She checked herself and hastily drew away from him. Mr. Hatchet-Ferrers, looking very determined, with a vague suggestion of the Napoleonic added to his general fat white Humpty-Dumptyness, had now joined them.

"Madge, Commodore Tribe," he began portentously, making an abrupt gesture with the cigar he had taken out of his mouth, "I have arrived at a decision. So kindly allow me to interrupt." He drew up a chair and wedged his enormous behind into it. "My plan involves the co-operation of Commodore Tribe." He did his nod-bow at the Commodore, then looked at Mrs. Bulfoss. "We need an intelligent and discreet intermediary. Otherwise this difficult situation, which is playing havoc with us all, may continue indefinitely. I may add, my dear, that Parkinson is now showing distinct signs of being aware of it."

"Parkinson? Oh—dear! He's the chauffeur, Commodore. A nice man really, but I'm rather terrified of him somehow."

"Parkinson," continued Hatchet-Ferrers gravely, "has been asking me what our plans are. Like all chauffeurs, he's anxious to know where we are going, so that he can look up the route and make what he calls 'good time' there. Of course I was unable to tell him, which I found extremely embarrassing."

"Yes—of course. Poor Arthur!" cried Mrs. Bulfoss. "I can just imagine what it would be like—trying to say something to Parkinson without telling him anything."

The Commodore felt tempted to say that Parkinson should be called into this conference—for Hatchet-Ferrers' manner turned it into a conference—to which he could probably make a formidable contribution.

"We need an intelligent and discreet intermediary," Hatchet-Ferrers went on, turning to the Commodore, "because there must be some discussion with Gerald Bulfoss, who in his present state of mind might be violent and create a scene. And Mrs. Bulfoss and I for various reasons do not feel equal to taking any adequate part in such a scene. She is highly strung and sensitive. So am I. Even in my industrial career I depend to some extent upon my solicitor, Strauss, of Parby, Parby, Dodgson, and Strauss, who has had a long experience of handling shareholders, to help me to—"

"Never mind about Mr. Strauss, please, Arthur," said Mrs. Bulfoss plaintively. "Go on about us."

"It was not irrelevant, my dear Madge. But Commodore Tribe is acquainted with Gerald, who is now interested in some plan for a Far-bridge Festival—"

"Oh—that ought to be amusing," cried Mrs. Bulfoss, giving herself away. For it was now quite clear to the Commodore that Mrs. Bulfoss regretted leaving her husband and preferred Hatchet-Ferrers, as well she might, as a distant adorer, occasionally sighing over her after a thumping good dinner, sending an expensive birthday present with a nice sentimental message. He was almost equally certain that Hatchet-Ferrers now shared this regret, and that, while still devoted to his Madge, he had found it impossible to fit her into his elaborate self-indulgent routine of luxury and cossetting, of pills and vintage wines,

and would like to see her safely back in Mayton Park Avenue, Farbridge.

"On the other hand," said Hatchet-Ferrers, without concluding his
previous sentence, "I hesitate to—er—embroil the Commodore in our
affairs, and naturally feel diffident about suggesting that he should act
not only as our intermediary with Gerald, but also, if necessary, as a
sort of referee, assuming of course that Gerald might be willing for
him to act in such a capacity." And he looked wistfully at the Commodore, who caught too an imploring glance from Mrs. Bulfoss.

"I'll make a bargain with you," said the Commodore briskly, and
saw Hatchet-Ferrers, who knew about bargains, brighten up at once.
"I'll undertake to talk to Major Bulfoss, to arrange a meeting between
the three of you as early as possible, this evening I hope, to do my best
to keep you from any scenes, and to arrive at a solution that will satisfy
all of you. Now if I do this, Mr. Hatchet-Ferrers, I shall ask nothing in
return for myself but only that you should perform a little public
service—make a handsome contribution to my Farbridge Festival
Fund. That's all."

"Oh—Arthur—you'll agree, won't you?"

"Of course, my dear Madge. Commodore, I must congratulate you
on your admirable clear-headed plan. I knew I was not mistaken in you,
as I told Mrs. Bulfoss. Now what do you propose to do?"

"I suggest that your car takes me at once to Mayton Park Avenue so
that I can speak to Major Bulfoss as soon as possible. You two stay here
or go for a stroll, and then as soon as I've arranged a meeting—or whatever suits everybody best—I let you know, either sending a message
with the chauffeur or telephoning you here. But you'll want the car
anyhow, so I'll send it back at once and telephone a message here.
Agreed?"

"Excellent, excellent," said Hatchet-Ferrers, extracting himself from
his chair, "I'll speak to Parkinson. Finish your brandy, my dear sir,
and then move off. Don't wait for your bill, I'll attend to that."

As the Commodore swallowed the last of his brandy, he discovered
that Mrs. Bulfoss had suddenly burst into tears. "There, there, there,
my dear Mrs. Bulfoss," he said soothingly, taking her hand and
squeezing it gently. "Now don't worry. We'll soon have everything
settled."

"You're such a comfort, Commodore. Actually I've been longing for

somebody like you to—to attend to everything, only I never thought
Arthur would agree. Do you think Gerald will?"

"I think I can manage him."

"If anybody can, I'm sure you can. You've got such a calm easy way.
Arthur's very clever but sometimes he's rather difficult—his health, I
expect. He's very fussy too—worse, I mean rather more than I thought
he'd be—but of course he's been a bachelor so long. Well, I *feel* much
better already." And she smiled at him in a foggy sort of way.

"You mightn't believe it," said the Commodore, smiling too, "but I
feel better. I'd had rather a bad morning—"

"You poor man!"

"And now I feel ready to cope with my own troubles again. Thanks
to *you!*"

"How nice!" Her enormous eyes, foolish but pretty, were now like a
June sky after a shower. Not a bad little woman, the Commodore reflected, and certainly preferable to that flouncing parlormaid. There
must be no nonsense from Bulfoss.

As soon as the Daimler had carried him out of sight of the Bull, he
tapped on the glass partition, and Parkinson, a solid, sensible-looking
fellow, drew up at the side of the road. By the time he was out of the
car, so was the Commodore, who said: "If you've no objection, I propose to ride in front with you. There's no hurry, and we might have
a talk."

"Yessir. Certainly, sir. Mind if I smoke?"

"Not at all," said the Commodore, climbing in. "Just drive slowly,
and we'll talk as we go along." He waited then until Parkinson had
walked round the vast bonnet and had seated himself again behind
the steering wheel. "It's about Mr. Hatchet-Ferrers and Mrs. Bulfoss.
If you don't want to talk, say so at once. But it's strictly between ourselves, and they've dragged me into it—I happen to know Major Bulfoss—and you might be able to tell me one or two things. I promise
they won't go any further."

"I'm on, sir," said Parkinson, as they moved majestically down the
road. "Suits me all right. Sooner they make their minds up, the better
I'll be pleased. Had about enough of this caper, if you see what I mean,
sir."

"I do," said the Commodore confidentially. "And I propose to act
on the assumption that they've had enough of it too. Am I right, Parkinson?"

"Don't know about her. Doesn't know whether it's Christmas or Tuesday, she doesn't, if you ask me. But the guv's had it all right. Won't admit it, of course, not after all this time he's been on the run-around with her. Won't admit it even to himself, but *I* know. Trouble is, he opened his mouth a bit too wide with her, after one of these fancy dinners they used to have, and then he found himself landed with her and fuss and palaver day and night. No good to the guv'nor. He likes a quiet life, all regular as clockwork, with just a bit of nice how-d'you-do on the side, if you see what I mean? Turn down here, don't we? Look at that bloke—no signal, nothing. I wouldn't give some of these blokes a sewing machine to look after. These young lorry drivers are the worst. Think they're chasing Rommel or something—proper baskets on the road, they are. But if you can get her to go back home and stay there, make no mistake about it, sir, the guv'nor'll be happy all right. And so will I. Another two or three weeks more like the last, and I'd be going back to the hire work, where I came from. Not that what you can't have the hire work for me. You see a bit of life all right, but I don't want to see a bit of life. I've seen enough, if you see what I mean, sir?"

"So have I," said the Commodore. "I'm with you there, Parkinson. Well, I'll do my best, and if there's anything you can do to back me up on the quiet, you do it."

"I'll do it. You mightn't think there's much you can do—just open-ing and shutting that door at the back and asking: 'Where to?' and keeping her steady on the road—but you'd be surprised. Just a look now and then. Putting a funny tone in your voice. Even the way you open and shut the car door. All works. Had 'em rattled this afternoon. Down there on the left isn't it? What do I do, sir? Wait for you or go back?"

"I don't want to be stranded here," the Commodore told him. "But if you see me go into the house, then you can go straight back to the Bull. This is it—Rosebank. Stop outside here and keep an eye on me, Parkinson."

Before he had time to ring the bell, he could hear the radio-gram playing dance music in the hall. A quick peep through the window on the left showed him the enthusiastic Anita in the clutch of a young man. He gave the spring bell a savage twist. The music had stopped by the time the bell had finished sounding its alarm.

"Major's not in," said Anita, regarding him sourly.

"Where is he?"

"Golfing."

"I'll wait for him." And the Commodore, determined to stand no nonsense from Anita, moved forward so that she had to give way.

The young man, who was very hot and looked horrible in a chocolate-colored suit, glanced up from the radio-gram. "I think it's all right now," he announced. "It was the valve. I'm from Pilcher's Radio Service."

"Don't mind me," said the Commodore. "I saw you dancing, and, if you're not too hot, just carry on."

"Only trying the set," the young man muttered.

"Nothing to do with him," said Anita, regarding her late partner with some contempt. "No excuse needed."

"Quite right, Anita," said the Commodore cheerfully. "Now where's the best place for me to be while I'm waiting for Major Bulfoss? I have to see him on very important business, so I'm going to wait. So where do I go?"

"Please yourself," said Anita. "Drawing room or study. Better make it the study. I ought to tidy up the drawing room before he comes back. Haven't touched it yet. Cook's gone, and it's murder trying to do it all myself." As she showed him into the study, which was small, dark, and melancholy, she continued: "I've given up trying to do this room. Anyhow he never uses it now she's not here. You're the chap that's trying to get this Festival going, aren't you? I remember now. Commander Somebody—well, Commodore then. Well, seeing it's you, I'll bring you a cuppa later on. Major won't want any tea. Not while they have a bar at the golf club."

The Commodore lowered himself into the big leather armchair, put his feet on another chair, thought for a few minutes about Major Bulfoss, Mrs. Bulfoss, Hatchet-Ferrers, heard Anita start up her vacuum cleaner in the next room, and sank slowly from Mayton Park Avenue into a bright phantasmagoria of tropical seas and islands, residencies and clubs, dazzling steps and cool shaded bars, crowded with shifting dream faces.

"Brought mine in too," Anita was saying, and reluctantly he awoke to find her standing beside him with a tray. "If you want to be snooty, I can go. But I thought it 'ud be company, and I hate to be by myself."

"No, I'm not snooty." He struggled up, yawning. "The tea and your conversation, which is frank to the point of brutality, ought to wake me up."

"I say what I think. Best way. Then if they don't like it, they can do the other thing. Sugar?"

"Thank you. No, nothing to eat." He gave her a solemn look. She was wearing the tight emerald-green dress again and a dashing make-up. "But is this brutal frankness quite in character?"

"How do you mean?"

"Well, if you're going in for this glamorous sex appeal, as you seem to be, oughtn't you to try for rather more charm, subtlety, feminine delicacy, that sort of thing? It's just a suggestion," he added hastily.

"That's what my friend thinks. But I say no." She took a noisy gulp of tea. "I bother about my looks. Have to with a nose like mine. But anybody that gets to know me has to take me as I am." She stared at him defiantly.

He sipped his tea and then began to fill a pipe. "Have you always been in domestic service?"

"What—me?" She was horrified. "Never would look at it before. I only came here 'cos he's an M.P. Thought they might take me to London and there'd be parties. What a hope! No, I've had dozens of jobs. Soon as I've had enough or anybody starts creating, I pack it up. Worked up at Whatmore's once. Too many girls there—get on your nerves. I'd six months at Jordan's—but it's murder on your feet, that job. Then I was a waitress at the Old Oak Nook. Not bad, lots of chaps coming in, but Mrs. What's-it said I was the wrong type. I could get a job at the White Hart if I wanted, chambermaid or waitress. Are you staying there?"

"Yes." And he added without thinking: "Mr. Hull's a friend of mine." Like hell he was, after what he said at the Three Black Boys that morning! And the Commodore began to wonder, as the girl rambled on, if he really had any friends left. Then they heard the Major arrive. She picked up the tray and went out, leaving the study door open.

"Oh—you're back, are you?"

"Yes—and what's the idea of the tea party?"

"Commander What's-it came and said he'd wait for you. So I gave him some tea. He's a nice old man."

"Do you mean Commodore Tribe? He's not an old man. You'll be calling me an old man next."

"Well," said Anita, "you're getting on, aren't you?"

"No, I'm not," said the Major crossly. "And put some whisky and soda and glasses in the drawing room."

"Say *please.*"

"Oh—for God's sake—"

"Language, language!"

"Don't stand there blathering," the Major shouted. "Get on with it."

"I might—and then again I might not."

"Oh—" It sounded as if Major Bulfoss might be threatened with apoplexy. The Commodore decided to stay where he was, giving the impression that he had not overheard this little interchange. He also decided that it ought not to be difficult to persuade Bulfoss that it would be better for everybody concerned if Mrs. Bulfoss came back. But he had still to make up his mind how he ought to put it to Bulfoss.

It was several minutes later when Bulfoss looked in. "Hello, Commodore." He sounded gloomy. "Been having an afternoon's golf. Had to do something for my liver. Let's go in the drawing room. More cheerful!" He led the way.

"That was a good show last night," said the Commodore cheerfully. "And young Seacombe managed to get us a line or two in a few of the important dailies."

"Did he now?" The Major brightened. "Do I come into it?"

"You do. And should be very useful."

"Much obliged for the tip you gave me about that. You and Mobbs were quite right." He said no more because Anita bounced in with the drink tray, banged it down on the small table, then banged the door behind her.

"By the way," said the Commodore, preparing the ground, "I don't want to tell tales, but when I arrived this afternoon, that young woman was dancing in the hall with the young man from the radio shop."

"She would be," said the Major, whose attitude toward Anita was clearly not what it had been several nights ago. "Cheeky little slut. Ought to boot her out, I suppose. But it's difficult, here on my own. Have a drink, old man?" As he mixed the drinks, he added: "Sorry if I didn't sound too pleased to see you. But that girl annoyed me, and I've had a stinking afternoon's golf—sliced like a lunatic. My golf's gone to pot. Well—cheers, Commodore!"

"Cheers, old man!" The moment was here. After staring reflectively at some fuzzy cattle against some improbable Highland scenery, he looked at the Major, who was stretched out on the sofa, still brooding over his golf and the hostility of the universe toward the soul of man, his features, empurpled by the wind and sun, screwed up in distaste.

"At lunchtime today, at the Bull in Tonks Cross," said the Commodore quietly and carefully, "I had the pleasure of meeting Mrs. Bulfoss."

"What?" And some of the Major's whisky jumped onto his plus-fours.

"A most attractive and charming woman, by the way," the Commodore continued, apparently ignoring the Major's goggling stare and wide-open mouth. "I gathered she'd made Hatchet-Ferrers bring her up here. In fact I had some talk with both of them."

"Do you mean to say," the Major demanded, almost a dark purple now, "that fat white pipsqueak's had the damned impudence to come up here. Why, I'll go and—"

"Wait," said the Commodore sharply, holding up a hand, like a traffic policeman.

"How d'you mean—*wait*?" the Major shouted. "What's the use of telling me to wait? If that chap's at the Bull, I'm going along there to give him a dam' good hiding." He hastily finished his drink and got up.

"And do more harm than good."

"Never mind about that." The Major glared at him suspiciously. "And anyhow this is no concern of yours, Tribe. I don't need your advice."

It was time to try a bluff. The Commodore stood up, large, calm, detached. "You're quite right, of course, Bulfoss," he said coolly. "It's no business of mine. I'll be sorry if you make an ass of yourself, if only because you might have been a help with our Festival. Also, I happen to like Mrs. Bulfoss. It's not my fault if both of them to some extent confided in me—people often do; I've never understood why—and seemed to think that I might be able to do something to settle this affair. But let's forget it." He picked up his glass and slowly drained it, giving the Major, who already appeared to be uneasy, a wondering look over the top of it. "Thanks for the drink. Incidentally I wouldn't go charging along to the Bull. I didn't say they were still there."

"Where are they then?"

The Commodore smiled and shook his head. "I'm disappointed in you, Bulfoss. Well—" And he began, very slowly, to turn away.

The Major came charging at him, grabbed his arm and shook it violently. "Look here, Tribe, you can't go like this—"

"What the devil do you think you're doing, man?" the Commodore thundered, releasing his arm and giving the Major a weighty push that sent him reeling back. "Why—you misbegotten piddling son of a seacook—old as I am, I've half a mind to plaster you against that wall. Put a hand on Horace Tribe, would you? God save us—in my time I've eaten better men than you before breakfast. By George—that little woman's worth ten of you—and God knows why she's worrying about you. Even that white slug of a businessman at least has the sense to talk quietly and reasonably to me and ask for my help. Mobbs and I were just beginning to haul you out of the mess you'd got yourself into. Now—stew in your own juice." After one last terrible bristling glare, immense, formidable, he marched to the door.

"What's going on here?" cried Anita, appearing there.

"Get back to the kitchen where you belong," the Commodore bellowed at her; and she fled. But this halt, as he had artfully foreseen, gave the Major just time enough to recover from this overwhelming onslaught, in which he had made most of the points he wanted to make, and to hurry forward, stammering apologies.

"All a mistake, old man," he was saying, not daring to put a finger on the Commodore's sleeve and yet anxious to prevent him from leaving. "I do assure you, honestly, Commodore. I'll do whatever you suggest. And I'm so worried I don't know what I'm doing."

The Commodore surveyed him coldly. "I want a plain answer to a plain question, Bulfoss. Do you want your wife back here?"

"Of course I do. All a mistake. I'd no idea—"

The Commodore cut him short. "Are you willing, as your wife and Hatchet-Ferrers have already suggested, to leave it to me? To see them here, to behave like a sensible man of the world, to be calm and considerate? If your answer is yes," he continued severely, "I might be able to arrange everything satisfactorily. No fuss, no scenes, no scandal, everybody happy. What do you say?"

To his astonishment and secret dismay, the Major, who by this time should have been thoroughly tamed, did not tell him at once to go ahead. What he did was to lean against a bookcase, gape blankly, and then mutter: "I don't understand this."

Another display of temper, the Commodore instantly decided, would be a mistake. He looked at the Major for a moment or two, shrugged almost in slow-motion, massively turned, sauntered across the hall. But before he could reach his hat, the Major had hurried after him.

"Well?" said the Commodore, who now thought that a chilly impersonal approach would be best. "What's the matter?"

"What's the matter?" And the poor fellow's voice rose to a squeak. "Everything's the matter. Look here—Tribe—you can't go like this—"

"You said that before."

"No, I mean—damn it—can't you understand? I'm all mixed up. Don't know where I am. If I've offended you, I'm sorry—"

"I'm not offended. Done with that. Now I'm just bored. Where's my hat?" And he looked carefully in the wrong place.

"You can't go," cried the Major in a frenzy. "Look here, old man—just think what it means to me. Of course I'll see them here. I'll do anything you want me to do. Leave the whole thing to you."

"No scenes, no nonsense?" The Commodore eyed him severely.

"No, I promise you. Not unless that Hatchet-Ferrers fellow starts anything."

"He won't," said the Commodore dryly. "But leave all that to me. They're willing to. In fact, they originally suggested it, of course."

"Come back and have another drink, old man. Then you can tell me what I ought to do, and fix everything. And don't think I'm not grateful. I am. I was confused, that's all. Been like it all day," he continued as they went back. "Topping my drives, slicing my approach shots, missing short putts."

Even when they were looking at each other over the whisky again, the Commodore was still the aloof organizer, the cold mastermind. "I'll ask them to be here at half-past six. You'll wait in this room. Leave me to stage-manage this business, Bulfoss."

"Yes, yes, of course. But do you think she—"

The Commodore cut him short. "If it's handled my way, and you keep yourself well in hand and do what I tell you to do, I believe with luck you'll have your wife back tonight. Now I'll telephone to them. But we don't want that girl here. Shall I tell her to clear out—or will you?"

"I think you'd better do that, old man," said the Major anxiously.

"With pleasure. You stay here. And go easy with the whisky. By the way, we may need some in the study after they arrive, but there's plenty of time to attend to that." A minute later he strode into the kitchen, where Anita jumped up and looked alarmed.

"What's the matter with you?" she demanded, not without some show of spirit, but shakily.

"Your best plan, my girl, is to rake yourself out of the way."

"Why should I? What's it got to do with you?"

"Don't talk to me like that," he began, bellowing as before and glaring at her.

"All right, all right," she cried, backing away.

"Can you go home tonight?"

"Yes, I suppose so. But what about—"

"Off you go then. Sharp!"

"Yes, but—"

"Do you want me to lose my temper again?" He asked it with a growl and a glare.

She walked across to the backstairs door, where she turned. A sudden grin appeared on her cheeky face. "My gosh, you're a fierce old chap, aren't you? Give me a thrill in a way. If the Major'd had a bit more of that, I don't know what would have happened by this time. Cheery-bye for now!"

His telephone call to the Bull brought Hatchet-Ferrers on the line almost at once. "It's not been easy," he told him, keeping his voice low, "but I've managed it. Be here, both of you, at half-past six. I take complete charge. Don't worry."

After the Major had been told what had happened, he said anxiously: "Do you think I ought to tidy up a bit?"

"On the contrary," said the Commodore. "We'll make it look worse still. I don't think that girl washed up, so bring a few dirty plates and cups from the kitchen. Yes, and some letters and any odd papers from the study. Go on. You'll soon see what I mean, Bulfoss." Left to himself, he emptied two ashtrays on to the hearth, rumpled all the cushions, scattered some ashes lightly here and there, and was busy tilting the pictures when he was interrupted.

"What on earth are you doing?"

And there was the Major's brother, Beverly Bulfoss, standing in the doorway, not merely bewildered but feeling outraged by the sight of these antics in the chief reception room of a gentleman's bijou residence in an admirable district.

"Just keep quiet, please," said the Commodore sternly, hiding his dismay. "We're rather busy here."

As if to prove the point, the Major now arrived, pushing past his brother, carrying some dirty crockery and cutlery and a mass of papers.

"Excellent, my dear fellow," said the Commodore, taking the papers and putting some of them on the floor and the rest along the sofa. "Now the plates." And as the Major came close, the Commodore, stooping a little, muttered: "Get him away or we're sunk."

"Look here, Gerald, what's all this?"

"We're busy, you know," said the Commodore reproachfully, giving the Major a chance to collect his wits.

"Don't keep telling me you're busy," cried Beverly, exasperated. "It doesn't make sense. Gerald, what's happening?"

"It's some kind of stunt," said the Major desperately. "See you some other time, Bev, old boy. Busy now."

"You're tight again," said Beverly in despair.

"Certainly not," cried the Major out of a clear conscience. "And look here, Bev, don't keep coming barging in here telling me I'm tight. Had quite enough of that."

"I should think so," said the Commodore, straightening himself up and giving the unhappy Beverly a sharp look. "I don't think you realize the harm you're doing."

"I'm not talking to you," said Beverly.

"You're not talking to anybody," said his brother. "And we've some people to see."

"What people?"

"Really," cried the Commodore, "this is too much." He wagged a finger. "I've arranged an important interview for Major Bulfoss—"

"An important interview! With dirty plates! And all that mess! I tell you, it doesn't make sense." He was jigging and screaming like a mad soprano. Clearly the Major was not equal to the situation, so now the Commodore took charge. He advanced massively upon the outraged Beverly, took him firmly by the arm, and marched him toward the front door. "Mr. Bulfoss," he said on the way, "you and I may have our differences, but we both have the interests of your brother at heart. Um? Good! Well, in the morning I've no doubt he'll be able to explain everything, but at the moment he and I are engaged in some very delicate negotiations and any interference, even from you, might ruin everything. Take my word for it, my dear sir," he said, opening the front door. "Now give him a ring in the morning."

"I believe you're a lunatic," said Beverly.

"I believe I am," the Commodore told him cheerfully, and then closed and locked the front door.

"Well, that looks better," he said, a few minutes later, surveying the drawing room, which looked as if several art students had been camping in it for a few days.

"But it looks terrible," the Major protested. "Madge will have a fit."

"That's the idea. We're creating an atmosphere. You're alone, helpless, in this forlorn and neglected room. What about a frying pan? Perhaps not. Mustn't overdo it. Now then, when she comes in, what are you going to say to her?"

"Oh—well," the Major began, with a certain hint of bluster in his tone, "I'll demand an explanation, of course, and then if she says she's sorry—well, I'll let it go at that."

"No good if you want her to stay," said the Commodore, helping himself to a drink. "Two minutes of that and she'll be back in Hatchet-Ferrers' Daimler telling the chauffeur to drive like blazes to Bournemouth. No, my dear fellow, you must begin by saying you're sorry—"

"Sorry! Damn it—it was she who—"

"Yes, yes, yes, but that's not how their minds work. You must begin by saying you're sorry, and that you've had a terrible time—you might push that eggy plate away then with your foot—but it probably served you right."

"I must say, Commodore, that seems a bit thick."

"It's a bit thick at first, but it gets thinner very soon. Once you've said it's all your fault and you've asked her to forgive you, then everything's set. But it's the only way. And don't forget," he added severely, "you promised to be entirely guided by me."

"I know. But I must say when a chap's wife—"

"And don't forget too," the Commodore continued with the same severity, "that Arthur Hatchet-Ferrers, though he may look like a spectacled goose egg and talk like an address to debenture holders, has been her devoted admirer for years, is lost in wonder and admiration at the fineness of her fiber, and is rich enough to keep her in Mayfair, Bournemouth, and Cannes, for the rest of her life without her ever setting eyes on a saucepan or a box of soap flakes again. Whereas here—"

"Yes, yes, old man," said the Major hastily and uneasily. "See what you mean. I'll say I'm sorry then. But suppose she asks me what I'm sorry about—eh?"

"It's not likely. But if she does, then you're sorry for your neglect, your lack of sympathy, understanding, imagination, for your—"

"All right, I get the idea. Think I might risk another drink?"

"Just one, to relax you. By the way, what about the study?"

"I've put some in there. Though I must say—if this fellow Hatchet-Ferrers thinks he's coming here to booze at my expense—"

"No, no, no. And remember our agreement. Keep calm, leave it all to me, and your troubles will be over. Cheers!"

"Happy Days!" said the Major thoughtfully.

The telephone rang in the hall. "I'll attend to it," said the Commodore, hurrying to the door.

"But dash it," said the Major, "it's my telephone."

"Yes, but supposing it's Hatchet-Ferrers. Too risky," the Commodore threw back over his shoulder. But it was Captain Mobbs.

"Better not bother him now," said the Commodore in a low voice. "Commodore Tribe here, my dear chap, and I'm hoping to have settled his domestic affairs within the next hour or so. No, leave us to it. Look in at the White Hart about nine, and I hope to have some news for you."

At twenty-past six Major Bulfoss, who had been wandering restlessly round the drawing room and would have straightened the pictures if the Commodore had not stopped him, came to a halt near the decanter, cleared his throat, and said: "Look here, Commodore, I really think I ought to have another drink. Just to relax me. I'm not relaxed. What do you think?"

"A small one, then. I'll do it." He gave his host a small one and himself a large one. "Happy Days! You know, Bulfoss, there's one thing about you that surprises and delights me—if you'll allow me to say so."

"Certainly, old man." The Major looked and sounded much gratified. "What is it?"

"It's the way you're able to lay your hands on all this excellent whisky."

"Oh—that. We've always done the estate business for Beggs and Morley, the brewers—they own a lot of pubs around here—and Freddy Beggs can always find me a case of good whisky. You ought to meet Freddy."

"Certainly I should," said the Commodore thoughtfully. "He ought to be a patron of the Farbridge Festival. Where do I find him? Or, better still, give me a note to him. It'll keep you nicely occupied for a few minutes."

And so it did. Just after the Commodore had slipped the letter of

introduction into his inside pocket, which was on the same large scale
as his coat and himself, they heard the urgent summons of the front
door bell.

"Here we go," said the Commodore. "Now remember. Keep calm
and leave all the moves to me. Stay here. Don't move. And as soon as
your wife appears, tell her you're sorry."

Hatchet-Ferrers was taking no chances. He had sent Parkinson to
the door. The Daimler was in the drive, but only just, and had been
driven round so that it was ready to be off at once. "Wants to know if
it's all right," said Parkinson. "If you see what I mean, sir? Bit on the
cautious side, the guv'nor is."

"All is well," the Commodore announced grandly, and was so
pleased with the phrase that he repeated it when he brought Mrs. Bulfoss and Hatchet-Ferrers into the hall. Mrs. Bulfoss was less nervous
than he had thought she might be, perhaps because she was entering
her own house, a familiar kingdom. But Hatchet-Ferrers was a
Humpty-Dumpty on the narrowest of walls.

"Where's Gerald?" she whispered.

"Drawing room," whispered the Commodore.

"Everything looks terribly neglected."

"Wait till you see the drawing room," he whispered. "Looks as if
the army had taken over. This way—we're going into the study."

Hatchet-Ferrers, a greenish goose egg, was trying to waddle on tip-
toe and was finding it far from easy. The three of them went along the
hall like an operatic trio of moonlit conspirators, with the voices and
orchestra missing.

"Now then," cried the Commodore heartily, when they were safely
in the study, "here we are. I don't say it's been easy, but now I have
the whole thing under control."

"Excellent, excellent," said Hatchet-Ferrers, dabbing at his enormous
face with a beautiful handkerchief smelling of eau-de-Cologne.

"I can't believe the drawing room looks any worse than this," said
Mrs. Bulfoss, who was at the moment more housewife than wife.

"Ten times worse," the Commodore told her briskly. "No comparison. Remember, there's no staff here now. I had to send that parlormaid home."

"Oh did you?" cried Mrs. Bulfoss, with a grateful glance. "I'm so
glad. You really are a wonderful man. But what happens now?" In
sharp contrast to her Arthur, who was obviously ill at ease and rather

apprehensive, she gave the impression now that she was almost ready
to enjoy the proceedings. Her cheeks were flushed a little; there was a
sparkle in her eye.

The Commodore gave her an approving nod. "You're looking splendid, you know. Very pretty. Now—your husband's waiting for you in
the drawing room. All set."

"And I hope," said Mrs. Bulfoss, taking out the sparkle and pulling
down her mouth a little, "that he's ready to say he's sorry."

Hatchet-Ferrers gave her a wondering look.

"Certainly," said the Commodore smoothly. "And he *is* sorry too.
He told me so. But please remember, he's paid heavily for it, poor
fellow. Now then, Mrs. Bulfoss." And he opened the door for her with
something of a flourish. After closing it after her, he moved Hatchet-
Ferrers gently into the armchair, mixed two large whiskies and sodas
with great dexterity, handed one over, then pulled up an upright chair
as close as he could, so that he sat towering above the other man.

"Your health, my dear fellow," he said softly.

"Thank you, Commodore," Hatchet-Ferrers closed his eyes, drank,
then opened them wide behind the giant lenses. "I must congratulate
you on the way you seem to be handling this business. Although, of
course, we're not out of the wood yet."

"Not far off," said the Commodore confidently. Then he stared
straight into the spectacles and spoke in a very deep quiet tone. "A
delightful woman. A charming woman. If I may say so, I admire your
taste there. The perfect friend, I have no doubt. But in confidence—"
and he hesitated.

"Yes, yes, strictly between ourselves, of course—"

"For a man with your responsibilities and commitments, with your
temperament, in your state of health, my dear Hatchet-Ferrers—a mistake. As one man of the world to another, I repeat, between ourselves,
a mistake."

"There's something in what you say, Commodore. And perhaps,
again very much between ourselves, I allowed myself to be carried
away, I was rather rash."

"I'd have done the same myself," the Commodore admitted. "Have
done, in my time. But there it is. Now let's change the subject. Has
your concern any office here in Farbridge?"

Hatchet-Ferrers looked surprised. "No. There's a small agency here
that handles our products. Why?"

"It's people like you we need to support our Festival scheme. To advertise Britain's recovery. To instruct and amuse the people. It seems to me that a handsome contribution to our Festival Fund might be regarded, for tax purposes, as a legitimate business expense."

A smile, the first he had ventured since he had arrived in the house, flickered on the pouting lips and behind the spectacles. "I had already considered that, naturally, my dear Commodore. And fortunately I always carry two checkbooks. One for my private account and the other for business expenses. You could let me have an official receipt?"

"By post, if you leave your address, my dear fellow. Our office is closed now, of course. It's still early days. Later we shall probably be working day and night. Music, drama, pageants, processions, exhibitions, lectures, flags, and fireworks." He waved an arm impressively. "As local Member, Bulfoss is supporting us. And I hope," he added, dropping his voice again, "that as our Member's wife, Mrs. Bulfoss will be able to play a prominent part both in our campaign and the actual festivities. She seemed rather excited about it, you noticed? Keep her interested —and amused." He took a drink, leaned back, and hummed a little.

"I wonder what's happening," the other said, after a pause. He gave the Commodore an anxious glance.

"I'll reconnoiter. Help yourself to another drink if you feel like one." The Commodore went out, but was back within a couple of minutes. "Everything going well, I think," he reported cheerfully. "But so far as I could gather, just at the moment negotiations are rather bogged down by some discussion, brisk but not unamiable, about a washing machine."

"He would never allow her to buy one," said Hatchet-Ferrers. "Not even on hire-purchase terms. Perhaps, if all goes well, I might—"

"A capital idea, only needing a little tact. If she's making a condition of it, I might tell her that you'll oblige there. Excuse me." He knocked on the drawing-room door, opened it an inch or two, without looking in, and called her outside. She came out looking flushed and tearful and excited, and, closing the door behind her, he took her arm, which was trembling, and led her a few paces into the hall. "I can arrange for Hatchet-Ferrers to buy you that washing machine," he told her confidentially. "Leave that to me. So don't make a condition of it."

"I nearly died when I saw that room," she whispered. "Poor Gerald! Is Arthur all right?"

"Yes, yes, in excellent form. But anxious for you to be happy. And, I fancy," he added, "rather anxious to get away."

"Yes, I know." She nodded, smiled, and returned to the Major.

"Going well, I think," said the Commodore, back in the study. "She asked about you. Rather worried, you know. I said you were anxious for her to be happy. And also would like to get away."

Hatchet-Ferrers looked grave—he could look graver than anybody the Commodore had met for years—pursed his lips, closed his eyes, did his Humpty-Dumpty nod-bow. "I must tell you, Commodore," he said, opening his eyes, "how much impressed I am by your handling of this business. At that hotel after lunch, as you will remember, I had one of my flashes and asked you to act as our intermediary. I simply said to myself: 'This is the man to do it.' Just as I knew when the moment had arrived to merge four companies into West British Chemicals. That too came in a flash. 'Hatchet-Ferrers,' some fellows say to me, 'you're a lucky man.' What they forget is that I happen to combine these flashes and sudden decisions, which terrify some of my colleagues, with a painstaking attention to ordinary day-by-day business. The fact is," he cried, almost in an ecstasy of self-appreciation, "I'm both methodical *and* intuitive, a very rare combination."

"Very rare," said the Commodore, firmly but rather mournfully as though he had been combing the globe for such fellows. "Very rare indeed."

"But what I was about to say—was that a man like yourself, capable of negotiating a delicate little affair like this with such skill, such firmness and tact, is wasting time organizing a Festival. We need men like you in industry—"

The Commodore checked him. "I'm stopping you, my dear fellow, not because I disagree but because whenever anybody talks to me like that somehow no good comes of it. I may be merely superstitious—"

Mrs. Bulfoss hurried in. "Everything's all right," she cried. "But I should hate you to go, Arthur, before you've just had a word or two with Gerald, even if you only shake hands and say hello nicely. I've told him that," she looked at the Commodore now, "but he's being rather obstinate about it. Could you do anything, please, Commodore?"

"Certainly." The Commodore waited a moment, then gave them their orders clearly and rapidly. "You two say goodbye here. I'll speak to Major Bulfoss. Then, while I'm bringing Mr. Hatchet-Ferrers and Major Bulfoss together, and the three of us are enjoying a friendly drink, you, Mrs. Bulfoss, will have your luggage removed from the car by Parkinson and then retire upstairs. This will avoid any awkwardness at the last moment, when Mr. Hatchet-Ferrers and I will leave you. Is that clearly understood? Right."

Major Bulfoss was busy tidying up the room when the Commodore joined him. He looked none too pleased when he saw who it was. "Thought you'd probably gone."

"I'm leaving in a few minutes," said the Commodore, "so don't trouble to thank me for all I've done for you."

"I wasn't aware," the Major began.

"Whenever anybody says that in that tone of voice, I always chip in quickly," said the Commodore firmly. "It merely signals the arrival of some pompous bilge. What I came in to say was that you're making a great mistake taking a high line about Hatchet-Ferrers."

"What? A fellow who—"

"Now, now, now! It'll take you five minutes, and cost you two smiles and a drink. Then what happens? First, you please your wife. Secondly, you please me, and though at the moment you seem to regard me as a nuisance, the fact remains I've tidied up your domestic life for you, perhaps your public life too. Thirdly, you please Hatchet-Ferrers, instead of leaving him feeling resentful, and I need hardly remind you that he's a man with a great deal of wealth and influence. Fourthly, you'll also please your better self by behaving like a big man and not like a small one." By this time his tone was easy and persuasive and he was smiling, and, try as he might, the Major could sulk no longer.

Five minutes later, they were shaking hands, Hatchet-Ferrers not without some signs of apprehension, the Major somewhat grumpily. Crying "Just one for the road, I think," the Commodore was hastily filling glasses.

"Rather warmer today," said Hatchet-Ferrers anxiously. "A touch of spring, eh?"

"Haven't noticed it," the Major grunted. "Dam' parky out on the West Farbridge course this afternoon."

A silence, during which the Commodore handed them their glasses. Something had to be done about it. "Well, let's have a toast," he told them. "I'll drink to anything except golf, cricket, or anybody's Old School."

"What's wrong with 'em?" the Major demanded, transferring his feeling of aggression from Hatchet-Ferrers to the Commodore, as the latter thought he would.

"Exactly. Just what I was about to say," said Hatchet-Ferrers, staring reproachfully at the Commodore.

"As soon as I came back to England," the Commodore observed loftily, his eye challenging both of them, "I find grown men talking like thirteen-year-old boys. Games and Schools. Schools and Games. 'Were you there in Stinker Brown's time?' 'He's the only chap who made fifty-seven, fourth wicket down, on a Thursday.' Schoolboy bosh! I drink to its confusion and damnation." And he drank what was in fact a rather weak whisky and soda as if he were downing a half-pint of vodka.

"You're talking rot," said the Major. "But then you might be a bit bottled, old man." And then he grinned and winked at Hatchet-Ferrers.

"I share your views and your suspicion, Major Bulfoss," said Hatchet-Ferrers, smiling.

"You're against me, eh?"

"Definitely, Commodore."

"Absolutely, old man."

"Then I must leave you. And I must take Hatchet-Ferrers away—or he must take me away—whichever you prefer. Shake hands, gentlemen. Goodnight, Major—and remember. Stand by the Festival, and the Festival will stand by you. We might even have you photographed together, standing by each other, the Major on the right, the Festival on the left. Goodnight, and sweet dreams."

"Are you all right, Commodore?" asked Hatchet-Ferrers. They were now sitting in the Daimler, and Parkinson was about to climb behind his wheel.

"My dear fellow, never felt better. But something had to be done. It was touch and go. When I went in, to suggest he should see you, he snarled at me like a hungry tiger. Ferocious chap, you know, Bulfoss. Threw out some prominent Conservative women the other Saturday— about half a ton of political womanhood. Then, one night last week when I was there, he began chucking things about and smashing 'em. Hell of a fellow. I tell you, it was touch and go. And something had to be done to ease the situation, so I did it, as you saw. Then you parted friends. And, as I promised you from the first, now everybody's happy. You're dropping me at the White Hart, I trust?"

"Yes, and I'll come in, just for a moment."

He stayed long enough to write a check at the reception desk. "For your Festival Fund, my dear Commodore," he said gravely, "and as a small token of my gratitude. You will, I hope, keep in touch with her, to make sure she's not too unhappy. She has great confidence in you, I know."

It was in the dining room that Laura came flying across to him, with Theodore moving massively in support of her.

"We've been looking for you everywhere," she cried. "It was all a mistake. Theodore made a silly promise to me about not lending you any money. I'm sorry—it was all my fault. And Mr. Hull's sorry too— he was only teasing you, and he's been awfully worried."

"My dear child," he said, smiling, "I've had such an amusing time since this morning that I'd almost forgotten what happened before. Sit down. You too, Theodore."

"We've started a Festival Fund," said Theodore. "It amounts to three hundred pounds."

The Commodore shook his head. "It amounts to five hundred and fifty pounds now, my boy. Look at this." They stared at the check he laid on the table.

"West British Chemicals?"

"Among the keenest supporters of the Festival idea," said the Commodore gravely. "And now what is there to eat? I had a very poor lunch—at the Bull at Tonks Cross. I don't recommend it, though I'm not sorry I went there. Hello, Seth! Come to apologize?"

"That's right," said Mr. Hull.

5

Sitting in the car with Mobbs was a tight squeeze for Theodore. He was large; Mobbs, though short, was fat; and the car was small. But when they rattled out of Farbridge, to begin their day's tour of the nobility and gentry, Theodore forgot his discomfort. He stared about him appreciatively. It was a fine morning, with everything clear and bright, except the distant hills which were hazy and bluish and nameless, the entrancing geography of romance. The road curved invitingly in the sunlight; under dazzling signposts the Automobile Association saluted briskly; there were shining clusters of primroses on the hedge banks, and young lambs frolicking in the meadows; the copses looked as if they were thinly veiled in green mist; roadhouses and ice-cream shops and filling stations were brave in new paint; and together with a reek of petrol and carbon monoxide, the infinite tender promise of spring was in the air.

"I can see that soon all this will be very beautiful," said Theodore. "It is all strange to me. Like a kind of dream."

"Like a what, old boy?" shouted Mobbs, busy at the wheel.

"A dream."

"Hardly ever dream," said Mobbs. "But when I do, it's always something dashed peculiar, bloody rum. Got a nice day for our little trip, haven't we? Glad to be running round a bit, for a change."

"Laura thinks we're wasting time, that it's not worth while getting these people's names as patrons and supporters."

"Never take any notice of what girls think—or what they say they think. All my eye, old boy. She probably imagines you're going to be tootling round to a lot of big houses full of dashing pretty wenches. I only wish she was right. But I know better. Just check the list again, old boy, will you? Start with old Lady Barth, don't we?"

Theodore examined the typewritten list of names and addresses. "Yes, Lady Barth first. Then Admiral Broadwater. Then we go to Brant-in-the-Hollow, where we're giving lunch to Sir Barclay and Lady Gishforth in the pub. Next, Field-Marshal Watton. Then, Barnleysale Castle—Lord Barnleysale, Lady Felicia—"

"Right, old boy—all present and correct. And I've got the route all worked out. Takes us round in a half-circle, about eighty miles roughly from my office and back again. We take a turn to the left somewhere along here to get to Lady Barth's place."

"She's the deaf old woman that Laura used to see in the Bulfoss office," said Theodore. "Do you know her?"

"Met her once, old boy, though I don't suppose she'll remember. Arranged a joint meeting with Crick, who's my opposite number for this part of the County, and she sat on the platform. Old crocodile. You'll have to soften her up, laddie. Knows we're coming, of course?"

"Yes, we wrote to them all. It'll be interesting to me to meet these people and see their houses. The only mansion I've visited so far had been turned into a factory." And he explained about Brant Manor and Mr. Hookwood and Group Captain Trevone.

"I like the sound of them better than these high-toned characters we're seeing today," said Mobbs. "For a Conservative Party agent, I'm not too strong on the nobility and gentry, old boy. One reason why I don't handle any rural constituencies. To be candid—the nobs don't take to me, and between ourselves I couldn't care less. I'm really depending on you today, especially with the women, who generally think I'm a common little sausage, just when I'm thinking they're a lot of painted maypoles and screaming old hags. But of course we've got a mixed batch today. And I'll probably manage the two Service blokes better than you will. Anyhow, it's a day out."

They had now turned off the main road, and after passing through a village they found themselves held up at a level crossing, where the gates were closed although there was as yet neither sight nor sound of an approaching train.

"These aristocrats who have no money now, aren't you sorry for them?" Theodore asked, as they waited.

"Only for a few quiet decent types," said Mobbs, "the sort who've always tried to behave like aristocrats. The trouble about most of 'em is that they haven't. They've wanted it both ways. Some of 'em would do anything for money—things you and I wouldn't touch with a barge-pole—touting and tarting and pimping round the place, yet suppose you ought to respect and admire 'em because of their family names. Not good enough, old boy. *Noblesse* without the *oblige*—you're out. Can't expect people to pay tribute to a night-club duke and countesses who are up for auction to the advertising agencies. But the quiet decent types, trying to keep an estate in order and do a bit of public service, I'm sorry for them. But they kept out of the gossip columns and picture papers. Here she comes. What do they call 'em *British* Railways for? We know we're not in Switzerland or Sweden, and we know they're railways. Dam' silly, I call it."

Farther along they turned to the right up a badly rutted lane that finally brought them to a dilapidated gateway. "This must be it," said Mobbs, swinging the car into a drive. "Don't suppose this old girl can keep anything up because she spends so much on lawyers. Always bringing actions or fighting 'em, my spies tell me."

Just before the drive curved up toward the house, which was a magnificent Queen Anne mansion smiling sleepily in the sunshine, they saw below the terrace a rock garden where two people were talking, both old and bent. The man was obviously a gardener. The old woman might be Lady Barth. Mobbs stopped the car and they got out. She was now approaching them in a queer kind of hobble-trot, like a witch. She was wearing old tweeds, rubber boots, a shapeless felt hat, but her rings flashed in the sun.

"Go away," she screeched, waving an arm. "Go on. At once. What next?"

"Lady Barth?" shouted Theodore, going to meet her.

"Go on. Hurry up. Get back in your horrible motor and go away. I've told you before," she yelled, pointing at Mobbs. Then, looking harder at Theodore, she hesitated, fumbled in her pocket, jammed some spectacles on her yellow beak, and stared again.

"Don't tell me you're one of these County Council men," she screamed at him.

He went closer, smiled, and said in a loud voice: "No, Lady Barth. Nothing to do with the County Council. Captain Mobbs and I have come to see you about the Farbridge Festival. Didn't you get our letter?"

"He's Captain Mobbs, is he? Well, he doesn't look it. Though I remember him now. Major Bulfoss' agent. Silly fellow—Gerald Bulfoss. Wife's left him—and I don't blame her."

"No," Theodore shouted. "She came back yesterday."

"Did she indeed?" Lady Barth's tone expressed the liveliest interest. "I must hear about this, young man. We'll go into the house. Hear better indoors. Come along, Captain Mobbs—don't stand there grinning." She scrambled into the car, and was screaming at them to drive on before they had had time to reach their seats. Then she kept silent until Mobbs had driven them up to the main entrance. "Come along, come along," she screeched, almost tumbling out, then leading them at a hobble-trot across the spacious paneled hall to a small room on the left. It was octagonal-shaped, with its panels painted a dark green, and must at one time have been very charming, but now it looked like a mad office. Once exquisite bookcases, desks, tables, were overflowing with broken-backed files, bundles of documents, letters tied with tape or jabbed onto skewers, folders bursting with newspaper clippings, dusty piles of periodicals, old directories; and in the middle of this mournful confusion, seated behind the largest and oldest typewriter Theodore had ever seen, was a plump, pink-and-white, silver-haired woman who looked like a rather old-fashioned advertisement for somebody's cocoa.

"Mrs. Wintle," Lady Barth screeched at her. And Mrs. Wintle produced a prim little nod and smile, as though somebody had gently whispered her name.

"My secretary," Lady Barth explained. "And deafer than I am. Deaf as a post."

Mrs. Wintle, behind her vast primitive machine, nodded and smiled again, this time not so prim but much sweeter, like everybody's Mother in technicolor.

"My godfathers!" Mobbs muttered. "This is going to be grim, old boy. Leave it to you." He looked about for a chair that was not stacked high with papers, could not find one, and compromised by leaning against a bookcase, with the result that a lot of stuff began sliding off the shelf in front of the glass doors. Fortunately, Lady Barth did not notice what was happening, for she was now leaning over Mrs. Wintle, resting her bejeweled claws on the top of the ancient typewriter.

"Major Bulfoss' wife," she was shouting. "You remember? Came back yesterday. God knows why. Silly woman, though."

Mrs. Wintle, wearing a fixed smile, was now wagging away like a clockwork figure. Theodore began to find her rather sinister and decided not to look at her again if he could possibly avoid it. Lady Barth was now scrabbling among the letters on the desk.

"Here it is," she screeched. "Captain Mobbs and Mr. Jenks. You Mr. Jenks? Good! But why do you want to give these Farbridge people a Festival? They get everything for nothing these days, and they're dreadful people, most of 'em. You don't know them. I do. Why give them anything?"

"Take over, old boy," Mobbs was muttering. "Can't face it."

Bending over Lady Barth, Theodore explained in the loudest and clearest tone he could contrive that the Festival would be largely paid for by the people of Farbridge, and then gave her a brief outline of what they hoped to do during the celebrations.

"I think," said Mrs. Wintle in a quiet spaced-out manner, as though a mechanical aunt had been wired for sound, "that this Festival would be very nice, Lady Barth."

"It's what?" Lady Barth shouted.

"Yes, I do think so," said Mrs. Wintle, smiling, nodding.

"My godfathers!" said Mobbs. "Blue murder, old boy!"

"Can't give you any money," Lady Barth screamed at Theodore. "Haven't got any, and if I had any, I wouldn't give those people a penny." She rushed to the wall, kicking away three old files that promptly burst open, and gave a jerk to a bellpull of dusty faded rose velvet.

"We don't want any money, Lady Barth," Theodore thundered. "Just your name as a patron and supporter."

"May or June?" asked Mrs. Wintle winsomely.

"God's truth," groaned Mobbs.

"Very well, you can have it," cried Lady Barth, smiling at Theodore.

A little old butler, almost a decayed midget, now arrived, carrying a gray cat with furious golden eyes. They gave the impression they were about to perform some circus act.

"Put him down, Fleming, put him down at once," Lady Barth screeched. "I've told you before. He doesn't really enjoy it. And bring some biscuits and sherry or something."

"No sherry, m'lady."

"Well, gin or something."

"No gin, m'lady."

"Well, something to drink. Hurry up."

The butler departed, leaving the cat with them. It made at once for Mobbs, who was now sweating hard. He moved away and brought down some more stuff from the bookcase shelf.

"And if you're giving any parties," Lady Barth told Theodore, "just see that I'm invited. Don't forget. I love parties, and hardly anybody seems to give them nowadays. Now tell me about Mrs. Bulfoss."

As he tried to tell her about Mrs. Bulfoss, the butler returned, shakily carrying a tray on which were biscuits, glasses, and a bottle of Swedish schnapps.

"Didn't know I had that," cried Lady Barth, rescuing the bottle from the tray. "Greville must have left it. Where had he been the last time he came here, Fleming?"

"Karachi," the butler boomed mournfully.

"Go on about Mrs. Bulfoss. And don't joggle, Fleming, or I can't fill the glasses properly."

The biscuits were very soft and stale. The schnapps, which Lady Barth had poured out as if it were lemonade, was very strong. Mobbs, after taking a good swig, was coughing and crying, and spilled some of his schnapps on the cat, who was clawing his trousers. Theodore, with a mouth full of biscuit, was still trying to answer Lady Barth's questions about Mrs. Bulfoss. And Mrs. Wintle's mechanical nods and smiles were now punctuated with loud hiccups.

"Well, I enjoyed that," Lady Barth shouted, as she stood in the doorway. "Put my name down. And don't forget about the parties."

Mobbs kept silent until they were nearly out of the drive. Then, after dividing his attention between driving and mopping his face, he observed: "We've got her name, for what it's worth. But if you ask me, old boy, that was bloody blue murder. Could never have tackled it myself. But you can leave the Admiral to me. Played golf with him not long ago. The night I first met the Commodore." And he gave Theodore an account of what had happened at the Bell at Tredberrow, and by the time he had concluded it they were miles away from Lady Barth and not far from the Admiral's house.

This turned out to be an enlarged old farmhouse, into which they were admitted by a tall nervous young woman who introduced herself as the Admiral's niece. "Uncle Hector's got lumbago again, but he's downstairs, waiting for you in the sitting room." They were standing in a narrow hall now; and she lowered her voice. "It's not anything that might upset him, is it?"

"Not in the least," said Mobbs heartily. "Won't take ten minutes, and he'll probably enjoy it." Mobbs was all confidence here, very different from the man he had been at Lady Barth's.

"Oh—well—that's all right then," said the niece. But as soon as she had shown them into the sitting room, she promptly departed. It was a low-ceilinged room, with squat bay windows, white walls, solid furniture, all very trim, and with just a suggestion of the battleship about it. The Admiral, a short, thick-set, brown old boy, was lying on a broad couch, with a copy of *The Times* across his knees.

"Can't get up, Mobbs," he grunted. "This confounded lumbago again. Been laid up for nearly a week. No exercise. Livery as the devil, into the bargain. What a life! Hope you've not come to drag me into one of your political jamborees. If you have, the answer's no."

"No, nothing like that, Admiral," said Mobbs in his most soothing tone. "A group of us in Farbridge are trying to organize a Festival there. Most people are in favor of it, but there's still some opposition. So Jenks and I are running round, persuading a few influential people like yourself, Admiral, to give us their names as patrons and supporters. We've just collected Lady Barth, who's very keen, and we're on our way to see Sir Barclay Gishforth, Field-Marshal Watton, and Lord Barnleysale. All good names."

"Humph! Don't quite catch on to the idea yet, Mobbs. And seems to me what we need now is more work and harder work and more attention to duty, and a bit less idling about and beer and skittles."

"I couldn't agree with you more," said Mobbs. "Just what I keep saying. But a Festival might help to ginger the people up. My Member, Major Bulfoss, is keen on the idea. And some of the Labour crowd—that chap, Muleford, for instance—are against it. Jenks'll explain what the doings will be."

Theodore told him what they hoped to do during the Festival.

The Admiral showed no sign of enthusiasm. "Not much in my line. A few good boxing shows—tug o' war—that sort of thing would do 'em more good. Show 'em how to keep fit. However, if you want to put me down as a supporter, Mobbs, I suppose you can, so long as you don't ask me to do anything. Who's running the show? You fellows?"

"Oh—no," cried Mobbs, looking pleased. "Glad you asked that, Admiral. The chap who's really got the thing going—and he's an absolutely first-class fellow—is one of your blue-water men—and you've met him already, the other night at Tredberrow, you remember?—Commodore Tribe."

If he had picked up the large brass ashtray, made out of a shellcase, and thrown it at the Admiral, Mobbs could not have created a more dramatic effect. Several things happened to the Admiral in quick succession. First, his eyes and his mouth opened wide. Then he gave a convulsive jerk, tried to sit up, was instantly reminded by his back muscles that he was suffering from lumbago, and was plunged at once into physical as well as mental suffering. Strange muffled oaths rolled out of the mahogany face.

"I've made some coffee," the niece announced brightly, entering with a tray.

"Bla—Bloo—Bluh—Take it away," he yelled.

"But, Uncle—"

"Take the dam' stuff away," he roared. He said nothing more for several seconds after she had gone. But this steely silence, during which he was pulling himself together, was if anything more terrible than the storm that preceded it. He looked at Mobbs. He looked at Theodore. He looked at Mobbs again. The hurricane itself had blown itself out, but there was something horribly treacherous about this calm, as if they were now in the center of the Sargasso Sea.

"Tribe," said the Admiral. "That's the fellow. Tribe. Horace Tribe." He spoke slowly, very quietly, but it was like a man beginning to sharpen a cutlass. "Calls himself Commodore Tribe now. Commodore! That's the fellow. I thought I recognized him that night at Tredberrow.

And I noticed too that he gave me a wide berth. So I made some inquiries, a day or two afterwards when I was in town. Asked old Buffy
Jones and one or two other men of my time. Looked up a few records.
In 1919, Portsmouth, he was severely reprimanded. In 1922, Malta, he
was yanked in front of a court of inquiry and only got off by the skin
of his teeth. Sent to India, got into trouble there, but managed to talk
himself into some poodle-faking billet in one of those dago South
American countries. More trouble—complaints to the F.O. and complaints to the Admiralty—has to resign his commission. Talks himself
into some longshore job with another of those dago countries, where
Buffy Jones, showing the flag, meets him covered with gold lace and
looking like a fellow opening cab doors outside a picture palace." The
fuse, which up to this moment had been quietly hissing, now went
spluttering and cracking into the main explosive charge. "Commodore!" the Admiral yelled. "Commodore my bloody backside! Fellow's
a charlatan, an adventurer, a brass-faced, monkey-faking scoundrel.
And if ever I set eyes on him again, I'll tell him so. Ought to be kicked
out of the country. And you fellows have the damned face to come
here and ask me to lend my name to one of his swindles!"

"Steady, old boy," said Mobbs uneasily.

"Don't *old boy* me," the Admiral shouted at him. "In another minute, if I hadn't asked you who was running this show of yours, you'd
have walked off with my name on your list. And Tribe would have
been laughing himself sick."

"No, he wouldn't," said Theodore.

The Admiral stared at him in pained surprise, as though a chair had
just made a remark to him. "I don't know who you are or where you
come into it," he began.

But Theodore cut him short. "The Commodore told us you weren't
worth bothering about."

"What?"

"And now I think he was right."

"Clear out." And the Admiral picked up his *Times* and shook it, to
prove that he had done with them. Mobbs had already risen, and now
Theodore stood up.

"I like Commodore Tribe." Theodore did not shout but spoke with
massive deliberation in a deep resonant tone. "You've called him a lot
of names. Perhaps he could call you some names too. What if he did
get into trouble? Haven't you ever been in trouble? If you haven't, it's

still not too late, you know. And let's hope you come out as well as he's done."

The Admiral gasped, flung down his newspaper, glared, and made a guggling noise.

His yellow mane almost bristling, his queer dark eyes glowing, Theodore was a huge formidable figure. "If he's a charlatan, then give me charlatans—and Buffy Jones, whoever he is, can take you. And if I'd been your niece, you'd have had that coffee tray thrown straight at your fat head. Good morning."

They found the niece in the hall, where she had evidently been putting an ear to the door. She was tearful but indignant. "How dare you talk to him like that!" she hissed at Theodore. "You ought to be ashamed of yourself. And now he'll only take it out on me. Silly idiots!"

They were back on the road, with the car turned toward Brant-in-the-Hollow, before either of them spoke. Then Mobbs said: "And you talk about girls thinking! Look at that one! Never know what line they're going to take, old boy. Might as well give it up. But I must say, you went over the top in fine style, laddie. Wouldn't have missed it for anything. Bingo!"

"What I'm wondering," said Theodore uneasily, "is whether we're going to regret that little visit. If he decides to start talking in Farbridge, he might make it difficult for us. You remember what the Commodore said about his session with Crandry and Whatmore and that editor? The Admiral might arrive with some good heavy ammunition for them."

Mobbs thought this over. "Not worth worrying about, old boy," he said finally. "If the mud's going to be thrown, the Admiral can give 'em another handful. But unless the Commodore's been in jail here— and I'm sure he hasn't—then it doesn't matter. Old Broadwater's stuff doesn't amount to anything—too far away and too long ago. Nobody cares except him and his pal Buffy Jones and similar old seadogs. After all I've had a spot or two of trouble with the War House in my time, if it comes to that. But who cares? Still, we'd better warn the Commodore, who, mark you, has undoubtedly been one of the lads in his day. *What's the use of worrying,*" he sang, "*it ne-ever was worth while—*"

It was about half-past twelve when they reached the main street of Brant-in-the-Hollow. Standing outside the pub was a long low car, and one glance at its lamps and gadgets told Theodore that it was the

Group Captain's. "There's a friend of mine here," he told Mobbs. "Group Captain Trevone. You'll like him."

And sure enough there was the Group Captain talking to George in the saloon bar. He was delighted to see Theodore, and no sooner had he been introduced to Mobbs than he ordered two large gins and ginger ales for them.

"Nice work," he cried, beaming. "George was just telling me you'd ordered lunch here for self and chum and the Gishforths. I'm here meeting Philippa and young Clare Thing, who are out of work, poor frippets, and are spending a day or two up at the Manor with us. Coming on the same train you took, Jenks. Not lunching here though. Hooky's laying something special on for 'em. Thanks, George. Down the hatch."

"Cheers!"

"Happy Days!" And Mobbs, after drinking, looked about him with great contentment. "My kind of place, this, old boy."

"What are you up to in Farbridge, Jenks? We've heard rumors, chiefly from Dulcie. Put me in the picture, chum."

Theodore told him about the Festival plan.

"Count us in," said the Group Captain. "I know Hooky'll be keen. We'll organize busloads of characters from the Manor. Might whack in with a subscription too. I'll talk to Hooky about it at lunch. And our two actress types will be interested, Jenks. Had you thought of that? Tell you what. I ought to see a bloke in Farbridge tomorrow morning. I'll bring the two winsome pin-ups with me, and we'll all have lunch and solemn palaver. Where do I find you?"

"We have a little office on the second floor of the White Hart. Have another drink."

"Just time for a very quick one. George! Where's he got to?"

The plump and smiling Maggie hurried in to attend to them.

"Hello, Maggie," said Theodore. "Do you remember me?"

"Of course I do. And so do all the girls up at the Manor. You ought to have heard some of 'em—oughtn't he, Groupie? Now—don't blush."

"You'd make anybody blush, Maggie. Wouldn't she, Captain Mobbs?"

"Making me blush all over, old boy," cried Mobbs, who was having a grand time, all hot and shiny.

The Group Captain looked at his watch. "I must meet that train, chaps. See you tomorrow then, Jenks. You too, sometime, Captain. We'll all have a hell of a Festival together." He dashed out.

"Must attend to your lunch," said Maggie, and hurried back to the kitchen. They heard the Group Captain's car roaring up the street.

"Just suits me, this, laddie," said Mobbs, beaming and steaming. "And if the lunch is anything like that Maggie, who's my idea of a wench, we should be in clover."

"I think Maggie is a wonderful woman," said Theodore, and told him how she had kept Sir Barclay Gishforth's cook for him. He had just come to the end of this story when Maggie returned with a tray and began laying a table for four in the corner where he and the Group Captain had lunched before.

"Ready as soon as they come," she announced. "Bit late, aren't they? Ten to one his old car's broken down again. But they'll get here somehow. Roast pork and apple pie today." And she bustled out, with Mobbs gazing after her, entranced. George returned and served a few customers, who stared at him, stared at Theodore and Mobbs waiting at their table, stared at their drinks, then departed. But no Gishforths. One-fifteen, one-twenty, one-twenty-five; and still no Gishforths.

"Looks as if they're not turning up, old boy," said Mobbs. "Something gone wrong."

"We'll give them another five minutes," said Theodore, who was feeling hungry and had been catching delectable whiffs of roast pork every time Maggie peeped in from the kitchen. Then, as usual, just as it looked as if nothing would ever happen again, everything began happening. First, Lady Gishforth, large, handsome, indestructible, came striding in, shouting her apologies. She was followed by Sir Barclay, a black-and-white pig, old Luffy, and a fat young man. It was like the outbreak of a bucolic revolution. The pig, which appeared to be very angry, charged Sir Barclay from the rear, and, as he went flying, was itself vigorously attacked, in an uproar of shouts, curses, squeals, and grunts, by Luffy and the fat young man. The pig made for Lady Gishforth, wisely thought better of it, then dashed at Mobbs, who tried to defend himself with a chair but somehow got himself entangled with the fat young man. Meanwhile, Sir Barclay, picking himself up, began aiming a series of kicks at places where the pig ought to have been but never actually was, and finally succeeded in booting old Luffy and sending him headfirst into Lady Gishforth, who hurled him back so that he fell over the pig, which squealed more than ever and tried to make its way into the kitchen. This brought George into the battle, with Maggie and three men from the taproom as powerful reserve forces. A strong flanking movement by Theodore and the fat young man, now disentangled from Mobbs, finally headed the pig toward the street door. In another minute the battle was won; and the pig, Luffy, and the fat young man vanished like a dream.

"Must have a drink, my dear chap," Sir Barclay gasped.

"Of course," said Theodore. "We'll all have something before we eat. George."

"It was that foul little car that broke down again," Lady Gishforth explained, when they were settled at the table. "We waited and waited on the road, and then finally Frank Mokes and Luffy gave us a lift. So sorry."

"Not our pig, you know," said Sir Barclay. "Beastly thing must have got out of the van when I did. However, here we are. Very jolly. I say, roast pork—wonderful!" He smiled at Maggie as she unloaded her tray. "You remember that woman, Mrs. Porter? Didn't stay, of course. So we've been living out of tins again. I keep telling Daphne, one of us will simply have to learn how to cook."

"Not me," said Lady Gishforth, who had been talking to Mobbs. "I know there's nothing in it. All sorts of idiotic women can do it perfectly. But I simply refuse to start now. It'll have to be you, Barky darling."

"Easier said than done," said Sir Barclay, rather gloomily. "How do you start learning, that's the point."

"Couldn't you go over to the canteen kitchen at the Manor," said Theodore. "Hookwood could probably arrange it."

"That's a notion," said Sir Barclay, brightening. "But I don't know how the women there would take it, don't you know."

"I do," said his wife firmly. "And it's quite out of the question. Now, Mr. Jenks, tell us what's been happening to you, and all about this Festival thing. And pass the mustard, Barky."

After he had told them about the Festival, they agreed to become patrons and supporters. Lady Gishforth was a little dubious, but Sir Barclay was enthusiastic.

"If you put me on some sort of committee, my dear chap," he said, "I could pop into Farbridge and give you a hand. What I'd suggest is meeting over a lunch table—say at the White Hart. I'd like that."

"We know you would, darling. But what use you'd be on the committee, I can't imagine. You don't know anything about festivals."

"I could learn. And in my time I've been a tower of strength at regimental sports and guest nights in the mess. Eh, Captain Mobbs? Same sort of thing really, eh?"

"Who have you been calling on?" asked Lady Gishforth. "Lady Barth? Quite mad, of course, but a useful name. I don't know Admiral Broadwater. Barky, do you know this Admiral Broadwater?"

"Met him once or twice, my dear. Devil of a temper. Probably all that cheap gin they used to have—about tuppence a go. Millions of pink gins—play hell with your liver. Did you say you were seeing old Barnleysale? That's a rum show, by Jove, very peculiar."

"He's been gaga for years," said Lady Gishforth in her loud clear voice. "And Felicia and her friends are most odd. I'd stopped calling even when we had the transport. How they keep up that monstrous old place, I can't possibly imagine. Apple pie? It looks delicious but I mustn't eat much."

"Like a touch of cheese with mine, please, Maggie. Sensible old custom." Sir Barclay's long mournful face was almost illuminated. "I must say, this is very jolly. Jenks, my dear chap, you seem to have a knack of brightening things up. That was a dashed good evening we had when you were staying at the Manor and we had the entertainment. I'll bet you're just the chap for this Festival thing. Must get in on it, Daphne can say what she likes. Run into Farbridge any time— just say the word."

"Did you hear the B.B.C. program from there the other night?" asked Mobbs.

" 'Fraid we didn't. Don't hear these things. Lead a very quiet life— too quiet. Different from the old days, of course, when we were dashing and splashing about all over the place. We'd be just rolling back from Cannes about this time—remember, Daphne?"

"Of course I remember, you idiot." It could not be said that she either sounded or looked really wistful, this not being possible within her range of expression, but no doubt she was feeling it. "You know, I have an idea I met this Commodore Tribe once in Cannes. He was with some absurd little black man—a rajah or sultan or something— wildly rich and quite ridiculous. Does that sound like your Commodore?"

"It does," said Mobbs, decidedly. "From some of the things he's told me, it does."

"A big, fattish man," said Lady Gishforth almost dreamily, "with an ingratiating manner—and probably no better than he should be."

"That's the chap," cried Mobbs. "Talk you into anything. Well, not you, perhaps. But you know what I mean?"

"By Jove, I say, Daphne old thing," said Sir Barclay. "I believe you're blushing. I really believe you are, my dear."

"Oh—don't be silly," she cried. "As a matter of fact, I was thinking about poor Maisie Fortune. If it's the same man—and I'm sure it is— she nearly went off with him. You remember, Barky?"

"Just remember some funny business. And if it's the chap I remember, he'd run a Festival as soon as look at you. The fact is," Sir Barclay concluded thoughtfully, "it's a dashed small world, people can say what they like. Last chap I'd expect to turn up in Farbridge, yet here he is. Can't explain it unless you admit it's a dashed small world. A lot of what-is-it, of course."

"A lot of *what*?" his wife asked.

"You know, the thing that brings chaps together when you never thought they would be. Or you think about somebody and you get a letter from him though you haven't had one for years. And you say: 'Well, that's a strange—what-is-it.' " He looked at them hopefully.

"Coincidence," Theodore ventured.

"That's it," cried Sir Barclay triumphantly. "Clever chap you are, Jenks. I said that to Daphne last time you were here. Didn't I, my dear? 'Clever chap,' I said. And you said you weren't sure."

"I never said anything of the kind. Yes, coffee for me—black, please."

"A cigar?" cried Sir Barclay, looking at Theodore's open cigar case. "Do you know—I think I will, my dear chap. And don't forget to put my name down. Better have my card to remind you. No, haven't got one. You must have one, my dear."

"I've only one of my own. But if you don't want to look him up in the books," she continued, addressing Theodore and Mobbs, "he's Rupert Adrian Barclay Gishforth, Sixth Baronet, D.S.O., M.C., Croix de Guerre, Justice of the Peace."

"Did you say you were calling on Wally Watton?" Sir Barclay asked hurriedly. "I was with the old boy for a time in France in the First War, and we were great pals for years. Then when he came to live near here, Daphne and he had a flaming row about some cups an' saucers—"

"Cups and saucers!" Mobbs was astonished.

"It was a lovely Chelsea set that he thought I ought to have offered him first," said Lady Gishforth.

Mobbs still looked astonished but said no more. Ten minutes later he and Theodore were saying goodbye to the Gishforths, who refused a lift and declared that the walk back would do them good. Even when they were several miles away from Brant-in-the-Hollow, Mobbs had clearly not recovered from his astonishment. Finally, Theodore asked him what he was pondering over. Was it something about the Gishforths?

"No, old boy. They're all right, specially him. Won't be much use to us, I fancy, but I like the way he enjoys everything, though you'd never think so from the look of him. Surprising how many of these old landed gents look like horses. No," he continued thoughtfully, "what I couldn't make out was this business of Field-Marshal Watton and the cups and saucers. I don't know him, but he took over our division in the First War—I was only a kid subaltern then, of course—and he was blue murder, old boy, the most bloodthirsty basket of 'em all. Started right off by saying we'd not had enough casualties. My godfathers! Put the wind up us poor sausages all right. Troops called him the 'Bloody Butcher.' And he wasn't old then—in fact, very young to have a division. But now—cups and saucers! I don't catch on, old boy."

It was about four o'clock when they arrived within sight of the Field-Marshal's house, which was a small Jacobean manor with clipped yew hedges and sunken gardens. The afternoon was darkening; low clouds were racing up from the west; and there had already been several flurries of rain. A man-servant who looked like an old soldier showed them into a small and rather dark library, where they introduced themselves to the Field-Marshal and to Miss Watton, the sister who kept house for him. The only difference between the two appeared to be that he wore trousers and she wore a skirt. They looked the same age and were exactly the same height; they were dressed in the same speckled tweed; they had the same iron-gray hair, bony and bloodless faces, pale angry eyes, and spoke exactly alike, in high, clipped, fantastic voices.

"Yaw'll have tay, af carse?" said the Field-Marshal.

"Ai've told them, Waltah," said Miss Watton.

"Thenk yoh, Barryl. Yoh fallows had a good day?"

"Tal us who've yoh've sin so fah?"

Mobbs, with some prompting from Theodore, told them about Lady Barth, the Admiral (very briefly), and the Gishforths.

"Gishforth's not a bed fallow," said the Field-Marshal. "Rathah stoopid, af carse. Ai'm not shah about Daphnay."

"No, Waltah, she's stoopid an' rathah greeday," said Miss Watton.

"Now yoh're bein' naughtay, Barryl," said her brother smiling. And when he smiled there seemed to be innumerable fine creases all over his face, like a dried river bed in a hot country. "But what is this Fes'val ideah?" And he looked from Mobbs to Theodore, with thousands of war graves in his pale eyes. And Mobbs, already sweating a little, left it to Theodore, who somewhat nervously produced his usual account of what they were trying to do. He had just finished when the tea was brought in, and there was a little break for inquiries about milk and sugar.

"Yoh sarve in the armay in the East?" the Field-Marshal asked Theodore, as though he had dismissed the subject of the Festival.

Theodore explained that he had fought in Burma, and had to answer several shrewd questions, all of them, it seemed to him, in sharp contrast to the Field-Marshal's rather absurd manner. At the same time, Mobbs, now sweating hard over his shaky teacup, was being closely questioned by Miss Watton. They were like a pair of junior officers making an Intelligence report at G.H.Q. But the tea was very good, as delicate and exquisite as the cups that held it. Finally, after the Field-Marshal and his sister had both lit fat Turkish cigarettes, the talk returned to the Festival.

"We don't care foh dramah an' pegeants an' a lot of beastlay noise an' fuss with fyahwarks an' thet sort of thing," said the Field-Marshal, with a smooth smiling contempt.

"But we adoah aighteenth-cent'ray musaik," cried Miss Watton with a faint sparkle of enthusiasm, like the first glimmer of spring in Greenland. "Don't we, Waltah?"

"Aighteenth-cent'ray musaik, lit'rachar, mennahs an' potteray," he replied, smiling. "It's our pairiod, when Westarn Europe was civilaized for a few years. An' don't tell us this house is all wrong. Jacobean, af carse. We know it only too well. It's our little trageday. But could yoh fallows pramise us some aighteenth-cent'ray musaik?"

"I think you were going to lay on some eighteenth-century music, weren't you, old boy?" asked Mobbs uneasily.

"We haven't planned all the program yet, of course," Theodore told them. "It depends to some extent on what grant we receive. But I know we're hoping to engage a string orchestra, probably to give concerts in the Corn Exchange, and they'd be playing a lot of eighteenth-century stuff, wouldn't they?"

"Af carse. An' we'd adoah it," cried Miss Watton. "No—if yoh made the propah arrangements, perhaps yoh could persuade my brothah to lend yoh some of his potteray for an exhibition."

"Good scheme!" said Mobbs.

The Field-Marshal frowned delicately. "Great care would have to be taken, yoh knoh. Impossible to show some of may best things. Daren't let them go. Fallows benging about—fraightful risk. Rahlly, Barryl, yoh're rathah naughtay."

"Waltah, yoh could spare enough for a chahmin' little exhibition—yoh knoh yoh could."

"Ai wondah." And the Field-Marshal looked elaborately dubious. But Theodore felt that he only needed a little persuasion and that this little scene between brother and sister might possibly have been almost rehearsed beforehand. They were now taken across the hall into a long and rather dark drawing room. As soon as the lights were switched on it looked like part of a museum. The walls were lined with glass-fronted cupboards and deep shelves filled with pottery and porcelain. Theodore had often heard of a bull in a china shop, but the nearest approach to that situation he had ever seen, or ever hoped to see, was little fat Mobbs, glistening and breathing hard, staring about him in that room. He was not in there as long as Theodore, for after half an hour he went off with Miss Watton to telephone to Barnleysale Castle, to explain the delay, and did not return. Theodore was there a full hour. He knew something about Chinese porcelain, as the Field-Marshal soon discovered, and now he had to appreciate the glory of the best old English, French and German potters. The Field-Marshal was a happy man, his eyes warm and alive at last. With delicate long white fingers, he brought out Chelsea plates and Bow mugs, Meissen cups and Chantilly figures, pointing out the beauties of texture, design, and color, absorbed and enrapt as if all the forty-ton tanks and heavy howitzers had never existed or had vanished from the world like an evil dream. The voice that had sent whole battalions to perish among the barbed wire, that had ordered artillery barrages to rip up wide farmlands and pound villages to dust, now lingered tenderly, like his long white fingers, over a Staffordshire teapot, a Sèvres nymph, a faïence vase with a blue ground like an eternal June.

"Well, we'll talk about the poss'bil'tay of includin' a small potteray exhibition latah," said the Field-Marshal, when he was seeing them off. "Meanwhale, if yoh fallows think M'name 'ud be any use to yoh—an' rahlly Ai'm on the shelf, yoh knoh—well, put it down, put it down. An' good lack to yoh! Maight as well anjoh ahrsalves whale we cen—" and his eyes, which were pale and angry again, glittered for a second "—because there prabably isn't much tahme. Goodday to yoh!"

It was now raining hard and Mobbs spent several minutes squinting through the streaming windscreen and silently piloting them out of the drive and back along the road. But when they were safely on their way to Barnleysale Castle, he suddenly exploded: "Cups and saucers! My godfathers! The old Bloody Butcher! Would you believe it? Don't you ask me why 'cos I don't know—may be the weather, old boy—but I'm beginning to feel rather down in the mouth. Do with a drink perhaps. But never like driving in the rain. Depressing!"

Certainly all the bright promise of the morning had vanished, it seemed forever. The roads they saw through the fine gray rods of rain offered no invitations. The hills were no longer there and the fields were so much sullen muck. The villages looked bedraggled and forlorn. No brisk salutes came from the Automobile Association. The signposts were hard to read and then appeared to offer doubtful information. Such glimpses as they had of the agricultural life suggested it was merely a short cut to bankruptcy and chronic rheumatism. Even the thought that they were on their way to a castle did little to cheer them; they wished they were going home.

"Although I must say," Theodore confessed, "that I'm curious to see what life in a castle is like. Somehow I can only think of *Ivanhoe*. Which, I know, is ridiculous. Is it really a castle?"

"As far as I know it is, old boy," said Mobbs cautiously. "But I've never been there and don't know much about it. All I do know is that Lord Barnleysale's an old man and a bit dotty. But there's a daughter, Lady Felicia. I seem to remember she used to be in the gossip columns a good bit, years ago. But I'd put *Ivanhoe* right out of your head, laddie. Name's worth having, though, because these are the real nobs of the County. Must have a good try here, but I'll probably have to leave it mostly to you."

As they went through the village and then roared up a short steep road leading to the castle, the rain was torrential, darkening and severely limiting the view. The shapeless bulk of the castle was looming above them before Theodore had a chance to see it properly. They dashed from the car into the shelter of a colossal doorway, where they rang the bell at a small door that had been let into the enormous iron-bound timber. Theodore had a vision of this door being opened by an ancient bowed retainer, bearded and suspicious; but after a long wait they found themselves confronted by an untidy-looking girl, about seventeen, cheerful, and impudent.

"Are you Captain Tubbs and Mr. Jinks? 'Cos if you are, that's okay."

"No, it isn't okay, not until you get our names right. I'm Captain Mobbs and this is Mr. Jenks."

"That's right," she said. "Well, they're expecting you. Better shove your coats down here." She pointed to an old refectory table at the entrance to the dusky cavernous hall, where one dim electric bulb was burning. "You want to keep close to me 'cos you can easily get lost here. Took me about a fortnight to know my way about. You want roller skates for this job."

"Bit saucy, aren't you, Gladys?" said Mobbs, as they began to move off.

"Well, I'm only helping my Mum out for a month or two. Just to oblige—and till me and my friend go to Llandudno for the summer. Hotel work. And it's all right talking, but you'd want to be saucy, as you call it, if you were stuck in this place. Gives you the creeps—and miles and miles from the kitchen to anywhere. Mind that armor."

She led them along a dusky stone corridor, as cold and damp as a cellar, then up a narrow staircase that brought them out into another corridor. They could now hear a tinny gramophone playing an old-fashioned jazz record. "That's them," the girl announced. "Keep that old gramophone going day and night—and all out of date. Better than nothing, though." A light from an open doorway showed a short curved flight of stone steps. With the sudden energy of youth, the girl bounded up these steps, pushed the door open wider, and cried: "They're here."

This round tower room seemed quite bright after the dusky corridors, and it was comfortably furnished and had some logs blazing in its massive old fireplace. On a table in the center were bottles and glasses and a portable gramophone. A tall fair woman in a long red dress was lounging on a settee, smoking a cigarette in a six-inch black holder. Another woman, who had a white face and short black hair and was dressed in a Russian blouse and green corduroy slacks, was standing at the table, mixing drinks. After a few moments of confusion, during which the fair woman behaved with admirable courtesy and the dark one seemed to be sulky and contemptuous, Theodore discovered that the fair woman was Lady Felicia, daughter of Lord Barnleysale, and that the other was her friend, the Honorable Pamela Fortpatrick. On closer inspection, both women were older than they had appeared to be at first; and Theodore guessed they were somewhere in their early forties. Lady Felicia had a haggard blonde beauty, like that of some attenuated Snow Queen; but everything about her, face and figure, voice and manner, seemed too sharp and brittle; and she lacked all the charm of bloom and fulfilment. Her friend Pamela was a coarser and more vigorous character; she had a hoarse sulky voice; and with her white and rather sagging face and her wide mouth covered with crimson grease, she looked rather like an embittered clown. Both of them seemed to him creatures who were not in their own time but had been preserved by some process of refrigeration or desiccation; and owing to some flaw in the process were already rotting inside. Perhaps the blinding rain, the castle, the dusky chill corridors and their armor, the stone steps, the round tower room, had combined together to make him feel unusually fanciful, but it did seem to him that these women were like characters in a sinister fairy tale.

"My God—that tune!" cried Lady Felicia.

"I know, darling," said Pamela. "Heavenly—and yet pure hell."

"Make two more Gimlets, Pam. You don't mind Gimlets, do you?"

Captain Mobbs, answering for the visitors, replied that Gimlets would be welcome.

Lady Felicia turned to Theodore. "Don't you find those heavenly old Gershwin and Cole Porter things desperately sad-making?"

"No, I don't," said Theodore, surprised.

"He's too young, darling," said Pamela, busy with her Gimlets. "You forget."

"Don't be a pig, Pam. And give him a lovely strong Gimlet. No Bacardi now—isn't it all just too bogus for words?" Again she appealed to Theodore, who again looked surprised. Pamela handed him a glass in an offhand contemptuous fashion, as if she were a superior barman compelled to work overtime serving very inferior customers.

After tasting it, Theodore decided his Gimlet consisted of a great deal of gin and a drop or two of lime juice.

"Ah!" cried little Mobbs, smacking his lips. "Just what the doctor ordered!"

"To coin a phrase," said Pamela.

"Pam sweet, do shut up," said Lady Felicia, giggling.

Mobbs caught Theodore's eye and made a mute appeal. "Hurry up and do your stuff with these nobs, old boy," his look said.

"We've called to see you, Lady Felicia," Theodore began firmly, "because we're trying to organize a Farbridge Festival—"

"My God!" Pamela muttered hoarsely.

"And we want you and Lord Barnleysale to give us your names as patrons and supporters. We've already got Lady Barth, Sir Barclay and Lady Gishforth, Field-Marshal Watton—"

"My dear, what a collection!" cried Lady Felicia. "But of course put me down. I don't know about Father. You'll have to talk to him yourself, and you won't find that easy, the poor sweet. What are you going to do—plays and things? Pam, it might be rather gay."

"Don't be silly, darling. It'll be all frightfully grim. My God—yes."

"Don't be *gruff* with us. And you don't know."

"I've seen the town, haven't I? I know it'll be pure hell."

"More drinkies, please, Pam."

Mobbs, fortified by the Gimlet he had now finished, stared aggressively at Pamela. "What's the matter with the town?"

"Everything, if you ask me," she told him sharply, mixing more Gimlets. "And if I were Felicia, I wouldn't touch your ridiculous Festival with a bargepole."

"To coin a phrase," said Mobbs.

Lady Felicia giggled again. "Don't be so discouraging, darling. Let's play some more of those heavenly old tunes, and try to forget how bogus everything is nowadays. We might dance." She looked at Theodore invitingly, but he smiled and shook his head.

"I must say, you have the foulest ideas," Pamela grumbled as she handed out the drinks. "And next time somebody else can mix them." She put a cushion on the floor, between the fire and the end of the settee, plumped down on it, and proceeded to light a short pipe.

"Let's finish these," said Lady Felicia to Theodore, smiling at him, "and then I'll take you along to see Father. And Pam and Captain Blobbs can have a lovely time entertaining each other. Come on."

Pamela turned and scowled. "That's one of your battiest bloody notions, Flissy. Captain Thing ought to go and see your father, or both of them—"

"No, darling, you know very well he couldn't possibly endure two of them—"

"And anyhow the girl who brought them up here can take him along—"

"Darling, it'll take hours. Don't be so *stubborn*. Come along, Mr. Jinks—I'm sorry, Jenks, isn't it? I'm desperate about names—always was. Captain Blobbs, be nice to Pamela. And do help yourself to Gimlets and things."

Once they were out of the room and going down the steep curved steps, she said: "I must warn you, it's miles—and if you don't know the way, you can easily get lost. We still make our own electric light— Father won't change because he says it would be encouraging Socialism—and our engine thing must be the first ever made. Look— hardly a glimmer. So we must keep close together." She put her arm through his and almost leaned on him, so that it was difficult to walk. "Do you mind our keeping close together?"

"No," said Theodore politely. "Of course not."

"You're rather sweet, aren't you? Where do you come from? Don't tell me Farbridge, it's not possible."

Slow as their progress was, for as they went along she leaned more heavily on him and sometimes at corners she hesitated for several moments, resting against him, they seemed to have left the tower room far behind by the time he had finished telling her where he came from and what he was doing in England. He had no desire to talk to her about himself, but it seemed a comparatively safe topic, and by apparently concentrating upon it he was able to ignore what seemed to him this leaning-and-resting business, which at best he found embarrassing and at its worst downright distasteful. At last, however, as he recognized with heartfelt relief, they arrived at the door of that gunroom in which it seemed that old Lord Barnleysale spent most of his time.

"It's me, Felicia," she cried, opening the door and replying to an inarticulate roar from within. "And I've brought a young man to see you."

It was a lofty, darkish room, and so full of stuffed heads that it looked as if half a zoo had battered its way through the walls and was staring in, astounded. In a leather chair as big as a throne, a colossal old man was sprawling. In the vast dressing gown he was wearing he suggested an untidy and dim Henry the Eighth.

"This is Mr. Jinks from Farbridge. He wrote to you about a Festival there."

"How de do? Sit down." Lord Barnleysale waited until they had found chairs. He appeared to be a character who existed in slow-motion. "Did you say Jinks?"

"No, Jenks," said Theodore.

"From Farbridge?"

"Darling, he wrote to you about a Festival there," said Felicia.

"In Farbridge?"

"Yes," said Lady Felicia and Theodore together.

"I don't see the point," said Lord Barnleysale, a look of despair slowly settling on his huge swollen face. "Chap in Farbridge comes all the way out here to ask me about a Festival there. But that's the way things are being done now. And of course I don't know anything about it. But it doesn't sound likely. Never heard of 'em having a Festival there. Not that sort of place."

"No, darling," cried Lady Felicia. "Mr. Jenks and his friends want to start a Festival—"

"Don't go on and on about it, my dear girl." Dismissing both her and the subject, he turned very slowly and massively to Theodore. "My other daughters were just the same. Go on and on and on if I didn't stop 'em. Now what can I do for you, young fella?"

Theodore did not know what to reply to this. Then he decided that it might work if he did not mention the Festival for the next half-minute. "I'm getting together a list of influential patrons and supporters. I've already got Lady Barth, Sir Barclay Gishforth, Field-Marshal Watton—"

"Quite right. Like a glass of sherry?"

"No, thank you, sir."

"Never touch it myself. Livery stuff, they can say what they like. Glass of whisky?"

"No, darling," Lady Felicia shouted at him, "we've been drinking gin."

"You're always drinking gin, you and young What's-her-name. Hetton was complaining about it this morning—or yesterday. Says it costs about thirty shillings a bottle—though he's lying, of course. Still, no reason to keep drinking the stuff day and night." He dismissed her again, and looked earnestly at Theodore. "How's your father, my boy? Fit as ever?"

"Yes," said Theodore in despair. "And we want you to be a patron of the Farbridge Festival."

Lord Barnleysale shook his head. "There isn't such a thing. Just some of Felicia's nonsense. They sit about drinking gin and say the first thing that comes into their heads. Wouldn't have thought you knew Farbridge. Beastly place nowadays—factories and so on—but when I was a youngster it was quite a pleasant little market town. Staying the night? We might have a rubber of bridge after dinner."

"No. I must get back to Farbridge," said Theodore, doggedly. "You see, sir, we're trying to arrange a Festival there, in connection with the Festival of Britain this spring. And I want you to be one of our patrons, with Lady Barth, Sir Barclay Gishforth—"

"And Uncle Tom Cobbley an' all," cried Lady Felicia, giggling.

Thoroughly annoyed now, Theodore jumped up.

"I'm sorry," she said. "But it'll be all right, so long as you don't expect a subscription or anything."

"What the blazes are you talking about?" her father demanded. "Uncle Tom Cobbley and subscriptions! Doesn't make sense. Now just keep quiet." He held out a hand to Theodore. "Can't get up. Bad for me. But look in here in the morning, when the light's better, and I'll show you my heads—dam' fine collection. Glass of sherry or whisky?"

"No, thank you," said Theodore, shaking hands.

"Well, enjoyed our little chat. Don't see many people nowadays. Where are you going, my dear fella?"

"Farbridge," said Theodore, trying to make it sound like a place that had not been mentioned before.

"Farbridge? Well, you tell 'em from me they ought to run a Festival there. Everybody's doing it, so why shouldn't they? Just an idea."

"It's a very good idea," said Theodore, not without an effort. And at least, he told himself as he and Lady Felicia began the return journey, he was now justified in putting Lord Barnleysale down as a patron.

"Captain Blobbs is rather a little tick, isn't he?" she said as they went along.

"I like him," said Theodore rather stiffly.

"Darling, you couldn't possibly," she cried, sliding her hand down his arm and then squeezing his hand quite hard. "And now you're cross. I'm desperately sorry." She waited a moment or two, and then, as he made no reply, she continued brightly: "Poor Pam was furious at being left alone with him. By this time they're probably throwing things at each other. Too blush-making. Do you like Pam, Jinks darling?"

"No," said Theodore, who saw no reason to disguise his feeling about her. "Not one bit."

"I suppose she is getting rather awful, poor sweet," Lady Felicia sighed. "But then you don't understand. Years ago, when everything was heaven, Pam was pure heaven—so gay all the time. We shared a tiny house she had just off Berkeley Square, and used to have the most divine parties—and there were all those heavenly shows and tunes, you know, and people were such fun. And then it all changed— and it's such hell pretending it hasn't. You don't understand, you *can't* understand— Oh God, I'll be crying in a minute. Let's hurry back and have a drink." And now she let go of him and moved so quickly, like a ghost, that he had to take long rapid strides to keep pace with her up and down the ancient stairs and along the empty sad corridors. But at the door of her room she stopped and put a finger to her mouth. "Listen to them," she whispered.

"Oh—rats!" Mobbs was shouting in disgust.

"And bloody rats to you!" cried Pamela hoarsely.

Lady Felicia burst in on them, screaming with malicious delight. Little Mobbs was scarlet and furious, while the lady looked more than ever like an embittered clown. Both of them gave the impression that hostilities had not checked the flow of Gimlets.

"Time we were off, old boy," cried Mobbs promptly. "Ready if you are."

"Of course he isn't," said Lady Felicia, hurrying to the table.

"Yes I am," said Theodore firmly. "I'm sorry, but we really must go."

"Quite," said Pamela, and she began to jerk a bellcord with savage energy.

"Darling, you can't," cried Lady Felicia among the bottles.

"I've rung now," said Pamela with some satisfaction. "Just give him one for the road. I'll put the gramophone on."

"Father was absolutely fantastic, poor sweet—"

"Let's push off, old boy."

"I'm ready."

"The girl will be here in a minute," said Pamela grimly, "to take you down."

"*Tell me more, tell me more,*" sang the gramophone wheezily.

"My God—that tune!"

"*Tell me more, I implore, tell me more,*" the tinny ghosts wailed.

"Yes?" said the girl from the kitchen.

"Take these gentlemen down."

"Goodbye. Thank you so much. Goodbye."

"Goodbye. Goodbye."

"Goodbye."

"*Tell me more,*" and it sank to a whisper from behind the closing door, "*tell me more, tell me more . . .*"

"Mind that armor," said the girl. "Gave myself a nasty crack second night I was here. Well, what do you think of it here?"

"I'll take Llandudno, Gladys," said Mobbs.

"That's what I say, though I wish you'd come off the Gladys. What they want here is a television set, never mind that rotten little old gramophone—out of date. My Mum started working here when she was younger than me—about thirteen, she says, four of 'em sleeping in a nasty little back place, bats and rats and God knows what. Catch me! Well, here you are. Better put your coats on—it's still raining. 'Night."

They rolled down the steep road to the village. "What with one thing and another," said Mobbs, "I'm going to take it slowly, if it's all the same to you. Got his lordship, didn't you? Good. But if you ever go there again, old boy, Archie Mobbs will not be in the party. Put the breeze up me. Still, we've now roped in the nobility and gentry, except for the Admiral, and he's not much loss. We've had quite a day really, old boy."

"Quite a day, Captain," said Theodore, slowly and with marked emphasis. The little car, still rather cold and inclined to splutter, moved uncertainly as if groping its way home. Other cars glared, dimmed, hooted, and went roaring past, leaving them to the rain and the sodden road and broken glimpses of forlorn wayside houses and villages without a name. Mobbs asked the world to pack up its troubles in its old kit bag; and Theodore began to think about Laura.

6

"Well, what happened yesterday?" Laura asked, with a challenging look. Theodore had only just arrived in the office, for although he lived in the hotel he was always later than she was, not out of grandeur, but because he slept heavily in the morning.

"I think we had a useful day." He gave her a very brief account of what had happened, wisely leaving the picturesque and dramatic details until some other and better time. "Anything happen here?"

"Certainly," she replied severely. "Councillor Gisburn, the youngish man who shouts rather, and Alderman Mrs. Coote or Mrs. Alderman Coote, or whatever she is, that nice woman, came in together and talked to the Commodore. Then Michael brought in a Miss Ayton from the Arts Council. And some posters." She pointed to them. "I was just going to put them up, to cover these beastly walls. Some of them are very gay."

They looked at the posters together and then began pinning them on the walls. "What was the Arts Council woman like?" Theodore asked.

"Miss Ayton? About thirty-five, and one of those smooth dark women who look rather like seals and always make me feel very young and untidy. The Commodore took charge of her—artful old monster. She was very pleasant but said that the Arts Council had already spent all its Festival money, and all they could give us was advice about getting off Entertainment Tax and where to find the sort of people we might want—musicians and lecturers and so on. I took a lot of notes."

"How's the Commodore?"

"He's in great form now there's all this money about. But we'll have to watch him, Theodore, because I think that having any money goes straight to his head. He can't bother with budgets and accounts. Already he says this room's not good enough, and we ought to find an empty shop or something to make a splash with. And we don't even know yet whether there'll be a Festival."

"What about the public meeting?"

"That's settled. And we're having some sort of committee meeting about it this afternoon. By the way there's some mysterious plotting going on about the Palace Theater and the Palladian Cinema. When

I was leaving yesterday, I saw Mr. Hull talking to that funny little man, Mr. Babley—you remember?"

"*Ah-ha?*"

"Yes—*ah-ha*! He comes into it somewhere."

"There's really quite a lot happening, isn't there?" said Theodore, looking pleased and rather important. Then he stared at the poster they had just unfolded. It advertised the Burmanley Festival, and did it chiefly by offering you, in the boldest coloring, two angular figures, presumably a man and a woman, whose heads had been split wide open either to receive or to emit brilliant rays of light. "What's this about? Doesn't make sense to me."

"I don't think posters have to make sense. And I like it. You have to look at it—and it makes you feel something exciting is about to happen. What more do you want?"

"Why have they to look like that?"

"It's just part of the design," she said impatiently. Even the smallest disagreement with him made her feel impatient at once, sometimes really angry. It was, she thought, just as if he were charged with one kind of electricity and she was crackling and sparkling with the opposite kind. Very exciting, but a bit much. "I don't believe you understand about these things at all."

"I don't believe I do," he replied mildly. He had that trick too, suddenly caving in just when she was ready to batter at him. Sweet in a way, but infuriating too.

"Well then," she said, in what she knew herself to be an insufferable tone, "you shouldn't talk about them."

He looked at her, just looked with no particular expression, but she felt her bones turning to jelly. Now what would he do? Shake her? Kiss her? Break something? After all, anything might happen. He was unlike any other man she had known because at times like this he seemed to turn into huge wild weather, which might darken and flash into a thunderstorm or thin out and quieten to reveal sunshine or clear starlight. But then he caught her out again, blast him.

"No, I don't suppose I should," he said humbly. "There are a lot of things I don't know. I haven't been around with them as you have, Laura. So I suppose I'd better keep quiet." He took the Burmanley poster and pinned it high on the wall, which had now very little of its pickled cabbage pattern left and was beginning to look very gay.

As she watched him, her eyes pricked sharply with tears, in the silliest and most maddening way. "You can do the rest," she told him, and went to bang and clatter on her typewriter. That was one thing about typewriters, especially old machines like hers: a girl could work her moods off on them. To complete the picture, she lit a cigarette she did not want, kept it in the corner of her mouth, and half-closed her eyes against the smoke, and became at once a knowing cynical type, like a girl reporter in a Hollywood film. Idiot!

The Commodore came in, wearing an immense brown velvet coat that was anything but new, yet nobody had ever seen it before. He was obviously delighted with it and himself.

"Good morning, my children," he cried, very much the whimsical old party. "Ah—the posters! Splendid! What a difference they make! Good work, children, good work!"

"I hate that coat," said Laura.

"You do, my dear? Why?"

"It makes you look like a seaside photographer in an old volume of *Punch*."

"My dear Laura, you ought to know by this time that I'm essentially a character in an old volume of *Punch*. About 1912. However, this coat is merely for office wear. I wouldn't take it to the Town Hall. Well, Theodore, I heard about your adventures yesterday from little Mobbs, rather late last night. He was in fine form, very graphic but perhaps a little on the fantastic side. Though, of course, it could have been that kind of day. We all have them."

"He told about Admiral Broadwater?"

"Yes—and Buffy Jones. I'll tell you all about that sometime—remind me. But at the moment I'm not worried about Broadwater. And I hope you're not?"

"I was a bit," said Theodore rather carefully. "But Mobbs seemed to think it was all right."

Laura had not been told about this Broadwater business, but preferred not to remind them. She merely said sharply: "I don't know why you imagine that little fat man has any sense. I'm sure he hasn't."

"Laura, Laura, you're really condemning him for being little and fat. Which won't do. After all, you're little too. And as for being fat, what's wrong with that? I'm fat, and in twenty or thirty years Theodore will be much fatter than I am."

"No," she cried in horror.

"Bound to be. And why not? The current prejudice against well-covered bones seems to me one of the idiocies of the age. Doctors—"

But he stopped there because, as if summoned magically, one of them now rushed in. It was Dr. Barr from the Town Hall, and he came in like a little red steam engine. "So this is your office, Commodore? Seth Hull told me where to find you. Ay, but Ah'm not staying—Ah just looked in for a minute."

"You must meet my assistants—Miss Casey and Mr. Jenks," said the Commodore. "Dr. Barr."

"It's a great pleasure," cried Dr. Barr, running round shaking hands. "It's a great pleasure. Which one of you will be looking after the music?"

"Miss Casey, I think," said the Commodore.

"Ay, ay—well, we'll have to have some talk about it, Miss Casey, that's what we'll have to do. But later on, later on. There's no great hurry about that." But he looked at her rather wistfully.

"I thought a good string orchestra," said Laura, "if there's one to spare."

"Ye couldn't do better. No, ye couldn't do better." He rubbed his hands together with tremendous vigor and enthusiasm. "Ah've two girls that are as daft about it as Ah am maself. Maybe ye'll come up to the house one night an' meet them, Miss Casey. Ay, that's what ye'd better do. An' just say the word an' we'll be playin' for ye ourselves—up at the house Ah mean, not at the Festival. We're not up to that standard yet. No, we're not up to that standard yet—an' Ah don't think we ever will be. But Ah didn't come to talk about that." And now he put on his cunning look, chiefly for the Commodore.

"You've news for us?" said the Commodore, taking a tone suitable for the cunning look.

"Ah have, Ah have," said Dr. Barr, slowly for him. "Ye're havin' this public meeting in the Corn Exchange next week. Who ye puttin' in the chair that night, tell me that?"

"We've got to settle that today," said the Commodore. "I thought we'd better have Major Bulfoss."

"Ay—an' no doubt that'll be wee Mobbs's idea. But this is what Ah came to tell you. Ask the Mayor. He hates to be left out o' anything, the poor old Mayor does—an' likes to hear himself talk—an' if ye ask him to take the chair—as a neutral, mind, not somebody on your own side—he'll be there an' ye've a great chance o' winning him over. Coverack, Tanhead, an' Muleford, they've all been pressin' him an' the Town Clerk, poor Meare—"

"Yes, I heard that," said the Commodore, jumping in. "And I gather that the Mayor and Town Clerk—to my surprise, because I didn't think they were men of such mettle—have been standing up to 'em, saying there's more demand for a Festival than they thought."

"Ay, they have, they have," cried Dr. Barr. "Though they go no further than that. But if ye get the Mayor into the chair at your meetin'—"

"I'll try it," said the Commodore. "And I'll put Mobbs onto Bulfoss to ask him to be one of our speakers. I'll see the Mayor this morning, if I can. No, I won't," he added hurriedly. "I'd better keep out of it. I'll put Jordan onto him. Or if Jordan won't, then Seth Hull."

"I think that's better than going yourself," said Theodore.

"It is, it is, it is," cried Dr. Barr. "Ye want local men to act against local men. Ah've found that maself. But Ah thought Ah'd explain about the Mayor. As a matter o' fact, Ah'd a word or two, all very cautious, wi' Meare, an' he's coming round to our side o' the question. He's a dithery wee fellow but he knows the way the wind's blowin'. Ahy, ay—well, Ah must be away to ma work, away to ma work."

"I'll go along and see Mobbs," said the Commodore, and left with the Medical Officer.

"And he's gone out in that awful coat," said Laura.

"But not to the Town Hall," said Theodore, returning to his poster job.

"He *looks* bogus in that coat, I suppose that Admiral What's-his-name told you yesterday he was?"

"Something like that," Theodore replied cautiously.

"Tell me. I hate it when I'm not told. Tell me exactly what the Admiral said."

He told her all he could remember. "But Mobbs said afterwards—"

"Oh never mind about Mobbs. Wee Mobbs." She began laughing. "I love Dr. Barr. I wonder what the daughters are like. What am I like, Theodore?"

He stared at her helplessly for a moment or two. Just as he was about to stammer out something, she checked him.

"I'm not asking for compliments. At least I don't think so. Though they're always welcome. Millions of us here just waiting for somebody to say something nice—it's pathetic. But when I said I wondered what Dr. Barr's daughters were like. I suddenly began to wonder what I was like. Because the queer thing is—I don't know. Sometimes I think one thing, sometimes another, quite different. So tell me, please." And she looked at him earnestly.

He had forgotten about his posters now, and had come closer, his dark eyes staring into hers. He drew a very deep breath. This was it, she thought—something wonderful at last.

"I'll tell you what you are like, Laura," he began. And there he stopped, and the morning was smashed to bits, for no sooner had he said her name, slowly and tenderly, than the place was invaded.

"Here he is," the burly man shouted. "Here we are, frippets." And then the room seemed to be full of gorgeous horrible creatures and smart clothes and Chanel Number Five and wonderful silk legs and painted smiling mouths and eyes glittering between lashes stiff with mascara and little delighted screams and *Darlings* and kisses—a feminine hell let loose. And what then was Laura Casey like? She knew only too well, blast it. Laura Casey was the poor shabby little thing behind the typewriter; a stray wet kitten; a quivering mouse; a furious nothing. And for some time after Theodore, half-protesting (or had she made that up?), had been whirled away, and nothing happened in the office except a scattering of papers after she threw the window open, she had ample opportunity to enlarge and improve upon these first wild comparisons. Just sitting there, apparently about six inches high, dressed in rags, ugly, unloved, and unwanted.

"Good morning, Laura," said Michael Seacombe, putting his head round the door.

"Good morning, Michael. Come in."

"Now do I wake or do I dream?" he inquired, once inside the room.

"I wouldn't know. Do you mean the posters?"

"No." He looked at them now. "It's a bit fierce—I mean the total effect—but better than that dismal wallpaper. But my original question referred to our friend Theodore Jenks. And the point is—did I or did I not see him below in the company of a rather gorgeous redhead and a slinky dangerous brunette? And another man too, but we can leave him out. And am I right in assuming that the golden tone and silvery laugh of these bright beings might originally have been acquired at the Royal Academy of Dramatic Art or the Central School of Speech Training?"

"Shrewdly observed, Seacombe," said Laura. "These are actresses, friends of a Group Captain Trevone, who was the other man and who's not unlike a talking bull in a blue suit rather too small for it. He's one of Theodore's mysterious buddies. The auburn-haired actress is called Philippa Hookwood and is the daughter of the Group Captain's partner. The dark one is called Clare Chesbey. Theodore saw them act once in London. And now I suppose you'll want to rush down and pretend to interview them."

"You suppose wrong," said Michael, settling down with a cigarette. "I much prefer talking to you up here. And now what shall we talk about? Me?"

"All right—you." Laura looked at him quite seriously. "I never understand what you're doing here. I don't know much about journalism, but I'm sure you're not the sort of man who generally hangs about a place like Farbridge picking up odd bits of news. And can I have a cigarette, please?"

Once he had made sure her cigarette was alight, he dropped back into the armchair, lying almost flat, with his long legs stretched out, his blue chin resting on the knot of that horrible yellow ocher tie of his. He had had his hair cut at last, and this made him look less ruffianly fantastic than usual, Laura decided, but even more impudent, for now his nose seemed to come out and turn up more than ever. But there was something definitely attractive about him. Perhaps it was his eyes, which were small but forever twinkling. Or his voice. Something, anyhow.

"It's a fair question, Casey," he began. "And it's about time you had a sketch of the Life and Times of Michael Seacombe. Born in the West Country, the son of a country doctor. A short but distinguished scholastic career at the University of Bristol. A military career, entirely without distinction, as a Desert Rat. Having already written this and that, including one bad novel, one of those novels in which you make the hero think everything you've ever thought yourself, arrived in Fleet Street in 1945. Continued there until '48. Incidentally, if that girl downstairs is called Chesbey, then I probably know her brother Lionel. We were on the *Echo* together. He has a column now, while I'm gathering bits and pieces here."

"Yes, and that's what I don't understand," said Laura. "Why you think it's worth it. How you make a living out of it."

"I'm coming to that," he told her. "I was sent down here to report a

by-election, not here in the borough but in the nearest county constituency. I was tired of London. I still wanted to write too, and I
didn't feel I could take a really good look at genuine English life and
character rushing to and from Fleet Street. So I stayed on here. One
place, outside London, seemed as good as another. A chap I worked with
on the *Echo* went back to Australia, and I write two newsy articles
a month for him. They pay for my room and breakfast, and the odd
news stories I sell, together with an occasional article, bring me enough
pennies to keep me going. Mark you, Laura, behind this mere façade
of newsgathering, I'm supposed to be really *writing*."

"And are you?" she asked, looking at him severely.

"Not a sausage. I could say I'm not ready yet, which would be true
up to a point. I could also admit I'm too lazy. To write and write—
when you don't know who's going to print it, who's going to pay for
it, who's going to read it—that takes some doing if you're a newspaperman, a bachelor with not too many expenses, and lazy into the
bargain. It might be different if the Little Woman were by my side,"
he added in the same easy light tone, but without looking at her now,
"and tiny footsteps could be heard pattering along the hall."

"It might," she said darkly, "and then again it might not."

"Why this skepticism, this cynical touch?"

"Some people think my father's crazy," she told him. "But I think
he's the most sensible man I've ever known. And he said to me—
not the last time he went away, the time before—that I must always
beware of men who suggest they need women to make something out
of them. It's very flattering, he pointed out, and appeals at once to the
maternal strain in a woman. But he said it wouldn't do, that happy
marriages were based on women's respect and admiration and not on
their pity, except in the sense that we're all sorry for each other.
Though that, of course, doesn't mean that a woman can't help. But
if she feels she's really doing it, then it's not right. My father used to
be fond of the theater, and he said that Shaw in *Candida* and Barrie in
What Every Woman Knows were flattering the women in their audiences and were not telling the real truth."

"Crikey, lady!" He stared at her with mock awe, but there was a
certain amount of obvious effort about it all. "I don't say your father
isn't right. But I don't think mine was the right instance. To begin
with, I wasn't crying out for help—"

"I know." She colored. "I didn't mean that. Sorry!"

"You asked me something, and I tried to tell you. The point I was making was—that having only myself to keep and being rather lazy— I wasn't making the effort I might make in other circumstances, or might make anyhow quite soon. I was also trying not to be pompous about myself, though I probably didn't succeed."

"Yes, Michael," she said rather humbly, "I know. And thank you for telling me."

"The Seacombe Service is always there, madam. Day and night—" But the knock on the door was imperative.

"I'll do it," said Michael, sliding out of his chair. "Sounds like the Inland Revenue."

This second invasion was very different from the first. Leading it, fully armored, was Mrs. Delacey, Questioner Number Three on the B.B.C. program and the proud mother of My Daughter the Entertainer. In support, representing the second line occupation troops, was a tentative dry-biscuit sort of woman, who was promptly introduced by Mrs. Delacey as her friend and neighbor Miss Fisby.

"Miss Fisby," said Mrs. Delacey, taking charge at once, "is a Talented Writer." She looked from Laura to Michael as if challenging them to deny this statement. "Miss Fisby has been wondering how to get in touch with the Festival Committee. We have had Great Difficulty in finding you, Miss Casey."

"Well, you know, Mrs. Delacey," said Laura apologetically, "there really isn't a Festival Committee yet. It hasn't even been decided if there's going to be a Festival."

"After Our Program the other night," said Mrs. Delacey, accepting the chair Michael offered her, "and then, I understand, the Public Meeting next week, there can be no doubt Farbridge will have its Festival."

"Hear, hear!" cried Michael, winking at Laura. "Won't you sit down, Miss Fisby?" She did, but only on the very edge of the chair.

"There is Not Much Time," Mrs. Delacey continued. "Otherwise, Miss Fisby would not have troubled you. But if a Pageant is to be part of the proceedings, as Miss Fisby says, then the Sooner The Better."

"The sooner what the better?" inquired Michael politely.

At this point Miss Fisby was seen to begin moving her lips, but she was stopped by Mrs. Delacey long before the other two heard a word she was saying.

"Don't try, dear," said Mrs. Delacey. "Miss Fisby has lost her voice. Some years ago she wrote a Pageant. I have read it and although I don't pretend to know about these things—My Daughter is an Entertainer in the Concert Party Line—it seemed to me Very Talented Indeed. This Pageant deals with Farbridge and Neighborhood. It was originally written for the Girls' Grammar School. And Miss Fisby says she could easily adapt it for your Festival. What, dear?" And Mrs. Delacey put an ear down to Miss Fisby, as if that talented writer were a watch that might have stopped. Laura ducked behind her typewriter to cope with a fit of the giggles. Michael looked on, as blandly solemn as a Harley Street specialist.

"Miss Fisby," Mrs. Delacey announced finally, "says that she could adapt her Pageant for your Festival in a few days. The question is— should she do so? There is Not Much Time. A Pageant requires a good deal of rehearsing."

She looked inquiringly from Laura to Michael; and Laura, who was still in no condition to talk, looked appealingly at Michael, who thereupon, with immense gravity, took command.

"Mrs. Delacey, Miss Fisby," he began, as if replying to a toast at a public dinner, "we're very glad you've mentioned this Pageant. But it's not in our respective departments. Miss Casey is responsible for— er—general organization. I am handling the public relations."

"Indeed," said Mrs. Delacey with deep satisfaction.

"The man you want is Mr. Theodore Jenks, who's in charge of the theatrical side of the Festival. And you'll find him downstairs, either in the lounge or the bar, where he's entertaining two well-known actresses from London."

"Known no doubt to My Daughter," said Mrs. Delacey, with a gracious little nod for everybody present.

"No doubt. Mr. Jenks is a tall good-looking young man with fair hair and dark eyes—you're bound to notice him. Now you explain all about Miss Fisby's pageant to him. If necessary, explain it to him scene by scene," Michael continued, with some relish. "Don't be put off by his manner. He's shy, that's all. If he suggests you see him some other time, don't agree. He's a very busy man, and now's your chance. It's now," he added, holding his hand out to Miss Fisby, who looked at it as if it were some exotic gift, "or never. Thank you. Good morning, Miss Fisby. Good morning, Mrs. Delacey."

"Most helpful," said Mrs. Delacey gratefully. "Come, Miss Fisby. I know these Busy Men, and I shall Stand No Nonsense from Mr. Jenks."

"And she won't, you know," said Michael, a moment or two later. "Friend Theodore will get a packet."

"He'll be furious."

"Serve him right for neglecting his work here, though what his work is, I can't imagine. Incidentally, have you any work you want to do?"

"Not before lunch," she replied promptly.

"Then I suggest that we wait a few minutes and then go below too. We can have a drink, and then lunch here, if you like."

"Do you think Theodore and his mob will be lunching here?"

"Almost bound to be."

"Then I'd love to, Michael," she told him; and saw herself laughing merrily while keeping an eye on these overdressed and affected Clares and Philippas. Especially the Clare one, who had bounced in as if she owned Theodore. "I wonder if I'd have time to slip home and change."

He stared at her. "Change? You don't want to change. You look all right. This isn't a party."

"No, of course not." Really, men! It was like dealing with Zulus.

Michael grinned at her. "I don't care. And I don't suppose he'd notice the difference. And if the actress types weren't impressed, you'd be worse off than if you went as you are; and there's nothing wrong with you as you are. Let's go down."

7

It was one of those early evenings when towns like Farbridge, sinking and drowned, like some Lyonnesse, in the pale underwater light that follows a clear sunset, and not achieving the sudden glitter of the cities at dusk, seem to be places where everybody has hurried home forever, where all life has gone washing out to the circumference, leaving the center untenanted, its streets as empty as they are in so many old drawings. But this apparent lifelessness is an illusion. On this evening, much was happening in or near the center of Farbridge. Behind dimming façades, like so many half-lit theater sets, there was plotting and counterplotting. The prejudices and passions of men went their unsleeping way. If there were few passers-by, mischief itself was still afoot.

For example, in a corner of the smoke room at the Unionist Club, which had remained unchanged since the eighties except for the price of its drinks, Colonel Whatmore, Mr. Crandry, Alderman Tanhead, and Mr. Corby-Smith, were seated round a table and nine shillings' worth of whisky and soda water and five-and-ninepence worth of dry sherry. Mr. Corby-Smith, who had the proof of an editorial in his hand, was looking as cunning as our tradition of a Free and Independent Press would allow him to look.

"I think," he was saying, "it will make people sit up. It's as strong as I could make it—"

"Not strong enough," said Mr. Crandry, who was in a bad temper. "You ought to have hit harder, Corby-Smith."

"Our law of libel is tricky, Mr. Crandry. But reading between the lines—"

"Nobody reads between lines," Mr. Crandry snapped.

"No, Mr. Crandry," said Alderman Tanhead. "It's as much as we could reasonably expect."

"Quite," said Colonel Whatmore, who was aloof and gloomy. "But it's a bit of a blow—what?—the Mayor agreeing to take the chair at this meeting. Bulfoss, of course—well, we know what to expect from him now—dam' fool!"

"It depends how the meeting goes," said Alderman Tanhead. "Herbert Walmer's cautious and timid, but he's a fair man with a good deal of experience, and he'll know how to interpret the feeling of the meeting."

"I might add a line or two to my editorial," said Corby-Smith, "referring to the meeting and—"

But Crandry seemed determined that the editor should never be allowed to conclude any statement. "Go on then. Pitch it stronger, man."

"Well?" And Corby-Smith glanced across at Colonel Whatmore, as if asking for help.

"Yes," said the Colonel dubiously. "I'm as anxious as you are, Crandry, not to let these people get away with it, especially that Commodore fella. But we haven't got the *Record* entirely in our pocket. Can't afford to go dead against public feeling—what?"

If people ever said "Pshaw!" Crandry would have said it then. As it was he made a noise that suggested he was thinking along "Pshaw!" lines. "They're bluffing. And I'm not going to stand for it, you can please yourself. Who's this?"

It was, in fact, that Labour stalwart, Alderman Muleford, who was for once allowing himself to be lured into one of the gilded haunts of the boss class. And his manner rather suggested that at any moment this dingy old-fashioned smoke room, hastily transformed to deceive him, would return to its fountains of champagne and troupes of dancing girls.

"Glass of beer'll do me," he announced defiantly in reply to Colonel Whatmore's inquiry. He lit his short pipe as if it were a beacon in honor of the Tolpuddle Martyrs. "I see they've got Walmer on their platform."

"It isn't their platform," said Alderman Tanhead.

"It's their meeting, isn't it? They fixed it up. We didn't. No necessity. Festival came up for consideration and was turned down. We all know that. Now they've got this meeting—and the Mayor into the bargain—piecan!"

"For once," said the Colonel, "I agree with you."

"What I meant," said Alderman Tanhead, who might be narrow and obstinate but was no fool, "was that it's a public meeting. We're allowed to speak, and I'm going to speak—and so are you, I hope, Muleford."

"Yes, I'll speak. Everybody knows where I stand. Hours and wages, better conditions—"

"Quite so." And Tanhead nipped in just in time. "So the feeling of the meeting will depend on the audience. And that—setting political differences aside, because we're agreed we don't want this Festival nonsense—is what we wanted to see you about." He gave a quick glance at Crandry and Colonel Whatmore, not for their approval but as a warning to let him manage Muleford. "Now we all know you've got a great deal of influence in Trade Union and Labour circles here. And we don't want your people to boycott this meeting. On the contrary." He looked hard at Muleford, who nodded. Corby-Smith nodded too, several times, all in an important fourth-estate sort of way. Whatmore and Crandry, who had been none too pleased to see Muleford, now brightened up and leaned forward.

Not very far away, in that office on the second floor of the White Hart, something like a committee meeting was being held. Present were the Commodore, Theodore and Laura (taking notes), old Jordan, Seth Hull, and Mobbs. They had just decided on their speakers for the public meeting.

"This is the list then," said the Commodore. "Major Bulfoss, Mrs. Coote—or, failing her, Councillor Gisburn, Mr. Jordan, and myself. And we're agreed that's enough?"

"Quite enough," said Mobbs. "Don't forget that at least three of 'em —probably Whatmore, Tanhead, and Muleford—will be speaking for the other side."

"And we're paying the expenses of the meeting," said the Commodore. "Providing them with a platform for nothing. Perhaps I was a fool to agree when they suggested it at the Town Hall."

"No, no, my friend," cried Jordan. "Much more sensible to hear both sides. Make a debate of it. Liberal democracy. Expensive and elaborate, but best in the end."

"What about an organist?" Mobbs asked.

The Commodore stared at him. "This is a meeting not a concert, my dear fellow."

"Can't tell me about meetings, old boy. That's something I *do* know about. And if the place is full, as it will be, nothing like the organ going and a singsong before the speeches to warm 'em up."

"Perhaps we don't want to warm 'em up," said the Commodore.

"Yes, yes, in this case, most certainly," cried Jordan. "Here we're the warm party, wanting something to be done. Our opponents are the cold party, against doing anything. Better then to warm up. *Hearts of Oak. Land of Hope and Glory.* That sort of thing. Oh, certainly."

"Leave it to me," said Mobbs. "I've done it before. Oh—hello, Seacombe!"

"Looks like business," said the new arrival. "Wouldn't interrupt, but this is important. This, Miss Casey and gentlemen, is a proof of an editorial that Corby-Smith has written for this week's *Record*. Never mind how I got it, though the Festival Fund owes me a quid. There it is." He tossed it on to the table round which they were sitting. "The first three paragraphs are the usual guff about hard times and high rates and not being able to afford a Festival. It's the next paragraph— you'll see I've marked it—that dishes out the dirt."

"Read it, one of yer," said Seth Hull. "Miss Casey."

" 'One or two members of the Borough Council and several fairly prominent residents,' " Laura read out to them, " 'were in favor of a Festival, but were willing to abide by the Council's decision, which won general approval, not to spend the ratepayers' money on any special celebrations—if that term is not too handsome for whatever is likely to be proposed—here in Farbridge. It is well to note that the persons chiefly associated with this new demand for a Farbridge Festival are neither members of the Council nor even prominent residents. A generous allowance of misrepresentation—and we appear to be encountering a good deal of it just now—cannot turn them into Farbridge citizens or give them any particular standing in our borough. Claims that there was some official backing from the central London authority for this mysterious Farbridge adventure, for which the ratepayer here will have to pay if the movement succeeds, have already been proved to be false. And no doubt other claims, if thought to be worth investigating, would meet with no better fate. We are staunch believers in private enterprise, as our readers know, but cannot admire the doubtful enterprise of self-invited and self-appointed Farbridge Festival organizers, amusing themselves at our expense. In fact, we suggest they take and use their wits elsewhere, and leave honest Farbridge townsfolk to conduct honest Farbridge business!'" She looked round the table. "I say, that's a stinker, isn't it?"

"It is, ducky," cried Michael cheerfully. "And a fairly cunning job, if you take a good look at it. Old Corby-Smith gave it all he knew. It doesn't contain a single actionable statement, yet it suggests you're a little gang of crooks, Con types living on your wits, who have just muscled into dear simple old honest Farbridge."

"That's about it," said the Commodore. "And it's me he's getting at, of course."

"Artful, cunning, difficult to answer." Jordan rubbed his nose hard. "What do you say, Captain Mobbs?"

"It's blue murder. And they'll all have read it by the time we have our meeting. My godfathers! It'll be the talk of the town by Monday."

"And I was the man," the Commodore groaned, "who told 'em if they wanted to play rough and tough, I'd show 'em something."

Old Jordan gave him a shrewd look. "You keep out of this, Commodore. Dignified silence. And the young people needn't worry. But we'll have to do something. Don't know what? Seth, I have an idea you're the man."

"That's right," said Seth Hull. "I'll fix it. Give it to me, Miss Casey. I'll have a word or two first with yer, Mr. Jordan. Then later on I'll look in at the *Record* office."

"Is that going to work, Seth?" asked Michael.

"Leave it to me, lad. I'll rough an' tough him."

Out at Mrs. Coote's, Huntley, the Chief Education Officer, and the rather beautiful and sad Helen Weeks, of Whatmore's, were drinking coffee. It was a queer time of the evening to be drinking coffee, but Mrs. Coote's was that kind of house, in which you might be given coffee when you arrived and soup or sandwiches two hours afterwards. It was a house full of children, homework, blue books and white papers and minutes of the last meeting, coffee and tea and odd bits of cake, and the clash of front door and telephone bells and sonatinas hammered out on a wreck of a piano. It was all a mess but had a happy atmosphere. There was a Mr. Coote, but he was a civil engineer who was away in Africa or India for months at a time, returning occasionally, loaded with inappropriate gifts, to a cheerful pandemonium, after which he made fruitful love to Mrs. Coote, who was equally glad to have him there or to see him go. It was not everybody's life, but the Cootes liked it.

Mrs. Coote had invited Helen Weeks and Huntley together, partly to talk about the Festival movement and partly because she believed they were vaguely attracted to each other and that something might come of it. (Here she was wrong, but then like many busy useful people, she was not clever about personal relationships.) All three were now smoking, trying to drink the coffee, which was horrible, and doing their best to talk, which was difficult because Prudence Coote, a grim little redhead aged eleven, was taking her turn at riveting a sonatina.

"I think that'll do now, darling," her mother shouted. "You played it very nicely. And isn't it bedtime?"

"No," said Prudence. But she left the piano and joined her brother Hugh, who was crayoning in a rather inspired fashion in the other corner of the room. Other Cootes could be heard on the floor above, which was clearly not carpeted.

This atmosphere was difficult for Huntley, who could not shout and scream like the women, and indeed could hardly raise his voice without ruining his mysterious intimate manner. But this comparative quiet gave him a chance.

"Erce," he said, although he had not been called upon to agree with anybody. "I think next week's meeting—if it goes well—may get us the Festival. Had a word or two with Meare this afternoon—he was cautious, of course—but I think that's his opinion too. Then there are two important questions—"

"Yes," cried Mrs. Coote, who never hesitated to cut into Huntley's murmuring. "That's what I want to talk about. And the first question is—what grant do we ask for?"

"Exactly." And Huntley closed his eyes, drew in the ether, quivered, and apparently lost consciousness.

"What was our original figure?" Helen Weeks demanded. "I remember we worked something out."

"I have it here," said Mrs. Coote, diving into some notes. "Yes, here it is. Three thousand five hundred pounds. That included seven-fifty for the organizer, who, if we'd passed it then, would have been working for us about eight months or so, perhaps longer."

Huntley joined them again. "Erce. If you remember, Mrs. Coote—I pointed out at the time—if that payment included office expenses, secretarial assistance, then it was not enough to tempt a first-class man—and too much for the sort of fellow who'd want to take it—familiar dilemma—"

"But I never felt," said Miss Weeks, who may have looked intense and melancholy but nevertheless had plenty of common sense, "that we needed an organizer for such a long time. I admit it's going to be a dreadful rush now. But I often think people prefer that—more dramatic and exciting."

"So do I," said Mrs. Coote. "Now I'm going to suggest that you two should be on the Festival Committee, with Mr. Jordan and somebody else—Gisburn perhaps. And I propose we ask for the original figure—three thousand five hundred. We also ask for private contributions, and I believe, with Jordan and Hull contributing handsomely, as I think they will, we ought to reach five thousand."

"Erce." Huntley had kept his eyes open ever since he spoke last, and was now looking deeply fatigued. "No great difficulty about the Committee—though the other side may want one or two of their own people on it—to question every item of expenditure. Where the trouble really begins—is with the organizer. Considerable prejudice against Commodore Tribe—must face it—and though he seems to be the right type of man, probably first-class—we may be told we can have our Festival—but not with Tribe running it."

"Well, I must say that's not good enough," said Helen Weeks warmly. "I happen to know little Laura Casey rather well—she's acting as secretary to Tribe, chiefly I think because she's fallen heavily for the rather mysterious young man, Jenks, who's working with them—"

"My dear," cried Mrs. Coote, "I've met him. And I don't blame her. And she's a nice child too. But go on."

"It's simply not good enough because there wouldn't have been a hope of a Festival if these three hadn't set to work here. And even quite apart from that, I don't believe we could possibly find anybody, especially now when there's so little time, to do the job half as well as they could. According to Laura, this Commodore man can almost persuade anybody to do anything, and this Jenks boy has terrific charm and knows all kinds of people in London, theater people and so on, and our only hope of having a decent Festival is to appoint these three as the organizing staff and to tell them to go ahead. I feel strongly about this."

"Helen's quite right, you know," Mrs. Coote told Huntley, who had ventured a short quivering nap.

"Erce, I think so." And now instead of closing his eyes again, he used them, in slow glances from one to the other of his listeners, to suggest illimitable complexities of Refined Back Room Boy intrigue. "We ask for the grant originally suggested—and for Tribe and the other two to be officially appointed—with a Festival Committee on the lines you suggest, Mrs. Coote. Erce. It means various little moves—having a word with certain people—anticipating certain possible countermoves— persuading one or two key people—" His murmur faded as he retreated farther and farther into some vision of Kafka-like ramifications and regresses; while the ladies, who had never been able to read Kafka and were suspicious of the Back Room Boy manner, frowned at him out of their impatience.

Meanwhile, a very different little meeting was being held in Paul Ravenstreet's sitting room at his lodgings. If this meeting had been challenged to describe itself—if, for example, representatives of the Special Branch, M.I.5, or the F.B.I., had come charging in—it would have declared itself to be a weekly meeting of the North Farbridge Philately Society, and in support of this statement Mr. Ravenstreet would have been able to produce three albums of later British Colonials, having been a collector himself during his earlier and escapist period. It is perhaps typical of a decaying bourgeois society and its miserable Liberal Democracy that these regular gatherings had never been required to explain themselves; all in sharp contrast, no doubt, to what would have happened to such deviationist types in a true democracy and under an ideal People's Government, which might have packed them off to cut timber in the Arctic Circle as an initial process of re-education. For this was, in fact, a meeting of Farbridge Communists, all five of them. Ravenstreet, though he provided the sitting room, was not the Leader, who was a short stern railway clerk. The remaining three consisted of a stringy youth who had worked in all the garages in the town, and two female comrades, an angry middle-aged teacher and an intellectual girl who was a typist at the Town Hall. Except the Leader, a man of iron, they were drinking tea, smoking, or eating rock cakes.

"At our last meeting," the Leader was saying, "Comrade Ravenstreet raised the question of this Farbridge Festival. I told him then what I thought the Party line would be on this question. I have now had a definite ruling."

He paused, but it was obvious from his tone that this ruling would be unfavorable, and already the other three comrades were giving Ravenstreet some hostile or contemptuous looks. Apparently a sound comrade was not only expected to obey orders but ought to be capable of knowing in advance what those orders would be, thus clearing himself of what might be called the charge of retrospective deviationism.

"Every effort must be made," the Leader continued, after glancing at his notes, "to prevent the workers from taking part in mock celebrations, of a counterrevolutionary type, which may be used to encourage Fascism, Imperialism, and Warmongering, threaten the solidarity of the revolutionary working class movement, and to increase among doubtful elements the tendency toward petty bourgeois escapism."

"Certainly," said the angry teacher, and then looked sharply at Ravenstreet.

"Party members," said the Leader, "whose work brings them into direct contact with Festival enterprises should endeavor to create disputes on wages, hours, conditions, call for strikes, and regard themselves as shock troops of industrial and other sabotage."

"That's it," said the stringy youth. "Let's 'ave a bit o' sabotage."

"That's quite clear, comrade," said the intellectual typist, who always talked and behaved like the heroine of a Soviet play. "Now we know what to do. And if I have a chance at the Town Hall, I shall take it."

"What will you do?" asked Comrade Ravenstreet, who was in a bad mood. "Put a letter in the wrong envelope?"

"Comrade Secretary and Chairman," cried the intellectual typist, now in the center of the stage at the Red Army Theater, Moscow, "I protest."

"Quite right," said the angry teacher, who had disliked Ravenstreet ever since he had refused the challenge of her honest, full-blooded Communist womanhood.

"I protest against a remark made in a deviationist and cynical spirit," cried the Heroine.

"That's it," said the stringy youth. "What's 'e goin' ter do? No idears, I'll bet."

"All right, comrades, I apologize," said Ravenstreet, who was beginning to feel an outcast. Then he added apologetically: "Naturally I accept the Party ruling. But I'd like to point out that we don't even know there's going to be a Festival here yet."

"Comrade," said the Leader with great severity, "it's our duty, as good Party members, to do all we can to stop this Festival, and, failing that, to do all we can to make it a failure."

"There's a public meeting about it next week," said the intellectual typist, almost an ordinary Farbridge girl again. "Do we attend that to make a protest, in the name of the class-conscious workers?"

"Some of us should be there, comrades," said the Leader. "If the Festival is agreed on, then I propose to put down on the agenda for our next meeting a discussion of what individual action members might undertake."

The teacher, angrier than ever, suddenly replaced the rock cake she had taken. "And I propose," she cried, with a furious glance all round, "that no further meetings should take place here, in view of Comrade Ravenstreet's unsatisfactory attitude. And I offer, for our next meeting, my own sitting room—perfectly quiet and with a nice gasfire."

"I second that," cried the intellectual typist.

"Now wait a minute," Ravenstreet began.

"Comrades," said the Leader-Secretary-Chairman, sitting bolt upright and looking such a man of iron that few of his colleagues in the Farbridge Station Goods Office would have recognized him at that moment, "in the name of Unity and Solidarity—" And the debate continued.

About half a mile away, in the editor's room at the *Weekly Record*, Mr. Corby-Smith, wearing his pince-nez, high stiff collar, spotted bow tie, but also an old alpaca office jacket, was sitting at ease, his long cigarette holder tilted at an angle, as he glanced rather negligently at some proofs. A morning paper man in the old days, he still liked to look in for an hour or two in the evenings, even if there was little for him to do, just to feel that he had not completely lost touch with those days. It was, in fact, part of his character performance. The adjoining rooms were deserted. There he was alone, perhaps deciding the fate of A. J. Balfour or polishing a witty retort to the Suffragettes.

The sharp rap on his frosted-glass panel was followed, while he was crying: "Come in," by the deliberate, impressive, vaguely menacing entrance of Mr. Seth Hull, who moved toward the editor's desk as if he weighed about half a ton. His great square face looked larger and a deeper shade of red than usual, and his little eyes were like pellets of blue glass.

"Oh—it's you, Hull," said Corby-Smith nervously. He was never at ease with Hull at any time, and now he suspected that the man was quietly but perhaps menacingly drunk. "Sit down. Anything I can do for you?"

"Yes," said Seth Hull, sitting down massively and never taking his indignant little eyes off the editor. "See that." And he threw on the desk a proof that Corby-Smith, first with astonishment and then with some alarm, recognized as his editorial on the Festival.

"How did you get hold of this?"

"Never mind," said Hull in his growling bass. "Beside the point." Then he leaned forward and tapped on the desk, making plenty of noise with his huge blunt forefinger. "What did yer write that for?"

"Well, my dear sir, it's a topical subject, and I considered that in the public interest—"

"Go on. I don't want any o' that stuff. I want to know why yer wrote that bloody poppycock."

"Come, come, we're all entitled to our opinion—"

"And I don't want any o' that neither," said Hull savagely.

"I really don't see why you should adopt that tone," said Corby-Smith, wondering whether to say that he ought to be going home.

"What about tone o' that?" And Hull pointed the table-rapping finger at the proof.

"It merely says what a great many people are thinking."

Hull brought his fist crashing down on the desk. "Now answer me. Who put yer up to it?"

"I'm responsible for what goes into the paper," said Corby-Smith hurriedly. "But I have policy meetings with my board of directors from time to time, chiefly Mr. Crandry, and occasionally Colonel Whatmore, who's Vice-chairman."

Hull was much quieter now. "An' Crandry told yer to write that, didn't he?"

"As a matter of fact, he did. Not that I—"

"We don't need that bit," said Hull, cutting in brutally. "Now look, Corby-Smith. Yer know me—or if yer don't, it's time yer did. An' when I say something, I mean it. Now I'll tell yer two things—for yer own good. Listening?"

The other left him in no doubt about that.

"Number One. Little Crandry won't be throwing his weight about so much soon. I'm not going to tell yer for why. Just take it from me, that's all." He stared so hard at Corby-Smith that although the latter did not know what to say, he felt compelled to say something.

"Well, I don't know about these things," he said hesitantly. "And no doubt you do, Hull."

"Number Two. Print that, an' it's bloody war between your paper an' me an' a lot more. Right off—bang!"

"But I must print it—"

"Now I'm tellin' yer. Print that, an' yer'll start something yer won't know how to finish. First, there's me—an' yer'd be surprised if I told yer how many things I'm connected with round here. Now print that muck, an' I take out—sharp—every advertisement of anything I'm connected with—hotel, pubs, garages, football, billiards, an' some more I've got up me sleeve. An' that's just a start. I'll go for yer—bang—bang—whizzbang! Next, there's old Jordan—"

"But he wouldn't—"

"He *would*. Told me to tell yer."

"But—but—this is sheer blackmail."

"An' I suppose what Crandry does is whitemail."

Corby-Smith had now taken off his pince-nez and was blinking as if at an unfamiliar sinister world. "It's not the same thing at all. Mr. Crandry, for all practical purposes, is more or less the proprietor of the *Weekly Record*. Naturally if there is anything about which he feels strongly—"

"Yer write it an' print it, an' we pay him for his paper an' make best of it. All right, that's what he does. Now I'm tellin' yer what me an' a few more's going to do. If your lot can do what yer like, then me an' my pals'll do what we like." He came up slowly out of his chair, still staring hard at the editor, and pushed his bulk against the desk, towering over the other man. "An' not so much o' that blackmail talk. Yer went far enough in that little packet o' muck there." He pointed to the proof. "Any more of it an' I'll slap an action on yer that'll keep yer awake for the next six months. Yer gettin' my monkey up, between yer. I'm sixty—wi' nobody dependent on me—an' some money to throw away. If yer want me to spend it knockin' hell out o' some o' you chaps, that's all right to me. It'll be a pastime. But not for you, it won't. Next thing yer want to do after you've printed that is to start packing your bags, mister." He lumbered to the door, where he turned slowly, pointing at the editor. "Leave that piece out—or your number's up."

"But—Mr. Hull—"

"I say no more." He stumped out, banging the door, but halfway down the stairs a wheezing sound, the rusty chuckle in the cave, came out of him. And by this time, Corby-Smith, no longer the Edwardian thunderer but a shaky oldish man, had picked up the telephone.

It was rather later still, about ten o'clock, when Laura heard the front door bell. She was alone in the sitting room, having volunteered to stay in when she knew the Saxons were anxious to visit some friends. To her surprise, this late caller was Theodore. "Is it too late?" he asked her.

"No, of course not. Come in. I'm on my own tonight."

As soon as they were in the sitting room, he said rather hurriedly: "I've just seen Seth Hull at the hotel. He'd been to the *Weekly Record* office, and he thinks he's bullied and bluffed Corby-Smith into washing out that attack on us. We can't be certain, of course, until the paper comes out, but Seth's pretty sure he managed it."

Laura almost shuddered. "If he says so, I should think it's all right. I'm glad that old meaty monster's on our side. Did you come to tell me that?"

"I thought you'd like to know."

"Oh yes—of course I'm delighted." She waited a moment. "Would you like something to drink, if we have it?"

"No, thank you. Unless you'd like to make some tea."

"I was just considering it when you rang." As she got up, she gave him an inquiring look. He tried to smile but was not altogether successful. "Just stay there. It won't be long."

It was not until each of them had taken several sips of the clear fresh brew, upon which he had rather laboriously congratulated her, that she asked him what was the matter. "If it's anything you can talk about," she added. "Because I know there's something." And it occurred to her then, for the first time, that perhaps inside she was much tougher than he was. Nothing to do with sex. Her father, who was rather small though strongly built, had told her more than once that little people were tougher inside than the big types.

"Two things," he replied. "First, about this morning. You probably think I ought not to have let those people sweep me out of the office like that."

"Nothing to do with me. You weren't doing much, anyhow."

"It was Festival business really. The Group Captain might be useful to us in various ways. And I wanted to ask the actresses about the theater side of the Festival. None of us knows much about that, and the Commodore says now that he wants to leave the drama part to me."

"Well, that's all right then," she said coolly. But then she began laughing. "What about Mrs. Delacey and Miss Fisby?"

But he did not even smile. "I've been reading that pageant, and I think it might do, when she's made it longer and brought it up to date. I've told the Commodore so, and he says, if they let us do the Festival, then you and I had better rope in Miss Fisby and her pageant."

"It seems to me that if we're not careful, you and I will find ourselves landed with all the work, while that lazy fat old fraud just sits about drinking with his chums. We'll have to watch that, my lad." She was all gay and matey, but he still did not respond. There was something flat and wooden about him tonight that irritated her and diminished him.

"Well, that's the other thing," he said slowly.

"What is?" She spoke sharply.

"I don't seem to be doing much. You can call the Commodore a lazy fat old fraud, but he's really carrying the scheme—"

"Yes, because it suits him and he's not making a bad thing out of it. Don't forget that." Laura was always more catty about the poor old Commodore than she felt or even intended to appear, but her anxiety to show Theodore that she had no illusions about the old boy always gave an edge to her talk in moments like this.

"And you've been far more use than I have," he continued, obviously determined not to be sidetracked into an argument about the Commodore. "So have Seacombe and Seth Hull. Perhaps even Mobbs—"

"Your colleague for calling on the County." Laura had one of those stubborn feminine prejudices against this trip.

But Theodore plodded on, like a man walking on a hot afternoon to some place he hated. "I'm beginning to feel I'm almost a passenger—"

"Don't worry. If this thing goes through, you won't feel that very long. You'll find yourself driving, steering, stoking, cooking, and doing all the other things that passengers don't do. Haven't I just told you that if we're not careful we'll find ourselves landed with all the work, except any that calls for a lot of booze and chat? And if all this stuff about not doing much has been making you feel depressed, Theodore, then you're being very silly."

"Well, it has."

"I could shake you."

"All right then. Shake me."

"You're too big. I'd just be shaking myself, and I don't need it. Look—let's be sensible," she continued briskly, as if she had no idea that what would do them most good was far removed from this sensible twaddle. "I can remember all we're proposing to do in this Festival, having typed it out umpteen times. Now if you've a bit of paper and a pencil, we'll decide what each of us ought to take on, always remembering that Marshal Tribe, our glorious leader, will dodge most of his share."

"That's a good idea," he told her, cheering up, and beginning to search his pockets. When he found a pencil and an envelope, however, instead of looking at her inquiringly, like a man waiting for a list, he looked at her quite unexpectedly in that special turn-your-heart-over way of his. "Laura," he began.

But she was holding onto her heart, just keeping it the right side up. "What? Aren't you ready?" All brisk and cool, the business girl, feminine—in fact, nearly as fresh and dainty as those in the advertisements—but hardened and streamlined for a career.

"You and Seacombe seemed to be enjoying yourselves at lunch today."

She raised her eyebrows, or hoped she did. "Yes, we were. Michael was in very good form. He can be very entertaining, you know." And now—what?

"Yes, I suppose he can," said the giant chump sadly.

Laura could have clouted him on one of his fat large beautiful ears. "Well, never mind about Michael. Festival activities. First then— music. I'm going to be responsible for that. With some help, of course. Dr. Barr and Helen Weeks chiefly, I think. Next—"

And they were still at it, and real life had hardly moved on an inch, when the Saxons returned, all smiles and nods and little glances, quite maddening. In the discussion about the future of Asia, Laura contradicted everybody, including herself, quite recklessly.

It would be pleasant to record that the foolish Theodore's rival, M. Seacombe, was pacing up and down the street outside or sitting in his lodgings dreamily endeavoring to recall some dark flashing image of Laura. The truth is, however, that he was up in Seth Hull's room, drinking large Scotches with Seth, the Commodore, and little Mobbs, and floating with them on a stream of reminiscence and disreputable anecdotes. Later, when Theodore looked in, the air was thick and reeked of smoke, spirits, lies, and nonsense. Did the bewildered lover turn in disgust from this crude masculine atmos- phere, instantly preferring his quiet bedroom and further meditation on the riddle of his dark lady? He did not.

CHAPTER THREE

Targets Are Reached, Missed, Even Passed

I

THERE is a fast train from London, complete with dining car in which anybody with a taste for gravy soup, fish bones, and tepid custard may have an excellent lunch, that arrives, usually rather exhausted, at Farbridge in the early afternoon. On the day of the Festival public meeting, among the passengers who alighted from this train were a woman and two men, all traveling separately, each of them carrying a small case. The woman was a pleasant-looking middle-aged creature, whose smart clothes were not quite in keeping with her innocent face and rather naïve manner. She was, in fact, the mysterious Grace who had dined with the Commodore and had then vanished during the performance of the revue. Now she asked a porter about hotels and was told to try the White Hart. There was only one taxi left, and as she prepared to take it, she found herself addressed by one of the two men, a prosperous, egg-faced, anxious fellow.

"Pardon me, madam," he said. "But do I understand that you are going to the White Hart? And if so, might I suggest, to save valuable time, that you allow me to share this taxi as I am going there too?"

"Oh—yes," said Grace, "that's quite all right."

As they climbed into the taxi, which was not one of your new squat vehicles and so had to be climbed into, the other man who had come from London now drifted nearer. He was such a vaguely dingy figure that at five years' range he vanished from sight in any vaguely dingy urban setting, but when closely observed he revealed certain individual features: he was badly shaven, had a rather long reddish nose, eyes of a dark pewter shade, shabby clothes, and a disgraceful hat; and he was one of those people who, by some private magic, always appear to have a half-smoked cigarette, always the same length, drooping from a corner of their mouths. The case he carried was very small and in a shocking condition.

"This White Hart, where is it, chum?" he said to the porter. "Far to walk?" As he spoke, he did not look at the porter but kept an eye on the taxi. "Turn right at the bottom and then second left and then right again," he repeated, hardly moving his lips. "Thanks, chum." And he began to follow the taxi.

Meanwhile, in the cavernous leathery interior of the taxi, its two passengers had not kept silent.

"My name," the man announced gravely, as soon as they had settled themselves, "is Hatchet-Ferrers." It may have been the Hatchet, the Ferrers, or merely the hyphen, but certainly his manner of announcing his name suggested that in his opinion it was a guarantee of impeccable behavior in any licensed vehicle.

"I see," said Grace, smiling vaguely. No guarantee, in fact, had been necessary. The man looked as harmless as the egg he somehow suggested. "It's not a bad journey from London, is it?"

"Well, I can't say I enjoyed it. But then I rarely travel by train these days. It happens, however, that my Daimler wasn't available."

"Fancy!" She was now glancing happily through the window. "I like these sort of towns, don't you?"

"I'm afraid not," he told her solemnly. "I don't pretend to know Farbridge well—although I have heard a good deal about it from—from a friend who lives here—but I don't imagine it's the kind of place I would care about. Neither one thing," he continued severely, "nor the other. Too small. Too provincial. A narrow life, I would say."

"I don't mind that," she said cheerfully. "Though of course they do get a bit nosey in towns like this." She gave him a smiling glance, and was rather alarmed to see that the eyes behind the enormous spectacles were closed and that a look of suffering had taken possession of his large white face. "I'm sorry—aren't you feeling well?"

"Yes, yes, thank you," replied Hatchet-Ferrers, who had in fact been alarmed by her remark about people being nosey in towns like Farbridge. "Although my health is not what it ought to be. I have to take care, considerable care. And I have a great many responsibilities and important commitments."

"Yes, I expect you have," said Grace, who decided that he was a rather nice but silly old fusspot. Wouldn't like to look after him, she reflected, fussing around and coddling himself.

"I think I saw you in the dining car," he said mournfully.

"That's right. Wasn't a very nice lunch, was it?"

His high voice quivered and then rose almost to a squeak. "A horror. An outrage. My dear madam, I can't tell you what I felt. I sent the fish away and tried the sausages. Appalling, simply appalling."

"Yes, well I hope they give us something better at this White Hart."

"Oh—I think so. I think you may depend upon that. I have a friend who is staying there and he speaks well of it, and he's a man of some taste and judgment in these matters, a man who has traveled widely and knows the world—a Commodore Tribe."

"Did you say Commodore Tribe? Well, I never did! You see," she continued, in a high state of excitement, "I know him. Not really well—but I do know him. In fact—" But then she checked herself. And unfortunately the taxi had stopped now, so that she had a good excuse for breaking off. "This must be it."

After she had asked for a room and had registered, as *Mrs. G. Robinson, Pelham Court, S.W.1.*, and while Mr. Hatchet-Ferrers, breathing heavily, was signing the register with a gold pen, as if it were a peace treaty, Grace rather timidly asked Miss Pratt at the reception desk if the Commodore was in the hotel. Looking up, Hatchet-Ferrers observed that he was about to ask the same question.

"No," said Miss Pratt, replying to them both, "the Commodore and Mr. Jenks have gone along to the Corn Exchange. They're having a big meeting there tonight about this Festival. I expect you could find him there. And anyhow he'll be back here long before the meeting starts. Shall I give him a message?" She looked at Grace.

Grace shook her head and said that she would go up to her room. Hatchet-Ferrers asked if there was a telephone in his room, and when he was told there was not, he allowed himself to be directed to a call box, where, not without some agitation, he put through a call to the Bulfoss house. But there was no reply, and then he too, feeling fatigued and remembering there were several pills and tablets that ought to be swallowed as soon as possible, followed Grace's example and went up to his room.

A few minutes later, Miss Pratt, who had been speaking on the telephone herself, was shocked to discover that a scrubby-looking man was peering down his long nose at the register. She hurried forward. "What do *you* want?"

"Want a room, miss." He spoke out of one corner of his mouth, keeping the untidy half-cigarette dangling from the other corner.

Miss Pratt, as she explained many times afterwards, took a poor view of him. "I'm afraid we're full."

"Now, now, now. Can't have that. Here on important business. Wouldn't like me to complain, would you, miss? No, of course you wouldn't. You must have some little back bedroom somewhere. That'll do me. Not choosy."

Remembering a little back room on the top floor, not considered good enough for the average guest, she reluctantly assigned it to him. Then, after registering, he took the key himself, waved away the porter, and drifted upstairs. As soon as he had gone, she examined the register, which now contained the simplest and least informative entry it had ever known: *A. Smith, London.* After staring at it indignantly for a moment or two, she went to the telephone, to report this dubious new arrival to Mr. Hull up in his private room; but then she remembered that Mr. Hull had an important visitor up there and had asked not to be disturbed.

Seth Hull, who at that very moment was saying: "Yer'll take a drop o' something," was in fact entertaining a notable Farbridge figure, namely, Geordie Pitts, once a star of First Division football and an international center half, and now the manager of the Farbridge club. He looked rather like a bald, friendly, pink gorilla.

"Yer'll be seeing most of our lads this afternoon?" said Seth, pouring out the whisky.

"I will, Mr. Hull."

"Me an' a few pals are very interested i' this meeting tonight at Corn Exchange. We want it to go well. An' if necessary we'd like to stop some folk who might be there to see that it won't go well. I dropped a hint to some of the lads, the other day."

"I heard, Mr. Hull. Best respects." And Geordie dealt with the whisky.

"It's just a favor, Geordie. If they don't want to go, I can't grumble. But as yer know yerself, I've tried to do my best for them, an' I thought some of 'em might like to do summat for me."

Geordie winked. "They'll be there, most of 'em. It's arranged. Some upstairs, some downstairs. Scattered—twos and threes. I'll be there myself, Mr. Hull, keeping an eye on 'em. I'll have a final word with 'em this afternoon."

"No rough work, Geordie. No, none o' that. Unless, of course, the other people start it—then we'll have to keep order."

"Must keep order," said Geordie, twinkling. "You're bent on having this Festival, are you, Mr. Hull?"

"Well now, I'll tell yer, Geordie lad. I wasn't so struck on it at first. Just seemed to me a goodish idea, which might help wi' trade an' so on. But some of 'em here's got so damned obstinate about not having it, an' been throwin' their weight about so much, they've got my monkey up, if you see what I mean?"

"I do, Mr. Hull. I'd feel the same way."

"I say to meself," Seth continued earnestly. " 'Well if it's last thing I do, yer'll have a bloody Festival an' like it.' Well, Geordie, much obliged, lad, an' get 'em there in good time—about half-past seven." He was about to say something else when Geordie put a finger on his arm to stop him. Geordie then held up this finger, in an obvious silent demand for no more talk, and the next moment moved quickly and quietly to the door, which he suddenly jerked open. Into the room fell the victim of this maneuver, A. Smith of London.

"Got him," said Geordie. "Thought I heard somebody outside. Very good hearing I have—always had." He was now standing with his back against the closed door, cutting off A. Smith's retreat.

"What the hell's the idea?" demanded Seth, glaring at A. Smith, who by this time had recovered himself and was smiling in a manner meant to be ingratiating but woefully lacking in charm, chiefly because the smile was as false as the extremely large regular teeth it revealed.

"Staying here," said A. Smith. "Looking round. Saw your door. Heard voices. Didn't want to interrupt, always polite, and then— whooshta!"

"Staying here since when?" asked Seth, still glaring away.

"Came on the London train, this afternoon. I've registered. A. Smith, London. That's me. All in order."

"All in order, is it? Just hold on a minute." And Seth telephoned down to the desk. "Has a Mr. Smith—of London—just registered? . . . He has, eh?" He listened for a moment or two to the doubts of the reception department, then said: "All right, love, don't yer bother. I'll manage." He put down the telephone, and addressed himself to Geordie. "I'll see you an' the lads tonight, Geordie. Off yer pop."

Left with A. Smith, Seth stared hard at him while maintaining a massive disquieting silence.

"All okay, I think," said Mr. Smith rather jauntily. "I'll be trotting."

"Hold on. Yer wanted to see me, didn't yer? If not, what were yer waiting outside that door for?"

"Do some other time. Could do with a bit of info. But it can wait. No hurry."

"Info?" Seth was still looking outraged when there was a knock and he shouted: "Come in."

"Mr. Hull," said the newcomer, who looked like money and was smoking a first-class cigar. "I'm Arthur Hatchet-Ferrers, Chairman of West British Chemicals. Commodore Tribe—"

"Yes, I've heard him mention yer, Mr. Hatchet-Ferrers," said Seth, who had heard the whole story of Mrs. Bulfoss' return, and treasured it. "Staying with us?"

"Yes," the other began, but said no more because now he noticed A. Smith, and there was something about A. Smith that made him open his eyes very wide and compress his lips, as if about to seal them.

"You're busy, gents," said A. Smith. "Some other time." And then he was gone.

Hatchet-Ferrers, his eyes still enormous and his mouth tightly shut, looked at the door that had closed so quickly behind Smith, turned and looked searchingly at Seth Hull, sat down, leaned forward, and unsealed his lips. "Mr. Hull, may I ask who that man is? I'm not inquiring out of idle curiosity. Who is he?"

"He's A. Smith of London, he is, an' we just caught him listenin' in behind that door when me an' manager o' Farbridge United was having a confidential bit o' talk. That's all I know now, but if I don't find out some more afore so long, my name's not Seth Hull. But I noticed yer gave a bit of a jump when yer saw him. What's up?"

"That fellow was on the train, Mr. Hull. I saw him pass up and down the corridor several times. Then I noticed him in the dining car, gobbling the atrocious food they gave us—in itself, I fancy, a suspicious circumstance. Finally, I saw him hanging about when another passenger, a Mrs. Robinson, I think she is, agreed to my sharing a cab with her to come here. And now I find him in here. Candidly, Mr. Hull, I don't like it. I have not a naturally suspicious nature—but I'm a man with heavy responsibilities who has to take care of himself—"

"That's right," said Seth, inwardly amused but looking like a wooden image. "Course yer have. Man i' your position. Go on."

"I didn't like the look of the fellow from the first, and now—frankly, Mr. Hull—I'm disturbed, seriously disturbed. Is he staying here?"

"He is tonight," said Seth grimly. "But if he stays longer than tonight in room he's been given, we'll know he's up to summat. He's up to summat anyhow, that chap is. Coming here with his A. Smith, London. Must think we're barmy. I'll show him. Just leave him to me, Mr. Hatchet-Ferrers. But yer didn't want to see me about him 'cos yer didn't know he was in here."

"You're quite right, of course." He cleared his throat and looked rather accusingly at the cigar he was holding. "I came to introduce myself. And—er—also, I was wondering if you knew whether Major Bulfoss and—er—Mrs. Bulfoss—"

"I can tell yer about them. They haven't gone away. He has to speak at our meeting tonight—an' it's ten to one he's either havin' a round o' golf or at their Estate Agent place. Now Mrs. Bulfoss—she's at a big Women's Institute do this afternoon. Trying a bit o' public life, Mrs. Bulfoss is. She'll be at our meeting tonight, on the platform."

Hatchet-Ferrers did his solemn nod-bow, carefully deposited an inch of ash from his cigar into the nearest ashtray, pushed himself up out of his chair, said: "Thank you, Mr. Hull," moved two steps, halted, and then pointed the glowing end of his cigar at Seth. "This Smith fellow. Do you think he could be employed by a Private Inquiry Agency?"

"If he is," said Seth comfortably, "it's a dam' bad firm. Coming here looking like that! Well, we'll see. Don't worry about him."

But as Mr. Hatchet-Ferrers slowly descended the main staircase, carrying but not actually smoking his cigar, he looked anything but carefree. And one of the first persons he saw in the entrance lounge was A. Smith of London, who was sitting in a fine tactical position, from which he had a clear view of the hotel entrance, the reception and porter's desk, and the staircase. Hatchet-Ferrers, after the first startled glance, ignored A. Smith, gave up his key at the desk, and waddled out into the High Street. It was a sunny afternoon, though not warm. Hatchet-Ferrers turned to the left, moved forward slowly, and then stopped outside the stores next door to the hotel. While pretending to examine a bedroom suite that looked as if it were made out of toffee, he kept glancing round at the White Hart entrance. But A. Smith never emerged. Retracing his steps, Hatchet-Ferrers paused long enough outside the hotel entrance to catch a glimpse of A. Smith still sitting in the same place. Much relieved, he sauntered away, had a look at the High Street, the Corn Exchange, the Town Hall, Peter Place, so that it was after four when he returned to the hotel. A. Smith was still there, with the magical inch of cigarette still smoldering and dropping ash on his coat. Afternoon tea could now be obtained in the lounge, and Hatchet-Ferrers obtained it. He was just pouring out his second cup when he saw the Mrs. Robinson of the taxi, now all fresh and trim, come from the direction of the lift and walk briskly along to the desk. After exchanging a remark or two with the head porter, she left the hotel. And about six seconds later, A. Smith of London was drifting, but at a fair turn of speed, toward the doorway. It was, as Hatchet-Ferrers assured himself with great thankfulness, as plain as a pikestaff, in fact plainer than any pikestaffs he ever remembered seeing: the man had followed Mrs. Robinson, and had come here to keep his horrible little eye on her.

Ten minutes later, when Hatchet-Ferrers had definitely decided against risking a cake with green icing, there came striding in, bulky and triumphant, Commodore Tribe, who caught sight of him immediately after he turned away from the desk.

"My dear fellow, this is an unexpected pleasure," said the Commodore, sitting down and taking a piece of buttered toast. "But nothing gone wrong, I hope?"

"I have had no news," said Hatchet-Ferrers in his most solemnly confidential manner. "And I felt I must know what is happening. So, acting on impulse—deplorable, no doubt, but understandable, I think, when you remember the state of my health—I rushed down here today, by train too. Have you—in confidence, my dear Commodore—had any talk with her?"

"I haven't. I've been very busy with this Festival business. But I understand they've been seen about together, and she's coming with him to our meeting tonight. You'd better come along too, hadn't you?"

"Frankly, is it wise? I'd already heard—from the landlord here, a decent fellow, I think, in spite of his manner—that she would be there. And I have been asking myself if I could risk it. What do you think? I trust your judgment, as you know."

"In your place, I'd risk it," said the Commodore, with a fair imitation of the other's tone. "After all, you have an interest in our Festival, being a prominent subscriber. That's a good excuse. You come with me tonight."

Hatchet-Ferrers looked happier, that is, more like an ordinary egg than an egg on which somebody had been penciling worried lines. "Very well, my dear fellow, I will. I had rather a shock this after· noon." And he gave a detailed account of A. Smith and his behavior. "Undoubtedly I was right," he continued, "when I told Hull that the man was probably some sort of Private Inquiry agent. Frankly, I thought he was following me, though I could hardly imagine that Bulfoss would go to such lengths—"

"I'm sure he wouldn't," said the Commodore, who was as positive as he sounded.

"Quite so. Then I discovered—by the exercise of a little ingenuity— that this man is actually following a woman who arrived here when I did, a Mrs. Robinson—incidentally I would have said a harmless kind of woman. I don't know whether I ought to say anything to her—what do you think?"

The Commodore made a shrugging motion. "Not knowing her, I couldn't say. Please yourself." Negligently he took a cake with orange icing and bit off two-thirds of it.

"She knows you, by the way."

The Commodore made a guggling sound, which might have been a startled "What?" struggling through orange icing, and stared at the smiling Hatchet-Ferrers.

"Yes, she distinctly said so, when I happened to mention you. She didn't tell me her name—although I gave her mine when we agreed to share a cab—but I saw in the register that she's a Mrs. Robinson. With some London address—S.W., I fancy."

"Is she," the Commodore began carefully, "a woman about forty-five, plumpish, gray eyes, brown hair, smartly dressed but with a rather unsophisticated provincial manner?"

"An exact description, my dear Commodore."

"By George!—it's Grace again. I'm infinitely obliged to you, my dear chap. I must look out for her. And for this Smith fellow. You know," he added, grinning, "what with one thing and another, this looks like being quite an eventful day."

"I don't know that I like eventful days," said Hatchet-Ferrers. "But then, of course, I have to take care of myself. Too much happening all at once is definitely bad for a nervous system like mine."

"Probably no good for mine these days," said the Commodore, his look still alight, "but—by George and Thunder!—now and again I still like to feel that anything might happen. And that's what I'm feeling now."

2

At five minutes to eight the Corn Exchange was full right up to the last two rows of the balcony, which are filled only when Farbridge is visited by the ballet or a swing band. The organ, which had been squeaking and thundering away for the last twenty minutes, was now playing that jolly old hunting song of the North, with the audience all singing: "*Do you ken John Peel tum tum tum tum, Do you ken John Peel dum dum dum dum?*" Up in the balcony and in the back seats below there were some dense little knots of young and toughish fellows, who might have been put there by Aldermen Muleford and Tanhead or by Seth Hull and Geordie Pitts, but certainly gave the impression that they had not merely drifted into the meeting. Among the mixed crowd nearer the platform were many familiar faces. Grace was there, looking rosy and excited, sitting next to Hatchet-Ferrers, looking pasty and anxious. There was a solid party from Brant-in-the-Hollow, including Mr. Hookwood and the Group Captain, Sir Barclay and Lady Gishforth, Fred and Liz and Dulcie. Maggie from the pub was there too, but was not sitting with the other Brant types, who had been invited by Theodore. It was Captain Mobbs who had persuaded Maggie to attend the meeting, and the empty seat beside her, at the end of the row, belonged to him, but he had not yet claimed it because he was still with the speakers somewhere out of sight, behind the platform. Dr. and Mrs. Barr and two heavily freckled daughters were present. So were Mrs. Delacey and Miss Fisby. The Communist Party was represented by the railway clerk, the angry teacher, and the intellectual typist, the stringy youth being absent. Ravenstreet was there too, but he was sitting with Helen Weeks and the Saxons, ignoring the rest of the Party and clearly showing deviationist tendencies. Eric Longshaw had brought a thin girl from the Tennis Club; and old Jordan's giant clerical lodger, Perkins, had brought four assorted specimens of Our Youth. Admiral Broadwater and his niece were there, both sitting bolt upright, refusing to sing, aloof, wary, as if called by duty to attend a tribal ceremony on the Congo. Mr. Corby-Smith was in the hall but was not sitting at the Press table, at which the best of a poorish lot was Michael Seacombe. Not far from this table, toward the end of the front row, were Seth Hull and several beefy sporting, drop-o'-something friends, giving a Smithfield Market look to that section of the audience. At the other end of the front row were two empty seats, and just as the organ spluttered and wheezed from *John Peel* to *Land of Hope and Glory*, these seats were occupied by Miss Laura Casey, in her best dark blue, and Mr. Theodore Jenks, who had slipped in through some mysterious pass door. They were followed by Captain Archibald Mobbs, who steered himself and a strong smell of whisky in the direction of the smiling, waving Maggie. The meeting was about to begin.

The speakers made their appearance on the platform, looking as usual like an underrehearsed and sheepish concert party. The Mayor was wearing his chain, a collar that might have once belonged to Gladstone, and an air of statesmanlike profundity; and he was accompanied by the Mayoress, who was wearing a fur coat that suggested no known animal and may have come from some other planet. Major Bulfoss, dark-suited and pink-faced, arrived with Mrs. Bulfoss, trim and fetching in beige under her leopardskin. Mrs. Coote was untidy, ripe, and reddish; old Jordan was beaky and tweedy; Colonel Whatmore was puce and stiff; and Alderman Tanhead and Alderman Muleford, coming on together, looked like a grim and ageing crosstalk act. The last but one to arrive was Commodore Horace Tribe, who had done something artful to his hair, collar, and tie, to suggest the elder statesman and Friend of the People. The very last was Chief Education Officer Huntley, who was not there as a speaker but as a symbolic figure of Knowledge and Culture. To prove that he could perform his self-anesthetizing feat in public as well as in private, he sank into his chair, closed his eyes, breathed deeply and quivered, and went under. At the sight of all these personages, the spiritual temperature of the gathering rose some twenty degrees. There was applause, of course, and mixed with it some cheers and hoots. These came from the back of the area and the balcony, where the humbler citizenry were sitting, and there was about these manifestations that flavor of irony and derision which lingers in the old Western democracies but has been eliminated in the truer democracies of the East.

"Very nice crowd, I'm sure," said the Mayoress complacently to Mrs. Bulfoss.

"Is it?" said Mrs. Bulfoss absently. The Commodore had just told her that Arthur Hatchet-Ferrers would be there, and now she was trying to discover where he was—poor Arthur. And surely he was over there, whispering to some woman—really!

"Get on with it, Herb," said Alderman Muleford, who was not in a good temper.

The Mayor began. It was a great pleasure to him—*Pzzzz*—to preside at this meeting, when an important discussion would take place regarding the question of the Festival for Farbridge, which—*Pzzzz*—they had thought at one time they had settled but which could still be thought of as an open question—*Pzzzz*—because of a considerable public demand for such a Festival, which—*Pzzzz*—some speakers would tell them had been exaggerated and others would say clearly showed that a Festival—*Pzzzz*—was wanted in the borough, which had always prided itself and rightly too—*Pzzzz*—on being a progressive community. And for ten minutes more, with many a *Pzzzz*, perhaps to show where he was, he hacked his way through dense thickets of relative clauses. When he finally emerged into the open, he was loudly applauded, just as many acrobats are enthusiastically clapped when at last they put an end to their unbearable antics. Above the applause could be heard a hoarse disreputable voice from the balcony, reminding the Mayor that he had other responsibilities by calling out: "Any old iron?"

Major Bulfoss, M.P., then led off for the Festival supporters. He repeated what he said in the B.B.C. program, but added that since the broadcast he had discovered that the demand for a Farbridge Festival had grown considerably, and that although he realized that as their Member it was no business of his to question the decisions of the Town Council, speaking as a Farbridge man—and a ratepayer—he was convinced that the Council should reverse its former decision as soon as possible, and that in his capacity as a Member of Parliament he promised to do all he could to ensure that the Festival would be a success and worthy of their ancient borough. All this was well received, although there were some hoots and catcalls, and a young man at the back of the hall advised the Major to put a sock in it. This was followed by the sounds of a scuffle, which the Mayor, after some hesitation, decided to ignore. He called upon Colonel Whatmore to reply to Major Bulfoss.

Addressing an audience of this kind, the Colonel saw himself as a military man and not as a manufacturer of artificial silk. The officers and men of some doomed regiment had been formed into a hollow square, flickeringly lit by bivouac fires and distant bursting shells; and the time was the Eve of Battle. Like many military orators, he gave the impression that he was attempting to combine the barking of the sheepdog with the baa-ing of the sheep. Although he made a good deal of noise, turning a dangerous purple in the process, it is doubtful if a large proportion of the audience heard what he said; and several members of it, whose delivery was unfortunately much better than his, kept announcing that they had no intention of listening to him. One of them, the loudest and most maddening, simply bellowed: "Fer-rom the Rer-hight, Num-bah!"

"In my opinion," cried the Colonel, struggling on, "it was most impropah for Majah Bulfoss to appah on this platform as a speakah—"

"Nonsense!" cried a voice suspiciously like that of Captain Mobbs.

"Quite right, Colonel," came from other voices.

"Gairt-cher!"

"Fer-rom the Rer-hight, Num-bah!" roared the tormentor-in-chief.

At this moment, while Major Bulfoss was on his feet, protesting against this reference to himself, and the Mayor had jumped up, trying to restore order, and the Colonel himself, about to burst, was banging the table in front of him and spilling the water thoughtfully provided for the speakers, a dirty cloth cap sailed down from the balcony and by an extraordinary chance actually landed on the table, whereupon the Colonel, in a blind fury, flung it back into the audience, not caring where it went. It may have been an old cap, a greasy cap, a cap no longer cherished by anybody, but it knew its way about, and on leaving the Colonel's shaking hand it made straight for the fat white face of Arthur Hatchet-Ferrers, and made contact before that gentleman realized what was happening.

"Really, I must say," cried Hatchet-Ferrers, grabbing the loathsome object as it dropped into his lap and tossing it away. "This is intolerable—absolutely intolerable. I can't possibly endure any more of this."

"It's all right," cried Grace, above the general din, not knowing whether to look concerned or to laugh. "It was just an accident. All over now."

"Well, I don't know," said Hatchet-Ferrers doubtfully. "Can't take this sort of thing—my nerves, you know—"

It was then that a large angry man appeared at the end of their row, leaned across several people, and roared at Hatchet-Ferrers: "What's the ruddy idea? You keep your ruddy caps to yourself, Fat Face." And then flung the cap at short range and with admirable aim so that for the second time it struck poor Hatchet-Ferrers fairly across the spectacles. This was too much, and, with a strange yelping sound, he got up and began pushing his way out, not going the short way, which led to the angry large man, but disturbing the whole row to his right. And as there was not very much room to pass, and Hatchet-Ferrers was so short-legged, round, and solid, his progress along the row soon became very difficult.

"Sit down there!"

"Turn it up, you lot!"

"Let me pass, let me pass," Hatchet-Ferrers was squeaking.

"I must insist," the Mayor shouted, and he glared down at Hatchet-Ferrers, now wedged between two loudly protesting women, "on the meeting keeping order—*Pzzzz*—and fair play for the speakers. You, sir—"

"Fatty wants to leave the room," shouted some anonymous wag.

"The speaker has made a reference to me," the Major was roaring, nearly the same color as the Colonel now.

"Come on, Whatmore," said Alderman Muleford, who was sitting near the Colonel. "Either carry on or pack it up."

"Mind your own dam' business."

"It *is* my business. And you're making a mess of it."

"Mr. Mayor, I appeal to you," cried the Colonel.

But the Mayor was still appealing for order, while the Mayoress was trying to talk to Mrs. Bulfoss, who had half-risen and was staring down at poor Arthur, wedged below but with his fat little arms free to gesticulate wildly.

"If you will give me your attention," the Colonel began, at the top of his voice, glaring at the audience.

"Fer-rom the Rer-hight, Numbah!" yelled the monster.

Colonel Whatmore made a choking noise, turned sharply, pushed past Alderman Muleford with such vigor that Alderman Muleford cannoned against Alderman Tanhead, and then left the platform, left the building, and went home in a temper that the Whatmore household remembered for the rest of the year.

Meanwhile, in the Corn Exchange the uproar had subsided, Hatchet-Ferrers had returned to his seat, and Mrs. Coote was speaking. She was heard in what appeared to be a respectful silence for some minutes, during which she explained how several of them had argued in favor of a Festival at the meetings of the special Committee, the year before, how they had felt that the decision of that Committee was wrong but that they were all too busy to make the Festival their particular concern. "But now," she continued, "the situation is different. We have some able and enthusiastic people—they organized this meeting—who are ready to make themselves responsible for the Festival as soon as the Council votes a suitable grant."

There was some applause, above which a man's voice could be heard crying: "How much?"

"The original grant that we on the special Committee proposed to ask for was for three thousand five hundred pounds. And I see no reason to change it."

Here she paused, before beginning the second part of her speech, and now a most unpleasant voice, not from the back but from one of the middle rows, cried raspingly: "Why don't you go home and look after your kids, instead of putting our rates up?"

There was some laughter, some applause, and many cries of: "Shame!" and: "Shut up!" and: "Turn him up." The Mayor was about to rise but Mrs. Coote, who had had plenty of experience of rowdy meetings, motioned him back.

"My children are quite well looked after, thank you. I only hope our friend's children—if he has any—are as healthy and happy. As for putting up his rates—well, I pay rates too. And I'd like to remind you that spending public money wisely, to improve our town, to encourage people to enjoy it more, to take more pride in it, might be one way—and not a bad way—of helping to look after our children."

This was well received, but it did not satisfy the owner of the unpleasant voice, who shouted: "You go home and improve that and—*uggle uggle uggle*—" At least it sounded like *uggle uggle uggle*, though that cannot have been what the heckler was actually saying. But unluckily for him, in order that his second observation should be clearly heard he had leaned forward, pushing his face between the shoulders of the two people sitting in front of him. One of these people was

Group Captain Trevone, who had taken a sharp dislike to the tone and manner of this heckler and had a very strong objection to the way in which this type bellowed about three inches from his left ear; so the Group Captain turned sharply in his seat, brought across his right hand, which was of uncommon size and weight, and pushed it flat against the type's face; whereupon, after the *uggle uggle uggle,* the heckling type aimed a wild blow at the back of the Group Captain's neck, thereby making a disastrous move, for the Group Captain though massive was anything but slow, and immediately his flat hand was transformed into a fist, and after withdrawing itself for a second to affect this transformation, it moved forward with appalling rapidity and connected with the heckling type's jaw, with the result that the heckling type went crashing back into his seat and lost so much interest in the meeting that a proposal from the platform to add ten shillings to the rates would have brought no protest from him. This was not the end of the matter, but for the time being it appeared to be; and the Group Captain gave his undivided attention to Mrs. Coote, who spent some minutes praising the Festival scheme, appealed for generous help, and sat down hearing far more applause than hoots and jeers.

Alderman Muleford now followed for the opposition. He was greeted with such enthusiasm from one section at the back that it was plain that he had his followers solidly massed there. He denounced the proposed Festival as Fancywork, and declared that he was not on the Council to encourage Fancywork. He was a Plain Man. ("You look it," a loud-voiced young woman in the balcony told him.) He had always fought for reasonable hours and conditions and decent wages, and would continue to fight for them. ("Off the point, sir," cried an old gentleman in front. "Off the point.") A lot of ratepayers—and he was one himself, he was ready to admit—didn't want the sort of stuff these Festival people would like to spend public money on; and he didn't see why they should be asked to spend a penny more in rates just to suit other people's whims. Those who had to have Fancywork should pay out of their own pockets for Fancywork. The Council had been right last year to wash out this Festival notion. He didn't really see any necessity for this meeting. ("Sit down then," somebody shouted.) He would sit down when he was ready to sit down, and not before. He'd been asked to speak, and these people who kept shouting at him hadn't been asked to speak. ("Hear, hear!" from twenty assorted types.) He had done his duty for a long time now, both in the Labour movement and in the Council, and he hoped to be able to continue doing it. ("Why?") Why? He'd tell them why. Because somebody had to look after the people's interests, honestly and fearlessly. And that was what he was doing at that moment. So no grant—nothing on the rates—no Festival—no Fancywork. That was Alderman Muleford's advice to them.

At about this time a great many different things were happening. The Group Captain had just received a fierce whispered message, telling him, in words even plainer than Alderman Muleford's, just what he was and that the heckler type's friends would be waiting for him outside. Maggie was squeezing the hand of Captain Mobbs, which was a size smaller than hers. Mr. Hatchet-Ferrers, despairing of leaving the meeting and still terrified of some appalling uproar in which he might be involved, had contrived to withdraw himself into a comatose state, so that now he was like an enormous newly laid egg; while Grace, who had stopped bothering about him, had succeeded in setting up a rough-and-ready signaling system with the Commodore on the platform. The two heavily freckled Barr girls had nudged one another into permanent giggles. The Rev. R. Perkins was compelling his four specimens of Our Youth to reseat themselves. The thin girl from the Tennis Club was pressing a bony shoulder against the upper half of Eric Longshaw's left arm. The Communist Party, which had so far withheld its fire, was preparing shortly to go into action. Laura Casey, who had been quiet, was now whispering to Theodore: "I hate meetings. I hate 'em, I hate 'em, I hate 'em. I don't think I'll ever come to another one, whatever it's about. I just *don't like people* when they're at meetings, and I hate not liking people. And now it's poor old Mr. Jordan's turn."

In spite of his age and little eccentricities, old Jordan was a refreshingly good speaker, partly because he was free from the rather dreary mannerisms of the political speakers. "Now I say," he cried cheerfully, "let's have a Festival. It'll do us good. Something to break the monotony. Something to work for. Something to look forward to, then to enjoy, then to remember. Alderman Muleford calls it fancywork. All right then, let's have fancywork. What's wrong with fancywork? And what's the use of Alderman Muleford and his friends obtaining the hours of work and the wages they want if so many people are feeling bored and stale? It'll cost a little money, but why not?"

Here a voice cried: "Yes, but it's not your money."

"A very foolish remark," said Jordan briskly. "Of course it's my money. I pay rates just as you do. And not only that, but I'm prepared to make a solid contribution to the Festival grant."

There was a good deal of applause here, but as he waited for it to subside, the Communist Party went into action. "To deceive the masses," shouted the intellectual typist. "To keep the Boss Class going," yelled the angry schoolteacher. And the railway clerk, who was good at it, made a loud hooting sound, to create a sort of general revolutionary atmosphere.

"Up the Commies!" cried a joker in the balcony.

Old Jordan stroked his little beard and said nothing until the hall was quiet. "I don't know who the masses are," he began. "Only know people—all kinds—not masses. And if there are masses, which I doubt, I still don't know how or why a popular Festival should deceive them. But never mind political catchwords, my friends. Let's look at this thing sensibly. Here's something—a Festival—that can't do anybody any harm and may do many people here a lot of good. Make a change, brighten 'em up, start 'em feeling and thinking. If that's bad, then life's bad. Perhaps it is. Sometimes think so. But while we're in it, better make the best of it. So try—among other things—a Farbridge Festival."

The Commodore listened carefully to the uproar that followed Jordan's speech. It mixed disapproval with approval, of course, but it seemed to him that a considerable number of people were now solidly applauding for the first time. And it was these people, and not the compact little groups that were there as a claque for either side, who were important. But now it was Alderman Tanhead's turn; and Tanhead, the Commodore guessed, was a far more effective and dangerous opponent than Whatmore and Muleford.

"We are always glad," said the Mayor, delighted to discover he was addressing an orderly meeting again, "to hear—*Pzzzz*—what our friend Alderman Tanhead has to say on any subject which concerns the welfare of Farbridge, which he has served for so many years— *Pzzzz*—in many different capacities, which now includes the chairmanship of our Finance Committee, which I need hardly say—*Pzzzz* —has a strong interest in this question of a Festival. Alderman Tanhead."

There was a tremendously enthusiastic noisy response from the anti-Festival groups, some scattered applause from the rest of the audience, and, the Commodore was relieved to notice, no loud signs of disapproval from his own supporters. He felt relieved about this because it seemed to him that it would now be better if Tanhead were given a fair hearing and the whole meeting quietened down toward its conclusion.

"So far we've had a lot of noise," Tanhead began, "but not a great deal of careful discussion." ("Hear, hear!") "With all due respect to previous speakers, I should like to make one or two points. In the first place, I should like to remind you that the special Committee appointed last year by the Council gave careful thoughtful consideration—much more than we've heard so far tonight—to this question of a Farbridge Festival. And this Committee recommended that Farbridge was in no position to grant adequate funds for a local celebration of this Festival of Britain, which, I must remind you, friends, has already received a very large—perhaps too large—government grant to which we Farbridge taxpayers have to contribute." ("Hear, hear!" and some applause.) "But now we're told that more people here want a local Festival than we thought, and that this demand has been steadily growing. In my opinion—and I've done my best to find out what people are thinking—there is no real evidence for this. We have our own newspaper here—the *Weekly Record*—and a very good newspaper it is too." (A voice: "Since when?") "It reflects local opinion. That's its business." ("Nonsense!" from Ernest Saxon.) "And the *Weekly Record* strongly supports my view that there is no such growing demand. We are, in fact, being bluffed, being hustled at the last minute into reversing the decision we arrived at last year. It's true that a few well-known Farbridge people—and we've heard three of them address us tonight—are supporting this Festival scheme, but they're mostly people who were disappointed last year when the special Committee rejected their advice. But up to a week or two ago, these people were content to abide by the Council's decision." ("Hear, hear!" and "No, no!") "What has happened then? Why is there all this fuss? Why are we here at this meeting?"

Tanhead paused, gave a meaning glance at the Commodore, who offered him an amiable smile; and then looked sternly at his audience.

"Because, Mr. Mayor and friends, one or two people who apparently had nothing better to do came to this town of ours—ours not theirs, don't forget—and began bluffing, hustling, and bullying us about this Festival business. What their motives were—or are—I don't know. But I must point out that their main idea was to persuade us to spend *our* money on *their* scheme, which, of course, is always very nice if, as

people say, you can get away with it." (Some laughter, and a few cries
of "Shame!") "I hear some people shouting 'Shame!' Well, that suits
me. Because I think it is a shame that now, when times are still hard,
when money is hard to find, people who are neither residents nor ratepayers in this borough, people who have no business of their own here,
whatever they may have or may do elsewhere, should come here and
try to bamboozle us into changing our minds at the last minute and
spending public money we can't afford to spend. And all I can hope is
that these people will now realize that they are wasting their own
time and that they might as well stop wasting ours. If they want a
Festival, let them go back to where they came from and have one
there. We've made up our minds. And our answer is still *No.*"

There was noise enough now, and although it included plenty of
loud protests, the Commodore did not like the sound of it. He felt
sure that a lot of the waverers who had applauded old Jordan's speech
were now giving themselves sore palms for Tanhead's, which had been
as artful and dangerous as he had imagined it would be. Hastily and
not too hopefully he began to sketch out his reply. Meanwhile the
Mayor was on his feet again, and this time was being rather long-
winded, explaining why Commodore Tribe should be given an opportunity to speak.

Laura and Theodore were furious. If she had been a man, Laura told
him, she would have jumped up and replied to that sneering brute at
once and at the top of her voice. To which Theodore, who was equally
angry but quieter and more controlled, retorted that the Commodore
would do it better than either of them could, and that he felt sure that
the Commodore would swing the meeting round to their side.

"And now—*Pzzzz*—I have great pleasure," the Mayor concluded, "in
calling upon Commodore Tribe."

"One moment, please," cried a voice, a crisp authoritative voice, from
the audience, while the Commodore was slowly rising. Theodore
swung round and immediately recognized Admiral Broadwater, who
was now standing up.

"*Pzzzz.* I am sorry, sir, but I cannot allow," the Mayor began.

"Mr. Mayor, I apologize for this interruption in your proceedings.
I'm Admiral Broadwater, and I've come here specially to protest against
—er—Mr. Tribe's assumption of the rank of Commodore—"

"Clear the decks, men," shouted Colonel Whatmore's chief tor-
mentor.

"Order! Order!" There was quite a chorus of it.

Theodore saw in a flash that the Commodore was looking desperate, and guessed at once that the poor old boy, though ready to face and outwit Tanhead, was really afraid of the Admiral. So something would have to be done, and Theodore Jenks would have to do it.

"Mr. Mayor," he cried, jumping up and making full use of his height and resonant voice, "as one of the organizers of this meeting—which has been paid for out of our private funds—I strongly protest against this deliberate interruption of our proceedings by Admiral Broadwater. We are not here to discuss naval ranks but the Farbridge Festival."

This brought all his friends to their feet, cheering, and most of the audience demonstrated their agreement. Admiral Broadwater and his niece began pushing their way out and were moving up toward the exit before the meeting was quiet again. The Commodore flashed a grateful smile at Theodore, who now sat down and had his forearm tightly and thankfully gripped by Laura's fierce little fingers. Everybody stared expectantly and in silence at the Commodore. With his massive head and bulk, he was easily the most commanding figure of the evening. Whatever he might be feeling, he appeared to be at ease; and as soon as he began speaking his rich and persuasive voice held his audience.

"Mr. Mayor, Ladies and Gentlemen, I realize that I am the only stranger who has spoken to you tonight, and I regard it as a great privilege to be allowed to speak to you. We have just listened to a very able speech from Alderman Tanhead. I won't call it a very friendly speech." (Some laughter.) "But I am sure it was an honest and sincere statement of Alderman Tanhead's views." (Some applause; and a voice: "We know old Tanhead.") "As it contained several references—and not very polite references—to bluffing and bamboozling and people coming here to spend your money, I should like to begin by pointing out that this meeting was organized by the Festival group, paid for out of its private funds, so that Alderman Tanhead was allowed to come here and attack us not at his expense, not at your expense, but at our expense." Here he waited for the audience to applaud his thrust, and they did.

"Now the point has been made that I am not a Farbridge man. Perfectly true. What you were not told is that I should like to be a Farbridge man." (Loud cheers.) "Nothing would please me better than to settle here, preferably as the man who helped you to run your Festival."

(More cheers.) "It has been suggested—and I cannot imagine why—
that there is something rather sinister, fishy, definitely suspicious, about
an outsider attempting to organize your Festival. May I remind you
that last year many of our cities were advertising for Festival organizers—paying out money to ask outsiders to help them? You may reply
that Farbridge didn't ask me. No, I saved you the trouble and expense
by coming unasked." (Some laughter, some mock cheers and hooting,
and some scuffling at the back.) "But of course I would never have
dreamed of trying to organize a Festival, particularly when there was
so little time, if I hadn't seen from the first that a lot of people here, including many of your most prominent and highly respected citizens,
personages like Mrs. Coote and Mr. Jordan and even your own Member
of Parliament, Major Bulfoss, were profoundly disappointed by the
absence of any Festival plans. It was felt in many quarters that the
Council had made the wrong decision. When the question was asked
at the B.B.C. program here, there was obviously an overwhelming and
enthusiastic majority in favor of a Farbridge Festival." (Loud cheers.)
"Your attendance at this meeting tonight, your response to the speeches
you have heard, prove my point. We have already raised, without any
public appeal, a Festival Fund amounting to several hundred pounds.
The National Press—which is free from the bias that afflicts one newspaper—I forget what it calls itself—I say, the National Press has already
commented on the eager demand for a Festival here. And in the face of
all this evidence, Mr. Mayor and Ladies and Gentlemen, it seems to me
sheer impudence to talk about any of us bluffing and hustling and
bamboozling the sensible people of Farbridge into holding a Festival
they do not want." (Much applause and "Bravo!") "If we're to talk
about bluffing and bamboozling, I can tell you where they're to be
found. Again, a slighting reference was made to our motives. Well, I
assure you there's no mystery about my motives in this business. I'd
like to settle in Farbridge—and as a man already well known and well
liked in the town. No harm in that, is there? And my other motive is
simple enough. I like to see people enjoying themselves. I believe, as
Mr. Jordan has already told us, that a Festival would do us good, break
the monotony, give us something to look forward to, then to enjoy,
then to remember. We can't be always counting and saving our pennies.
We can't live by carefully keeping ourselves half-dead. Perhaps we
can't afford a Festival, as some of these overcautious people think. But
it might be truer and wiser, in the position we're in now, to think
that we can't afford *not to have a Festival,* can't afford to see another

big blank where there might easily have been color and fun and life. And believing all this, and liking Farbridge itself, and finding many good friends, I stayed here to help. I've been told tonight by Alderman Tanhead I've nothing better to do. All right, I'll accept that with all that it implies. Because, my friends, perhaps there really isn't anything better to do—for I can't think of anything better than to come to a place I like, to make new friends, to help people to enjoy themselves, to make something that will be remembered with affection. That's all —and thank you for listening so patiently."

"He's done it," cried Laura, as the heart-warming roar and thunder of the meeting's approval surged over them. "The lovely old monster's done it, Theodore. Listen to them." And indeed it was several minutes before the Mayor could make himself heard, calling upon Mr. Huntley to propose a vote of thanks to the speakers.

It might be imagined that Huntley, with his murmuring and eye-closing and refined Back Room Boy manner, would not be able to propose a vote of thanks, especially at such a large meeting; but he had proposed hundreds of votes of thanks, had an effective public manner as well as a private one, and was in fact a cunning old hand.

"Sure you'll agree," he cried, somehow turning his audience at once into fairly bright youngsters about fifteen years of age, "we've had a splendid meeting. Capital speeches—great interest and enthusiasm. On your behalf I should like to thank all the speakers—and, of course, our distinguished Chairman. Of course, it's not for me to say which team won the debating match—that's for you to judge. All I can say is that I hoped last year there would be a decision in favor of a Festival, and that now I'm hoping harder than ever." (Laughter and some applause.) "I should like to stress too that it was the supporters of the Festival scheme and not its opponents who organized this meeting, and so gave us this splendid opportunity of hearing both sides and making up our minds—if they are not made up already. And now will you please show your approval in the usual manner."

And as they clapped, the organ began grunting and wheezing, like a brassy dinosaur clearing its throat, and then ground out the National Anthem. The meeting was over.

3

Not far from Seth Hull's office, on the first floor of the White Hart, was the Palmerston Room, used for small public lunches and dinners, committee meetings, wedding parties. It was a darkly crimson mid-

Victorian room, not very large but full of enormous things, as if giants had once used it, peeping at themselves in a mirror nine feet by six, lumbering across to a ten-foot sideboard to remove a cruet weighing fifteen pounds. It made Laura feel like a happy midget. All the Festival group were in this Palmerston Room after the meeting. Seth Hull's bovine look concealed a deep understanding of what the ordinary sensible human being needs at such times, just after a crisis, and so he had not only provided the Palmerston Room, where they could congratulate each other, but had also hospitably furnished it with food and drink.

Seth himself was in fine form. "What yer drinking? Try a drop o' this. An' summat to eat with it. Meeting put it across 'em, didn't it? Yes, I thought one time Tanhead might ha' swung 'em, but Commodore put paid to him all right."

Huntley had accepted an invitation, and one or two of the knowing types said that his presence there, following upon the little boost he gave them in his speech, was fair proof that the Council would decide now for a Festival. He was busy preparing to turn pressed beef, salad, and a little whisky and water into Knowledge, Culture, and Refined Intrigue; and was also discussing the meeting with Mrs. Coote and old Jordan. "Erce," he was murmuring, clean off the record and between those four walls, "Tanhead went too far. I thought he might—I said so to Barr, this afternoon—but, of course, if there'd been no reply from your side, Tanhead might have carried them—erce. I shall tell the Town Clerk tomorrow he must push this thing through quickly now. Any chance of your looking in, Mrs. Coote? Capital—capital! You had a word with the Mayor after the meeting, didn't you, Mr. Jordan? First-class—absolutely first-class. Erce."

"Who's that man Mrs. Bulfoss is talking to?" asked Mrs. Coote, with a curiosity that belonged to her sex rather than to the Chairman of the Education Committee. "And where's Major Bulfoss?"

Mrs. Bulfoss was sitting in a corner talking earnestly to Arthur Hatchet-Ferrers, who was now only just recovering from his shattering experience with the cap during the meeting. After it was over, he had been torn between his desire to avoid any further nerve-torturing experiences, such as an encounter with a suspicious Major Bulfoss, and his hope of having some talk with Mrs. Bulfoss, his Madge, his joy and his despair, his candle when he turned himself into a two-hundred-pound moth. Without some rapid and adroit assistance from Grace,

Mrs. Bulfoss herself, and the Commodore, he would have been helpless. But they had arranged for Captain Mobbs (who had to allow his
Maggie to return with the Brant-in-the-Hollow party) to persuade
Major Bulfoss to go along with him to the Unionist Club for a sandwich and a drink or two, thus leaving Mrs. Bulfoss free for an hour to
attend Seth's little party and there to meet Hatchet-Ferrers. So now,
here they were, in a corner with a mysterious dark marble pedestal,
eating ham and tongue ("My dear Madge," Hatchet-Ferrers had said
gravely, "I realize I have no longer any right to interfere, but I implore
you not to risk the lobster"), and deep in intimate talk.

"It was weak of me, I acknowledge it," Arthur had said, "but I had
to know if you were happy, my dear Madge. Are you? Tell me
frankly."

"Dear Arthur!" And Mrs. Bulfoss, who was having a lovely time,
tried to give him a wistful little smile. "It was sweet of you. And I'll
try to explain." It was hard work not looking gay, for here she was at
a party, eating tongue and salad and drinking gin and orange, sitting
in a corner with her devoted admirer who had dashed across the country to ask if she were happy, and what more could a woman want?—
yet she would have to look rather sad not to offend poor Arthur, who
had already had a shattering time with that cap and all those beastly
people at the meeting. "In a way I'm quite happy," she continued,
plunging in, "and then again in a way I'm not, if you know what I
mean. Actually it's been difficult." And off she went.

Laura and Theodore had got themselves tied up with one of Seth's
meaty, sporting chums, a Mr. Pladd, who assumed that they were married, never heard their shy protestations that they were not married,
and insisted upon refurnishing their bedroom for them in the style of
his own, which was very cozily nuptial indeed. The fact that Mr. Pladd
in his nonsporting hours was in the furniture trade did nothing to
restrict his fine free style of reference, especially in the matter of double
beds, and long before he had done, Laura was staring at him watery-
eyed, pressing her lips together to restrain the giggles, and Theodore
was a scarlet pillar of embarrassment.

In another corner, sharing a high sofa and half a veal and ham pie,
the Commodore and Grace were deep in talk, oblivious of the others.

"I was terribly ashamed," said Grace, referring to her disappearance
in London. "Disappointed too. We were having such a lovely evening.
Didn't you think we were having a lovely evening?"

"I did," said the Commodore. "And I waited until all the rest of the audience had gone, hoping you were about somewhere, and then one of the attendants told me he'd got a taxi for you. I wouldn't have minded so much if I'd known who you were and where you lived—"

"Oh dear—yes! I felt just the same. Though I did know your name, thank goodness."

"It's no business of mine, Grace," said the Commodore. "But I think of you as a friend—"

"Oh yes," she cried eagerly, her pleasant gray eyes alight, "so do I. Why—when I read in the paper you were here, trying to do this Festival, I made up my mind I'd come and see you. Just think of that."

"Well, then, my dear Grace, what made you disappear like that?"

Her face clouded at once. "I'd seen somebody. I suddenly heard him laughing, then I turned round and saw him. And I had to go."

"Without saying a word to me—?"

"I couldn't explain. And I was in a panic." She shook her head and looked stubborn.

He knew it would be a mistake to press her now. "Never mind," he said softly. "You're here now. I've thought about you a lot. Too much."

"You haven't." She was delighted. She placed her hand on his impulsively, and cried: "If they let you do this Festival—and I'm sure they will—I want to give you five hundred pounds for it."

"Five hundred pounds?" He was staggered. "But that's a lot of money. Are you sure you—"

She cut in hastily: "I've plenty of money. That's one thing I have, perhaps the only thing. Don't worry about that."

"All right then, I won't." Another surprise. This was an astonishing woman. "Thank you very much, Grace. But you must be here to see how we spend it."

She looked wistful. "That would be lovely. And I'm sure you'll do it very well, I mean this Festival. I'm glad you said you like this place—in your speech, which was ever so good—everybody praised it. Because I like this sort of place too. I was saying so coming on in the taxi to Mr. Hatchet-Ferrers." She smiled. "He's an old pussy cat, isn't he?"

"I know what you mean," said the Commodore with mock gravity. "But he's an egg really. Humpty-Dumpty in the money."

She went off in a sudden peal of laughter. "Oh, you're such a nice man to be with, even better than I remembered. I oughtn't to say that, ought I? Ought to be more reserved like. And I used to be, but I'm so tired of it and things are in such a mess that I can't help letting myself go a bit with you, Commodore."

This was all very pleasant, but her mention of Hatchet-Ferrers had reminded him of something important that he felt he had been a fool to overlook so long. "Grace," he began, giving the back of her hand a little tap, then continuing in a low urgent tone, "there's something I ought to have told you before. Hatchet-Ferrers thinks there's a man here who followed you from London. He noticed him on the train and then here, and thought at first this chap was following him. But then he saw him leave the hotel this afternoon just after you did. Shabby little man who might be a private detective. Put himself down in the hotel register as A. Smith, London, which says exactly nothing."

"Oh good gracious me!" Grace was clearly alarmed. "They're at it again, though I don't remember this one. Where is he?"

"I didn't notice him downstairs when we came in," said the Commodore. "Hatchet-Ferrers pointed him out to me before the meeting, but when we came back I forgot about him."

"Here you two," and Seth was standing over them, "about time yer had another drop o' something, isn't it?"

"It is, Seth, but this is more important." And the Commodore told him about Grace and A. Smith.

"And I can't feel easy now I know about him," said Grace fretfully. "Gone and spoiled everything. Do please go and find out where he is and what he's up to."

"I'll go," said the Commodore.

"And I'll come with yer," said Seth grimly. "This is my hotel an' I've had a do wi' that chap already. Him an' his A. Smith, London! Must think we're soft. I'll show him."

But A. Smith had to be found before he could be shown. He was not downstairs in the entrance lounge, and had not been there for the past hour, they were told.

"Well, we'll see if he's up in his room," said Seth. "Though I'll bet a pound to a penny he's not. Hell of a room it is an' all. We don't let it as a rule. It's up at top."

"Do you think he is a private detective?" the Commodore asked as they went up.

"Of a sort, I dare say," said Seth. "But decent ones are usually retired bobbies, an' this chap looks like something they swept out of stand on a race course. But this Mrs. Robinson—though I'll bet that's not her name neither—looks a decent sort o' woman. Fancy her a bit, don't yer?"

"Yes, I do, Seth. Between ourselves. But don't ask me anything about her, because, beyond the fact that she's an unusually nice woman, I don't know anything about her."

"Well, happen this Smith does," said Seth dryly.

They stopped at a door near a cistern at the end of the top landing. Seth knocked several times, but nothing happened. He tried the door, but it was locked. "He's not there. An' he didn't go out else old Frank'ud have noticed him. If yer ask me, Commodore, he's some-where here, on the job. An' he wasn't outside Palmerston Room, that's a certainty."

"Could he be keeping an eye on Grace's room?" asked the Commodore. "No reason why he should, of course, but he might think there is. Do you know which room she was given?"

"Yes, I noticed when I was looking at register. Have to take notice o' them things when you're running a hotel. Yer'd be surprised what yer have to take notice of. Second floor it's on—other end from your office. Come on."

Finally they arrived, two large quiet men, round a corner that brought them facing a short corridor, where there was apparently nothing to be seen but a selection of English footwear, mutely inviting brushes and cloths. It was very quiet along there, not a sound beyond a faint snore and the occasional tinkly drip of a tap somewhere. Never-theless, Seth Hull laid a warning finger on his companion's arm and then held that finger up to his mouth, to caution silence; after which he moved forward stealthily, with the Commodore, feeling rather ridic-ulous, following close behind him. Halfway along the corridor, Seth pointed to a bedroom door, and the Commodore judged from his silent signal that this was Grace's room. Seth moved forward a few more paces, suddenly stopped, caught the Commodore's arm, and then pointed. All the Commodore could see was merely another door, but clearly there was something about it that turned Seth into a large rough imitation of a dog scenting a rabbit. They crept on again, halted out-side this door, which was not quite shut, and then Seth drew in a deep triumphant breath. "Got yer, lad," he said softly, and flung open the door. And there, blinking among pails and mops and brooms, was A. Smith.

"Yer coming with us to my office," Seth told him grimly, "an' any monkey tricks an' I'll dot yer one."

Nothing more was said until all three were safely out of the hotel's sight and hearing, behind the closed door of Seth Hull's office. Then A. Smith closed his eyes, lifted his long reddish nose, and loudly sneezed.

"Excuse that," he said. "Cold in there. Got any whisky? Or rum'll do. Just a touch for a warm up."

Seth stared at him severely. "I'll give yer full marks for bloody cheek an' impudence. An' that's all. I spotted that door moving. Just like Geordie heard yer outside here this afternoon. Always giving yerself away, aren't yer?"

"That's right. No good for this class of work. Told 'em so. Much better at gathering info. Psychological stuff too. Pretty hot at that, you'd be surprised. No drink, Mr. Hull?"

"I could do with one, Seth," said the Commodore, giving him a wink.

"Well, I was just going to ask if yer'd like a drop o' something," said Seth amiably, and went to his cupboard.

"Well, Mr. Smith?" said the Commodore sternly.

There was now a half-smoked cigarette dangling from the corner of A. Smith's mouth. "Live and let live, gents. You've rumbled me? Okay. Doing no harm, y'know."

"How do we know?" asked the Commodore.

"Well, use your loaf."

"Don't tell me to use my loaf," the Commodore thundered. He was not really angry but he felt that this fellow might be easier to handle if he were given a jolt or two as well as a drink. "I'm asking you to explain yourself."

"No offense, Colonel. Don't forget you've pulled me off the job. Might be awkward. Don't blame you, in the circs. But take it easy. For me, Mr. Hull?" He took the whisky. "Ta, muchly."

"I've half a mind to ta yer muchly downstairs into the street," said Seth, glowering at him. "Coming here—A. Smith, London—spying around—hiding in cupboards. Gives hotel a bad name. Everybody's noticed yer."

"Don't believe that. Bit much." Smith's professional pride was hurt. "I don't say I'm good. Admitted I'm not. But I'm not that bad."

"Don't kid yerself, lad. Yer ought to be advertising summat, not on a detective job, if it is one."

A. Smith, still looking grieved, produced a soiled card, which read: CHARING PRIVATE INQUIRY AGENCY.

"All right then," growled Seth. "What's the idea?"

"Can only give you a bit of info. All confidential. First rule of the business. Well, then. Followed a party here from London. Having taken over from colleague early this morning. Party's here. Admit that. There you are. All above board."

Seth gave an inquiring glance at the Commodore, who promptly took over. "You followed a lady here. Why? And who's employing you?"

"Not poss." And Smith shook his head, almost pityingly. "Couldn't spill it. Much as my job's worth."

"Well, I wouldn't put that at much, from look of yer," said Seth brutally. "Suppose I put yer out in street?"

"Now, now, Mr. Hull. Booked a room."

"I know, but yer haven't booked that cupboard an' all." Seth sounded exasperated. "Tell Commodore what he wants to know—or I'll have yer out i' two twos."

"And I'll give him a hand," said the Commodore grimly.

This was evidently a crisis, for Smith now removed his smoldering tattered cigarette, looked at it with some surprise, as if he had just discovered that he was a smoker, and then, without glancing up, muttered: "Can't tell you much. Not my case really. Party left her husband. He came to our agency, first to find her, then to know what she was up to. All I know, Colonel." He now looked up and stared hard at the Commodore, who guessed at once that he was lying."

"What do yer think?" asked Seth.

The Commodore made a shrugging motion. "Leave it at that, I suppose, Seth."

"All right then," said Seth, wagging a finger at Smith. "Off yer go, straight upstairs to bed. No more landing an' cupboard work, lad, or yer out on your backside."

"Suits me, Mr. Hull. Up early this morning. Had a long day and could do with shut-eye. Ta for the drink. 'Night." And he drifted out.

"Well, that's that," said Seth. "Didn't get much out of him, an' it's my opinion he knew more than he let on to know."

"Yes, of course," said the Commodore rather gloomily. "I knew he was lying when he looked me straight in the eye like that. Most liars have that trick. I'd better tell Grace what's happened. She was worried. By the way, she offered me five hundred pounds for the Festival, if it comes off."

Seth was impressed. "She must have plenty o' money then."

"She told me she had. And she's not the type who'd say she had if she hadn't."

"She's gone on yer, Commodore. I spotted that right off."

"I like that woman, Seth." The Commodore was very serious. "Money or no money. I liked her from the first. I can't say exactly why. Something simple and friendly and restful about her—"

The telephone on Seth's desk gave him a buzz. "Yes, Frank," he said to it, and then listened, all astonishment. "Well, I'll be damned! All right, Frank." He put down the receiver, and gaped maddeningly at the Commodore.

"What is it, Seth?"

"She's gone."

"Grace?"

"That's right. Must have phoned for a car, 'cos one came for her, an' she went down with her bag, Frank says, told him she had to go, left him two pounds to cover her bill—an' of course he knew she didn't owe us that much—an' off she went."

The Commodore was on his feet. "By George—I'm going up to that detective and I'll get more information out of him if I have to half-kill him."

"That's the idea. Come on."

They went hurrying up to that little top landing again, rapped on the door, charged into the tiny bedroom. A. Smith was not there, and neither was his case. A. Smith had vanished.

"What's going on?" cried Seth. "Like a lot o' bloody conjuring!"

Old Frank, the night porter, could tell them nothing they did not know already. He repeated his account of Grace's hurried departure; but he had never seen A. Smith leave the hotel.

"I give it up," said the Commodore in despair. "We might as well go back to your Palmerston Room, Seth. I'm hungry again."

Laura, Theodore, Mrs. Coote, Jordan, Mrs. Bulfoss, and the rest had all gone, and the party now consisted of Hatchet-Ferrers and little Mobbs, who had come along from the Unionist Club after detaining

Major Bulfoss there. These two, so much white fat and so much red fat, were sitting close together, immensely solemn and far from sober.

"Been telling Cap'n Mobbs," said Hatchet-Ferrers, almost tearfully, "I'm very very grateful to him for what he's done for me tonight. Very very very *very* grateful."

"An' I've been telling Mr. Hachel-Fellel," said Mobbs, shaking his head slowly, "that's it's nothing at all—nothing—nothing—nothing." He paused, focused carefully upon the Commodore, and said: "You having a good evening, Commodore, ol' boy?"

"A very fine type of man, the Commodore," said Hatchet-Ferrers. "Very very fine type."

"My godfathers—yes! But," said Mobbs with deep solemnity, "has he had a good evening? That's point, ol' boy. Face issue." He then repeated: "Face issue," several times, and then concluded severely: "Sounds silly."

"I've had a most peculiar evening," said the Commodore who had been helping himself to food and drink. "What with one thing and the other—a most peculiar evening."

"Quite so," said Hatchet-Ferrers, very knowing. "By the way, I thought your friend—Mrs.—Mrs.—Mrs. Er—a very very nice woman. Where is she?"

"She's gone."

"T-t-t-t!" And Hatchet-Ferrers shook his head. "Pity! What about Brown—Jones—Smith—inquiry agent fellow?"

"Gone."

Both the solemn fatties now looked reproachfully, with their mouths wide open, from the Commodore to Seth, who was grinning at them.

"Too many people going," Mobbs finally announced. "It won't do, ol' boy, won't do at all. Careless."

"Quite so," said Hatchet-Ferrers, with the same reproachful melancholy. "An' what does it mean, gen'l'men?"

"Hanky-panky," said Seth.

"Hanky-panky?" They both repeated this as if it were some strange password out of the *Arabian Nights*.

"Best thing you two can do," said Seth briskly, "is to try a good glass o' sharp bottled beer—to wash it all down—an' then pop off to bed. Isn't it, Commodore?"

"It is, Seth. They couldn't do better."

"So what do yer say?"

"Hanky-panky," they said, shaking their heads very slowly. "Hanky-panky."

4

Two days later, on the Thursday morning, Laura was typing some letters that the Commodore had dictated to her when it occurred to her there might be somebody knocking on the door. She stopped her typing, and then distinctly heard three timid little knocks. "Come in," she shouted rather impatiently.

The woman who ventured in was exactly like her knocking. She was a mousy little woman, probably between forty and forty-five, neatly dressed but wearing a straw hat that was a definite mistake. "I'm so sorry," she gasped. "I'm disturbing you, aren't I? I really wanted to see Commodore Tribe. Is this the right place?"

"Yes," said Laura. "He's gone along to the Town Hall. They want to talk to him there about the Festival. And I think that means they've decided to have one and to let him run it." She smiled.

"Oh—I'm so glad. I can't tell you how glad I am. I'm Miss Church—Lettice Church, and when the Commodore was at Tredberrow, with M.F.A., I was there too, you see, and he said when he left—and I was so sorry when he had to go—that he might possibly send for me. You do see, don't you—Miss—er?"

"Casey. And I don't quite understand, Miss Church. While you tell me, I'm going to have a cigarette. Like one?"

"Oh—no, thank you, Miss Casey." She was all in a flutter about this cigarette business. "If I smoked, I'm sure nothing would be more enjoyable than our having a little cigarette together, making it all very cozy and companionable, I'm sure. But—apart from the expense—I don't like the taste and they make me cough—so stupid, of course, but there it is. Can I sit down over there, do you think?"

"Yes, of course. Now tell me all about it, Miss Church." And for the next ten minutes she listened to an account of how the Commodore had arrived at Tredberrow, and worked there with Mr. Thoken and Miss Church, and how Mr. Crandry had burst in one afternoon and the Commodore had left, after telling her that she too ought to look round for something else to do. "And he was quite right," Miss Church continued. "Mr. Crandry—such a horrid little man really, Miss Casey—has finished with the review now. And I'd already heard about the

Commodore and this Festival through my cousin, who lives here in Farbridge, Una Fisby—"

"Miss Fisby? The one who wrote the pageant?"

"Yes, she's extremely clever. So I'm staying with her, Miss Casey, and I thought I'd come and see Commodore Tribe to find out if there was anything for me to do."

"You know, there might be," said Laura. "I think we shall need at least one more secretary—if that's what you want to do."

"Shorthand, typing, simple accounts," said Miss Church eagerly. "And receiving people and listening to their complaints. I'm quite good at that. I've a sympathetic nature, you know, Miss Casey, and I do think that makes such a difference. I'm sure you've a sympathetic nature too—haven't you?"

"No, I don't think I have, Miss Church. I soon begin to lose patience with people. And I seem to be getting worse."

"I don't believe it for a moment, Miss Casey. And I can tell. But what shall I do? Go away and come back—or wait? I don't want to interrupt your work, and I know how precious time is some mornings."

"I'd stay, if I were you. But, if you don't mind, I'll just finish this." She resumed her typing, occasionally throwing a remark at Miss Church, who was all eager attention when spoken to but otherwise effaced herself. A fluttery, twittery old thing, thought Laura, and probably useless in a crisis, but not bad to have around in the ordinary way. But how much ordinary way there would be, and how much crisis, it was difficult at this stage to say, she concluded. She looked across at Miss Church. "You like the Commodore, don't you?"

"Indeed I do, Miss Casey." The little woman was pink with enthusiasm. "He's very naughty sometimes, of course—as you must know—I mean, leaving letters unanswered, postponing work, and sometimes, I'm afraid, drinking far too much—but somehow I never really *minded* —and when he was working with us at Tredberrow it made *all* the difference. Oh—yes, Miss Casey, I like him very much. It's not *really* necessary I should find other work at once—I have a little money saved —but I should love to work for the Commodore—and doing a Festival too. All kinds of things going on, I suppose, Miss Casey, in this Festival?"

"That's the idea. Theater and music and exhibitions and perhaps Miss Fisby's pageant—"

"Gracious me, it sounds so exciting. And it would be such a nice change from those foreign affairs. Oh—you've no idea how tiresome they become, Miss Casey, those foreign affairs. I never want to know anything about them again. I wish they'd just stop having foreign affairs."

"I've often wished that," said Laura.

Then in came Theodore, smiling, and the Commodore, who looked like an old Roman Emperor returning in triumph. "All settled," he cried, and then noticed Miss Church. "Why, Miss Church—this is very pleasant. Crandry give you the sack?"

She told him what had happened and why she was there.

"Well then, now you're on the Farbridge Festival staff," said the Commodore. "Settle terms with you later. Too busy now. Take that hat off—it's not right anyhow—and get a pencil and notebook or something. This is Mr. Theodore Jenks, my chief assistant—Miss Church. Now we're all set."

"Very Napoleonic, aren't you?" said Laura dryly.

"Certainly. Have to be. Now that it's settled, there's a hell of a lot to do all at once." He sat down, lit his pipe, and continued briskly: "They had a meeting yesterday, as I thought. Festival agreed upon. A fortnight. Last week in May, first week in June. Take notes, you girls. Mrs. Coote's suggestion was accepted—a grant of three thousand five hundred. Must pay for everything, including all our expenses."

"It isn't much, you know," said Laura rather sharply, for she thought the Commodore too vague and optimistic about money, "not when you think what we have to do."

"That's what I've been saying," Theodore told her. And they exchanged a quick look that expressed their conviction that the old boy would have to go easy with the money.

"We'll have to do some preliminary budgeting, of course," said the Commodore. "Theodore can start on that, this afternoon. Don't forget there's more to come than that three thousand five hundred. Old Jordan will give us a thousand. That's four thousand five hundred. Then my friend—er—Grace promised me five hundred if this thing went through. That brings it up to five thousand, right off."

"Yes, but where is she?" said Theodore.

"Oh—she'll turn up. And she knows where to find us. By the way, I must get hold of young Seacombe, to put out some publicity. Grace'll see it then. She did before."

"You know, I didn't see much of this Grace woman the other night," said Laura thoughtfully. "And she seemed quite pleasant—rather sweet in an innocent sort of way. But isn't it possible she might be quietly mad?"

"Certainly not," the Commodore thundered. "Monstrous idea. I'm surprised at you, Laura."

"But you never know—"

"Of course I know. No more off her head than you are. Less, in fact. And you'll oblige me by not talking like that again, my dear girl."

"Why, I do believe—"

"That's five thousand," said the Commodore, cutting her off sharply. "And with what we've got in hand, plus a few more private contributions—from Seth, for one—it'll be nearer six thousand than five."

"I shall budget on five," said Theodore firmly.

"Please yourself—but don't starve anything for the sake of a few extra hundreds. Next. They've arranged for a Festival Committee, to whom we're responsible. Not finally settled who's on it, but probably Mrs. Coote, Jordan, Huntley, Miss Weeks, Councillor Gisburn, and that fellow Coverack, to handle the finance. Pity about him, but I couldn't do anything about it."

"We shall have some trouble with him," said Laura darkly.

"We shall have all kinds of trouble before we've finished," said the Commodore rather airily. "But we'll meet it when it comes. Next—program. Some things they insist on. You made a note of 'em, Theodore, my boy."

"A Farbridge Pageant," said Theodore, glancing at his notes, "to be performed in the football ground, probably for three nights. A Festival Ball—"

"Crikey!" said Laura.

"Probably in the Corn Exchange, date to be arranged. On the middle Saturday—a procession, gala in the park, fireworks. That's what they insist upon having, and we've agreed. And we undertake to organize some concerts in the Corn Exchange, a good company, doing more than one play, at the Palace, some special films, two or three small exhibitions, and half a dozen lectures at the Central Library—both Mrs. Coote and Huntley are very keen on them."

"And you two go up to London tomorrow," said the Commodore masterfully, "to see what you can do about the music, drama, lectures, and so forth. Can't afford to waste a day now. But we'll discuss that later. Next thing is premises. Are you with us, Miss Church?"

"Well—yes—in a way," she gasped. "But really I can't see how you can possibly—"

"Yes, we can," he told her. "You don't know us. This isn't guessing about the Politbureau in Tredberrow. Now—premises. We must have them and I've had my eye on the perfect place, that empty shop on the other side of the High Street, nearly at the end. Good position, several rooms—"

"But do we really want a place like that?" Laura asked, with a protesting note in her voice.

"Certainly," said the Commodore. "Told you that before."

"We do, you know, Laura," said Theodore. "I've been working it out. It's not just offices—though this room wouldn't be big enough, and it's not easy to find—but we want a central inquiry place where people can ask us what's happening and book seats and obtain tickets. And that shop's just right, as the Commodore says."

"I know the place. Bulfoss' are the agents. Don't forget I was there. And those are very valuable premises. Why, it would cost us the earth."

"We're only going to rent 'em for a couple of months," said the Commodore. "I'm not sure the Council couldn't requisition 'em. Laura —you're going there this afternoon."

"Where? To the Council?"

"No, back to Bulfoss'. To make an offer to rent that shop."

"Why, I couldn't begin—" And then she broke off. After all, perhaps it was time she did something cheeky and preposterous for the good of the cause. She smiled. "All right, I'll go this afternoon. But that means I must have time to go home and change."

"Change? You'll do as you are," said the Commodore. "This is a business visit not a social occasion."

"I'm not going back to Bulfoss', even for five minutes, unless I'm looking my smartest."

"Miss Casey is quite right," said Miss Church, with what was for her an astonishing firmness. "I should do the same myself."

"Bless you, Miss Church!" cried Laura, smiling at her. A feminine alliance had instantly come into being. The remainder of the morning was spent by the four of them doing letters, telephoning, and sending off telegrams to the people Laura and Theodore would have to see in London the next day.

At three o'clock a very trim little Miss Casey brightened the dingy entrance to Messrs. Bulfoss and Sons. The last person she had spoken to there had been poor old Linny, the ghost, and he was the very first person she met there that afternoon. He was haunting the rather dark stairs that led up to the main offices. Seeing her, he removed the empty old pipe he had been sucking.

"Here, miss, you're not trying to get back to this lot, are you?"

"No, Mr. Linny," she told him brightly. "I'm working for the Festival Committee now, and I have to see Mr. Bulfoss on business."

The dim sad wonder vanished from his face, and he gave her the same grin he had given her before. "Mean old stinker—that was it, wasn't it?" he whispered. "Cheered me up that did. Every time I look at his lordship, I remember what you called him. Have you thought of anything else?"

"No I haven't. I haven't come here to call him names, you know."

"You might get round to it, though, miss," he said rather wistfully. "And if you do, I'd like to know. I could do with another bit of cheer-up. Just think of something tasty for him. Do him good, and make a lot of difference to me."

Joyce Benson, Myrtle Tetlow, and Miss Thring were all in the general office.

"Well, look who's here!" cried Myrtle, stopping work at once. "And aren't we smart?"

"Mr. Bulfoss is engaged at present," said Miss Thring severely. "He knows you're coming to see him. Perhaps you'd like to wait outside, and then I'll let you know when Mr. Bulfoss is free."

"Oh really, Miss Thring," Joyce protested. She was a mild creature but not entirely spiritless. "It's silly talking to Laura like that."

"I should think so," Myrtle muttered. Then she brightened up. "Listen—bell. Mr. Bulfoss wants you."

Miss Thring hurried out, and immediately the atmosphere was different. The three girls went into a cozy huddle.

"What's it like here now?" asked Laura.

"Just the same," said Joyce.

"No, it isn't. It's worse," said Myrtle, despair in her huge silly eyes. "He's been in a rotten temper nearly every day since you left. Not because of you, of course, but because of the Major, I think."

"Mostly, yes," said Joyce. "Is it true you're mixed up with this Festival business, Laura?"

"I'm working for the organizer."

"Well, I'll bet I'm not here much longer," cried Myrtle. "Boy I know says I can get a smashing job where he works, if I like. Something to do with electricity. I couldn't make out what they do exactly, though he went on hours and hours about it—you know the way some boys do. Either they're messing you about," she continued, regarding her ample curves with some complacency, "or they're yapping for hours about cars or machinery or something. I get fed up with 'em sometimes."

"No, you don't," said Joyce.

Myrtle laughed. "Well, you know what I mean. Here," and she stared at Laura, "you've got two other boys now, haven't you, as well as that chap at the Bank? Now, don't pretend—we know, don't we, Joyce? Because Joyce has seen you twice with a very tall fair boy. And I saw you one night—last week it was, Thursday, I think—with a dark chap, smashing type, I thought. Who's he?"

"His name's Michael Seacombe. He's a journalist."

"Oo—is he? I don't know where you find 'em, Laura." Myrtle sounded quite aggrieved. "I suppose it's this Festival thing. Asked a question on the wireless too, my mother said. I must say, some girls have all the luck. I've stuck here too long. I'll try electricity or something."

There were sounds, from behind the partition, of a visitor taking his leave of Mr. Beverely Bulfoss. A moment later, Miss Thring returned.

"You two girls get on with your work," she said sharply. Then she stared at Laura through her thick glasses, which magnified the cold hostility of her look. "Mr. Bulfoss will see you now, Miss Casey. But I may as well tell you that I'm certain Mr. Bulfoss will not want you back with us again. We gave you your chance, and you refused to take it and you were also extremely rude to Mr. Bulfoss. Too late to apologize now, I'm afraid."

Laura smiled with great sweetness. "You don't understand, Miss Thring. I've come here to see Mr. Bulfoss on business, as he knows very well, because we rang him up this morning about it. I'm surprised he didn't tell you. I'm here," she concluded grandly, "on behalf of the Farbridge Festival Committee, to make an offer for some premises." And so far as it is possible for a girl of five foot three, not even wearing a long skirt, to sweep out, she swept out.

"I don't understand this business," said Mr. Beverly Bulfoss fretfully, making full use of his high whinnying voice. "The lease of the shop premises at 121 High Street—extremely valuable premises, as you ought to know—has been acquired by Waterson and Fowler, who, after making certain alterations, for which the necessary permits have been applied for, hope to open a branch there in the early autumn. That is the position. And there is nothing more to be said." He had not asked Laura to sit down, but by this time she had sat down, and now Mr. Bulfoss stared indignantly at some point about two feet above her head.

"Then you think we ought to ask Waterson and Fowler about them?" She did not feel cool but hoped that she appeared to be.

"I thought I'd made myself clear," said Mr. Bulfoss in his grandest manner. "I cannot see there is anything more to be said."

"Oh—yes, there is."

"I beg your pardon!" He sounded like a peer of the old school whose coronet had been whipped off his head.

"I said: 'Yes, there is,'" cried Laura. "We only want those premises until the middle of June, at the latest. I don't believe the permits for the alterations will be through by that time. So we might as well use the place, and of course we'll pay a reasonable rent."

"Out of the question."

"Well, it wasn't out of the question when I was working here, a couple of weeks ago. You were thinking then of trying to let the premises for two or three months, but gave it up because it wasn't likely anybody reputable—and that was the very word you used, Mr. Bulfoss, *reputable*—would want them for such a short time."

"All that," said Mr. Bulfoss, who had a large store of such phrases, "is beside the point. Quite beside the point."

"Oh—don't be silly," cried Laura, losing her temper.

He rose, yards and yards of him, businessman and country gentleman and all. "I don't propose to listen to any more impertinence from you, Miss Casey. Good afternoon."

"We might even get the shop temporarily requisitioned," said Laura.

"Nonsense!" he shouted. "Leave my office at once."

It was then that Major Bulfoss arrived. He had probably been told that it was Laura who was with his brother, for he marched straight in. "Hello, hello! What's all this about?"

Beverly Bulfoss was already looking as annoyed as he possibly could look, otherwise he might have looked still more annoyed. "Never mind, Gerald," he said testily. "Just leave this to me. All a lot of nonsense."

"What sort of nonsense, Bev?"

"Really—Gerald—!"

"It's quite simple, Major Bulfoss," Laura began, but was not allowed to proceed with her explanation.

"*Will you go away?*" And the harassed Beverly fairly screamed it at her.

Miss Thring looked in. "Lady Barth's here," she announced urgently.

"Oh—my God!" And Beverly collapsed into his chair, and began opening and shutting his hands in the oddest fashion, as if there were dozens of invisible insects buzzing over his desk.

"Take it easy, old boy," said Major Bulfoss, regarding his brother anxiously.

"Now, Bulfoss—" and Lady Barth came jangling and screeching in, as if late for a Witches' Sabbath "—this is utterly too preposterous —and if you can't put it right I must find somebody who can. Speak up. Oh—hello—Major Bulfoss! Hear your wife's back."

"Come into my room," said Major Bulfoss desperately, seizing Laura by the arm. He hurried her into the little far room, hastily shut the door, then leaned against it, drawing a long breath. "My hat— that woman terrifies me," he muttered. "Poor old Bev! Mustn't mind him, by the way. Very worried these days, poor old boy. Got a cigarette, Miss Casey? I'm clean out."

After they had lit their cigarettes, they sat down companionably, and pretended not to hear the screeching of Lady Barth and the whinnying protestations of Beverly Bulfoss in the next room. Laura explained about the premises in High Street. "Your brother was just being obstinate about it, Major Bulfoss," she added. "What I ought to do now is to go straight to Waterson and Fowler and explain to them we want this shop for the next two months as a Festival office. They'd probably let us have it for a nominal rent, just to work up some local goodwill."

"No, no, Miss Casey, we'll do it," said the Major hastily. "Look much better coming from us. And you mustn't mind poor old Bev. Gets on his high horse—"

"Well, he ought to come off it," said Laura lightly, but with the unconscious brutality of youth.

The Major shook his head at her. "All right sitting there—pretty girl your age—talking like that. Everything looks easy—"

"No, it doesn't. A lot of things seem very difficult to me."

"They'll seem worse when you get older. Poor old Bev has his troubles, business and otherwise. Like me. By the way, I suppose you met Hatchet-Ferrers, the night of our meeting?"

Laura hesitated, remembering that the most elaborate arrangements had been made to prevent the Major from knowing that Hatchet-Ferrers had been anywhere near Farbridge that night.

"Oh—I found it out," said the Major, observing her hesitation. "That's not the point. But you met him, didn't you? Right. Well look, Miss Casey, you're a sensible sort of girl. Now, between ourselves, what would a woman find in a fellow like that? Remember, I described him to you, roughly, that Saturday night? And I was right, wasn't I?"

"Well, he's certainly fat and moon-faced and doughy," said Laura thoughtfully, "and obviously rather fussy and silly about himself—"

"Exactly. Couldn't have put it better myself."

"But at the same time, though he's a kind of untouchable, there's also something rather sweet about him."

"Why, blast it!" cried the Major exasperated. "That's just what Madge says. Now what the blazes is sweet about him? Just tell me that."

"She's gone, thank goodness!" said Beverly Bulfoss, putting his long narrow head round the door. "And I don't think we need to detain Miss Casey, Gerald."

"Don't interrupt, Bev, old boy." The Major waved him away. "Just tell me now—what's sweet about him?"

"What's sweet about who?" cried Beverly irritably, bringing a further length of himself round the door.

"Well, he seems rather kind and—sort of helpless," said Laura.

"I don't see it," said the Major.

"What *is* this?" demanded his brother, whinnying now.

"Oh—for the love of Pete!" cried the Major jumping up. "Can't a man have a little private conversation—?"

"Upon my word!" Beverly yelled, glaring at him. "With business as it is—"

"Yes, business as it is!" shouted the Major. "That's rich, that is."

"What's rich?"

"Don't keep on whatting like that. Enough to drive a man barmy. And just look what happens, after all your talk to me. We've a chance of a nice little let of those Waterson and Fowler premises, a chance

to oblige the Festival people and the Town Council and to do ourselves a little bit of good all round. And what were *you* doing when
I came in? Telling Miss Casey here to go away."

"I don't consider," his brother began, with wounded dignity.

"Don't start that," the Major shouted, doing a little stepdance. "High
horse stuff. And we've had too much of it already."

"I believe," said Laura, getting up, "we could get those premises
requisitioned—"

"You hear that," the Major shouted, and for a moment Laura felt
he might pick her up and wave her in Beverly's lengthening face.
"That's what happens. And then you talk to *me*! With all my troubles
and responsibilities! Miss Casey, please leave this to me. I know
Waterson and Fowler and I'll fix it with them."

"A nominal rent," said Laura sternly.

"Yes, yes, of course," said the Major eagerly.

"I wash my hands of the whole business," said Beverly in an
embittered tone. "Only pointing out that before we commit ourselves
we need some guarantee from these Festival people—"

"You chump," roared the Major, "they've got a grant from the
Council. The whole thing's official now."

"I was not told that," said Beverly reproachfully.

"You never gave me a chance to tell you anything," said Laura
sharply.

"Pop off, old boy," said the Major. "I'll deal with this."

"Very well," said Beverly, with immense dignity. "I'm going across
to Hartley, Foster and Graves. For Lady Barth. Urgent." He withdrew, closing the door gently.

"Got another cigarette, Miss Casey? Halfday closing or I'd have
sent out for some. Thanks so much." He lit the cigarette and pulled
on it slowly. "Poor old Bev. Gets rattled so easily these days. Now
would you say there was something rather sweet about *him*?"

"No, I wouldn't." Laura was very definite.

"Madge says the same. Funny how you women seem to agree. Now
I'd have said there was. Whereas—Hatchet-Ferrers—not a glimmer.
Well, there it is. Now I'll get on to Waterson and Fowler. What are
your people prepared to pay?"

"A nominal rent."

"Yes, but what? Three hundred pounds for—say—nine weeks?"

"A hundred and fifty," said Laura promptly.

The Major regarded her mournfully. "Nice eyes you've got, Miss Casey. Noticed them before. Unusual. Very nice."

"I know," said Laura. "They're very special. But not a penny more than a hundred and fifty."

The Major did not sigh—it is extremely difficult for a middle-aged Englishman to sigh—but he blew out cigarette smoke in such a way as to suggest a sighing effect. "I'll try, Miss Casey. Just leave it to me."

And that was how the Festival organizers, a few days later, found themselves occupying the central and commodious premises situate at 121 High Street, on payment of the nominal rent of fifteen pounds per week.

5

While Laura was revisiting Bulfoss and Sons, the Commodore was returning to the scene of one of his major defeats, the registered office of the Farbridge Theater Company, Limited. The Palace did not look quite so forlorn and tawdry at this time, a dullish afternoon too, as it had done on that bright mid-morning. The attraction of this week was another touring revue, entitled *Stop It, Girls!*. After glancing at the photographs of the cast, the Commodore decided that it had the same horrible mixture of brassy youngsters and decayed old troupers that he and Mobbs had found there before.

"Not a big attraction," said the manager sadly. He looked more than ever like the last surviving member of the House of Usher. He had had the ghastly inspiration to wear an ancient dark-green suit; the dye on his hair and mustache reflected the light with the strangest hues; his flesh was waxier still, and now had great veins apparently filled with blue embalming fluid; he seemed fairly to glitter with putrescence. "No, not a big attraction."

"Is it worse than the show I saw here?" said the Commodore.

"Not quite up to it," the manager admitted in his Usher whisper.

"Good God!" The exclamation came before the Commodore could check it. He had no desire to vex this aged man. "Well, you've heard that we're having our Festival?"

The specter of a smile haunted the indigo mustache for perhaps a second. "Yes. I was very pleased to hear it, though of course it won't do us much good."

"It will. You'll be in it, my dear sir. You remember what I told you, the evening I was here?"

The manager risked shaking his head. "Mr. Crandry won't have it, you know. I'm very sorry, but there it is."

"There it isn't," said the Commodore briskly. "I'm here, as you know, to have another talk to Mr. Crandry about our Festival."

"No use," said the manager wistfully. "I'd better take you up to him. But I might as well warn you, Commodore, Mr. Crandry doesn't seem to like you."

"That's not news," said the Commodore cheerfully. "He doesn't like me, and I don't like him."

They were now going upstairs. "I must confess," the manager whispered through the gloom, "he's a bit sharp and apt to put his foot down. But then he can afford to, can't he?"

"We shall see. I suppose he's condescending to see me again, after saying he wouldn't, so that I can watch him putting his foot down."

A strange sound suggested that the manager was laughing after his own fashion. "You have to go carefully with him. It wasn't easy at first, but I manage all right now."

"Is Colonel Whatmore with him again?" asked the Commodore.

"No, he's alone. Might ask me to stay, this time. He often does."

The manager was right. He was commanded to remain, which he did in the humblest possible manner, sitting on the very edge of the chair nearest the door. Meanwhile the Commodore had settled himself in an armchair and was now lighting his pipe.

"Well," said Crandry in his peculiar harsh scream, "you've got your Festival, such as it is."

"And you told me I wouldn't, remember?"

"All right, I was mistaken. I knew there were plenty of fools round here—in the Council too—but I didn't think they were silly enough to give somebody like you a few thousands to play with. But don't think you can do what you like with that money. Don't get that into your head. You'll be carefully watched, Tribe. Won't he?" And he glared, for confirmation, at the manager.

"Yes, Mr. Crandry, I suppose so," the manager stammered. His dim old eyes gave the Commodore a glance of apology, and the Commodore smiled at him reassuringly.

"And while we're remembering," Crandry then continued, prepared now to enjoy himself, "you might remember that I also said that we wouldn't let you come near our theaters. And I agreed to see you this afternoon just to remind you about that. Didn't I?"

"Yes, you did, Mr. Crandry," said the manager mournfully.

"Well, don't sound so down in the mouth about it," said Crandry brutally. "Too down in the mouth altogether, you are. Time we had a few smiling faces round here."

"Perhaps they *are* here, only you always just miss seeing them, Crandry," the Commodore suggested comfortably.

The manager made a noise that rapidly became a cough. Crandry glared at him suspiciously, then looked at the Commodore.

"That's all I have to say to you, Tribe," said Crandry. "So you needn't waste any more of my time or your own. You don't get this theater or our cinema. That's final." He noticed now that the Commodore was glancing at his watch. "All right, you can go. No more to be said."

"Hasn't it occurred to you," said the Commodore, "that even if you feel you've no duty to Farbridge itself, you've a duty to your shareholders?"

"That's my business," Crandry snapped. "I know what I'm doing."

"But do you? This Palace Theater is half-dead now. If the Festival brought it to life for a week or two, it might stay alive, whereas if you persist in keeping us out, merely because you happen to dislike me, you may soon have a decayed empty theater on your hands. And what are your shareholders going to say then?"

"There's something in that," said the manager, thereby qualifying for the George Cross.

"What did you say?" If his inkwell had suddenly contradicted him, Crandry could not have looked more astonished.

There were still a few drops of blood in that ancient body, for a faint flush stained the waxy cheeks. "I—er—just ventured to say, Mr. Crandry, with all respect, that—er—there was something perhaps in Commodore Tribe's argument. I mean—" And there followed a dim mutter about attractions and the public.

"When I want your advice, I'll ask for it. And you be careful. Perhaps you've been here too long."

The old man, who looked as if he might faint, began wretchedly stammering an apology. But it was broken by an imperative knocking, followed at once by the impressive entrance of Seth Hull and the smiling little Mr. Babley with his dispatch case.

"Sorry we're late," said Seth.

"Sorry you're late? What do you mean?" Crandry demanded sharply.

"I'm not talking to you," said Seth in his loudest and flattest tone. He turned to the Commodore. "How's it going?"

"It isn't," said the Commodore. "He's told me we can't have this theater, and when I pointed out he had a duty to his shareholders, and the manager here ventured to say there was something in my argument, Crandry threatened him with the sack. I take it, that's what you meant, Crandry—um?"

"Look here, what *is* all this?" Crandry cried harshly. "What are you doing here, Hull? If you want to see me, why didn't you make a proper appointment?"

"Just giving yer a chance," said Seth coolly. He and Mr. Babley were sitting down now, and were looking very much at home.

"Not a hope," said the Commodore, smiling.

"I told yer, didn't I?" said Seth.

"Ah-ha!" said Mr. Babley merrily.

While the fingers of Crandry's left hand scrabbled in his thin little beard, the fingers of his right hand beat an exasperated tattoo on the desk. "Either tell me your business or get out."

"Fair enough," said Seth massively. "But afore I come to business, Crandry, I want to tell yer this. Yer've been playin' boss round here a bit too long. An' like a lot more, yer've got careless. For instance, I'll bet yer've not noticed what's been happening to Farbridge Theater Company shares just lately. Have yer?"

Crandry kept still now. "What are you talking about, Hull?"

"Yer see, them shares have been changing hands just lately. Haven't they, Mr. Babley?"

"Ah-ha!" said Mr. Babley, looking up from his dispatch case and twinkling away.

"Mr. Babley ought to know 'cos he's been buyin' 'em for us. An' when I say *us*," Seth continued, "I mean old Jordan an' me. An' I'm interested i' this talk about duty to shareholders, 'cos me an' Jordan have become shareholders in a pretty big way. Haven't we, Mr. Babley?"

"Ah-ha! Between you, of course, you have a controlling interest." And Mr. Babley laughed merrily.

"I don't see anything to laugh at," said Crandry sourly.

"I do," said the manager, rising shakily.

"Gentlemen," said the Commodore, also rising, "I leave you to your business. Good afternoon, Crandry."

As they went down the stairs, the manager said: "Does this mean you'll use this as your Festival theater now?"

"It does," said the Commodore grandly. "My two assistants go up to London tomorrow, and one of them, young Jenks, will be discussing the possibility of bringing a London company here. As a matter of fact, I'll send him along here tonight so that you can give him all the information he may need for tomorrow—all the usual details—"

"Yes, yes," said the old man eagerly. "I'll tell him everything. I only hope I'll still be here in two months' time."

"Of course you will. I'll see to that."

As they stood in the foyer, near the deserted advance booking office, the manager said: "Did you know when you came this afternoon that Mr. Hull and Mr. Jordan had got a controlling interest in the company?"

"Certainly I did," the Commodore replied. "Seth Hull was late, so I thought I'd give Crandry a chance to be reasonable. Well, I'd better get back." But he glanced round the foyer. "We'll make this look like something during the Festival."

"I'll do *my* best, Commodore," said the old man.

"I know you will. But start now." And the Commodore patted his shoulder. "Go into training for it."

6

Laura and Theodore caught the early London train. Unfortunately, it did not start from Farbridge and was almost full when it arrived there, so that although they found seats in the same compartment, they were not actually sitting together and could not talk. However, they could exchange glances, and Laura felt it was both exciting and cozy to be rushed toward London with Theodore smiling there, so close. It was almost like a happy dream. Last night, Laura had gone to bed early, after a very hot bath and some warm milk, but she had been too excited to fall asleep quickly, and then she had wakened at five. After an hour or so in the train, she began dozing and really dreaming; and it was all rather confusing but very pleasant.

They were both staying the night in London, Theodore at Renders Hotel, Laura with her aunt in Knightsbridge; and they had already arranged that Theodore should call for her and take her and her aunt out to dinner. He had the Knightsbridge address carefully written out in his pocket diary. They would have a wonderful evening, being gay about the people they had met during the day: it was all planned, all set. "If you're likely to be late," Laura said as they moved with the crowd along the platform, "just telephone, won't you?"

"Yes, I will," he assured her. "But I shan't be late. I can do all I have to do long before eight."

That is what he actually said, but Laura never heard the last sentence, never knew he had spoken it, because just as he was saying it, a porter, in a hurry to claim a taxi, dived between them, and by the time they came together again, that sentence had been lost. And Theodore, in all the bustle, did not know that she had never heard him mention that fatal "eight."

There were too many people waiting for taxis. Laura decided to take the Underground to Knightsbridge while Theodore thought he could find a bus that would drop him not far from Renders. So they parted at the entrance to the Underground.

"Tonight then," said Laura smiling. It seemed silly to remind him again they were meeting at seven o'clock.

"Wonderful!" he cried, smiling too.

"Lovely!" she breathed. Then she raced down the stairs to the ticket office, all excited and gay. She wondered all the way to Knightsbridge why so many people looked so miserable and if it was life or just being underground in London that did it to them. When she returned to the surface of the world, Knightsbridge seemed marvelously rich, varied, sparkling, like an enormous genteel fair. And the hairdresser recommended by her aunt kept his word and began making her beautiful with only the least possible delay. Wonderful, Lovely!

But there was work to be done. At quarter to twelve she was at the concert agent's, just off Wigmore Street, where she explained to an elderly man and a nice middle-aged woman, Mrs. Prince, her scheme for a series of modest orchestral concerts in the Farbridge Corn Exchange. "I know there isn't much time," she added, "and that with all these Festivals nearly everybody must be booked up, but I thought you might be able to think of something for us."

"Jimmy's Number Two, if he's going on with it," said the elderly man to Mrs. Prince, and then left them.

"An excellent idea," said Mrs. Prince. She summoned a secretary and gave her some instructions that Laura did not hear. Laura, in fact, was busy trying to puzzle out what Jimmy's Number Two might be.

"It's Jimmy Fettercairn, you know," said Mrs. Prince, beaming. She was delightfully unlike Laura's idea of a concert agent. Laura had expected to meet somebody Central European, mysterious, temperamental, and, if feminine, with a white face, short iron-gray hair, a scarlet cigarette holder, and a cupboard full of fantastic liqueurs. Mrs. Prince was very English, cheerful and robust and motherly, and would have been perfect in any advertisement of invalid food, shown offering it to some daughter who had crept home to be cherished. "You've heard his string orchestra, Miss Casey?"

"Only on the air. But it sounded heavenly."

"Jimmy's very good, and if, as we think, he's starting a Number Two—because of course his Number One is fully booked—then it would be just right for you at Farbridge. They'll be mostly young players, but Jimmy's a superb trainer of string players. That's his great thing—not conducting. So it wouldn't matter very much if he couldn't come to Farbridge himself, though no doubt he would for a night or two. Well, we'll see. I've sent a message."

They chatted for several minutes, and then the secretary returned to say that Mr. Fettercairn was at that moment rehearsing his Number Two at the usual place, where Mrs. Prince and Miss Casey were welcome to call upon him. Mrs. Prince hustled Miss Casey down to the street, into a taxi, talked concerts for ten minutes in the vast sluggish river of London traffic, rushed Miss Casey out of the taxi, up a flight of stairs leading to wholesale dress goods, up another flight ending in wholesale toys and novelties, up a last and dingier stairway that left commerce behind, contrived a bare sad landing, and then took Laura, entranced, into the eighteenth century. It was, of course, not the room itself, which was a mere box of dirty wallpaper and grimy windows, but the music of the strings that whisked her back into the eighteenth century. Laura loved violins, so fiercely alive and yet so delicate, all that she herself would like to be. And there they were, cutting elegant eighteenth-century patterns out of the very air. What a miracle music was, she told herself all over again: we only just deserved it. She smiled at Mrs. Prince, who beamed back, almost as if Laura were a nerve-ridden and half-starved daughter who had returned to be cherished.

Mr. Fettercairn had a masterful nose, fanatical gleaming eyes, and

a hair and beard that had turned gray too early. He looked like a
younger Don Quixote, although he was wearing baggy old flannel
trousers and a mustard-colored sweater. His sixteen instrumentalists
were mostly young, and half of them were girls, all eager and warm
and adoring him. Laura adored him too, right off. He was the kind
of man who would be a terrible nuisance to have in your life, she
decided; he would be rude when he ought to be polite; he would
forget everything that, from a woman's point of view, he ought to
remember; he would be still asleep when he ought to be up and out,
and would be up and out and lost when he ought to be safely in bed;
he would wear his horrible flannel trousers at a smart party and only
put on his best clothes when he decided to take a motorcycle to
pieces; and he would remain infuriatingly and gloriously adorable.

"No, children, no," he would shout at his players, after stopping
them with a great cry of agony. "Make it sing—sing—*sing*. It's like
old codfish, last week's rice pudding, tombstones—we're all dead. Now
let's have it again—*Dum-dee-dum-dee-tah-de-dah*." He made a horrible
sound when he did that. "Once again—and this time we bring it all
to life—and make it sing—*sing*. Firsts well up—and you seconds—
down a bit." And off they would go again.

He had seen Mrs. Prince and Laura and had given them a welcoming wave of the hand, but he did not stop his rehearsal to talk to
them, much to Laura's relief. She felt she could have stayed there
for days, listening to the Bach and the Handel make a number of
little jumps nearer to perfection. However, at about quarter to one, he
dismissed the players until two o'clock, and then came down the room,
rubbing his head vigorously with the ruin of a towel.

"Early days, early days," he cried to Mrs. Prince, "but they're coming
along, Edith my own true love. Violas are the trouble, really. I'll have
to do better but how—God knows. Well now?"

"The place for that towel, Jimmy, is the dustbin," said Mrs. Prince.
She introduced Laura and told him about the Farbridge Festival.

"We could probably manage that," he said. "But let's eat and drink.
You can pay, Edith. You're rich. Are you rich, Miss Casey?"

"I haven't any money at all," said Laura.

"Neither have I. But Edith has a lot, and anyhow will put us down
to expenses, under the heading of entertaining the musicians and
customers. We'll go round to the pub. If we hurry, we'll be able to
grab a table for three. It'll probably be boiled horse—but nourishing."

The pub was only just round the corner, and Mr. Fettercairn was clearly a regular and favored patron of the establishment, where they were given a corner table in a small crowded dining room on the first floor. After they had ordered food and drink, he suddenly stared speculatively at Laura and said: "Farbridge? Farbridge? You wouldn't know a girl there called Helen Weeks?"

Eagerly and proudly Laura said that she did.

"How is she?" he asked. "Still beautiful?"

"She's rather lovely, yes," said Laura. "But sad too. She was engaged to a man who was killed, and she doesn't seem to have got over it even yet."

"It was a mistake though," he said. "I knew him. What does she do?"

"She's the personnel manager at a large factory," said Laura. "And she's a member of our Festival Committee."

"Edith, you must fix up this Farbridge thing. May's out, but we could give you the first week in June. Number Two, of course. The players you've just heard, with a few improvements. But you won't know them by June, I promise you. Very rough now—all over the place—but they're young and mad keen."

"They seemed to be," said Laura. "It was one reason why I enjoyed your rehearsal so much. Just to see a few people who are so eager and enthusiastic about what they're doing."

"You know, it's a rum thing about our island race," said Fettercairn. "And after you with that chutney stuff, Edith, please. A very rum thing. Either we're changing fast or we never were what we were supposed to be. All the politicians, when they're telling the truth, and the businessmen and the shopkeepers complain we're all so dim and lackadaisical, don't want to work hard, don't even want to earn extra money. Isn't that so?"

The ladies said that it was so.

"Right. A dim, dreary, slovenly, lackadaisical lot, that's what we are. Yet I raise another orchestra—offering minimum salaries, hard work, rissoles in Warrington, campbeds in Hanley—and the youngsters fight to get in and slog away day and night. Arnold says it's the same with ballet. The people I know in the Theater say it's the same there. Terrific enthusiasm everywhere. We're becoming a nation of fiddlers, dancers, and actors. Well, have we changed our character, or were we always like that really—and now that nobody gives a damn the youngsters come out in their true colors? I don't know the answer. I only know it's rum. How big is this Corn Exchange of yours, Miss Casey?"

Laura described it, and Mrs. Prince, who had some recollection of the hall, said it could hold more people than were likely to want to listen to Jimmy's Number Two on any one evening. By the time the coffee came, they had agreed that the orchestra should give six or seven concerts, of which three would be conducted by Fettercairn himself, for a guarantee of two hundred and twenty-five pounds on the week, and fifty per cent of any receipts above that figure. The Fettercairn Orchestra, with no mention of Number Two ("By the end of May they may be the better bunch," their master declared.), was definitely engaged for the Farbridge Festival. Or would be when the Festival Committee had formally approved the engagement, and the Commodore had signed the contract that Mrs. Prince would send on to him. Laura felt splendidly important, and, what with music, business, Fettercairn, a sherry and a bottle of cider, rather giddy.

"Shall I tell Helen Weeks about you?" Laura asked, when Fettercairn was about to rush back to his rehearsal room.

"I should think so," he cried, his dark-gray eyes on fire. "Tell her I'm coming to conduct specially for her. Tell her—no, leave it that. I must go." And off he went, charging out.

"I adore him," said Laura happily.

"So do I," said Mrs. Prince smiling. "And so—probably—does your friend Miss Weeks."

"Is he married—or anything?"

"No, not even anything at the moment. So there's a chance for one of us. And don't worry about those boys and girls you heard. He'll have them in splendid shape in another few weeks, and they'll have been playing in public for about three weeks before they come to Farbridge. You'll see, my dear. Well now, can I drop you anywhere? You must have other people to see."

"I have to go to the Tanson Lecture Agency," said Laura. "But I'm not due there until three, so please don't bother about me. I have some shopping to do. I'm afraid this lecture business is going to seem awfully dull after the music."

It was a fine afternoon, and staring and shopping and staring again was a pleasant change from Farbridge, although, of course, being London, there were too many people. But there was also the warming thought that one of the people might be somebody famous or, today, better still, Theodore. However, after an hour of shop windows and crowds, she was rather glad to arrive at the Tanson Lecture Agency, which consisted of two rooms above a lot of lorries, baskets, and decaying vegetables in Covent Garden. In the outer office was a severe-looking middle-aged woman, who told Laura that Miss Tanson was free to see her. Once inside the private office, Laura was pleasantly surprised, for Miss Tanson was a girl only a year or two older than herself, not smart or forbidding but just a lively and rather plump young woman in a tartan skirt and a cream blouse.

"My father's away," she explained, "but I'll do just as well. Better probably, because Dad's a bit long-winded. And I know all about it."

"Well, I don't," said Laura. "I'll be quite frank, Miss Tanson. It's one of the conditions of our grant that we have to arrange some lectures. Personally, I'm against it. I can't see that lectures are part of a Festival. And I don't think I like them anyhow. You don't mind my saying so?"

"Not a bit," said Miss Tanson heartily. "But the point is, you've got to have some, haven't you? What kind do you want? We've all kinds."

Laura had to laugh. "It's like buying little presents—or sweets. I suppose they ought to be rather mixed—but more or less educational and cultural, because that's the idea, I think."

"Well now," and Miss Tanson began rummaging among the files and papers on her desk, which was very untidy, "what about somebody like Rufus Grope? He's done a lot of lecturing and sometimes talks on the Third Program. Here he is." She handed over a large photograph, and Laura found herself staring, without enthusiasm, at the likeness of a rather gloomy invalidish man. "He lectures about Art and Life and all that," Miss Tanson continued cheerfully. "We've booked him quite a lot this last season, chiefly for a lecture called *I'm a Fierce Gay Anarchist.* Fifteen guineas and expenses. Look, I'd better make a little list of possibles with their fees. I don't know how much you want to spend altogether, but we can see. If we book one or two of the more expensive ones, then I could let you have one or two of our old regulars at a reduced fee, particularly as it's summer. Mildred Sawkins, for instance, who does *I Know the Gipsies* with songs to her guitar."

"Is she good?" asked Laura, struggling with a giggle.

"Do laugh if you want to, my dear," said Miss Tanson, in the friendliest fashion. "I rarely meet another girl on this job. It's a nice change, so let's enjoy it. Well, Mildred Sawkins isn't bad. The trouble is, she's been doing it so long. She once spent a few days with some gipsies—and personally I wouldn't be found dead with them—and she's been going round for the last thirty years talking about them. But let's bear her in mind, shall we, as a possible fill-up? Now, going to the other extreme, here's Derek Ogle. Everybody knows him, of course, through his articles and broadcasts. Forty guineas—but I might get him for thirty-five in May or June. My dear, they rush to hear him. He calls his lecture *Just People*—you know, all about the dear ordinary people he's met—"

"I can't bear him," said Laura.

"Neither can I, but that's neither here nor there, is it really? Apart from the Radio Plumber—and he's death, if you like, though I wish we handled him—dear Derek was the biggest hit of this last season. But you'd rather not bother about him?"

Laura shook her head. "What about Dan Cobbley? When the B.B.C. did their Question program at Farbridge, he seemed popular and he was helpful about our Festival."

"Dan Cobbley, certainly. *Country Days and Ways*—fifteen guineas. I'll put him down. We can settle the exact dates later. Look, if you'll take Rufus Grope, I'll get him for twelve. All right? Cobbley and Grope then. Now how do you feel about old Lily Fawcitt and her *Beautiful Speech*—theater chat with bits of Shakespeare thrown in—not bad—ten guineas in summer—humph?"

"All right. That's three. Possibly four, with Gipsy Sawkins and her guitar. But I feel—" she hesitated, thinking of Hilda Saxon, who was waiting for these lectures "—we want—I don't know—perhaps something—"

"What you want, my dear," said Miss Tanson briskly, "is what you suggested at first—a nice mixture. On the educational cultural level, naturally. Now let's see." She began turning the pages of a large file. "Poets? Plenty of them. All kinds. There's a heavenly Scotch boy with dark-red hair, who's supposed to be a wonderful poet, though I can't understand a single thing he writes. But he's unreliable on the lecture platform. Either he gets tight and talks for hours, or he sulks and marches off after about quarter of an hour. I wouldn't risk him. You see, I'm being just as frank with you as you were with me."

"Yes, you are," said Laura, "and I'm very grateful."

"Art critics? Do you want slides or film?"

"I think we'd better not," said Laura. "The room at the Farbridge Central Library is a queer shape, and it wouldn't work."

"Music—with illustrations. Quite popular as a rule. And here's a nice man—Peter Gulval. Third Program and *Listener* and all that—but a sweet creature, you'll enjoy looking after him. Fifteen guineas. I might get him for less, but I really think I ought to stick out for fifteen for my nice Peter. Shall I put him down?"

"Yes, I think so. Could he lecture on music for strings?"

"My dear, on *anything*. But I'll make a note—music for strings. Now we've got Cobbley, Grope, Fawcitt, Peter Gulval, and Mildred Sawkins if you want her. And what I'd suggest now is something literary and on the heavier side. And, my dear, I've got just the man. As a matter of fact, he wrote to say he'd be looking in this afternoon, so he might be here any moment. I'll tell you about him quickly. He's Leonard Mortory, the very distinguished critic who also lectures at Cambridge. He's very modern and academic too, so he gets it both ways." She was now rapidly turning pages. "You probably know his books."

"No, I don't. But I know his name, of course," said Laura, who did, for she had heard Hilda Saxon discussing him.

"Here they are." And Miss Tanson read out their titles. "*Disavowals. Rejections. Exclusions*. And a new one just out—*Refusals*. He's terribly fastidious, of course, and hardly likes anything."

"Is that a good idea?" asked Laura.

"My dear, I haven't the foggiest. But I gather it's fashionable. And I do advise you to take him, although you may have to go up to twenty-five. He doesn't lecture often, outside Cambridge, and Dad and I between us had quite a time persuading him to accept a few special engagements. He'll give a tone to your little series, and if you feel twenty-five is rather high, I'll throw in Mildred the Gipsy and her guitar for eight and expenses—and you can be quite firm with her about her expenses—no need to stay at the best hotel when you're telling people how wonderful it is to be a gipsy. What do you say?"

"All right, Miss Tanson. That's six now, isn't it, and that's all we need. I'd better make a note of them."

"Don't bother. I'll have a list typed out for you. Have a cigarette while you're waiting—here you are. Shan't be a couple of minutes."

Left to herself, Laura smoked contentedly, feeling that she had done rather well with these lectures. She could not pretend that she had put herself to very much trouble about them; but then she had warned everybody from the first that she was not interested in lectures.

"Well, there you are," cried Miss Tanson, handing over a typed list. "If you don't mind waiting, then as soon as Mr. Mortory comes, we'll have tea."

"They look quite an impressive mixed lot," said Laura, surveying her team.

"Oh—yes. Very good. Now what about dates? It's always tricky fitting people in, I must warn you."

So for the next few minutes they discussed dates and the sequence of the lectures. When Mr. Mortory finally arrived, he had Mrs. Mortory with him. He was a dusty-looking man, who stared hard through heavy tortoise-shell spectacles and kept tightening his lips as if some dreadful crisis were on hand. He had an odd trick of beginning a speech in a confident booming tone and then fading away, as if he were a faulty wireless set. Mrs. Mortory was younger than her husband; a haggard woman with untidy auburn hair and angry eyes, and badly dressed. Laura rather liked her, but did not know why. They all had tea.

"I shall give you a lecture on *The Novel*," said Mr. Mortory.

"Good," said Laura. "I think people will like that."

"Always popular," said Miss Tanson. "Try the cake, Mrs. Mortory."

"I must warn you, however," Mr. Mortory continued, "that I take the view that life is too short for any intelligent reader to waste his time reading most so-called great novelists . . . Fielding, Sterne, Dickens, Thackeray. . . ." He faded out.

Laura wondered why time that was too precious for Fielding and Dickens should be devoted to reading and listening to Mr. Mortory; and she nearly said so. As she hesitated, she happened to exchange a glance with Mrs. Mortory, who suddenly smiled. "What's the matter with them?" she asked.

"They're no longer significant," Mr. Mortory replied bitterly, as if all these old novelists had done him an injury. "They don't offer us the organized correlation of critical experience and fantasy we demand. They lack the absolute integrity we insist upon. . . ." He was fading rapidly now. ". . . structural properties . . . technical insights . . . closer critical methods. . . ."

"Leonard," said his wife, "drink your tea. We can't hear you properly and don't know what you're talking about."

Mr. Mortory ignored his wife's remarks, charged up his batteries, stared severely at Laura, and continued: "We have been accused of being formalists. Very well. But some cultural tradition must be preserved in a world like this . . . decay of values . . . mass communication. . . ."

"I couldn't agree with you more," cried Miss Tanson cheerfully. "Do have some cake."

Mr. Mortory accepted some cake and ate it very quickly and without any sign of enjoyment. As if it were *David Copperfield* or *Vanity Fair,* Laura told herself.

"Shall I come to Farbridge too?" said Mrs. Mortory.

"Yes, do," said Laura. "It's a Festival, you know, and among other things we're having Fettercairn's orchestra. I met him this morning and fell for him heavily."

"So did I, when I met him," said Mrs. Mortory, no longer looking angry but smiling.

"He won't lecture," said Miss Tanson. "Dad tried to persuade him. Then he sent me, and I did my best, but it was hopeless. Such a poppet too."

"I shall go to Farbridge with you, Leonard," said Mrs. Mortory. "It might be fun. Do you have some fun there, Miss Casey?"

"I'm just beginning to," Laura replied. "But don't you find Cambridge amusing?"

"No, I don't."

"Now, Frances," said Mr. Mortory in a warning tone.

"Leonard, I shall say what I like for once," she retorted sharply. "Of course, Cambridge is all right really, but I seem to have been there too long. It's a tiny fortress of culture, in which Leonard and his friends are busy assessing and ignoring and rejecting, and keeping at bay the vulgar swarming mob outside. Isn't it, Leonard?"

"Well, my dear," said Mr. Mortory, with a faint gleam of humor, "you could call it that, if you liked."

"And there are times," Mrs. Mortory went on lightly, but with an undercurrent of almost bitter earnestness, "when I'd like to steal out quietly, open the gates, and let the mob come charging in, singing awful songs and eating fish and chips. Just sometimes—when I find I'm getting rather tired of clever people, sound intellectuals, men who have complete integrity and nothing much else. I begin to feel then," she added rather wildly, "that I'd love to go to Blackpool or Brighton with a gang of bookmakers, retired prizefighters, boozy comedians, and jolly fat women with dyed golden hair who keep pubs. And that, of course, is silly."

"Quite," said Mr. Mortory. "And we must go, my dear. We meet at Farbridge then, Miss Casey."

Five minutes later, Laura departed for her aunt's flat in Knightsbridge, no longer worrying about musicians and lecturers for the Festival but increasingly conscious of the splendor of the evening in front of her. Theodore and London. She had a long dreamy bath, and was only just out of it, at six-thirty, when her aunt came in.

Miss Olivia Casey was the younger sister of Laura's father. She was a trim and handsome woman about fifty, not much taller than Laura herself, with the Casey eyes and two very effective white streaks in her neat dark hair. She did something quite important at the Board of Trade. Laura never knew what it was. She had looked her up once in *Whittaker's Almanack*, which unblushingly announced that Miss O. Casey, M.B.E. was paid £1750 a year but did not specify her duties. Laura admired her enormously and was very fond of her too. Olivia was great fun, as well as being very intelligent and attractive, and it was a mystery to Laura, in spite of that impressive £1750 a year, why her aunt had never married. She suspected there had been some wonderful secret romance, but had never discovered any real clue to it.

"What time is your young man coming?" said Olivia.

"Seven," Laura replied happily. "But he's not exactly my young man."

"You can explain that later, Laura darling. And try to be ready for him at seven—I'll put the gin and sherry out now—because I may not be quite on time."

At five to seven Laura went into the sitting room, all set for the evening. There were drinks on a small table. Laura sat down, looked at an evening paper, made no sense out of it, threw it down, thought it looked untidy lying there, picked it up and folded it and placed it on the table with the drinks and then removed it to another table, pulled a face at herself in the mirror, turned the top lights on and then switched them off again. At five-past seven her aunt came in, all set too.

"We look two very elegant females, I must say, Laura."

"Don't we! I love this room."

"I like it too, but I hope your What's-his-name—Theodore—arrives soon to take us out of it."

"He had much more to do today than I had," said Laura. "And then he doesn't know London as well as we do."

"Oh there's plenty of time," said Olivia. But I think we might give ourselves a drink. Sherry—or gin and something? And what's happened today?"

Explaining about the music and the lectures took ten minutes or so, and answering questions about the Festival in general swallowed another ten minutes.

At half-past seven they stopped pretending everything was all right. "I'm terribly sorry, Olivia. It's not like him to be late. And I told him exactly how to get here, and saw him write down the address."

"I booked a table at the Laurel. I'll ring up and tell them we'll be later than I thought."

At a quarter to eight, Olivia was impatient and rather cross, and Laura was biting her lip and blinking back tears. At ten to eight, when they decided to wait no longer, Olivia was suddenly patient and tactful and Laura was in a white raging temper. At three minutes to eight they were in a taxi, after Laura had angrily forbidden her aunt, who was still being patient and tactful, to leave any message with the porter for a Theodore who might possibly have been held up somewhere. At the Laurel they ordered an excellent dinner that only one of them enjoyed; and although they exchanged some droll anecdotes about life in Farbridge, London, and several foreign parts known to Olivia, and laughed from time to time, they knew they were sitting there eating and drinking among the ruins of an evening.

"And I don't care," cried Laura, when they were back in the flat and she was caring enough to blow the place up, "I don't care. I'll never forgive him for this—never—never—never."

"No, darling," said her aunt, who knew that young women who stormed away like that were ready to forgive almost anything.

But the porter, when he had assured them that he had been on duty continuously and that no young man had called for them, had not been speaking the truth. For at one minute to eight, when all seemed quiet, he had slipped out at the back and popped into a public bar only twenty yards away, where a sporting character of his acquaintance was waiting to see him. And so he had never seen Theodore, who had arrived exactly at eight o'clock.

7

When Theodore rang and rang the bell of Miss Olivia Casey's flat, and nobody appeared, first he was disappointed, then rather alarmed, and finally extremely annoyed. All day he had been looking forward eagerly to this dinner. In fact the idea of it had taken much of the color and sparkle out of the day's events. He had lunched at Mrs. Hungerford's together with Archie Mossat and Clare Chesbey. Most of the talk had been between him and Mossat, who had agreed to bring a company to the Farbridge Palace Theater for two weeks for the Festival. This company, which would be called the Mossat Repertory Company, would perform three plays, Derek Boon's *Why Should the Nightingale?* and two classics, a Shakespearean comedy, probably *Twelfth Night,* and an eighteenth-century comedy, perhaps *The Rivals.* Philippa Hookwood, Clare, and the others at the Mermaid Club would be in the company, but Bettison Phelps would be replaced by a younger leading man. Mossat's terms were sixty-five per cent of the gross, at ordinary Number One theater prices, with a guarantee of twelve hundred pounds for the two weeks; to which Theodore agreed. During these negotiations, which took time, much rich food and drink was served by one of the two Austrian women, Mrs. Hungerford bounced and gasped, and the dark luscious Clare made enormous eyes at Theodore and gave him sleepy seductive smiles.

"An' Ah've got an idea for this leading man we want," said Archie Mossat. "A big name. A tremendous pairsonality. An', properly produced, a guid actor too. Juist occurred to me this vairy meenute." He waited.

"My dear, I give it up," cried Clare.

"Archie," said Mrs. Hungerford smiling, "this is one of your moments, I can tell. He has these extraordinary flashes, you know, Mr. Jenks. Wonderful! Daring! Sometimes downright *terrifying.* I can see it in your eye, Archie."

Mossat held it a moment, with excellent professional timing. "Patrick Gorebarry," he announced.

"I knew it," cried Mrs. Hungerford triumphantly. "Quite mad—this idea—but dazzling too—quite dazzling—"

"Darling Archie, you simply can't," cried Clare. "He was marvelous, of course, but he's been impossible for ages. He's never been sober since about VE Day. Darling, you're mad to think of it." She turned to Theodore. "Don't you agree, Jenks darling?"

Jenks darling said that he could neither agree nor disagree as he had never heard of Patrick Gorebarry. It was then explained to him by the other three, all more or less speaking at the same time, that Mr. Gorebarry was a romantic youngish leading man, handsome, graceful, with an exquisite voice, whose enthusiasm for alcohol, or for a world softened and mellowed by its influence, had floated him out of stage doors and studios and finally out of the public eye and hearing altogether. All this was common knowledge to the three of them, but Archie Mossat declared that he had been reliably informed that Pat Gorebarry was sober and repentant, after a long cure, and so anxious to make a comeback that he would probably agree to play for two weeks at Farbridge, where his name would undoubtedly attract the public. And if Pat would agree to join them, then Archie, who after all would have the responsibility for producing him, was ready to risk it. Mrs. Hungerford was doubtful, and made as much of her doubt as she did of her enthusiasm, chiefly by covering her eyes with her hands and then slowly shaking her head. Clare, who had played in a company to which the wild Patrick had brought disaster, was decidedly against engaging him.

"Jenks man, it's up tae you," cried Mossat. "Ah'm no saying it's no reesk. But if ye tak' it, ye get a fine actor, a pairsonality, a big name. An' if ye give him a chance, ye give your Festival theater a chance too. What d'ye say, laddie?"

"Careful, darling," said Clare.

"Well, if he's sobered up and wants to start again," said Theodore slowly, "I think we ought to give him a chance." So it was agreed that Patrick Gorebarry should be approached to grace the Farbridge Festival; and many strange wheels and curious devices, as Theodore realized later, were set in motion.

He and Clare had tea in her flat, where brother Lionel joined them for half an hour, during which he took some notes about the Festival and promised to pay it a visit on one of its gala nights. After Lionel had gone, Clare spoke of her ambition to play the part of Viola, without quite asking Theodore to see that she obtained it, and appeared to be reluctant to let him go. But he explained that he had more Festival business to attend to, and hurried off to the New Half Century Club, where the Commodore had arranged for him to see Bilst and some documentary film people.

"We have the Palladian Cinema for the Festival period," he explained, "and we thought we might show some really first-class documentary films there." In addition to Bilst, who was rather like a highbrow official Mobbs, there was a young woman called Claudia Peck, who had a fat gloomy face but magnificent eyes, an untidy

gangling chap called Rogers, a nameless silent man resting behind a
beard, and a girl with a white face and short hair who looked like
a romantic stage Victorian street arab. They were all drinking gin in
the bar of the New Half Century Club, which was new and shiny,
comfortless and very crowded. Somehow it suggested a bar in some
ramshackle city that was besieged or in the middle of a revolution.
Theodore kept feeling that at any moment the shelling would begin
or somebody would arrive screaming a desperate message. But all that
happened was a lot of gin and talk about festivals and cinemas and
documentary films. Theodore was made quite a fuss of, and they all
wanted him to go with them, later that evening, to a party given by the
great Donavan, who was apparently the emperor of the documentary
film world. But Theodore, although he accepted Donavan's address,
which Mrs. Peck wrote out for him, said firmly that he had another
engagement, for which he silently thanked heaven. Rather weary of all
this talk and fuss, and a bit dizzy with the gins he had been drinking
absent-mindedly, he hurried from the club to Renders Hotel, changed
his shirt and tie, and arrived outside Miss Olivia Casey's flat exactly at
eight o'clock.

When he returned, exasperated, to the little entrance hall of the flats,
he looked about for a porter but could not find one. He hung about for
a minute or two, feeling more a stranger to London than he had done
any time since he had first arrived there. A little farther along, across the
road, were two telephone call boxes. Though he knew it was idiotic,
he rang up the flat, as if by some obscure magic the telephone bell
might be answered when the door bell had been ignored. The melancholy futile ringing he listened to only made him feel worse. Nearby
was a taxi rank, and when he made inquiries there, he learned that ten
minutes before, a taxi had been summoned to the flats and had been
seen taking two ladies away. With anger flaring now in the dark wastes
of his depression, he rang Clare, without much hope of finding her in
so late. But she was in, and pretended for a moment or two that she
could not leave what she had elaborately planned to do at home that
evening, but then allowed herself to be persuaded to join him at
Renders for dinner. He had ample time to drink two large pink gins,
lolling in one of Renders' faded plush chairs like one of the old bucks,
before she appeared, dressed in a neat artful black that made her look
more creamily luscious than ever.

She guessed something had happened to disappoint and anger him, but she was clever enough to ask no questions and to make an effort to keep him amused. And the restaurant at Renders, with its enameled Edwardian dowagers, their creaking escorts, the pantaloon and old-clown waiters, the huge dishes and cruets like pantomime props, offered her plenty of material. And they were both young and hungry, and the wine was good, so the dinner passed easily enough.

"And now what shall we do?" said Clare, when dinner was over.

"Those documentary film people wanted me to go to a party," he told her. "A man called Donavan's giving it. Do you know him?"

"No, but I've heard of him. The great white chief of documentary. Shall we go? I adore parties, almost any kind. Let's go, darling."

They found the party in a spacious first-floor front in Bloomsbury. The walls were covered with immense enlargements of film stills, which seemed much more impressive and exciting than the human beings there, who were the New Half Century Club lot all over again. After a few minutes, Theodore lost Clare but was discovered by Mrs. Peck, who took him to their host. Donavan was a long knobbly Irishman, with no sense of humor but with the usual Irish capacity for sustaining a character part. He combined the accents of the Abbey Theatre and Broadway, for he had spent some time in America. For years he had been writing and lecturing about documentary films—on any subject: *How Buttons Are Made*; *A Postman's Day*; *Save Your Water*; anything—with a mixture of Marxism and mysticism much rummier than the rum punch, which tasted of lemon and turpentine, that he now ladled out for Mrs. Peck and Theodore.

"Claudia tould me about yor Festival show, Jenks," he said, "and—begod—you're a lucky man. We're putting together a program for you, me boy, that *is* a program—*period*. Of what? Of *Film*. Isn't that so, boys an' girls? Check?"

The assorted stooges, who included the man with the beard and the Victorian stage street arab, agreed with enthusiasm.

"Film," Donavan continued, almost in an ecstatic chant. "Documentary. Film. Documentary. Rhythmic construction imposed upon the reality o' the modern world. None o' your lousy pampered actors," and he glared at Theodore as if Theodore represented a casting agency, "an' none o' your plaster sets. Reality. The world we live in. The environment. Our whole goddam' society in our own time. That's our

raw material, me boy. But we bring to it our ideas of rhythmic construction, dynamic visuals, aural patterns. And then we get Documentary, Film. The real thing. Even little Claudia here can do it, can't
you, me darling?"

Mrs. Peck, blushing and almost beautiful in this moment of glory,
told the master that she had tried.

There was a great deal more of this, and of the peculiar rum punch,
but after quarter of an hour or so, Theodore drifted away.

"Hello! You look rather mournful." It was the middle-aged woman,
the film critic whose name was Agnes, whom he had met at the party
for Ilba Cram at the Savoy.

"I'm feeling mournful," he told her. "I wasn't too happy when I
came here, but I'm afraid this party's made me feel worse. Not that
there's anything really wrong with it, I suppose, but it just doesn't
make anything happen to me."

"The only party spirit we seem to have left," she said, "is the political
party spirit. When I was a girl in an ugly poverty-stricken provincial
town, we had parties that cost fourpence but they were *parties*. You
enjoyed 'em. You laughed, you danced, you sang, you saw everybody
there absurdly enlarged—not like these stills on the wall, which are
inhuman, but in the firelight of affection. This isn't a party. It's just
a lot of documentary types whistling in the dark. Who's that voluptuous
young woman over there? She doesn't seem to belong."

"She's a friend of mine, Clare Chesbey, an actress."

"You brought her, did you? She keeps glancing this way. In your
place, I'd take her away again. You won't have any fun here. My God,"
she muttered, "there isn't any fun anywhere. And not even any whisky
here. Or have you spotted any? This punch they're dishing out is like
their little films—pretentious and feeble. I've got a car. Would you two
like a lift?"

"Yes, please." And Theodore moved toward Clare, who gladly met
him halfway. The sardonic Agnes dropped them at Clare's flat and
refused to go up with them. "I haven't much sense," she said, "but I've
sense enough not to make a third with a pair like you two. Go on.
Enjoy yourselves."

"And how do we enjoy ourselves?" asked Clare, a minute or two
later.

"I don't know," said Theodore mournfully, for at that moment he

FESTIVAL

saw the whole dismal wreck of the evening round him, and he was not directly replying to Clare's question.

"Well, I must say!" She laughed, but rather nervously. "No, don't apologize, darling. It was that boring party. My fault. Sit down. You're too enormous standing up." And as soon as he had sat down, she went and wound her arms around him and brought the smooth oval of her face close to his.

It was very late indeed when he got back to Renders, and he was too tired to bother leaving a call, so that it was also very late indeed when he woke that Saturday morning. The train that he and Laura had agreed to catch had left for Farbridge before he was out of bed. He had to wait until the afternoon, and, after a miserable journey, in a world so different from the one he had enjoyed the morning before, on the way up to London, that it might have been another planet, he arrived in Farbridge about dinnertime. In fact, the Commodore was just finishing dinner, in the dining room of the White Hart, when Theodore joined him.

"We have to go along to old Jordan's," said the Commodore, eyeing him rather sharply. "You don't look too brisk, my boy. Had a thick night?"

"I was up late."

"Laura come back with you?"

"No. I haven't seen her since yesterday morning."

The Commodore raised his eyebrows but made no comment. "What happened yesterday? Festival business, I mean."

Theodore gave a brief account of what he had done. Even to his present jaundiced view, it seemed a satisfactory day's work, and he was still pleased with his agreement with Mossat.

But the Commodore, who was rather grumpy, criticized this transaction. "Don't pretend to know about these things. But then, you don't, do you? Seems to me, though, that we're guaranteeing 'em too much. I don't object to their percentage of the takings, but with this guarantee we're really banking on the theater taking about a thousand or so a week."

"Well, it ought to take more than that. And after all, as Mossat pointed out, they're giving us three productions. He couldn't have afforded to do that unless he felt fairly certain he could get an Arts Council tour afterwards."

"In that case," the Commodore grumbled, "you ought to have waited and then got 'em on a lower guarantee. I have an idea they slipped one over you, my boy. Good lunch—pretty women—bit of flattery—"

"Rubbish!" said Theodore sharply. "It wasn't like that at all."

"You don't know these theater people. Very artful."

This annoyed Theodore all the more. "If I hadn't known this particular group, you'd never have had a hope of persuading a company as good as this to come to Farbridge. The point is, they can afford to take risks because Mrs. Hungerford is always ready to subsidize Mossat. And instead of grumbling, Commodore, you ought to thank me for remembering this group and grabbing them for the Festival."

"Well, we'll see." The Commodore lumbered to his feet. Then he gave Theodore a sly infuriating grin. "Don't forget I saw you the other day here with those two handsome wenches—and they're in this company, aren't they? Well, I'm off to Jordan's. You'll be along later, I suppose?"

"I suppose so," said Theodore sulkily. Throughout his dinner he brooded over the unfairness of the Commodore's criticism. He might not know much about the Theater, but he was certain that the Commodore knew even less. What was the matter with everybody? First, Laura, and now the Commodore. He began to feel a stranger, somebody from a long way off, which indeed he was.

When he arrived at old Jordan's, and was admitted by his fellow giant, Perkins, he found that Dr. Barr and his two freckled daughters were performing a trio. There were about a dozen people there, including Mrs. Coote, Huntley, Miss Weeks, and of course old Jordan himself and the Commodore—and Laura who was sitting in a corner with Michael Seacombe. Several times during the music he tried to catch Laura's eye and failed. As soon as it was over, he went across to her.

"Laura," he began, speaking as if they were alone, which indeed at that moment he felt they were.

"Oh—hello!" she said coolly, and then instantly turned away and began talking to Seacombe. The next moment she had moved away with Seacombe. And it happened then, simply by pure chance that nobody had a greeting or a smile to spare for Theodore, who stood there alone, very large, a quarter of him belonging to a different race altogether, with everything familiar and friendly now thousands of miles away, let down, snubbed, unfairly criticized, not wanted any more. He stood there for a half-minute that was like a whole burning year of ignominy, and then hastily left the house.

8

As time was so precious now, they had agreed to hold the first Festival Committee meeting at five o'clock the next day, Sunday, not in the little second-floor office but in the Palmerston Room, where Seth Hull had provided tea. Present were Jordan, Mrs. Coote, Huntley, Gisburn, Helen Weeks, the Commodore, Seacombe, and Laura, looking very unhappy.

"Well," said Jordan, who was acting chairman, "we're all here, I think. Coverack's a member, of course, but didn't want to come today. No reason why he should. Make a start, then. Call on the official organizer, Commodore Tribe, to report progress."

"Jenks isn't here," said Seacombe.

"No, so he isn't. Still, manage without him, I suppose. Sorry to, though, nice lad. Commodore?"

"Mr. Chairman," the Commodore, unsmiling, began slowly, "before I ask Miss Casey, who has all the details, to explain to you what has already been arranged, I must say something about Mr. Jenks. I'm sorry to say—he's left us."

There was a murmur of surprise round the table, and something sharper, more urgent, from the other end, where Laura was sitting.

"He didn't come and see me," the Commodore continued gravely. "I wish he had have done. I could have persuaded him to stay. But he left early this morning and I found this note from him after he'd gone. It's very short, so I'll read it. *Dear Commodore, I am returning to London this morning as I feel you no longer need me in Farbridge and from now on I might be only in the way. I hope the Festival will be a great success. I am certain that it has every chance now. With best wishes, Yours sincerely, Theodore Jenks.*" He paused.

"Laura!" cried Helen Weeks, alarmed.

"No, I'm all right," said Laura, who clearly wasn't. She looked piteously down the table. Then added, faintly: "He stays at Renders Hotel. He'll be there now. You could talk to him."

"I'd thought of that, my dear," said the Commodore gently. "And I rang up Renders an hour ago. He wasn't there and they weren't expecting him. So we don't know where he is. I'm very sorry about this, Mr. Chairman, as I feel it's partly my fault—something I said last night." Laura said something inaudible, but he shook his head at her and continued: "Perhaps Miss Casey would rather not explain what we've all arranged—"

"No," said Laura sharply, her face very small and pinched, very white, "of course I will." She waited a moment, collecting herself. "The—the—following arrangements—for the Festival—have already been—been completed. First—" And she went through the list: music, drama, lectures, documentary films, dust and ashes.

PART THREE

CHAPTER ONE

Tuning Up

I

IT WAS Maytime now in Farbridge's High Street, and every blue and gold morning it seemed to flower into prettier and gayer displays of millinery and sportswear, ties and shirtings. Even the implements in Walmer's, with their stainless steel and red paint, seemed brighter every day. Jordan's Stores looked subtropical, riotous. The front of the White Hart had been repainted and was blooming with window boxes. But to arrive at the peak of the street's interest, on these May days, you had to cross the road from the White Hart and then turn to the left, which brought you to Number 121, now the Festival Center. The town had never seen anything like it before. You could hardly believe you were still in Farbridge.

To begin with, the old shop front had been painted an exciting pink, a pink that defied the tradition, the elements, the whole economic and aesthetic outlook of the South Midlands. It was a little festival in itself, this pink. It was also a challenge, as Laura Casey and Helen Weeks, who had carried that pink through against much opposition, had thought it would be. The people who did not want a Festival—Crandry and Whatmore, for instance, or Aldermen Tanhead and Muleford—gave that pink one glare and then hurried past. The people who had always been in favor of a Festival found their curiosity, eagerness, enthusiasm, mounting and bubbling and coming to the boil every time they looked at the Center. And the doubters and waverers began to be drawn by the sheer impudence of that pink, and once they were brought close to the window, then the posters caught and held them: they were trapped.

To all except those people who exist to save money and to keep themselves *to* themselves (which is where they belong), those posters, so various in their appeal, so boldly printed and artfully colored, were a delight and a snare. And the window was filled with their multi-colored promises. There, for instance, was the Palace Theater bill, announcing that for the two weeks of the Festival, with the *Free List Entirely Suspended* (it was the ancient manager who had insisted upon that), the Mossat Repertory Company, direct from the West End, starring Philippa Hookwood and Patrick Gorebarry, would perform *Twelfth Night, The Rivals,* and the new play by Derek Boon, *Why Should the Nightingale?* And seats could be booked at once, if necessary at the counter inside, not two yards away. Then musical citizens were trapped immediately by the statement, in red and black on a cream paper, that the Fettercairn String Orchestra would give six performances in the Corn Exchange. Enthusiasts for the spoken word were caught by the long narrow intellectual poster, black on primrose yellow, that offered them six lectures in the Central Library, at five o'clock on Mondays, Wednesdays, Fridays, beginning with Rufus Grope, poet and critic (*I'm a Fierce Gay Anarchist*) and ending with Leonard Mortory (*The Novel: A Revaluation*). Then people who longed for a large picturesque view of local history were caught by the dashing poster, designed by an art master and a colleague of Ernest Saxon's, declaring that a *Farbridge Pageant,* by Una Fisby, would be staged at the Farbridge United A.F.C. ground on the Wednesday, Thursday, and Friday evenings of the first week. And why not on Saturday? Because, as another exciting bill proclaimed, on that first Saturday, after a Grand Procession, there was to be a Gala followed by firewords at Mayton Park. And on other nights, except Sundays, in this same park there was to be Dancing and a special Festival Café. And if you cared for none of these things, if you wanted a little very quiet culture during the day and nothing more, there were still the Exhibitions—Arts and Crafts, Ceramics, Old Farbridge. But if you pined for roistering and a touch of high life, there was the grandest event of all, announced in a rather severe, almost snooty, little poster, the *Festival Ball* at the Corn Exchange on the final Friday. And if the mind, as well it might, reeled at the sight of all these competing posters, then the owner of the reeling mind had only to pop inside the Center and there, at the counter, buy for threepence a *Complete Official Program* of the Festival.

Behind that counter, where tickets for all the various attractions could be obtained, Miss Church was now assisted by her cousin's friend, Mrs. Delacey. They made an admirable team, their styles being in sharp contrast. Following a suggestion by Laura Casey, who was now Assistant Organizer and very important, these two ladies tried to divide the work so that Mrs. Delacey dealt with any of the Festival enterprises for which there was a large demand, and Miss Church took over all those to which people had to be coaxed a little. "Now I'm sure you'd enjoy that," Miss Church would say, like an eager mouse, referring perhaps to Miss Mildred Sawkin's lecture *I Know the Gipsies*. But should some fellow come bouncing in, bluffly demanding six seats in a row for one of the most popular nights at the theater, then Mrs. Delacey would stare at him and announce, with severity and many capital letters: "We are almost Sold Right Out. Six seats together are Only Possible on Some Other Night." And any man who had not made up his mind, who was merely flirting with this Festival idea, was bound to be impressed one way or the other, either by Miss Church's eagerness, which suggested that the Festival was altogether so wonderful that it was a privilege to sell tickets for it, or by Mrs. Delacey's immense condescension, which told the inquirer he was fortunate to be attended to at all.

This combined Inquiries-and-Box-Office department had been newly painted, and its side wall and temporary partition had been covered with posters, so that it looked very inviting and gay. Beyond the partition and the public eye, there had been little attempt to brighten up the old shop premises. At the back, on the ground floor, was a narrow darkish room, smelling of boot polish, that served as the office of the honorary director of publicity for the Festival, Michael Seacombe, and of its honorary (but with expenses) Social Organizer, Captain A. Mobbs. For the Whatmore-Tanhead group in the local Conservative Party had been too strong for little Mobbs, and so, in spite of the protests of Major Bulfoss, he had lost his job as the Far-bridge agent. So while he was waiting to decide what he would try next, he had turned Social Organizer, whatever that might be, and shared with Seacombe this room at the back, together with a deal table, two chairs, some posters and programs, a telephone, three tumblers, a corkscrew and bottle opener, and rapidly diminishing supplies of vermouth, gin, and whisky. As yet there had been little social organizing for him to do, but it was generally held that he would be very busy and useful once the Festival began. Even now he was co-operating with the Town Hall—and not every man can co-operate with a town hall—to organize the Festival Civic Lunch on the opening Monday. In his new suit, a dark blue with a faint crimson stripe that set off his regimental tie very artfully, he looked much smarter than he had done when in political life. He allowed it to be thought that these changes in his appearance had been made in his capacity as Social Organizer. The truth was, however, that Archie Mobbs, though fat and into his fifties, was now in love, and spent many an hour daydreaming in that back room, especially in the afternoon when the gold Maytime crept in and the smell of boot polish was almost intoxicating. And Maggie, though friendly enough, was coy; and there were disturbing rumors from Brant-in-the-Hollow of a persistent dairy farmer and an insinuating suitor who owned the garage across the road from the pub. But she had promised to pay several visits to the Festival, which would lend a certain glamour to its Social Organizer.

In the front room on the first floor, with a fine old bay window, the Commodore had his office, with furniture borrowed from the room they had originally in the White Hart. The Assistant Organizer, Miss Laura Casey, worked in a smaller room at the back on the first floor. And as everybody, even the Commodore in his private thoughts, agreed, this was where the real work had been done. Laura had in fact worked much too hard, and now she was altogether too fine-drawn and too much on edge, as brittle as paper out of an oven, and was in danger, some of them thought, of cracking up very soon, perhaps before the Festival actually began. Often she would suddenly lose her temper and then be tearfully apologetic. She would work herself to a white-faced, bleary-eyed standstill, and then be angry if it was suggested she should go home and forget about the Festival. Ever since that Sunday meeting, when the Commodore had announced that Theodore had left them and Laura had taken Theodore's work and piled it on top of her own, she had torn into the job in a queer emotional feminine fashion, without any sensible masculine letting up and relaxing and yarning and yawning; and now, as the Commodore began to admit to himself, she had turned herself from a godsend into a problem, perhaps the most serious of his problems.

For she had the whole thing at her fingertips, knew everything and everybody, and if she broke down now, with the Festival almost on top of them, the Commodore, as he told himself, would be in a devil of a hole.

Now she had come charging in again, staring at him accusingly and storming away. "I told you what would happen. And now it's happened. Coverack's better, and he's probably coming in this afternoon."

"All right, my dear," he told her. "I'm sorry he's back on the job again. I wish him no harm, but that illness was very useful to us. But if he's coming here, that's no great matter."

"Of course it is. He's going to·tell us we've been hopelessly overspending. And you can't say I didn't warn you."

"I can't," he said comfortably. "Though I'll venture a word of advice. Never tell people you warned them. Never say: 'I told you so.' It does no good, merely gets you disliked. Not that I dislike you, my dear Laura—"

"Oh, never mind that stuff," she said impatiently. "This is serious. You know very well we've hopelessly overspent. All those ridiculous prizes, for instance. I said at the time we couldn't afford anything like that."

"Well, if we can't, we can't. We cut 'em down, that's all. Meanwhile, they look well on the bills and attract plenty of attention."

"And that's only the beginning," she continued, waving some papers at him. "Just look at these figures. They're only rough—I don't pretend to be good at figures—"

"Neither do I," he said cheerfully. "Some people are and others aren't. We're the others."

"But Coverack isn't. And I had to send everything over to his office this morning. Commodore, please—" She stopped, and there were signs of a quick change of mood, more disturbing to the Commodore than her angry reproaches.

"My dear," he began, speaking very slowly and gently, "just listen to me for a minute. There's only one thing worries me now about this Festival. It's not the money, not Coverack, not the whole dam' Town Council. After all, they're in it now, up to their neck, and they'll have to see it through. No, what worries me is you, my dear girl."

"I'm all right. Don't worry about me."

"No you're not, and I do, we all do. I'll tell you something I oughtn't to tell you. I had a visit yesterday, when you were out, from your landlady and friend, Mrs. Saxon. She told me that she and her husband were worried about you, that—"

"Hilda had no right to come here," she began indignantly. But he stopped her.

"They're fond of you, as we all are. And they think, as I do, that if you're not careful now you'll break down. And just when we'll need you. My dear, take it easy."

"It's all very well saying that—"

"Why not pack it up for a day or two? Then you'll be ready for anything by next Monday."

"It wouldn't work," said Laura. "There's nowhere I particularly want to go and nobody I particularly want to be with. My aunt in London, who's at the Board of Trade, is abroad just now. And if I went away, I'd only worry and fuss. Not only about the Festival. There are other things too. I haven't heard from my father for weeks and weeks, and I can't help wondering about him. Oh—I expect he's all right—it's happened before—but when I can't sleep, then I begin to wonder about him." She hesitated.

He waited for her to continue. When it was plain that she would not say any more, he looked hard at her but tried to make his tone sound casual. "I suppose you know that Theodore's still in London—or was a few days ago?"

"Yes. Michael told me. A man called Lionel Chesbey told him. But it's nothing to do with us, has it?" Her voice was quite steady.

"Hasn't it?" And he stuck out his heavy lower lip as he looked at her inquiringly.

"He left us. He ran away. He didn't stop to have it out with us, which would have been the fair sensible thing to do, but just ran away."

The Commodore had been filling his pipe and now he lit it. "This running away," he began slowly, between ruminative puffs, "we seem to have had more than our share of it here. Remember Grace? Never heard a word from her since she disappeared after our meeting, y'know, Laura, although she knows where to find me. Not a word. Not a sign. Clean gone. Last time I was in London I went to the address she gave in the White Hart register, but she wasn't there. And of course her name wasn't Robinson."

"You liked her rather a lot, didn't you?" said Laura who was now perched on the table, swinging one leg, and looking less harassed.

"Devoted to her, you could say, although I really hardly knew her. Nothing romantic, y'know—I'm too old for that. But there was a woman I could have settled down with, cozy as you please. Can't explain why I felt that, but I did. And I have an idea she felt the same about me. And then—off she goes—and there's no finding her. She might be anywhere now. Not like Theodore. We could soon put our hands on him if we wanted to."

"But we don't want to," she said. "He ran away. He spoiled it. Oh yes—I'll admit that. I've worked my blinking head off but it's never been the same since. Just because three of us began it, and then one of us behaved stupidly—and ran away." She had got down from the table and was leaning against it now, no longer calm.

He pushed himself out of his chair. "I think we all behaved stupidly. I know I did. That lad was deceptive, Laura."

"In what way?"

"He looked so large and calm and self-confident that you were apt to forget he was a stranger here, not really sure of himself—"

"I know, I know. I've thought of that. But—"

"But what?"

Her reply was to burst into tears. He put a heavy comforting arm round her and she buried her face in his coat like a child. A moment or two later, Michael Seacombe looked in.

"Coverack's downstairs asking questions," he declared. "Fortunately he started on Madame Delacey—and is already losing on points."

"Take this child out, my boy," said the Commodore, "and fill her full of tea and cake. No, no, my dear, you leave Coverack to me. Off you go with Michael. Is Mobbs below?"

"He is," said Seacombe. "Shall I tell him to come up? Okay, chief. Laura, powder the nose, and let's go."

"I ought to be here if Coverack—" she began.

"No you oughtn't," said the Commodore masterfully. "Off you pop."

The Commodore had a minute alone with Mobbs before Coverack came upstairs. Mobbs was looking very spruce, and already suggested social organization on a fairly high level. "Anything I can do, old boy?"

"Want you in support while I tackle Coverack," said the Com-

modore softly and hastily. "Need a witness too. A certain amount of
fat may be in the fire. But we don't see it go in, don't believe there's
any fat or fire about, if you see what I mean. Our motto is *All
Serene.*"

"Ay, ay, skipper!" cried little Mobbs.

Coverack arrived. Whatever his three weeks' illness had done to
him, it had not warmed his eye, shortened his nose, or brought any
generous curve to his pale lips. He looked shaky and yellow but no
milder than before. And he was wearing black, as if already in
mourning for the Festival balance sheet.

"My dear fellow," cried the Commodore, "glad to see you about
again. Sit down, sit down. You know Captain Mobbs? Since we
last met, he's joined us as Social Organizer."

"Why?" said Coverack, sitting down.

"Because we need one," the Commodore explained genially. "And
Mobbs was free for a few weeks, and very kindly took the job on,
without pay, just for out-of-pocket expenses. Well, well, things have
been moving, as you must have gathered."

"Quite a brisk business downstairs today, old boy, Miss Church
tells me," said Mobbs, drumming on his fat little thighs.

"Good, good!" cried the Commodore. "But only to be expected,
of course."

"Naturally," said Mobbs.

"And, mark my words, there'll be a devil of a rush the next three
days."

"Good for you, Archie! That's the spirit. But then, you're all the
same. Keen, keen, as friend Huntley says."

"Everybody must be in a show like this," cried Mobbs with immense enthusiasm.

During this duet the Borough Treasurer, in a kind of sinister slow-
motion, had been opening his brief case and taking out of it a number
of papers. He gave no sign whatever that he had heard anything the
other two had said, although their dialogue had been aimed at him.
Now he looked up, and fixed the Commodore with a stare that he
might have just brought out of a refrigerator.

"I've had twenty-five years' experience," he began in his most
hostile grating tone, "and this is the worst ever. I warned you before
I was ordered to bed. I also warned the Town Clerk. Nobody can
say I didn't warn you all."

"Of course not," said the Commodore. "Don't worry about that, my dear fellow. You've done your share of warning. We all know that. What's this all about, by the way?"

"What's it all about?" Coverack almost screamed it out. He began tapping the papers on his knee. "It's criminal negligence, if not worse. You—"

"Just a minute, Mr. Coverack." The Commodore's tone was icy now. "I thought I heard you say that something was criminal negligence, if not worse." And he gave him a bleak stare.

"That's what I said," cried Coverack angrily.

"Don't forget that, Captain Mobbs," said the Commodore, over his shoulder. "Criminal negligence, if not worse."

"I got it, Commodore," said Mobbs severely. "Like you, I didn't believe my own ears at first." He stared reproachfully at Coverack.

"Go on, Mr. Coverack," said the Commodore. "Unless you'd prefer to give yourself time to think what you're saying."

"And not a bad idea," said Mobbs.

"Don't stage this performance for me," cried Coverack. "I'm doing my duty. And I know exactly what I'm saying. According to these figures, you've already committed the Festival Fund to an expenditure of between seven and eight thousand pounds. It's lunacy. And as I don't propose to sanction more than half these payments, you can decide as soon as possible what must be cut out."

"My dear sir," said the Commodore smoothly, "we can't possibly cut anything out, except a few prizes here and there. That's our Festival program, and we're committed to it."

"No question about that," said Mobbs cheerfully. "And a dashed good program too, as everybody is saying."

"How many towns—yes, towns four times the size of this," the Commodore demanded with rhetorical emphasis, "can show a better one?"

"You're wasting your breath and my time," said Coverack. "Whatever happens to your program, you can't be allowed to spend more than twice our grant to you. The whole thing's childish. I can't imagine what the Festival Committee has been doing while I've been away. Look at these commitments."

The Commodore took the paper, stared at it a moment or two, then looked severely at Coverack. "Childish, eh?"

"That's what I said," the other repeated, but with less assurance now.

"You'd hardly think it possible," said the Commodore, addressing Mobbs, "that a responsible official could come here and use such language. Especially when he doesn't seem to have given any thought to the subject under discussion."

"Thought!" cried Coverack. "How much thought do you think it requires? Including private subscriptions, you've less than five thousand pounds at your disposal. Already you've undertaken to spend more than seven thousand five hundred—"

The Commodore, still addressing Mobbs, cut in massively and smoothly. "A little thought would soon have shown what these figures mean. For example, you'll see here the guarantees to the theatrical company and the orchestra—let us say, between them, roughly fifteen hundred pounds. But to assume we shall have to pay out that fifteen hundred pounds is to assume that nobody will go near the theater or the concerts."

"Which is just childish, old boy," cried Mobbs. "They're booking seats now."

"I'm quite aware," Coverack began, stiffly.

"There's no reason, unless we're very unlucky," said the Commodore, booming away, "why we should have to pay out a penny of that fifteen hundred pounds. In fact, on the concerts, which we're running ourselves, we may easily make a profit. It's the same with the Pageant. The costs are here but not the returns. The same with the dancing in the park, and the Gala. Are we to assume that nobody'll go near them, that the park will be empty?"

"It's safer than assuming that everybody will go and that the park will be full," said Coverack angrily. "Of course, I'm quite aware that you'll have various receipts to set against this expenditure. I'm not a fool. But you don't know what might happen, and in the meantime you're undertaking to spend money that you haven't got. It's my duty to see that that doesn't happen." He leaned forward and twitched the paper from the Commodore's hand, and then began to put everything back into his case. "I shall make a strong recommendation tomorrow morning that this program should be drastically cut—"

"And I shall make an equally strong recommendation," the Commodore thundered, "that either you stop trying to wreck this Festival, which I was asked to organize, not you, or you resign from our

Committee. If it were not for the fact that you've been out of action for several weeks, Coverack, we'd never have been able to plan a Festival of any size and interest. By George!—if it comes to that, you're more likely to lose public money, out of sheer timidity, than I am, trying to give the people a good show. And if I didn't think you were still a sick man, I'd go straight to the Town Hall and demand an apology for all this talk of criminal negligence and lunacy and childishness. And another thing. I understand you spent some time downstairs asking questions, where the public could hear you."

"Quite right, old boy," cried Mobbs. "I heard him. Miss Church and Mrs. Delacey couldn't get on with their work."

"In future," the Commodore continued grandly, "if you've any questions to ask, bring them to me and don't interfere with my staff."

"I shall resign," said Coverack, getting up. "I refuse to accept any responsibility for this nonsense."

"Much better," said the Commodore. He turned to Mobbs. "Now about the Festival Civic Lunch on Monday—"

Coverack stumped out, which was as well because the Commodore had not the least idea what to ask about the Civic Lunch.

"I don't know that we worked the *All Serene* touch," said Mobbs grinning, "but what you did do settled his hash all right."

"And I'll tell you something," said the Commodore softly, and as he spoke a huge mischievous smile illuminated his massive face. "Those figures he's got don't include the fireworks. I ordered the fireworks myself, Archie. Asked for a fellow to come down and see me, and locked myself in with him and a hell of a great catalogue. Are you fond of fireworks?"

"Every time, old boy."

"So am I. Never had enough of 'em. But this time there'll be no complaints. I let myself go, my boy, on the fireworks. You'll see. And now, I think, we've earned a little refreshment—um?"

"A spot, I think, old boy. Just a spot."

2

At about the same time that the Commodore and Mobbs were celebrating their defeat of Coverack, Theodore was standing in Charing Cross Road, near Cambridge Circus, waiting for a block in the traffic to thin out so that he could cross the road. He had been attending a rehearsal of the Mossat Repertory Company in a basement room just off Drury Lane; and had slipped away as soon as it was over, feeling that he had had quite enough theatrical society for one day. As he stood there, busy with thoughts that were none too cheerful, he heard a tapping and then a voice calling him. It was a woman in a taxi; and after a moment's bewilderment he recognized her—for now she had stuck out her head to call him better—as the Commodore's friend who had arrived in Farbridge for the Festival meeting and had then disappeared. She seemed eager to speak to him and was now holding the door open for him. He leaped forward, just as the traffic was about to move on, and flung himself in the cab beside her.

"You do remember me, don't you?" she inquired anxiously. "I recognized you right off. Mr.—er—Jenkins, isn't it?"

"Jenks. Theodore Jenks."

"Yes, that's it. And I'm—well, you can call me Grace, if you don't mind. Then I'll just call you Theodore, if that's all right to you. Because 'Mr. Jenks' is a bit standoffish, isn't it?"

Theodore said it was, and asked where they were going, for by this time the taxi had churned its way round Cambridge Circus and was proceeding down Shaftesbury Avenue.

"Well, it was taking me back to my flat," said Grace apologetically. "It's a little furnished flat just off Piccadilly. Very central, of course, but stuffy and not too clean—I don't care what they say—and not very homely. But then it's awkward—I have to keep changing," she added mysteriously. She put a hand on his arm and gave him an appealing look out of her nice gray eyes. "I wonder if you could spare a few minutes, Theodore."

"I could spare a few hours," he said, with a touch of bitterness. "And you needn't be apologetic about it, because I'm really very glad to see you, Grace."

"That's very nice then. We'll let him take us to this flat—I can't call it mine, it doesn't *feel* mine—and then we'll have a little talk. Let's not start yet, though. It'ud spoil it. All this noise and commotion. One time I'd have thought it wonderful to be living right in the middle of London like this, but now I can hardly wait to have done with it. Just shows you, doesn't it? I feel ashamed often to be so sick of *people,* when I know they're just as good as I am, perhaps better. But I can't help it—I do. There just shouldn't be so many all in one place. It was never meant to be, that's my opinion. Makes people too cheap, an' then you don't like 'em, an' that's all wrong, not what was intended for us at all."

They stopped in a little street somewhere in the St. James's region, and then went creaking up to the third floor in a reluctant old lift. She showed him into a small sitting room that looked so impersonal that it might have come straight from the window of a furniture shop. "It's Service," she said, "and—oh!—I'm so sick and tired of 'em, with their Service. It's not human, even if it was good an' willing, which it isn't. I'd give anything to get back into a nice kitchen of my own. I've nothing to drink, though I suppose they could get you something, but I was going to order some tea, even if it is late for it. Could you do with some?"

Theodore said he would rather have tea than anything else, so Grace summoned a melancholy Levantine waiter, who received her order for tea as if it were the latest piece of bad news in a long campaign of defeat.

"But why aren't you in Farbridge?" she asked.

Staring hard at an *Old London Street Cry* on the opposite wall, Theodore explained what had happened just before he left Farbridge. "I felt they didn't want me any more, that they could get on better without me, so I cleared out." An apologetic note had crept into his voice.

"I think you were very silly," said Grace warmly. "It doesn't sound like either of them to me. That was a nice girl, that little Miss Casey—and I know a nice girl when I see one. Fond of you too, she was—I saw that. And I don't believe for a minute the Commodore wanted to get rid of you. Why should he? He thought a lot of you. He told me so. He just happened to be sharp with you for a minute, that's all. And why shouldn't he—a man of his age and experience, and you just a young fellow? Now—weren't you silly, Theodore? Go on—admit it?"

"Yes, Grace," he muttered, "I suppose I was. But I've suffered for it. They haven't."

"How do you know they haven't?" she demanded rather sharply. "All that work to do and you not helping, like you promised! And Miss Casey—Laura—what about her? Probably cried her eyes out. I'll bet you've no idea how girls take on when they're alone. Women too. Me for one—silly old thing!"

The melancholy Levantine brought in the tea, and they said no more until he had gone and she had poured out two cups of something you could stain a floor with. "And what are you doing now?"

"Well," and he looked and sounded rather embarrassed, "I'm helping this theatrical company that's going to the Festival."

"I didn't know you were an actor."

"I'm not. But I know them—and it was something to do—and it would give me a chance of seeing what happens at Farbridge without bothering anybody. I'm just one of the two assistant stage managers, and I have two little parts."

"Well, I never did!" She shook her head at him over her cup. "Go and walk out—and now you're going back with this theater lot. Not got yourself mixed up with one of the actresses, have you?"

"I suppose I have in a way," he confessed.

"Enough said!" she cried. "And you don't care tuppence about her, I can see that. It's that nice little Laura all the time, isn't it? And you went an' ran away! T-t-t-t-t!"

"What about you and the Commodore?"

"Now, now, now! We're not talking about me."

"But he's very fond of you—and twice you just vanished." His tone and look were half-humorous, half-accusing.

"I don't suppose he cares."

"Well, you're quite wrong. He does, I know, though of course he doesn't say much about it."

"Go on with you!" For a moment or two she looked radiant. "Would you like another cup?"

"Yes, please." He hesitated. "Look, Grace, I've told you what I did, and admitted I've probably been a fool. What about you? Hadn't you better tell me? Perhaps I could help in some way."

"Perhaps you could," she said slowly. "And then again—I don't know." She waited a moment. "All right, I'll tell you. Not every bit of it, of course—take hours and you'd be bored stiff—but just enough so you'll understand. Finish my tea first, though."

"I come from Nottingham way," she began briskly, "but we needn't bother about that. The point is, I've been married twice. I was very happy the first time, except we couldn't have any children. He had a nice little road transport business—two big lorries, a light lorry, and a van—and we were doing quite well. Then, a year before the war, I lost him. One of his drivers was off, so he drove himself, when he had a heavy cold on him, and there was a terrible accident. So I sold the business, what there was of it, and bought a hotel, just the other side of Nottingham, pretty little place it was. Well, I was there a few years, building up the business and coping with the war and all that, and gradually coming to life, you might say. I mean inside myself, where there wasn't anything just after Tom had gone. When a woman's happy with a man, inside herself she builds everything round him, and then if she loses him and he's not there, well it's all silly. If you see what I mean." She looked at him earnestly.

He told her that he did.

"I doubt it, a young chap your age, thinking it's all just getting your arms round 'em, when that's only a small part of it, though very nice, of course. Well, then I did something silly—silliest thing I've ever done. I married again when I never ought to have done. My sister warned me and so did her husband, and perhaps if they hadn't, I wouldn't have done, but I was a bit tired of them telling me what I ought to do and oughtn't to do, you know how relations are. His name was Rudfort, so that's my name—worse luck—Mrs. Rudfort. He was a London man but had some business up our way, so he kept stopping at my place and being very gentlemanly and attentive. And so he talked me into it, which I ought to have known was all wrong because when a woman's found the right chap, she doesn't need to be talked into it. She meets you halfway if it's all right, and just remember that, Theodore, and don't let anybody tell you anything different. Wouldn't you like to smoke?"

"I'd like to smoke a cigar," said Theodore, "but I thought you might not like having this room full of cigar smoke."

"Then you thought wrong. I'd like it, so you smoke your cigar. I ought to keep some cigars. I could afford to, the best if I wanted, but it hasn't occurred to me. Smells lovely. Tell me what they are, later, and I'll get some. Well, I married Mr. Rudfort—and that's how I think of him, so you can tell—and then I knew right off I'd made a mistake. We weren't right for each other at all, no more than a cat and a dog are. For six months I kept my hotel going, though I was going to sell it, and of course he kept on with his business, which was chiefly in London. And then—you'll never guess—I was left a lot of money, nearly two hundred thousand pounds. Yes, I'm rich—though I have to keep reminding myself. I'll tell you how it happened, and it just shows you. I had an Uncle Peter, my mother's oldest brother, a queer old stick who'd gone to be a clerk in London and then got on, something to do with lending money. Well, in the war he didn't like the bombing, so he asked if he could come up and stay with me, 'cos there wasn't much bombing round our way. So he stayed whenever he wanted, and he insisted on paying, though he looked a shabby old thing and never spent a penny more than he had to, so I just charged him what he cost me, which wasn't much, and made him comfortable though he didn't need much looking after; he was one of those dried-up little old men that nobody bothers about, though he'd got a sharp tongue, and sometimes when everybody'd gone to bed he'd sit up and tell me about his experiences in London. Then when the war was over, he didn't come up any more. It was after that that Mr. Rudfort came on the scene, of course. Well, Uncle Peter died, quite sudden, and he went and left me all this money. And then I guessed something." She paused, dramatically.

Theodore smiled. "And I know what it was. Your husband—Rudfort—knew you were going to inherit this money."

"That's clever of you," she cried. "And you're quite right, though, mind you, I can't prove it. But it's my belief—and I'm certain of it—that he knew all along. Because just before we got married he asked me to sign a paper—he said it was just a little fancy of his—saying that if one of us divorced the other, then the one who got the divorce took everything the other had. It seemed just a piece of silliness to me at the time, and he pointed out that it was worse for him than for me—because if I went off with a man, he'd keep me anyhow, this new man would. But once I'd come into this money and I couldn't live with Mr. Rudfort any longer, then there was nothing silly about it. Mind you, I'm not mean, but he'd done the dirty on me, right from the start, and I made up my mind he wasn't going to have a penny of it, not if I could help it. You can't blame me, can you?"

"No, of course not," said Theodore. "It sounds a queer arrangement, probably not legal—I don't know. But that's why the detective followed you to Farbridge?"

"Yes, and as soon as I knew about him, I lost my head, and rushed off. And then moved. I keep moving, that's the worst of it. Have to, 'cos of all this horrible spying on me. And that time when I first met the Commodore and we went to the theater, I left in such a hurry because suddenly I heard him laughing—for once—a few rows behind me. Just like me to choose the one night he was there! And of course I didn't want to run into him after the show and drag the Commodore into my old mess. I was ashamed too. So off I ran."

"But if you've got the money," said Theodore, to whom her story was far from clear, "why do you stay in London? Why don't you go abroad somewhere, out of the way?"

She seemed rather confused. "Well, I couldn't, earlier on, because there was still some of the money to come and I had to keep seeing solicitors and signing things. I still have, now and again, but I suppose I could go away if I wanted to. But I don't now." She looked defiantly at him. "All right, I'll admit it, though I'm old enough to know better. Yes, it's the Commodore. There's something about him, I can't explain just what it is."

Theodore said that there was undoubtedly something about the Commodore, that he knew exactly what she meant.

"In a way," she continued, rather hurriedly, "it seems to me we're in the same boat. You ran away from Farbridge—and I still think it was very silly of you—and now you're going back, though you're not sure what good it'll do."

"And are you?"

"Yes, detectives or no detectives. I've written to Mr. Hull at the White Hart booking a room from Monday, as Mrs. Robinson like last time, but I begged him not to say anything to anybody, not even the Commodore. Oh dear! You've no idea what a relief it is to tell somebody all about it. Look—you wouldn't like to have some dinner here with me, would you? I'd be ever so glad if you would. I'll ask 'em to do their best for us. Will you?"

"I'd like to," he told her, "if you really want me to."

"Of course I do," she cried gaily. "I'll talk to them on the telephone and see if they can make a special effort for us."

After the special effort had been promised and the time for it fixed at seven-forty-five, Theodore said he would slip along to his hotel, a much newer and less expensive place than Renders, and return about half-past seven. This he did, after changing into a darker suit.

It was toward the end of the meal, which was a minor triumph of the canning industry, that Grace made her astonishing request. It astonished him when it actually arrived, although for some time before he had begun to feel that there was something she wanted.

"Theodore, I wonder if you'd do something for me," she began, looking wistful. "It's very important to me, or I wouldn't ask it.

You see, he's got some things of mine—oh!—papers, bits of jewelry, souvenirs—that I kept in one of those fancy old inlaid Eastern boxes, about so big." Apparently it was about eighteen inches long, a foot high, and perhaps a foot thick. "I oughtn't to have left it behind, but I did, up at the house we had—it's really his house, not mine—in Highgate. He won't give it me, though it's mine not his, and I won't set foot in that house, never again. Do you think you could get it for me—tonight?"

He gaped at her. "Do you mean—go and ask him for it?"

"No, he won't be in, not when you go tonight."

"How do you know he won't, Grace?"

"Because," she replied coolly, "he's coming here to see me. I've agreed to that. And I don't mind him knowing where I live this time because I'm leaving on Monday morning, going to Farbridge. He's to be here at ten. He won't be here long, of course—no fear—but it'll give you plenty of time to get the box."

"But I can't break into the house."

She laughed. "No, you don't need to do that. I wouldn't think of asking you to start burgling for me. I've still got a key. So you just walk in and take the box. First door to the right off the hall—that's where it was—in that room. You can't miss it."

"But suppose there's somebody there—a servant?"

"There won't be. He's only got a daily. All I'm asking you to do, Theodore, is to fetch something that belongs to me. Now will you, just to please me? I might be able to do something useful for you soon— you never know—and I shan't forget. Will you?"

He would have liked to have refused, but it seemed impossible so rather reluctantly he agreed. Grateful, jubilant, she explained in detail how he could find the house, which was a semidetached villa between West Hill and the Heath, and exactly what he had to do when he arrived there. It seemed simple enough, and by the time she had given him the key and a careful description of the box itself, his early doubts had almost vanished and he had begun to feel that he was in fact merely about to perform a trifling service for her.

It was just after nine when he left the flat. Following her instructions, he took a bus that took him to the bottom of West Hill. He had to walk nearly to the top of West Hill before turning down to the left, toward the Heath. The night was heavily overcast, with a low indigo ceiling of cloud. As he turned down the narrow lane, thunder was already rolling in the southwest. Not a leaf stirred; the darkness was oppressively close; and although he had not brought a raincoat, his suit was rather thick and he found himself sweating inside it. The house took some finding, and it was a little after ten when, feeling like another Macbeth, he tiptoed along the short paved walk to the front door. As he hesitated a moment, the key in his hand, the thunder rolled nearer and there was a sudden glare of lightning somewhere beyond the Heath. He had time to notice that the curtains had not been drawn in the bay window of the front room, where, if Grace was right, he would find her box. He wished he had brought a torch with him, although it was obvious that the house had nobody there, for all was silent and dark. He slipped inside the hall, closing the door behind him, and then struck a match.

Hastily deciding that speed was more important than caution, he switched on the lights in the front room, darted forward and drew the curtains. It was not a large room and was very plainly furnished, and in less than half a minute he realized that it contained nothing even remotely resembling the box that Grace had described to him. If it was still in the house, then it had been removed to another room. At the back were a dining room and a kitchen and a strong smell of beer and cabbage—but no box. He dashed upstairs, looked in a dusty airless front bedroom and found nothing, then tried another bedroom, a rumpled place reeking of face powder and unwashed sheets, and was about to leave it in despair when he caught sight of the box, which was exactly as Grace had described it, perched on top of a wardrobe. As he took it down, discovering to his relief that it was not heavy, there was a crash, there was a flash, and the storm broke, with the noise of a hundred kettledrums.

With the box under his arm, he ran downstairs, only to halt in dismay just before he reached the hall. For there, standing just inside the door, with her mouth wide open, ready to scream, was a plump middle-aged woman. As he hesitated, the scream came, high above the drumming of the rain. He saw her turn and fling open the door, to scream into the night. There was no getting out that way, so he jumped down and raced toward the back, then wasted a few precious seconds by charging headlong into a pantry. As he recovered himself, made for the kitchen, and, in the darkness there, tried to find the back door, he heard more screams, some vague cries, and other disturbing sounds. He wasted more time tugging at a door that was bolted; and then, just as he finally unbolted the door, he heard high above the growling of the thunder, the battering of the rain, the screams and cries, the piercing urgent note of a police whistle.

Through the rain and the dark, occasionally split by lightning flashes, he ran and ran, still clutching the box, making blindly for the Heath. After five minutes, soaked and gasping, still hearing or seeming to hear the police whistles, he had left all the lighted windows behind, and was slipping and plunging in a black wilderness. He had known nothing like this since he had left the Burmese jungle. He seemed to be hours and hours battling his way toward the lights of Hampstead, with his fine thick suit a chill pulp, his shoes so much squelching, and cold riverlets flowing down his back. But when he finally arrived at the Belsize Park station, looking and feeling like a man who had been pulled out of the Heath ponds, it was only about eleven o'clock. He steamed away in the Underground, feeling a hunted man, and grimly made up his mind to deliver the wretched box to Grace that night. If, when he emerged from the Piccadilly Circus station, he had caught sight of an empty taxi, he would have claimed it, dropped the box at Grace's, and then had himself driven straight back to his hotel. But there were no empty taxis, and it was a very weary wet man who rang the bell to summon Grace.

"My goodness me!" she cried as she let him in. "But you're wet through."

"Of course I am," he told her. "I was crossing Hampstead Heath in all that storm. Well, here's your box. But it wasn't where you said it was."

"Did you have any trouble finding it?"

"Trouble! I had almost every possible kind of trouble." And he began to explain what had happened. Then he started sneezing.

"Now look, Theodore. If you keep those clothes on another minute, you'll be catching your death of cold. Get straight into that bathroom, get those clothes off, and give yourself a nice long hot bath. And if you throw your clothes out, I'll take 'em straight down to the drying cupboard they have here. No—no argument, young man, or you'll be getting pneumonia. Go on. In you go. Always plenty of hot water here, that's one thing. And take the things out of your pockets before you give me your clothes."

So he filled a bath, undressed, emptied his pockets, and dropped his soggy clothes for her to pick up and take away. As he got into the bath,

he heard her say again that she would herself take his clothes down to
dry as she did not trust the Service, particularly at that hour. Not two
minutes afterwards, as he gratefully accepted the warmth of the water
and began to feel deliciously relaxed and drowsy, he heard a tapping
at the bathroom door.

"Yes, Grace," he called, "what is it?"

He had not troubled to lock the door, and now it slowly opened, to
admit a long nose, a smoldering cigarette, suspicious dull eyes. And he
had seen this face before, but could not at that moment remember
where. But if either Seth Hull or the Commodore had been there, he
would have been told at once that these unprepossessing features belonged to A. Smith, London, operative of the Charing Private Inquiry
Agency.

"What do you want?" Theodore yelled at the face. "Go away."

It nodded and closed one eye. "Not staying, chum," it said. "Saw a
chance and popped in. Popping out now."

"Well, pop out then," said Theodore angrily.

"Remember you," it continued, with another wink. "White Hart,
Farbridge. Had my eye on the wrong bloke there. Just shows. Like to
give the name? Just for info."

"Go away," cried Theodore, and threw a large sponge at the face.

"Now, now," it said reproachfully. "Live and let live. Get the info
at Farbridge. Easy, Nice trip too. Ta ta for now." And it vanished.

Theodore listened, decided that the intruder had left the flat, and
completed the bath at his leisure. Quarter of an hour later, wrapped in
a blanket, he was enjoying a cup of tea with Grace, who listened quite
coolly to his account of the man who had looked into the bathroom.

"That must be the little man who followed me to Farbridge," she
said. "Long-nosed, ratty type. That's him. Oh—well—he doesn't matter
now."

"Doesn't he? I'd have thought he did." Theodore felt rather annoyed
by the cool way she was taking it all.

"No, not really. You remember I told you about the paper I signed—
the one about the divorce? Well, I've got it now. It was in that box."
And she pointed at the box, which she had opened. Then she smiled
at him. "I'm ever so much obliged. Have another cup of tea—do you
good."

Even after he had accepted the fresh cup and had taken several sips,
he still kept silent.

"Penny for them," she said gaily.

"Do you ever feel," he began slowly, "that you're lost in a vast madhouse, that everything's stopped making sense, that life's got out of control like an idiotic dream?"

"No, I can't say that I do," she said, cheerful and interested. "Do you?"

"I'm feeling it now," he told her pointedly.

"Go on with you!" And she laughed. "I'll pop along and see how your clothes are. You'll feel all right in the morning. You'll see."

"I won't until I've passed a few policemen and nothing's happened. But I should like my clothes, please. I seem to have had rather a long day."

3

On the Saturday morning the Commodore stayed in the White Hart to make a final check of the catering arrangements with Seth Hull; so Laura moved into his room and found herself in charge of the Festival Center until he returned. She had just gone through the morning mail when Mrs. Delacey marched in.

"My friend Miss Fisby is here," she announced.

"Oh—really, Mrs. Delacey," Laura cried, "I can't bother with Miss Fisby this morning."

"She is here At My Suggestion," said Mrs. Delacey in her grandest tone. "She did not want To Cause Any Trouble. Though Gifted, as we all know, she is Shyness Itself. But she is Deeply Distressed."

"About the Pageant, is it?"

"It is. Mr. Capperton, the Producer, has Taken A Great Liberty."

"All right, I suppose I'd better see her. Bring her up, please, Mrs. Delacey."

There could be no doubt that Miss Fisby really was deeply distressed. She looked as if she had been crying for hours. Mrs. Delacey put her into a chair and then stood bolt upright behind her.

"What's the matter, Miss Fisby? Are you having some trouble with Mr. Capperton?"

Miss Fisby nodded, blushed, watered, choked.

"I'm so sorry. Do tell me," said Laura, drawing heavily on her rapidly diminishing store of sympathy for her fellow creatures.

"Bonnie Prince Charlie," Miss Fisby faltered.

"Bonnie Prince Charlie?"

Miss Fisby nodded, then fairly burst into tears. Laura looked inquiringly at Mrs. Delacey.

"Mr. Capperton insists upon the Bonnie Prince Charlie episode Being Removed," said Mrs. Delacey.

"Oh, I see," said Laura. "Well, he told me the other day that something would have to be cut, and after all I suppose it might as well be Bonnie Prince Charlie. He'd nothing to do with Farbridge, had he?"

"No, not really," Miss Fisby stammered, "but—oh!—it's such a shame."

"Miss Fisby is Very Devoted to Bonnie Prince Charlie," said Mrs. Delacey severely. "And so feels that he ought Not To Be Tampered With."

Miss Fisby looked hopefully at Laura in a watery sort of way. "Everybody loves Bonnie Prince Charlie, Miss Casey."

"No, they don't," said Laura, rather brutally. "I don't, for one."

"Miss Casey," cried Mrs. Delacey in an awful warning tone.

"I'm sorry, Miss Fisby. I didn't mean to be unkind. But really everybody doesn't feel about Bonnie Prince Charlie as you do, and I know Mr. Capperton was worried about that episode particularly as it meant hiring some rather expensive costumes."

"My Daughter always says, 'Don't Try To Save On Dressing The Show,'" said Mrs. Delacey.

"That's all very well," cried Laura, "but we're spending far too much money as it is—"

"It's all my fault," Miss Fisby wailed.

"No, it isn't, Miss Fisby. And I believe the Pageant will pay for itself. But you must allow Mr. Capperton—"

"I'd rather give up Cavaliers and Roundheads," cried Miss Fisby.

"No, we can't cut the Cavaliers and Roundheads," said Laura impatiently, "otherwise it leaves too big a gap."

"Miss Casey is Quite Right There, dear," said Mrs. Delacey.

"You know, Miss Fisby, I did feel when I read your script that Bonnie Prince Charlie had rather been dragged in. Now—listen—why don't you cut him out of this pageant and then write a special Scotch pageant with a lot about him? People are sure to want you to write pageants for them after this. What do you say?"

"An Excellent Suggestion," Mrs. Delacey added.

"Very well," said Miss Fisby faintly, getting up. Then she looked wistfully at Laura. "Do you really think it's going to be all right, Miss Casey—the Pageant, I mean?"

"Of course it will."

"As My Daughter says," cried Mrs. Delacey, "It Will Be All Right On The Night. Come along, Miss Fisby. Remember, you have promised to Help Us Below."

Several minutes later, just when Laura had recovered from this interruption, Captain Mobbs came in with a fantastic old man whose hair and mustache were dyed an outrageous blue-black.

"This is Mr. Fotheringay, manager of the Palace," said Mobbs. "We're checking the list for Monday night. Miss Casey, our assistant organizer, old boy. Knows it all."

"How is everything at the theater, Mr. Fotheringay?" Laura asked.

The old man rubbed his hands. "Shaping well. Shaping very well. Splendid attraction, of course. London company. And Patrick Gorebarry will be a big draw, a very big draw. Mr. Mossat came down last night with his stage manager and electrician. They're putting in a temporary extra switchboard tonight. Like old times. I'm having the front specially cleaned and decorated first thing on Monday. Some nice frames outside already, very nice. Splendid attraction."

"Mrs. Whatmore—you know, the Colonel's wife—rang him last night and wanted to know why she hadn't had any tickets for Monday. So Mr. Fotheringay referred her to us."

"Couldn't say anything myself," said Mr. Fotheringay apologetically. "Didn't know what the situation was."

"Well, it's quite simple," said Laura sharply. "If Mrs. Whatmore wants some seats for Monday, she can go and buy them. She's not included in the Civic or the Festival group. Why should she be? Cheek, I call it."

The old man rubbed his hands again. "That's what I thought it, but couldn't say so. Now about this list. I make it fourteen pairs altogether —seven pairs in the stalls, and seven Front Circle. Lot of seats to give away, but we shan't be quite out on Monday and it always looks well— with the Mayor and Mayoress and so forth."

When they had finished checking the list, old Fotheringay said: "They'll be rehearsing late tomorrow night, Miss Casey, and in the old days I always liked to see they had coffee and sandwiches. I'll arrange that, shall I? And of course on Monday there'll be a little refreshment in my room for your party and the Mayor's."

"My godfathers—yes," cried Mobbs.

At that moment Mrs. Delacey, who had turned herself into a kind of herald, appeared in the doorway. "Mr. Johnny Jolly," she announced, "Of The Jollyboys Band."

"Come on, old boy," said Mobbs to Fotheringay. "We're off."

"Excellent attraction too," said old Fotheringay as he followed Mobbs.

A young man with carefully waved dark hair, a lilac sports shirt, and a mustard-colored jacket, burst into the room, crying: "Where's the Big Boss?" He was followed by a languid silvery blonde, who gave Laura and the whole room one disgusted glance and then, leaning against the wall, examined her writhing lips in a compact mirror.

"The Big Boss isn't here this morning," said Laura, "so you'll have to put up with the Little Boss. And that's me."

"Johnny Jolly in person," he said, holding out a hand. "And that's Mrs. Jolly, professionally known as April Bond—you've heard her on the air. Who'm I talking to, Miss—er—?"

"Casey."

"You can't beat the Irish. Say hello to Miss Casey, April sweetheart."

"Hello!" said April in a tired voice, without looking up.

"Hello!" said Laura, longing to slap her.

"Well, now we're all acquainted," said Johnny Jolly. "Just ran over from Brum, where we're playing this week. Got eighty out of the little old bus—nice going."

"Nice going, my foot!" said April.

"Now, sweetheart—"

"Oh—shut up!"

"Here, here, wait a minute," cried Johnny, suddenly aggressive. "You had to get up in the morning, for once. All right. You had to take a ride with me. All right. So what?"

"What d'yer mean—so what?" demanded April in shrill disgust.

"Don't give me that," he shouted.

"Give you what?"

"Don't do it, that's all."

They were now glaring at each other, as if they were at home, reacting against a long weary session of playing and crooning the sloppiest love songs.

"Just a minute," said Laura sharply, feeling that it was about time they were reminded of her existence. "I'm rather busy, you know, and if you're really going to have this out, would you mind going some-where else?"

"Snooty, aren't we?" said April.

"Possibly," said Laura icily.

"I'm gonna getta cuppa coffee," April told her husband. "In the ca-fay down the street. Say what you've got to say an' don't take all morning."

"Ten minutes, sweetheart," he said as she went swaying out, "or might be less." He turned to Laura. "Got her up too early this morning. She's temperamental. But a lovely artiste—a lovely artiste—ask any-body."

"I'm sure she is. And I didn't mean to be snooty. But I really am rather busy."

"Natch," said Johnny. "Well, I've just been up to this Mayton Park, where me an' my boys are playing next week, an' it's a nice set-up so long as we don't have rain. But soon as I saw it, I said to April: 'We gotta have a bigger brass section, sweetheart.' That's what I said, an' she says: 'You're dead right, Johnny,' though she hasn't wanted to agree with me this morning. So there it is. If I'm going to give you people what you want," he continued earnestly, "I'll have to have a bigger brass section." He gave her a beseeching look out of his treacle toffee eyes. "And as I can't save on the saxes an' woods, that means more money."

"I see," said Laura.

"I'm not trying anything on, Miss Casey. Don't think it. I'm not greedy. Ask anybody. All I want is to give you people what you expect from Johnny Jolly an' his Jollyboys, an' up there, believe me, with the combination we quoted you it's going to sound thin. I could do with another six, to make it rich an' lovely. But I'll tell you what I'll do. I'll manage with two more trombones, another trumpet, and perhaps a bass sax. An' if I get 'em for another sixty on the week, I'll be lucky. But some of the boys'll come for me where they wouldn't for another leader. They know I treat 'em right, natch. Well, what do you say?"

"The trouble is, Mr. Jolly, we're short of money. We've had to make a little go a long way. And we're already committed to spending quite a lot on the dancing in Mayton Park. There's your fee, the shell thing you play in, and the dancing platform. We're only charging sixpence to listen and two shillings to the dancers, and we don't know how people will respond—"

"Listen," cried Johnny, perching on the table, leaning toward her, and almost drowning her in the scent of eau-de-Cologne, "if I get the right combination, and you've got the right publicity, we'll have 'em tearing the railings down to get in. Don't take my word for it, Miss Casey. Ask anybody. But, mind you, I've gotta work fast to get those extra boys. Natch."

"Natch," said Laura, who had been longing to try it. "Wait a minute, please, and I'll ring up our chief organizer, Commodore Tribe. I must have his authority.

"Natch," said Johnny, and dropped off the table to go and stare out of the window while she telephoned. Fortunately the Commodore was in Seth Hull's private office, and she was able to tell him what the band leader had said.

"Well, Mr. Jolly, we'll pay you an extra fifty pounds just for the first week, and won't decide about the second week until we know how popular the dancing is. And that really is the best we can do."

Johnny nodded gloomily and obviously began thinking, which he did by closing his eyes and moving his lips soundlessly. After a few moments of this, there was a noise from outside, where two women appeared to be exchanging loud angry remarks. Johnny stopped thinking and rushed to the door.

"Keep it quiet," he shouted.

"I beg your pardon."

"And I beg yours," cried Johnny, "but keep it quiet, that's all. I wanna think."

Mrs. Whatmore was wearing a beige costume this morning, but there was no mistaking that massive figure, that purple face, that outraged look and tone. And Laura, remembering Major Bulfoss and that fantastic Saturday night, found herself wanting to giggle.

"Look here," Mrs. Whatmore began, ignoring Johnny and staring hard at Laura.

"Lady, for Pete's sake, keep it quiet a minute and let a man think. Fifty quid. It means Charlie doubling on the bass sax. Well, that's okay but—"

"Where are my tickets for Monday?" asked Mrs. Whatmore in a loud firm tone, still staring at Laura.

"If you don't pipe down, you won't get a show on Monday," cried Johnny, frowning at her. "Know who I am?"

"I've not the slightest idea," said Mrs. Whatmore, looking at him with undisguised disgust.

"Johnny Jolly, that's all. Trying to get the combination right for you people, that's all. So never mind about the tickets. Let's get the show right first. If you wanna dance—"

"I don't want to dance," Mrs. Whatmore shouted at him. "I'm talking about tickets for the theater." She looked at Laura. "Who is this man?"

"Mr. Jolly," said Laura very quietly, "is the band leader who has been engaged to play in Mayton Park. And when you interrupted us, he and I were trying to settle some rather important business."

"Natch," said Johnny, looking indignantly at Mrs. Whatmore. "So either keep it quiet or take a walk."

Mrs. Whatmore gave no sign of having heard him, but nevertheless she said no more but went and sat down in a heavily determined manner. And now above the noise of the thick Saturday morning in the High Street there came an impatient hooting from just outside the Center.

"That's the ball an' chain out there," said Johnny with a rueful grin, "tooting the horn of the old bus. Better cut it short. Okay, I take the extra fifty for the first week, an' then we see. But we'll wow 'em. Ask anybody. Be seeing you, Miss Casey," and he held out his hand, "an' if there's anything special you want me to play, it'll be a pleasure, so just name it. Bye-bye for now." He stopped just long enough to give Mrs. Whatmore a parting glance. "Cheer up, Ma. An' come an' shake it in the park next week."

"I must say—if that's the kind of person you're bringing to Farbridge," said Mrs. Whatmore. But like many people who announce in that tone what they must say, she failed to say it.

"About the theater tickets for Monday," said Laura quietly, "I think you don't quite understand the position. There are two small groups who have been invited. One of them is headed by the Mayor. The other consists of members of the Festival Committee. You're not a member of the Festival Committee. And if, on the other hand, you haven't been invited by the Mayor, then I'm afraid I can't help you."

"Do you know who I am?"

"Yes, you're Mrs. Whatmore—"

"Exactly, and our position here—"

"Colonel Whatmore was never in favor of our having a Festival, and did everything possible to prevent it."

"And quite right too," said Mrs. Whatmore angrily.

"The performance on Monday at the Palace," Laura reminded her sweetly, "is part of the Festival."

It was at that moment that Mrs. Bulfoss came tripping in, wearing a new flowered pink dress that set off her type of prettiness. "Good morning, Miss Casey," she cried gaily. "I hope you don't mind. Actually—I'm only looking in for a second." And then she noticed Mrs. Whatmore, who was slowly rising out of her chair in a miraculously smooth and majestic manner, as if an illusionist were at work in the room. "Oh dear!" said Mrs. Bulfoss.

"On the evening that Major Bulfoss behaved so outrageously," said Mrs. Whatmore with immense deliberation, "there was a young woman in the house who had obviously been drinking with him. You may be interested to learn, Mrs. Bulfoss, that that young woman is here." And she pointed dramatically at Laura.

"I know she was," said Mrs. Bulfoss. "Don't be silly."

"Am I to understand—"

"You're just being silly," said Mrs. Bulfoss, shaking her head at her.

"I am not being silly," Mrs. Whatmore thundered. She looked from Mrs. Bulfoss to Laura. "I had no idea that this young woman had been given, probably through your husband's influence, an official appointment in connection with this Festival. And in my opinion, it is nothing less than an outrage."

"Oh dear!" cried Mrs. Bulfoss. "Actually you've got it all wrong, you know."

"Nothing of the kind. And at the earliest possible moment, I shall speak to my husband and to the members of my Women's Executive Committee. Moreover, I believe that Miss Weeks holds a very responsible post, as personnel manager, in my husband's works. Am I right?" And she glared at Laura.

"Quite right. But I don't see the point—"

"The point," said Mrs. Whatmore, cutting in sharply, "is that if Miss Weeks has consented to these various unsavory arrangements—and that's the least one can call them—then she's not fit to hold the post—"

"Oh no," cried Laura, jumping up, "you couldn't be as mean and stupid as that."

"Actually," said Mrs. Bulfoss, "you've got everything wrong, Mrs. Whatmore, you really have."

"I know exactly," Mrs. Whatmore began, but stopped short because Mobbs now bounced into the room, beaming and sweating. And the next moment, Mobbs, seeing her, had stopped short too.

"Don't tell me, Captain Mobbs, that you're one of these Festival people too," said Mrs. Whatmore, regarding him with marked distaste.

"Honorary Social Organizer," said Mobbs, standing his ground well. "Good morning, Mrs. Bulfoss. Nice day."

"And may I ask, Captain Mobbs," Mrs. Whatmore continued in the same tone of elaborate disdain, "what you're supposed to do?"

"Social organizing," said Mobbs promptly. "The theater party on Monday night, for instance. The Festival Civic Lunch on Monday too."

"What Civic Lunch is this?" cried Mrs. Whatmore angrily.

"It's the one we're having on Monday," replied Mobbs.

"And I must say I'm looking forward to it," said Mrs. Bulfoss, smiling at Mobbs and then at Laura. "Is Patrick Gorebarry going to be there? My dear, he's heaven."

"Yes, he's been invited," said Mobbs, "and I'll make sure you're sitting next to him, Mrs. Bulfoss."

"Now that's a promise," and she wagged a finger at him with tremendous archness, "and you won't go back on it."

"My godfathers—no."

Mrs. Whatmore, who throughout this playful little exchange had been standing in the middle of the room looking like some savage ancient monument draped in beige dress goods, now appeared to explode. It would hardly have been surprising if she had filled the room with little planetary Mrs. Whatmores all furiously circling round the central sun of righteous indignation. No words were audible at first. And then, before they arrived properly, Laura began laughing. She collapsed into her chair, and laughed and laughed. Instantly infected, Mrs. Bulfoss and little Mobbs began laughing too.

Mistakenly assuming they were laughing directly at her, Mrs. Whatmore in an ungovernable fury sprang at Mrs. Bulfoss, seized her by the shoulders, and shook her violently, crying: "Stop it, you stupid fool of a woman!"

But Madge Bulfoss, foolish and vaporing though she was at times, was not entirely without spirit, and now she twisted herself free of Mrs. Whatmore's grasp, screamed defiance, and then landed a resounding slap on the nearest purple fat cheek. Mrs. Whatmore tottered back a pace or two, her eyes bulging with horror. Mrs. Bulfoss, bursting into tears on the way, flew round the table to cling to Laura, who shouted to Mobbs to take Mrs. Whatmore away.

"Come along now," cried Mobbs, sounding like a small anxious policeman, "come along. We've had quite enough of it. My godfathers—yes!"

He laid a tentative hand on Mrs. Whatmore's arm. She pushed him away, announced that the last had not been heard of this, and marched out, with Mobbs, putting a handkerchief to his steaming pate, at her heels.

"Oh dear!" cried Mrs. Bulfoss, still clinging to Laura. "Oh dear!" And the pair of them could not decide whether to laugh or to cry.

"What goes on?" said Michael Seacombe, standing in the doorway.

"Oh—Michael!" said Laura, delighted to see him.

"My dear," cried Mrs. Bulfoss, straightening herself, "I must fly. Actually I only meant to look in for a second, just to see how things were going."

"All right, I think," said Laura as soberly as she could.

"I'm so looking forward to Monday." Mrs. Bulfoss looked at Michael. "Is it true that Patrick Gorebarry drinks all the time?"

"He used to," said Michael. "But they say he's off it now."

"Isn't that wonderful?" cried Mrs. Bulfoss. "Goodbye, my dears. See you on Monday."

Michael strode across the room, stretched long arms across the table, and held Laura lightly by the shoulders. "Whatever you think you're going to do, just don't do it. You've had it, this morning."

"I have," she began. But he stopped her.

"Tell me later. I've got various odds and ends of news too. But they'll keep."

"I've still got—" she began again, looking at the stuff on the table. But again he stopped her.

"Come out and have a quick short drink and then an early lunch. Can't do any good in here. I can tell. Come on now. No nonsense."

She smiled at him. "All right, Michael." She walked round the table. "Golly, I must look a mess. I know I feel one."

He put two fingers under her chin and gently tilted up her face toward his. "Terrible. Hair all over the place, nose shiny, eyes hollow and red-rimmed, lipstick gone, ink smudge on chin." He kissed her lightly. "Tidy up, and let's go. You need cherishing."

"Of course I do," she said in a rather uncertain tone, blinking a little.

"And I'm the chap to do it. Come on now."

"Give me two minutes." And she fled.

While he was waiting, Mrs. Delacey appeared in the doorway. "There's a Person wishing to see Miss Casey," she said, rather like a dubious butler.

"You tell that person to pop off, Mrs. Delacey," said Michael firmly.

"Aren't you Taking A Good Deal upon yourself, Mr. Seacombe?"

"I am," he told her cheerfully. "And I'll take more before I've finished." He waved her away.

"Who was that?" asked Laura, a few minutes later.

"Nobody. Forget it." He was masterful. "Come on now. Don't give that table even a look."

"No, Michael," she replied demurely; and together they went below and out into the busy street, the sensible sunlit world.

4

No doubt there was still much to be done on that last Sunday before the Festival opened, but the Commodore and Captain Mobbs, Chief Organizer and Social Organizer respectively, were certainly not doing it. The middle of the afternoon, a warm and windless afternoon with that extra density, that curtaining and cushioning of earth and air, which Sunday seems to bring, found them returning, in Mobbs's little car, from Brant-in-the-Hollow, where they had been lunching in the pub. Their guests had been Sir Barclay and Lady Gishforth, who had still neither acquired a cook nor any elementary knowledge of the art itself. Full of food, ripe with drink, a little somnolent, they moved at no great speed to Farbridge, through the vast sleepy hollow of Sunday afternoon.

"You were quite right, of course," said the Commodore, who was still enjoying a cigar. "I'd met Daphne Gishforth before."

"Knew her very well, I'd say, old boy."

"No, not really, though she might give you that impression. She's bored, poor woman, and meeting me again reminded her of old triumphs and glories, lost kingdoms. Very natural, my dear Archie. But not my type. Certainly not these days. Too hard. Too brittle."

"Same here," said Mobbs. "But then I never fancied the nobs, and they never cared for me. Maggie's my style. How do you think I stand there, old boy?"

"What are your intentions?" the Commodore inquired gravely.

"Oh—marry her like a shot. No hanky-panky there, old boy. All above board. Oh—yes, marriage every time, though of course at the moment, with no job in sight, I haven't much to offer, much less than that damned farmer and the other fellow with the garage. And it's getting me down a bit, that thought."

"Nonsense, my dear chap," said the Commodore. "She's taking her holiday these next two weeks and coming to the Festival, isn't she?"

"Got it all laid on," said Mobbs proudly. "Even got her a room at my digs."

"Then the rest ought to be easy—"

"But the other two chaps are coming in on various nights, to take her out. They insisted, and so did she. Fair-minded girl, Maggie."

"There isn't such a thing," said the Commodore. "It merely means that her emotions aren't involved yet. And it's your business, my boy, to involve 'em. If you can't do it, as Social Organizer too, I'm ashamed of you. But whether it's wise," he added reflectively, "is another matter."

Mobbs was so surprised that he gave his wheel a twist in the wrong direction so that the car moved to the right. Much angry tooting and shouting from a car that was about to overtake him made Mobbs pull in to the left and finally bring the car to a halt. He wiped his glistening forehead. "Just stop a minute, if you don't mind, old boy. You gave me quite a shock then. Why isn't it wise? Something about her—or me?"

"Neither, so far as I know," the Commodore replied thoughtfully. "I just happen not to be very fond of the married state, myself. Except for youngsters anxious to be parents."

"Ever tried it? Marriage I mean, old boy."

"I have," said the Commodore coolly, "and officially I'm still married. But I wouldn't call myself a marrying man. However, that's not the point. Do you feel like driving on now, Archie? Good! I can talk as we go. No, the point is that marriage doesn't seem to me to bring out the best in women. Love does, up to a certain level. But not marriage. There's something, I fancy, about its very legality," he continued slowly, "that secretly irritates them. They lose the lover in the husband."

"But I thought they all wanted husbands," said Mobbs, with the air of one willing to be instructed.

"Most of 'em do because that's the way, they feel, that things have been arranged for 'em. But they don't want a husband as they want a lover. It's a different kind of wanting. And this husband-wanting, as I see it, really annoys them. So when a man turns into a husband, he's not the complete man a lover is. He's a social front, a job, a legal document, a responsibility in the wrong sense, and a prize silver cup that's only plated. And all this doesn't bring out the best in 'em. Or so it seems to me, Archie, though I must point out that my experience during the last thirty years has been mostly gathered outside England, mostly in places where there are as many mature lovers and mistresses as there are husbands and wives."

"Not quite the same thing here, old boy," said Mobbs with more confidence. "Dead keen on marriage here even yet. I know Maggie is. But what I offer with it, God only knows."

"You couldn't put your hand on about five thousand pounds, could you?" the Commodore inquired dreamily.

"Draw it mild. I wish I could put my hand on five hundred. I'd feel better. Why? Got a scheme, old boy?"

"Not worth the name," said the Commodore wistfully. "A dream not a scheme. But did Seth ever show you the Three Black Boys?"

"No, but I've had a drink or two there. Nice old place but terribly run-down."

"And I could run it up, if I could find the money to buy the whole property. There's a snug little wines and spirits business goes with it, part of the property. You take that over, I run the pub and restaurant, with your Maggie helping us out—and there you are."

"Bob's your uncle!" cried Mobbs. "Perhaps Seth would lend us the money?"

"No he wouldn't. I'm sure of that." The Commodore yawned. "And I don't suppose between us we've enough to pay for the paint and varnish, let alone the property itself and the good-will of both concerns, we'd better forget it." He yawned again. "Sorry, but Sunday afternoon always does this to me, always did."

The Commodore dozed a little and it was not until they were turning into High Street, like a huge empty stage-set in the heavy sunlight, the muffled air, of Sunday, that he struggled back to full consciousness. "You know, Archie, when I told 'em at our Corn Exchange meeting that I wanted to stay on here, I wasn't just flattering 'em. I've got fond of this place. Can't exactly say why, because there's nothing very special about it—but there it is. And if I have to clear out, I'll be sorry."

"My godfathers!—but I feel just the same," cried Mobbs, delighted by this similarity of tastes and views. "I've not had an easy time here— Bulfoss was never any great shakes, either as a candidate or a Member —and I wouldn't say I'd made many friends—and quite a few enemies —but whereas I used to like moving on, now I'd like to settle here, if I could find anything. And, as you say, old boy, there's nothing special about Farbridge. Even my digs are only fair. But I like it here and don't want to leave."

"We must do something about it, my boy," said the Commodore solemnly, as the car drew up to the White Hart. "Coming in?"

"No, thanks. I'll run home and have a nap. Yes, old boy, we must do something about it. Going to Huntley's place tonight, aren't we? Pick you up, shall I?"

"Do. Then we can have a drink or two, because I don't imagine that Huntley'll be well provided. A light ale and cider type, I fancy. Be here about seven, Archie."

The Commodore went blinking into the dusky deserted cave of the White Hart lounge. Before he noticed anybody at all, he heard a charming clear voice calling him, and then saw it came from an alcove in which a man and a woman were taking tea. Going nearer, he recognized the woman as Philippa Hookwood, the actress.

"A-ha, Miss Hookwood," he cried, holding out a hand. "All ready for us?"

"Not quite, Commodore," she said, smiling and motioning him to a chair, "we've a long night's rehearsal in front of us. This is our leading man, Mr. Gorebarry. Patrick, this is Commodore Tribe, who's running the Festival here."

"Splendid!" said the actor smiling. "Have some tea or something."

The Commodore, who already knew Miss Hookwood's opulent good looks, examined Patrick Gorebarry with some curiosity. Much might depend on this fellow's power of attraction. What he saw was a tallish lean man, forty perhaps, almost gipsy dark, astonishingly handsome in the half-melancholy, half-sulky romantic style, with a personality at once reckless and weak. His voice, like the shoulders supporting the careless linen coat, was magnificently masculine; but the fingers that held his cigarette were like a girl's; and something that was neither man nor woman but perhaps a bewildered child peeped out of his eyes. If his acting came anything near his appearance, the Commodore decided, Gorebarry would soon fill their theater.

"Anybody here interested in us, do you think?" the actor asked.

"The advance isn't too hot," said Philippa.

"Too early to say what'll happen," said the Commodore, who knew little about the Theater and cared less, but felt he had to sound as if he did. "We're doing a sort of special Civic performance tomorrow night, and that ought to help. But we'll know more when you come to Sheridan and Shakespeare. You're doing this new play tomorrow, aren't you? What's it like?"

"I love it," cried Philippa. "And it plays quite well."

"So you say, darling," said Gorebarry. "And I'll take your word for it. But it seems bloody tedious to me so far."

"Wait until you have an audience, darling."

Already it was clear to the Commodore that these two darlings had not in fact any great liking for each other, that they were just sitting in this corner together because they had nothing better to do, and that any trouble that might arise later in the week would come from their dislike of each other rather than from any romantic passages between them.

"You very fond of the Theater, Commodore?" said Gorebarry.

"No, not very."

"God, how right you are!"

"Pat, don't pretend," cried Philippa. "You know you adore it."

"I don't. Never did really," he said moodily. "Can't decide which I detest the more, film studios or theaters. A plague o' both your houses!"

"Wait till you try television," said Philippa darkly. "It's the end, darling, honestly the end. And anyhow, what would you like to have done or been?"

"Anything but an actor," he replied, in a tone that only an actor could have used. He looked quickly from one to the other of his listeners, then gazed searchingly at nothing in particular, while Philippa made a secret little derisive face at the Commodore. "I ought to have been a jet pilot. Or a racing motorist. Or a yachtsman. Or even a writer, sitting at home in a dressing gown. Or the leader of a revolutionary party, swaying the mob. Or a smuggler. I could have been an explorer if there'd been anything left worth exploring. Or a surgeon. I wouldn't have minded owning a damned great shop, running like hell from floor to floor selling anybody anything. Or I might have been happy on a little farm somewhere—"

"Not on the little farms I've seen," said the Commodore dryly.

"He doesn't mean a real farm," said Philippa, her eyes bright with malice. "It's a stage farm, with a few nice rural props—"

"Oh—for God's sake!" he exclaimed angrily, and jumped up and strode away.

"Pat, don't be silly," she called after him.

He swung round, returned in three quick long strides, took her hand and bent over it, and gave her an exquisite smile. "My dear Philippa, I wasn't being silly. I was merely going to call the theater.

I suddenly remembered something." And he released her hand, and this time did leave them.

"When he does that to me—just looks and sounds like that—even I can feel myself going mushy," she told the Commodore. "And I don't even like him. What he'll do to some of these women here these next two weeks, you can't begin to imagine. That is, if he keeps moderately sober. You know about him, of course? Yes, well, it's a frantic risk but so far—touch wood—we've had no trouble. It's one reason Archie Mossat took your young friend on, to help him to look after poor Pat."

"What young friend?"

She stared at him, surprised by his question. "Why, didn't you know? The boy who was helping you here at first—Theodore."

"Theodore Jenks?"

"Yes, of course. And another fatal charmer, only—thank God—unlike Pat Gorebarry he doesn't know it yet. All the girls in the company adore him, but Clare, who's very quick and artful, grabbed him first."

The Commodore was thinking hard. "Where's Theodore now?"

"At the theater, of course. He's one of our assistant stage managers, among other things. What's the matter?"

"I remember this Clare—she came here with you—a very attractive wench—"

"Yes, if you happen to like that type. Coarse dark hair, thick white skin, short-legged and busty. But a sweet girl—of course."

"How far has this gone?"

"What—between Theodore and Clare? My dear, don't ask me, but at a guess, knowing Clare, I'd say as far as it could go."

"But no engagement, no talk of marriage?" the Commodore persisted.

"Not that I've heard of, but I wouldn't know really. But why all this curiosity? You don't seem that kind of man, if I may say so."

"You may say so as often as you please," said the Commodore hastily. "It's not Sunday newspaper curiosity. Quite different. You see, my assistant on this Festival job is a girl called Laura Casey, who's very hardworking and dependable—and a delightful child—but who's been in a queer state ever since she and Theodore, who seemed to be in raptures about each other, had a quarrel."

"Oh, that's why he left you, is it, Commodore? I'm so glad you joined us here. I love this sort of cozy talk about people one knows. Don't you?"

"No, not much. But I think that's chiefly why he left us." He waited a moment. "You see, young Laura has another admirer here, a journalist called Michael Seacombe—"

"Oh he came to see us in town, for some publicity stuff. He's rather attractive, isn't he? But go on. I like this."

"Well, the point is," said the Commodore carefully, "if both Laura and Theodore are sufficiently attached elsewhere, then all's well. Or if they suddenly forgot about their Clares and Michaels and fell into each other's arms—which isn't likely, I'm afraid—all would be well too. But if, which is most likely, they're both in some messy state of mind in between these two happy extremes, and they're running round this town worrying about each other, then poor little Laura might go and break down altogether, and I'll have this Festival entirely on my own hands. Now do you see why I asked those questions?"

"My dear, I saw it minutes ago. Quite clear. But I don't believe in this breaking down business. Girls are much tougher than that, and if there's a lot of emotion roaring round, exciting young men coming back, quarrels and reconciliations and whatnot all over the place, then, my dear man, they simply thrive on it. Yes, I know. When he left, she was suddenly miserable and edgy. That was because everything suddenly went dull, lifeless. I know. I've had some."

"You may be different," he objected.

"Nonsense. I'm just about average. Look. If she's still in love with him—and I'll bet she is—then she'll do no breaking down just because he's around again. No fear. If she's fallen out of love with him—and decides to take What's-his-name—Michael—then she'll keep going just to show Theodore what a fool he was to run away and how little she cares now. And either way she'll be bossing the Festival like mad, just to show off. I know I would."

"But don't you see, Miss Hookwood, that there's something in between—"

"No, there isn't," she said firmly. "It's either one or the other."

"I'm afraid I don't agree," said the Commodore, who would have saved himself and others a lot of trouble afterwards if he had agreed. But now Patrick Gorebarry came sauntering back.

"Any news?" asked Philippa.

"We've to be there at seven," he replied, "so I propose to rest for a couple of hours. We're the only two staying here, aren't we?"

"Archie Mossat's here, and of course our dear Mrs. Hungerford

arrives here tomorrow. But nobody in the company. Most of them—
and that includes your Theodore—" and she looked knowingly at the
Commodore"—*and* Clare—are staying at a pub near the theater. I
think it's called the Albion. Well, I must rest too. We'll meet tomorrow
at your Town Hall lunch, Commodore, if not before."

The Commodore, who was now standing just outside the alcove, lit
his pipe, then watched the players moving beautifully toward the
stairs. He was about to follow them when once again he heard his
name being called. He turned to discover a thick-set, glum-faced fellow
crossing the lounge. It was Frank York.

"Want to talk to you," said York.

"Possibly. But do I want to talk to *you*, that's the point."

"Better sit down somewhere quiet," York continued.

"I don't want to sit down somewhere quiet," said the Commodore
easily. "I'm going up to my room to have a nap."

"Well, I suppose this'll do," said York sulkily. "Now look, I need
twenty-five pounds—sharp."

"Not interested," said the Commodore.

"I dare say. But I'd like to remind you that I've got a good idea about
what went on at the Bell when you were there and I wasn't. And if
you'd like to keep out of trouble, then twenty-five pounds isn't much
to ask, is it?"

"There's a name for this, you know," said the Commodore pleasantly.
"It's called blackmail."

"Not what I'm doing isn't. I'm just asking you to lend me twenty-five
pounds. That's all."

"And I," said the Commodore in the same easy pleasant style, "am
just telling you to go to hell. That's all."

"I've been told," York went on, keeping his dull brown gaze fixed on
the Commodore, "that if I sued for divorce, I could get heavy damages
from the other chap. But I don't particularly want to do that. Unless,
of course, somebody puts my back up. Like you, for instance."

"Just a minute," said the Commodore, who had seen a massive figure
approach the reception desk. "Seth, can you spare a moment?"

"I can," Seth called. "Hold on a sec."

"What's the idea?" asked York rather uneasily.

"He's the landlord here," the Commodore explained, "and a great
friend of mine." He waited a moment or two, and then Seth came

across to them. "Seth, this is Mr. York, whose wife keeps the Bell at
Tredberrow, where I stayed before I came here."

"Met her once," said Seth, and then to York, rather abruptly: "How
d'yer do?"

"Now Mr. York," the Commodore continued smoothly, "is under the
impression that while I was there and he was away, I was making love
to Mrs. York—"

"Here, steady!" York cried indignantly.

"And he's come here today to ask me for twenty-five pounds, which,
he says, I'd better pay if I want to keep out of trouble. I've told him I
call that blackmail."

"Every time," said Seth with marked severity. "And if yer paid that,
in a week or two he'd be coming for another packet."

"Exactly," said the Commodore. "And I don't think that kind of
thing should be encouraged."

Seth poked a thick stiff forefinger into the lapel of York's coat. "Outside—sharp. An' don't come here again on a job like this. Now—hop
it."

"I've warned him," York began.

"Don't start any bloody argy-bargy here," cried Seth with passionate
emphasis, "or yer'll get my monkey up. Outside."

As they watched him go, Seth said: "I've heard tell o' yon chap but
nowt in his favor. Wife's all right. Keeps a good house. And he wor
away when you wor there, eh?"

"He was, fortunately," said the Commodore.

"Ay. A fairly ripe an' tasty piece, Mrs. York, from what I remember
of her. Of course yer wouldn't have got up to anything, would yer,
Commodore?"

"Naturally not," said the Commodore blandly, looking him in the
eye.

"What an idea!" said Seth, looking the Commodore in the eye.
"Can't think where some chaps get their notions from." He looked
round the room. "Quiet, isn't it? But it won't be like this tomorrow
at this time. Every room taken till a week on Saturday. Could have
let some of 'em three times over. Might have a surprise for yer
tomorrow. No, I'm not telling. Wait an' see, lad. Are yer in tonight?"

"No, Seth. Huntley's giving a little party, and Mobbs is coming
for me at seven. We'll have a drink or two first."

"Happen I'll join yer."

"Do. I'll go up and have a nap now. Sleepy sort of day. Thanks for helping me with York, Seth."

Refreshed by a short absence from this world, the Commodore, promptly at seven, went down into the bar, and there joined Seth and little Mobbs in a very pleasant session of whisky, opinion and reminiscence that lasted until eight-thirty. Dutifully but reluctantly, the Commodore and Mobbs then descended from these golden high pastures of fellowship, and drove to West Farbridge in search of the large corner house in which Huntley, a bachelor, had rooms. They were in a ripe but not eagerly expectant mood.

"My guess is," said the Commodore, "that it'll be one of these thin, coldish, cultured parties. Tomato sandwiches, cider cup, and sonnets or sonatas. Lot of women with long blue noses and colossal collar-bones. You know the sort of thing, Archie?"

"No, I don't really, old boy. But I think I see what you mean. I remember now that this chap who's lecturing for us tomorrow, Grope, will be there. He's staying with Huntley, who's giving this party for him. Chap who calls himself a fierce gay anarchist, y'know, old boy?"

"I'll lay eight to one he's a solemn ass," said the Commodore.

"I'm not taking you," said Mobbs. "But we can always push off after an hour or so."

"We can. So watch for my signal."

Huntley met them in the hall. "So glad you could come along," he whispered. "Erce. Most of our Festival group are here—and some of my teachers—all absolutely first-class types, keen as mustard. And Grope's here. Erce. Fascinating fellow, of course. I persuaded him to read some of his latest stuff—very modern, of course—difficult—but thoroughly worth while, I think—erce. And do help yourself to every-thing that's going—sandwiches, buns, beer, cider. In you go. I'll be back in a minute."

There seemed to be about thirty people in the room, with many earnest schoolmistresses sitting on the floor; and Mr. Grope, who was standing with his back to the fireplace, was reading aloud. He stopped for a few moments while the Commodore and Mobbs pushed their way in and found a corner where they could lean against the wall; and then, after a solemn nod in their direction, he continued his reading. The fierce gay anarchist, who was dressed in neat blue serge, was a man about forty-five with patchy gray hair, a jaundiced com-

plexion, and sepia-shadowed pouches under his eyes. He had a curious
voice, sad and hollow and yet booming, that suggested a giant calling
to be let out of a zinc box.

"This next poem," he announced, looking at Mobbs, "is called
Menippus on Half-day Closing—"

"Called what, old boy?" cried Mobbs, baffled but anxious to show
some interest.

"*Menippus on Half-day Closing*. It's rather gay, I think."

"Good," said Mobbs. There was a slight stir among the listeners,
and a hastily suppressed giggle that sounded like Miss Laura Casey.
Grope raised his little book, scowled at it, then boomed hollowly:

Utter mendacities
Are almost suppressed,
Except in the case of the girl with too many shoes.

All the vanilla avenues,
With blood on the blinds,
Are closed
To centaurs
And leading technicians in small bicycle factories.

When shall we meet
Flamingoes in the maze?

There was a murmur of wonder and admiration as Mr. Grope
slowly lowered his book and closed his eyes. A plump woman with
eyeglasses and immense coils of hair round her ears declared that she
had loved that poem for years and had never imagined she would
have the privilege of hearing Mr. Grope read it.

"I didn't quite get it, old boy," Mobbs muttered to the Commodore.

"You didn't, Archie?" said the Commodore. "Shall we have it
again?"

But already it had been decided by a small group of admirers led
by the plump woman, that Mr. Grope's final reading should be of
his *Twenty-seven Teashops*, which a young man with a cold in the
head described as one of the masterpieces of our age.

Grope raised his book again, scowled at it again, then dropped to
a still lower and hollower booming, as if the zinc box containing the
giant were now partly underground:

Undulating circumstances
And the tired funeral
Of my oldest aunt,
Who had always wondered about Turkestan,
Brought ambivalence,
No consternation,
But sugar, if you don't mind.

To eat choc ices
With Iphigenia,
The roof gone
And a new pattern of stars,
Without Pascal
Or Kierkegaard,
No benefit of clergy
And never a flit-gun for ambrosial bees.

My cousin the Colonel
And his almond unicorn
Joined us every Tuesday
And one,
And then two,
And then three,
Girls with long pointed blue hats
Danced up, danced down, danced away

Past the cash register.
Pay at the desk, please.
Pay at the desk.
Pay at the.
Pay at.
Pay.

And then the poet slowly lowered his book and closed his eyes again. "Bravo!" shouted the Commodore, and then loudly applauded, so that many of the others there followed his example.

"Still didn't get it, y'know, old boy," said Mobbs.

"You're not in the movement, Archie," said the Commodore. "You've neglected your literary tastes, I'm afraid, my boy. This kind of evening is wasted on you. Let's go and talk to Grope."

"What about?" asked Mobbs anxiously.

"God knows. But he's lecturing for us tomorrow, and you're our Social Organizer, so stir yourself, my dear fellow." He pushed through the throng.

"Erce," Huntley was saying to Grope, "it makes such a difference to hear you read them. The whole inner structure, the emotional undertones and overtones, become more obvious. Erce. Ah—you must meet our Festival organizer, Commodore Tribe. And Captain Mobbs."

"I think," said Grope, with deep solemnity, "you seemed to enjoy my little poems, Commodore Tribe."

"My dear fellow," cried the Commodore, shaking the other's limp hand, "it was magnificent. We won't forget this evening in a hurry, will we, Mobbs?"

"My godfathers, no!"

"Some beer," said Huntley gaily, "or cider—if that's your tipple? A tomato sandwich? Or a cheese sandwich?"

"Now," said the Commodore to Grope, "have you met my assistant, Miss Casey? She's looking after our lectures. And very keen."

"Erce," said Huntley. "Absolutely first-class."

"And Michael Seacombe, who does our publicity," the Commodore continued, giving Michael a quick wink. "A journalist at the moment, but devoted to literature and one of your most ardent admirers. And so is Miss Casey, who'll be looking after you tomorrow afternoon at your lecture."

"A pleasure," said Mr. Grope sadly. "You'll find it a provocative talk, I think. On the light side perhaps—one has to be on these occasions—but making a good many sound points."

"I'm sure it does," said Laura demurely.

"I admire the title very much, Mr. Grope," said the Commodore, with all the appearance of earnest enthusiasm. "Your own, I take it? I thought so. Very happy."

"Erce," said Huntley. "And you're giving our lectures a capital send-off—capital." He breathed, quivered, went under.

"No doubt about that," said the Commodore heartily. "And I'm very sorry indeed that I shan't be able to be there. The first day of our Festival, Mr. Grope—it means a tremendous rush of work for some of us."

"It does," said Mobbs. "Tomorrow—it's over the top and the best of luck! But you're coming to our Festival Civic Lunch, Mr. Grope, aren't you?"

"Of course he is," said the Commodore hastily. "And I think he ought to say a few words. Eh, Mr. Grope? Nothing fierce or gay or anarchical, but just a few words to wish us luck—eh?" He felt Laura tugging at his sleeve and allowed himself to be pulled away.

"Will you stop it, you wicked old man," she whispered fiercely. "It's all right for you and Fatty Mobbs, filling yourselves with whisky and then marching in here, saying any nonsense to that man. But I've got to look after him tomorrow, don't forget."

"Don't worry about him, my dear," said the Commodore. "He'll swallow anything."

"Can't I tempt you?" said the plump woman with eyeglasses, holding out a large plate of buns.

"No, thank you," said the Commodore. "I can't think about food yet. Not after those twenty-seven early closing teashops."

"A wonderful experience," said the plump woman.

"Wonderful, wonderful!" said the Commodore. "I should try Captain Mobbs with those buns. With a couple of buns and a glass of cider, he's happy anytime anywhere. Yes, the fat little bald man." He turned to Laura. "I want to talk to Seacombe for a few minutes. Festival business but you needn't bother about it. Is there another room where he and I could talk?"

"I think there's a little dining room across the hall," said Laura. "I'll tell him to join you there. Sure you don't want me?"

"Positive, my dear," said the Commodore, who was. As he moved off, he ran into Huntley, flushed and triumphant, with a jug of orangeade in one hand and a plate of very pale cheese straws in the other.

"You're not leaving us already?" cried Huntley. "What about another drink—orangeade—awfully good, I believe? Something to eat? Some cheese straws—or a paste sandwich?"

"No, thanks, my dear fellow." The Commodore now assumed a conspiratorial manner, which, he knew, always worked with Huntley. "I have to have a quiet word or two with young Seacombe," he said out of the corner of his mouth. "Just about one or two things— you know. So I'm popping across the hall."

Huntley became the Refined Back Room Boy at once. "Quite, quite," he murmured, closing his eyes. "And you're perfectly right to be careful. There are one or two people here—no, I'll say just *one*—you know —who—"

"Exactly," said the Commodore, and left him happy.

In the dining room, the young man with a cold was talking to a
thin young woman with enormous earrings and a general air of being
one of the Borgias out of school hours. His interruption of their eager
talk appeared to annoy them.

"Mr. Huntley was asking for you two," said the Commodore coolly.
"I think he wants you to talk to Grope."

"Of course," cried the thin young woman. "He's rather marvelous,
isn't he?"

"Wait until you've had some talk with him," said the Commodore.
"The wit, the insight, the fire!" Left to himself, he glanced round the
room and then noticed, on the sideboard and in the shadow of a soda
siphon, a coy half-bottle of whisky. He was helping himself rather
hurriedly when Seacombe came in.

"Hoy, hoy!" cried Michael, spotting the whisky at once. "That's
what I've been looking for. Is there another glass?" He found one.
"I'm also damned hungry."

"So am I," said the Commodore. "I've had no dinner and I can't
start feeding myself buns at my age. However, I shall clear out soon,
though of course it's too late to find any hot food anywhere."

"Did you really want to see me about something? Laura said you
did."

"Yes. Won't take a minute. Young Jenks is back—with the Mossat
Company at the Palace."

"I know he is," said Michael, "though I haven't told Laura."

"That's the point. She's bound to find out, probably by tomorrow
night at the latest. Now, as you know, I've been worried about little
Laura. Doesn't matter to me—" But he stopped there. An elderly
woman came in, through a doorway obviously leading to the kitchen,
and with her arrived a most tantalizing smell, for she was carrying a
dish of fried sausages.

"Mr. Huntley can say what he likes," she said to them, smiling, "but
I think they ought to have something hot."

"Absolutely," cried Michael, at her side at once, with his hand
on the dish.

"An admirable thought," said the Commodore. "Now don't you
bother—"

"We'll attend to them," said Michael, taking the dish.

"Thank you so much," she said. "I might manage a few more."

"I should do that at once," said the Commodore, who was now looking for the mustard on the sideboard.

"You were saying?" said Michael, a few moments later when they were eating the sausages.

"I was saying that it doesn't matter to me—though of course I'm very fond of Laura—which of you she falls in love with or gets herself engaged to. It would if I disliked one of you, but then I don't."

"I can see that," said Michael. "But what you don't want is an unhappy Laura, who doesn't know where she is. That's it, isn't it?"

"It is," said the Commodore, overlooking the excellent advice Philippa Hookwood had given him. "Let's have another drink, shall we? These sausages are welcome—but hellishly hot. So what I suggest—and this is why I wanted to have a word with you—is that if you feel you're making any headway with her, then you'd better rush her into an engagement at once. If you could work it, we might even announce it at the Civic Lunch tomorrow."

"The idea had occurred to me," said Michael thoughtfully, with half a hot sausage six inches from his mouth. "I'd also wondered whether it wouldn't be rather a dirty trick."

"It would if you were rushing her into immediate marriage," said the Commodore. "But, after all, it's only an engagement."

"Then what's the point of the move then?" Michael demanded shrewdly. "Either we're rushing her or we're not."

"I'm not rushing her. I'm merely trying to keep her busy and happy during these next two weeks." The Commodore was not quite as easy and confident as he sounded.

"Well, I'll see how it goes," said Michael doubtfully.

Mobbs burst in at that moment. "Look, old boy," he began, "I've had enough of this. Nothing to—" And then he saw what they were eating and drinking. "My godfathers! So this is what goes on. Give me a glass and a fork."

"You go back, my boy," the Commodore said to Michael, "and look after Laura. Take her home, and don't let her go near the theater, which is where Archie and I are going, as soon as he's had two sausages and one small drink. Yes, that's all you're having, my friend. No time for more. Besides, you can't skulk in here, hogging the only decent bit of food and drink the party has. How's Grope?"

"Well tangled up with some rather dreary types," said Mobbs grinning. "And serve him right—him and his forty-seven teashops! My godfathers, what a party, old boy, what a party! I say, this isn't a bad sausage. Hot, though. Well—here's luck to the good old Festival!"

5

An hour later, that same Sunday night, and a mild radiance of stars could be seen above the darkening town. The pubs and cinemas had closed. The last bus had rolled out of Peter Place. There were still a few raised voices in the main roads, and some echoing footfalls down the side streets; but already the night's long silence was invading Farbridge, which now gave no outward sign of being on the eve of its Festival.

In his private office at the White Hart Seth Hull had fallen asleep over the sporting pages of the Sunday press. Out at Mayton Park Avenue, Major Bulfoss was sitting in his study with a drink and *The Case of the Tall Albino,* Mrs. Bulfoss, at her dressing table upstairs, was pulling little faces at herself in the mirror, and Anita, the parlormaid, was at the back gate, locked in the arms of the young man from the radio shop. Not far away, Colonel Whatmore (vulnerable), playing against his wife and Beverly Bulfoss, was vainly trying to make Five Diamonds Doubled and to avoid the reproachful stare of Mrs. Beverly Bulfoss. Old Jordan was in bed, reading Gibbon. Helen Weeks, who had returned early from Huntley's party, was curled up in her largest chair with the later poems of W. B. Yeats and three chocolate mints. Huntley himself, supported by a few first-class keen people of his, was still entertaining Grope, who had begun to yawn. Mrs. Coote, alone at last and with the house quiet, was writing to Mr. Coote and trying to appear more sprightly than she felt. The Mayor and Mayoress were asleep, and so was Alderman Tanhead. Alderman Muleford was playing solo whist in a back room at the Labour Club. His colleague, Councillor Gisburn, together with Mrs. Gisburn and four neighbors, was playing a very noisy game of Newmarket, to the accompaniment, which nobody noticed, of a Schumann song recital from the loud-speaker. Myrtle Tetlow, of Messrs. Bulfoss and Sons, was telling a young man, from Jordan's gramophone department, to stop it and behave. Dr. Barr, after a good go with the girls at old Haydn, was sitting up to taste a drop of Malt and the *British Medical Journal.* Comrade Railway Clerk was walking home with Comrade Intellectual Girl from a meeting at Comrade Teacher's, where Ravenstreet's expulsion from the Party had been finally declared. Mrs. Delacey, Miss Church, and Miss Fisby, feeling moved already by the Festival spirit, were drinking tea and eating sponge fingers. Corby-Smith was still trying to do the *Observer* crossword. Eric Longshaw, after returning from a stroll with the thin girl from the Tennis Club, was staring rather sleepily, over a glass of milk and four digestive biscuits, at his textbook of Commercial Spanish. Meare, the Town Clerk, and Coverack, the Borough Treasurer, who were neighbors, were playing chess. Crandry was sitting in the library of his large sad house, totting up figures in a small sad book. Hilda and Ernest Saxon had gone to bed early, retiring when Laura arrived with Michael Seacombe, and had taken with them Jugoslavia, Atomic Energy, Co-Education, and Nature Cure.

"No, Michael," Laura was saying, "you've made all the difference these last few weeks. And I'm terribly grateful. I really mean that."

"I know," he told her. "But that's not what I'm talking about, is it? Something quite different. Something I felt from the first."

She shook her head, slowly, rather miserably. "I'm all confused. I can't help it. I suppose it's partly because I'm so worried about my father. But you know about that. I won't go on about it. But I don't know what to say."

"Don't say anything," he said. "Not yet. Just listen to me." And off he went again.

Outside the Palace Theater was Mobbs's little car, and a few yards away, nearer the stage door, and looking as if it had just completed a journey from Stamboul, was the car owned by Group Captain Trevone, D.F.C., D.S.O. Both owners were inside the theater. Mobbs was standing at the back of the Pit with the Commodore and Fotheringay, the manager. The Group Captain was slumped down in the stalls, where he had no business to be, where he had not been made welcome, not even by Philippa Hookwood, who had told him sharply that she had no time to bother about him, that he would only be in the way and bored stiff by the rehearsal, and that if he had any sense he would drive straight back to Brant Manor. But the Group Captain was an obstinate man; so there he was, sitting massively and gloomily in the stalls, while the rehearsal went on forever.

"No, no, no," cried Mossat, who seemed to lose his Scots accent at these times, "Take the pink out of your floats."

"Charlie," the stage manager, George, could be heard calling wearily, "you've still got your pink in your floats."

And from somewhere hidden and remote Charlie replied that he had never been told to take out his pinks.

"You've got it there, Charlie," cried George.

Mossat wriggled and moaned in the darkened aisle. "God save us all! George, give him the cue, and while you're at it, make sure he knows when to check his border and to bring up the two perches. And I want that baby spot in, if it takes all night. Let's get it right, George, once and for all. And hold it, everybody, hold it."

There were mysterious cries from both Charlie and George about circuits.

"Don't talk to me about circuits, boys," Mossat screamed. "I don't understand. I never did. I'm just an old actor who's had no dinner. Just get on with it, boys, quick as you can, for God's sake." And he sat down, to give a performance, although nobody was looking at him, of a man eating a beef sandwich in an agony of frustration.

Through the passdoor and into the vacant dusk of the auditorium came an entrancing glimpse of a medieval lady, who became Miss Hookwood. The Group Captain hastened to her side.

"Trevy, you *are* an idiot," said Miss Hookwood, but not so sharply this time. "Why don't you go home? This'll last hours and hours."

"Damned play's not worth it," he growled.

"Yes, it is, and don't start arguing, I can't bear it. I ache." She leaned wearily against the wall, and then immediately felt the support of the Group Captain's thick hard right arm.

"Wish I'd brought a drink for you, Phil," he muttered.

"So do I," she confessed. "I need something stronger than watery coffee tonight."

"I'll fix it." He brought her gently away from the wall and put her into the nearest seat. "Take it easy a minute. I'll try the manager bloke. He's standing at the back there." And he hurried up the aisle.

Mr. Fotheringay was telling the Commodore and Mobbs, with ancient but genuine glee, that this was like old times.

"Well, it may be," the Commodore observed, "but a little of it would go a long way with me. Like some kind of all-night obstacle race. Hello!"

"Why, it's Group Captain Trevone," cried Mobbs. "How are you, old boy?"

"Miss Hookwood needs a drink," the Group Captain announced sternly. "Poor girl's all in. Can't anybody do anything about it?"

"Mr. Fotheringay?" said the Commodore.

"This way, gentlemen. I was just about to suggest it." Up in his room he first poured out a generous whisky that the Group Captain, after promising to return, rushed down to Miss Hookwood.

"I must say, darling," the beauty confessed, "you're rather a comfort at times."

"Well, that's something," said the Group Captain gruffly, seating himself in the stall in front and twisting round to stare at her.

"Though I still think you were an idiot to come here tonight. Why did you?" She looked at him over the glass, in the queer half-light that kept changing as George and Charlie checked the lighting cues.

"Couldn't stay away. What about this Gorebarry chap?"

She laughed. "Well, what about him?"

"I've heard about him. Knew a chap who knew him. And I don't like the sound of him. Mows down you frippets and leaves you weeping by the dozen. So my chap said. Anything funny about that?" He sounded serious.

"Yes, I'll tell you a secret, Trevy, you ape," she whispered. "I can't bear him."

"Charlie," cried George, "you've taken the ground rows out. The ground rows, Charlie. Yes."

"What's the matter with you tonight, Trevy? Now, don't be absurd. And finish this. I've had enough."

But it was Archie Mossat, who had suddenly come down the dark aisle, who grabbed the glass. "Philippa, go back at once. We'll be off again in a minute. And if there's any whisky to be finished, I'll finish it." Which he did, and then began shouting to George to clear the stage.

"Run along now, Trevy," said Philippa as he walked with her to the passdoor. "I'll see you tomorrow night, when it'll all be different."

"I'm not sure you will," he muttered.

"Why, Trevy!" she cried, genuinely startled. And then, with the passdoor half-open, she laughed. "Don't be silly, darling. Of course I shall."

He looked at her steadily, a formidable man. "It doesn't follow. I may have had as much as I can take. You never know. So don't count on me, just for once. Goodnight, Phil." And he turned away before she did, leaving her staring after him a moment.

"I'll just take a quick one for the road, thanks," he said up in the manager's room.

"What's this play about?" asked Mobbs. "Anybody know?"

"Saw it in town," said the Group Captain gloomily. "It's about a cardinal getting up to something."

"Sexy?" inquired Fotheringay hopefully. "Used to do wonderful business with *The Garden of Allah*."

"I got the impression it was on the hot side," said the Group Captain, "but I never knew quite what they were talking about. Well—cheers for your Festival, chaps!" But he put no heart into it.

"Not quite up to your usual form, old boy," said Mobbs, regarding him with some concern. "Anything wrong?"

"One or two things on my mind. I'll take 'em to bed. Thanks for the drink."

"I'll let you out," said the manager. And they went off together.

"Very lively bloke as a rule, the Group Captain," said Mobbs. "Something wrong with him tonight. Very devoted to this Hookwood girl, and perhaps she's upset him."

"Might be in love, might be money," said the Commodore, "or it might be the old melancholy of Sunday night seeping through. There's no stopping it, do what you like. Feel it myself. Just another small one, and then we'll go, Archie."

"But look who's here," cried Mobbs.

It was Theodore, untidy, hot, embarrassed. "Hello! I heard you were up here."

"My dear boy," said the Commodore cordially, shaking hands. "I knew you were back there, but didn't like to disturb you. Well, you couldn't keep away from us."

"No," said Theodore, trying to smile. "I couldn't keep away from you. How's—everything?"

"All in good trim," said the Commodore. "Ready for action tomorrow, beginning with an official lunch in the Town Hall."

"And—how's Laura?"

"Been working like a little steam engine. Done too much really. But all right, I'd say. Wouldn't you, Archie?"

"No, I wouldn't, old boy. Not altogether."

"Oh—come, come!" said the Commodore rather sharply.

Theodore looked from one to the other, rather slowly: a big simple fellow, bewildered, rather sad. "I only looked in to say hello. Must get back. I'll be seeing you both soon, I hope."

"Well," said the Commodore, a few minutes later, when he and

Mobbs came out into the mild and spacious night, with silence everywhere and the theater now a mere dark bulk, "I've got my Festival and it starts tomorrow. With all set. And what am I feeling at this moment? I'll tell you, Archie, my boy, off the record. I feel about seven hundred years old, as lost as when I came into this world, old and lost, homeless and empty, and altogether bloody sad. Now, why is that?"

"I don't know, old boy," said Mobbs. "But I feel just the same."

"As that producer chap is probably still saying," said the Commodore, squeezing himself into the little car, "God save us all."

Ending with Fireworks

I

ON THE ground floor of the Town Hall, Farbridge, just behind the Council Chamber, there is a rather long, narrow, high room that looks not unlike a dry swimming bath. It is this room that is used for official receptions and civic banquets. On these occasions it is closed on the ground-floor level to all but invited guests. The general public, however, can assert their democratic rights by climbing to the first floor, where there is a door leading to a little balcony that offers an excellent view of the junketing below. There are very few students of municipal oratory in Farbridge, but in that little balcony they can pursue their studies. There are no fixed seats up here, merely a couple of dozen small wooden chairs arranged in three tiers. And when, on that first Monday, the Festival Civic Lunch was being chewed, washed down, swallowed, one of the chairs in the middle row was occupied, somewhat precariously, by Theodore Jenks.

The guests had found their way there through streets already gay with bunting. The Festival had begun. The banqueting room itself did not look very festive, and indeed still suggested a disused swimming bath; but the long table down one side and the short table at each end were almost bright with guests and flowers, food and drink. The Mayor himself, wearing his chain, was seated in the center of the long table, and making a most convivial *Pzzzz*. Waitresses, mostly with flat feet and enormous hips, were serving tomato soup, roast chicken, mashed potatoes and cauliflower, and ices. There was red wine, a fiery Bordeaux from Algiers; there was white wine, Sauterne style but sweeter still; there was beer. And a lively buzz of talk ascended to the balcony, where Theodore, who had been sent by Mossat (too busy himself to attend the lunch) to keep an eye on Patrick Gorebarry, was staring down hungrily not at the roast chicken but at Laura Casey, sitting between the Commodore and the detestable smiling Michael Seacombe. For Gorebarry, wedged between Lady Barth and

Mrs. Bulfoss, Theodore hardly had a glance to spare, which was, as he was shortly to discover, a pity. Not, as he pointed out afterwards more than once, that he could have done anything. Mossat couldn't expect him to jump up and shout: "Stop!" or leap down from the balcony and take the glass out of Gorebarry's hand. The fact remains, however, that it was Laura he stared at, a Laura who did not even know he was up there, remotely devouring her with more zest than she could find for the chicken.

When the lunch began, Gorebarry had had a brief difficult session with Lady Barth. "Well, what do *you* do here?" she screamed at him.

He gave her a despairing glance, and then, pitching his voice admirably, he replied: "I've come to arrange the fireworks." At which Mrs. Bulfoss, on his other side, began giggling.

"Did you say fireworks? You don't look that sort of man," said Lady Barth, rather annoyed. "Though I must admit you can't tell who anybody is nowadays." But she looked at him suspiciously.

"I was a ballet dancer before I came into the firework business," said Gorebarry blandly. "But one night I jumped clean into the orchestra pit and badly injured two trombone players—"

"Two what?" she shrieked at him. "I don't know what you're talking about. Wretched bit of fowl they've given me—like india-rubber. Kindly pass the wine. If I can't eat, I'll drink. What about you?"

"Allow me," he said, filling her glass.

"Thank you. But I don't like to see a man not drinking anything." And she turned to her other neighbor, who was that fierce gay anarchist, Rufus Grope.

"Poor man!" said Mrs. Bulfoss, smiling into his exciting dark eyes. She felt she was looking very attractive, and that actually life was marvelous. "Now don't start telling me ridiculous things about yourself, Mr. Gorebarry, because I know who you are. I've admired you for years, and I'm terribly excited about tonight."

"How nice of you!" he murmured, regarding her with a melancholy approval. "Let me fill your glass. What's it like, this stuff?"

"I never know about wines," she confessed prettily. "But it seems rather strong. Have you got a good company?"

"My dear, I wouldn't know. Difficult to say, really. Are there to be speeches here?"

"Oh, sure to be."

"Yes, of course, sure to be. My God! Either I must leave early or have a drink."

"I know exactly how you feel," she told him. "My husband's the Member of Parliament here, and I've had to listen to hours and hours of speeches, until sometimes I wanted to scream."

"You ought to have screamed. Perhaps we might scream together. But no wonder I detected in those pretty eyes of yours, my dear lady, a hint, a touch, a remote suggestion, of suffering."

"You didn't?" She was delighted.

"Very well, I didn't then," he replied moodily, offering her his tragic profile. He said no more but pushed his food about, just as Arthur Hatchet-Ferrers so often did; but of course he did it somehow in a grander, nobler way. But something had to be done to keep his attention.

"There!" she cried recklessly. She had filled his glass.

He looked at it, fingering the stem irresolutely. He looked at her, a huge dark question in his eyes. She could feel herself melting under that look. What a terribly exciting man! Gerald and Arthur, poor Arthur, seemed a pair of dim dummies.

"You think I ought to drink this?" he asked her.

"Well, why not?"

"Only sensible thing I've heard today. Blessings!" He drained the glass in one gulp. "I've tasted worse, though if that's claret, then I'm Edmund Kean." He filled his glass, then smiled at her. "What do I call you?"

"I'm Mrs. Bulfoss—"

"Nonsense! I can't call you Mrs. Bulfoss. I wouldn't call anybody Mrs. Bulfoss."

"Madge then."

"That's better. Madge, I drink to that absurd inadequate nose, those limpid blue eyes."

"What are you saying?" cried Lady Barth, who had now had quite enough of Mr. Grope.

Goreberry emptied his glass first, then stared balefully at Lady Barth. "I was saying that before I was in the ballet I was a traveler in whole-sale confectionery—"

"You were saying nothing of the kind," said Lady Barth sharply. "But I see that you're drinking now."

"I'm drinking," he declared emphatically. "And so is she—Madge—

and so are you." He began to fill all three glasses, found the bottle inadequate, and called imperiously for another.

"I don't think I want any more," said Mrs. Bulfoss, beginning to wonder if she had been wise in encouraging him to drink.

"My dear Madge, of course you do. And very shortly I shall demand some brandy, enough for both of us."

"There probably isn't any."

"Then we'll send out for some, Madge. In the meantime, kindly ask your neighbor to make a long arm for the bottle of white wine along there. It can't be worse than the red."

All this glass-filling and bottle-passing went unnoticed by Theodore, who was still staring at Laura. He was feeling miserable. After returning very late from the theater, he had slept badly; he felt out of it up there in the balcony; and he had had no lunch. There were several other people staring down with him, but he could not have described one of them. Another man came in and sat down in front of Theodore, who merely gave him a quick glance and then resumed his sad staring.

The coffee had arrived below; the Loyal Toast was drunk, and tobacco smoke drifted above the tables; and now the Mayor addressed the company. He was very glad that it had fallen—*Pzzzz*—to his lot to preside at a gathering—*Pzzzz*—of this kind, which was unique—*Pzzzz*—in the history of their town, which—*Pzzzz*—had never before had a Festival. And on he went, for the next ten minutes, *Pzzzz*-ing and *which*-ing, glazing all eyes. The next speaker was Mr. Huntley, not in his Refined Back Room Boy manner but giving a straight little talk to the Fifth and Sixth Forms. He thanked the Mayor and welcomed the Festival, which, thanks to the work of some absolutely first-class keen people, ought to be a great success; then he called upon that distinguished man of letters, Mr. Rufus Grope, to say a few words. Mr. Grope, who was looking very bilious, reminded his listeners that he had a lecture to deliver later that afternoon, announced his belief that the world was rushing headlong into political, economic and cultural ruin, and hoped that everybody in Farbridge would enjoy the Festival. Mr. Huntley then pointed out that among the guests present were the star players of the Mossat Repertory Company, Miss Hookwood and Mr. Gorebarry, who no doubt could be prevailed upon to say a few words. Lovely, gracious, but perhaps a trifle wan, Miss Hookwood thanked everybody concerned for the wonderful lunch (and did it with such an air that you felt she could never have tasted tomato soup and chicken before that day), expressed her pleasure at the prospect of performing at the Palace Theater during these two weeks, and was sure that her distinguished fellow player, Mr. Gorebarry, would prove to be more eloquent than she could possibly be. And here at least she was quite right.

"Mr. Mayor, Alderman, Councillors, Members of the Festival Committee, Festival Organizers, Fellow Guests," cried Mr. Gorebarry in a magnificent style, his tone rich and warm, his features gravely composed but his eyes glittering with devilment, "I thank you. From the bottom of my heart, I thank you. You have seen the players well bestowed. Astonishing food, ripe wines both red and white, beauty, charm, intellect, all have been with us today. And for all this, a poor player, still a lonely vagabond at heart, thanks you. We have come to Farbridge, of which we have all heard so much, to entertain you, and to make friends. Already I have made friends." And here he clapped a hand on the shoulder of Lady Barth, who was staring at him openmouthed. "In days to come, sitting by the fire remembering such triumphs as come the way of an actor, I hope to recall these two weeks in Farbridge, now gorgeous in Festival array, as a highlight, a shining peak, ladies and gentlemen, in the career of a poor struggling mountebank. Sir—" and he pointed to the Mayor, who looked startled "—you see us, as I hope you will tonight, in our paint and multi-colored costumes, in the artificial sunlight and moonlight of our lamps, and little do you realize—" and here he turned and glared at Messrs. Grope and Huntley "—the long desperate struggles, the ignominies, the secret heartbreaks, of our fantastic calling. You stare with admiration, as well you might, at Miss Hookwood. He pointed dramatically at her, and everybody did stare; and Miss Hookwood, though furious with him, found her eyes filling with tears. "What beauty! What exquisite grace and charm! What melting pathos! What delicious comedy! That is what you say, or what you ought to say. But what do you know, even you, here in Farbridge, of the real Philippa Hookwood, the real Patrick Gorebarry? Nothing." He paused, one delicate hand still raised, and there was not a stir, not a cough, as he wondered what the blazes to say next. Then he allowed his raised arm to droop and falter; a smile of strange childlike sweetness lit up his dark face; and very quietly and beautifully he spoke Hamlet's dying speech:

Horatio, what a wounded name,
Things standing thus unknown, shall live behind me.
If thou didst ever hold me in thy heart,
Absent thee from felicity awhile,
And in this harsh world draw thy breath in pain,
To tell my story . . .

He waited a moment or two, then, Patrick Gorebarry again, he cried: "Mr. Mayor, Ladies and Gentlemen, most gratefully, most warmly, I thank you."

Even Theodore, up there in the balcony and convinced by this time that Gorebarry had started drinking again and that a nightmare of trouble might now threaten the Mossat Company, found himself applauding with all the others.

"You devil!" Lady Barth screamed at him, fastening a jeweled claw on his arm. "I ought to have known. But I think I did. You and your fireworks! Go on," and she released him, "talk to her, though she's a very silly woman."

"Mr. Gorebarry," cried Mrs. Bulfoss, her little nose quivering, her large blue eyes brilliant with unshed tears, "that was so beautiful, I can't tell you. Really divine."

"My dear Madge," said Gorebarry coolly, "it's uncommonly nice of you to be taken in by such bosh. What about some large brandies now?"

The Commodore had been asked to reply for the Festival organizers, and was now on his feet, genial and easy. "I want to say thank you too, though I can't do it with Mr. Gorebarry's grace and style." He told them how hard his assistants had worked, and then singled out for special praise his chief assistant, Miss Laura Casey. "And now I've a pleasant announcement to make," he continued. "For even though Miss Casey and our director of publicity, Mr. Michael Seacombe, have been working so hard for us, the old romantic spirit has not been idle, nor neglected. And so I know you will be all delighted to learn that Miss Casey and Mr. Seacombe have given me permission to announce their engagement."

"No," cried Miss Casey, jumping up, but her cry was lost in the applause. Then things began happening in the balcony. The large young man sitting precariously on the second row of chairs had pitched forward on the first row, making a terrific clatter. As he tried to disentangle himself, he was helped by the short elderly man who had come in late and had sat almost in front of him. And this man, taking a good look at the embarrassed Theodore, had tapped him smartly on the shoulder, saying: "Look here, young man, I want a word with you." Now Theodore, although courageous enough and not unusually apprehensive, had never felt easy since the moment when he had been seen with Grace's box and the woman there had raised the alarm for the police. For all he knew—and he was a stranger in this country and so never quite sure of his ground here—a graphic description of him might have been given to Scotland Yard, and detectives might be looking everywhere for him, especially as he could not be sure that Grace had told him the truth about that box. And there was about this abrupt and rather masterful elderly man in the front row, to Theodore's confused mind, shocked by the announcement of Laura's engagement, a definite suggestion of Scotland Yard and detectives and sudden arrest, and that smart tap on the shoulder and that authoritative: "Look here, young man, I want a word with you," were almost like the jingle and click of handcuffs. So he pushed the man away, jumped up the two tiers like a colossal mad frog, sending chairs clattering down, and dashed out into the first-floor corridor, without noticing that nobody was following him.

While Theodore was hurrying out of the Town Hall, the short elderly man was leaning over the balcony rail, waving to Laura, who had left her seat at the table. Then, as she came nearer, she recognized him, and cried: "Dad. Dad!"

In the general confusion, for the Commodore's announcement and the commotion that followed it had broken up the lunch party, Mrs. Bulfoss and Patrick Gorebarry, who had not moved from their places, were still engaged in intimate talk.

"My dear Madge," Gorebarry was saying, "if you have some brandy out at this house of yours, then it's all quite simple. We go there, drink it, and continue without a break to build up, to consolidate, to crown, our beautiful friendship. Will your husband be there?"

"No, he won't. But oughtn't you to rest or rehearse?"

"Certainly not," he said decidedly, in a tone that would have terrified Archie Mossat. "Come along now. Let's get out while we've a chance." And he pulled her up after him.

"Pat," cried Philippa Hookwood in some alarm. "Pat. Just a minute." But she was too late.

"Anything wrong?" asked the Commodore.

"There might be," she said darkly. "Pat Gorebarry's gone off with that woman. That doesn't matter—that's up to her—but I've an idea, from his general behavior, speech and all, that he's started drinking again. And if he has, then the fun begins. Who was the woman? Mrs. Bulfoss? Somebody'll have to go after him."

By this time Laura had met her father at the bottom of the stairs from the balcony, and was telling him tearfully how worried she had been about him.

"Got home quicker than I thought I would," he told her. "Then came straight here. But what about these young men, Laura? Surely the fellow you described so enthusiastically in your letters was the fellow up there in the balcony, who went off like a shot when I spoke to him? What's the matter with him? What's happened?"

"I don't know," she wailed. "It's all got into a terrible mess. Oh!"

"Now, now, now. Come along. Let's get out of this."

Mobbs and Michael Seacombe came out of the banqueting room together. "Lunch went off like a rocket, I thought, old boy, didn't you?" said Mobbs.

"It went off like a very small rocket tied to a hell of a great stick," said Michael gloomily. "And no sooner had the rocket gone up than the stick came down—wollop!"

"Captain Mobbs," Lady Barth screeched. "Enjoyed myself immensely. Have some more. Make it dinner next time."

2

After Theodore had hurried out of the Town Hall, he made for his hotel, the Albion, after first making reasonably sure that the short elderly man was not following him. It was only about half-past two, and now, recovering from his shocks, he felt very hungry indeed. There was no hope of a proper lunch at this time, but the Albion had a snack bar where there might still be something left. And once in the Theater, he reflected, you seemed almost to say goodbye to solid hot food and to live on drinks and cold scraps. The only people standing at the counter of the snack bar were Archie Mossat and George, the stage manager, who were eating pork pie and potato salad in a vague exhausted manner, as if they had been recently shipwrecked. There was nothing left for Theodore but brawn sandwiches, and before tackling them he hastily downed a large gin and ginger ale.

The other two broke off their unending technical talk to stare at him. "Ye look peculiar to me, ma laddie," said Mossat.

"Anything wrong?" asked George, a little round man who looked like a child that had been allowed to stay up late for about forty-five years. He and Theodore were on excellent terms.

"Yes, George, all kinds of things," Theodore muttered through his sandwich, which was very dry and had a peppery flavor.

"Was Pat Gorebarry there?" said Mossat. "And did he mak' a speech?"

"He did," said Theodore gloomily. "Rather fantastic, but went down very well."

"Guid!" cried Mossat. But then he stared at Theodore. "Did ye say it was rather fantastic? Don't tell me he had any drinks."

"I'm afraid he must have done. It sounded like that sort of speech to me. Very effective, but not quite sober."

"He's off," said George, not in despair because for some days now, with three productions on his hands and the Palace stage and the temporary switchboard to cope with, he had passed through the valley of the shadow and was out of reach of despair.

"Ma Gord!" cried Mossat, putting down his pork pie and turning into a mask of horror. "If he's started, he'll never stop. Why did ye let him start, Theodore?"

"How could I stop him?" asked Theodore indignantly.

"But what happened? Where's he now?"

"I don't know."

"But it's your business to know."

"I fell over some chairs in the balcony," said Theodore, "and then I thought a little man was going to arrest me. So I had to clear out. For all I know, Gorebarry may be back at the White Hart now, resting."

"He may, and then again he may not," said Mossat.

"Well, wherever he is," said Theodore firmly, "I'm staying here to finish these sandwiches and then have another drink. What happened there, what with one thing and another, was no fun for me, let me tell you."

"George, we'll awa' to the theater, an' maybe do some phoning from there," said Mossat.

Left to himself, Theodore remained at the counter, mournfully chewing his sandwiches. The place was deserted now except for the woman behind the counter, who was busy clearing up, and a man sitting not far away, with his face hidden behind a newspaper. Theodore gave him one look and then abandoned himself to mastication and gloomy reverie. He was sorry now he had come back to Farbridge. He would leave at once if it were not for the fact that he couldn't possibly let down Mossat and the company. Or so he told himself.

Then he saw that the man sitting down was no longer hiding his face behind a newspaper. And the last time he had seen that face he had been taking a bath in Grace's flat. Yes, it was the little private detective, A. Smith of London. Theodore stared at him angrily.

"Now, now," said A. Smith, coming across, "don't look like that. Mr. Jenks, isn't it?"

"Yes," said Theodore rather sulkily.

Smith winked. "Trust me to get the info. Every time, chum. But you're staying here, and she's gone to the White Hart again. Right?"

Theodore decided to keep his temper. "Would you like a drink?"

"Can a duck swim? Ta, muchly. Pint of bitter."

"Now look," said Theodore, after Smith had dipped his long nose into the pint glass, "you're making a mistake. I don't blame you, after finding me in that bath, but the fact remains that I'd never been in that flat before that night and I've never been there since. There's absolutely nothing between us. I hardly know her. And that's the truth."

"I believe you, though thousands wouldn't." Smith winked again. "But didn't I hear you saying you thought some little man was going to arrest you? Or did my ears deceive me?"

"That's something quite different."

"How different?"

Theodore found this question difficult to answer, and so he shrugged it away.

"Can't answer that one, can you, chum?" said Smith cheerfully. "Okay. Try another. Would a box come into it? Ah—got you there. No need to reply. Face did it for you."

Theodore felt that it was useless to deny this. So he finished his drink and said nothing.

"Give you a bit of info, Mr. Jenks. A nice woman that, I dare say, but a terrible liar, like most of 'em."

"Well," said Theodore reflectively, "she may be. But I hardly know her, and there's absolutely nothing between us. Do get that into your head."

"Here with the theatricals, aren't you?"

"Yes, just helping them for these two weeks."

Smith nodded. "Gorebarry. He's not staying here, is he?"

"No, he's at the White Hart. Do you know him?"

"I know him but he doesn't know me. See what I mean?" And Smith winked again. "Had to tail him once. What a job! Mustard, that bloke."

George came hurrying in. "Theodore," he cried, and then stopped, clearly embarrassed by Smith's presence.

"Leave you to it," said Smith. "Be seeing you, Mr. Jenks. And ta for the drink." He sauntered out.

"Now listen, Theodore," said George earnestly. "Philippa's just telephoned about Pat Gorebarry. He didn't go back to the White Hart after that lunch, and Philippa thinks he went off with a Mrs. Bulfoss, perhaps to her house, and Archie told me to tell you that you must go straight up there and see that Pat's all right, otherwise we may have had it for tonight. I know, old man. You don't want to go bursting into somebody's house. But it's just got to be done or we're sunk. Archie and I would do it, only we're still up to our necks. Now off you go, like a good chap. Pat likes you too, so you'll do it better than we would."

Theodore decided that he needed help and that the best person to give it to him was Mobbs. So he walked round to the Festival Center, and there wasted twenty precious minutes, sitting in the office at the back, waiting for Mobbs to appear. The Commodore was not there, and, to his relief, neither were Laura nor Michael Seacombe. However, as soon as Mobbs arrived, he agreed to take Theodore out to the Bulfoss house in his car. But it was nearly four o'clock when they rang that fierce front door bell.

Mrs. Bulfoss herself answered it. "Oh dear—yes! Mr. Gorebarry *is* here. He insisted on coming because he said he had to have some brandy, and so I had to give him some. He's—rather excited, though very sweet, I must say."

"Theodore's supposed to be looking after him, you know," said Mobbs softly, as they followed her into the hall.

"I hope he won't mind your coming here," Mrs. Bulfoss whispered anxiously.

"So do I," said Theodore rather grimly.

But Gorebarry, lying on the sofa and nursing a glass of brandy, gave no sign of resenting their intrusion. "Welcome, welcome," he cried. "Madge, my dear, two more glasses. Theodore, my boy—and Captain Tubbs—"

"Mobbs, old boy."

"It should be Tubbs, but Mobbs it shall be. Well, Captain Mobbs, Theodore my boy, here we fleet the time carelessly as they did in the golden world."

"Very nice too, old boy," said Mobbs dubiously, "but—"

"But what, brave heart?"

"Don't you think you ought to be resting, Pat?" said Theodore.

"Resting? Resting? Why? Here am I, in the very pink and prime—"

"Yes," said Theodore doggedly, "but don't forget we're opening tonight."

"Important performance too," said Mobbs. "With the Mayor and a lot of the nobs specially invited."

"A fig for the Mayor and your nobs!" cried Gorebarry. "And what a deadly old bore that fellow is!" He sat up and turned himself into the Mayor. "I am very glad—*Pzzzz*—to preside at a gathering, which —*Pzzzz*—is unique in this town—*Pzzzz*—which has never had a Festival—*Pzzzz*—which—*Pzzzz*—which—*Pzzzz*—"

"Oh you are naughty," cried Mrs. Bulfoss, laughing. "And it's exactly like poor Alderman Walmer."

Gorebarry emptied his glass, and, before anybody could say a word, had begun filling it again. "As for this damned old cardinal I have to play tonight," he said carelessly, "I wouldn't take a ten-minute nap to create such a character. The truth is, hearts, he's bosh. He won't bear thinking about. The less I rest today, the more we fleet the time carelessly, the better I'll play him. The thing to do is to forget about him until about ten-past seven. I know. Trust Pat. He knows." He drained his glass, stared at them rather wildly for a moment or two, then closed his eyes and apparently went to sleep.

Theodore signaled to Mobbs to remain and to Mrs. Bulfoss to follow him quietly out of the room. "The point is," he said to her in the hall, "to decide how much more we can safely let him have. He must have started at that lunch."

"It was my fault," she confessed unhappily, "though of course I didn't realize he'd go on and on."

"Apparently he always does, once he starts," said Theodore grimly, "and that's been the trouble. But I think he'd have started anyhow today, even if there hadn't been you and that lunch. He's pretending not to care about tonight, but I know he's been anxious and nervous about it, not having acted for some time."

"He's such a heavenly man," she sighed. "Don't you think so?"

"No, I don't. But on the whole I like him." He listened for a moment or two. "Well, if he sleeps, we needn't worry."

But ten minutes later, Gorebarry was wide awake, and had another brandy, and was explaining exactly what was wrong with Philippa Hookwood's acting. "And she's only got three tones," he concluded. "Like a traffic light—red, amber, and green—take your choice." He tilted the brandy bottle above his glass, but only a few last drops fell out of it.

"But you must admit she's very attractive," said Mrs. Bulfoss.

"Certainly not," he replied severely. "And this bottle's empty. We must get another."

"Couldn't now, old boy," said Mobbs hastily.

"And you promised to take me to Mr. Grope's lecture," Mrs. Bulfoss told him reproachfully.

"Did I?"

"Of course you did. And we ought to be going. Captain Mobbs can take us in his car."

"Very well," said Gorebarry gravely, struggling from the sofa to his feet. "If you insist, my sweet Madge, we'll go to Mr. Thing's lecture in Captain Tubbs's car. Where is Mr. Thing functioning?"

"At the Central Library."

"Good God! I haven't been in a Central Library since I was fourteen. Come, my coach! Bustle, my boys, bustle!"

They squeezed themselves into Mobbs's little car and arrived at the Central Library just after five. "I'm not coming in," said Mobbs. "I've several things to do, and I'd quite enough of Grope last night. See you at the theater."

A small platform had been erected in the main hall of the Library, and in front of it were about two hundred little chairs, of which a hundred and fifty or so were occupied. Huntley, who was in the chair, was already introducing the lecturer. Gorebarry's performance of an anxious latecomer making the quietest possible entrance was excellent up to a point, but after that it was ruined by his knocking down two chairs and then shushing angrily at Mrs. Bulfoss and poor Theodore, who was scarlet with embarrassment. And just as he was sitting down, Theodore caught a glimpse of Laura's furious little face, for she had jumped up at the end of the front row to see what was happening; and this completed his humiliation.

"And now," said Huntley, "I will no longer stand between you and our distinguished lecturer."

"Hear, hear!" cried Gorebarry.

"I am sure we are all in for a tremendous treat, a talk that is both provocative and wise, witty and profound. Mr. Rufus Grope."

The applause that greeted Mr. Grope as he came forward to the table, shuffling his notes, was led by Gorebarry, who was so enthusiastic that several people sitting near—including, as Theodore saw to his shame, Laura's friend, Mrs. Saxon—began to regard him with some suspicion. Acknowledging the applause with a few solemn nods, Mr. Grope did not cut a very attractive figure. His drooping shoulders, his awkward little movements, his sad pouchy face with its bilious look, were unprepossessing even for a lecturer.

"Mr. Chairman, Ladies and Gentlemen," he began, once again the giant calling from a zinc prison, hollow but booming, "I am a Fierce Gay Anarchist—"

"A what?" cried Gorebarry, apparently unable to believe his ears.

"A Fierce Gay Anarchist," said Mr. Grope, staring reproachfully in the direction of the actor.

Gorebarry rose unsteadily, pointed at the lecturer in an ecstasy of derision, and shouted with laughter. There was an uproar of protest. "Keep quiet there" and "Turn him out," they were crying. "He's a Fierce Gay Anarchist," yelled Gorebarry. "Angels and ministers of grace defend us!" And pushing past a dozen people who had jumped up to voice their protests, then knocking over several chairs on his way out, Gorebarry fled, still shouting with laughter. Theodore went in pursuit of him at once, but being very large and unwilling to push other people out of his way he could not escape from the hall as fast as the actor did. And just as he reached the door he found his arm caught and held by somebody who said sharply: "Now look, young man, I've got to have a word with you." It was, of course, the same short elderly man who had tackled him in the Town Hall balcony.

"Not now," cried Theodore, wrenching himself free. "Some other time." He dashed down the short flight of stairs that led to the main entrance of the Library, but neither there nor outside in the street could he see anything of Gorebarry. Breathless and despairing, he stood outside the Library, wondering what to do next.

"It's awful, isn't it?" said Mrs. Bulfoss, suddenly appearing at his elbow. "Though I must say, I wanted to laugh. Didn't you?"

"No, I didn't," said Theodore rather savagely. "Don't you realize that in just over two hours he's got to be at the Palace, playing an important part for the first time. And God knows where he's gone, and what he's up to."

"I know," said Mrs. Bulfoss, with a sigh. "Actually I can see it's awful for you. For him too, probably. And he's such a heavenly man really."

"You'd better go home, Mrs. Bulfoss," Theodore told her. "He just might have gone back there. And I'll go on to the White Hart, where he's staying. If he's not there, I'll have to search the town for him. If only he hadn't gone to that lunch!"

"My fault, my fault. I'm so sorry. And it's such a bad beginning for the Festival for you."

"Damn and blast the Festival!" cried Theodore from his dark morass of anxieties and disappointments. "I wish I'd never heard of it."

3

At the White Hart, the Commodore was taking tea with Grace, whose appearance there had been a wonderful surprise, and Philippa Hookwood and Mrs. Hungerford, who had joined up with them. Philippa was still worrying about Patrick Gorebarry, and nothing that the other three could say would reassure her.

"You don't know him," she told them darkly. "And you haven't to play opposite to him tonight, and I have. I ought to be resting now— I'll have to go up soon—but what's the use when I'm wondering all the time what's happening to that idiot?"

"My dear, I'm certain it'll be all right," cried Mrs. Hungerford. "Won't it, Commodore? He couldn't possibly let us down now."

"Oh—couldn't he?" said Philippa.

"No, not when it's all so—" Mrs. Hungerford was all breathless enthusiasm again. "I mean, as soon as I arrived this afternoon, I felt the whole thing was just—Such a genuinely festival atmosphere, I felt at once. Didn't you?" She appealed to Grace, who replied promptly that she did.

"And as soon as I met Commodore Tribe," Mrs. Hungerford continued, "and of course I'd heard our dear Theodore talk about him, I knew that the whole scheme was absolutely—oh!—just—you know."

"Thank you, Mrs. Hungerford," said the Commodore, with a twinkle. Then he looked grave, and lowered his voice. "But I'll let you into one little secret, ladies. If this Festival isn't a wild success, there'll be hell to pay here in Farbridge. We've overspent. The Borough Treasurer's walked out on us. And unless the public packs us out—theater, pageant, concerts, park dancing, everything—we're broke, ruined, and some of us may have to run for it, leaving by the back door at two in the morning. No, I mean that. I've taken a huge gamble." He looked at Grace, who smiled at him.

"There's Theodore," cried Philippa, waving.

"And he doesn't look very happy, does he?" said Grace, also waving.

Theodore came hurrying up to them. "Is Gorebarry here?"

"No," said Philippa in dismay. "I thought you'd know about him."

"I do know about him," said Theodore grimly, dropping into a chair, "up to ten minutes ago." And he gave them an account of what had happened since lunch.

"And that," said Philippa tragically, "just about tears it."

"We could organize a search," said the Commodore.

"I'm rather good at looking for people," said Grace cheerfully.

Theodore, remembering the box episode, gave her rather a sour look. "Some of them are good at looking for you too. I met that shabby little detective chap again. Yes, he's here."

"A. Smith of London, do you mean?" cried the Commodore.

"Yes," said Theodore sulkily, "and there's another chap about who seems to be chasing me around." He looked accusingly at Grace, who colored and then, meeting the inquiring stare of the Commodore, looked more embarrassed still, in fact, quite guilty.

"Oh, there's poor dear Archie at last," cried Mrs. Hungerford, rising and darting away.

"She seems very devoted to Mossat," said the Commodore.

"The boy friend," Philippa murmured, "though what goes on and how it works, I can't imagine. And just now, I don't care. Theodore, you'll have to find Pat."

"I know," he replied wearily. "I know. I sent Mrs. Bulfoss home to see if he'd gone back there. You say he's not here. The pubs aren't open yet, so he can't be drinking anywhere."

"Oh—can't he? He can be drinking, once he starts, at any time."

"In London perhaps," said the Commodore. "But not here. I wouldn't know where to find a drink at this hour, and I know Farbridge better than he does. He must be wandering about, or back in the theater, or in some teashop."

"Or buying a motorbike or chasing a girl in the park," said Philippa bitterly, "or giving a false name at a police station." But then she jumped up and waved frantically across the lounge, which was rapidly filling. "Thank goodness! There's Father and Trevy. And Trevy'll have his car."

"Darling Trevy," she cried, a minute later, after kissing her father, "I'm so glad you're here."

"Oh you are, are you?" said the Group Captain, obviously steeling himself against these blandishments. "Well, I've heard that before, Phil. Too many times."

"Darling, don't be silly. You can tell me about that afterwards. But you've just got to help Theodore and me." And she explained about Gorebarry, with some help from Theodore, and finally the Group Captain agreed to take Theodore in his car to search the town.

"What's the matter with Trevy?" she asked her father, as they stood watching the Group Captain and Theodore hurry out.

"You'll see, my dear," said Mr. Hookwood dryly. "Ought to be resting now, oughtn't you?"

"Yes, come up with me a minute." She turned to the Commodore and Grace. "I'll see you tonight—and pray for us."

"Quite a commotion," said Grace cheerfully, when she and the Commodore had the corner to themselves. "I'm going to enjoy this. I like plenty happening, don't you?"

"I used to think so," he told her. "But now I'm not quite so sure."

"Go on, you love it. I can tell. Wouldn't like you if you didn't."

"Oh! So you like me, do you?" And the Commodore looked hard at her.

"Wouldn't be here if I didn't. You ought to know that." She was genuinely reproachful.

The Commodore did not avoid her glance, but, after having met it, he looked idly round the lounge. It was only Monday, and yet apart from one or two Saturdays he had never seen the White Hart so busy before. Was it the Festival? "It must be the Festival," he said aloud. "And Seth said he was full. We may pull it off yet."

"Of course you will," said Grace. "Knew that all the time."

"How long are you staying, Grace?"

She looked surprised. "Why, for all the Festival, of course. Two weeks. What a question!"

A man came up then and asked if he might take two or three chairs from their table. After he had gone, their corner seemed more isolated and intimate than before. The Commodore lit his pipe and looked over it at his companion's open pleasant face. No eyes could have been more innocent and candid.

"What happened about Theodore?" he asked.

"I met him accidentally in London, last week," she replied, rather hastily, "and he did something for me—got me something I wanted. He was wet through when he came back. There was a storm that night. He wasn't too pleased about it. What about him and that nice little girl—Laura?"

"Nothing. And don't let's change the subject. Now, Grace," he continued, in a rather masterful manner, "you're here again, and I'm delighted. You say you like me, and again I'm delighted—proud too. But twice you've run out on me, without a word of explanation. I don't think it's good enough, you know."

"No, I know it isn't." She was troubled, and avoided his look.

"Even young Jenks seems to know more than I do," he went on. "I could see that when he began talking about that detective. You were blushing. Doing it very nicely too. But I think it's about time you told me something. Don't you?" he asked gently.

"I meant to tell you," she said hurriedly. "But not here, not now. You've lots to do, including finding me a seat for the theater—remember? And we're having dinner early, and I must have a bath and put some nice clothes on." She put her hand on his. "When it's all over tonight, if we can find a quiet corner, then I'll explain everything. I promise. And no more running away—honestly."

So he let her go, and then he strolled along to the Festival Center, where Miss Church, Mrs. Delacey, and Miss Fisby were still selling tickets and answering inquiries. In the back room, where the smell of boot polish seemed stronger than ever, he found Mobbs and Michael Seacombe about to refresh themselves with gin and vermouth.

"Six o'clock, old boy," said Mobbs, "so we need something. Join us? Good! Any news?"

"Apart from our leading actor nearly wrecking Grope's lecture," said Michael. "We know about that."

"My godfathers—yes."

"Theodore and Group Captain Trevone," said the Commodore, "are now out combing the town for him."

"Even if they find him," said Michael, "he'll probably be reeling all over the stage tonight as Cardinal Who's it. And I've just had a pair of dramatic critics in here who've come specially from town—they're friends of the author, Derek Boon—a couple of wriggling pansies—"

"Eric and Charles," cried Mobbs in an astonishing falsetto.

"Stop it, you naughty man," said Michael. "But they'll write us up, if we give 'em a chance. Damn Gorebarry—and also that fool of a Bulfoss woman, who apparently started him off on this binge."

"I want another seat for tonight," said the Commodore, "for my friend Mrs. Robinson, who, incidentally, has money and promised to help us if necessary. And if we're unlucky, some of us may need a little ready cash to make a getaway before this Festival's over."

"You don't surprise me," said Michael, who appeared to be in a somber mood.

"No, old boy, nothing like that," cried Mobbs. "And I'll find her a seat. About the last. Had to find one for Laura's father."

"Where is Laura?" asked the Commodore.

"Rushed out of the lecture in a fury," said Michael. "Blames poor Jenks for that barney. Apparently he pushed her father away. But Father Casey, who seems a very sensible chap, thinks Jenks mistakes him for somebody else."

"A detective, I fancy," said the Commodore thoughtfully.

"Why a detective?"

The Commodore picked up his glass and shook his head over it. "Don't know, though I propose to find out. Unless it's all fantasy." He finished his drink. "Peculiar vermouth that, if it *is* vermouth, which I doubt. Well, comrades, I must go. We're eating early, and I propose to put on a dinner jacket. You too, I hope."

Michael detained the Commodore. "You know, if you were a younger and less likeable fellow," he said slowly, "I'd be inclined to give you a poke on the snout for making that lunch announcement of my engagement to Laura. I've not had one civil word or look from my dear fiancée since."

"But she's on her mettle, isn't she?" said the Commodore. "Active, lively, full of go and fight? That's the great thing. Until we're through with this Festival."

"Oh—burn the bloody Festival!" shouted Michael in sudden and quite genuine rage. "Go away, and let me finish this gin in peace and misery."

4

For the first time for many years there was a crowd outside the Farbridge Palace Theater on a Monday night. The playgoers themselves of course made up quite a crowd, but they were surrounded by genuine lookers-on who with the sure instinct of their kind knew at once that this was an occasion. Here at last was an audience that had its own audience. Already the Festival spirit was quickening Farbridge. There were no police linking arms, no mob rushes, no wild demonstrations of enthusiasm, for it was not that sort of occasion, and the sergeant and the constable, though they made pretty heavy weather of it, had no difficulty keeping the front of the theater clear; but the crowd was there, three or four thick, and from it came definite murmurs and buzzes of interest and approval, punctuated by those derisive chuckles and loud sniggerings that are part of our democratic heritage. There was indeed much to see, to wonder at, to admire.

There were Alderman and Mrs. Walmer, in full mayoral splendor, symbolic figures of Farbridge citizenship; and if Mrs. Walmer's shoes were too tight, condemning her to hobble wincingly, as much might be said of our citizenship. Commodore Horace Tribe, in an immense dinner jacket with something outlandish, almost piratical, about its cut, looked very imposing indeed; and the lady with him, in silver and blue, demurely feminine, very sweet. Perhaps Captain Mobbs' evening clothes were rather too small for him, and his soft shirt was badly rumpled; and perhaps the fine figure of a woman, Maggie, by his side, might have been more artfully and less showily dressed (the large flowered pattern overemphasizing her curves); but the general effect was not bad. Old Jordan wore a tail coat with a black waistcoat and a very narrow black tie, and somehow this was all in character; and it helped to set off the dark sad beauty of Miss Helen Weeks, in a new saffron dress she could not afford but had wildly bought as soon as she heard that Jimmy Fettercairn would be coming to Farbridge. Mrs. Coote's emerald dress was not new and perhaps a mistake, but she looked happy and healthy, which is more than can be said of most of us. Major Bulfoss looked correct, pink, and sulky; and Mrs. Bulfoss pretty and excited in turquoise, with tiny silver slippers out of a fairy tale. Three hobbledehoys whistled at the sight of her, as they did too when Miss Laura Casey appeared, in cherry red, accompanied by her father, who was still wearing his tweeds but looked trim, brown, rather distinguished, a confident little man from far places. There was Mrs. Hungerford, gasping in old gold. Screeching in the middle of a group of tall, mysterious County types, there was Lady Barth, looking like an old witch roughly disguised as a Christmas tree. Dr. and Mrs. Barr and the two girls were so clean and so Scotch that they might all have been scrubbing one another for a couple of hours. Mr. Huntley, whose dress tie was unfastening itself, brought a headmistress who was all amber beads and Paisley shawl. Michael Seacombe brought nobody, had not changed, looked sulky and rather tight, like a journalist hero of an American film.

Up in the foyer, which was brightly lit and gay with flowers, the old manager, Mr. Fotheringay, was in full evening dress, with hair and mustache dyed a richer blue-black, and fantastically pink about the cheekbones. He looked ready to tie any heroine to a railway line at a moment's notice. There was, of course, the usual confusion about tickets that there is on all these special occasions; and Mr. Fotheringay, although appealed to, badgered, even abused, was enjoying it all. He had already told a select number of important patrons that refreshments would be provided during the interval in his room; and now he was dropping a hint to a few people like the Commodore and Mobbs that if they wished to look in his room or visit the bar before the performance, they could safely do so, even though the orchestra was already playing, because the curtain would not rise at the advertised time. "Always happens on these big evenings," he added proudly. "Just like old times." And he rubbed his hands and chuckled away.

But there was no hand rubbing and chuckling backstage. For it was now twenty-five minutes past seven, and Patrick Gorebarry was still missing. Theodore, who was still out with the Group Captain, had returned to the theater twice and telephoned since to report their failure. Archie Mossat was pacing up and down in the wings, cursing and moaning and clutching his gingerish curls. Philippa, who had been called down for consultation, while the rest of the Company were told sharply to stay in their dressing rooms, was there too, looking like a beautiful medieval princess about to explode.

"Ma Gord!" cried Mossat, stopping, "look at the time. What are we to do. Phil?"

"You'll have to play it, that's all, Archie," she said in despair. "You must know most of the lines and the moves."

"Ah doubt it, Ah doubt it," he moaned. "Ah've been so busy wi' *Twelfth Night* and *The Rivals*, not only producing but learning Malvolio an' Sir Anthony again. An' Ah'm a comic character actor not a romantic leading man. Nobody wants to see me as Cardinal anybody. We can't go up, that's all."

"They might want to see me even if they don't want to see you," she said rather sharply. "And in any case, we can't let these people down. We were mad to engage Pat Gorebarry. And both Clare and I warned you. You can't say we didn't."

"Ay, ay, ay, but there's no use recriminating. Does no good."

"It does me good," said Philippa. "I've got to do something besides sitting here waiting for a drunk leading man. God!—I could kill him."

"Ay, ay, but what are we to do before we kill him?"

And then they saw Theodore, who cried: "We found him. He's here."

They hurried round to Gorebarry's dressing room, which was the star dressing room, on the stage level, on the O.P. side. He had flopped down, white-faced, hot-eyed; and his dresser, a foolish old man, was vainly trying to remove his collar. He was very drunk, but he could talk after a fashion.

"He can't possibly go on," cried Philippa, angry and disgusted.

"I don't think he can," said Theodore, standing in the doorway. "We found him in a little pub, the other side of Peter Place."

"Ah wonder," said Mossat, "Ah wonder."

"Go on?" cried Gorebarry, sitting up and glaring at them. "Wha' hell you mean? Cer'n'ly go on. Li'l late, tha's all. Didn't know time. No watch. Ready give won'ful p'form'ce Car'nal Who's-it—won'ful p'form'ce."

"Look at him. My God!" And Philippa burst into tears.

"Look at him!" Gorebarry shouted. "Wha' hell you mean? Go 'way, silly woman. Stan'in there—insults—bawlin'! Go 'way. Li'l late, tha's all. Ready—in—in five—ten—minutes." But the effort he had to make in order to announce this clearly, so that they would understand, was too much for him, and he swayed forward and looked as if he were about to pass out.

"Gangway!" cried a loud cheerful voice outside.

"Trevy," cried Philippa, filling the two syllables with wonder, hope, and joy.

"Leave this to me, chaps," said the Group Captain, who had a jug of coffee in one hand and a fizzing glass in the other. "I'll fix it. Done it before. Just give me quarter of an hour with him. Make a speech or something to amuse 'em."

Gorebarry pointed to him waveringly but solemnly. "Now here's a man. An' they're gettin' bloody uncommon."

"I think he's right too," said Philippa, as she and Mossat and Theodore walked away. "And I believe Trevy'll do it—the angel. I must do my face again."

"Theodore," said Mossat excitedly, "nip round fast to the front, lad, and ask the Commodore or one of 'em to come back here and mak' some kind o' little speech, welcoming the company, anything, to pass a few minutes. Off ye go."

Theodore raced round from the stage door to the main entrance and was lucky enough to find the Commodore still in the foyer, where he was talking to Mobbs and the manager. All the other people had now taken their seats.

"Come round to the back," cried Theodore, grabbing the Commodore's arm. "I'll explain as we go." Which he did, adding a few details about the play.

So just as the audience were becoming restless, the commanding but genial figure of the Commodore appeared between the dusty rose curtains. He lifted a hand, and there was quiet. "Mr. Mayor, Ladies and Gentlemen," he cried in his warmest tones, "before the curtain rises, I am sure you would like me, on your behalf, to welcome to Farbridge this special Festival Repertory Company that Mr. Mossat has brought from London." There was a heartening round of applause from all parts of the house. "Allow me to add that it is a considerable tribute to our Festival policy that Mr. Mossat should be presenting such a distinguished company in Farbridge. And I think he will find that we appreciate it." There was more applause. "May I remind you that on Thursday evening and for the remainder of the week, he is giving us a brand-new production of that old favorite, *The Rivals*, and that a week tonight we shall have *Twelfth Night*, in which Mr. Mossat himself will be playing Malvolio." They clapped again. "I have been asked to say a special word or two about tonight's play—*Why Should the*

Nightingale?—a romantic play in verse, by a prominent member of our new school of romantic poetic dramatists, Derek Boon. This play had its first production, at the—er—Mermaid Club Theater in London, only a few weeks ago, when it had a most enthusiastic reception. I believe it will be received with equal—if not greater—enthusiasm here in Farbridge. Thank you, Mr. Mayor, and Ladies and Gentlemen— thank you." And he bowed, smiled, and retired.

He walked across the Cardinal de Cortrai's peculiar garden where the young actor with butter-colored locks and the pink-and-white costume was preparing to loll and wriggle, and into the wings where Clare Chesbey, now a luscious medieval maid, was ready to make her first entrance. Mossat dashed up. "Commodore, that was fine, an' juist what was needed. Passed a bit o' time an' warmed them up nicely. George, cue the orchestra, and tell everybody to stand by. Ma Gord, what a life!"

Just behind the back cloth the Commodore ran into Theodore, who came from the other side, carrying a bound script. "How's the leading man now?"

"The Group Captain's pouring coffee into him," said Theodore, "while his dresser's putting his clothes on. It'll be a peculiar perform- ance at the best, but then it's a rum play and a fantastic part, so perhaps nobody'll know the difference. I have to follow him round, as far as I can, at the back of the set, and keep prompting him."

"A lovely evening," said Philippa, joining them at that moment. "What a time I'm going to have!"

"I'll go back," said the Commodore. "I don't want to miss any of this."

"You brute!" cried Philippa to his retreating back. Then she looked earnestly at Theodore. "You must have been with Trevy for about an hour and a half at least, looking for Pat?"

"Yes, I was. We went all over the place. Mostly in and out of pubs after six o'clock."

She hesitated. "He seems to be in a rather queer mood these days. Did he—say anything about me?"

"Well, not exactly."

"Oh!" She sounded disappointed. "Well, I suppose I ought to be thinking about doing a little acting. There's the opening music."

"There's still a minute." And Theodore put a hand on her arm so that she turned to face him. His tone was urgent, though quiet. "He's not the kind of chap to say much about a girl he's seriously in love with. But I gathered he's feeling rather desperate, that he can't go on allowing you to have him on a string—"

"But I don't—" she began.

"Listen, please, Philippa. Because of something that's happened to me, I talked to him. And I told him not to make the mistake I did, but to grab hold of you and tell you what he felt about you and no nonsense—"

"You didn't?"

"Stand by," said George. "Curtain going up."

Sitting with her father in the front row of the dress circle, Laura watched the curtains parting and rising, and felt a mixed sense of relief and eager expectation. She wanted to sit there, with her father so close and safe, and yet be in Avignon or anywhere else that wasn't Farbridge, to lose herself and all her sad muddle among cardinals and princesses and serving maids and pages. She wanted to laugh and cry over other people's lives, not her own. The theater might have been invented specially for her that very night.

Nevertheless, the play began badly for her. She recognized the maid who came swooping into the garden as Clare Chesbey, the girl Theodore knew, and now probably knew only too well. And she could not think of any reason why a young man who was horribly thick with this Clare, quite ravishing and with a lovely low voice, should ever bother his head about Laura Casey, even a Laura Casey who had shown herself to be completely devoted to him, let alone a Laura who had been bad-tempered and silly. Feeling very small and miserable, she stared at this peculiar garden in Avignon and began to wish she had stayed at home.

Then the Princess and the Cardinal entered, and it was much better. Miss Hookwood was even more opulent and ravishing than the Chesbey girl, but Laura, out of a true intuition, refused to associate her with Theodore. And then Patrick Gorebarry proceeded at once to give an odd but very exciting performance as the Cardinal. He roamed about in a strange but fascinating way, as if he had discovered some new and more flexible style of acting. Sometimes he hesitated or muttered odd words or phrases that could not be properly heard; and at other times his magnificent voice rang out like a trumpet or went curving down into melancholy and defeat like a muted violin, so that as she listened she would feel her eyes hot with tears. What a wonderful thing such acting was! He made the others, even Miss Hookwood, seem only half-alive. Some of his speeches, like most of theirs, were often rather vague and faintly silly, but now and then, when he was most vivid and challenging, he would bring out passages of great beauty, which Laura could not help feeling she had heard somewhere before. After he had left the stage, and the act was concluded by Miss Hookwood and Clare Chesbey and the pink-and-white youth and a comic drunken steward, who finally sang a song, it was all mildly entertaining, and the audience loved the funny bits; but Laura, who had not expected to admire Gore-barry so much, felt that the play's exciting quality had vanished with the Cardinal.

"Want to go out?" said her father, after they had done applauding the act.

"No, I think not," she told him. "But you go and have a drink. I'm rather tired."

"Yes," he said, with one of his kind but sharp glances. He had always known what she was feeling; they were very close. "Well, I'll hang on a bit." They were now alone in their section of the dress circle. The orchestra was playing a waltz. He smiled at her, his leathery brown face crinkling delightfully. "Enjoying it?"

"I'm not sure about the play," she said, "but I think Patrick Gore-barry's absolutely wonderful. I'd no idea he was like that. What's the matter?"

"He's a good actor," said her father, who when he returned from his far travels always did a good deal of playgoing. "But shall I tell you a secret? Two, in fact. Better not, perhaps."

"No, you must, now you've started."

"Well, then." He grinned at her. "First, he's tight, and hardly knows what he's doing. Second—but this needs an introduction. Years ago, your Aunt Olivia gave me a pocket edition of Shakespeare in three volumes. And I've carried them around ever since, read them all over the place. So now I know my Shakespeare. Well, so far you've not only heard part of a play by—who is it?—Derek Boon, but you've also heard bits and pieces—and very good too—from *Hamlet, Henry the Fourth, Richard the Second, Richard the Third, Macbeth* and *Othello.* And with any luck, in this next act, we ought to have some quotations from *Much Ado, A Midsummer Night's Dream, Antony and Cleo-patra, Lear* and *The Tempest,* all great favorites of mine." And then, in his engaging boyish way, he suddenly roared with laughter, and she had to laugh too. He stood up and pulled her up beside him. "Come on now, Laura, let's have a drink. I'd like to meet some of these new friends of yours."

In her dressing room, Philippa Hookwood was storming away to Mossat and Theodore. "It's all very well saying they're adoring it, but it's just making nonsense of the play and absolutely ruining my performance. No, it's not your fault, Theodore—you've done all you possibly could. But honestly, Archie, it's murder. I never know where he's going or when my cues are coming, if at all. And—my God—this next act, at any moment, he may turn round and give me the *To be or not to be* or *Tomorrow, and tomorrow* or *Our revels now are ended*. And what do I do? Sit down and then applaud at the end?"

"Yes," said Mossat. "Why not?"

"Oh, don't be a dam' fool, Archie," she cried crossly. "It's not funny. You're not there, trying to act with him."

"Ah know," said Mossat apologetically. "But it might ha' been a lot worse, darling. And they're loving it."

"That's not the point."

"I think it is," said Theodore. "No, please listen to me, just for once. When we talked about this play at Mrs. Hungerford's, after the first night at the Mermaid, I was told that my objections didn't matter, that the sort of play I wanted was dull and difficult for the actors, who were happy in plays like this, wearing fancy costumes and spouting gorgeous lines. It was all bringing the Theater back to the actors, restoring the old magic. Well, that's what Pat Gorebarry's doing tonight, better than any of you. The audience think he's wonderful, that's obvious. So what does it matter if his Cardinal is nonsense and he keeps remembering bits of Shakespeare instead of Derek Boon's lines? I'll see how he's getting on. The Group Captain's looking after him."

He found Gorebarry begging the Group Captain, who had allowed him one small glass of brandy, to let him have another drink. "Just one," he pleaded, "and then I'll give you a performance in this act that'll make your hair stand on end."

"I don't want my hair to stand on end," said the Group Captain, "and you're not having any more."

"Now look, old man—"

"Turn it up," said the Group Captain sharply. "You're not having another drink until the show's over."

The actor would have resented this tone from anybody else, but he was so much impressed by the Group Captain that now he only smiled his exquisite wistful smile. "But you ought to talk like that to our Philippa, not to me."

"Drop that," the Group Captain growled. He looked at Theodore. "Want a drink?"

"No, thank you. Pat, I hear they think you're wonderful."

"They must be half-witted. Not that I didn't bring off one or two little things. Do better in this act."

"Second Act beginners," came the cry.

Up in the manager's room, the warning bell had sounded, and everybody had gone except Maggie and Mobbs, Grace and the Commodore.

"We ought to go back," said Grace. "I hate to miss anything."

"So do I," said Maggie. "And I think it's lovely, though I don't quite understand what they're all talking about, do you?"

"No, but it makes me want to cry," said Grace, "and I always like that. Come on, let's leave these old boozers."

"Perhaps a quick one," said Mobbs, as the ladies left them.

"Yes, just a small quick one," said the Commodore, with a judicial air. "Did I tell you that Seth phoned from the park? Very poor attendance there, though of course it's Monday. If we're unlucky, we might drop a packet up there." The Commodore picked up the drink that Mobbs had poured out. "Very much between ourselves, my dear Archie," he continued, looking solemn, "if we don't have rather a lot of good luck this week, we may find ourselves in a very nasty hole by the end of the week."

"Be all right, old boy," cried Mobbs. "Feel it in my bones."

The Commodore gave him a droll glance. "What bones? No, don't tell me. We'd better go in. It's going quite well, you know."

"Seems to be," said Mobbs as they moved out. "But candidly, old boy, I'm not getting it. Like that stuff Grope was reading last night. Don't get it. Either I'm stupider than I fancy I am, or these chaps nowadays are half off their rocker."

"The trouble with you, Archie," said the Commodore, patting him on his fat shoulder, "is that you don't belong to our intellectual and cultural elite."

"I dare say, old boy. But do you?"

"Deep down I believe I do, Archie. But not of course to that collection of prigs, bluffers, and pansies who advertise themselves as members of it. Hello—curtain's going up."

An hour later it came down, hiding a noble ruin of a Cardinal who had added to Boon some delicious scraps from *Troilus and Cressida, Macbeth, Antony and Cleopatra, Lear* and *The Tempest,* to a rattling storm of applause. The full company took five curtains, after which Miss Hookwood and Mr. Gorebarry took three, and then the others returned, bringing with them Mr. Mossat, who briefly expressed his thanks to the audience. But they would not leave until Gorebarry had made a speech. "Ladies and Gentlemen," he intoned grandly, "I can only join our gifted producer in thanking you most warmly for your generosity toward us here tonight. Already, here in—er—Farchester—Farbridge—we feel we are among friends. Already, your charming Lyceum—Grand—Palace Theater seems like home to us. Please remember that we are with you for—er—some time—playing—er—Shakespeare and—er—Goldsmith, I beg his pardon, Sheridan as well as Mr.—er Boom. And what a chance for you! What happiness for us. Thank you—thank you—on behalf of us all."

Five minutes later, after a rather savage exchange with Miss Hookwood, who could no longer control her feelings, Gorebarry was holding a crowded reception in his dressing room, where he insisted upon holding the hand of Mrs. Bulfoss, greatly to the astonishment of Major Bulfoss, who kept muttering something about "a jolly good show." Mrs. Hungerford was there, bouncing and gasping and never finishing a phrase. Mr. Huntley and the Paisley-and-amber headmistress had ventured in, and in the doorway, wedged between County types, Lady Barth was screeching away. Theodore was hanging about in the corridor from the stage door, hoping that Laura might come round.

"She's gone home with her father and the Saxons," said Michael Seacombe, without being asked by Theodore where she was. "Where do I find Clare Chesbey? I thought I might get a little story out of her, and I know her brother, Lionel. You don't mind if I talk to her, do you, Jenks?" There was a touch of insolence in his tone.

Theodore glowered at him. "Why should I? And don't talk to me like that, Seacombe, or I might lose my temper."

"And then what?"

"You'll be sorry." And Theodore went in search of George, to eat and drink with him at the Albion.

There were admiring visitors in Philippa Hookwood's dressing room too, but somehow they soon melted away shortly after the arrival of the Group Captain, who looked very grim. He put his great back against the door, and watched her covering her face with cold cream.

"You'd better go now, Trevy," she said, not looking at him. "You can wait outside while I change. Shan't be long. I'm dying for food and drink."

"Wipe that stuff off your face," said the Group Captain. It was an order, very sharply delivered. She raised her eyebrows, but said nothing. After she had wiped off the cold cream, she turned and looked at him inquiringly, her rather large handsome face quite pale, a trifle worn. "I'm not supposed to be looked at like this," she said rather uncertainly, "and after such a hell of a day too. What—what's the matter, Trevy?"

Before she could no more than squeak some sort of protest, he had pulled her out of the chair, and, snorting away, with blue fire in his little eyes, he took hold of her so that she was quite helpless in his huge thick arms. And then he was kissing her, and it was wonderful. "But a bit much," she gasped. "Honestly, darling, you're just a bear."

"Bear, my foot! I'm a man."

"Well, yes, you are, darling."

"And I can't stand any more of it, Phil. Either I clear out or you move in. I mean it. I'm serious."

"What do we do then?" she said softly. "Live in sin?"

"No dam' fear. We get married—and pronto!"

"But I don't want to leave the stage, Trevy. I'm sorry, but I don't."

"All right, please yourself. I won't beef. We'll work something out." He let her go now, looking rather shamefaced. "That is—if you could somehow manage to feel something for me—just a bit of what I feel all the time. I know I'm not one of these fascinating types you're always meeting—"

"You daft great gorilla!" she cried, not knowing whether to laugh or to weep. "You would start this tonight of all nights—"

"I know—but I'd had it, Phil, I'd had it. And if you only could—"

"You idiot, I adore you—and have done for ages. And I'll marry you as soon as you like—next week. And now go away and let me change."

And that was how the first Festival pair came together, a situation plain to everybody when they arrived in the Palmerston Room at the White Hart, which Seth Hull had turned into a supper room for his Festival guests. One glance at the radiant Philippa, at the beaming though rather dazed Group Captain, told the whole story; and all the others crowded round to shake their hands.

"And about time too," said Mr. Hookwood, after kissing his daughter. "I think he'd have walked out on me if you'd said no, my girl."

"Best bit o' news today," said Seth, who had been feeling gloomy after his visit to Mayton Park, where the attendance at the dancing had been far below what he and the Commodore had hoped. "We'll have a drop o' champagne."

"Get cracking with it, Seth," said the Group Captain. "But it's on me."

"Darling, it's just perfect," cried Mrs. Hungerford, bouncing away. "And it simply makes the whole thing—just—absolutely—I mean—the performance—and everything—"

"You've said it," the Group Captain told her.

"And please don't forget," said Philippa, after making sure that Patrick Gorebarry had not yet arrived, "that if it hadn't been for Trevy, who devoted all his evening to it, we'd never have seen Pat Gorebarry on that stage tonight."

"Young Jenks was on the job too," said the Group Captain. "Where is he?"

"Yes, where's poor Theodore?" cried Grace, flushed and clearly excited by all these proceedings.

The Commodore led her away as he replied: "Theodore's not staying here and has probably had enough of it all today. Now don't forget, Grace, what you promised earlier tonight—that you'd tell me at least as much as you told him about yourself. Preferably more than you told him."

"Oh—well, that wouldn't be hard to do. I just had to tell him something," she said crossly. "And I've not forgotten my promise." She smiled at him. "But don't you start ordering me about."

It was then that Gorebarry made a big entrance. There was no sign of Major Bulfoss, but Gorebarry was still holding Mrs. Bulfoss by the hand, rather as if she were some small but charming prize he had just been awarded. As for poor Mrs. Bulfoss, she was still hovering between terror and enchantment.

"And here we are," cried Gorebarry, very much the guest of honor, "longing for rich food and drink. What news, hearts, what news?"

When he was told, he embraced Philippa, who submitted with a swift sideways glance at the frowning Group Captain, and then he seized the first glass of champagne. "To Philippa, our golden lass, and Group Captain Trevone, a Man—by heaven! And may they breed ripe wenches and great scowling lads—"

"That'll do for you, Pat," said the Group Captain in his sharpest tone of command. "Come on, let's eat."

They were still eating, some standing at the central table, others sitting at small tables, when Major Bulfoss appeared, looking annoyed. "Oh, there you are," he cried to his wife. "Couldn't make out where you'd got to."

"All's well, Major," said Gorebarry. "Wipe the cares of state from your brow and join us in our innocent revelry and friendly mirth."

"You'll take a drop o' something, Major?" said Seth.

"Oh—well, thanks, Hull. Just a spot, perhaps." And the Major sat down, staring now with bewilderment rather than annoyance at his wife.

The Commodore had been having some talk with Mobbs and Mr. Hookwood, leaving Grace happy in a corner with Maggie, with whom she had established a sound alliance. Now he decided that the time had come when he might hear Grace's story. But there was Maggie, telling Mobbs it was time he took her to her lodgings; and no Grace.

"She said she was tired, like me," said Maggie, "and so she'd just slip out."

"By George—I believe she's done it again," cried the Commodore. He hurried below, to find out the number of her room, and then went up and knocked at her door.

To his relief he heard her call out: "Yes? Who is it?"

"I thought you'd run out on me again," he told her, as quietly as he could through the door.

It opened about an inch. "I'm sorry but I suddenly felt very tired," she whispered. "Now off you go or you'll be giving me a bad name round here. Goodnight."

As he walked away, the Commodore for once found himself feeling unsociable, with no desire to return to the party in the Palmerston Room. Suddenly weary and rather melancholy he went along to his bedroom, where he lay awake in the dark for several hours, trying in vain to forget the Festival and to ignore the future.

5

The Commodore, who as a favored resident was still able to break-fast in bed, even though the hotel was full, came down late next morn-ing. He inquired about Grace—for he was still feeling uncertain about her—and was told she had gone out. He sauntered out into High Street on his way to the Festival Center. The morning was fine but heavy, close, not promising for the second day of a Festival; he did not like the smell of it. Staring without enthusiasm into a haberdasher's window was a short shabby figure that seemed familiar. It was A. Smith of London.

"Terrible prices," said Smith, indicating the haberdashery. "Glad I'm not dressy. How's tricks, Commodore? Festival going well?"

"Too early to say," said the Commodore. "Staying with us long?"

"Depends," replied Smith, with a wink. "Party's gone off in a car—hired—with female friend, strapping roly-poly piece. No luggage. Out for the day."

So Grace had gone off with Maggie. The Commodore felt relieved. "Not much for you to do then, Smith?"

"Not enough. Like to keep busy, specially in a place like this. Differ-ent in London. Amuse myself there, every time. If she stays here, might do a little job for you on the side. For cash, and no word to the agency. Anything doing?"

"Not at the moment," said the Commodore, eyeing him thought-fully. "But I'll bear it in mind."

"I'm versatile," said Smith, "and a wizard at getting info. Calling me Nosey when I was ten. It's a gift. Either you have it or you haven't. I have it."

"You don't surprise me. What about a little information to be going on with? Just as a sample. For instance, what did young Jenks do for—you know—Mrs. Robinson, your subject, party, or whatever you call her?"

Smith tapped the end of his long nose with a very dirty forefinger, while his eternal smoldering cigarette transferred itself to the other corner of his mouth. "Worth a quid?"

"I doubt it," said the Commodore. "It's just idle curiosity on my part. Still—just as a little retainer—and in case I might want you later, when of course you'll be paid handsomely—" And he handed over a pound note.

"She got him to pinch a box for her," Smith mumbled out of the corner of his mouth that did not hold the cigarette. "Client told us. Police job really, 'cos his housekeeper complained, after seeing Jenks. But he's not pressing it."

"Is this chap her husband?"

"Had your quid's worth. But I'm not mean. Put it like this. Bet she told Mr. Jenks he was. Bet she said the box was hers."

"Well, wasn't it?" the Commodore demanded rather sharply.

Smith winked again. "Matter of opinion. She's artful, y'know, Commodore, very artful."

"I don't believe it. There's a mistake somewhere."

"Matter of fact, they all are. Make rings round us blokes. Not me, except just once—a red-haired piece in Kilburn. Specially artful round there. And don't ask me why 'cos I don't know."

"Well, I'm glad there's something you don't know," said the Commodore. "But about this box. Why should she ask young Jenks to get it for her?"

"I'm stretching that quid's worth. Must be getting soft. However," said Smith, "here it is. The client's seeing her that night. She thinks it's safe for Jenks to go up to Highgate and get the box. Doesn't know about the housekeeper, see? When the client leaves her flat, I take over again. She pops out. Door open. I pop in, to take a decco. Jenks in the bath. Nothing doing between 'em though. Take my word. In fact," he concluded, "she hasn't got a bloke. Not yet. But keep Gorebarry away from her. He's mustard. But I'm opening my mouth too wide. Not like me. Now don't forget if there's a little job for me on the side. Info, tailing, and nice psychological touches—that's me. 'Morning."

On his table at the Center the Commodore found a rather curtly worded message from Meare, the Town Clerk, asking that a daily report of the Festival, giving details of attendances, takings, expenditure, should be sent to him. This did not sound like Meare, who was a mild fellow, and the Commodore did not feel happy about it. He summoned Laura.

"I don't like this," he told her. "Apart from the extra work it gives us, I don't like the smell of it."

"It's Coverack, of course," she said. "Shall I do it—or will you?"

"I'll do it—or at least I'll dictate a rough draft, giving 'em the general picture, and then you can fill in the figures. Take this down, please, my dear." He waited until she was ready, then dictated: "The

Festival made an excellent start, following the Civic Lunch. In spite of some initial difficulties about seating arrangements, the Library Lecture by Rufus Grope was well attended and successfully delivered. The sale of tickets amounted to whatever it was. The Mossat Company opened to—whatever it was—and the theater could have taken more money if a number of tickets had not been given away. There was great enthusiasm at the end of the play. The advance bookings are—"

"I can get those," said Laura, "but I'm afraid they're rather disappointing so far."

"We don't mention that." He continued dictating. "The attendance at Mayton Park, both of dancers and spectators, was somewhat below what we expected, and the café-buffet did very little business; but undoubtedly this is chiefly due to the fact that the younger people rarely go out and spend money very early in the week. At the same time, as we are spending a good deal of money on this dancing, we ought to ask ourselves whether it would not be wise to spend more on publicity for this particular attraction. A more detailed report on our Mayton Park activities will be included in our next general report. The advance sale of tickets for all activities—" He broke off. "Well, you can fill that in later. All right?"

"Yes, I suppose so," said Laura. "We'll have to put something in about expenditure. Day by day, I suppose they mean?"

"I don't know what they mean, and I doubt if they do." He paused to light his pipe. "One of us will have to take a look tonight at the dress rehearsal of the Pageant, while the other goes up to Mayton Park. Take your choice. They're equally unpleasant to me."

"I'll go to the park then," said Laura, with no show of enthusiasm. "Michael can take me. I don't know if he likes dancing."

"You don't sound as if you care either," said the Commodore, giving her a sharp look.

She ignored both the look and the remark. "You'll have to do the Pageant rehearsal then. One of us must be there. Let's hope it doesn't rain. The weather forecast isn't very optimistic."

"Then it's like me at the moment," said the Commodore. "Hello! You leaving us already?" For Laura's father had come in, carrying a small case.

"Going back to town for a couple of days," said Mr. Casey. "I'll be back on Thursday to see your production of *The Rivals*. Old favorite of mine. Well, Laura, like to see me off—or are you too busy?"

After the Caseys went off together, the Commodore tried his hand at adding up a few Festival figures, took a great dislike to the totals he achieved, and decided that his arithmetic was probably at fault. Then he smoked his pipe in the bay window and stared idly down at the High Street's late morning bustle, framed in the Festival bunting, bright in the sun. He liked the look of what he saw, so delightfully free from that shadow of disaster and ruin which seemed to grow somewhere at the back of his mind. Then a little cough turned him round. His room was now decorated by the presence of a slender blonde young woman, who looked as if she had conjured herself out of a technicolor film.

"Good morning," he cried cheerfully. "Won't you sit down?"

She swayed across to a chair, carefully deposited herself in it, crossed her legs with equal care, and then focused upon him an immense azure gaze. "April Bond."

"I beg your pardon," said the Commodore.

"That's my professional name—I expect you know it. But I'm really Mrs. Johnny Jolly. Are you the Commodore gentleman who's running this Festival?"

"I am, Mrs. Jolly. Or do you prefer Miss Bond?"

"Just call me April. I'm more used to it."

"Then just call me Commodore, April. I'm used to it too. And the gentleman part is very doubtful." He smiled, and she smiled back at him, though it was obvious that she did not realize he was being funny. Perhaps he wasn't, he told himself.

"Well, Commodore, I'm glad it's you this time and not that snooty little dark girl who was in here last time."

"You mean Miss Casey, my assistant. She's not really snooty, you know. She's been working too hard, and she's worried."

"Who isn't? I asked for you last night."

"Oh, did you, April? Where—at the White Hart?"

"Yep. We're staying there. But they said you must have gone to bed. That was in that private room where we'd something to eat and drink after the show. Wasn't it nice those two getting engaged—both ever so attractive I thought, though she'll have to watch herself! But Johnny and that Patrick Gorebarry nearly had a fight."

"What about?" The Commodore was fascinated. Her face never lost its slightly blank hauteur, and her voice, with its queer Cockney-

American drawl, just went on and on: it was like having a chat with a lifesize talking doll.

"Well—about me, in a way. Not that I wasn't behaving, but that Gorebarry was plastered. And talk about bedroom eyes! Johnny's not so bad in that line, but that Gorebarry chap—boy, it's murder!"

"It is, is it?" cried the Commodore heartily. "Well now, what did you want to see me about, April?"

"You went to the theater last night, they said, so you weren't out at the park."

"No. They had a rather quiet night, I'm afraid."

"A quiet night? Listen, Commodore, it was dead. Poor Johnny couldn't believe it. And when he asked me to sing, I says: 'Who to? Or have we come out here to rehearse?' I oughtn't to have said it, but my pride was hurt same as his, so I had to take it out of him a bit, you know."

"I do know, April. I've had it taken out of me in my time. Why do you do it?"

"I've asked myself that," she replied, shaking her head about an inch each way. "I'd do anything for poor Johnny—honestly I would. Look at me coming to see you like this. But if anything goes wrong, even if I'm sorry for him, I have to take it out of him a bit. Like last night. That's why he knocked a few back—and he doesn't as a rule—and wanted to start a fight. It was that Group Captain that stopped 'em. Boy, is he tough? Trying to take it out of him 'ud be something."

"It would," said the Commodore. "But though I'd hate to spoil any delicious reverie inspired by that notion, April, I still don't quite understand what it is you want to see me about. Is there something I can do for you and your husband?"

"Well, that's it. We gotta contract—and if you people say we must play up in that park till Saturday week, we'll have to do it. But if you ask me, Commodore, either you get some people there or wash it out. Mind you, it's just me that's talking—Johnny doesn't know I'm here— thinks I'm shopping. But this is going to get him down, an' do the boys no good—and as for me, if anybody thinks I'm going to vocalize into a mike for ten people, four kids, and two dogs, they can think again. It might have looked a good idea—seemed all right to us—but it seems it isn't. Don't ask me what's the matter with these people here 'cos I don't know. Never happened to us before. It's—it's—" she searched for the right word, and then produced it with a gleam of triumph "—it's mortifying."

The Commodore nodded gravely. "I know how you feel, April," he began; but then a young man in a salmon sports shirt and a grass-green coat came bounding into the room, holding out a hand and crying: "Johnny Jolly himself! Good morning, people!" But at the sight of his wife standing there, he stopped dead, and the wide smile vanished.

"All right, Johnny," she said. "I came to see him myself. So what?"

"So what?" he cried angrily. "Thank you for nothing, that's what. Kindly mind your own interference, that's what."

"I suppose I'm not here in this dump," she said, with withering irony. "I'm somewhere else. I'm at the Finsbury Park Empire. I'm at the Manchester Mecca. I needn't worry."

"Did I say I'd come and see him or didn't I?" shouted Johnny. "And is this shopping or isn't it? And am I running this outfit or are you?"

"Ask me another. I'm beginning to wonder."

"Don't give me that," he shouted.

"Nobody could give you anything, Mr. Big."

"What again?" said Laura, who was inside the room before any of them saw her come in.

"Miss Snooty's back," said April in deep disgust.

"That's manners, isn't it?" Johnny yelled at her. "That's clever, isn't it, insulting the management?"

"How long does this go on?" asked Laura wearily.

"It stops now," said the Commodore, suddenly taking charge. "Laura, don't bother about this. I'll see you in a few minutes." She nodded and went out. He went round the table and approached the other two, dominating them. "My dear April, please sit down. And you sit down too, Johnny." Rather sheepishly they obeyed him. "Now then," he began, after lighting his pipe, "April—who came to see me because she was worried about you, Johnny—has explained what you're both feeling. I sympathize with you. And after all, it's disappointing to us too. But don't worry. In a night or two we'll have that park packed for you. In the meantime, if there's any stunt you'd like to work—dancing competition, that kind of thing—we'll back you to any reasonable amount. Last night meant nothing. A Monday and only the first night of the Festival. The theater was a big counterattraction too."

"Natch," said Johnny. "But you've got this Pageant starting to-morrow night, I see. What about that?"

"Finishes just after nine," said the Commodore. "We tell the audience about the dancing. We run special buses from the football ground to Mayton Park. The Pageant will do you far more good than harm."

"It might at that," said April. "But supposing it rains?"

"We agreed to take a chance on that, my dear," said the Commodore. "But if it should look as if we're in for a really bad spell, then I'll arrange to transfer the whole thing indoors. There's an old skating rink we might use. Now stop worrying, both of you. By the end of the week, you'll be having the time of your lives, I promise you. Take a stroll—show the people how fine and handsome you look—talk over a few possible publicity stunts—and then come and lunch with me at the White Hart. Eh?"

"Thanks, boss," said Johnny, getting up. "We'll do just that."

"Commodore," said April, putting her hand in his, "you're a lulu. See you later." And off they went, taking most of the technicolor with them.

Laura returned; Mobbs and Michael Seacombe came up; the coffee arrived; and the four of them settled down to their daily conference. The Commodore explained the visit of Johnny Jolly and his wife.

"Well, we can't use that old skating rink," said Laura. "We inquired before and found that it's being used as a warehouse. Quite hopeless. And there's no other place. If it's wet, then the dancing has just had it, that's all."

"And I'm not sure about these publicity stunts," said Michael Seacombe. "If we had a daily paper, it would be different. But with one weekly—that doesn't like us—we can't do anything. Yes, we can make announcements at the Pageant, use a loud-speaker van, rush a few bills out—but I'm not wildly optimistic about the result."

"Besides," said Laura firmly, "we just can't afford to spend money on publicity and prizes—"

The Commodore held up his hand. "In one sense, we can't. In fact, we haven't got it to spend. On the other hand, seeing that we're in so deep, we might as well go a little deeper."

Laura was staring at him accusingly. "It sounds to me now even worse than I thought. Is there something you've not told me about?"

"Let's keep to the point," said the Commodore hurriedly, hoping that Mobbs would not say anything about those fireworks. "All I'm saying is that small economies won't help us now, whereas if we spend a little more, it may make all the difference. Anyhow, I'll see if Jolly has anything to suggest. Now tonight we needn't worry about the theater, though one of us might look in. I'm going to attend the dress rehearsal of the Pageant, which will probably need cutting. Laura—with you, Michael—is going out to Mayton Park. No lecture this afternoon, but there's something—"

"Opening of the Old Farbridge Exhibition at Charity House," said Laura. "Three o'clock. By Lord Barnleysale."

"He's one of the County nobs that Theodore and I visited," said Mobbs, sounding rather uneasy. "As a matter of fact, I never actually saw him. Theodore saw him, and said he was old and a bit barmy, but he's a tremendous name round here and ought to attract people to the opening. He's going straight to Charity House from his castle, but I'll be on the job to look after him."

"Good, Archie," said the Commodore. "Who's taking the chair for him? Major Bulfoss? Right. I'll try to be there. How's the exhibition looking?"

"I've just come from there," said Michael. "Thought there might be a story in it. Doesn't look too bad—some nice old bits and pieces—but it's dull, very dull. Unless it's me." He yawned. "Sorry!"

"You're livery," said Laura severely. "I suppose you drank too much last night. The trouble with this Festival is that all you chaps drink too much, we haven't any money, too many important people are against us, and the public—so far—isn't sufficiently interested. Otherwise, it's grand."

"Soundly stated, my dear," said the Commodore. "By the way, your father seemed to me very observant and shrewd. What did he think of our chances?"

"He thinks we planned it on the right lines," Laura replied. "He was most complimentary about that. But he thinks too that having to rush it as we did, we haven't given people enough time to take it all in and that without a daily local paper, or local radio as they'd have in America, we're not really in constant touch with people, building up interest and excitement. We talked a long time about it last night after the theater."

"He's dead right, of course," said Michael, rather gloomily. "We might have brought out a little Festival daily—"

"Well, why don't we?" cried the Commodore.

"Too late now. And pretty expensive unless you carry plenty of advertising."

"How's business downstairs this morning?"

"Rather slow so far, old boy," said Mobbs. "Though it's early, of course. And no great rush at the Palace. They're a bit disappointed in the box office, after last night."

"Well," and the Commodore paused a moment, "any other bad news?"

"Yes," said Laura. "I had to look in at the Bank this morning, and although nobody said anything, I couldn't help feeling that the atmosphere there was rather chilly. And I'm sure that manager doesn't like us, that secretly he's one of the Enemy. Nice, isn't it, when we may need their help at any moment?"

"Now, Laura," the Commodore began.

"Oh, don't start that," she cried angrily, shaking her head as her eyes filled with tears. Then she ran out of the room.

"Let's face it," said Michael softly. "I'm making that girl about as happy as a stiff dose of flu. I thought your little scheme, Commodore, was all wrong when you first mentioned it, on Sunday night, and now I know it was a real stinker. Incidentally, I had rather a valuable chat last night, after the show, with Clare Chesbey, the pretty dark girl in Mossat's company. I used to know her brother rather well."

"What did she say?" asked the Commodore.

"Some other time, if you don't mind," said Michael, and walked out.

"On the whole," said the Commodore reflectively, "I like young Seacombe, but there are moments—and they seem to be on the increase—when I should like to kick his backside. By the way, your Maggie seems to have gone out for the day with Grace. Did you know?"

Mobbs nodded. "They arranged it last night, old boy. Shan't see her today, because this chap who runs the garage at Brant-in-the-Hollow is taking her to Mayton Park tonight. A very fair-minded girl, Maggie."

"And as I've told you before, there isn't any such thing." The Commodore pushed himself up from his table rather wearily. "I'm going out. I want to think, and there's something about this shoe store that stops me thinking. See you this afternoon at the Exhibition, Archie."

"We're taking a chance, having old Lord Barnleysale to open it," said Mobbs, following him out. "That is, if what Theodore told me was true. Though the atmosphere of that castle may have rattled him a bit. I know it did me. But old Barnleysale is the King Nob of the County—

and hardly anybody sees him now—so he ought to attract a nice crowd."

And here Mobbs was quite right, as the Commodore saw for himself when he arrived at Charity House just before three. Charity House was a small, restored fifteenth-century building in a turning off Peter Place, not far from the Old Oak Café. It had one room a little above the street level, and two smaller rooms on the first floor. The room downstairs was nicely filled, mostly with middle-aged women. Old Jordan and Huntley were there, standing near the little platform.

"It seems to me," said the Commodore, joining them, "that so far you two are getting most out of this Festival. Never a dull moment for you."

"Certainly," cried Jordan. "Kind of thing I like. Said so from the first. Look worried yourself, Commodore. Anything wrong?"

"Yes, but I won't bother you with it now. Good crowd. Hope they've paid something."

"Erce," Huntley murmured. "A shilling. And we're arranging for parties of senior schoolchildren to come at sixpence a head. You know that an ancestor of Lord Barnleysale actually built this place? Extraordinarily interesting." He closed his eyes, quivered, went under. "I must remind Major Bulfoss. He ought to refer to it in his opening remarks." He opened his eyes. "Here they are."

A little procession was making its way towards them. It was led by Major Bulfoss, who was looking nervous and pop-eyed. Then came the vast ruin of Lord Barnleysale, who was leaning on the arm of his daughter, Lady Felicia. And little Mobbs, scarlet and moist, brought up the rear. Lady Felicia and Major Bulfoss hoisted Lord Barnleysale on to the platform, where he collapsed into an unusually large chair, and, after some slow-motion fumbling, put two pairs of spectacles on his huge swollen nose, and stared rather blankly at some notes. Huntley mounted the platform too and whispered to Major Bulfoss. Lady Felicia sat close to her father and regarded him anxiously. Mobbs, dabbing his forehead and breathing hard, retired with the Commodore to lean against an old refectory table, the nearest exhibit.

Major Bulfoss, opening the proceedings, said that it was a great honor for him to take that chair that afternoon, at the opening of the Old Farbridge Exhibition, and to introduce somebody who really needed no introduction, Lord Barnleysale, whose—er—forefathers—ancestor—had actually built Charity House and presented it to the borough of Farbridge, which had an—er—older history than a lot of people imagined. "And—er—now I have great pleasure in calling upon Lord Barnleysale," he concluded, and sat down. Everybody clapped.

Although sharply nudged by his daughter, Lord Barnleysale gave no sign of having realized that he was now being called upon. He just sat there, a mountainous old gentleman in an Edwardian black-and-white tweed coat, still staring through his two pairs of spectacles at his notes. "Eh? What?" he rumbled, after a further nudge or two from his daughter. "Oh—I see." And then he dropped his notes. "No, leave 'em there," he could be heard saying. "Lot of nonsense." And then, as Lady Felicia was helping him to hoist himself out of the chair, he could be heard muttering gigantically: "Who's that fellow who spoke? Major What? Bullfrog? Nonsense, Felicia!" And there were one or two hastily suppressed giggles from the audience.

"Well—er—Major—er—Chairman—Ladies and Gentlemen," his lordship began, in an enormous bass rumble, removing his spectacles. "Had some notes, but we won't bother about 'em. Never really cared about speaking from notes. Mistake, actually. When I first took my seat in the Lords, old—er—Who's-it warned me against it. 'Cramps one's style, my boy,' he said. And quite right. Better to speak out, say what you think." He stared about him, then put back one pair of spectacles, and stared again. "Charity House, eh? Ancestor of mine built it. Got into trouble with the Church—kidnapped some fella's wife or something—so had to build this place. Not used when I was a youngster. Except for storing corn. Came ratting here many a time—fine sport. Only a youngster, of course—still at school really. Liked Farbridge in those days. Nice little market town. No beastly factories and that sort of thing. Quite different nowadays—can't stand it. However, sensible idea to open this old place again."

There was some applause, keenly led by Huntley.

But for some mysterious reason this applause did not please his lordship, who looked annoyed. "All very well, clapping," he grumbled, "but ought to get something done. All right as far as it goes to reopen this old place, tidy it up, stick a few things in it, as you seem to have done. But why stop there? What you want's some sort of exhibition. Old Farbridge, that sort of thing. Why not? What's wrong with that? Why be slack about it? Only needs some enterprising fella to get it started. Do it myself if I was twenty years younger. So beg to move, Mr. Chairman, that when you get round to this Festival of Britain business, if there's anything in it, we hold some sort of exhibition here

in Charity House. Thank you." And he sat down, grinning triumphantly at his daughter and patting her on the arm.

Huntley, a quick thinker, was on his feet at once. On behalf of the
Festival Committee he thanked Lord Barnleysale for opening the
Old Farbridge Exhibition in such a spirited and original manner, and
asked the audience to show their appreciation in the usual way, which
they did, noisily encouraged by the Commodore, Mobbs, and old
Jordan.

"My godfathers!" cried Mobbs, as he escaped with the Commodore.
"Theodore was quite right."

"And so were you to ask him here," said the Commodore, chuckling. "I feel better after that. Couldn't we persuade the old dinosaur
to open something else? Or better still, to close it, then perhaps he
really would open it, if you see what I mean. This must be his car."
It was an enormous and very old Rolls-Royce.

"It is. Lady Felicia drove him in. She's taking him home and then
coming back tonight to go to the theater. I've fixed her up with a seat,"
Mobbs continued, "which was only too easy. She says she used to know
Gorebarry—and as she seems to be nearly as bad as he is—very hot
stuff, I gather—then if they get together, it's over the top and the best
of luck! You'll be up in the Palmerston Room again, Commodore,
after the Pageant dress rehearsal? Right, then see you there. Must wait
here for the nobs."

The Commodore spent the rest of the afternoon in his office at the
Center, returned to the White Hart just after five, and found Grace
and Maggie having tea in the lounge.

"We've had a lovely day in the country," said Grace brightly. "I like
the country so long as I don't have to live in it. And if you live there,
you can't visit it, can you?" She prattled away for the next ten
minutes.

"I must find Seth Hull," said the Commodore. "He and I are going
to attend the dress rehearsal of the Pageant. It's at the football ground,
and as Seth's the great man there, I want him with me. Like to come
with us, Grace? I know Maggie's not free. She's going out dancing
tonight with an admirer."

"Yes, I know," said Grace, with a sparkling glance at Maggie. "She's
told me all about them."

"Unlike some people," said the Commodore, "who promise to tell
and then don't."

"That's right," said Grace cheerfully. "Well, I'll come with you. What time? About six? I'll be ready."

Seth drove them himself out to the football ground, which was in East Farbridge, surrounded by rows of little houses built about the beginning of the century. He led them to a central section of the grandstand, where the directors of the club and their friends could easily slip in or out of their seats, to or from a room that smelled strongly of a drop of something. And indeed no sooner had they arrived than the manager of the club, Mr. Geordie Pitts, suggested that a drop of something should be taken. Grace, fascinated by all the figures in fancy costume milling around the playing area, refused to leave her seat in the stand, but the three men decided for a drop.

"You're missing nothing," said Geordie, when they were standing round the table, lighting Seth's cigars. "Proper bloody muck up out there. Mr. Capperton won't get started for another twenty minutes. I told him to come in here. He needs anything we can give him, that poor chap does."

For the next five minutes they discussed the arrangements for handling the spectators on the following evening, the opening performance; and as they did not expect more than two or three thousand, at the most, and Geordie Pitts and his staff frequently had to cope with twenty-five thousand, these arrangements presented no great difficulties. Then Mr. Capperton arrived, and with him, white and trembling, was the author, Miss Fisby.

"Oh, Commodore Tribe," she cried shakily, "I can't tell you. It's all so difficult."

"Miss Fisby," said Seth, regarding her with some concern, "what you want's a drop o' something."

"Oh, thank you, but I couldn't possibly, Mr. Hull. I think—I really think—" and her voice sank to a tragic whisper "—I'd be sick."

So she was sent up to join Grace in the stand. Meanwhile, Mr. Capperton hesitated, explaining that he rarely drank spirits. He was the English master at the County Boys' School, and a large sweaty man, with moist tufts of hair coming out of his nostrils and ears and above the front of his sports shirt, as if he were an enormous hair pillow that had been slashed in various places. Fortunately, he had a very loud voice, which had boomed across many sports grounds.

"If yer ask me, Mr. Capperton," said Seth gravely, "this is a time when yer'll start drinking spirits. Beer an' lemonade an' suchlike'll never see yer through this job. Yer've got some trade on tonight, lad. Geordie, a good stiff un for Mr. Capperton."

"Well, thank you, Mr. Hull," said Capperton. "Perhaps you're right. It took us five hours to get through it last night."

"And what about tomorrow's performance?" asked the Commodore. "Because I must tell you, here and now, that I want you to finish not later than quarter-past nine. I'm very anxious to collect some of these Pageant spectators for the dancing at Mayton Park, and I've arranged for special buses to take them out there."

Capperton stared at him in despair. No doubt it was an illusion but suddenly he seemed hairier than ever, as if he were sprouting hard as a kind of protection. "But with a quarter of an hour interval, which we need," he cried, "that means we can only run for two hours."

"Well, that's long enough for any pageant," said the Commodore firmly. "In fact, with all due respect, Mr. Capperton, it's a good hour more than I've ever been able to take of any pageant."

"I know," Capperton moaned. "Don't tell me. I know. Why the devil I ever agreed to take this thing on, I can't imagine. But it means we'll have to cut and cut."

A voice, vaguely familiar to the Commodore, was now heard calling urgently for Mr. Capperton. Then there burst into the room a very strange figure indeed. It was Ernest Saxon, still wearing his spectacles and looking like a conscientious science master, dressed to represent one of Cromwell's Ironside generals.

"By gow," cried Seth, staring, "now we're seeing summat."

"I'm sorry to intrude, gentlemen," said the scholarly Ironside, "but this must be settled. Capperton I've been sent to appeal to you. No, nothing to drink, thank you, Mr. Hull. There are five of us in the Cavaliers and Roundheads episode who habitually wear glasses, and Miss Thackery, who's responsible for our costumes and make-up, says that we can't wear them. Now it's bad enough for me, and it's much worse for two or three of the others—old Mortimer, for instance, is as blind as a bat without his glasses—and already we nearly had a very nasty accident with one of those absurd pikes. Really if we're all groping about—and with that horse too, which as you know I thought a mistake from the first—anything may happen."

"Yes, yes," said Capperton, absent-mindedly accepting a second good stiff one from Geordie, "yes, yes, yes, yes. I don't know what to say. You don't look too bad, Saxon, old man—"

"Very impressive," said the Commodore smoothly.

"But old Mortimer and one or two of the others wear quite heavy tortoise-shell rims. And, honestly, Saxon, can you see a Cavalier wearing tortoise-shell spectacles?"

"If I take my glasses off," said Saxon, "I can't see anybody wearing anything. I think you'd better come round at once, Capperton. Some of those chaps of ours from the Sixth who are playing Druids are having trouble with their beards and beginning to lark about. As usual," he added bitterly, "young Webster can't keep order."

"Yes, yes," said Capperton. "I'll come along." He swallowed his drink hastily, choked a little, looked wildly at the Commodore and Seth and cried: "If ever I take on anything like this again, may I be certified. My wife warned me. I warned myself. Now I warn you—what you'll see and hear tonight out there will be a screaming chaos."

A few minutes later, even down there, they could hear his voice booming angrily through the loud-speakers, which had been installed to carry the speeches of the performers from the center of the pitch. They finished their drinks and went up into the stand, where the Commodore sat beside Grace, keeping her between him and poor little Miss Fisby.

"It's such a pity that the programs aren't ready for tonight," said Miss Fisby, "because, of course, they explain what's happening and who everybody is. But the audience will have them tomorrow, thank goodness!"

"And you can explain it to us, can't you, Miss Fisby?" said Grace. "I was just saying, Commodore, how clever she is to be able to write a pageant. I wouldn't know how to start. Would you?"

The Commodore said that he wouldn't. "But I hope Capperton does," he added. "They ought to get on with it now, or he'll be all night. And look at that sky." For though the sun still shone, and everything looked clear and bright, there were dark clouds massing above the opposite stands.

Capperton now roared through the loud-speakers that the run-through was about to begin, without music as this had already been rehearsed and some adjustments were being made to the panatrope. A tall stout woman in purple, covered with gilt stars, came forward and had a conversation, in rhymed couplets, with a rather cheeky little boy who seemed to be dressed in sacking. Miss Fisby explained that this was the Spirit of History talking to the Spirit of Farbridge. It was difficult to hear what they were saying because sometimes they were too near the microphones and sometimes too far away. However, it was fairly clear that the Spirit of History was promising all manner of good things to the Spirit of Farbridge.

"And I'll bet he's a cheeky little monkey," said Grace. "Now who are these funny men with beards? And what are they going to do with that girl."

"They're Druids," said Miss Fisby, "and they're sacrificing a maiden at the sacred oak."

"Make a wider ring, Druids," cried Capperton through the loud-speaker. "Don't bunch together, you fellows."

A beard fell off, and there was some giggling from the other Druids, so that it was hard to hear what the doomed maiden was saying.

"Erce," said Huntley, suddenly making an appearance two seats away from the Commodore. "All Sixth Form boys from the County School. First-class, most of them. Very keen. And Capperton's done a splendid job, don't you think? Absolutely first-class."

"Taking their time, though, aren't they?" said Seth, from the row behind. "Bit on slow side, this Druid business. Now who's this chap? I know him, of course—it's young Billy Jackson, who had a trial at center half with our reserves—but who's he supposed to be?"

"A Roman officer, I think," said the Commodore.

"Erce," said Huntley. "Traces of a Roman camp just beyond West Farbridge."

"You're too soon, Jackson," Capperton boomed at him. "Go back, go back. And who told you Anglo-Saxons to move? We don't want to see you for ten minutes yet. Druids, Druids—come along, Druids."

"Oh dear!" cried Miss Fisby. "It's all so difficult. And they all seem so much *stupider* now they're wearing their costumes. It's not going to rain, is it?"

"Looks like it," said Grace.

"Where's the Spirit of History?" boomed Capperton, now nearing despair. "Mrs. Giggleswick, come along *please*. She's *what*? . . . Well, she can't have anything sewn now. I don't care if everything falls off, we must get on. Don't move, Centurion, don't move."

"Keen as mustard, Capperton," Huntley murmured. "Did a capital production of *A Midsummer Night's Dream* last December—absolutely first-class. I've complete confidence in him."

"He'll have to cut it," the Commodore muttered. "Any suggestions, Huntley?"

"Between ourselves," Huntley whispered, "I think the Anglo-Saxons might go. They're not Miss Fisby at her best—and they're being played by the East Farbridge Youth Group who are not—in confidence —a very brilliant lot—though desperately keen, many of them."

"Could you suggest it tactfully to Miss Fisby?"

"I think so," Huntley murmured. "I think I might, you know." And he went along to sit by Miss Fisby and to murmur and quiver and close his eyes at her.

"That ginger-haired lad who's waving a horn or summat," said Seth earnestly to the Commodore, "has been playing ouside right for our reserve team this last season—he's nobbut eighteen—an' in two or three year, if he'll keep at it an' train properly, he'll be as good on the wing as any player i' this country, mark my words."

"But if there aren't any Anglo-Saxons, Mr. Huntley," Miss Fisby could be heard crying in despair, "how do I bring my Normans in? It's all linked up, you see."

"Perhaps just a word or two from the Spirit of History," said Mr. Huntley. "Mrs. Giggleswick could easily learn a few extra lines. She's very intelligent—and a ripping actress."

The Anglo-Saxons were now making merry, drinking imaginery mead out of imitation horn tankards, and one of them appeared to be singing a song. It was raining, and already the Anglo-Saxon roisterers looked damp and peculiarly dismal.

"Norman Knight," Capperton boomed. "Norman Knight, come on. And listen, everybody. Never mind this drop of rain. Unless we're in danger of ruining the costumes, we're going straight on. Well, come *along*, Norman Knight."

"He oughtn't to call his name out like that," said Grace.

"No, that's what he is," said Miss Fisby. "Actually, it's young Harold Stephenson, the son of the pork butcher. It's the Norman Conquest, you see, and the poor Saxons haven't a chance against the heavily armored horsemen."

"Flourish of trumpets," shouted Capperton. "*Tan-tan-ta-ra.* Now then, gallop up to them."

It was a very large horse that was carrying Harold Stephenson and his armor, but it was also very old and showed no sign of entering into the spirit of the Pageant. Very slowly and unwillingly, it ambled about a quarter of the way across the ground, and then it stopped. And it seemed beyond the power of the mailed rider, who was beginning to show signs of distress, to make it move another yard.

"Well, that'll do turf a bit o' good," said Seth, as the horse dropped a fine supply of manure.

Grace began giggling. It rained harder. The damp Anglo-Saxons, displaying more animation than they had done throughout their wassail, scampered for cover. Mr. Capperton made strange moaning sounds through the loud-speaker. The horse turned slowly in a circle, and the knight dropped his spear. The Spirit of History appeared in a mackintosh, but just as she had announced the Norman Conquest into the microphone, a number of sprightly little figures in Lincoln green dashed onto the ground, followed by a stalwart young woman in gym costume, who bustled them into some kind of Morris dance, seeming to create in the drizzle a midget and lunatic Merrie England.

"No, Miss Fawcett, no," yelled Capperton in an agony of protest. "No Robin Hood yet. Take them away. Get back, all you Sherwood Forest lot. Hurry up. Now—Mrs. Giggleswick—"

The Spirit of History sneezed into the microphone.

"Anybody take a drop o' something?" Seth inquired, as the rain began to drum hard on the corrugated iron roof of the stand. Miss Fisby, almost in tears, begged Mr. Huntley to go with her to talk to Mr. Capperton. The miniature Sherwood foresters, with Miss Fawcett after them like a gigantic indigo sheep dog, scampered toward shelter, dodging past retreating Anglo-Saxons and Druids clutching their soggy cottonwool beards. The horse and his knight were still circling slowly in the torrent, but the Roman centurion and a strange new figure who might have been the Sheriff of Nottingham were converging upon the pair, while Mr. Capperton, soaked and screaming, could be seen gesticulating along the touchline.

Grace consented to have a little drop of something while the Commodore and Seth had large drops. Then Seth went off to talk to Geordie in the managerial office. "What this place wants," said Grace, looking about her with housewifely distaste, "is a good clean up."

"And what I want," said the Commodore, with less than his usual tact, for he hated this rain and was feeling grumpy, "is you to keep your promise and tell me at least as much about yourself as you told young Jenks."

"Oh, don't be silly. I had to tell him something. And what a time and place to ask me anyhow! I'm surprised at you, Commodore, really I am."

"I had a talk with that private detective this morning," he continued, ignoring her remarks. He had been tactless but it was too late to dismiss the subject now. "A. Smith, the info man."

"Well, you needn't take any notice of *him*. And surely you didn't ask him about me?"

"No, not exactly. But—er—I gathered one or two things."

But they were interrupted by a highwayman, who was wearing a raincoat and smoking a pipe. "Mr. Huntley round here?" he asked.

"No," said the Commodore. "He went down with Miss Fisby a few minutes ago. Who are you? Dick Turpin?"

"More or less," said the other gloomily. "And if we don't have a rehearsal tomorrow afternoon, school or no school, we can't possibly perform at night. You might tell Mr. Huntley that." And he vanished in a cloud of Navy Cut.

"Well, I must say," cried Grace indignantly, "talking to that awful little detective—and gathering things about me—you ought to be ashamed of yourself. If you want to know about me, then ask me— and don't go asking people like that. Really!"

"But confound it all!" the Commodore roared. "Every time I do try and ask you, you disappear or go to bed or go off for a day in the country."

"And what if I do?" demanded Grace sharply. "You don't expect me to stand about just waiting to answer your silly questions. And I thought we were real friends." Her lip trembled.

"Now, Grace," and he took her hand, "if I didn't worry about you, I wouldn't bother you like this. Ever since we first met—"

The door burst open again, and this time it was a boy about fifteen wearing a black coat, a frilled stock, and damp gray side-whiskers. "Please, sir—"

"Go away," the Commodore yelled at him.

"Yes, sir," and he went.

"As I was saying—ever since we first met—"

But Grace began laughing, and laughed and laughed until the tears ran down her scarlet cheeks. "I can't help it—I'm sorry—but I just can't help it—"

Mr. Capperton, soaked and apparently hairier than ever, came in and brought with him Mrs. Giggleswick, the Spirit of History, who was blowing her nose hard. "I've told Mrs. Giggleswick she must drink a little whisky and keep herself warm," said Capperton, "or she won't be fit to appear tomorrow night."

"Of course she must," cried Grace, and began fussing over Mrs. Giggleswick while the Commodore poured out two whiskies. He then took Capperton on one side. After all, he was the Director of the Farbridge Festival and it was about time he asserted himself.

"Now, my dear fellow," he began, "drink your whisky and please listen to me for a minute. I'm going to be quite frank with you, and I know you'll respect my confidence. We're running into difficulties with this Festival. So far we've spent too much and not taken enough. A lot depends upon this Pageant. Now you must rehearse all tomorrow morning and afternoon. We'll get Huntley's permission for all the teachers and boys and girls to be free for the day—and that accounts for most of you—and it ought not to be difficult for the others to spend the day here. Eh?" Capperton nodded. "Right. Then, don't hesitate to cut out everything you're doubtful about. Don't spare anybody's feelings. If you cut the whole show down to an hour and a half, I shan't grumble. Better be too short than too long. You've done a wonderful job—and we're all very grateful—but for all our sakes from now on be ruthless, my dear fellow. You could be, I can see that. Now—tell everybody to be here at ten in the morning and then send them off home."

"But what if it's still raining tomorrow?" said Capperton.

"It will not rain tomorrow," said the Commodore. "Trust an old sailor. You'll have a fine day and then a wonderful night."

"Listen to him," cried Grace, with that peculiar mixture of admiration and derision which is characteristic of her type. "Knows it all, doesn't he? For all that I'll bet he's right. You'll see. Can we go now? I'm hungry."

Half an hour later, Seth drove them through the pouring rain back to the White Hart, where, since it was not late, they did not go up to the Palmerston Room but dined downstairs in the ordinary way. But the dining room was quiet, and Grace and the Commodore had a corner of it to themselves. Over the Scotch broth and the roast lamb, Grace chattered away, but the Commodore, who was still feeling grumpy, said little.

"I suppose you're not going to ask me anything now," she said finally.

"No, Grace, I'm not."

"Not interested now—um?"

"Of course I am, but obviously I must leave it to you," he told her. "You've made that pretty plain."

"You're really worried about your Festival, aren't you?"

"I am," he admitted. "Tonight'll be a dead loss all round. The park washed out. I rang up the theater, and tonight's returns are disappointing. And anything may happen to that confounded Pageant, on which we've already spent a lot of money."

She nodded. "Have you forgotten I promised you some money?"

"No, I remember. And I'd have asked you for it if you'd been here. But now—it's different. We may be thousands down. I took a big gamble. If I've lost, I'll have to run out of this town, and I don't want to do that. I like it here."

"So do I. But you won't have to. I'm certain you won't."

He shrugged his shoulders, and then, feeling rather boorish, he said: "I hope you're right. But you can't help us now. Only the weather and the public and a bit of good luck can pull us out. Forget about it, Grace."

She looked at him a moment, with a queer little sparkle in her eye. "I'll tell you about me," she began. "And if ever Theodore tells you anything, don't take any notice. I was making most of it up. It amused me, and didn't do him any harm. You're different, of course."

"I'm glad to hear that." He eyed her rather sharply, noting again that queer little sparkle. "But please go on."

"Do you know the Peak District?"

"No, not really. Is that where you come from?"

"Yes, I was brought up on a farm there. Lovely place it was, all among the green hills. Then I married a young man who had a good job in a steelworks in Sheffield, and we were very happy, except we couldn't have any children. You can't have everything, can you? But Bob and I were very happy. Then there was a horrible accident—I never understood it properly—something to do with one of the furnaces." Her eyes filled with tears. "And I lost Bob. You know what it's like then—you're only half-alive. I went back home—just to be with my own folks—and among those lovely green hills."

"You said earlier tonight," he reminded her gently, "you liked the country so long as you didn't have to live in it."

She looked at him reproachfully. "What are you trying to do? Catch me out?"

"My dear Grace," he protested.

"All right. That's what I feel now, but I didn't then. Well, I came in for a share of the farm, and my brother bought me out. Then the husband of a friend of mine wanted to start a catering business in Sheffield, so I went in with him, because I'm interested in catering, and we did very well. Then I got tired of it—"

"No more marrying?"

"No, though I'd my chances, of course. So I sold out of this catering business, and bought a half-share in a lovely hotel about twenty miles out of Sheffield, back in the Peak District. It'ud been an old country mansion, and it was all beautifully furnished and got up and it did a high-class business. And then—this was just before the war—I took it over entirely. Well, the war came, and we were well out of the bombing, all nice and quiet and safe, so a lot of people wanted to stay, whatever we charged, though, mind you, I always tried to be fair. One of these people was a Mr. Gruberlin, who was a refugee who'd had big silk businesses in Vienna and Prague and must have got all his money out somehow because he was very rich. And he was terribly frightened of the war and the bombing—he was getting on and not very strong and altogether a funny old thing—and I let him stay as long as he liked, and did my best for him, just because I was sorry for him, though a lot of people weren't and tried to make trouble. You can imagine how it was, can't you?"

The Commodore said he could, though he had certain reservations that he decided to keep to himself. The waiter brought them sardines on toast, and was told they would have their coffee later, up in the Palmerston Room.

"Well now, I come to the queer part," said Grace earnestly, as soon as the waiter had gone. "Mr. Gruberlin was very grateful to me, and very much attracted as well, and he told me that if he wasn't married already—and his wife had gone to America, he said—he'd marry me. Well, he couldn't do that—not that I'd have had him—but after a lot of talk he said we ought to live together—he was getting on, but you know what these foreigners are like. Promised me anything I wanted too. 'No, Mr. Gruberlin,' I told him, 'I like you very much, as you ought to know by this time, but I couldn't do that. I'm not that kind of woman and I don't feel about you like that, if you see what I mean,' I told him. 'Well,' he said, 'you're a good true woman, Grace, and you've made me as happy as you could and I shan't forget,' he said. Only he had one of those thick foreign voices, you know. Then of course after the war was over, he began his traveling again, and wasn't frightened any longer, but he came up and stayed with me once or twice a year. I was getting rather tired of my hotel because it was such a business getting staff. But I stuck it. Then, last autumn, poor Mr. Gruberlin died—quite suddenly—and—what do you think?"

"He'd left you some money," said the Commodore, promptly.

"That's right. But it's not so simple as you think."

"Perhaps I'm not thinking it *is* simple," said the Commodore, who wasn't.

She gave him a quick look. "Oh—well—it was all very peculiar, and the solicitor said he'd never known anything like it. I got a few thousand pounds anyhow, whatever happened. But I got a lot more—oh—at least a hundred thousand pounds—if—well, if at the end of twelve months, the solicitor was satisfied I was the kind of woman I'd told Mr. Gruberlin I was—a nice respectable woman. Because if I wasn't, you see, then I hadn't told him the truth—and he wasn't going to let me have all that money. Did you ever hear of such a thing?"

"Never until now, Grace," said the Commodore.

"Neither did I," she said gaily. "That day we first met, and I left you in the theater, I suddenly heard the solicitor laughing and then saw him—and got in a panic."

"And does this solicitor employ our friend A. Smith of London? And where does the box come in—the box that poor Theodore brought to you?"

"Oh—no, that's my cousin. You see, like a fool I told him about all this—it was just before I first met you, after I'd sold my hotel and come to London—and it was a silly thing to do because I've never really liked him, but I had to tell somebody. And he's trying to find out something about me and then—don't you see?—blackmail me. Yes, that's what he's after. And I'd left that box in his house, so when I knew he was coming to see me, I asked Theodore to get it for me. But I think that's quite enough about me just now. Let's go up to the Palmerston Room and see if anybody's there yet." She rose and moved away from the table, but then stopped, laid a hand on his arm, and stared at him with those clear gray eyes, candid as a child's. "I'm trusting you," she whispered. "You won't talk about it, will you?"

"No, Grace," he told her solemnly. As he followed her out of the dining room, he thought with some surprise, I simply don't believe that yarn. And he wondered what she had told Theodore.

There were only two persons in the Palmerston Room, Laura and Michael Seacombe, who were eating cold tongue and salad and looking cross.

"Don't tell me," said the Commodore. "You went up to the park and were rained off. So was our Pageant dress rehearsal, which was looking like hell anyhow. And the theater's badly down tonight. Any other bad news?"

"Yes," said Laura. "I'm in a bad temper. So is Michael. And Johnny Jolly and his awful blondie will be here any minute now, and they're in a bad temper too."

"And I hate this furniture-polish dressing they've put on the salad," said Michael, putting down his knife and fork. "I'm going to telephone a story. I'm probably wasting my time—but who cares?" He left them, without a smile for anybody.

Grace looked at Laura, who was still eating. "You're no more in love with that chap than I am," she said, rather sharply.

"Probably not," said Laura, who was curt but not unfriendly. "But I don't fancy that subject tonight. Tell me about the Pageant. How bad was it? And what have you arranged?"

There was time to discuss the Pageant and to drink some coffee before Johnny Jolly and his April, who had had to change, interrupted them.

"Now this time, let *me* talk," said April, who gave the impression that she had been arguing angrily for half an hour or so.

"Just a minute, just a minute, sweetheart," shouted Johnny.

"Now why? Just tell me why?"

"Because I say so, that's why. Because I can do the talking, that's why."

"Oh no," cried Laura. "Not again."

"Hold it, Johnny," said April. Then she went and stood over Laura. "Now look, Miss What's-it. Just tell me—once and for all—what you think gives you the right to be so snooty. Who are you? What have you done?"

"Take it easy, sweetheart," said Johnny.

"You shut up." She looked at Laura. "Go on. Tell me."

"I'm nobody," said Laura. "I haven't done anything. And I'm not snooty, as you call it."

"Of course you aren't," cried Grace indignantly.

"But I just can't bear these boring quarrels that you and your husband have in public as if—"

"Oy, oy!" cried Johnny. "Turn it up."

"And I should think so," cried April.

"Now that'll do," said the Commodore sharply. "I'll have no more of this. You asked Miss Casey some questions, April, and she answered you. Now let's drop it, and try to be friends. We're all disappointed and on edge—"

"Don't waste the big manly charm, Commodore," said April icily. "It worked this morning. But it won't work tonight, not after that wet graveyard. Contract or no contract, we're packing it up. Aren't we Johnny? Go on, you wanted to talk. Tell 'em."

"Johnny," that band leader announced, in quite a different tone from his usual one, very quiet, rather precise, "is now going down to the bar, where he wishes to be alone."

"No, Johnny!" his wife shouted in alarm. But Johnny stalked out. She burst into tears. "You can't do anything with him when he talks like that."

"I'll have a good try," said Grace surprisingly. "He's got such a nice band too, I've heard it. Leave him to me, dear." And she hurried out.

"Laura," said that young woman, getting up, "is now going home, and will insult anybody who tries to stop her. Goodnight."

"Goodnight," said the Commodore, feeling rather dazed. He stood looking hopelessly at April, who was struggling through her tears. "I wasn't nice to you, was I?" she said, trying to smile.

"No, you weren't. And I'm very disappointed in you, April. I've done my best for you all—"

She swayed forward, weeping afresh, and gently collapsed against him, so that he had to put an arm around her. And a moment later, before he had any chance to disentangle himself, an Easter Island statue, dressed in an old-fashioned dark suit, came clomping in, glared accusingly at the Commodore and the sobbing April, and said in an enormous and terrifying voice: "You are Commodore Tribe, Director of the Farbridge Festival?"

"Oh crumbs—what's this?" cried April, turning to stare at this astonishing new arrival.

"My name, sir, is Abel Stang," he intoned. "An old resident in this borough, a substantial ratepayer, well known in Methodist circles here and equally well known as an advocate of the Single Tax and the noble efforts of Henry George. I was told I would find you here, sir, and I have found you—*and* this unfortunate young woman."

"What d'yer mean—unfortunate young woman?" cried April, before the Commodore could say anything. "Listen—you've got the wrong idea—"

But she had no chance against Mr. Stang, whose voice could easily have cut in against the whole Jollyboys band. "Tonight for once I have visited a theater, to discover for myself what manner of entertainment you and your associates have provided for our thoughtless young people. And what I saw and heard tonight so disgusted and alarmed me that I rose in my seat to make a public protest and then left the building. Tonight I shall write a letter to the local newspaper, expressing myself with all the force at my command. The editor has not always printed my letters, but I imagine that on this occasion he will be glad to give my protest full publicity, as his paper, quite rightly in my opinion, has never supported your Festival." He stopped, and it was as if a full military band had triumphantly ended its concert.

"Mr.—er—Stang," said the Commodore, who now that he was no longer supporting April felt that he might be able to cope with this monster, "you're making a lot of noise."

"I'll say he is," said April. "He ought to be up in that park—him and a good drummer."

"I'm expressing my feelings, sir—"

"Yes, yes, yes," the Commodore shouted. "No doubt about that. But you're not the only person with feelings. Other people have 'em too."

"I'll say," cried April.

"Now, Mr. Stang," the Commodore continued, this time in a quiet reasonable tone, "what does all this amount to? You've been to the theater and seen a play you don't like—"

"Don't like?" thundered Stang. "I've not been so deeply shocked, so utterly revolted, for years, sir."

"And probably done you good too. You look to me like a man who could do with a shock or two, if I may say so. Well, you didn't like the play—I didn't care for it much myself, by the way—so you had to stand up and make a nuisance of yourself, after which you charge in here roaring and bellowing—"

Mr. Stang held up his hand, and a very heavy leathery sort of hand too. "And what did I see when I came in here?"

"Probably fifty naked dancing girls swooning among the wine and roses," said the Commodore. "That's where you fellows are luckier than most of us, who only see what's actually there. In this case, Mrs. Jolly, having a good cry on my shoulder because her husband's disappointed and angry, and myself—a harassed elderly man, sober and depressed, wondering how to make Farbridge enjoy itself. In addition—" he waved a hand towards the center table "—some portions of cold tongue and salad, with the wrong dressing on it, some empty coffee cups, and a few dregs—if the term doesn't flatter the stuff—of light ale. That is what's actually here," he cried, warming up, "but of course it won't do for you, who want something out of *Petronius Arbiter* or the unexpurgated *Arabian Nights*. No, Mr. Stang, that's only my little joke. But I hope you'll accept my assurance that this is a room used by a few hard-working conscientious entertainers who need some late refreshment, and that it's as harmless and respectable as a vestry."

"Well, Commodore Tribe," Stang rolled out with immense solemnity, "I wish to be just, to be fair, and I must confess that so far—"

It was then that the Palmerston Room was invaded. First came Seth and the waiter, carrying trays loaded with bottles and glasses. They were followed by Mobbs, who looked pickled, and Mrs. Hungerford and Archie Mossat, who were cheerfully screaming at each other. Philippa and the Group Captain came next, and they were all right, from a Stang point of view, except that she looked too ripe and blooming and he looked too happy. But then came Grace, who was clinging desperately to the arm of Johnny Jolly and dragging him with her, clearly because Johnny, already disheveled and goggle-eyed, was trying to stop and have it out with somebody behind him. And that somebody was Patrick Gorebarry, lit up like a Coronation Fleet, arm in arm with Lady Felicia, an exquisite reeling specter; and together they were singing with much feeling *I've Got You Under My Skin*.

"Why, darling," Lady Felicia screamed, pointing at Stang, frozen in an appalling Easter Island disapproval, "that's the man—I swear it is."

"My godfathers!" cried Mobbs. "So it is."

Gorebarry, turning himself at once into the tragedian, tottered a pace or two nearer Stang, lifted a trembling finger, and cried in a sepulchral tone:

> *Let's talk of graves, of worms, and epitaphs;*
> *Make dust our paper, and with rainy eyes*
> *Write sorrow on the bosom of the earth.*
> *Let's choose executors, and talk of wills . . .*

But then he made the mistake of venturing too near the outraged Stang, who, a true Ironside (and Capperton could have done with him at the Pageant), never hesitated to use force to defend himself against the unbeliever and the wine-bibber; and now the actor received a stout blow on the chest, which sent him reeling back against Lady Felicia, all too insecure herself, so that the pair of them went sprawling against Johnny Jolly, who was now struggling with both Grace and his wife; and then the place was a hideous pandemonium of misplaced arms and legs, shouts and screams, and the crash of breaking glass. From all of which, with the look of a man who had been right all the time, Mr. Abel Stang promptly retired.

"Well, old boy," said Mobbs who smelled like a bar parlor and looked like a small active volcano, "and how do you think the Festival's going?"

For once—and to the astonishment of Mobbs—the Commodore did not speak like a man and a brother; he snarled, like one of the Enemy: "The Festival be jammed and buttered!"

"Be what, old boy?"

"Anything you like," came the snarl. "Please yourself. But don't talk to me about it. I'm going to bed." And the Commodore stalked out, without a look, without another word to anybody.

6

Ever since that horrible Sunday, when they had the first meeting and the Commodore had announced that Theodore had gone, Laura had hated Festival Committee meetings, and always felt at her worst at them. Now, on Thursday afternoon, looking round the table in the Commodore's room, she told herself that this would probably be a particularly disagreeable meeting. It was not that anybody would try to be unpleasant, for now that Coverack had gone, they were all friendly; but the atmosphere, already heavy with disappointment, would be all wrong, and tempers—including her own, as she knew only too well—might easily be lost. They were all there—Mrs. Coote, Helen Weeks, Mr. Huntley, Councillor Gisburn, the Commodore, Mobbs—except old Mr. Jordan, for whom they had waited a quarter of an hour.

"Well," said the Commodore, rather wearily, "we'd better begin without Jordan. It's annoying because, frankly, I'd rather counted on his advice this afternoon. Perhaps he's losing interest in us."

"He could be," said Gisburn, who did not sound as loud and genial as he generally did. "I propose Mrs. Coote acts as chairman and we make a start."

"Capital," murmured Mr. Huntley, closing his eyes.

"Very well," said Mrs. Coote briskly. "Now tell us what's happening, Commodore. But first I think I ought to tell you that Councillor Gisburn and I don't feel very happy about the way things are going."

"That's right," said Gisburn, putting on a rather obstinate look, for which Laura felt like slapping him. She hoped that these two were not going to be official and pompous, so that instead of the usual informal talk there would be a lot of stuff about *agendas* and *proposals* and *amendments*.

"I'm not wildly happy either," said the Commodore, with a rather pathetic little smile that made Laura long to comfort the old scoundrel. "We've done our best here, but we can't work miracles. However, we can talk about that later. The position isn't as bad as I thought it was two days ago, but it isn't very grand. Miss Casey can give you the figures, if you want them when I've spoken my little piece. The Pageant opened last night, and there was a fair audience, about what we expected, and it was very well received. They rehearsed all day, and Capperton made a lot of useful cuts—"

"Absolutely first-class job, I thought," said Huntley, opening his eyes very wide as if he had just discovered how to work his eyelids properly.

"I'm sure he did," said Mrs. Coote. "It seemed all rather silly to me, last night, but people were liking it."

"Quite so," said the Commodore, rather dryly. "A pageant was insisted upon, you'll kindly remember, and there it is, and if it keeps fine tonight and tomorrow we may get larger attendances. Let's hope so. Next, the theater's been disappointing so far, I must confess, and unless it improves enormously we can lose money on our guarantee to the Mossat Company. Sorry, but there it is."

"Who fixed that lot?" Gisburn demanded.

"Actually, it was young Jenks, just before he left us," said the

Commodore. "But of course I accept full responsibility. It seemed an excellent chance—and the only one in sight—to bring a really good company here."

But he sounded too apologetic for Laura. "And so it was," she cried hastily. "I don't believe we've anything to be sorry about." And then, as several of them looked rather hard at her, she felt her cheeks burning. Defending Theodore now, was she?

"Maybe," said Gisburn. "But you can't blame people for not liking that play. I couldn't make any sense out of it, and neither could the wife, who's very fond of plays."

"Well," Laura began hotly, but was checked by the Commodore.

"They're playing *The Rivals* tonight," he said, "and *Twelfth Night* opens on Monday. And they've been considered good plays for quite some time now. I've still hopes of the Palace venture being a success. Our real failure so far has been the dancing in Mayton Park. The attendance on Monday was disappointing. Tuesday was a complete washout—heavy rain. Last night wasn't much better than Monday. And of course that means that the buffet's running at a bad loss." He hesitated.

Golly, thought Laura, this sounds dismal, and the poor Commodore's behaving as if a spring was broken somewhere inside him, as if he were only just another weary oldish man.

"Supposed to be a good band too," said Gisburn. "But I paid 'em a short visit last night, with the wife, and we both thought they all seemed down in the mouth."

"We can't call it off, I suppose?" said Mrs. Coote. "They have a contract."

"Yes, and don't forget we spent a lot of money up there, staging the dancing and putting up the café-buffet place." The Commodore hesitated again. "As a matter of fact, Johnny Jolly and his wife have been so depressed about the whole thing—and I'm hanged if I can blame 'em—that they were quite anxious to call it off, but I refused to let them go."

Mrs. Coote frowned at him, though not unpleasantly. "Do you think that was wise in the circumstances?"

"Exactly what I was wondering, Madam Chairman," Huntley murmured.

"Same here," said Gisburn.

"Yes," said the Commodore shortly.

"That's not telling us much," said Gisburn, clearly annoyed. "why was it?"

"Because, as I told you, we've already spent a lot of money in that confounded park." The Commodore spoke sharply, and came to life now, much to Laura's relief. "Because on Saturday we have a big gala and fête up there, which have already cost us a good deal, and we must have a band. Also, there's the ball tomorrow week. Now look here." And he sent a defiant glance round the table. "I thought we all agreed from the first that this Festival must be done as well as it could be done in a place this size, that if it meant taking risks— and obviously it did—then we must take those risks. And so I've taken them, and am still taking them."

"And I absolutely agree," cried Laura with some heat, although she suspected that the Commodore had gambled far more wildly than he should have done, and indeed she had warned him over and over again. "If people won't respond properly, that's not our fault."

"And I agree too," said Helen Weeks. "That was the policy of this Committee, and we can't turn round now and blame the organizers."

"Well," said Mrs. Coote slowly and dubiously. She looked at the Commodore. "Anything else?"

"The two exhibitions are just ticking over," said the Commodore, "but we needn't worry about them. Miss Casey has made herself responsible for the lectures, so she can tell you about yesterday's."

"It was Dan Cobbley," she told them, "on *Country Days and Ways,* and of course it was very popular because he's so well known on the air. It paid for itself, and everybody seemed to like it—except me. But then I think he's rather an old fraud, doing a character act. However, he filled the Library, and we've had about forty more bookings for all the other four lectures."

"What about the Fettercairn concerts?" Helen Weeks asked, carefully avoiding Laura's eye. "How are the bookings for them?"

"Not very good so far, I'm afraid," said Laura.

"I don't know what's the matter with people," cried Helen angrily. "If it had been a dance band, they'd have been screaming to hear it."

"Would they?" The Commodore was very dry. "We've a very

good dance band out at Mayton Park, and so far I haven't noticed any frantic rush to hear it."

"Perhaps we've been wrong about Farbridge people," said Laura, who felt less inclined than usual to keep quiet. "Perhaps the Tanheads and Mulefords and Coveracks and the local paper were right all the time."

"I won't accept that," said Mrs. Coote rather sharply. "Just remember this Festival was rather rushed, and people weren't given much time to think about it. And then again, perhaps you—we—haven't done enough to make them excited about it."

"Just what I've been thinking," said Gisburn promptly.

The Commodore emptied his pipe into the ashtray with unnecessary vigor. "First it's suggested we've been taking too many risks. And now, I gather, we may not have taken enough."

"No, no, Commodore, that's not fair," cried Mrs. Coote, but more in anger than in sorrow, with a dangerous sparkle in her eye.

Now we're off, Laura told herself, and wondered whether to jump in and create a diversion.

"What is it then that we haven't done that we ought to have done?" demanded the Commodore.

"If you ask me—nothing," said Mobbs stoutly.

"And I'll confess that I don't know," said Mrs. Coote.

"You thought you could do it properly in the time," said Gisburn, his obstinate look back again, "and we find you couldn't."

"Or we imagined people were alive here," Laura flashed at him, "and we were wrong."

"And if that's all you've got to say, Miss Casey," said Gisburn, really annoyed now, "you might as well keep quiet."

"Which, incidentally," said Mrs. Coote with a smile that did not take out all the sting, "is what you're supposed to do, Laura, unless asked to speak."

Hot-eyed in her humiliation, Laura half-rose from her chair. But the Commodore waved her down, and took charge of the situation.

"Madam Chairman," he said with grave formality, "please allow me to take this opportunity of saying that so far as it can be assumed that a Farbridge Festival exists, most of the credit belongs to Miss Casey, who has worked so hard and spared herself so little that she might be forgiven a spark or two of temper, particularly when the rest of us are far from being calm and reasonable." He looked round, gave them a grin. "You know, before I came to Far-bridge, I spent some months writing a lot of stuff, mostly rubbish, about foreign affairs. I hoped for a change of atmosphere. But—by George—I'm almost beginning to feel I'm back where I was. But—here's Mr. Jordan—at last."

"Sorry I'm late," said the old gentleman in his brisk staccato manner. "Meeting doesn't look too happy either. Tempers, eh? I know—disappointed. Feel it in the air." He did not accept the chair that Mobbs was offering him. "Been detained on Festival business, though. Decided you needed help. Um—um?" He gave them a beaky inquiring look. "Quite so. Do it in my own way, though. Old shopkeeper, you know. Fifty years of it. Artful. Know the public. Thanks, Captain Mobbs. Sit down a minute while I give you a short lecture. Don't interrupt, please. My turn."

He sat down, buried his sharp nose in an enormous red-and-yellow handkerchief and blew vigorously, and then chuckled a bit. Whatever he chose to do or say now, Laura felt grateful to him, for he had changed the atmosphere of the meeting.

"Most of the time people behave like a lot of jackasses," he began. "And worse now than they used to be. Less individuality. More crowd mentality. Eh? Quite so. That being so, my friends, let me tell you why so far we're not succeeding. Been discussing that, haven't you? See it in your faces. No result too. Well, we're not succeeding just because we're not succeeding." He stopped, looked at them.

"I don't get it, Mr. Jordan," said Gisburn.

"We live in an internal-combustion-engine world," old Jordan continued, stroking his beard. "Engine hard to start, won't move at first. Then once it starts, it'll go faster and faster. People like that now. Internal-combustion jackasses. So what have I done? Spent this morning for once in my store. Closed this afternoon. Arranged for a lot of young people to buy tickets. One ticket at a time, then back in queue. Priming pump. Start demand. Big queue —must join it, that's how they think now. Not only that. Had to make arrangements this end. Artificially cut down supply. Further bookings refused for this evening or that. Large notices saying SOLD OUT. Both ladies downstairs to be haughty and difficult. Every ticket now a favor. Had them told at theater, Corn Exchange, every-where. Now come and have a look."

They all crowded into the bay window with him. There was a

queue, three or four deep, extending fifty yards down High Street. Old Jordan chortled at their astonishment. "Some of 'em my people, of course. Going round and round. But already most of 'em genuine new customers. All cylinders firing. Success succeeding. Come away, come away, mustn't see us. We don't care. Sold out. Take it or leave it."

"Mr. Jordan," cried Laura, "you're heaven."

"Nonsense. Tall fair young man with dark eyes your heaven. And time you told him so. Now then." They did not sit down again but stood about listening eagerly to him. "First think. At five o'clock sharp we sell no more tickets but bolt the door in their faces. No matter if the queue's half a mile long."

"Oh, but surely," Mrs. Coote began; but he cut her short.

"No, Mrs. Coote, we do it my way. All those people who are turned away will come back. Bring others with 'em. Last chance. Tickets by hook or crook. You'll see. Second thing. Mayton Park. It'll be fine tonight. Crowd from Jordan's going. Hookwood and Group Captain Trevone sending in their employees in special buses. Seth Hull's sending a lot of young men. All arranged. And at a certain time we turn away all newcomers. No, no, too late, too late!"

"It might work, you know," cried Helen Weeks.

"My dear young lady, no *might* about it. Guarantee it. By Saturday engine running as fast as you like. Full speed all next week. But no interference downstairs, please. Leave it to me. Artful old man. And run away, all of you. Off you go."

Laura told her father all about it, later that afternoon, when they were having tea at the White Hart. He had returned from London by the afternoon train, and this time she had been able to get him into the White Hart, by asking Seth to offer her any bedroom that might unexpectedly fall vacant. "I don't know whether heavenly old Jordan has saved the Festival—though there was an enormous queue when I left—but he certainly saved our meeting, where we were all losing our tempers. Though the Commodore was angelic about me, when I was suddenly ticked off for talking at all. But the last two or three days do seem to have got him down rather, as if he'd lost nearly all his bounce and cheerful impudence."

"He's not young, you know," said her father. "And we lose our resilience. Like old indiarubber."

"I have an idea," she went on slowly, "that he's spent—or committed us to spend—even more than he'll admit. But on what, I can't imagine."

"Is there anything he's handled entirely by himself?"

"I can't thing of anything." She stared into her cup for a moment or two. "Except fireworks. He did the fireworks entirely by himself. I never even saw the man they sent. Dad, it couldn't be fireworks, could it?" She was very solemn.

Her father roared with laugher. "I'll bet it is. I know it would be with me. Of course—fireworks. What a glorious opportunity! Look —Laura—isn't he sitting over there with Miss Hookwood and that other older woman? Catch his eye, my dear, and bring him here. Fireworks!" And he began laughing again.

But when the Commodore joined them, Mr. Casey looked quite serious. "Commodore," he said gravely, "there's a question Laura and I would like to put to you, if you don't mind. You don't? Good!" He leaned forward and whispered: "How much have you spent on fireworks?"

The Commodore adopted the same confidential manner. "I don't quite know the figure yet," he muttered, carefully not looking at Laura, "but a devil of a lot. In fact, far too much. They sent a most persuasive fellow with a wonderful catalogue, and I'm afraid I let myself go."

"Well, really!" cried Laura, vexed.

"Dozens and dozens of everything?" said her father. "Rockets? Huge Catherine wheels? Giant Roman candles?"

"Yes, of course," said the Commodore. "But that's just the beginning. I've got things you've never heard of, my dear fellow—colossal things."

"I envy you, Commodore, I envy you."

"But you'll be there on Saturday night?"

"I couldn't be stopped."

And then both of them were roaring with laughter, so that people were staring at them.

"It's not funny," said Laura severely, "and you're like a pair of idiotic schoolboys. And don't you realize we may be ruined by this firework silliness?"

"Of course I do," said the Commodore. "But I just couldn't resist it."

"And it's just what I'd have done," cried Laura's father.

And off they went again, two sixty-year-olds rocking and roaring over their wretched fireworks, and now Laura had to laugh too, though she still protested as she laughed.

"My dear Casey," said the Commodore, preparing to leave them, "I must tell you that you're a man after my own heart."

"And the same to you, Commodore. The very same to you. And I'd have done it myself—like a shot."

"Well, see you both at the theater," said the Commodore. "By the way, Laura, I gather from Philippa Hookwood that you may have a surprise tonight. No, no, you must wait."

"I'm looking forward to *The Rivals*," said Mr. Casey. "Old favorite of mine. What about your leading man? Will he be drunk again?"

"Apparently not. Miss Hookwood says they've kept him rehearsing too hard. He's playing Faulkland, not Captain Absolute as they originally planned, so they've kept him at it. Well, we'll see."

When they arrived at the theater, it looked even livelier than it had done on Monday night, and Laura felt immensely relieved, ready now to enjoy herself. For, try as she would, it was hard not to feel responsible all the time for this blinking Festival.

"Good evening, Miss Casey. Good evening, sir," cried Mr. Fotheringay, the manager, who was standing in the foyer, rubbing his hands. His shirtfront was dazzling white; his hair and mustache were a fine midnight blue. "Wonderful business tonight. Very big attraction. Yes, madam?" And he turned away, delighted to be badgered.

"You wouldn't know him for the same chap," said Mobbs, who had come up with Maggie. "Used to get me down just to look at him. Made you feel they'd dug him up just in time for the First House."

"Now you stop it, Archie," cried Maggie, who was wearing her flowered dress again and somehow reminded Laura of a Harvest Thanksgiving.

"If those two marry," Laura said to her father as they found their seats, "it'll be like roast pork marrying a lovely plum pudding."

"There's nothing wrong with that," he told her. Then he waited a moment. "By the way, what about you?"

"Not now, Dad, please. Let me enjoy myself."

The orchestra was playing some sort of eighteenth-century jig, which began to die away as the house lights faded and the magical golden glow illuminated the fringe of the curtains. Then the curtains had gone, and they were looking at a sketchy kind of street in Bath. There, shambling about very uncertainly, was a fantastic figure, a huge bewigged coachman, at whom Laura stared in astonishment and a wild wonder. No, surely it couldn't be! On came neat little Fag, crying: "What—Thomas—Sure 'tis he—What—Thomas—Thomas!" To which the strange coachman, after a pause and an audible gulp, replied in a hoarse strained voice: "Hey! Odds life, Mr. Fag, give us your—er—your hand, my old—er—fellow servant." And Laura did not know whether to laugh or to cry. For now she knew that peering unhappily beneath that wig was Theodore Jenks.

The old comedy went off like one of the Commodore's most extravagant rockets. Gorebarry was magnificent as the self-tormenting Faulkland; Philippa was a stately Julia, Clare Chesbey a charmingly silly Lydia Languish, and Archie Mossat a genial tornado of a Sir Anthony; and if Acres and Sir Lucius O'Trigger and Mrs. Malaprop were not as funny as they thought they were, or as young Dick Sheridan hoped they would be, they did well enough; and altogether the piece rollicked along, and the audience loved it. Laura would have enjoyed it more if she had known the text of the play, for she kept hoping for—and yet dreading—the reappearance of Theodore as Thomas the coachman; and when he never returned, not even at the final curtain, she did not know whether to be glad or sorry. But when it was all over and Gorebarry and Mossat had made speeches and the company had taken its last bow, she felt in a state of happy excitement, and better than she had felt for weeks and weeks.

"A good evening," said her father, who was taking her to the Palmerston Room for some supper. "It may not be as clever as *The School for Scandal*, but I've always preferred *The Rivals*. There's a freshness about it, a rush of young high spirits, that the other play hasn't got. And what a tremendous acting part Faulkland is, when it's properly tackled! I must say that Gorebarry, drunk or sober, was superb."

"Yes, he was," said Laura. "But in a way, more tragic than funny. I felt desperately sorry for him, torturing himself like that. But I suppose we all do sometimes."

"Oh yes," said her father, rather dryly, "it happens. Possibly even now. Or would you say—not now?"

"No, I wouldn't. And you know jolly well I wouldn't. Next subject. I wonder how the other Festival things have gone tonight?"

They soon learned, in a Palmerston Room that had a new atmosphere, that the Pageant had done very well and that there was quite a large crowd, both dancing and listening-and-looking, out at Mayton Park. It may have been the better weather, or some of old Jordan's artful devices, or the fact that it was now Thursday of the First Week; but it seemed certain now that the Festival had turned a corner. Laura ate heartily, drank some claret her father had ordered, and then went from group to group, being gay and rather silly, hardly knowing what she was saying because she was so impatient for the theater people to arrive. For though Theodore was not staying at the White Hart, she felt sure he would come along to the Palmerston Room tonight. Then, at last, she saw Gorebarry, Clare Chesbey, Mossat and Mrs. Hungerford, and Philippa Hookwood with her Group Captain. After the least possible decent interval, she worked her way round to Miss Hookwood, congratulating her on her performance.

"And I must say," she cried gaily, after a minute or two, "I was absolutely staggered when I saw Theodore Jenks as that coachman. I must tell him so—he's somewhere about, I suppose."

Philippa, with a quick touch on the arm, contrived to turn her aside, away from the noisy group. "I'm afraid he isn't tonight, my dear," she said quietly. "He's dashing—or has already dashed—up to Town as he hasn't to rehearse tomorrow. Something about arranging his air passage to Singapore, because he wants to go back as soon as we've finished. Oh—I'm sorry." But Laura had gone.

"Where's that daughter of mine, Miss Hookwood?" Mr. Casey asked, a few minutes later. "I thought she was talking to you."

"She was, Mr. Casey." And Philippa told him what had happened. "And she didn't give me a chance to say something I've been wanting to say to her for several days, ever since Monday, in fact, when poor Theodore said something very significant to me."

"What's that boy like?"

"He's a darling. And you'll simply have to do something about those two, who are behaving like idiots."

"I start tomorrow," said Mr. Casey firmly. "Though how or where, I'm not sure."

"The Bulfoss party, after the show tomorrow night," said Philippa. "You make certain that Laura's there, and I'll guarantee poor Theodore, even if my Trevy has to hit him with a blunt instrument and drag him there."

In the end house in Alma Street, Ernest and Hilda Saxon, triumphant after a successful evening respectively as a spectacled Ironside General and a Mother with a Son at Trafalgar, were finishing a modest supper of wholemeal bread, processed cheese, and cocoa, accompanied by Monteverde on the Third Program, when there flashed through the sitting room, like a distressed little comet, the figure of Miss Laura Casey declaring that she wanted nothing but her bed. When it had vanished, Hilda looked at Ernest, who returned her look anxiously through his spectacles, which were already beginning to have something vaguely Ironside about them. "Upset again, I'm afraid," he said. "Not good enough, you know, really not good enough."

"I'd like," Hilda declared, to his astonishment (he overlooked the Trafalgar influence), "I'd like to take one or two of those young men —and—and box their big fat ears."

7

The Commodore strolled into his office at the Festival Center, on Friday morning, humming *Tell Me, Pretty Maiden.* There he found Mobbs waiting for him. "Message from Laura, old boy, saying she's not feeling very bright this morning, but hopes to be along later. So I wondered if there was anything I could do."

"Sure to be, Archie, sure to be," cried the Commodore cheerfully, picking up his letters. "Notice the people down below—queue already. Old Jordan was quite right. Notice the weather—pure gold. My boy, our troubles are over. From now on, we enjoy ourselves. Except, if Laura's off, you'll have to look after our today's lecturer, Miss Lily Fawcitt, who is to talk to us—though not to me, if I can help it—on *Beautiful Speech.* Otherwise, the prospect is bright. Ah—what's this? Mr. Watchbold would like to have a word with me at the Bank. That, perhaps, isn't so good. Nevertheless, this morning I feel I could cope with a dozen Watchbolds. You'd better come along with me, Archie."

After a little delay, they were admitted into the presence of Mr. Watchbold, who had to be convinced that the Director of the Farbridge Festival had no secrets from his Social Organizer, Captain Mobbs. The bank manager was a fat, pasty-faced man with a mustache that looked false and a hearty genial manner that certainly was false. "Sorry to have dragged you here," he cried, laughing merrily. "I know you're a busy man these days, Commodore. But then we're all busy men, aren't we? Ha ha ha!"

"Ha ha ha!" went the Commodore and Mobbs, though they had not quite the trick of it.

"Just a little formality really," Mr. Watchbold continued, almost bursting with merriment. "But I thought you'd want to know that your account is drawn as far as we can go, so that unless you make a further and substantial payment into the account, we can't undertake to meet any drafts upon it—um? Ha ha ha!"

"Ha ha ha!" the other two tried, but without gusto.

"And so, gentlemen," Mr. Watchbold went on, as if he were running a game at a children's party, "please don't write any large checks until you've let us have five hundred or so—or shall we say a thousand, just to be on the safe side—um?—ha ha ha! And that's all, I think. Festival going well?"

"Terrific, old boy," said Mobbs.

"A gigantic success," cried the Commodore. "Ha ha ha!"

"Capital, capital!" said Mr. Watchbold, holding out a hand that looked rather like a large helping of boiled apple pudding. "Then it's simply a matter of being a little brisker on your financial side—um?"

"That's all it is," said the Commodore. "The money's there, of course. Ha ha ha!"

"Of course, of course. Ha ha ha! Well, good morning, gentlemen, *good* morning."

"Ten to one," said Mobbs as soon as they were outside, "he's been got at. He's very thick with Whatmore and Crandry."

"Just a big merry rat, no doubt," said the Commodore, rather dreamily. "But his ultimatum doesn't worry me. We can get along nicely until Monday, by which time we shall have plenty of money to pay in. Let's forget him." They had now turned into a short narrow street that was unfamiliar to him, probably Early Victorian, with some pleasant old shops in it, a secondhand bookseller's, a watchmaker's, a seedsman's, an old-fashioned tobacconist's, all trim, if a trifle sleepy, in the sunlight of the late May morning. The Commodore glanced about him appreciatively. "Nice little street this, Archie. Don't remember noticing it before. I suppose keeping a shop here would be damned dull, but probably somebody could persuade me to chance it, this morning."

"I had a good look at the Three Black Boys property the other morning," said Mobbs. "And you were quite right, old boy. That's it. And what a hope!"

"Yes, but let's keep it in mind. Fix it firmly there. After all," the Commodore went on, half-serious, half idly humorous, "even your Fairy Godmother can't give you what you want if she doesn't know, just because you don't know, what you want. People forget that. So let's concentrate on the Three Black Boys, Archie. And never mind about Watchbold, Crandry, Whatmore, Coverack, and all the forces of darkness, my boy. Our Festival's in full swing."

Not long after they were back in the Commodore's office, a Mr. Atcham, from the company that was supplying the fireworks, was announced. He was quite different from the genial and enthusiastic salesman who had conjured such a magnificent order from the Commodore. Mr. Atcham was a small clerkly sort of man, who had one real and very busy little eye, and a glass eye that was fixed in a perpetual blue glare of indignation. The effect was disturbing, rather sinister. It was as if the busy little real eye was forever reporting, unfavorably too, to the indignant glass eye. The Commodore guessed at once that no good would come of this interview. However, he assumed a confident jovial air.

"Well, Mr. Atcham, I hope you've come to tell me that your people are now making their preparations here for a magnificent display tomorrow night."

"I have, Commodore Tribe," said Mr. Atcham very carefully and with a tiny smile. "And one of our best men is in charge. I need hardly add that we've given your order our very best attention."

"Splendid, splendid," cried the Commodore, looking at the glass eye and then hastily switching to the other. "We're having a very successful Festival, but I believe the fireworks will be my favorite item in our program."

"The same here, old boy," said Mobbs. "Always been fond of a good firework display."

"You will not be disappointed," Mr. Atcham assured him gravely.

So far, so good. The Commodore, shrinking a little from Mr. Atcham's blue glare, began to look like a busy man, poking his letters about. This move was not lost on the little busy eye.

"I have the bill here," said Mr. Atcham, producing a formidable document, "and it includes everything except a few minor expenses, which can be settled later."

"Yes, well, of course we'll settle the whole thing shortly," said the Commodore, accepting the bill with a fine careless air, not even glancing at it.

"I should like your check in settlement today, if possible," Mr. Atcham continued, as if the Commodore had not spoken. "But if that's not convenient—"

"And I'm afraid it isn't." The Commodore cut in like lightning.

"Then I must have it in the morning in time to clear it before the Bank closes. Saturday hours, of course."

The Commodore stared at him rather haughtily. "I'm afraid I don't understand. This isn't a private transaction, you know, Mr. Atcham. Your fireworks have been bought by the Farbridge Festival Committee."

"I'm quite aware of that, sir. And no offense intended, naturally. But we have a very strict rule that our accounts must be settled and customers' checks cleared before the display. Fireworks aren't like most other goods. Once they've been let off, we can't take them back. So we have this rule. A mere matter of form so far as a civic concern like yours is concerned—"

"Oh—quite—quite," cried the Commodore carelessly.

"Quite," said Mobbs, who liked to make some contribution.

"But do you mean to tell me," said the Commodore, avoiding that fixed indignant glare, "that if by any chance you hadn't cleared our check by tomorrow noon, there'd be no display tomorrow night?"

"That is our rule, Mr.—er—Commodore Tribe."

"Laughable," said the Commodore. "Don't you think so, Captain Mobbs?"

"I go one better, old—er—Commodore," said Mobbs. "It's potty." Mr. Atcham made no reply to this but simply kept the sinister eye effect working hard.

"Still, there it is," said the Commodore, waving a hand. "Now then, Captain Mobbs, what about Miss Casey?"

"Not here, and may be away all day."

"What a nuisance!" The Commodore looked at Mr. Atcham's busy eye. "Miss Casey is my chief assistant and looks after finance. I *could* give you a check, of course, but the way we do things here it might lead to a dreadful muddle, and my Committee might be annoyed. What do you suggest, Mr. Atcham?"

"It's not for me to suggest anything," said Mr. Atcham rising.

"You know your own arrangements. I'm sorry to cause you any inconvenience. But I must assure you, sir, that I can't possibly break our rule. Which is—no payment, no firework display. I'll call again this afternoon." And he seemed to walk out rather like a cat.

"Bit of a teaser, old boy, isn't it?"

"A teaser? My dear chap, it's a thunderbolt. This bill is for about eight hundred pounds, and unless it's paid by noon tomorrow there'll be no fireworks at the Gala—except for us."

"My godfathers! But did you say eight hundred—"

"Never mind about that. I thought I'd do the thing well. And the damnable irony of the whole business is that we'll probably have a whale of a crowd there tomorrow night, and money to burn, but no fireworks to burn. Now, Archie, think—think hard."

"I am thinking hard, old boy. But eight—"

"Stop that. Be bold, creative, ingenious. Don't let's waste time and energy on mere negative emotions." And then the Commodore let out a howl of dismay. "I've just remembered. Old Jordan's gone away until tomorrow night. Grace has gone off for the day again, though whether she really has a lot of money or is just romancing is an open question. Now who else has any money?"

"Young Jenks? But he's away until late this afternoon."

"There must be somebody."

"All the people with money here are against us, old boy. And you heard Watchbold at the Bank—"

"Yes, yes, of course I did," cried the Commodore impatiently. "Sorry, Archie, but let's think." So they thought, the Commodore pacing the room, and Mobbs patting his fat little thighs.

"I suppose," said Mobbs slowly, after several minutes of thigh patting, "we couldn't let him have a check tomorrow morning, make some mistake in it—"

"I've thought of that," the Commodore cut in. "But if he gets to the Bank, they'll tell him we've no funds, and we're sunk. If he spots the mistake, comes back and can't find us in time, then he hasn't cleared the check—and there'll be no fireworks."

"Laura's father—what about him?"

"Probably hasn't the money on tap—how could he have? Though I wouldn't mind telling him. He's a nice fellow, no fool, and likes fireworks. We'll bear him in mind—"

And then A. Smith of London walked in, with the eternal half-cigarette smoldering under his long nose. "If intruding, say the word."

"Consider it said," the Commodore told him sharply.

"I bought it," said Smith, turning away.

"Just a minute," cried the Commodore. "Come back, Smith. I wasn't thinking when I spoke before. I want to talk to you." He turned to Mobbs. "Archie, it might be better if you don't hear this. And anyhow you might try to find Mr. Casey, tell him frankly what we're up against, and see if he has any ideas."

"Righto, old boy." And Mobbs bounced out while Smith sidled farther in, looking rather like an anteater on the prowl.

"Sit down," said the Commodore. He waited a moment or two, then said sharply: "What about Mr. Gruberlin?"

"Mr. Who?"

"Gruberlin."

Smith shook his head. "Sorry. Never heard of him. Good memory too. You'd be surprised."

The Commodore felt certain that Smith was telling the truth. Now he tried again. "Your subject or party or whatever you call her has gone out for the day again, hasn't she?"

"That's right," said Smith. "With me left behind here. Looks silly, doesn't it?"

"Why don't you tell her cousin that he's wasting your time and his money?"

"Cousin? What cousin?"

"He's your client, isn't he?"

"No cousin comes into it," said Smith. "Likewise, no Mr. Gruberlin. She's been telling you the tale, Commodore. Warned you she was a liar, didn't I? Better change the subject. Looked in to see if there was any little job I might do for you. On the side, of course. Unofficial. Like we said, the other day."

"There might be something," said the Commodore slowly. "In strict confidence. Festival business." And he explained about Mr. Atcham and the fireworks.

"I got it," said Smith. "Nifty little problem too. And down my street. But I want two quid as a retainer. He waited until the Commodore rather reluctantly handed over two pound notes. "Ta, muchly. Now to work. And notice the professional touch. Point One. Fireworks are here, and they'll get 'em ready 'cos they're expecting the money. Oke. Point Two. Does their foreman wait till he gets the all clear from this Atcham? Or does he go an' let 'em off unless Atcham goes an' stops him? Which I think is more likely. About three to one on."

"Well, I don't know," said the Commodore rather impatiently.

"Never said you did," Smith went on, unperturbed. "Leave it to me. I'll find out. That's where the professional touch comes in. Now if they let 'em off unless Atcham stops 'em, we can work it. But if it comes off, I want twenty quid. Festival exes. Professional services. But unless you promise me that twenty, I say no more."

"All right. We pay you twenty pounds if your plan works. That's a promise. Now what do you suggest?"

"He comes in the morning for his check. You give it to him. You get a receipt. That's to show the foreman, if he's fly. We tell him we don't know where Atcham is, but here's the receipt all okay. Call that Point Three—Point Two B, if you like."

"Don't be so damned pedantic, Smith. Never mind what point it is. What about Atcham? We can't let him take that check to the Bank."

"Now, now, Commodore. You're not talking to your little fat chum." Smith was genuinely indignant. "Even the real wide boys say I know my business. Of course we can't let him go to the Bank. As soon as he gives you that receipt, something happens. Say he has to get out of the way—quick. He's locked in a big cupboard or a little room. Want a nice set-up, of course. And then you forget to let him out till all those rockets are up in the air. What can he do? You forgot— that's all. You've paid him for his fireworks. Got his receipt. He can take the check round on Monday. You were doing your best for him. He might have been attacked by toughs or a dangerous lunatic. There could even be a drink or two and some grub in the room he's locked in. Might even be something in the drink that gives him a nice long nap. Only you want the right set-up. No easy windows. What about the back room here? Better have a decko."

"You know, Smith," said the Commodore, whose grin had been broadening, "there's rather more in you than meets the eye."

"That's right. Heard that before. This Atcham bloke—would he be the sort who'd take a drink in the morning, when you'd given him his check?"

"No, not that type, I'd say. A quick cup of tea perhaps," said the Commodore. "Or coffee."

"Not easy then. Better leave him something in the room. You say he's coming this afternoon? I'll take a peep at him."

"But then you say *something happens* while he's here tomorrow—"

"Leave that, leave that," said Smith hastily. "Give me time to work out something juicy. And I'm in charge—see? No amachure interference, chum."

"No, no. I've every confidence in you now, Smith," said the Commodore, giving him a winning smile. "By the way, you wouldn't like to tell me why you're following my friend Grace—um?"

Smith winked. "It might spoil it for you, cocky. You're happy. She's happy. And I'm happy. So leave it. And let me get on with this firework job. Very tasty."

8

Although Theodore made only one brief appearance in *The Rivals*, as Thomas the coachman in the opening scene with Fag, he was kept very busy helping George during the rest of the performance, which made heavy demands on the stage management. So on Friday evening he had little time in which to brood upon his private life, especially as Gorebarry, who had been cold sober the night before, when he opened anxiously as Faulkland, was now taking to the bottle again and had to be watched and coaxed. Moreover, the midnight dash to London, the early and hasty visit to the B.O.A.C. office, the heavy-eyed return journey on the lunch train, had left Theodore feeling rather weary. And also somewhat foolish, because the visit to London had not been really necessary, as he knew very well; it had been merely one of those impetuous and quite senseless moves that young men in his state of mind make as a kind of idiotic protest, a gesture of defiance at the rational world. So the less said about it, the better; and all Theodore wanted to do, after *The Rivals* had been put to bed for the night, was to slink away and put himself to bed, regretting not for the first time his impulsive decision to assist the Mossat Repertory Company at Farbridge.

So he said to Philippa Hookwood: "I'm sorry, but I don't want to go. I'm tired. And I don't particularly care for those Bulfoss people."

"But, darling Theodore," she protested, still an exquisite eighteenth-century lady, "I definitely promised you would, last night, and you can't let me down now. Can he, Trevy?" For, the play being over, the Group Captain had now loomed up, massive and beaming, and apparently quite indifferent to light industry production in Brant-in-the-Hollow. "Look, you tell him, darling. I must fly."

"Absolute fact, Jenks, old man," said the Group Captain. "She definitely promised you'd be there. Can't let her down. A lot of these frippets don't care what they've promised, but Phil's different. Keeps her word every time." He laid a heavy hand on Theodore's shoulder, almost as if arresting him.

It was no use pointing out to anybody in the Group Captain's infatuated and bemused condition that it was Philippa Hookwood and not Theodore Jenks, longing for solitude and bed, who had done the promising. It was so useless, in fact, that Theodore had to laugh. "All right, I'll come along, though I shan't stay."

"Nice work. You come with Phil and Gorebarry and me in my car. You might hurry him up, Jenks, old man. He's inclined to linger in his dressing room with a few admirers and a bot. Get him cracking while I do a steady knock-knock on Phil's door. Incidentally," the Group Captain added, with a huge hard grip on Theodore's forearm, "take my advice—pick the right frippet and get yourself tied up to her—and you're skating two miles high with a full band."

So they went roaring out to Mayton Park Avenue in the Group Captain's car, with Theodore and Pat Gorebarry packed uncomfortably among mysterious hard objects in the back seat. "Machine parts is my guess," said Gorebarry, who had now arrived at the stage where he never stopped talking. "Probably covering us with oil. And nothing this side that feels like a bottle, unfortunately. However, it's just occurred to me that I'm on my way to meet my charming little Madge again. I've missed her. Or have I? Not a clever woman—if you like clever women—though there's a kind of permanent wit about that tiny nose of hers. Husband—the majah—is a dull dog, but hospitable, I imagine, willing to open a bottle or two. What do you think, Theo, my lad?"

"I'm not thinking," said Theodore, and yawned to prove it.

The Bulfoss hall had been cleared up and was brilliant with lights and flowers. Their little party made an impressive entrance into it. "Major Bulfoss," cried Gorebarry, shaking the limp hand with extravagant warmth, "what a pleasure this is—to see you in your delightful house! And Madge—my dear Madge—" he seized both her hands and held them wide apart "—how beautiful you're looking for us! Never wear anything else but this—whatever it is. But I'm feeling desperately cold after that brute of an open car. A little brandy, perhaps? Good, good!" He turned her round deftly, tucked her left hand under his right arm, and led her, blushing, toward the nearest table. "How gay everybody seems! The Farbridge Festival is a success? Of course it must be. Commodore, your servant, sir. Odds borough and arts councils!—but I think we're taking the town, sir."

And then Theodore found himself confronted by the short elderly man with the brown face and sharp eyes. This time there was no possible escape. "Mr. Jenks, come with me. I want to talk to you." He guided Theodore to a small shabby study, which was empty. He locked them in, looked hard at Theodore, and said: "I tried to get hold of you on Monday."

"I know you did."

"Well, do you know who I am?"

"Scotland Yard?"

"What a dam' silly idea!" cried the elderly man testily. "You ought to know better than that. They're big fellows in rather tight blue suits. No resemblance. My name's Casey. I'm Laura's father."

"Good lord!" Theodore gaped at him. "But why didn't you tell me?"

"Never gave me a chance. What's this Scotland Yard nonsense? Not wanted by the police, are you?"

"Probably not. You see—"

"No, some other time, then. Sit down. You're too big to stand there. Now then," said Mr. Casey sharply, "I'm going to ask some questions. Don't tell me to mind my own business. I never do, and anyhow this *is* my business. Why did you leave this place some weeks ago?"

"Chiefly because of Laura," Theodore mumbled, very red and staring hard at the photograph of some bewhiskered Bulfoss. "I only stayed in the first place to be near her. Then I felt she wasn't really interested. She was very thick with Seacombe. She didn't keep the appointment we had in London. She snubbed me next time we met. And—"

"Fiddledy-diddledy-dee! Why did you come back then for this Festival? You're no actor."

"Because I was a fool. I couldn't stay away."

"That's better. Now you're talking sense, my boy."

Theodore looked at him. "What's the point of all this?"

There was a knock at the door, and Mr. Casey told it severely to go away. "What were we saying? Oh—the point."

"Yes. She's engaged to Seacombe."

"Nothing of the kind. All off. Never was on, really. Lot of nonsense. Can't you see something I spotted at once, four thousand miles away? She's in love with you."

Theodore shot up from his chair and brought down a pile of Tory pamphlets. "Are you sure? Has she told you? Where is she? Is she here?"

"Wait a minute. I didn't say I was in love with you, and there are several questions—"

"Some other time, Mr. Casey, please. They'll keep, like my police story."

"Now I think of it, so they will. Wait here—keep the door locked— and I'll send her along."

"Perhaps she won't come."

"Don't start that nonsense again. Of course she will. But guard the door."

Several years, lit with wonder, dark with despair, shining with hope, appeared to pass. And then she was there, looking uncertainly at him, strained and rather white-faced, blinking, quivering about the lips, hardly pretty—but the dark little darling of all time. And he made some daft hoarse noise, moved, blindly clutched, and there she was, where she ought to have been weeks ago, in his huge enraptured arms. And several more years, crammed with rockets, champagne fountains, moons, bursting stars, and a salty flavor of wet cheeks, appeared to pass.

Then, because they had forgotten to lock the door, Major Bulfoss and Mr. Hatchet-Ferrers walked in, carrying a bottle of whisky, a siphon of soda, glasses, and a plate of sandwiches. The lovers sprang apart. Major Bulfoss was purple with indignation, and Mr. Hatchet-Ferrers whiter than usual with it.

"A howling cad, that's all he is," said Major Bulfoss. "And why Madge can't see it beats me." He was now busy with the whisky. "Soda, Arthur?"

"Not too much, Gerald," said Hatchet-Ferrers gravely, staring at the glass through his enormous spectacles, pure Humpty-Dumpty. "And you're right, of course. The worst type of theatrical mountebank. I saw it at a glance. I must say I feel most bitterly hurt. It was a profound nervous shock for which I shall probably pay dearly. I have to be careful, you know, Gerald."

"I know you have, old man."

"Your health, Gerald."

"Cheers, Arthur," said Major Bulfoss. They were in such a close huddle over the whisky that apparently Laura and Theodore did not exist for them. "A fellow of your type—" the Major continued "—well, I could understand the attraction—"

The lovers began to edge away.

"Exactly what I was about to say myself," said Hatchet-Ferrers solemnly. "I mean as regards yourself—a solid public man, and a gentleman, whom any sensible woman would appreciate. But this posturing buffoon, half-drunk, still reeking of grease paint—bah!"

"Let's go," Laura whispered.

"Outside," Theodore muttered. "Not back to the party, please, Laura."

"No, darling." And they fled, and as they went, hand in hand, she cried: "You know, I've always wanted to hear somebody say *Bah*. And now I've heard it. Everything's happening tonight." And there went flashing through the hall, through the chatter and gossip and grumbling, like a strange glittering bird down some back street, that rare sound, a voice bubbling with happiness.

"Party or no party, old man," said Major Bulfoss, "I'm half-inclined to kick him out."

Hatchet-Ferrers winced at this suggestion of violence, his cheeks like junket in an earthquake region. "I sympathize, my dear Gerald, but I think that would be a wrong move. You know what I think about the fellow—but—to create a scene—no, I don't advise it."

"You may be right, old man," said the Major gloomily. "Possibly playing right into his hands—what?"

"They're here." And the voice from the doorway brought them round sharply. "Why, hearts—and golden lads," continued Gorebarry, entering with Mrs. Bulfoss upon his arm, "how is it with you?"

"Now come along, you two," said Madge, flushed and giggling happily, "let's all have lovely fun."

"I must say," said Hatchet-Ferrers bitterly, focusing his giant spectacles upon the pink tip of her nose, "I'm most disappointed, and after an unusually tiring journey too."

"A bit thick," the Major growled, glaring at Gorebarry.

"Now don't be silly, you two," cried Madge.

Gorebarry came out of a dream, to reproach them in his richest tones. "Lads, lads, you're dry and in a sad humor. Brace up, and cheerily now, my boys! Especially you, my noble heart—Arthur, first in the field though not in tournament, or words to that effect. Come, Arthur!" And he tried to pat Arthur's shoulder with a hand that still held a glass, with the result that a generous helping of brandy went over Arthur's collar and down his neck.

"Stupid idiot!" cried Hatchet-Ferrers in an astonishing high soprano, and then hurriedly waddled out like a hunted duck.

"Look to your fat white friend, my dear Major," said Gorebarry earnestly. "I think he needs you. Any brandy in here? We're all a cup too low."

The party was now at its height. Some of the younger Mayton Park set, together with Philippa and the Group Captain, Clare Chesbey and the actor with butter-colored hair, were now dancing. The Commodore and Grace were in a corner with Mrs. Malaprop and Sir Lucius O'Trigger, sharing a dish of lobster mayonnaise, which Sir Lucius had cunningly appropriated. Mr. Casey, having seen his daughter pass through the hall like a blazing torch, was cheerfully explaining to Mrs. Coote exactly when and where he had met Mr. Coote. Mr. Mossat was entertaining three dazzled West Farbridge matrons with reminiscences of the Theater. Mr. Huntley was exchanging murmurings, nose quiverings, and eye closings for Mrs. Hungerford's exclamations and gasps. Looking beautiful and sad, Helen Weeks was pretending to listen to a man who was very angry about import regulations in Iraq or Uruguay or somewhere. Seth Hull was showing Bob Acres and George, the stage manager, a trick with three florins and three pennies. Mobbs, almost a little blast furnace, was arguing passionately about cheese with a mysterious couple who were rather tight, did not appear to know anybody, and had probably come to the wrong party. Dr. Barr, with the help of four wineglasses, two ham sandwiches, and a macaroon, was demonstrating to a small intellectual circle how he once dealt with a sudden outbreak of typhoid. Eight wives, and five husbands belonging to different wives, were glowering on the sidelines of the party, waiting to go home. Anita, the maid, and her sister and her cousin were hurrying in and out with food and drink and occasionally rushing into a corner to giggle; while the hired waiter, drunk, was singing a popular Irish ballad in the pantry. And outside in the garden, where the party sounded like a monkey house on fire, in the sweet-smelling companionable old night, were Laura Casey and Theodore Jenks, sometimes talking it all over, sometimes locked and silent in an embrace, busy defying a whole world of power politicians, mad propagandists, atomic scientists and experts on biological warfare, pessimistic philosophers, despairing sociologists, soured moralists, gravely concerned leader writers, by daring to be happy. . . .

9

On Saturday morning, after leaving his room rather earlier than usual, the Commodore went into Seth Hull's private office.

"Nice morning," said Seth, "an' it'll keep nice for your Gayler this afternoon an' for fireworks tonight. Luck's changed, eh?"

The Commodore sat down and lit his pipe. "I think it has, but I don't want to shout too soon, Seth." He hesitated a moment, wondering whether to tell Seth about his fireworks problem and to ask him to lend the Festival nine hundred pounds over the week end. But he decided against it. Seth had been very helpful, very friendly, but the Commodore did not want to confess to him that he had landed himself in such a mess, just as the Festival had turned its corner. "Just been looking at the *Weekly Record*. Very nasty article about us."

Seth's massive face darkened. "I've seen it. And it never ought to have got in. Young Seacombe ought to have told me about it, before paper come out, like he did afore. What's he playing at?"

"He's finished with us, Seth. Gone up to Town, I think. As soon as Theodore came back here, Laura knew Seacombe wasn't the right man for her and told him so. It was partly my fault," the Commodore admitted, "because I encouraged him to rush her. However, she and Theodore made it up last night, and all's well."

"Good for them," said Seth grinning. "Always liked young Jenks. He'll carry corn better nor Seacombe an' all. She picked right chap, little Laura did." Then his face darkened again. "But if yon Corby-Smith thinks he can print that muck, I'll show him. I warned him afore. I'll Corby-Smith him—you wait. And anyhow it'll do Festival no harm now. Too late. We're off. Here—" and now he grinned again "—somebody else is off too—"

"What? Not—"

"Ay, your pal Mrs. Robinson—Grace. Left early this morning."

"Seth," cried the Commodore, pushing himself out of his chair, "I give it up. She never said a word to me about going, last night. Not the slightest hint." He moved restlessly. "Seth, I'll be frank with you. I like that woman. And she seems to like me. And yet, without a word, she does this vanishing trick again. What's it all about?"

"Well," said Seth slowly, "poor woman can't help it if she's got a husband who's—yer know, lad—ninepence in the shilling, a bit barmy."

The Commodore stared at him. "Is that what she told you?"

"She let it drop, as yer might say," Seth replied with some complacency. "Didn't like to say owt to you. Yer know how they are."

"I give it up again," cried the Commodore, rubbing his cheek with the stem of his pipe. "I believe she tells a different story every time. And yet she seems a nice sensible woman. But she told me—" but he stopped short, shrugged his shoulders "—oh well, what's the use? I just give it up. But why the blazes did I, at my age, have to go and fancy a woman who keeps disappearing and seems to give a different account of herself to everybody she talks to?" Then he remembered something, and stared at Seth in dismay.

"What's up, Commodore?"

"If she's gone, then Smith, that little private detective, has gone too."

"Well, I can't see that doing anybody any harm. We could spare that little weasel. But if yer want to know, he's not gone after her this time, Smith hasn't, an' I saw him downstairs, not twenty minutes since, talking to Laura's father, Mr. Casey. If he hadn't been, I'd have told him to sling his hook."

"Seth," said the Commodore hastily, "I'll see you later. Urgent business now."

Mr. Casey and Smith were still talking in the lounge. "I'm in on this fireworks plot, Commodore," said Mr. Casey, smiling.

"Good." He turned to Smith. "I was afraid you might have left, when I heard that she'd gone—you know—"

"Assignment finished," said Smith. "Nothing new for yours truly. So staying here for private work. Suits you. Suits me. Going through with it this morning?"

"I'll have to. No alternative," said the Commodore, who always found himself at these moments reproducing Smith's telegraphic style.

"All set then. All set at your end. Just leave it. All set at mine. Mr. Casey gives me a hand, if necessary." All three were standing, and now Smith came closer and did a ventriloquial act, keeping his cigarette smoldering away and his lips almost closed. "If nobody turns up to see you, Mr. Casey does it. If somebody else comes all the better. We're watching, see? All you got to do, Commodore, is keep him there at top of the stairs, till I give the alarm. Then, in he goes. That little room's all fixed. Miss Casey won't be there. Doesn't know what it's about. But she's been told to go off for the morning with her bloke, Jenks. All set, see? Easy as pie."

When Mr. Atcham, looking rather worried, was shown into the Commodore's room by Mobbs, he was warmly greeted. "A beautiful day, Mr. Atcham," the Commodore boomed at him, "and I think we can hope for a fine night for your fireworks. Everything in good order out at the park?"

"You may depend upon our man there, Commodore," said Mr. Atcham. "But now—"

"Of course, of course. And I must apologize for keeping you waiting so long, Mr. Atcham. These formalities, eh? Now I have the check here—and we're in good time—and all I want from you is a receipt."

"Well," said Mr. Atcham dubiously, "I have to take the check along to the Bank—"

"Of course you have. But just as you have your little rules, we have ours. And I can't hand over a check for this amount without obtaining a receipt. That's only reasonable, isn't it?"

"You must see that, old boy," said Mobbs.

Mr. Atcham looked rather unhappily from one to the other of the large smiling faces, then said: "Very well, gentlemen. Let me have your check, and I'll give you a receipt." He stared hard at the check for nearly half a minute, while the Commodore hummed *The Lily of Laguna*, and then carefully wrote out a receipt. "There you are, sir. And now, if you'll excuse me—"

This was the ticklish part. With a warning glance at Mobbs, who hurried to open the door, the Commodore put a heavy arm on Mr. Atcham's shoulder and kept it there until they reached the top of the stairs. The door of Laura's little room was open and inside the light was on, for the window had been boarded up. On the table was a covered plate of sandwiches, a glass, and a bottle of whisky, about a third full. "Now we've done our part," said the Commodore, still keeping a hand on Mr. Atcham, "but are you certain you've done yours?"

"Everything is in order, sir," said Mr. Atcham, clearly anxious to get away.

"All ready for eleven o'clock, eh?"

"Yes, yes. Now if you'll excuse me—"

"The set piece. What about the set piece? I'm told they often go wrong," said the Commodore hurriedly. "Can't have anything going wrong tonight, my dear fellow."

"I assure you," said Mr. Atcham, wriggling out of his grasp.

And then Smith appeared, a frantic figure at the bottom of the stairs. "Look out, Commodore," he yelled. "He's here again. Can't stop him. Get out of the way—sharp."

"What—" cried Mr. Atcham.

"Take cover while we deal with this fellow," the Commodore shouted, and thrust Atcham into the little room, locked the door, and pocketed the key. Mobbs did some stamping and vague shouting, for atmosphere. At the bottom of the stairs, behind the grinning Smith, appeared the large white anxious face of that desperado, Arthur Hatchet-Ferrers. "I just wondered, Commodore," he called. But he was not allowed to say any more.

"Coming, coming," the Commodore shouted. "Hold everything there. I'll be with you." And as he and Mobbs went clattering down the stairs, with Hatchet-Ferrers gaping up at them, a loud-speaker below began playing dance music.

"We keep that going, see?" said Smith, while Mobbs was reassuring the bewildered Hatchet-Ferrers that nobody had gone mad. "Till this front office closes. Nobody hears him hammering to be let out. Sounds good too. Festival touch. Bloody artful, eh? But get Fat Face out or he might rumble something."

"Too early for a drink, I'm afraid," said the Commodore, sweeping Hatchet-Ferrers, who still looked dazed, through the crowd buying or waiting to buy tickets. "But we could have a cup of coffee. There's a place along here."

"It must be my nerves, I suppose," said Hatchet-Ferrers, when they were waiting for their coffee, "but there seemed to me the most extraordinary commotion in there. Everybody shouting—and that horrible little man with the long nose." He shuddered, turning himself into a jellied egg.

"You must be careful, my dear fellow," said the Commodore. "What you need now is a quiet chat—perhaps over a cigar. I don't seem to have my case—oh—well, thank you, I will. I know your excellent taste in cigars. And now what can I do for you?"

"I've had a word with Madge—Mrs. Bulfoss—on the telephone this morning," said Hatchet-Ferrers with enormous solemnity, "and she tells me she has to judge the—er—decorated floats, or whatever they're called—in the Gala Procession this afternoon—and then present the prizes. Now Gerald—Major Bulfoss—has definitely refused to accompany her. There was some—er—trouble last night. And I was wondering if you'd have any objection to my coming along with Mrs. Bulfoss, and doing what I could to help."

"My dear fellow, of course not. I regard you," said the Commodore with equal solemnity, "as one of our earliest and most distinguished patrons."

"I appreciate that," said Hatchet-Ferrers. "And it's uncommonly good of you, I must say. There's some sort of lunch, isn't there?"

"One-fifteen at the White Hart. And I'm looking forward to seeing you there, with Mrs. Bulfoss. Sir Barclay and Lady Gishforth, who are also judging and prize-giving, will be there too."

"Delightful," cried Hatchet-Ferrers. Then he hesitated. "This—er—actor chap, Gorebarry—he's not going to be about this afternoon, is he?"

"At the theater all day. Which is, of course, where he belongs. You fond of fireworks, by the way? Not very? A pity, as with any luck we ought to have a magnificent display tonight."

That is, if Atcham could not make his escape from that little back room. The Commodore stayed away from the Festival Center for the remainder of the morning. While he was buying the Gishforths some pink gins at the bar of the White Hart, he saw a long nose and a smoldering cigarette appear round the door.

"All lovely so far," Smith muttered. "Hammering like hell an hour ago. Quiet now. Just been up to listen. Might be taking the lunch I left him. If so, he'll go to bye-bye for the next eight hours or so. A drink? Every time. Ta, muchly. Report later."

Neither the Commodore nor Laura had had anything to do with the Gala Procession, which had been organized by a subcommittee under the chairmanship of Councillor Gisburn. A little stand had been erected in front of the Town Hall, and there the Commodore and his lunch party joined the Mayor and other notables, to watch the procession. Later, the judges would go out to Mayton Park, to take a final look at the competitors before making their awards. The Commodore, who had done himself very well at lunch, took his seat on the stand and felt better than he had done ever since the Festival began. He remembered,

of course, that Grace had vanished again, that there was this fishy business with Atcham and the fireworks, that his future only extended,
with luck, to the next seven days; but in his after-lunch mood, finishing
his cigar in the delicious sunshine, these unpleasant matters faded to
mere shadows in the golden haze. Glancing from the Gala program
to the crowd, which was thick around the Town Hall, he felt for the
first time a definite and proud sense of achievement.

"By George!" he cried to Sir Barclay Gishforth, who had also lunched
very well. "These people said we couldn't give 'em a Festival. And now
look at this."

"A jolly good show, Commodore," said Sir Barclay. "Like this sort
of thing. Always did. Think I can hear a band. Jolly good—Daphne—
what?"

And then there came, more or less swinging, round the corner the
Silver Band of the Farbridge Fire Service, booming and clashing away,
bringing the expectation of the crowd up to the boil. Close behind came
some boy scouts, of assorted sizes, and some girl guides who appeared
to have just been taken off a grill. There followed the first of the floats,
on which the Farbridge Co-operative Women had staged their tableau
The Arts of Peace, with eight maidens and matrons, all in white, spinning and weaving and playing a harp and smelling flowers and smiling
and wobbling.

"Bit long in the tooth, some of 'em," said Sir Barclay. "But the one
with the bread is rather an attractive gal."

The East Farbridge Social Club had conjured some sort of pirate
ship out of a coal lorry, and six enthusiastic members, glistening with
paint, were buccaneering like mad. The Combined Girls' Clubs were
doing a Morris dance on their cart. The Farbridge and District Allied
Trades Association offered *Dick Whittington,* with an immense pantomime cat that ran about and scratched itself and made menacing
gestures at the younger spectators, who screamed with pleasure. The
Farbridge Institute, whatever that was, had an impressive but mysterious tableau entitled *Today and Tomorrow,* which seemed to consist
of some angry people in raincoats gesticulating at some smiling youths
and girls in peculiar bathing costumes.

"Have to take another look at that, Daphne," said Sir Barclay, a
conscientious judge.

"Why?" she inquired in her hard clear voice. "Nonsense, I call it.
Now who are these people?"

Nobody knew. They were mostly middle-aged men in suits rather too tight for them—though there was a sprinkling of severe-looking females —and they carried banners about Peace and Prosperity and that sort of thing; and by the time they reached Mayton Park some of them would have to take off their shoes.

Then Sir Barclay rose several inches out of his seat, and made a whinnying noise. "It's our crowd from Brant. Oh—jolly good!" And so it was. Messrs. Hookwood and Trevone (who was sitting by the driver and waved to the stand) offered *Light Industry*, with Liz and Dulcie and Fred, and other keen types in smart overalls busy doing something to something in a very keen fashion. "And as far as I'm concerned, definitely a winner," said Sir Barclay. "Another band now. Really, I must say, Commodore—a jolly good show."

Yes, the Farbridge Police Brass Band, led by a large boiled sergeant, came thumping and clanging along, preparing the spectators for the delights of the North Farbridge Women's Institute, which was actually bottling fruit, and clearly was ready to bottle its way right up to Mayton Park. This was followed by a number of stern little girls in gym costume. The next tableau had been organized by the Brewery: *Ye Olde Pigge and Whistle,* in which some very red-faced eighteenth-century characters were dealing manfully with ale and churchwarden pipes. A contingent of small boys in white shirts and blue shorts heralded the next dramatic item, which was received with a huge roar. For this was *Another Goal for the United,* in which several actual members of the first team, netted in, could be seen scoring goals, to the joy of everybody except one embittered supporter, who bellowed: "Let's see you do it next season."

There were some children in *Snow-White and the Seven Dwarfs,* with the smallest dwarf being sick. Young men from the Y.M.C.A. performing gymnastic feats. Merry maids round a Maypole. And somewhere about there, in spite of his pride and pleasure and all the excitement, the Commodore fell asleep.

He awoke to find the procession gone, even the sound of it reduced to a remote drumming, the crowds melting away, the stand deserted except for Laura and her father, who were quite close, looking up at him smilingly, obviously waiting for him to wake up. He rubbed the dreams out of his eyes. Yet this too, for all its clear sunlight and the warmth of the afternoon, was like a dream. He had then a strange moment of insight, feeling profoundly that life was altogether different from all our common accounts of it; but that too vanished like a dream.

"I don't know how you could fall asleep," said Laura rather reproachfully. "Gisburn and his gang made a very good job of the procession, I thought."

"Capital, capital," he said, struggling with a yawn. "We'd rather a heavy lunch—and then the warm afternoon, you know—"

"You're an old monster," she said affectionately. "Well, you must come up to the Park and see what's happening."

"I suppose so." He got up. "What about transport?"

"I've got a taxi," said Mr. Casey. "That's why we waited for you. Come along."

"Look here," said Laura, in the taxi, "what's happening in my little office? Why am I kept out of it? Dad only grins in a maddening way. What are you two up to?"

"It's a long story," said the Commodore, with mock solemnity. "And I'll tell you later—not today."

"Quite right," said Mr. Casey. "Some other time, Laura."

Laura then proved that feminine intuition is something more than a mere legend. "Fireworks," she suddenly announced. "I'll bet they come into it. You both have a silly firework look on your faces."

Nothing more was said until they were approaching the main entrance to Mayton Park. The traffic, mostly buses and coaches, was thick, and on each side the crowds were streaming along. The Commodore looked out approvingly.

"I get awfully mixed up when I see a lot of people," said Laura rather dreamily. "Sometimes I hate them, and long to run away. Sometimes I love them, they seem so sweet. I do today."

"I'll admit," said the Commodore, "that today, for the first time, I've been feeling that you and I, my dear, have really accomplished something."

"And Theodore," she said quickly.

"Yes, Theodore too. How is he, by the way?"

Laura laughed. "Wishing he could get out of that theater, poor darling. And he has to rehearse Twelfth Night tomorrow and Monday. He's playing both Curio and Antonio, the sea captain—he kept saying his lines to me this morning—thank goodness he hasn't much to do."

"It'll all be very Curio, I suspect," said her father. "Well, you've certainly attracted a crowd today."

Once afoot in the park, they made their way past stalls and tea tents and cocoanut shies and little roundabouts for the children, all of them already doing a brisk trade, to the large space in the center where the decorated floats and carts were drawn up in a ring, for the inspection of the judges, and various other competitions were being held. Here Mobbs, an old hand at this sort of thing, was being very busy and important.

"Isn't your Maggie here?" Laura asked him.

"Yes," he replied, mopping himself, "but she's not with me today. It's the farmer's turn. Big gawky bloke. I'm more afraid of him than I am of the garage chap, because she's sorry for him. It's all still touch and go, you know, Laura. Yes, coming." And off he went, like a little steam engine.

The most solemn and conscientious of the judges was undoubtedly Hatchet-Ferrers, who had somehow acquired an enormous notebook in which he scribbled away with a gold pencil, after many a searching glance through his formidable spectacles.

"Actually," Mrs. Bulfoss declared, "Arthur's being rather tiresome about it all. You'd think it was his precious West British Chemicals or something. And now he's offered twenty-five pounds as a Beauty Prize, and all the girls are madly competing."

The Commodore stayed just long enough with Hatchet-Ferrers to accept one of his magnificent Havanas, and then drifted away from the harassed note-taking Humpty-Dumpty to smoke it in peace. Later he strolled up to the high ground where a policeman and about a hundred small boys and girls were staring at the fireworks in their roped enclosure. Atcham's foreman was still working away. Here the Commodore was joined by Laura's father.

"Very impressive," said Mr. Casey. "I congratulate you, Commodore."

"Not yet, my dear fellow," the Commodore muttered, "not yet."

"No news, I suppose?"

"Not since lunch."

They talked idly for half an hour or so, preferring to remain up there away from the bustle and noise. And then a familiar figure appeared.

"Oke, so far," said Smith. "Just come from there. All shut up of course, that Center. But got a front door key. Yale job. Went up to that back room. Listened. He's out—lovely shut-eye."

Was he sure, they asked.

"Don't be ridic. Ear to the keyhole. Hear him sawing wood."

"Sawing wood?" The Commodore was startled.

"Now, now! Snoring—shut-eye—ever dreaming of thee. All oke. Neat job so far. But keep the fingers crossed. And watch it here to-night. Allow him eight hours out—no more. Give you ten guesses what I'm going to do now."

They refused even one guess.

"Hoopla," said Smith, with that smiling complacency with which a man mentions his little weaknesses. "A sucker for it. Always was. Always will be. Show me a hoopla stall and I'm throwing good money away. Well, you can't be wide all the time. Ta-ta for now. See you later."

The crowds swarmed round the stalls and tea tents or applauded in the competition ring, and the afternoon withered away. The Commodore and the Caseys, feeling sticky and rather stale, returned to the White Hart and there, after a refreshing interval, dined with Seth, who stood them champagne. "That caffy-buffit I'm running up there didn't do so bad Thursday an' last night," he said gleefully. "But tonight'll be a bobby-dazzler, my chap says. I've rushed a lot more stuff up, but I'll bet there's not a drop nor a crumb left time fire-works starts. Hey!" he shouted across the dining room. "Come here, you two."

Johnny Jolly, in a purple dinner jacket with cream lapels, and his April, blonder than ever and shimmering like a mermaid in her seagreen evening gown, came sauntering over.

"You'll take a drop o' something afore you go up there," said Seth. "I've heard yer complaining, but yer'll be lucky tonight if yer can get to your bandstand." So they condescended to take a glass or two of champagne, and April, deciding that Laura was no longer snooty, not only smiled at her several times but actually described what par-ticular combination of hot and sweet numbers she proposed to "vocalize" with her Johnny.

Not long after Johnny and April had gone, Laura said that she was going along to the Palace, where they were giving *The Rivals,* to wait for Theodore. "We shall be in good time for the fireworks," she added.

"We hope so," said her father, with a droll glance at the Commodore.
"You keep your eye on that young man o' yours," said Seth.

"Why?" she asked sharply.

" 'Cos he might easily melt an' fade away, poor little chap." And Seth gave a huge guffaw. Laura made a face at him, and hurried out. "Never mind," Seth continued, with a wink at Mr. Casey, "we know some that seems to fade away, don't we, Commodore?"

"If that wink puzzles you," said the Commodore to Mr. Casey, "I'd better explain that Seth is referring to my friend, Grace, who certainly has an odd habit of disappearing suddenly."

"So Laura tells me," said Mr. Casey. "Pleasant woman, I thought, but what an odd history she's had, hasn't she? She was telling me something about it at tea the other day. That old skipper just coming for the night to her place, and then falling ill, when she thought he was broke, and then afterwards leaving her a fortune."

"Probably King Solomon's mines," muttered the Commodore, who had exchanged a look with Seth.

"Think it's a bit steep, humph?"

"Don't ask me, my dear fellow," cried the Commodore in despair. "I give it up. Well, I suppose we ought to be having a look at that park."

"I'll run yer up," said Seth, who not only ran them up but also, after telling the police at the gate who he was, drove them within twenty yards of his illuminated "caffy-buffit." The whole place was packed. In their glittering shell, Johnny and his Jollyboys were nodding and swaying, wailing and drumming; into the microphone and out of the numerous loud-speakers, April poured the woes of deserted colored girls as lavishly as it could be done by a young white woman who had never set eyes on the Old South and had a happy husband beaming at her bare back; on the dance platform there would not have been room even for Beverly Bulfoss wearing nothing but his pyjamas; and, all around, the starers and listeners, dwindling into faint pink blobs in the dusk, whispered and giggled, hummed and sang, by the thousand. Standing in the lighted entrance to the café-buffet with Seth, the Commodore was recognized by some of the folk patiently queuing for supper. "Three cheers for Commodore Tribe and the Festival!" some young man shouted, probably remembering him from the meeting. And up the cheers went, the Commodore's heart swelling with them.

"Now that's summat to be proud about," said Seth. "Don't often do that round here."

"First time it's happened," said the Commodore. "And I *am* proud, Seth, believe me."

"Awkward now, though," Mr. Casey whispered, "if our firework scheme doesn't work."

"You needn't remind me," the Commodore groaned. "As Smith said, I'm keeping my fingers crossed. And I shan't feel comfortable until I see those rockets going up."

"What about having them earlier?"

"I've thought of that," the Commodore muttered, "but we couldn't work it now. Let's stroll round. It'll help to pass the time."

So they strolled and strolled, pretending to be interested in everything but Mr. Atcham and his fireworks, but at twenty to eleven they found themselves pushing their way through the crowd assembling near the high ground where the fireworks were roped off. Here the illuminations of the dancing place and the lights of the stalls were left behind, and it was nearly dark. The roped enclosure had an entrance, which a policeman was keeping clear, and the Commodore and Mr. Casey, now reduced to conspiratorial hurried whispers, moved slowly nearer and nearer to this entrance. About twelve minutes to eleven, they were joined by Laura and Theodore.

"In spite of all this," said Theodore happily, "we had a full house tonight."

"Good, good," said the Commodore. "Crowded here too."

"We know that," said Laura. "What's the matter with you two?"

"No, no, Laura," said her father hurriedly. "Some other time."

"By thunder, Casey," cried the Commodore softly, "I'm in a cold sweat. I really am. Hello, who's this? Smith? Any news?"

"Have a heart," said Smith very quietly. "Went up and listened about eight. He was awake then all right. Hammering again. I pushed off—sharp. Left him to it. Daren't go back. Either he's out or he isn't."

"Yes, yes, yes," the Commodore whispered impatiently. "I'm well aware of that. What time is it?"

"About seven minutes to go," said Smith. "Take it easy, chum. Nearly zero. Got a pink comb and a packet of fags out of the hoopla—and cost me nearly ten bob. That's me an' hoopla."

"Oh—damn your hoopla!" the Commodore muttered.

"Manners, cock," Smith said reproachfully. "Mind them nerves."

The policeman guarding the entrance to the enclosure had now taken it into his head to flash a torch about, for no reason that the Commodore could imagine. But the idiotic flashings somehow increased his anxiety and the tension. The crowd was thicker than ever, although there was some vacant space near where they were standing, perhaps because of the entrance and the policeman. Up near the fireworks, some figures could be seen moving around, and a flicker or two of light. Three minutes to go.

Then they could hear a commotion and raised voices, all rapidly coming nearer. The policeman flashed his torch, and there, crying to be let through, pushing and squirming toward them, was a disheveled figure hard to recognize as natty little Mr. Atcham. Finding a few yards of open space at last, he came running with great audible gasps towards the policeman's torch and the entrance to the enclosure. But he had to pass close to the Commodore and his group, just outside the narrow beam of light, and as he came up, a foot, belonging to A. Smith of London, shot out, and down he went.

"Is it Mr. Atcham?" cried the Commodore, helping the exhausted man to his feet but at the same time winding a great arm round him. "My dear fellow, what on earth has happened? Where have you been?"

"Take it easy, chum," said Smith, giving a hand. "You're all in. Heart's going something terrible."

"Gug—gug—gug," cried Mr. Atcham, the glass eye glaring horribly.

"Easy does it, chum."

"Lean on me, my dear fellow," cried the Commodore.

"Gug—gug—lemme—lemme—gug—locked room—"

Then with a wonderful swish and a zoosh the first rockets went up, and then seemed to vanish, so that for a moment there was silence and nothing happening up there at all. But just when everybody was beginning to feel that perhaps nothing would ever happen again anywhere, the sky burst into vermilion, blue and silver particles. A huge "Ah!" like that of an awakening giant rose out of the crowd. A thousand lads whistled the rockets to greater heights and more glorious explosions.

"My dear Atcham," the Commodore was saying, "I take the blame entirely. As soon as we got rid of that fellow, I was called away and clean forgot about you. By George!—you might have been there until Monday if that policeman hadn't finally heard you. My fault, my fault. However, here you are, safe and sound, with our check in your pocket. And what a fine show! Magnificent, my dear fellow, absolutely magnificent!"

Above a chorus of *Ahs* and *Oohs* that seemed to go sighing out far beyond the boundaries of the park, the rockets went streaking up fierily, and cascades of pale gold and silver tumbled and dissolved in the upper air and multicolored meteors flashed and faded. Great wheels went whirling and flaming until they became blossoms of fire. There were things that banged and winked and vanished and then out of nothing seemed to spill shining cartloads of rubies and emeralds. Mysterious monsters belched and roared, bombarding the sky with sullen missiles that were transformed far above into amethyst and saffron fountains.

Like many other lovers there and perhaps for miles around, Laura and Theodore kept still and very close together, warmly conscious of each other, while they gaped happily up at this brief magical springtime of fire and air, with its jeweled rain, melting green willows, crimson roses that blazed and withered in a few seconds, and the trumpets and lilies etched in white fire against the midnight, the long branching fingers of a pure shining whiteness, that were the most entrancing of all. "And I don't care what the Commodore spent," murmured Laura. "It's worth it—bless him! Oh—look!"

They looked, and all the crowd behind them looked; and children who had been sent to bed hours before ran to magically illuminated bedroom windows; and perhaps even Crandry and Colonel Whatmore and Alderman Tanhead took a peep or two and felt vaguely disturbed. So the fireworks burst high above the darkening town; and the first week of the Farbridge Festival ended in rapturous *Ahs* and thunderstruck *Oohs,* in gold fountains hanging in mid-air and a million insubstantial gems that nobody could buy or sell, in color and fire, a sudden wonder, a glimpse of glory.

CHAPTER THREE

Take Your Partners

I

ON SUNDAY morning, a warm morning, close and sleepy, Laura's father, crisp as a chilled lettuce, arrived in Alma Street and insisted that she should go with him to church. So she floated dreamily by his side along Inkerman Place and into Baldwin Road to the newish church on the corner. It was a yellow and waxy sort of place, smelling of polish; there were only about thirty people there; the hymns were all in such high keys that Laura found it easier to giggle than to sing; and the sermon seemed a queer mixture of a Bible story and an angry editorial from the *Daily Telegraph*.

"Not good, I agree," said her father, back in Baldwin Road again, "but nevertheless I feel better for it, perhaps because I'm so rarely at home. Now I'll tell you what my program is. Lunch with you, I hope. Look at the papers and fall asleep. Take a brisk walk until dinner, which I shall probably eat with the Commodore and Hull, who doesn't say much but is a good listener. Now what's your program? Work or young man or both?"

"Both," said Laura. "We'd have gone out for the day, but he has to rehearse this afternoon, and I'll have to look after these Fettercairn people. The Saxons have some friends for lunch, so Theodore and I arranged to meet at the White Hart, where you can lunch with us too. You can pay, if you like. Oh!—I've been meaning to ask you for days, Dad—did you find any treasure in Central America or wherever it was?"

"Not the kind you mean—pieces of eight and doubloons. But I sold an American some valuable information and half an option for three thousand dollars. Not bad."

"I like us Caseys, don't you?"

"Always did, but try to hide it. I like this kind of Sunday too, until evening. Never fail to enjoy my Sundays every time I come back.

Sounds, smells, even the sunlight, all different on an English Sunday. But by seven in the evening, I've had enough."

"We keep straight on," said Laura, for now they were walking toward the center of the town. "I propose to spend most of this afternoon and evening dashing between the theater and Theodore and the Corn Exchange and the orchestra, and if you think I'm not going to like it, then you're wrong."

Theodore was waiting for them at the White Hart.

"What country, friends, is this?" cried Laura.

"This is Illyria, lady. Hello, Mr. Casey! Lunching with us? I may have to keep saying *Twelfth Night* lines. I can manage the first sea captain pretty well, but I'm still shaky with Antonio, the other sea captain."

"They're both very dull chaps, darling, though no doubt you'll make something very odd out of them as you did out of that *Rivals* coachman. Oh—look—that's Mr. Fettercairn."

Proudly she brought him across and introduced Theodore and her father to him. He did not look quite as disreputable as he had done in the London rehearsal room, but his tweed coat and trousers did not match and there was a button or a stud missing from his shirt, so that it flapped open behind his rather loose tie, which was a horrible plaid with egg on it. Nevertheless, he looked astonishingly handsome and distinguished, and Laura found herself still adoring him.

"How's the orchestra now?" she asked him.

"You won't know them, just as I promised you wouldn't. We're rehearsing this afternoon. Come and listen. Is this your young woman?" he said to Theodore.

Confused but delighted, Theodore admitted that it was.

"A queen poppet," said Fettercairn. "I told Mrs. Prince so, next time I saw her after I'd met you," he said to Laura, all smiles and blushes. "And I owe you something for engaging us to come here. Chiefly because of our friend, Helen, who's lunching with me here."

"That's the beautiful but rather sad girl, isn't it?" said Mr. Casey.

"Yes," said Laura, "though she's been less sad lately. Ever since she knew you were coming here, Mr. Fettercairn. Though I oughtn't to tell you that. She'd be furious."

"We've exchanged messages," said Fettercairn, "but haven't met yet—I mean, not since several years ago." He looked at his watch. "She's late, though, whatever you say she may be feeling, Miss Casey.

I really think," he declared to the other two men, "they live in a different sort of time—an older, vaguer sort of time, with no minutes in it."

"Like the East," said Theodore.

"We have so many things to do before we meet you," cried Laura. "You've no idea. But isn't that Helen coming now?"

"God's truth," muttered Fettercairn, staring. Then he hurried toward her, and they saw her stop, smile, kindle, and flame.

"Come away," said Laura's father softly. And as they moved toward the dining room: "There's an astonishing amount of falling in love behind the scenes of this Festival, isn't there?"

"That's what a Festival's for," cried Laura gaily. "And then there's a still better one going on inside your head."

There were not many people lunching, but among them, sitting at one table, were Philippa Hookwood, Mrs. Hungerford, the Group Captain, Mossat, and Gorebarry, quite sober for once.

"And he's not going to have a drink, he says," Theodore told the other two, "until he's finished playing Sir Toby tomorrow night. When he plays a cardinal or sober miserable Faulkland, he's tight, and now that he's cast for a roaring drunk, he's determined to keep sober."

"Well, that's acting," said Mr. Casey. "Will he be a good Sir Toby?"

"He was wonderful the other day, rehearsing," Theodore replied. "He made even Archie Mossat and George laugh."

"What a pity your two sailor chaps aren't funny, darling!" said Laura, smiling at him. "Golly, I'm hungry all of a sudden."

"So am I," said Theodore, beaming across at her. "And you wait— my two sailor chaps may be much funnier than Sir Toby and Ague-cheek and that gang. Archie Mossat is playing Malvolio with an Edinburgh accent. It seems to suit him too."

It was the happiest kind of meal for Laura, who ate a lot and felt both proud and cozy between her men. Afterwards, rather sleepy, she walked to the Palace with Theodore and went backstage with him for a few minutes. Early though it was, there already seemed to be a lot of noise and confusion, with men moving things, and shouts for George and Charlie and "Props." It did not seem possible that the palaces and gardens of Illyria, and all the beauty and fun of Viola and Olivia and the Duke and the romping drolls, could ever come out of that dreary mess of canvas and electric lamps and wire and confused bellowing. And she was just somebody in the way, so she was rather glad to leave, after telling Theodore she would be back in the hope of joining him in the tea break.

Feeling sleepier still, but important and very much behind-the-scenes, she walked slowly up to the old Corn Exchange, deserted and drowsy in the sunshine. But at the top of the stone steps leading to the main entrance, she found Dr. Barr and his two daughters tip-toeing about.

"Ay, ay, ay," cried Dr. Barr in a high gleeful whisper. "Ye've met ma gairls, of course? Of course, of course. Well, we juist had to mak' sure the orchestra had arrived, an' then we heard them rehairsing. Ay, we heard them rehairsing. Faintly, ye know, Miss Casey, not properly at all—och no, not properly at all. An' I want the gairls to watch the bowing—ay, to watch the bowing." He looked at Laura wistfully, ably supported by the girls, all bone and freckles, who eyed her not only wistfully but almost hungrily. "Would there be a way into the rehairsal, d'ye think, Miss Casey? There would, eh? Ay, ay, ay. Well, the three of us'll be as quiet as mice, I promise ye. Alison, Elspeth, careful the way ye put your feet down, an' follow Miss Casey an' me."

She led them into the hall through a side door that she had been told would be unlocked. The only other person listening to the rehearsal was Helen Weeks, who saw Laura and the Barrs, waved, then apparently fell again into a happy trance. Leaving the Barr family to watch the bowing, Laura crept to a seat near the aisle and dreamily abandoned herself to the hour, the place, the music. She had never been inside the Corn Exchange before in full daylight, with sunlight and blue sky outside the square windows above the balcony. It gave the place a noble and gracious appearance, with something rather dramatic about its lighting, like a hall that had come out of an old Dutch painting. The musicians on the platform, the men in their shirtsleeves, the girls in summer dresses, were in a subdued light, delicately lit and shaded below a great gold arrow of sunshine. And now they were playing dances from Purcell's *Fairy Queen*, exquisite but remote, haunted by that strange sadness which gathers like mist over the revels of past ages . . . wasn't *Greensleeves* once a jolly rowdy song, bellowed out by Sir Toby and his fellow sots late at night, and now didn't it seem a heartbreaking whisper and ghost of a tune . . .? and how beautiful the strings were, so fierce and yet so delicate, as she had thought before, but better now, as Jimmy Fettercairn said they were . . . and here was Theodore . . . and they were in some other place. . . .

"Laura," said Helen Weeks rather reproachfully, "you were asleep." The orchestra had stopped. Some of them were smoking. Fettercairn was mopping his head.

"I heard a lot, Helen, but it's that kind of afternoon. And I shall be here part of the time tonight. He's quite right about them. They're much better than when I heard them in London. Wonderful, in fact."

"Aren't they?" Helen cried softly, very proud and, even after one lunch, obviously part of the Fettercairn Orchestras. "And I think he ought to stop now. Do you want to talk to him about tonight, Laura?"

"Just one or two things," said Laura, getting up and trying to look like an alert assistant director of a Festival. "Come with me. After all, you're on the Committee. You look after him."

"I'm going to," she said, and then they laughed. "And you attend to your Theodore and the theater people."

By the time Laura was back in the theater, they were within quarter of an hour of breaking. The stagedoor keeper said there was "a caff" open only two streets away, and she and Theodore found it, and it was one of those places, common in London but not often seen in towns like Farbridge, that had an urn and stale buns and thick chipped cups and too many flies buzzing round sticky tables. But they sat in a corner happily, sipping very sweet stewed tea, exchanging afternoons, and occasionally squeezing each other's warm moist hands. And while distant church bells were ringing, who should march into the place, bearing down on them like the Provost Marshal of some Amazonian force occupying the town, but Mrs. Delacey? And with her was a toothy, busty girl with blue eyelids, in pink and apple green. My Daughter?

"I was Informed you were here, Miss Casey, Mr. Jenks," said Mrs. Delacey. "This is My Daughter. As a gentleman friend was driving from Colwyn Bay, she Took The Opportunity of being dropped here, to spend a night with Her Old Mother."

"Isn't that nice?" cried Laura, and smiled at My Daughter, who thereupon answered with a smile so wide that she seemed to have lipstick all over her teeth. Then, keeping the smile at full stretch, she opened her eyes, which were like Mrs. Delacey's only gone mad and put in a blue enclosure, right at Theodore, who did not know where to look.

"We were wondering," Mrs. Delacey continued, "if it might be possible for us to attend the rehearsal of *Twelfth Night* this evening. After all, My Daughter is a professional artiste herself, and In My Humble Way I am a member of the Festival Staff."

"Of course you are," said Laura. "So come along, though I don't know what it'll be like."

"I do," said Theodore with no enthusiasm. "It'll be very long and horribly boring for you. But of course you can always go when you've had enough of it—unlike me."

"Poor you! And don't I know it," cried My Daughter, sparkling away at Theodore. "Got Patrick Gorebarry in the company, haven't you? He was playing in Brighton one time when I was there with a show, and he got going with one of our girls who was sharing digs with me —soprano, very refined, and a lovely girl too. And what she told me about him!"

"Clarice!" said Mrs. Delacey. "None of That Loose Talk—especially here." And her warning glance seemed to suggest that the tea urn was too young and innocent.

"Now, Mumsie!" cried Clarice, with an immense playfulness designed for pier pavilions. "I've heard you go on."

"Perhaps it's time we all went on," Laura suggested. All the way to her seat in the stalls, Clarice compared—and most unfavorably too— the Straight Theater or Legit with Concert Party Work Plus Panto, which according to her was almost an endless Christmas Party, with Wonderful Pals on both sides of the curtain and Loads of Lovely Gifts. And to this Mrs. Delacey listened with a sort of stern pride, occasionally prompting or adding a Pleasant Little Memory of Skegness or Bognor Regis or *Puss in Boots* that time in Sunderland.

From then on Laura had a most peculiar evening, like a daft dream. Archie Mossat (half-turned into Malvolio) stood in the aisle shouting at George in the wings, and George shouted up to Charlie on the switchboard. Part of the Duke's palace got stuck. Theodore, a monstrous Elizabethan sea captain, kept popping in and out. Clare was very angry about her tights, a situation that promptly uncovered a rich seam of reminiscence in Mrs. Delacey's Daughter. Gorebarry and the yellow-haired actor as Sir Toby and Aguecheek were very funny, and then very bored, and finally rather cross. Laura dashed up to the Corn Exchange, where there was quite a good audience, and saw Jimmy Fetter-cairn, astonishingly correct in white tie and tails, juggle his strings through dazzling patterns of sound. Then, with her head full of Handel and Mozart, she returned to the theater, to intervene in a quarrel between Mrs. Hungerford, who had come bouncing down from the Dress Circle, and Mrs. Delacey and Daughter; to agree with Philippa Hookwood, a yawning Olivia, that Clare was too coarse and strident as Viola; to fetch sawdusty pies and beer from the little pub opposite the stagedoor for Theodore and chums. She was back at the Corn Exchange in time to congratulate Fettercairn, half-dressed and dripping wet, and to kiss Helen Weeks because she was not sad any more. Then once more in the theater, where there were no Delaceys, and Mr. Fotheringay was snoring over a plate of sandwiches in the back row of the pit, and Mossat and Mrs. Hungerford and Gorebarry were arguing in a corner, and there were such great mournful gaps in the rehearsal that it seemed as if there could not possibly be any Illyrian palaces and gardens and poetry and fun all ready for the next night. Then all at once it was altogether much too long an evening, and she was kissing this absurd brick-red whiskery Theodore, and then hurrying home through silent streets under the sensible wide old night sky.

She went to the Festival Center fairly early next morning, for she knew there would be a great deal to do, and to her astonishment she found a shabby little man with a long nose in her room. He seemed to be doing something to the window, which was partly boarded up.

"What are you doing?" she asked him.

"Shan't be a sec," he told her. "Smith's the name. Commodore knows about me."

"But what happened to the window?"

"Ask me no questions," said Smith, "I tell you no lies. Just forget it. Funny business."

"Do fireworks come into it?"

"Girlie, I wouldn't be surprised. There you are. You can see lovely. Giving us a nice Festival, aren't you?"

"Yes, we are," said Laura, watching him stack the boards from the window in a corner. "And I'd like to get on with it. I'm very busy."

"That's right. Busy little bee, that's you, girlie. And remember me to the boy friend. Big fine bloke, that. You've got something there, Miss Casey. Toodle-pip!"

She worked hard all morning, settling accounts, seeing the various people who were responsible for the money they had taken at Mayton Park on Saturday, and it was not until after twelve that she went in to see the Commodore in the front room. He was talking to Mobbs.

"One of you will have to come to the Bank with me," she told them. "There's an awful lot to pay in. Saturday was a huge success. Look." She showed them her rough statement. "Isn't it wonderful? We're actually making money now."

"Archie," said the Commodore, "we're all going to the Bank. To see Mr. Watchbold."

"Wouldn't miss it, old boy," said Mobbs beaming. "Come on, Laura, divide the dibs among us."

So the three of them marched into the Bank and demanded to see the manager. After some delay they were shown into his office, and there, seated grimly by his side, was their old enemy the Borough Treasurer, Coverack. And between them on the desk was a check, which the Commodore recognized at once as the one he had given Atcham.

"Just arrived at the right moment," cried fat pasty-face. "Don't you agree, Mr. Coverack? Ha ha ha!"

"We're off," muttered Mobbs.

"This is the kind of situation that was bound to arise," said Coverack regarding all three of them with profound distaste. "Mr. Watchbold tells me he gave you a definite warning last Friday."

"Oh—certainly," cried merry Watchbold. "Couldn't do anything else, could I? Ha ha ha!"

"Just a minute," said the Commodore sourly. "What's funny about it? Tell me that."

"Nothing is funny about it," said Coverack bitterly.

"I'm not talking to you," said the Commodore. "I'm talking to jolly Mr. Watchbold with his *ha-ha-ha.*"

"That tone," said Mr. Watchbold, pained now, "is quite unnecessary."

"And returning our check, which is what you were going to do, is quite unnecessary too," said the Commodore. "Look—money." And he began dumping their packages of it on the desk. "Money. Money. Money. We hit the jackpot on Saturday night. There's nearly two thousand there, and more to come."

"Well, that's very satisfactory, I'm sure," said Mr. Watchbold, not yet back to his ha-ha-ha. Coverack looked annoyed.

"I'm sorry I can't pay this into some other bank," said the Commodore, who was not his usual genial self at all. "If I could, I would, like a shot. Now just have that counted and give us a receipt. And you needn't stay, Coverack. You hoped we'd fail, but we haven't done, though no thanks to you two. We're not only giving people here what they enjoy but we're also, at last, even paying our way. Now laugh that off—ha ha ha!"

"But I think you were wrong, Commodore," Laura said to him, after they had left the Bank. "You oughtn't to have snarled and gloated like that. It was all wrong somehow. I know they were against us, but you ought to have just smiled and been rather polite. I'm sorry, but I do think you were wrong."

"Perhaps I'd better leave it to you next time, Laura," said the Commodore, clearly annoyed. He stopped, frowned, hesitated. "Do we start quarreling among ourselves, now that everything's coming right?"

"No, of course not, old boy," said Mobbs anxiously. "Though I know what Laura means."

"So do I," he muttered. "Not in a good mood today. You two go on. See you later."

Fortunately the afternoon was better for Laura because Peter Gulval, who was giving the lecture, *Music for Strings*, that day, proved to be the pleasantest and most intelligent lecturer she had to deal with, and an old friend of Fettercairn's. She had a little time with her father too, who was leaving the next day, but only had a quick word with Theodore, who was still rehearsing *Twelfth Night*. After the lecture, which she enjoyed, she rushed home to have a bath and change for the theater, the last performance she would see with her father and the last, she hoped, in which she would have to worry about poor Theodore's very dubious capabilities as an actor. Not that she blamed him, for, as he had explained more than once, he had only joined the company for her sake, to have an excuse to come back to Farbridge. But she was very nervous, for him and for the whole production (which had seemed such a mess the night before), as she entered the crowded foyer again with her father, and saw fantastic old Mr. Fotheringay rubbing his hands.

It was wonderful. Not Viola, for Laura would never like that girl, Clare Chesbey. Not poor sweet Theodore, whose sea captains were a very awkward pair, who sometimes shouted and sometimes mumbled and never knew what to do with their enormous and apparently quite useless hands. Not some of the smaller parts, which had to be doubled and fitted in anyhow. The Duke was smaller and older than he ought to have been, like his palace. The Clown was not quite the bitter-sweet zany that Shakespeare had had in mind. But Mossat's Malvolio from Edinburgh way, bowing before the lovely stately Olivia, indignant and outraged among the drunken drolls, was a superb creation. And so was the stuttering Aguecheek of the young actor with the yellow hair. And, best of all, bringing shouts from the gallery and making her cry with laughter, was the dropsical wheezing Sir Toby Belch, in whose apoplectic glare and sodden roaring and muttering there seemed no trace of the Gorebarry she knew; and for the first time her heart went out to him, and she forgave him everything, for here, lighting up the whole Festival, was that rare thing, about which we talk so easily and yet can never explain, the authentic flash of genius. And it blazed, of course, divinely like another sun, in the mind that created this glorious old comedy, with all its lingering sweetness and uproarious antics, its wistful lovers and strange clowns, its golden Illyria that never was or could be in this world, its seacoast of Bohemia that so rightly chose Theodore for its captains. The voice of the Clown came faintly as everything round him faded:

A great while ago the world begun,
With hey, ho, the wind and the rain ...

and she listened in happiness but close to tears. And everything that followed, going behind the scenes to see Theodore and to tell Gorebarry, weary and embittered now as if he hated to find himself again in this world, how wonderful he had been, going with Theodore and her father up to the Palmerston Room and eating and drinking and shouting at people there, and watching Gorebarry and Mossat and Fettercairn do a mad clowning act like three great boys, and walking home afterwards with Theodore, both of them tired, quiet, almost as solemn as the huge night, it was all like a dream, an Illyrian dream, all full of happiness and close to tears.

2

At the Festival Center on Wednesday morning, Laura marched into the Commodore's room, followed by Theodore. "We want to talk to you," she announced firmly.

He smiled, not without difficulty. "Well, children, here I am. Talk away."

"I don't want to talk here. Do you?"

The Commodore gave a little shrug. "I'm not sure I want to talk anywhere. What is it? Festival business?"

"No," Laura replied. "The Festival's all right. There are one or two little things, but they'll keep. No, Theodore and I want to talk to *you*. About you. Now, you chaps, no nonsense. Follow me."

Grumbling a little, the Commodore followed with Theodore. "Know where she's going?" he asked as they descended into High Street, a few yards behind her determined little heels, fiercely striking the pavement.

"I've no idea, Commodore," said Laura's young man, who had already begun to realize that small women, however passionately devoted they might be to their large males, are compelled by their inner being to assert themselves almost at all times. "We agreed last night that we must talk to you, that's all. Where she's going now, I can't imagine. But that's all right. Leave it to Laura." And he gazed tenderly at the little figure ahead of them, and indeed was so tender about it that he bumped into somebody.

"Man, you're clumsy," cried Dr. Barr. "Och—it's you two. Busy aboot the Festival, eh? Ay, well you're doing fine, you're doing fine, you're doing fine. Yon Fettercairn—"

But already they had left him behind. Along High Street, then down Turton Street, then cutting through Leather Walk, they followed her into Peter Place, where all the buses were throbbing and growling to be off. Then they saw her reach the entrance to the Old Oak Nook, stop for a moment and turn, to make sure they had seen her, and then disappear into the café.

"Where it all started, you see?" cried Theodore out of the wonder and delighted amazement in which he had existed almost permanently ever since the Bulfoss party, last Friday night. "Isn't that just like her? Perfect idea!"

The Commodore, who was remote from this mood, said that he hoped the place would not be too full. Actually, although the town was busy and had a vaguely Festival air even so early in the day, the Old Oak Nook was nothing like full. They found Laura in the far room, already seated.

"Is this the same table?" said Theodore, still all wonder and delight.

"The very same," she told them, rather solemnly, like a child. "And it suddenly occurred to me that this is where we ought to be. Just where it all began. Three coffees, please. Any cakes?"

"Not for me," said the Commodore, settling his bulk. "I've almost every bad habit known to man, but I don't eat cakes at eleven in the morning. And I don't believe anybody can talk properly and eat cakes. No cakes, thank you," he told the waitress, and watched her go. "Now then, what's all this about?"

The lovers looked at one another, and the Commodore left them to it and filled his pipe. Then they decided they would wait until after the coffee had arrived. The Commodore lit his pipe and stared at nothing in particular, while the other two now looked at one another just for the exquisite pleasure of looking. The coffee came; the waitress departed.

"You see," Laura began, "we're worried about you, Commodore darling. And we don't want to be worried about you. If we weren't, everything would be perfect. Now here we are, where we all first met. We said we'd run a Festival here, and we've done it, and whatever happens now, nobody can say it hasn't been a great success. Theodore and I—after being very silly—"

"Yes, yes, yes," said the Commodore hastily. "You're very happy. And soon you'll be popping off to Malaya or somewhere. And I'm very glad."

"Well, you needn't rush it like that," said Laura. "We're not going to talk about *us*, though it seems to me the most fascinating subject there's ever been. I told you, we want to talk about you—you grumpy old monster."

"Seriously too," said Theodore. "We're really worried, as Laura says. We can't imagine what's the matter—"

"Well, I wouldn't quite agree with that," Laura put in hurriedly. "But we know the Festival's all right now. It won't make much money—why should it?—but everybody's having a lovely time. And people here know you've done it—and they're grateful and admiring, really they are—and the ones who don't like you don't matter now. So that's all right. Yet you're not your cheerful monster self at all now. Something's gone wrong. Theodore thinks it's money—"

"Probably, I thought," he said, but got no further.

"I think it's your friend, Grace," Laura continued firmly. "Her disappearing again—after telling everybody quite different stories about herself. And she did, you know."

"I know she did," said the Commodore slowly. "I've got quite an

interesting collection now. The Thousand and One Nights of Grace."
He produced some sort of grin.

"But you don't think it's funny, do you?" cried Laura, challenging
him.

"Not very. I don't like any of this. Not pride, I think. Never had
much. But I don't like the idea of you two youngsters worrying about
me—"

"But why not? We're your *friends*."

"Of course we are," said Theodore. "And we know that none of this
would have happened without you. Don't we, Laura?"

She nodded, but kept her brilliant gaze fixed expectantly on the Commodore.

"All right," said the Commodore reluctantly. "No reason why you
shouldn't know. First, about Grace. I liked her a lot, and she seemed
to like me—"

"My dear, she *adored* you. Admitted it."

"So what? She tells six more unlikely stories, and vanishes again, this
time for good apparently. Well, that's that," he went on wearily, "but
I'll confess I had hopes of something different. Not just her money—
if she really has any—though I'm not pretending it wouldn't have been
useful. But I liked *her*. Liked having her around. It seemed to keep
things more settled and yet easy and cheerful, all very important at my
age. But she's gone. The Festival's been a success—I agree we can
assume that now—but in a few days it'll be over And then what? A vote
of thanks for Commodore Tribe. Come again, Commodore, if we
ever think of having another Festival." He broke off, frowned, pushed
out his thick lower lip. "I don't like this. Whining old party. Let's
drop it."

"No, please, Commodore," cried Theodore.

"You're just being proud and grand," said Laura reproachfully. "I
forgot to tell you that my father, when he left yesterday, sent his best
wishes to you and hopes you'll meet again. And that means quite a lot,
because he's terribly hard to please. Now tell us. Are you worried
because Grace has gone and the Festival's nearly over and you don't
know what to do next?"

He nodded. "That's about it. And just remember that at my age,
when things are not opening out but narrowing and closing in, what to
do next is quite a problem. Especially if you're beginning to want a
settled life and find yourself rather tired of scheming and using your

wits. I thought there might be something here for me, but there isn't. Oh—at the worst I might scratch some little job out of Seth or old Jordan, if I refuse to move on to the next pitch, like some damned old Punch-and-Judy man. Or try some bit of nonsense with little Archie Mobbs, who's as broke as I am. But I've had other ideas, usually too late at night, I fancy—and now I see I oughtn't to have encouraged myself. Well, you asked for it, and there it is. Now forget it."

"Of course not," cried Theodore. "If you feel like that, then come with us—"

The Commodore stopped him. "No, my boy. Thank you for suggesting it. But it wouldn't work. And Laura knows it wouldn't. Don't you, my dear?"

She moved her head gravely. "No, it wouldn't work. But, Commodore, I feel there's something else. Don't you want to tell us?"

"Why not?" he replied, not looking at either of them but taking his pipe out and staring into the bowl. "It completes the picture. A man called York came to see me yesterday. I've had trouble with him before. When I was in Tredberrow I stayed at a hotel that his wife ran. He was away—they'd separated temporarily. It was when he came back that I came here to Farbridge. Somebody told him tales about his wife and me. On the basis of them, after he heard I was going to run the Festival, he tried to blackmail me. Seth and I kicked him out. Now he says he's going to divorce his wife, cite me, and claim damages. So this time there's no kicking him out. He's kicking me out. Well, now you have the whole thing—Grace gone—future dubious—and now this fellow York, who is, of course, a most unpleasant type. You asked for it, and there it is. And now let's go—a little new Old Oak goes a long way with me."

As they left, the Commodore continued: "By the way, I shan't be about until evening. Archie Mobbs and I feel we need a break, so we're having a run round in his car. Perhaps I'll be a different man next time you see me. Time I was." He grinned, hesitated, then put one hand on Laura's shoulder and grasped Theodore's upper arm with the other hand, and transformed his grin into a smile of great sweetness. "Stop worrying about me, you two. I've had my turn. Now it's yours. Enjoy yourselves. And, don't forget, I'd never have done anything here without you. I don't forget it."

He turned away, and they let him go. Then they walked slowly round Peter Place, on their way back to the Festival Center. It was impossible, of course, they agreed, to take the Commodore's advice; and in fact now they found themselves worrying harder than ever. But what could they do for him? Find Grace? Run round getting him the job he deserved? Or what?

"This York business ought to be tackled first," said Theodore, as they walked back along High Street. "If we could settle that for him somehow, the rest mightn't be so bad."

"Yes, but what do we do?" said Laura. "Go and see this York man? I don't believe that would work. We aren't the right sort of people. I wish Father hadn't gone, he'd probably know what we ought to do. Darling, think hard."

"I am doing," he told her, rather helplessly. And then just where the queue for Festival tickets began, he startled her and at least half a dozen other people by exclaiming: "I know. Come in here a minute." And he took her into the doorway of a suitcase shop. "Smith—or whatever his name is, that's the man we want, if he's still here. I caught sight of him yesterday. I'm going to try to find him. Meet me at the White Hart about one. I love you." He kissed her, and then was gone.

Laura collected some Festival letters and accounts from her own room and took them into the Commodore's, where she always worked if she knew he would be out for several hours. Trying hard not to think about Theodore and Smith and York and the poor Commodore, she worked until about half-past twelve, when she was disturbed by the entrance of a woman with no hat, a lot of peculiar dark curls, a rather short puce frock, plump bare legs, and sandals. She looked a very sprightly forty-five or so. She put her head on one side and smiled very broadly to reveal a tremendous dimple in the cheek that was winsomely tilted up.

"Mildred Sawkins," she announced. "The Gipsies, you know. And I'm sure you're Miss Casey. Am I right?" She spoke in a kind of contralto coo that Laura found maddening at once.

"Oh dear, I'm so sorry, Miss Sawkins," cried Laura, going forward to her. "You ought to have been met and looked after. But our Social Organizer, Captain Mobbs, has had to go off somewhere, and I've been desperately rushed this morning. Have you got a room?"

"At the White Hart, my dear," she replied, to Laura's dismay. "Expensive. But of course your splendid Festival. I'm so glad. And I've already had just a tiny peep at your lecture room in the Library. Perfect for me, simply perfect. Isn't this *fun*? Don't you think it is? Of course you do."

"Well," Laura began.

"Of course, of course you do," Miss Sawkins sang, seizing both of Laura's hands and swinging them. "I can see it in those lovely lovely eyes of yours. Now don't say I can't, my dear, because you know I can."

Gosh, this one's murder, thought Laura, as she escaped from this hand-swinging business. Help, help! But having put herself at a disadvantage by opening with an apology—and she genuinely felt rather guilty at having completely forgotten that Miss Sawkins was arriving —she now found herself unable to stand up against this cooing persistence, with the further result that at five minutes to one she also found herself weakly accompanying Miss Sawkins into the White Hart. She did not exactly remember inviting Miss Sawkins to lunch with her there, and perhaps she never did invite her, perhaps Miss Sawkins in her gipsy fashion had invited herself; but there they were. And Mildred—for she just had to be Mildred, it appeared, simply refused to be Miss Sawkins—would have a teeny drink before lunch, and it turned out to be a socking great double gin and Dubonnet.

It was then that Laura had her inspiration. For there, not far away, solitary, deep in melancholy introspection, a vast unwanted egg, was Mr. Hatchet-Ferrers. Hastily excusing herself to Mildred, Laura hurried across to him.

"My dear Miss Casey, I beg your pardon," he cried, coming out of his sad trance. "I didn't notice—you know, what with one thing and another. In point of fact," he added solemnly, "much as I appreciate the various excellent attractions that you and the Commodore have provided for us, I was wondering whether it was really wise of me to stay here any longer. I have to be rather careful, you know, Miss Casey— and—"

"Yes, I know, Mr. Hatchet-Ferrers," she broke in urgently. "But would you like to do something kind for me—and for the Festival— and perhaps for yourself too? Thank you, I knew you would. Well, you see that very attractive woman over there? That's Miss Mildred Sawkins, the famous lecturer on the gipsies, who's lecturing for us this afternoon, and I ought to be looking after her, but I can't, and both the Commodore and Captain Mobbs have gone off somewhere. Do you think you could possibly give her lunch and generally look after her for me? You'll find her enormous fun. Could you? How wonderful!"

"Miss Sawkins—Mildred—" she cried triumphantly, a minute later, "this is one of our most enthusiastic patrons, Mr. Hatchet-Ferrers, who's dying to meet you. I have to—"

But it didn't matter what she had to do. Mildred no longer cared. There was something about Hatchet-Ferrers, his solemnly deferential manner, his massive Humpty-Dumptyness, his air of wealth and expensively cushioned ease, though all far removed from the gipsies, that engaged all Mildred's attention at once. And clearly Hatchet-Ferrers, still nursing the wounds that Madge Bulfoss and the fantastic Gorebarry had inflicted upon him, was equally fascinated. All Laura had to do was to leave them alone, which she did just in time to meet Theodore entering the lounge, followed by the long-nosed, seedy Smith.

"We'll go into the bar," said Theodore. "The sooner we talk to Smith, the better, so lunch must wait."

"Yes, of course. And I've just been very cunning. I've got rid of a terrible woman, and probably also provided Arthur Humpty-Dumpty with a soul mate. And it'll serve Madge Bulfoss quite right for neglecting him and running after Pat Gorebarry."

They found a quiet table and provided Smith with beer. "Terms first," said Smith, after drinking their health. "All exes, of course. Might have to move around a bit—sharp too. Then twenty-five quid, lose or draw. Fifty quid for a win—that is, if I stop this York bloke. Take it or leave it, people. No argy-bargy."

"All right," said Theodore, who then proceeded to give Smith "the info," which was very sketchy. "And I wish now I'd asked the Commodore to tell us more about it," he concluded ruefully, "but it was difficult at the time."

"I'll manage," said Smith, finishing his beer and preparing to leave them.

"But, Mr. Smith, what can you do?" asked Laura, heartened a little by his superb self-confidence but still bewildered. "I mean, I wouldn't know where to start."

"Easy," said Smith, with a wink. "But no job for an amachure. I go straight out to this pub at Tredberrow. Ask questions. Try the wife. Where was York when he was away? I nip down there. Ask more questions. A bob gets you half a quid he was up to something down there. A bloke like York, bound to be. I get the info. Back here with it. Soon as I can, of course. Work fast too, though I don't look it. Never see me in a hurry. Old hand and artful, see?"

"It's like a detective story," said Laura, fascinated.

"Can't read 'em. Made up stuff. Like a bit of nice sentiment. Ever read *She Married an Earl*? Lovely book that. Ta, muchly, for the wollop. Cheery-bye."

The first person they saw in the dining room was Mobbs, who was lunching alone and looking rather gloomy.

"But I thought you were going off for the day with the Commodore," said Laura. "That's what he told us."

"That's what we arranged," said Mobbs, looking surprised now. "But he never turned up. I thought some Festival business must have caught up with him."

Laura and Theodore exchanged troubled glances. "No, I don't think it could have done. He left us to find you." She looked at Theodore. "Darling, I think he must have gone off somewhere by himself. And I don't like it."

"He'll be all right, Laura," said Mobbs. "Sometimes a chap feels like that. Try the oxtail. You won't do better today."

As they found a table, Laura saw that Mildred Sawkins and Hatchet-Ferrers were lunching together, and having a lovely time, with Hatchet-Ferrers solemn and deferential, and Mildred shaking her peculiar curls, winsomely tilting her head, and sparkling away like ten gipsy princesses. No need to worry about her any more, with Humpty in attendance.

"Oh," said Theodore, as they sat down, "there's Sir Gervais over there, with Clare. He's her uncle, you know, and it was through him, when I was staying at Renders, that I got to know Lionel and Clare."

"Well, I don't know that that makes me one of the old gentleman's most enthusiastic admirers, darling," Laura told him, smiling but a little sharp. To her Clare was "that girl" and best forgotten.

"Then you're wrong," said Theodore, beaming at her. "Sir Gervais introduced me to Clare, who made me go to the Mermaid Club, where I met Mr. Hookwood and the Group Captain, who asked me to visit them at Brant, and if I hadn't gone to Brant, I shouldn't have come to Farbridge and walked into the Old Oak Café and met you. And what a waste and a misery that would have been!"

This fascinating topic, with all its equally fascinating ramifications, lasted them through most of lunch. When they were finishing their pudding, Sir Gervais, purple and wheezy and still in slow-motion, came across with Clare, who was wearing a ravishing dark-yellow dress and giving a fine performance as a simple, devoted, wide-eyed niece.

"Mind if we join you, m'boy?" said Sir Gervais, demonstrating what complex movements are required to place a heavy human body accurately into a chair. Laura, after being introduced to him, exchanged with Clare smiles and sundry remarks of a terrifying sweetness.

"Stayin' a few days with the Wattons, m'boy," Sir Gervais wheezed. "Met him, didn't you? Motored me in to see their exhibition of ceramics—some dam' fine pieces too, of course. Sheer loot, half of 'em—wonderful opportunities these soldier fellas used to have—an' Watton never missed a chance. Coming to see you perform tonight, m'boy. *Rivals,* isn't it?"

"I'm only on a minute, and I'm awful," said Theodore.

"And, let's face it, not much better in *Twelfth Night,*" said Clare, smiling.

"I thought *you* were very good as Viola," said Laura carefully. "Most of the time, anyhow."

"Where's Pat Gorebarry today?" asked Theodore hastily.

"Dreadful fella—what?" said Sir Gervais, who had been giving a slow-motion demonstration of how a good cigar should be pierced. "Though Clare doesn't think so."

"My dear, he's off somewhere, I think, with that Bulfoss woman," cried Clare. "Not that he really cares tuppence about her—because—"

"Sh-sh!" Laura went sharply, for she saw that Hatchet-Ferrers, who had just escorted Miss Sawkins out of the dining room, was now returning and was almost within earshot. With many grave apologies he drew Laura away from the table, saying that he had an urgent message.

"Miss Sawkins," he began, pronouncing the name as if it were that of some world celebrity, "has now gone to rest before her lecture, and she asked me to tell you, my dear Miss Casey, that there will be no necessity for you to worry about her at all. I will see that she arrives at the Central Library in good time, with her guitar and whatever she needs. No, not at all—a great pleasure, I assure you. Indeed, I was about to thank you, Miss Casey, for the rare privilege you have given me in making me known to Miss Sawkins and allowing me to entertain her. A woman of wide experience," he almost chanted, "intellectual and high-spirited, yet truly feminine, deeply sensitive, as I realized almost at once. The lecture, I know, will be a rare treat, as audiences seemed to have found it everywhere. But the privilege of her acquaintance, which I owe to you, Miss Casey, is a still rarer treat. Thank you."

Golly, thought Laura as she rejoined the others, Sawkins ought to forego even the reduced fee we're paying her, and Madge Bulfoss won't have a look in now. At this rate Humpty will be buying some gipsies soon, giving his Mildred a small tribe for a birthday present. She grinned at Theodore, who looked wonderfully handsome and adorable sitting there with the fat old Baronet and that girl.

"Like to meet this Commodore chap," Sir Gervais was saying.

"You can't just now," said Theodore, suddenly looking worried. "He seems to have gone somewhere."

"And I ought to be thinking of doing some work," said Laura.

But she did not go straight back to the Center, for she had to call at the ticket office of the Corn Exchange, and Theodore went along with her. To reach it they passed between the old stone pillars, out of the warmth and bustle of the street, climbed some worn steps that brought them onto the same level as the main doors in the hall, only a few yards away from the ticket office. Here it was cool and had the dusk of shadowed old stone about it, throwing into relief the blaze and stir of the afternoon outside. When she had finished her business at the ticket office, which lasted only a few minutes, Laura found herself wanting to linger in this deserted and shadowy place. She put a hand on Theodore's arm to keep him by her side, and together they stood there, looking down into the street, so brilliant, warm, alive, with every passer-by on the pavement caught in that brief clarity which is at once beautiful and melancholy, as if it were an image of Time itself. And then, while they were as silent and motionless there as figures in some old painting, and a great tenderness took possession of her, one thing after another happened, all unexpected and yet somehow not surprising, like some fragment of a happy dream, or a perfectly rehearsed incident in a play made out of real people and actual scenes and without beginning or end.

Old Jordan appeared on the bright pavement below, looking like a marvelous portrait of himself as he hesitated and peered up at them. With an untidy thin parcel under his arm, he came up the steps, recognized them and smiled, tore the brown paper from his parcel and showed them another water color by his man, Yardlow, even better than the one he had given them when they had first gone to his house to lunch. When Laura had given a soft cry of delight, then without a word he made her take it; and before she could thank him, he touched her on the arm and pointed toward the doors of the hall behind them. They turned to stare. One door was open now, and Helen Weeks was standing there with Fettercairn, and as these two looked and smiled at each other, there was such warmth and life and beauty in their faces that Laura could have cried out with wonder. Nor was that all. There came stealing through the open doorway, from the orchestra waiting to rehearse on the platform far down the hall, the sound, remote but clear, of the first violin, and then the viola, idly playing the second theme of Elgar's *Introduction and Allegro*; and it was as if faraway voices, noble and dreamy, were pronouncing the benediction she had already vaguely felt, were blessing forever, so that she could never forget, the brilliant warm street and its image of Time, the dusky old stone place where she stood so close to Theodore, old Jordan's smile and his gift of the enchanted cartridge paper with its own sunlight and shadow, the faces of her friends in the doorway, the drama of real things without beginning or end, the clear dream that she saw with eyes so wide open. And she never did forget it. Many a time afterwards, in a dark hour, with hope fading, existence a salt desert, she returned in memory to that time, that place, caught and held once more that very moment, and felt the stream of life running free again, flashing in the sun, as it had done in that high summer of the Festival. . . .

3

All Friday morning Theodore was busy, not at the theater but at the Festival Center, helping Laura (now in charge, the Commodore not having returned) and little Mobbs. Just before twelve Laura went off to meet Mr. Mortory, who was lecturing that afternoon, and his wife, leaving Theodore and Mobbs to decide if it would be safe to sell a few more tickets for the Festival Ball, to be held that night in the Corn Exchange. Officially the list was closed, but some people, including a few influential types ("nobs" to Mobbs), were still fiercely demanding tickets. At a quarter to one, Mobbs, looking like a baked ham, declared that he had done enough for one morning. "We've earned a spot, old boy, and it'll just run to one apiece," he said, getting out what remained of his gin and vermouth. "So we'll relax. Wearing a white tie tonight?"

"No, I haven't got one," said Theodore, perching himself on the Commodore's table. "Just a dinner jacket. Are you?"

"Felt I ought," said Mobbs gravely. "Cheers, old boy! You know, Social Organizer an' all that. So hired some tails. Not a bad fit either. Maggie'll be there—and I want to impress her because the other two blokes are coming too."

"What?" cried Theodore, wanting to laugh. "All three of you with her tonight?"

"That's the way she wants it, old boy. Overdoing the fair-play touch perhaps, but there you are. Matter of fact," he added confidentially, "as far as I can see—tonight it's over-the-top-and-the-best-of-luck. Bound to be. My godfathers—yes! And couldn't be a worse time for me to pop the question. Nothing to offer her—not a sausage. The Commodore and I had a vague scheme or two, but of course no capital. And now he isn't even here. Trying to raise some capital in Town perhaps. I don't know. Nobody knows. But I'd feel a lot better if he was around."

"So would I," said Theodore, who was anxiously awaiting news from Smith, not heard from since lunchtime two days before. "In fact, Laura and I are really worried about him."

"Me too, old boy. My godfathers—yes!" And his round red face was wrinkled in distress so that he looked like a colossal baby about to cry. "Miss him like blazes. Not the same here without him. However. You won't be at the Ball until late, I suppose?"

"No, I'm not going to the theater at all tonight," replied Theodore, standing up and stretching. "They're doing Boon's play so they don't really need me, and I've two shows of *Twelfth Night* tomorrow—worse luck. Why, Archie?"

Mobbs finished his drink, smacked his lips, then gazed earnestly at his friend. "Have a dance or two with Maggie, old boy, will you? Cuts out the other two blokes. And you can put in a word for me. She likes you. And it was you who introduced us, you remember, that day we visited the nobs? So just say a word for poor old Captain Archie Bloody Mobbs, out of a job and nearly broke and no catch at all as a husband, I'll admit. Lunching at the White Hart, aren't you? No, I'm not. Can't afford it every day. I've just realized that—a bit late."

"Archie," said Theodore firmly, taking him by the arm, "you're the Social Organizer, and it's your duty to lunch with Laura and me and these Mortory people. He's our most important lecturer, Laura says, and you must help to entertain him with some solid high-brow conversation. So come on."

The lounge of the White Hart was crowded, and, perhaps because of the Ball, had very much a Festival air. "Some nobs here already, old boy," Mobbs muttered, as they looked round for Laura. "You can hear 'em. Always shout their bloody heads off, I can't think why."

When they found Laura, and she had introduced them to the Mortory couple, she said they ought to go straight in to lunch, as tables were much in demand. Theodore had had from Laura a full account of her visit to the Tanson Lecture Agency and her tea with Miss Tanson and Mr. and Mrs. Mortory, and now, as they sat down in the dining room, he examined this Cambridge pair with some curiosity. Clearly they had had a drink or two with Laura out in the lounge. Mr. Mortory, staring through his heavy spectacles and tightening his lips, appeared to be almost tortured by his intellectual and cultural responsibilities, and gave the impression that by the time he rose to lecture at five o'clock he would be ready to revalue The Novel out of existence. Mrs. Mortory still had the untidy auburn hair that Laura had described, but now her eyes were not angry but sparkling away, she was charmingly dressed and gay, so that she seemed a much more attractive woman than Theodore had expected, though he remembered that Laura had liked her. He was sitting between her and Laura, while Mr. Mortory was on the other side of Laura, with Mobbs next to him and on the other side of Mrs. Mortory.

"Darling," Laura whispered, while Mobbs coped rather desperately with the visitors, "has one sherry gone to my head or is there a lot of excitement about here today?"

"It's not the sherry," said Theodore. "I feel it too. Look—there's Philippa and Pat Gorebarry lunching with Lady Barth and some nobs. And if Pat's not pickled now, he soon will be."

"I know. And—don't look now—but over on your right Humpty-Ferrers is entertaining his Mildred, who insisted on staying on for the Ball, *and* Major and Madge Bulfoss, which is pretty daring of him, you must admit." She giggled a bit, then checked herself. "What about Smith, darling? Any word? Oh—dear! However, let's try and enjoy this lunch." She raised her voice. "What would everybody like to drink?"

"A sound claret perhaps," said Mr. Mortory severely, then turned to Mobbs again. "Well, say Stendhal, Flaubert, Proust, Gide," he boomed, then faded out, the battery still at fault.

"You're probably quite right, old boy," said Mobbs. "But I wouldn't know. Don't read these foreign types myself. In fact, don't read much at all really, though now and again I like to settle down with one of these rattling good Western yarns—you know, old boy, sheriffs and cattle rustlers and everybody shooting from the hip. Not much in your line, I fancy."

"Not at all in my line," said Mr. Mortory, with a faint smile.

"Well, tastes differ, old boy," cried Mobbs heartily. "And wouldn't do if we were all alike, would it?"

But Mr. Mortory now turned to Laura, while Theodore brought Mobbs into his talk with Mrs. Mortory. "The fact is," he continued, "we're all in love here. Captain Mobbs is in love."

"Steady, old boy."

"All sorts of people I see in this room are in love. Even our old Commodore, who runs the Festival though he's disappeared these last few days, is in love, I fancy. More people in Farbridge, Mrs. Mortory, have fallen in love or thereabouts, just lately, than at any other time in its history. Perhaps it's in the air."

"I'm very glad to hear it," cried Mrs. Mortory gaily. "Oh—look— isn't that Jimmy Fettercairn?"

"It is. He's in love too—with that beautiful dark creature with him. She doesn't look it, but she's a member of our Festival Committee."

"A pity about Jimmy Fettercairn," said Mrs. Mortory reflectively, "though I can't say I blame him. Duck? Oh—I love duck. By the way, who's that very dark attractive man facing us, at the table where that old woman's screaming so hard? I feel I've seen him before. Is he an actor?"

After Theodore had explained about Pat Gorebarry, Mobbs said: "You steer clear of that chap, Mrs. Mortory. Barmy—lifts the elbow all day and most of the night—and asks for trouble."

"Well," Mrs. Mortory murmured, still looking across at Gorebarry, "I've never asked for trouble, but I seem to have had plenty—of a rather dreary kind. But what happens—what does he do?"

"A small, distinct, self-conscious elite," Mr. Mortory boomed sadly at Laura, "entirely separate from the large public . . . and its new mass culture. . ." He faded out.

"But I don't want to be one of a small, self-conscious elite," cried Laura. "It sounds awful. Just an arty-smarty little gang, dreadfully pleased with themselves, out of touch with most of life."

"It's a question of the preservation and survival of certain cultural values. . ."

"Help yourself, old boy, then pass the bottle," said Mobbs.

"A few genuine artists . . . a few small groups here and there capable of appreciating. . ."

"I'm sorry, Mr. Mortory," said Laura, "but it sounds to me all so small and select and undernourished, not pushing down any fat roots or producing any juicy fruit. I fancy I must be just one of the other lot, the stupid mob. Anybody want any more vegetables? No? By the way, you are coming to our Ball tonight, Mrs. Mortory, aren't you? I've kept tickets for you, and tell me quick if you don't want them, because they're very much in demand."

"My dear," said Mrs. Mortory, who was looking younger and more cheerful every minute, "I don't know what Leonard feels about it but I'm certainly coming to your Ball. And bless you for remembering!"

"I've come prepared for this occasion," said Mr. Mortory, unpressing his lips into his faint smile, "and so I propose to escort you . . . my dear. . . . Kind of you . . . tickets . . . Miss. . ."

"That's the stuff, old boy," cried Mobbs, when the battery had obviously run out. "With all due respect—do you a power of good. Can't be reading Thingumtibob, worrying about What's-it, all the time—can you? You just give 'em all the thick stick in your lecture, an' then come and shake a loose leg."

"Captain Mobbs," cried Mrs. Mortory, who was delighted, "if it could be managed, would you like to come to Cambridge and deliver a course of lectures? You'd be wonderful."

"Pulling the old leg, eh?" said Mobbs, after a short pause. "But I'll tell you. No Cambridge for me. I've been there twice—in a summer when it was baking hot, in winter when it was perishingly cold— and each time there seemed to be nobody about and nothing to do. Opposite of Oxford, where there always seem to be so many people, you can't walk on the pavement and have to queue up for a sandwich and a glass of bitter. Give me Farbridge, though so far I've not had any offers, not a sausage."

"Captain Mobbs," cried Mrs. Mortory, who was drifting into a reckless mood, "I adore you."

Mr. Mortory looked up, raised his rather dusty eyebrows, then stared gloomily at the menu, did some Rejecting, Excluding, Refusing of puddings and ices, and finally decided on a little cheese.

Shortly afterwards, they found a corner in the lounge, and Theodore ordered coffee, cointreau for the ladies, brandy for himself and the other two men. Then Pat Gorebarry arrived. He was pickled, as Theodore saw at once, but at the stage when he carried himself with immense dignity and did everything with an elaborate air of old-world courtesy and charm. "Miss Casey, my dear Theodore, may I join you? Captain Mobbs, your servant, sir. First, I need a brief respite from the screechings and sharp nudgings of Lady Barth. Secondly, I gather you are entertaining the eminent, the distinguished, the famous literary critic, Mr. Leonard Mortory. Sir," he said to the bewildered Mortory, "this is a great privilege for a poor player, an uneducated buffoon, an illiterate mountebank. I have read several of your books, sir, and have been equally astonished by their scholarship, their grand integrity, their entire lack of insight. And this," he continued, moving round and taking her hand and bestowing upon her his heartbreaking smile, "is Mrs. Mortory. I was wondering, if you will pardon the impertinence, exactly what color your eyes are. I see now they're a kind of cinnamon shade with a flicker of green, very rare and extraordinarily fascinating—"

"Did you say *lack* of insight?" Mr. Mortory demanded, more flustered than indignant.

"I did, sir," Gorebarry flung over his shoulder, still bending over Mrs. Mortory. "We'll discuss it some other time. Mrs. Mortory," he continued in his most exquisitely melancholy and ravishing tone, "is it possible that you are coming to the Ball tonight? You are? And what are you proposing to wear, if again you'll forgive the impertinence?"

"Well," said Mrs. Mortory, blushing like a schoolgirl but with a dancing light in her eyes, "it's a wretched old thing but I still like it—cream-colored heavy silk, with a very full skirt—"

"My dear," said Gorebarry, as if he had known her for years, "you'll look wonderful—and I shall be there, as soon as our play is over, to see you—"

"Leonard," she cried, "perhaps we might go to the theater first. There'll be plenty of time afterwards for dancing."

"Perhaps," said Mr. Mortory. "I think I'd better have a rest . . . glance over my notes . . . lecture at five. . . ."

"We poor performers," Gorebarry murmured, now helping him to rise. "A great privilege, Mr. Mortory." He turned and smiled again at Mrs. Mortory, who had never taken her eyes off him. "Cream-colored heavy silk, a very full skirt—cinnamon with a flicker of green. We meet at midnight. Now back to the wife of Barth." Steadily but with great care, he walked across the lounge.

"Well," said Mrs. Mortory, with a suspicion of a sigh, "I'd better go and look after poor Leonard. Thank you so much, Miss Casey." She hesitated. "I see what you meant about that man Gorebarry. All kinds of trouble. But—oh dear!"

"Yes," said Laura, laughing, "oh dear!"

"Don't quite get this *Oh dearing*," said Mobbs, when Mrs. Mortory had gone. "Do you, old boy?"

"I think so," said Theodore, "though I don't like to hear Laura say it."

"Darling, I was just echoing her," cried Laura. "I knew what she was feeling, but that doesn't mean I feel it too. And I don't, not the tiniest bit, so don't worry. But already she looks ten years younger than she did when I met them in London."

"I don't feel squiffy," said Mobbs earnestly, "but honestly I don't know what you're talking about. Though you seem to have got it, old boy."

But Theodore was staring at two men standing near the reception desk. "Laura—look—that's Smith talking to Seth Hull. I think you'd better let me look after this. Or would you rather be here, Laura?"

"No, we'll go back to the Center, darling. But let me know as soon as you can what happens. Come on, *Capitaine*. More work. And I'm feeling horribly sleepy."

Theodore walked toward the entrance with them, then joined Seth and Smith. "I don't know what's on," said Seth, "but I was just saying this York chap was in here this morning, asking for Commodore, an' said he'd try again this afternoon. If yer want to see him, Theodore lad, yer'd better see him up in my room. I'll tell yer what—you an' me'll go up there now, an' leave Sherlock Holmes here to nab him an' bring him up."

"Oke," said Smith.

"Have you got anything?" Theodore asked eagerly.

"In the bag," said Smith. "Leave it now, though, till he comes. Why boil cabbages twice? See you later."

Up in Seth's private office Theodore found him rather mysterious about the Commodore. "I don't understand you, Seth," Theodore said finally. "You don't seem to be interested."

"No," said Seth comfortably, "I'm not bothering."

"Then you must know where he is."

"No, I don't. But my guess is—he's trying to find Grace. He'll be back—tomorrow at latest—happen tonight."

Theodore stared in some exasperation at Seth's huge meaty slab of a face and the twinkling little eyes that gave it life. "I can't make you out. I know you like the Commodore, yet you don't seem to care."

"Ay, too bad, isn't it?" He twinkled away.

"I suppose it doesn't matter to you that this man York is trying to blackmail him."

Seth's manner changed abruptly. "Nay, that's summat else, lad. We're having none o' that. And yer were right to get that little 'tec after him. He doesn't look up to much, Smith or whoever he is, an' I took against him when he first come nosing round here, but he managed that firework job all right last Saturday. Aaa—" and Seth now contrived those rusty grandfather clock noises that suggested he was amused "—I had to laugh when Commodore an' Mr. Casey told me about that caper. Well, lad, how many more are yer letting into this dance tonight? I'll have my work cut out catering for that lot."

So they discussed the Ball, telephoning the Festival Center for the final figures, and they were still at it when York arrived with Smith.

"Here, what's this?" said York uneasily. "I came to see Commodore Tribe. I don't want a meeting."

"Sit down an' shut up," said Seth, an ideal chairman for this type of proceeding. "Nobody asked yer to come to my hotel, an' if yer don't like this, yer can lump it. Now Theodore, lad."

"You told the Commodore you'd drag him into a divorce case and claim damages."

"Well, what if I did?" said York sulkily. "That's between him and me. Nothing to do with you people."

"Except that we happen to be friends of his," said Theodore, "and we don't see why he should be blackmailed."

"Who's talking about blackmail?"

"I am, cock," said Smith. "All you wanted was to be bought off. Old game. So old it smells. When you start claiming damages in any divorce court, I'll do a trapeze act at the Palladium."

"What are you talking about?" York demanded belligerently.

"You chum. Got all the info. Want it? Oke. From last October to March this year, where were you and doing what? Living at Number Five, West Row, Granston. With a Mrs. Tross—Evie to pals. Little woman, reddish hair, about thirty-five. And wondering where her Frankie's gone. Want any more?"

It was clear that York, who was now standing up and staring at Smith open-mouthed, did not want any more.

"Got to be clever to play your game, chum. And if you're clever, I'm Ginger Rogers." Smith wagged a finger. "Turn it up. Or next time somebody'll put you inside. Got a good pub too. What more do you want?" Smith now appealed to all the rational powers of the universe. "Got a lovely pub, a nice little trouble-and-strife, and yet wants to start putting the black on people! All comes of backing losers! What a twerp!"

In a blind fury York aimed a blow at him, but Smith, with his inch of cigarette still smoldering away, coolly dodged it. The next moment, Seth had taken a huge grip on York's collar and was saying: "Now listen, York. If ever yer come here again, I'll put my foot to your backside. An' another thing. Next week, when I've a bit o' time, I'll run out to Tredberrow an' ask a few questions at the Bell an' if I don't like what I hear, then I'll have a word or two with your missis an' tell her a few things. Now take yerself off—sharp as yer can."

"Fifty quid," said Smith briskly, after the door had closed behind York. "Plus exes." He produced one of the dirtiest pieces of paper Theodore had ever seen, and handed it over. "Twelve pounds fifteen and six. All there. Call it sixty-three quid. But no check, Mr. Jenks. Cash every time for yours truly."

"I'll go halves i' this," said Seth. "Give me a check for thirty-one pound ten, Theodore, an' Smith, come here in the morning and I'll give yer cash—sixty-three pound."

"Oke, Mr. Hull," said Smith. "But I'd like to sub a bit. On account of paying out the exes. Any objection?"

Seth produced a fat wallet and gave him twenty pound notes. "I wouldn't say you're owt much to look at, Smith, but seemingly yer can do a smart job when yer want to, I'll say that for yer, lad."

"Ta, muchly. But you're all wet about the looks. Where'd I be if I looked like Patrick Gorebarry or Mr. Jenks here? Wouldn't have an earthly. But I can look smart if I'm not on a job. You'd be surprised. And look—do me a favor. Want to go to this Festival Ball tonight. Do you no harm to have me there neither. You never know. And I can hire some lovely clobber. What do you say?"

"We can manage that," said Theodore, who had been writing his check and now gave it to Seth. "Thank you very much, Seth. I only wish we could get in touch with the Commodore or that he'd come back here. But then you think he will. Come on, Smith. I want you to do me a favor now."

He waited until they were out of Seth's office, and then continued: "It's about this woman you were following—Mrs. Robinson or whatever she calls herself—Grace. You seem to have finished with her now—"

"Right," said Smith, as they went down the stairs. "Agency told me to take a holiday. Don't want me to spill anything though, do you, Mr. Jenks? Not supposed to, you know. All confidential. First rule of the game. Has to be."

"I can understand that," said Theodore. "And if it was just curiosity on my part, I wouldn't ask you to tell me anything about her. But we're worried about the Commodore, who's probably gone to London to try to find her. And he knows she's told everybody a different story about herself—"

"He can't say I didn't warn him," said Smith. "Told him she was a liar. Over and over I told him."

"But what's the point of her telling these stories? Why does she lie?"

"Can't help it. No point at all. Not playing a con game. Nothing like that. Decent nice woman. But gets carried away. Lots do. Tell you anything for tuppence. Going out?"

"Yes," said Theodore. He did not speak again until they were out in the High Street. "You must tell me more about her. After all, you've done very well here this week. Haven't you now? And I believe the poor old Commodore's more than half in love with her. So—as you say—have a heart."

"Oke," said Smith. "What about a cuppa?"

"All right, a cuppa. There's a place along here."

Over his cuppa, Smith, though still cautious, was more forthcoming.

"Won't give you details. Wouldn't be right. No names, no pack drill. Must keep it sketchy. Take it or leave it. Oke." He removed his ashy stub of a cigarette, blew hard into his cup, took a noisy drink, then continued. "She was married. Up North. Husband died. No children. Ran a hotel. Did very well but just after the war had a breakdown. Not barmy but starting on the way to it. Then she marries again. Wrong bloke and it doesn't take. Don't blame her, knowing him. She comes into money, through an uncle who made pork pies and what-not. Not as much as she tells people—but a tidy bit. Leaves the husband. So he says she's not responsible, see? Can't prove it so puts us on to it. Follow her round, get the evidence. Get it?"

"Yes, I think so. But why were you called off?"

"Can't say for certain," said Smith, who had now mysteriously acquired another half-smoked cigarette. "Being here, not on the spot. I can guess, though. A quid to half a dollar she got browned off and paid hubby to turn it up. A thousand or two, and she goes her way, he goes his, and nice work if you can find it."

"The Commodore could never marry her then," Theodore mused regretfully.

"Come off it. Don't be ridic. I'll bet he's got about six wives, all colors, as it is. And didn't do badly for himself out at that pub at Tredberrow, I heard. Some blokes know where to find 'em, and he's one. Reminds me of a case I had last year. A woman comes to us—"

By the time Smith had concluded his reminiscence it was time for Theodore to hurry off to the Central Library, to find Laura at the lecture. He found her, looking out for him, just inside the lecture room, which was crowded. Huntley, in the chair, was making his intro-ductory speech. "'Erce," he declared, "I think we may justly congrat-ulate ourselves on the splendid series of Festival lectures that have been given here. But Miss Casey, who organized these lectures, has been very clever about them, and, good though they all have been, she arranged to keep the best for this final day. Mr. Mortory is known to us all as one of our most distinguished literary critics, the possessor of a fastidious mind, a penetrating—er—judgment, the author of *Disavowals, Rejections, Exclusions, Refusals*. And now here he is, to give us a talk—*The Novel: A Revaluation*. Mr. Mortory."

Mr. Mortory acknowledged the applause with a grave nod, picked up a sheaf of notes, looked at them with some distaste and put them down again, moved a glass of water six inches to the right, stared hard at the ceiling, cleared his throat, and began. "It has been obvious for some time to some of us who care about literature," he boomed angrily, "that the art of fiction, so far as such an art can be said to exist, should be intelligently examined, assessed, revalued." He was beginning to fade. There was some coughing. "What are its significant patterns?" he demanded severely of the coughers. "What tests should we apply?" He was fading again. ". . . The few intelligent readers . . . those capable of appreciating . . . form. . . . correlation . . . awareness. . . ."

"Speak up, sir," cried a sharp elderly voice, which sounded as if it might belong to old Jordan.

"What kind of awareness do we postulate in the novelist?" Mr. Mortory asked at the top of his voice.

"Let's go, darling," said Laura, plucking at Theodore's sleeve. "Then you can tell me what happened about Smith and that man York. And there won't be any danger of your becoming one of the small self-conscious elite and we can just go on enjoying ourselves." They went. "And I'll tell you who isn't at that lecture," Laura continued. "Mrs. Mortory. She's having her hair done, and between us we had to bribe the girl like mad to get her the appointment."

4

When Laura and Theodore talked about the Festival, as they often did afterwards, in places thousands of miles from Farbridge, Laura could never be certain which part she liked best of all, but Theodore, though he always hastened to praise the Bulfoss party (because of Laura) and the Saturday night fireworks, plumped every time for the Festival Ball. And not, he would add, because of the dancing, nor the grand appearance of the old Corn Exchange on this occasion, nor the music of Johnny and his Jollyboys (who put on some ordinary evening clothes and produced some violins for the waltzes), nor the supper and drinks that Seth had done very well; and no, not even because it was really the last—just as it was the grandest—event of the Festival, with everybody there, like a well-arranged finale. No, the great thing was that it had a very special atmosphere, some secret oxygen of its own, that set the mind and heart dancing as well as the feet. It was that kind of evening, that sort of time, when the world is not a cinder rushing through the icy dark but a bubble, floating in blue air. But, of course, a chap has to be in the mood, and Theodore was very much in the mood. So was Laura, naturally, but although she may have started off feeling gayer and more excited, as girls generally do, perhaps some undissolved lump of feminine sense and responsibility remained with her and she could not quite abandon herself to the glorious silliness of everything, like a child keeping a birthday with mad uncles, as he could and did. But then, she did not drink as much as Theodore and the chaps.

Everybody was there, except the unfriendly types, who were probably plotting and biting their nails somewhere in dark back rooms. (And Grace, of course, about whom nobody seemed to know anything, although Laura sometimes wondered if Seth Hull was as blankly ignorant as he pretended to be.) Yes, everybody was there, and within an hour everything was going splendidly, both on the dance floor, which took up about two-thirds of the hall, and in the buffet, which was about a third of the floor, screened off, and then overflowed into various small rooms round the entrance. The Mayor appeared and performed a stately waltz with the Mayoress before disappearing, presumably to discuss municipal affairs with many a *which* and *Pzzzz*, in one of the smaller rooms. Huntley, with all the appearance of being anesthetized, danced very carefully with the Paisley shawl headmistress, Mrs. Coote, and the Barr girls. Mr. Hookwood and the Group Captain (waiting for his Philippa to arrive from the theater) danced with Liz and Dulcie, the Mayoress and Mrs. Gisburn, and other matrons and frippets. Old Mr. Jordan, very energetic but never varying his step, danced with anybody who could not avoid him. Hatchet-Ferrers was there, looking enormously rich, unhealthy, and solemn in the fullest possible evening dress, and divided his attentions between Mildred Sawkins, all peculiar curls, spangles, and gipsy devilment, and Madge Bulfoss, in pale pink and very much on the lookout for Pat Gorebarry. Major Bulfoss kept popping into the buffet but would return, stiff and rather goggle-eyed, to do his duty on the floor, where he took his partners round as if they were mobile petrol pumps. Mr. Mortory, still looking dusty, had a desperate quarter of an hour with Lady Barth, glittering and jangling and screeching out awful remarks about everybody; and then he retired, gloomily, to eat sausage rolls. Mrs. Mortory, cinnamon eyes watching for Gorebarry's arrival, wore her cream-colored heavy silk with the full skirt, looked very handsome indeed, danced with anybody who claimed her, and smiled a tiny secret smile. Maggie, looking

like a great warm apple, jigged round in turn with the garage proprietor, the farmer, and Archie Mobbs, not one of whom ever danced
with anybody else when she was not available but departed hastily
to refresh themselves. Sir Barclay Gishforth, a notable performer in
the early night-club style, circled the floor with Lady Felicia, an adept
at the same style. After singing a foxtrot chorus or two into a microphone, Johnny's April, as slim, bright, and hard as a platinum watch,
condescended to mingle with the dancers; and then she was claimed
at once by a short, mysterious man with a distinguished nose, who
said little but had a most masterful haughty way with him and really
did suggest that figure so often met in fiction, so rarely in real life, the
man in immaculate evening dress.

"But, darling, it can't be," said Laura, as Theodore swung her closer
to this impressive couple.

"I tell you, it's Smith," said Theodore, and brought them alongside.

"What did you say you are?" April was asking.

"M. I. Five," Smith muttered out of the corner of his mouth. "Keep
it to yourself."

"But what's that?" April was bewildered.

"Wasting it on you, Toots," said Smith reproachfully, and then,
as they passed, he winked at Theodore, and Laura, who had already
laughed a lot at nothing in particular, began laughing again. And
Helen Weeks, dark and lovely in soft damson velvet, who was in
Jimmy Fettercairn's long arms, looked at Laura, and laughed too,
just out of happiness.

But how could everybody be there when the Commodore was missing? It was like an illusionist's trick. At one moment he was still
missing, and then the next moment he was there, in a rather greeny
old evening coat and outsizes in collar and white tie, dancing with
Lady Gishforth, calling her Daphne, and roaring over old times. As
soon as the music stopped—and this time the Jollyboys refused an
encore and plainly wanted a drink and a smoke—Theodore led Laura
across to the other two, and all four went into the buffet. After they
found their partners some refreshment, the two men had some private
talk.

"Went off looking for Grace, of course," said the Commodore.
"Didn't find her, though. Had to come back tonight. Couldn't leave
poor Laura with the Festival on her hands." He looked at his glass.
"Not very good tipple, this. I believe Seth has something much better

in one of the small rooms. We'll try it later. I'm not feeling gay, my boy. I'll confess it. Doing my best, but I'm devilish worried."

"Well," said Theodore, "I've disposed of York for you." And he explained what Smith had found out and how York had been finally routed.

"My dear Theodore," cried the Commodore, who was genuinely moved, "I'm eternally grateful. By George—I am. It's a pity about Grace—and I don't know why, but that woman, with nothing extraordinary about her except her ability to give false accounts of herself, had a fascination for me—but there it is. My boy, I shall cheer up. I shall endeavor to be my old self. Waiter," he called sharply, looking and sounding the most important personage for miles around, "I'm Commodore Tribe, as you probably know—"

"Yes, sir. Anything I can—"

"Give my compliments to my friend, Mr. Hull, and tell him that if he has anything better and stronger than this stuff in one of his back rooms, Mr. Jenks and I will be glad to taste it." He stared about him. The buffet was filling up now. "Seems to be going well so far, eh? Good. We must see that it goes even better. Now who the devil's this with Mrs. Jolly?"

"Bubbly for you," Smith was saying as he came up. "Bubbly for me. George, two bubblies. Anything to eat? Name it, girlie."

"Smith," said the Commodore, astounded.

"Now, now, Commodore," said Smith. "Incog here. Know my friend?"

"Mrs. Jolly and I are well acquainted. You're looking very beautiful tonight, April. And Johnny and his boys seem to be playing very well. Tell them so from me, my dear."

"Johnny can put on a bit of class with anybody," said April proudly. "Nice change after that park too. And the boys haven't a bad string section neither, have they? I say," for now Smith was foraging farther down the table, "who's this Mystery Man? Don't get him at all."

"*Sh*," the Commodore went, looking at her gravely.

"Why? What's the idea?"

"*Sh*," went Theodore, shaking his head at her. "Quiet now."

"I am glad you were able to be with us tonight, sir," said the Commodore to Smith, who now arrived with food and drink.

"A great honor, sir," said Theodore. "Is there anything we can do for you, sir?"

"No, thanks all the same, men," said Smith loftily. "A very nice little place you have here. Quite decent. Here you are," he said to April, who was gaping at him. "Looks like tinned salmon to me, though. But always tasty, I say."

"If you'll excuse me," said April, still gaping, "I must have a word—"

"Certainly, certainly," cried Smith, waving her away. "Thanks for the lovely build-up Commodore. Smashing piece to look at, that one, but got nothing upstairs. Wasted that M. I. Five gag on her. Never heard of it. Have to look 'em over a bit now. That one in pink might do. Know her?"

"I'll introduce you," said the Commodore. "But give me a moment alone with her first." He went across and detached Mrs. Bulfoss from her group. "Madge," he said softly, "there's a certain man here tonight who's very anxious to meet you. Don't show any surprise if I call him Mr. Smith. That's what he prefers. And I think it would be tactful not to ask any questions. You understand, my dear Madge?"

"Well actually, Commodore, I don't quite. But of course it's very exciting. Do you mean—"

"Careful. He's here." The Commodore took a step forward. "Mrs. Bulfoss, may I introduce—er—Mr. Smith—?"

"How d'you do?" cried Mrs. Bulfoss, very pretty and gay.

"Charmed," said the mysterious man, hardly moving his lips, "very charmed." And then, as she confided afterwards to several friends, he looked straight into her eyes with a strange, penetrating, wistful yet masterful, enigmatic look that actually she felt going right through her.

"I'll leave you, sir," said the Commodore deferentially.

"Do, do. Some other time, Commodore. If I can spare it." And he turned to give Madge Bulfoss another of those strange right-through-her looks.

Meanwhile, Theodore had been joined by Laura, and after a few minutes the Commodore returned. "With Seth's compliments," said Theodore, indicating the bottle in front of him.

"Now don't you chaps start boozing," cried Laura. "Lady Gishforth left me because she said she didn't want her Barky to get tight too early. Later on, apparently, it didn't matter. Only he insists then, she says, on doing some special dance of his own, which is all right if everybody else is rather pickled. Listen, the band's back again. No more drinks for you, darling, until you've danced again."

"I promised Archie Mobbs I'd dance with Maggie," said Theodore, "so that I could sing his praises to her. But she seems to have a sort of syndicate of partners, including Mobbs, who work nonstop."

"This," said the Commodore, after emptying his glass, "is something very different." He took up the bottle. "I'm much obliged to Seth. I suppose he's here somewhere."

"Yes," said Laura, "and here's Humpty-Ferrers, by himself too. Keep hold of me, Theodore, because I simply couldn't dance with him. He'd be like a giant egg—a bit poached now too."

"Stick to me," Theodore told her. "We'll dance again in a minute."

"I'm looking," said Hatchet-Ferrers gravely, "for Miss Sawkins."

"And who's she?" the Commodore inquired, filling his glass again.

"She was our Wednesday lecturer," cried Laura. "*I Know the Gipsies*. And Mr. Hatchet-Ferrers very kindly looked after her for me and they're now great friends."

"A most delightful woman, Commodore," said Hatchet-Ferrers. "A trifle too high-spirited at times perhaps, but that's the artistic temperament. I left her trying to persuade the bandleader to play some gipsy dance music—the situation was somewhat embarrassing as the man did not appear to be co-operative—and now I can't find her."

"Well, there's Madge Bulfoss over there," said the Commodore mischievously. "Talking to that man everybody's wondering about. Very much absorbed too. See 'em?"

Hatchet-Ferrers stared, adjusted his enormous glasses, and stared again.

"I overheard him on the dance floor saying something about M. I. Five," said Theodore carelessly. "Let's dance, Laura." And they hurried out.

"My dear fellow," said the Commodore, giving Hatchet-Ferrers a glass, "I think you need a little of this. Seth Hull's special brand."

"I think I do. Thank you, Commodore." He sampled it, then took a longer drink. "Excellent indeed." But his mind was not on it. He stared again at Madge and her companion, his moon face, which might have been designed for it, deeply troubled. "Commodore, I've seen that man before. Where or when, I cannot remember, but the memory, vague as it is, remains distinctly unpleasant."

"Ah!" said the Commodore, making the most of it. "Not that you surprise me."

"And Madge, between ourselves, can be indiscreet at times," Hatchet-Ferrers continued, troubled now at the greatest possible depth, somewhere among the giant squids. "I'm thinking more of official and political matters, not of personal relationships. Should I have a word with Gerald Bulfoss, do you think?"

"I think you ought," said the Commodore gravely. "But have another drink first. You may need it." He began pouring again. "I have a feeling that a lot of strange things may happen tonight. Don't ask me why, my dear Hatchet-Ferrers. I have these feelings, just as you do, I remember. Now, who's this?"

"Miss Sawkins," the other replied, swallowing his drink so hastily that he nearly choked. Miss Sawkins and the Commodore patted him on the back, and then were introduced to each other. "Perhaps you'll have a talk with the Commodore, Mildred, for a few minutes. I have a rather urgent errand—official and political rather than personal."

Miss Sawkins tipped her head to one side, produced the dimple, shook the peculiar curls a little, and smiled winsomely up at the Commodore, who made up his mind at that very moment to be rid of her as soon as possible. "Commodore Tribe," she began in her best dove tones, "I've been hearing so much about you, though I don't suppose you've ever heard of humble little me. Now have you?"

"For years and years," said the Commodore. *I Know the Gipsies*. As soon as I was told we could have lectures at the Festival, I said: 'Then get Miss Sawkins.' Cost what it may, I told them, they had to get you."

"Oh—how sweet of you! I wonder if I might have the teeniest sip—"

"Not of this," the Commodore cried hurriedly. "Beastly stuff. I'd be ashamed to offer it to you. Now there's the man you want. Huntley," he called. Huntley came across, smiled vaguely at Miss Sawkins, declared that everything was going awfully well, closed and quivered and went under.

"I was just about to offer Miss Sawkins a little claret or cider cup," said the Commodore, "and then persuade her to give me the next dance. But I see young Jenks looking for me—probably on urgent business—so reluctantly, my dear Huntley, I must hand Miss Sawkins over to you. And you couldn't ask for a better partner, Miss Sawkins—first-class—absolutely keen—so off you go. Now, Theodore, my boy?"

Theodore had brought Maggie with him. "Sir Barclay grabbed Laura. Maggie doesn't want to dance again just now, so I've brought her here for a drink and to talk to her about Archie Mobbs."

"Ah, yes, Archie Mobbs," said the Commodore, shaking his head at Maggie, who was like some rosy symbolic figure of plenty. "How is our poor friend taking it, Theodore?"

"Badly, very badly. Here's your drink, Maggie, though you don't deserve it."

"I like him very much," said Maggie. "But after all there's the other two chaps—one with a lovely farm and the other with a nice car business—and Archie is the oldest—and the fattest."

"There's nothing wrong with age and fat," said the Commodore. "And I ought to know because I have an ample supply of both. It's a compliment to be courted and loved by the oldest and fattest. Go on, my boy. Tell me about poor Mobbs."

"He was talking to me about it, this morning," said Theodore, pretending to ignore Maggie. "He felt it was tonight-or-never. 'And what have I to offer her?' he said. 'Not a sausage,' he said. There were tears in his voice."

"I'll bet," said Maggie.

"There you have it," said the Commodore. "No lovely farm. No nice car business, if there is such a thing. Not, as he said, a sausage. Only an affectionate nature, courage and kindness, humor and a cheerful outlook, and a romantic soul. That's all."

"He ought to be telling me this, not you," said Maggie, who was not unmoved, however, by this recital.

The Commodore put an arm round her, and dropped now into a persuasive whisper. "Maggie, he's afraid to say what's in his heart because at the moment, like me, he has no plans, no immediate prospects, many enemies in high places, having sacrificed nearly everything for the Festival and the people of Farbridge. Theodore, my boy, pass the bottle, and then leave us. Maggie, my friend loves you. Poor brave little Archie Mobbs—"

"Oh, stop it," cried Maggie, much moved now.

"Not a sausage to offer you—"

Theodore arrived on the dance floor just in time for a Paul Jones. In the outer ring of males he found himself grasping the hand of Pat Gorebarry, who had just come from the theater, and they had a chance to talk as they first shuffled round, before the thing speeded up. "Well,

I've played that idiot Cardinal for the last time, my lad," cried Gore-barry, who was looking ravaged and reckless. "That Mrs. Thing—the don's wife—never came to see us, for which I'm thankful. Is she here? Or has she taken fright? By Heaven—no—she's over there, and smiling at me." And as soon as the two rings broke, ignoring all the rules, he flashed across and claimed her.

Theodore drew Mrs. Bulfoss out of the pool of females, and as they fox-trotted sedately, she talked about Smith. "Actually I know he's *somebody*—because of what the Commodore said—but he talks in the oddest way—quite common, though I suppose he's putting that on. And then Arthur Hatchet-Ferrers—who, I must say, has been rather tiresome lately—had to come and warn me against saying anything to him—I mean, Mr. Smith, though of course I know that isn't his name actually. Do you know where he comes from?"

"Yes. London." And then he was back with the circling males, going faster this time, so that what with one thing and another the whole Corn Exchange seemed to be rapidly turning itself into a merry-go-round; and the next minute he found himself waltzing frantically with Lady Barth, who was astonishingly energetic and yet never stopped talking or screeching. "Remember my secretary-companion, Mrs. Win-tle—deaf as a post? Still talks about you. Got yourself engaged to that busy little dark girl, I hear. Nice little thing but you could have done better than that. Seen Felicia? All skin an' bone nowadays. Drinks like a fish too. Barky Gishforth's enjoyin' himself. Where's Daphne? Poor as mice these days. Wouldn't be much better myself only I don't stand any nonsense from anybody. Well, thank you for the hop. Back to the hens now."

More galloping round with the men, then a stiff shy little dance with a Barr girl, another gallop, the last, and this time he was within reach of Laura and before anybody could intervene they were away. "You look a bit peculiar, darling," she began. "Are you tight? Or am I just feeling giddy? Both probably. What's happening apart from Pat Gore-barry grabbing Mrs. Mortory every time and her adoring it? Where's Mr. Mortory?"

"He was eating sausage rolls in a thoughtful way, last time I saw him. Lady Barth calls you a busy little dark girl. And I left the Commodore melting Maggie for Mobbs. But where is Mobbs? And where's Smith?"

"Smith's here. I had the waltz with him, and he smells of camphor or moth balls or something, but he was sweet about you in his Smithy way. And he says Humpty-Dumpty-Ferrers and Major Bulfoss keep trying to talk to him, but that Humpty's too slow and the Major's blotto—that's his word for it. Do you love me?"

"Yes, more than ever."

"So do I. I mean, love you. Let's keep together from now on, shall we, and blow being sociable and letting other people butt in?"

When they returned, later, to the buffet, Gorebarry and Mrs. Mortory were with them. No sooner had they found some food and drink and a corner to sit in than Mr. Mortory appeared, looking very untidy and rather odd. "Why, Leonard, where have you been?" his wife asked.

"I ate a lot of sausage rolls," he said vaguely, "and then sat in a little room behind there and a man talked to me about Argentine Railways . . . not important. . . ." Then he stared hard at Gorebarry through his rather thick glasses. "Why 'lack of insight'?"

"Why what?" asked Gorebarry.

Mr. Mortory wiggled a finger at him. "After lunch, you said my criticism showed a lack of insight. Why?"

"An interesting question," said Gorebarry. "But allow me to put one to you, before I answer yours. What is the relation between the individual in the existentialism of Sartre and his school and the central self in Kafka?"

"I shall have to think that out," said Mr. Mortory, looking cross. And left them without another word."

"I didn't imagine you'd know about those things," Mrs. Mortory said to Gorebarry.

"I don't. I happened to hear something like it one night on the air, and I thought it might make him happy."

Mrs. Mortory laughed, and Gorebarry took her hand, looked into her eyes, and said tenderly: "Come to the theater tomorrow, my dear, and I'll show you the best Sir Toby Belch since Ralph Richardson or Cedric Hardwicke played him. Perhaps better. Now when you laugh, those little flickers of green in your eyes seem to expand and flash—"

Laura jumped up. "Let's find out about Mobbs or somebody, Theodore. Goodbye, you two." As they pushed their way through the crowd, for the buffet was full now, Laura went on: "I was against Mr. Mortory this morning, but I'm not sure I am now. And anyhow those two had better be by themselves. Is everything becoming rather peculiar, or is it just me, darling?"

"It's both. Here's Smith."

"Fat Face has rumbled me," said Smith. "So bang goes the incog. Major won't have it, though. Says we met in some West End Club. Blotto, of course. The wife's a disappointment. Doesn't use her loaf. Danced with Lady Gishforth. Got class but the cold type. Frozen horse. Commodore says he's fixing me up with a Miss Sawkins. Gipsy type and full of go. But he's plastered and could be wrong. But I'm liking it. All experience. So ta, muchly, for the invite."

Farther along, where Theodore had left the Commodore, they found an uproarious group, consisting of Philippa Hookwood and her father, the Group Captain, Sir Barclay, the Commodore, Maggie and Mobbs, who was rounder and redder and hotter than they had ever seen him before. "What's happened?" cried Laura.

"I've taken him," said Maggie.

"My godfathers—it's true, old boy," said Mobbs, shaking hands with Theodore. "And I know you helped."

"It was that about you not having a sausage that got me," said Maggie, who still could not decide whether to laugh or to cry. "It just got me, that did. And take that grin off your face, Groupie. You tell him to stop, Miss Hookwood."

"Behave, Trevy, you monster," cried Philippa.

"No, no, you've got it wrong, Maggie and Philippa, my dears," cried Sir Barclay, who was now very ripe. "The Group Captain and I were comparing notes as to how to put the finishing touch on this extremely jolly party—"

"Which the more respectable types are now leaving," said Philippa.

"All the better, of course," Sir Barclay continued. "And, in comparing jolly old notes, we both hit on the same thing—a sort of general round dance called this an' that—according to where you happen to be—"

"It's called *Ring-a-ring-a-dub-dub*," said a cold clear voice, for Lady Gishforth had joined the group. "And we'll be lucky if Barky and Trevy don't shed most of their clothes. I suppose there's no stopping you now, Barky?"

"Certainly not, Daphne. Trevy and I—"

"Then I shall join in," said Lady Gishforth.

"And I must bribe the band with whisky," said the Group Captain. "Always have to about this time—and we need plenty of *zing* and *boom* for this act. Commodore, you and Barky pick sides while I liberate the band."

"I'll give you a little advice, Miss Casey," said Lady Gishforth. "And please remember it. Whenever your husband decides to do something idiotic and rowdy, insists on making a fool of himself in public, always join in. Don't forget that. You'll find it very useful."

"Thank you very much," said Laura demurely.

"I'll tell you something," Maggie whispered to Theodore, "it was Archie all the time. But you don't want to make it too easy, you know. The first time you brought him, for lunch that day, remember, he looked so pleased, I took a fancy to him right away. And everything the Commodore said about him is true. And we'll manage somehow— him and his no sausage!"

"What side, old man?" Major Bulfoss asked the Commodore, glaring but not unamiably. "Don't want sides do we?"

"Yes, for some *dub-dub* thing," said the Commodore vaguely.

"Don't think I could touch it." The Major wagged his head slowly, then suddenly looked indignant and grabbed the Commodore's arm. "Look here, about this M. I. Five chap—bit thick, isn't it? I mean, whether he is or he isn't—an' Arthur Hatchet-Ferrers says not—seems to me still a bit much. Half a mind to raise it in the House. Would you raise it in the House?"

"Only a few inches on a dull day," said the Commodore, leaving the Major to work it out. "Ah—Miss Sawkins, Huntley—you're on Group Captain's side for *Ringing the dub-dub*—or whatever it's called."

"One of those dear old folk dances?" cried Miss Sawkins.

"Probably—erce," said Huntley. "Absolutely first-class—some of them."

"It's more Ancient British than Old English," said Theodore carelessly. "Clothes are shed by the leaders, I'm told."

"Hatchet-Ferrers, my dear fellow," said the Commodore, "I claim you for the Group Captain's team. I don't know how you'll be in the *ring-a-ring-a* part but for the *dub-dub* you'll be superb."

"I'm afraid I'm not familiar with this—er—game or dance," said Hatchet-Ferrers. "But I must tell you, Commodore, that I've now recognized that fellow—he's that little private—"

"*Ch-ch-ch,*" went the Commodore rather severely. "Here to keep an eye on things for the Festival Committee. Ask Lady Gishforth about your dub-dubbing. She knows."

"But you're not in their team, don't forget," said Theodore. "Now here's Mr. Mortory, Commodore. He gave a brilliant lecture, this afternoon."

"In existentialism," said Mr. Mortory gloomily, "the ego may be said—"

"You're in Sir Barclay Gishforth's team, my dear sir," said the Commodore. "And I advise you to fortify yourself with a drink or two first. Theodore, a glass of Seth's special for Mr. Mortory, who's at least half a bottle behind us."

"I don't quite gather," Mr. Mortory began, as Theodore took charge of him.

"It's the new folk dance school," said Theodore, pouring him a full glass. "The expression in movement and rhythm of certain basic conflicts in the contemporary Unconscious."

"The central self in Kafka," said Mr. Mortory, "can be described—briefly—"

"Drink up," cried Theodore. "Then report to Sir Barclay—over there —doing something to his collar."

"Come along, my side," roared the Group Captain, who looked now as if he would not need to remove any clothes but at any moment might simply burst out of them. "Chaps and frippets alternately in a line. Get weaving. Nice co-operation from the band boys. Listen—*ring-a-ring-a-dub-dub*."

Ring-a-ring-a-dub-dub went Johnny and his Jollyboys. *Ring-a-ring-a* went Sir Barclay and his side, and *dub-dub* replied the Group Captain's team. Theodore never had a clear notion of what they were doing, and was never able afterwards to reconstruct the pattern and the movements. But sometimes he was part of a long snaky line, shuffling forward, wriggling and stamping, sometimes advancing toward the other group, sometimes whirling Laura round and round. *Ring-a-ring-a-dub-dub*—and he caught an astonishing glimpse of Seth, puce and gasping, twirling round Lady Gishforth, still cool and unruffled; *ring-a-ring-a-ring-a-ring*—and there were Miss Sawkins and Huntley (eyes closed), Madge Bulfoss and Smith, swaying and prancing; *dub-dub-dub-dub*— and the Commodore and Hatchet-Ferrers advanced upon Lady Felicia and April; *ring-a-ring-a-ring-a-dub-dub-dub-dub*—and Sir Barclay and the Group Captain, now without coats, now without collars, ties, waistcoats, sweating and roaring, circled and stamped; *ring-a-ring-dub-ring-a-dub-dub*—and Johnny Jolly was with his April, and Pat Gorebarry was hurrying a flushed and laughing Mrs. Mortory off the floor, and old Jordan and Mr. Mortory and the Paisley shawl headmistress and Lady Barth were performing a foursome on their own, and Mobbs and Maggie were spinning round and round like pink tops, and Jimmy Fettercairn seemed to be conducting what were left of the Jollyboys, and somehow Helen Weeks was playing the piano up there, and—yes it was—Smith, no other, banging the drums, bringing out a tremendous *dub-dub* to everybody's *ring-a-ring*. And then, really before he knew where he was or had sorted it out properly, it was all over, something gone and done with, streaking away and mistily dwindling on the time track; and he and Laura were going home, the night vast and cool, very old but capable yet of swallowing and digesting another few million Festival Balls, and perhaps a shade more ironical than usual. But the memory of it remained, with a light or two never contributed by the Farbridge Electricity Department, to defy time and darkness.

5

Rather late on Wednesday morning the Commodore reluctantly got himself out of bed, accompanied by the mournful thought that it would be all the same if he stayed there. Before he began shaving, he stuck his head out of the window. There had been some light rain earlier, but now the midsummer sun was climbing high in a clear sky, and all was fresh and gay. Except Commodore Horace Tribe, who was suffering from a slight headache, a sour mouth, and a profound sense of anticlimax. The Farbridge Festival had come and gone; the Mossat Repertory Comany, the Fettercairn Orchestra, Johnny and his Jollyboys, all had departed; the Festival Center had seen its last meeting of the Committee, and all its posters and notices had gone for wastepaper; and his final report had been delivered to the Town Hall. He had been congratulated. Votes of thanks were in the air. There had arrived this very morning an invitation to be a guest of honor at a special Ladies' Night Dinner of the Farbridge Lodge of the Ancient and Noble Order of Stags. But he could not live on congratulations, votes of thanks, or, except for one evening, on a dinner of the Noble Stags. On Monday and Tuesday he had not had much time to think about himself, for he had worked hard helping Laura to clear up the accounts, knowing that she was anxious to get away from Farbridge as soon as she could, to buy her trousseau. But now he had plenty of time to think, and what he thought gave him no satisfaction whatever. He tried to assure himself that he was no worse off than when he came to Farbridge, nearly broke and with no plans, less than three months ago. But this would not do. He felt much worse off, simply because he had dared to entertain large hopes, and now they had vanished like the Festival. And now not only had he no plans, but what was much worse, shocking and quite frightening, was that he could not summon up sufficient energy and interest in things even to begin making any plans, contriving any kind of future for himself. "By George, Horace, my boy," he muttered at his lathered reflection, which made him look like trimmed-down Father Christmas, "you're getting old."

He would have to talk to somebody. Laura and Theodore were no use, although—bless their hearts—they were ready to worry about him. Archie Mobbs, more or less in the same position as he was but younger and with at least a few little irons in the fire, was out at Brant-in-the-Hollow, staying with his Maggie. So it had better be Seth, friendly enough but not an easy man to talk to with your heart in your boots. But Seth, as he had admitted very late a night or two ago, had done very well out of the Festival, so he might be ready to listen to some melancholy confidences from Commodore Horace Tribe, late Director of that Festival, now about to be sent off with a vote of thanks and a Noble Stags' dinner.

After putting on his oldest suit, he went downstairs and knocked at Seth's door. Seth was in but not alone. Old Jordan was with him, looking rather like an Arab elder plotting against the Caliph. The Commodore was not sorry to find Jordan there, for after all the old boy had plenty of money and, unlike most people with plenty of money in Farbridge or elsewhere, he had a friendly regard for poor Horace Tribe.

"Sorry to break in," he began. And then he stopped, for it was sickeningly clear—and the fact hit him like a hammer—that his presence there was not merely inconvenient but a definite embarrassment to both these men.

"Can't do with yer here just now," said Seth gruffly. "Some other time."

Old Jordan shook his head. "Spoil everything, Commodore. Very important private talk. Not Festival business, of course. Festival's all over."

"Yes, the Festival's all over and done with," said the Commodore very slowly but not quite steadily. "I must remember that." And he began to move away.

"Some other time," Seth called, and almost made one of his wheezy noises. "Later, later."

"Why?" said the Commodore bitterly, and left them. It may have been a morbid fancy but just as he went he seemed to hear Seth's deep rusty chuckle. So not only didn't they care a rap, but they found it funny. So much for all good friends in Farbridge.

Poppy, the chambermaid, was doing his room when he returned there. "Don't bother making the bed, Poppy. I'm going."

She opened her eyes very wide, and her mouth opened by itself. She was a hefty simple young woman, who looked rather like a dairymaid in a children's picture book. "You don't mean you're leaving?"

"I do. Just going to pack."

"But you'll be coming back, won't you, Commodore?"

He shook his head, and then turned away to take a suitcase down from the top of the wardrobe. There was a sniffling sound. He glanced round in time to see two large tears welling up in Poppy's velvety brown eyes. "Now, now, Poppy. Can't stay here forever, can I?"

"No—only—" and as she wagged her head in a bewildered fashion, the tears rolled down her plump red cheeks "—I didn't expect—somehow—you'd go off sudden like this."

"Neither did I."

She caught his mood now. "Whatever's made you decide to go off sudden like this? An' just when everybody's making such a fuss of you too."

"I haven't noticed the fuss," he told her as he opened the suitcase on the bed.

"Where are you going? Is it something special you want to do, Commodore?"

"No, Poppy. I'm just going—that's all. And I want to start packing. So off you go, there's a good girl."

"I think it's all wrong," she cried indignantly. Then she went bustling out, as if to tell the world.

He began his packing. There was a time when he had enjoyed cramming his things into trunks and cases, preparing for the next adventure. But not now. He had packed and unpacked far too often. He had wandered too long, and now, getting old, with the wits he had lived by rusting and dulling, his heart no more in the game, he

found himself a homesick man without a home. Except, of course, the
long home in the ground; and it might come to that very soon. But not
here, not in Farbridge. He would never accept willingly that final defeat
here, where in his own way he had fought for life.

After half an hour or so of listlessly opening and emptying drawers
and tumbling some of the stuff into his cases, Fred the porter came up
to tell him that Miss Church was below, asking for him. So he followed Fred downstairs. The lounge was very quiet these days, dusky
and somnolent in comparison with the June sunlight and the bustle of
the street outside, and without a trace of the high jinks of the
Festival period. All gone, hurrying to be forgotten. And little Miss
Church looked very small indeed, waiting there.

"Oh—Commodore," she began, as breathless as if she had been
talking for an hour, "I thought I ought to tell you that tomorrow
Mrs. Delacey and I are going for a little holiday to Colwyn Bay. Mrs.
Delacey's daughter is there, you know, with the entertainers. And we
both felt we needed a little holiday—"

"Of course you do," said the Commodore, desperately trying to be
his old self with her. "Laura and I were only telling each other last
night what a wonderful job you did for us and the Festival. So go and
enjoy yourselves. Sea, mountains, Colwyn Bay, Mrs. Delacey's daughter
—what could be better?"

"I'm so glad you think so," cried Miss Church. "And it was such
a splendid experience working for the Festival, and I feel I've made so
many new friends. *So* very different from Tredberrow—and that
horrid office in the barn. Then everything going off so well in the end
too—and everybody so pleased. You must be so proud—"

"Oh—I am, I am." And he tried to look it.

"And I do want you to feel, Commodore, that if there's *anything* I
can do—you only have to ask. Even if it means coming back from
Colwyn Bay, though I'm afraid Mrs. Delacey would be rather disappointed, and her daughter too because she's booked very nice rooms
for us—"

"I wouldn't dream of it, my dear Miss Church. But thank you all the
same. And if there ever should be anything—"

She looked at him, and suddenly it was as if there was a glimmer of
ageless wisdom in her rather foolish eyes. "Commodore," she began,
and then hesitated.

"Yes, Miss Church?" And now his tone was no longer falsely hearty, perhaps a trifle patronizing.

"Please tell me. What's the matter? There's something, isn't there? You don't mind my asking, do you?"

"No, why should I? We're friends, aren't we?"

"Oh—Commodore!" She was scarlet and was blinking rapidly. "Thank you for that. But do please tell me."

"Well," he replied slowly, "I suppose I expected too much and now feel disappointed. I'd hoped—never mind, but I'd apparently done too much hoping. Don't you bother your head about me, Miss Church. You go and have a gorgeous holiday."

She looked at him in silence for a moment or two, an unusual air of dignity about her, and then said quietly: "Commodore, you probably think I'm very foolish, and I suppose I am sometimes. But I notice people and try to understand them in my own way. And you're a better man than you think you are, Commodore. Please remember that. I know you've done a lot of things you oughtn't to have done, but really you're a good man." She looked at him steadily, wisely, for another moment, then broke into her usual uncertain little smile, blinked hard, hurried out of the hotel.

Very slowly he returned to his room, sat down among the litter of clothes still on the bed, lit a pipe that he never tasted, and stayed there, neither packing nor unpacking. Poppy looked in once, gave his face a quick apprehensive glance, then said something he did not catch, and withdrew. Though heavy with doubt, time passed.

A sharp rapping on his door began it all. Wearily he answered, but then, when Laura and Theodore came bursting in, perhaps he already suspected that the open door behind them led to a world quite different from the one he had been thinking about.

"We were told to bring you," cried Laura. "So hurry up and change that awful suit."

"Why should I?" he inquired rather sourly. "And what are you talking about?"

"They really haven't told him," she said to Theodore, who nodded and then pointed significantly to the suitcases and the clothes. She was horrified.

"What were you up to, Commodore?" she demanded.

"I was packing and then clearing out," he confessed. "I suddenly felt nobody wanted me here any longer—and this morning Seth wouldn't even let me talk to him about it—so I thought I might as well go."

"Go?" cried Laura quite angrily. "Go where? Just tell me that."

He gave her a mournful little grin. "My dear, I hadn't—and still haven't—the foggiest idea. London, I suppose."

She grabbed the lapels of his coat and jerked them up and down furiously. "You barmy old idiot monster, I could shake you and shake you and shake you. There you sit glooming when everybody's been—"

"Laura!" And Theodore for once checked her.

"I'm sorry, darling. You were quite right to stop me. I'll be waiting downstairs. Make him change his clothes—and don't be too long." And out she went.

"Look here, my boy, what is all this?" the Commodore inquired testily.

"A lunch, chiefly for you."

"I don't think I want a lunch chiefly for me. Not in the mood for it."

"Commodore, this is a surprise so I can't tell you about it. But please take it from me that when you arrive at this lunch, you *will* be in the mood for it. Also, believe me that everything you've been thinking this morning—unless I'm guessing badly—is all wrong. Now hurry up and change, just to please Laura. And I'll put some of these things back."

"No point in doing that."

"Yes, there is. Come on, now." He waited a moment or two, until the Commodore, vaguely grumbling, began to change; and then he started clearing the bed of clothes. "Have you received your invitation from the Ancient and Noble Order of Stags? Friday night, isn't it? Laura and I go to London on Saturday morning." And he chattered away until the Commodore was ready.

As soon as they appeared in the lounge, Laura, bursting with impatience, rushed up and began bustling them out of the hotel. "Not the Old Oak Nook again, is it?" the Commodore growled, as they steered him in the direction of Peter Place.

"No, it isn't the Old Oak Nook," said Laura sharply, "and don't start sneering at the Old Oak Nook just because there's no drink there."

"Well, I must admit I could do with a drink," said the Commodore mildly, not feeling able to cope with this feminine ferocity.

"Where we're going, I imagine, you can booze yourself silly. And now don't let's talk any more."

Still thoroughly mystified, he allowed himself to be marched into Peter Place and then round two sides of it until they came within sight of the little old wine and spirits shop, Inchbald and Wainfleet (perfect for Archie Mobbs, he remembered with a stab of regret), and the entrance to Saddler's Row. He was about to pass it, with some wistful exclamation, when to his astonishment the youngsters turned him into the little cul-de-sac.

"The Three Black Boys?" he said ruefully. "Well meant, but I think I'd rather not have seen it again."

"Just don't talk," said Laura severely, "until you know what you're talking about. I suppose this is the way in, isn't it?"

They went into the little dark entrance, past the snug, into the long central bar, where a good many fellows, and some women, were drinking their beer. The Commodore was recognized by several of them, and there were cries of "Good old Commodore!" and "Up the Festival!" Feeling rather dazed now, the Commodore, with Laura digging her fingers into his arm, followed Theodore into the old Coffee Room which had not changed at all. But the open door in the far long wall and the four windows there showed him a walled garden that had been marvelously transformed. All was trim. There were tables shining in the sun. And people, all his Farbridge friends—and he realized in a flash now they were his friends—Seth, old Jordan, Mobbs, Maggie, Mrs. Coote, Huntley, Dr. Barr, Mrs. Bulfoss, and a dozen more.

"Here y'are," shouted Seth, grinning. "Now then, you say it, Mr. Jordan. Silence all!"

"Commodore Tribe," said old Jordan, grave and impressive but with a tiny Arabian Nights twinkle, "before we sit down to lunch, I have to inform you that the Three Black Boys, together with the old-established concern of Inchbald and Wainfleet, has lately been acquired by—er—a new and progressive proprietor, on whose behalf I have been asked to offer you, on terms to be agreed upon later, the post of general manager of the establishment. I may add that it is the wish of all of us here—and of many many others who cannot be here—that you remain with us in Farbridge. Do you accept this offer?"

"By George and thunder—yes, I do," cried the Commodore, his heart thumping away.

Everybody began clapping but old Jordan held up his hand. "There is one further point," he began, contriving to be at once graver and more twinkly than before. "The proprietor wishes to live on the premises. This means that your—er—duties, as resident manager, may bring you in constant and—er—intimate contact with the proprietor. Have you any objection, Commodore?"

He looked from old Jordan to Seth, who was beginning to wheeze and turn purple. Another noise suggested that Mobbs was probably drumming away on his little fat thighs. "No, I've no objection. Though of course I'd like to know who it is."

"Proprietor," bellowed Seth, thus saving himself from exploding altogether. "There y'are, lad."

Some people stepped aside and there she was coming toward him —Grace. She smiled in a rather wobbly fashion; the long look she gave him was brilliant and then uncertain; the smile began to wobble hard; and by the time he reached her, the rosy face had begun to crumple and pucker.

"Why—my dear," he said gently, as if they were alone, "this is the best news of all, the best I've ever had. Never run away again." And he kissed her, while everybody else there pretended to be noisily anxious to sit down and get on with lunch, and Seth did a lot of bossy shouting about it.

"It'll be weeks and weeks and perhaps months before we get the place as we want it," she said to him a little later, as they lunched at a little central table, flecked with sunlight and the trembling shadows of leaves. "I've got a lot of plans to show you. I've been very busy, what with one thing and another. But Seth knew. He's been very kind. I used to telephone to him. He told me how worried you were. I'm sorry, Commodore. I shall always call you Commodore. Not that Horace isn't all right, but I like Commodore best. And there's just two more things—at least for now. Don't ever tease me about the silly stories I tell. They don't really do any harm—and I can't help it—and I'm not so bad as I used to be."

"My dear, I'm looking forward to 'em. But no teasing. I promise. What's the other thing, Grace?"

She hesitated a moment. Then in a very low voice she said: "Would you marry me if you could?"

"Certainly," he replied. And meant it.

"Well, we can't, you know. I did my best about it—but he's cleared off now—after I gave him that money. I'm sorry. Do you mind?"

"I'm in the same boat. So if it wasn't you, it would be me. Both alike."

"Well, I never!" And she suddenly broke into a delicious peal of laughter, and her clear gray eyes danced with the leaves in the sun as she looked up at him. "Aren't we awful?"

6

The special Ladies' Night Dinner of the Ancient and Noble Order of Stags was being held at Charity House, where Lord Barnleysale had opened the Old Farbridge Exhibition in such a peculiar manner. At the entrance, the Commodore ran into Huntley. "Hello, are you a Stag?"

Huntley quivered and closed. "No—a guest. But not a guest of honor, like you and Laura Casey and Jenks. Actually it's a thing they very very rarely do." He was murmuring now, the Refined Back Room Boy. "Very interesting old society, of course . . . keep the old traditions . . . you'll enjoy it, I think."

"But who are they, these Stags?" said the Commodore.

"A few business fellows and professional men," said Huntley, almost going to sleep on the Commodore's shoulder, "but mostly the better-class tradesmen—very decent keen fellows, all of them. Let's go in, shall we?"

One of the first persons they saw was the Mayor, Alderman Walmer, but, as he hastened to explain, he was not there in his official capacity. "Here to do you honor—*Pzzzz*—being an old Stag and a past Surroyal—"

"A what?" said the Commodore, taking some sherry.

"Rather interesting," Huntley whispered, as if he had curled himself up in the Commodore's left ear. "The Order calls its members and officers after the branches of the Red-deer antlers—old tradition, I imagine—"

"Allow me—*Pzzzz*—to introduce you to our present Surroyal," said Alderman Walmer, producing a small anxious man with eye-glasses who was wearing a kind of red cape with antlers embroidered on it. The Commodore recognized him as the High Street chemist who had sold him shaving soap and liver salts.

"The Ancient and Noble Order welcomes you, Commodore Tribe," said the chemist, with immense solemnity. "Your health, sir."

"Your health—er—what do I call you?"

"The full title is Grand Master Surroyal," the other replied proudly.

"Then your health, Master—I mean Grand Master Surroyal," said the Commodore. The sherry was terrible.

A muffled giggling noise behind him made him turn his large broad back on past and present Surroyals. The other two guests of honor had arrived. "And she's got the giggles," Theodore muttered.

"I can't help it," said Laura, her face crimson, her eyes watery. "I'll stop in a minute, I promise."

"Come, come," said the Commodore severely, "we can't have that. Guest of honor too. I don't advise the sherry," he added in a whisper.

Noble Stags and their ladies, mostly middle-aged and plumpish, milled around them, drinking the light sherry with an appearance of reckless abandon. "Please remember, young Laura," said the Commodore, "that this crowns all our Festival work. So be careful. Besides, you may have to make a speech."

"I couldn't possibly," Laura began, but was interrupted by an unexpected, discordant and shattering call on a horn, which the Commodore, looking over the heads of his neighbors into the hall, saw was being blown by a lank spectacled fellow wearing a bright-green coat.

"Known in the Order as the Forester," murmured Huntley, who apparently was still in the Commodore's left ear. "A sort of herald originally, I imagine . . . acts as toastmaster . . . very interesting . . . all so keen. . . ."

"Grand Master Surroyal," the Forester roared—and he had a colossal rusty bass—"Guests of Honor, Ladies and Guests, Noble Stags —kindly take your seats, for dinner is about to be served."

"Follow me," said the Surroyal chemist, and led them in and then round to the top table where he halted in the center, facing some enormous antlers. The Commodore was on his right, and Laura, small and desperate, was between the Commodore and Theodore. There were about two hundred Stags and guests in the room, and already it was very warm. On the other side, on a dais, three anxious middle-aged women were playing something that might have been *The Roast Beef of Old England*. The Forester, after silencing the trio and everybody else with a blast of his horn, called upon the Abbot of the Noble Order to say grace, and a little clergyman at the end of the top table said it quickly and rather angrily, and then they sat down. This was not too easy because the top table appeared to have more diners than it could comfortably seat, and the guests of honor found themselves packed close together, with the enormous antlers, which tipped to one side too easily, already a nuisance.

"Well, well," said the Commodore, making the best of it, "this is very pleasant, and very kind of you to have us here, Grand—er—Surroyal."

"A pleasure," said the chemist, taking off his eyeglasses and wiping them, for the thick red cape was making him very hot and sweaty. "We go in for a bit of ceremonial—old customs—on these occasions. I hope you don't mind."

"Delighted," said the Commodore. "Nothing like a few old customs and a touch of ceremony."

"Everybody look this way," cried a photographer, standing on a little table at the far end of the hall. "Your attention, please! Everybody look this way. And top table please stand up. Now keep perfectly still for five seconds."

So they stood up, kept still, sat down again, with somebody swiveling the monstrous antlers, and they seemed to be packed together closer than ever. Laura began making queer choky noises. The three middle-aged women began playing *The Pirates of Penzance*. Waitresses, out of breath and nearly out of temper, dumped rather meager helpings of tinned tomato soup more or less in front of them. Bottles of Beaune, almost steaming, arrived. Trying to fill Laura's glass, the Commodore caught his sleeve on a point of the antlers.

"Will you tell your friends, the other two guests of honor," said the Grand Master Surroyal, "that our guests of honor at these special dinners always stand up with the Grand Master Surroyal when he takes wine?"

"I will," said the Commodore, and did, only to be told by his friends, who were having some difficulty with their spoonfuls of soup, that they did not understand what he was talking about. "Well, kindly remember," he went on, "that I am now a Farbridge man, and am not bolting out East, and that the Noble Stags are paying us a handsome compliment. In short, behave yourselves. Incidentally, they've practically mulled this wine."

"Golly, but this room's hot," said Laura.

"And I'm hungry," Theodore muttered.

"Quiet now, children, quiet," said the Commodore. And then nearly fell backwards for at that moment the confounded Forester chap, who must have crept up behind him, blew a horrible blast on

his horn. Then he began, at the top of his appalling voice: "The
Grand Master Surroyal and Guests of Honor will be pleased to take
wine with all past Surroyals."

"Up you get," said the Commodore, with some difficulty rising himself and lifting up his glass. About a dozen old boys had also risen and
were raising their glasses. The Commodore drank to them in his
mulled Beaune. Laura made some choky noises. Sitting down was
even more difficult than before, because now the waitresses, angrier
than ever, were trying to remove the soup plates. The Commodore
pushed the nearest branch of antler farther away, with the result that
the other end, on the far side of the Grand Master Surroyal, swung
round and knocked over a glass of wine.

"I suppose we couldn't have this thing removed, Grand Master?"
the Commodore inquired in what he hoped was an easy genial fashion.

"Grand Master *Surroyal*," said the chemist, correcting him. "No—
it's the custom at all our dinners—to have the Great Antlers—"

"Yes, yes, quite so," said the Commodore hastily, moving just in
time to escape having his fish course plastered over his ear. Not that
it would have done much harm because there was very little of it,
perhaps about two inches of fish covered with white sauce. He poked
a fork at it tentatively.

Then the horn went again. "The Grand Master Surroyal and Guests
of Honor," roared the monster, "will be pleased to take wine with
all Trez-tines."

There were about thirty Trez-tines, fattish chaps mostly and looking
as hot as the Commodore felt. Some of them had pints of beer, which
the Commodore envied them, for the Beaune did not improve upon
acquaintance. He tried to solve the sitting down problem by pushing
his chair back, to avoid bumping against Laura or the Grand Master
Surroyal, but while this made his descent easier it also took him far
from the table, and when he moved forward he found that his
neighbors had not left him enough space. Finally he turned a little
sideways and disposed of his bit of fish very quickly. But then when
he tried to reach his bread, after dropping his fork and then using the
right hand again, he got entangled with the nearest branch of the
antlers once more. He was just disentangling himself, sweating away,
when one of those smirking jackasses who must say something got
up, two tables away, and cried: "Grand Master Surroyal of the Farbridge Lodge—a few of us here from the County Lodge—beg the

honor of taking wine with you, sir, the guests of honor, and past
Surroyals." There was some applause; the insane Forester blew his
damned horn; the Commodore wrestled with the antlers, and then
just got up in time and had a mouthful of dregs.

"I'm terribly sorry," Theodore was crying to his neighbor on the
right, a hot jam roly-poly sort of woman who had tried to spread
herself while he was standing and had then been severely bumped
when he sat down again. Another steaming bottle of Beaune arrived.
The three women, probably desperate now, took an uncertain shot at
The Entry of the Gladiators, and the 'cellist either broke a string or
snapped a suspender.

The tiny space between the Commodore's right shoulder and
Laura's left cheek was suddenly occupied by Huntley, who, from
some mysterious kneeling position, whispered: "Rather interesting.
I've just learned that the Farbridge Lodge is the third oldest in the
Order. Thought you might like to mention it in your speech. . . ."

"Look out," a waitress yelled furiously, and after some scuffling behind, very large hot plates, with very small helpings of chicken, cauliflower, and potatoes, were banged down on the table. The Commodore tried to fill glasses, though Laura, now in a perilous state, chokily
protested. An outlying branch of the nightmare antlers now began
teasing Theodore, who, losing all patience, gave the thing a powerful
shove so that it went sliding back on its wooden base, wobbled a
moment, and then went crashing off the table. The horn gave its
loudest and most horrible blast. The green-coated maniac then roared:
"The Grand Master Surroyal and Guests of Honor will be pleased to
take wine with all Bez-tines and Brow-tines." And up sprang Noble
Stags by the score, lifting their glasses and pint mugs, waving and
cheering.

But this time they were not joined by the three guests of honor,
who simply could not rise to their feet. The Commodore was leaning
back, Laura had crumpled down in her chair, and Theodore was
collapsing on the table with his head in his hands, all three of them
helpless with laughter.